GUARDIAN

DIVISION ZERO BOOK 4

MATTHEW S. COX

DIVISION ZERO PRESS

Division Zero: Guardian

Book 4 of the Division Zero series.
Second Edition

Original release © 2015 – Matthew S. Cox
Second Edition © 2018 All Rights Reserved

A DIVERGENT FATES NOVEL

ISBN: 978-1-949174-18-2 (Ebook)

ISBN: 978-1-949174-19-9 (Paperback)

CONTENTS

REPRIEVE

Content to follow Evan's lead, Kirsten let him pull her along a hallway packed with loud children, frustrated chaperones, and glowing holographic displays of technical concepts. His baggy blue jacket rustled as he squeezed his way past the crowd to the console of a three-dimensional depiction of Mars terraforming. He twisted around to look at her, bright green, blue, and pink light from holograms glinting in his awestruck eyes from animated models of machines.

Each time he got close to a station, the display came alive, demonstrating the workings of each device or scientific process. She kept within arm's reach behind him, every so often allowing his exuberance to lift her out of her gloom. Whenever her hair tickled at her collarbones where her short, coral-hued dress didn't cover, she grasped at the spot as if a fly landed on her. Kirsten held her silver purse tight to her hip and stared down bare legs at her pink Nomz, which meowed a few times as she tried to keep up with his rush to the Mars exhibits. Her sneakers' electronic cat sounds mostly drowned in the din. No matter how much she tried to stretch out their trip to the West City Science Center, the day marched on toward its inevitable end.

For the first time in her life, she felt like a child on the last day of summer vacation: happy in the now and dreading tomorrow.

"That's the machine that makes the air better." Evan pointed at a processing tower in cutaway view. Oversized 'molecules' cycled around an endless animation demonstrating how the machines converted carbon dioxide to other gases. "It's gonna take a long time. That's the bad air coming in, and that's the catalyst chamber, and that's where they send it back to the sky." He grinned up at her. "Most almost all of Mars' air was carbon dioxide, like ninety-something percent before we started. And that's bad 'cause we can't breathe it."

Kirsten smiled, despite feeling ashamed of herself since a nine-year-old knew more about space science than she did. She gestured at a tall, narrow lattice easily the size of a ten-story building, scaled to the little holographic figures at its base. The top consisted of an octagonal array of panels, fanned open like a high-tech flower. "What's that thing?"

"That's one of the field emitters." He put his finger through it, and a thin blue energy beam shot skyward. "Mars doesn't have a magnet anymore, so the air will blow away into outer space." Evan waved at another screen on a panel to the right of the cubby containing the display. "There's satellites around Mars that focus the force field the tower sends. It won't stop missiles n' spaceships, but it's enough to let the air stick to the planet."

"Wow." Kirsten squeezed his shoulder while staring at all the animated models. Her feelings of inadequacy gave way to pride, in both watching his curiosity run wild, and knowing that if not for her chance call to a little cyberware shop, he'd still be cowering in some filthy locked bedroom—or dead. She wiped at her eyes. "You, uhh… you're really into that space stuff."

He looked up at her again and tilted his head. "What's wrong? Are you sad 'cause you gotta go back to work tomorrow?"

"A bit, yeah." She brushed his hair off his eyes. "I was thinking about how happy I am that I found you."

Evan spun to face the railing and moved to his right, approaching the next display, which focused on the construction of the first Mars cities underground. Animated drilling machines crawled back and forth like enormous plastisteel moles. "Why do people cry when they're happy?"

"I'm not sure, hon. Good question. Maybe when you grow up and become a scientist, that'll be the first mystery you solve." She winked.

He stuck his tongue out. "Scientists have more important things to do."

"Oh?" She leaned back with an appraising raised eyebrow. "What's my little mastermind going to work on then?"

Evan poked her in the side. "I'm not a mastermind. They do *bad* things like make big weapons and try to control the world." He moved on to the next display, a 'simple' demonstration of an ion engine that left Kirsten feeling like a dog mesmerized by bright flashing lights. "Im'a make a machine that lets everyone talk to ghosts… and see them too."

"There's some things like that. Well, at least the talking-to part, but they're not reliable." She smirked. "Most people think of them as toys."

"Abernathy said the government has electronics that work with psionics." He poked a button that made the drilling machine speed up. The animation opened to an 'X-ray' view showing how the broken rock flowed within the driller to collection pods in the back. A man's voice, barely audible over the crowd, narrated what it had been like for the crews working ten-hour shifts with only eleven hours of breathable air in the tanks.

Kirsten thought of the rumors surrounding Division 9. Everyone in Zero received the warning not to attempt telepathy on any of them, especially doll operatives. Rumors about psionic-feedback devices that could turn the most innocent surface thought read into a nosebleed migraine—or worse—ran rampant. Dorian had once mentioned something he'd overheard in a meeting of the Command Council. Of course, as soon as he said 'alien life on Mars,' a species they'd referred to as Ixylid, Kirsten tuned him out. He had either been messing with her, in which case she refused to bite, or overheard a secret of the sort that caused lifespans to experience sudden shortening.

"Do you believe him?" Evan glanced back and up at her. "Abernathy knows stuff."

"Well, there's psi inhibitors." She tried to think of how they worked, if they functioned on a purely technical level or operated in a way beyond what pure science could explain.

"They send stuff into the brain so you can't concentrate. Not the same." He tapped the side of his head, his orb of mouse brown hair so dense it concealed his entire finger. "They're cruel 'cause they can make a person go crazy." His eyes widened. "I'm gonna make something better someday."

Kirsten shivered at the memory of the school's demonstration of psi inhibitors. At age fourteen, each resident of the dorm headed for a non-Admin role with Division 0 got a brief taste of one as 'encouragement' not to abuse their powers. Since the brain had a tendency to interpret the random information based on past experiences, the distractions the device forced into her head took the form of her mother's screaming voice for the thirty seconds they left it turned on. As embarrassing as it had been to have a bad panic attack in front of six of her peers and three adults, at least none of them had ever teased her about it.

"They didn't use one on you did they?" Kirsten squeezed her fists, trying to hide the anger leaking from her stare.

Evan shook his head. "No. 'Tenant Daniels said we're too small. Not 'til high school." He stopped by a hologram model of one of the massive air scrubbers used on Earth to make up for the atmospheric damage caused by plant die-off. "Is it scary? Kira said 'couple years ago, this one girl wound up having a accident right in class when they put one on her."

Kirsten looked at the drilling display, some fifteen feet past them, hoping he didn't notice how red her face felt. "Inhibitors make you think of the worst things your brain can conjure."

He held her hand. "You saw your mom, huh."

"Yeah."

Evan wrapped his arms around her and squeezed. When he leaned back, his cheeks had lost noticeable color, leaving him pale. "I'll see Mick, won't I?"

She patted him on the back. "Maybe. Depends on how your head works. You might hallucinate a world without any Monwyn stuff."

He gasped, feigning horror. She winked and poked him in the ribs until he smiled. They followed the tunnel around past a few more holographic displays devoted to early Mars mining efforts, hydroponic farming, and some of the first-generation ships capable of taking passengers between planets. At a horseshoe end, a life-sized diorama of the Mars landscape (as it existed in 2149 when a joint UCF/Japanese team landed to perform a colonization study) contained sub-sentient synthetic humans dressed in period space suits. They resembled the original thirteen-person crew, and conversed with a large group of kids from part of some organized tour group.

Four weary adults waited by the railing separating the Mars exhibit from the rest of the museum. Their arrangement, visible fatigue, and demeanor screamed 'teachers' to Kirsten. A few feet to their right, a woman with the same general type of ID badge on a lanyard around her neck squatted to chat in harsh whispers with a little dark-skinned girl in a beige dress. Her black hair hung in a shoulder-length bob; she looked about Shani's age and halfway between terrified and angry enough to hit someone.

"Ankita, please… you need to calm down," said the woman.

"But, Miss Martinez, I wanna go home." She sniffled. "It's not fair we have'ta go here after school."

"You haven't even given the Science Center a chance." The teacher forced a smile past her exhaustion and general sense of 'so done with this.' "It's fun."

The child looked around at the crowd. Kirsten's gut clenched at the fear in the girl's eyes, and she slowed to watch. Evan looked up at her when she tugged at his arm. He zeroed in on the girl a second later.

"I don't like it here. I'm scared." Ankita glared at the teacher. "Take me *home*."

On the word 'home,' the child's eyes flickered with a hint of amber light.

"Home," said Miss Martinez. "I should take you home."

Kirsten rushed three steps forward and put her hand on the teacher's shoulder. "A moment?"

The woman startled and leaned back with a hand on her chest; they made eye contact. "I'm sorry. I have to take Ankita home."

Kirsten dove into the teacher's thoughts, finding a weak surface-level suggestive implant. The little girl's face and the concept of home swirled around and around… from the way it felt, the teacher had misinterpreted and was about to take the child back to her own apartment. Kirsten erased the suggestion, leaving the woman blinking and dazed.

"Ankita?" asked Kirsten. She smiled and took a knee. "Why are you so frightened? Did you do that on purpose?"

"W-what?" The twig-thin child took a step back, raising her hands. "Who are you? *Away.*"

Kirsten braced herself to resist the command, but it brushed over her mind with little strength. *I wonder if this is how Renee would've felt if I tried to use suggestion on him.* "I'm not going away, sweetie. We need to talk."

"Who are you?" asked a male teacher in dark blue. He inserted himself between Kirsten and Ankita.

Evan opened his mouth, but decided to keep quiet.

Kirsten held up a finger, reached into her purse, and flashed her ID. "Agent Wren, NPF Division 0. I need a moment with this girl."

"Oh…" The man's face exuded perspiration. "Psionics…"

"Is something wrong?" Kirsten narrowed her eyes.

"I… Uhh. No. It's, I mean, not that there's anything wrong with psionics." He scratched his head. "I'm not comfortable near them." His eyes shot open. "I mean it's great they're what they are… I just prefer not to be around that sort of thing."

She frowned. "I'll try not to get any on you."

"*Home!*" yelled Ankita.

"Home," said the male teacher. "I'm going to go home now."

He turned as if to walk away, but Kirsten grabbed his arm. "*Stay with the tour. Ignore that command.*"

The white glow from Kirsten's eyes glimmered back at her from the teacher's. Ankita gasped. He seemed to forget the past thirty seconds and returned to where he'd been standing with the other three educators. Rather than take off running as Kirsten expected, Ankita flung herself into a trembling hug.

Evan glanced up at Kirsten. *She's got suggestion, right?*

She nodded. "What's made you so scared that you're doing that to people?"

Ankita flashed wide puppy eyes at her. *I'm sorry. I know it's bad, but I wanna go home. I'm scared. I don't like being here.*

Loud telepathic whining in such a tiny voice caused the muscles in Kirsten's back to lock up. "Of what? Are you having problems with your parents?"

The girl blinked. "No. My mom and dad are great." She sniffled. "Yesterday, I was playing an' a strange man wanted to give me a bear. I started walking away, and he said he wasn't trying to kidnap me. He put it on the ground and told me I can have it. I looked at his head. It was a bomb. He didn't like us 'cause we're psionic."

Kirsten suppressed a growl. "Can I see him in your memory?"

Ankita nodded and stared into her eyes.

The child's surface thoughts contained blurry images of a small park in front of an apartment tower. A pale man, warped by a six-year-old's fear into the proportions of a giant or troll from the Monwyn movies, shambled over. Gaunt, he had a few days' worth of beard stubble and a blue ball cap. He held up a small brown teddy bear in pink overalls and smiled. Kirsten dove in a little further. The man set the bear on the plastisteel walkpath and backed away, gesturing at it. Ankita peeked at the man's surface thoughts, certain he meant to kidnap her. When she saw the truth, that the stuffed bear would explode, that this man wanted to send her to some place called Hell, she ran screaming to where her parents sat on a bench.

Piece of shit. Kirsten glared.

Ankita covered her mouth with both hands, looking shocked.

"Oops. Sorry. Don't repeat that word." Kirsten fished her NetMini out of her purse and snapped a picture of Ankita's face. "You understand that it's wrong to use that ability on people unless you are protecting your life or the life of a third party?" *What am I doing? She's little.* "Ankita, it's not nice to use your abilities on your teachers like that. You can get in trouble."

"Huh? I don't wanna go to a party." Ankita scrunched and released her dress with both hands. "I don't wanna get blowed up."

The girl had such a strong desire for the safety of home that Kirsten wanted to go hide in her own bedroom. She started a search in the Division 0 archives with a quick image-capture of the girl's face, and delved into the child's mind a little more while waiting for it to run. *Modest telepathy, weak suggestion... thankfully no telempathy. Those eyes are bad enough.* She couldn't find any memories of her using her abilities beyond the vague notion that sometimes people did what the girl wanted when she became upset. *No conscious awareness of her suggestion ability.*

The NetMini beeped. A fist-sized hologram of the child's face, a little younger and in a pastel yellow shirt with a daisy-shaped collar smiled at her next to a bank of text.

Ankita Ravi [CFFE:0A1F]

    Age: 06Y 04M

    Status: Registered

    Completed P-APT Initial Assay Panel 1 - 2417-NOV-02.

    Astral:(negative)

    Clairvoyance:(negative)

    Kinesis Group:(negative)

    Metabolic Group: (negative)

    Precognition:(negative)

    Suggestion:(latent)

Telepathy:(Grade 1 / dominant)
Parent1: Mother (Positive – Record: CFFD:904A)
Parent2: Father (Positive – Record: CFFD:904B)
Notes: Parents registered, declined recruitment. Cooperative/friendly.

Kirsten skimmed over the rest of the notes from the Division 0 Admin liaison handling the family's case. She clicked on the two file references to check out the parents, both average telepaths. The mother had a modest rating in telekinesis while the father had an eyebrow-raising note of Grade 6 in accelerated healing within the metabolic group. The man could likely recover from a bullet striking anything other than his heart or brain in a matter of a minute. Their records looked clean, despite their not wanting to join Division 0, even as Admin. The file mentioned their beliefs being incompatible with violence, even violence necessary to deal with criminals.

They registered her about a year ago. I don't need to do anything here... except. Kirsten added a note to the girl's file to trigger a follow up from the Admin rep handling her case. The child needed a little training on how to resist 'excited manifestations' happening again, especially in less benign situations.

"Am I in trouble?" asked Ankita.

Kirsten bit her lip and took a knee to bring herself closer to eye-level with the girl, deciding to respond telepathically for privacy. *No, sweetie. Not this time. Do you know what psionic suggestion is?*

Ankita shook her head.

You have a psionic skill that can make people do stuff. Using Suggestion on purpose can get you into trouble, but I know you weren't doing it to break the law, and I don't think you even wanted to use it.

"No." The girl looked down. "I just wanted to go home."

Kirsten took her hand. *I can do it too. That's why you didn't make me go away. It's one of the talents that gets people in trouble when it is used wrong. If you ever use that ability on purpose without a good reason, you can get in a lot of trouble. Even if you use it on your parents to stay up past your bedtime or get out of doing homework.*

Ankita's eyes widened. "I'd never do it to Mom or Dad... I'd get in *so* much trouble. I'd be grounded for like ever."

"Don't be afraid." Kirsten smiled. "I do think you should work with someone to learn how to control it."

Evan looked down at the floor, wobbling his right sneaker back and forth on the toe.

Damn. Kirsten sighed in her thoughts. *He thinks I'm going to cut our trip short and go to work right now.* "I don't think that man is going to try and harm you here where there are so many people. He wants to hurt people like us, not everyone else. You should be safe with your class, but I your parents should report what happened."

"Okay. I didn't mean to *make* Miss Martinez take me home. Am I have'ta gonna go to jail?" asked Ankita.

"Nope." Kirsten patted her on the shoulder. "You were scared and it happened accidentally. People with our gift have to be extra careful."

"He's not gonna try to hurt me?"

"I don't think you're in any danger here. That man wanted to hurt psionics. He won't try anything in a crowd this big. I'll have them send a patrol unit to your house, okay?"

Ankita nodded. She looked to the side as the teachers started the process of collecting their charges from the false Mars surface. "Can I go?"

Kirsten nodded and stood.

Miss Martinez smiled at her. "Sorry for the trouble. Umm, what happened?"

"Ankita has some abilities that she hasn't learned how to control yet. When she is scared, they can sometimes manifest on a subconscious level. It should be nothing to worry about. She seems like a sweet kid."

The girl blushed.

"Sorry to be a bother." Miss Martinez guided Ankita away and rejoined the group.

Kirsten flicked open her email client and started typing in a request to send a Tactical unit to do a sweep of the area around the girl's home, and talk to the parents about what happened.

"Hey, check out that dumbass typing," said a mauve-haired teen girl with black lipstick, four lip rings, and a black and white striped long-sleeved shirt. "Why don't you catch up with the rest of the world and get a plug?"

Her apparent boyfriend laughed.

Evan glared at them. "Don't make fun of my mom."

"That's your mother?" The girl gawked. "Damn, what'd you have him when you were ten?"

Kirsten stared at a mangled line of text… too many typos for even auto-correct to fix. She tried to focus on the meditative lessons Gabriel had been teaching her to channel anger. *Not worth it.*

She left the two to their debate about how she had a boy that old at her age, and finished her email. Evan's mood improved once it become clear their evening wouldn't be interrupted. By the time they reached the next station, all trace of worry had left him.

He talked to the 'original colonization crew' for about fifteen minutes. Naturally, Evan *had* to ask them how they coped with farts in a spacesuit. After, they made their way out the other end of the horseshoe past more exhibits dedicated to the workings of various spacecraft. The first detailed how the life support systems worked, next came an interactive map of the migratory breathable zones on Mars, and finally, Evan spent a while at a two-booth-wide section showing off what colonization efforts looked like in the modern age. New expeditions in 2418 were a world apart from what the Mars expedition had to live with. Between drop boxes for buildings and advances in suits, a viable colony could be set up on a new planet within months, even before the terraformers finished with it. Living among all those trees, plants, and ponds would've been almost tempting... if not for the any of a thousand unexpected ways to die.

A wall of fragrance hit them when they emerged from the 'space' portion of the Science Center. Each breath brought something different: spices, sweet, Indian food, Chinese, searing steak, and buttery... something. Evan stood on tiptoe sniffing the air. He grinned, grabbed her hand, and pulled her along the central concourse around a slow-motion battle playing out between full-size dinosaur skeletons. Some sixty yards later, past several souvenir shops and media stores, he led her into the food court.

Two steps past the end of black gloss exhibit floor to somewhat slippery dull red tile, he stopped. "Can we eat?"

"I've been starving for the past hour." She winked. "Wherever you want."

He looked around. Numerous food vendor counters lined the walls of a large rectangular chamber. The two far corners had doors leading into sit-down restaurants: Japanese hibachi place on the left, and a 'Kowboy Kut' steakhouse on the right.

She squinted at it. *Why do they always think spelling stuff stupid will sell more crap?* Tables and chairs took up the middle of the room, arranged around hexagonal planters with exotic trees that looked stolen from rainforests. Four-inch holographic ships flew about in a simulation of interplanetary trade, docking with physical model space stations hung on wires from the ceiling.

Evan seemed most drawn to a large cartoony panda over a food vendor that smelled about as Chinese as the steakhouse. Kirsten followed him, fingers crossed his nose sensed something her eyes didn't. He sidled up to a metal trackway used to slide trays past the vendors, and peered through the glass partition at the food.

"Hi, welcome to Happy Panda," said a youngish teen girl who appeared at least partly Chinese.

Evan ignored her and made faces at the food, as though he couldn't decide if he wanted it.

Kirsten didn't pay much attention to the girl until she waved at him and frowned. "Sorry, kid, are you visually or hearing impaired?"

Evan leapt back and yelped. "It spoke to... Oh, crap. She's, uhh, not a doll." He blushed. "Sorry. I thought you were a doll."

True enough, surface thoughts did swirl around in the clerk's head... about how sick and tired she was of being mistaken for an android. Kirsten flashed a conciliatory smile. "I'm sorry... I don't remember the last time I've seen a real person working a fast food place."

"It's okay." The girl rolled her eyes. "I get that a lot. The museum has this thing about 'taking it back to an older time' or something. Hard to get in here... so many kids, so few jobs. Apparently, dumping food on plates is educational."

Evan shot Kirsten a shocked stare, still blushing. "Uhh, can I have the sweet and sour chicken please?"

"Sure," chirped the girl. She looked at Kirsten. "Can I get you something?"

She eyed the serving bins behind the glass, most of which contained the 'cardinal eight': Chicken with Broccoli, Lo Mein, Sweet and Sour, Pepper Steak, Mei Fun, Fried Mustard Wings, Chinese Spareribs, and General Tso's chicken.

"Lo Mein for me."

"You both have a choice of soup."

Evan and Kirsten said "Wonton" at the same time.

"Do you want to add any meat to your noodles?" The girl's smile seemed more genuine. "Chicken, Pork, Beef, or Shrimp."

"Is the meat real too?" Evan gawked.

"Vat grown actually..." The clerk struck a proud pose.

"Chicken please," said Kirsten.

The tab came to ₡156. *Ouch. Bit steep for a hot buffet, but I guess the museum gets a cut.* Evan led the way to a table set in a patch where a dense jungle tree offered some shade from the glaring overhead lights. He sat under branches that would've rested on Kirsten's head, leaving her the seat facing the tree. Hunger got the better of both of them for a few minutes. Despite the look of it, the food tasted far better than she'd expected. While the noodles were a tad mushy—no doubt from sitting—the chicken had been cooked to order and surprised her with its quality.

Evan made faces while gnawing on a tough bit of sweet and sour.

"Is that chicken or pork?" Kirsten tilted her head.

He shrugged. "Can't tell. It's fried."

A faint rustle in the leaves made her glance up. A bright green snake, as big around as her arm, dangled out of the tree, its snout less than an inch from Evan's right ear. She set her fork down and raised her hand in a slow, controlled motion.

"Evan. Don't move."

He kept eating. "It's not a real snake."

The snake chuckled. "Hello."

Kirsten leaned her left elbow on the table and her forehead in her hand. "Synthetic."

"Of course." The snake made a *tsk tsk* sound. "I'm afraid *Morelia viridis* has been absent from this country for over two centuries now. Live animals in this area are quite rare, and usually pets."

Kirsten pictured her eyebrows joining in a cavewoman unibrow. "Huh?"

"Green tree snake," said Evan. "And of course it's synthetic. They wouldn't have live snakes in the food court. Besides, even if he was real, they're not venomous."

"Would you like to know about me?" asked the snake. "And technically, I'm a python."

Kirsten smirked. *Technically, you're plastic and silicon.*

"Okay." Evan shoveled rice into his mouth.

The serpent rambled on about its usual habitats in what used to be Florida, as well as New Guinea and Australia, including how rumor had it a few surviving biological ones remained in more remote jungles. It spoke of its behavior and diet, of being popular pets before the price of a real one rivaled that of a car. Despite never having heard of the animal before, Kirsten couldn't find interest in it. After giving its speech, it looped itself over a low-hanging branch to 'rest.'

"You okay, Mom?" Evan leaned down to get a better angle at making eye contact. "You look sad."

"They only gave me a month." She pushed half a plate of noodles around. "I've got to report tomorrow."

"I know." He stabbed his fork into a piece of sweet and sour. "It's not like you're going to disappear off the planet."

She exhaled. "I like having the whole day to be with you."

"Me too." He smiled.

"I hate it when I'm caught late and you get stuck."

He held a finger up while he finished chewing. "It's okay. People need help. You're like the only one who can help with the spooky stuff." Evan gulped iced green tea. "And the, umm, un-Harbingers picked you, right?"

She let off a wistful chuckle. "Yeah, something like that. Seraphim." *Not going to be talking about that any time soon. They'll think I've cracked.*

"I'm glad the spirits were quiet. You didn't get called back early." He grinned. "And Sam's pretty cool. Are you gonna get married?"

A sharp intake of air led to her failing in her experiment at breathing lo mein. She pounded her fist on her sternum until her throat cleared, and wiped tears from her eyes. "I don't know. I suppose it's always possible, but I've only known him a little while and something like that shouldn't be rushed into."

Evan leaned close. "I like him. Sam's a lot nicer than that old man. He was creepy."

Kirsten dropped her fork. *Goodbye appetite.*

"Uhh, sorry." He stared down for a few seconds. "You acted all funny around him. Didn't feel like you were you."

"I'm so sorry." She reached across the table and took his hand. "I don't understand how he did it, but that bracelet made me... it made me feel, I dunno... helpless without him. Like some weak little girl who couldn't do anything without a man holding her up." She scowled. "You were right. He *was* a liar."

"Did he wanna hurt us?" The worry in his eyes made her want to kill Konstantin all over again.

"I'm not sure. I don't think I'll ever know. He wanted me close, probably to watch."

Evan gasped. "He's the one who made all the demons."

"Yeah." She grimaced. "More called than made."

He nodded, his mouth curled into an imperious frown of admiration. "I'm glad you kicked his ass."

She burst out laughing, drawing several glances. Her appetite decided to come out of hiding. "You don't have to worry about him ever again. Well" — she glanced at her NetMini—"it's almost one. The school wanted me to make sure you spent at least an hour in the botanical wing."

He seemed a few shades less than thrilled. "Plants are boring, but okay."

"After that, I have something special in mind for our last day of vacation." She winked while twirling noodles on her fork.

"There isn't a new Monwyn vid out?" He furrowed his eyebrows, deep in thought.

She shook her head.

"Funzone?"

"Nope."

Evan tapped the fork on his chin. "Uhh, Lunar tour?"

She examined her fingernails. "Nope. Not enough time. That's like an eight hour flight, so that would be a weekend trip."

He whined, swinging his feet back and forth. "Not a movie?"

"Nope."

"Are you taking me somewhere?"

"Yep."

"Fun?" He tilted his head. "Or mushy?"

She giggled. "Oh, you'll probably think it's fun."

Evan all but vibrated in his seat out of frustration.

She took an extra-long time chewing a mouthful of lo mein. "I booked a two-hour reservation at Penumbras VR."

His jaw hung open. *"Two hours!?"*

"Mm hmm. And I'm going to try playing too."

He bounced in his chair. "That's gonna feel like... like... eight or nine hours in Monwyn! Oh, you gotta take Asara the Huntress. You look like a Sun Elf."

She blinked. *Damn network people call me an elf all the damn time.* "What does that mean?"

Evan grinned. "Elf women are short, thin, and really, really pretty." Her cheeks went hot. "Sun Elf 'cause you're blonde. Moon elves have black or white hair, and the ones from Penumbras Forest have purple, blue, or black hair—and glowing eyes."

"What about Xiana, the sorceress?" She entertained a not-so-fond memory of running around Konstantin's manor house in nothing but a black silk robe, mind-blasting people.

He shook his head. "No way, Mom. She's like evil and stuff. An' she's not a playable character anyway."

"Are there any girl wizards?"

"There's Izra, but she's not really a wizard. She's an elementalist. Most of her spells are combative, but she's got a couple shields and walls in Earth."

"Hmm." Kirsten finished off her lunch. "I suppose I'll pick something when we get there. Don't forget you're gonna have a quiz on the botanical stuff, so pay attention."

"Okay." He jumped to his feet and gathered his trash.

Kirsten couldn't help but eye the crowd looking for a man similar in appearance to that little girl's distorted memory while they walked out of the food court. Dread at going back to work tomorrow ebbed and surged. *I have to get back into my stride. Maybe a month off was too much? He's going to get sick of having me around.* She grinned.

At the entrance to the botanical sciences exhibit, he stopped and whirled to face her. "Mom? If I get a hundred on the quiz, can we go back to the VR place again?"

"Okay, Ev. You got yourself a bet." She smiled.

2

ALL HANDS

Kirsten's new apartment had one huge advantage over her old one—
two bathrooms.

She teetered at the precipice of sleep while standing in the
autoshower, smiling at the weak echo of Evan reciting lines from one of the
Monwyn movies coming out of the drain. Her bedroom's attached bath
must've shared plumbing with the shower unit in the hallway bathroom.
Gravity started to pull her over backward, but she grabbed the handrail to
steady herself.

Ugh. Theodore could walk in on me and I'd barely notice. She yawned.

A plastisteel ring slid up and down the outer wall of the clear plastic tube,
rotating as it sprayed her with warm water, rinsing the soapy morass away
from her body. She leaned back, trying to sneak a few more seconds of sleep
on her feet, and closed her eyes as the fans in the base whirred to life. In
seconds, her hair whipped around amid a tornado of hot air, standing straight
up. After the dry cycle died down, she stepped out of the tube—and straight
into Theodore.

His scraggly, permanent-wet hair hung in a curly mess down to the middle
of his chest, matted to his prewar olive drab trenchcoat. A black tee shirt and
greenish fatigue pants dripped water, though at least he'd masked the bullet
wounds that took his life.

Kirsten drew in a breath to scream, mostly out of being snuck up on.
Having spent a lot of time hopping in gel tanks lately took much of the shame
out of being caught naked; she didn't even think to cover herself. "Dammit
Theo!" She fumed, and balled her hands into fists at her sides. "You scared the

shit out of me."

He leaned to the side and eyed the floor. "Not quite."

Grumbling, she stormed to the white box on the wall and pulled a set of plastic-wrapped underwear from the bottom slot. Warmth swam over her face, but she refused to give him the satisfaction of showing embarrassment at having a man (even a dead one) staring at her nakedness. Unlike the medics and the soldiers, *he* had lust on his mind. "Something wrong, or are you back to your old self?"

Theodore chuckled and sauntered over to the mirror, examining his face. "Scarin' ya was a little happy surprise... I just wanted ta check up. Knowin' tis yer first day back."

She gave him a sidelong glance, wondering what had possessed Theodore of all ghosts to afford her a modicum of privacy by not staring at her. After stepping into her panties, she pulled them up and unpacked the soft sports bra. "I haven't been this nervous since I was sixteen and Lieutenant Prost said 'here's a badge and an E-90, you're active now... and oh yeah, we have a paranormal serial killer out there you need to stop.'"

Theodore laughed. He waited for her to wriggle into all of her underwear before peering over. "Crazy bastards givin' a laser to a teenaged girl. My sister barely let her kid have a cell phone at that age."

Kirsten glanced at him before walking out into the bedroom. "Cell phone? Is that some kind of primitive implant that worked on human tissue?"

His laughter echoed behind her. "No, kid. It's a... aww hell, Google it."

"That sounds dirty." She sighed at her uniform laid out on the bed. "I'm not googling anything when there's a ghost around to watch."

A meaty slap accompanied his hand meeting his face. "Ugh. Never mind. I keep forgetting how much the Internet has changed in 400 years."

"The what?" She stepped into her clingy black pants and grabbed a clean uniform top from a drawer.

"Forget it." He shook his head. "Look, we're all grateful for your help with that abyssal. No tellin' how many of us that thing would'a snacked on. The Kind appreciate your effort."

"You're welcome, Theo." She smiled while putting on the rest of her gear. The duty belt and left forearm guard both felt heavier than she'd remembered them. Kirsten fidgeted at everything and sighed. "Well, here I go."

"Hey." He tossed his hair over his shoulder with a quick nod. "We like you, but we don't want you to join us—yet. Keep your head down."

"I'll try." Confidence and nerves warred in her gut. "Thanks, Theo."

"*De nada.*" He vanished into a smear of luminescence, and the water that had leaked all over the rug went with him.

She walked into the hall, where Evan waited, dressed except for shoes. His

baggy blue Monwyn tee shirt concealed his lack of weight, as did his pants—
though his big smile chased away her worries.

He ran into a hug. "You look badass, Mom."

Kirsten squeezed him. *He's still so skinny.* "Get your shoes on, we're a little late."

"Okay." He zipped off to his room.

She headed to the kitchen and poked the food reassembler until it spat out a small apple-stuffed pastry and a decaf coffee. After a quick prayer seeking forgiveness for sinning against the sacred bean, she turned to present them to Evan as he entered. *He's too little for caffeine, but he likes the taste.*

"Cool!" He grabbed the treat and stuffed it in his mouth.

They made it to the elevator before he coughed. "Ugh. Decaf?"

Kirsten laughed. "I don't know whether to laugh or be horrified you can tell the difference from the first sip at nine."

He shrugged one shoulder. "It's okay. You don't want me to get sick, so I think the coffee gods will let it go." He squinted up at her. "I trust this crime against coffee will not continue when I'm eleven."

She ruffled his dense mop of mouse-brown hair. "Come on."

The elevator opened at the roof-level parking deck, revealing a glimmering expanse of parked hovercars and air laced with the smell of metal. The Division 0 patrol craft stood out like a black smear on white curtains. Evan glanced up at her.

"Don't be scared."

Kirsten raised her left forearm and tapped the button on the wearable computer. The patrol craft responded by opening both gull-wing doors. "I don't know if I'm scared so much as…" *Okay. Time to grow up. Vacation over. I can't just wrap myself around him 24/7 for the rest of his life.* "Ugh. Work… I got used to being lazy."

He hopped in the passenger seat, munching on his apple pastry.

She settled in the driver's spot and stared at the controls. The car felt *wrong;* it took her a few seconds to realize the cause—no Dorian. *Oh, no… did he…* Her eyes watered at the thought he'd let go of his attachment to the mortal world since she'd found Sam. Granted, a couple of dates hardly a happy ever after made, but still, where was he?

Evan mumbled with a mouthful of sticky crumbs, gave up, and resorted to telepathy. *Why are you crying?*

"I'm not crying. I'm misty-eyed." She wiped her cheek. "Wondering where Dorian Went."

He slurped the fake coffee. "You haven't gone near the car in a month. He probably got bored. I bet he's at the station messing with Morelli."

She laughed. "Yeah. He would've told me if he was going to leave."

Kirsten brought the car online, grabbed the sticks, and pulled straight up into the air. After a quick turn, she pushed forward on the left stick and the vehicle lurched into motion, ascending into a hover lane. Seconds later, they joined a stream of other vehicles moving like blood in the virtual veins of the city. Evan finished the pastry and licked apple jam from his fingers. After, he sat up straight and 'monitored' other cars, on the lookout for anyone breaking a law.

After an uneventful ride to the Police Administrative Center, she deployed the wheels and pulled into the underground garage. Samir waved from the gatehouse. She returned it, despite his not being able to see her through the armored electronic 'windows.' As soon as she stopped in her designated space, Evan leapt out and sprinted past a row of similar patrol craft, his backpack flopping.

Kirsten hurried to shut down the car, then gave chase, catching up where he waited for her by the interior door. She walked him to the school wing near the Division 0 dormitory, gave him a quick hug, and went up two floors to her squad room. Most people along the way greeted her with friendly smiles and nods, barring the usual ones who darted off at the sight of a mind blaster.

She'd long ago given up trying to explain that her rating wasn't strong enough to blank someone's head; of course, she got off relatively light. People feared Lieutenant-Commander Ashford for his ability to destroy memories and even any sense of personality within a brain. His pallor and bad hair didn't do much to help his creepiness, but she felt bad for him.

The stark, hospital-white corridor leading to her squad room felt foreign, yet at the same time familiar. An eerie sense of being out of place came on, as though she wandered the halls of a school years after graduating. At any moment, she half-expected someone to pop out and yell at her for being there.

Dorian occupied the chair behind his old desk, feet up and head forward as if napping. Relief spread over her, but flashed to a fit of poorly-suppressed giggles at the frazzled look on Officer Morelli's face.

"K!" Nicole leapt from her chair and ran over, hugging her like a tween reunited with her best friend. "Wow that was a fast month. How are you doing?"

"Fine. You know how it is... first day—"

"Evan's okay?"

Kirsten headed to her desk. "Oh, yeah... he's doing great. Little thin still, but—"

"Something's going on." Nicole walked with her. "All Tac units are on FS."

"Whoa." Kirsten blinked. *What the heck happened that they have everyone on flash standby?* "Any idea what—"

"I decided not to try blonde." Nicole pulled her NetMini out. "You want a berry latte?"

Kirsten slumped in her chair and propped her face up in her hands. "Yeah, sure. Feels like I'm going to need it."

"Logan," yelled Captain Eze. "Armor."

Nicole rolled her eyes, careful to keep the gesture hidden from him.

"You better." Kirsten smiled. "You might need to fly out of here any second."

"Yeah, yeah…" Nicole headed for the lockers, grumbling.

Captain Eze lingered in the doorway to his office. Once Kirsten made eye contact, he beckoned her with a wave.

Well, at least I know I can't be in trouble… I haven't been back long enough to do anything. She pushed off the desk to stand, stretched, and walked over. "Morning, sir."

"Welcome back, Wren." He smiled on the way to his desk. "How are things?"

"A little somber at being out of vacation time, but I'm okay."

He brought his hands together in front of his chest, steepling his fingers. "If there is anything you need to talk about, I am here. We've had three different clairvoyants study that bracelet. None were able to determine how he influenced your mind."

For the second time that morning, warmth flooded her cheeks, though this reddening came from anger. "Bastard. I… don't know. The only explanation that makes any sense doesn't make any sense."

He chuckled. "Ahh yes. Magic. They've developed a theory that he somehow managed to embed a latent psionic effect in that bracelet."

She rubbed her right wrist, mercifully free of the gold ouroboros. "It was a demon, sir. A minor abyssal that he somehow infused to the trinket. I think it's something like the way a poltergeist isn't a 'real' ghost. They don't have true awareness, more like random energy. The whole time, I sometimes felt like I had an entity following me, but I could never find it. The damn thing was hanging on my arm."

"Demon." He rubbed a finger back and forth over his upper lip. "They'll like that about as much as they like the M word."

"I didn't believe it either… but how else do you explain funny marks on the ground opening a hole to the afterlife?" She raised her arms to the sides and let them drop.

His eyebrows rose, creasing his shiny dark brown forehead. "Above my pay grade. Though with any luck, it shall not be a future worry. You are certain he is dealt with?"

She shivered. "I don't think it's possible to get any more dead than he is."

"Very good. Doctor Loring's report was favorable. I am glad to hear you are coping well."

"Yes, sir. A lucky call interrupted and stopped things from going too far." Kirsten sank into the chair facing the desk. "I can't believe it made me forget Evan. That's worse than anything he almost did to my body."

He bowed his head for a second. "I'm sure your protective feelings toward him helped you break the control."

"He's still too thin." Kirsten glanced at her knees. "I'm feeding him well, maybe a little too much."

"You did examine his P-APT report, didn't you?"

She grimaced. "Actually, uhh… I was afraid to look at it. He's said some things that make me wonder if he's a precog."

Eze nodded. "He is, but nothing strong enough to get the attention of the Council. Grade 1."

A boy who could see only flashes of imminent harm to himself or those he truly loved wouldn't be of any use to the military or government. Kirsten exhaled a sigh of relief. "That's good."

"He tested at a surprising rating in accelerated healing. Grade 4." He paused. "He must've been using it constantly."

Kirsten glared. "I should've killed that bastard."

"Last I heard, you effectively did. The man's been catatonic since. Don't worry about it, Wren. That was as justified a use of force as one can ask for. He attacked you."

"I know, sir. Thank you."

"You know Evan's particular skill set puts a high drain on the body's resources."

Using it constantly… Her eyes shot wide. "Son of a bitch. If he couldn't regenerate himself…"

Captain Eze gave her a stern look, though he retained a hint of a smile. "Kirsten, don't trouble yourself with what-ifs. We can't know if his accelerated healing abilities saved his life or merely made it tolerable. The important thing is that he is safe now, with you."

"Is inflicting a normally fatal wound on someone with that ability who survives because of it still chargeable as murder?" Her fingers dug into the armrests.

"That is a debate for more learned people than I." He shook his head. "Don't waste thought on it."

Kirsten pictured the man who'd locked Evan in a room and beat him: unshaven, unwashed, drunk, laying on the floor with a nosebleed bad enough to cause a pool of blood under his head. That, in turn, brought a brief pang of a headache. The aftershock from such a powerful mind blast had haunted her for days.

"Are you all right?" asked Captain Eze.

"Yes, sir. Just another bad memory on the pile." She let off a sad chuckle.

A klaxon sounded in the ready room. Nicole and Morelli, both in armor, ran out.

She swiveled from the window to glance at Eze. "What's going on?"

He frowned at his terminal, reading for a few seconds. "A hot mess. Looks like we're going, too. All hands."

Dread weighed on her gut. "W-what happened?"

Captain Eze rose from his chair. That he looked more exasperated than worried lessened her fear some. "A political mess more than anything. An unknown number of psionic individuals have taken hostages, but that's not the worst part."

"Oh, no." She stood. "Kids? I'll grab armor."

"We don't believe so. The victims are members of a sect run by that wingnut Reverend Harris."

Kirsten scowled. "That piece of shit calling for all psionics to be rounded up and burned?"

"The very same." He flicked his terminal off and walked to a private armor cabinet in the office. "I'm half tempted to think this is a stunt. The psionic individuals may already be dead."

She paused at the door. "Is that why they want me there?"

"It's not just you." Captain Eze swiped his terminal locked and started for the door. "They want everyone."

3

DAMAGE CONTROL

Kirsten carried a helmet under her arm, jogging toward an elevator full of strong light that spilled into the hallway when the doors opened. Dorian's apparent solidity faltered as he passed through the closing doors, trailed by wisps of ethereal plasma and a hint of cologne. Once at her side, he again looked no different from the living as he faced front. Chrome strips at the four corners of the cube-shaped capsule tinted black with the reflection of her armor. She jabbed a finger into the holographic icon for the parking level and stepped back, letting her arm drape at her side.

She exhaled. "This isn't going to end well."

"Nice to see you back to your old self." He smiled.

"Thanks." She glanced at him.

"What?" He raised an eyebrow. "I can't tease you for not listening to me when it wasn't your fault."

Small favors. "Thanks. You gave me little scare this morning when you weren't in the car."

The elevator opened, and she hurried to the patrol craft, Dorian at her side.

"I didn't want to intrude, and it got rather boring out there." He stretched into a streak of color that melted into the armored windscreen before reforming in the passenger seat. "Though, I dare say Morelli may be visiting that Doctor Loring of yours soon."

"Bad." She shook her head, chuckling as she brought up the NavMap, which already showed the incident area marked with a flashing red pin.

Triangles swarmed around it. "Wow… it's like everyone but the Council went there." She activated the bar lights and headed for the gate.

He grumbled. "They're more worried about bad press than body count."

"Only a little cynical."

Dorian pursed his lips, pondered, and shook his head. "You're still young enough to confuse pragmatism with cynicism."

Damn Harris… "Has religion ever been used for anything other than an excuse to hate?"

"Some people use it to get rich." Dorian laughed. "But seriously, yes. Many people use it in noble ways, but they're not the ones the NewsNet cares about."

Once she cleared the ramp leading up from the sunken garage, Kirsten hit the 'quick shift' to hover mode, catapulting the patrol craft skyward in a climb that crushed her against the seat. Dorian sat as calm as if they hovered at a standstill.

Kirsten flew up over the civilian hovercar lanes, leveled off, and accelerated to 340 mph, headed due north. If the situation were more critical, she'd have gone high enough to cut across the century towers, but the military frowned on that—no sense risking an unplanned meeting between a hovercar and an aircraft. Voices murmuring on the comm channel spoke of a standoff and hostage negotiators.

"How do you think this is going to play out?"

Dorian shrugged. "Either way, that little church is going to spin this to their favor. Even if we manage to save every single hostage, psionics are going to be 'horrible.' It wouldn't surprise me if they brought Ashford in and nobody winds up remembering any of it."

Kirsten gawked, staring down the length of the twin yellow lines on the windscreen that outlined a virtual 'road' to follow. "That's… unethical."

"More unethical than letting a small group of closed-minded bigots incite a backlash that could claim the lives of hundreds of psionics and anyone else caught in the middle?" He drummed his fingers on the console.

Kirsten found the noiseless motion unnerving.

She deflated. Surely, the National Police Force wouldn't resort to altering memories to suit its own public relations interests. *That's so wrong… we're the good guys.*

Dorian glanced over. "I can tell by the look on your face you're seeing some of the tarnish under the veneer. With the possible… make that *probable* exception of Deputy Director Burkhardt, I'm sure they are thinking in terms of doing the most good."

"You're just saying that to make me feel better." She slowed to under 200 and hooked a left around a black glass tower, passing close enough to disturb a small army of spherical window-cleaning bots. The head-sized machines strayed, drawn away in the wake of the passing patrol craft for a few seconds before their ion jets flared cyan and they returned to their task. "You think they're as corrupt as any corporation."

A mile and change ahead, the street below shimmered with the emergency lights of an uncountable throng of Division 0 vehicles... as well as a tractor-trailer sized mobile command post. The legion of hovercars blotted out the ground as though some malevolent deity had spilled night all over the road, tinting the upcoming edge of a grey zone black. Any usual trepidation at being in the grey faded with the sheer number of police personnel in the area. They had to outnumber citizens four to one in this sector.

"It comes and goes." Dorian sighed. "I like Carter. Things have been better with her at the helm."

A navigation pointer popped up, directing her to set down at a point a block and a half from the site. The electronic windscreen displayed a marker, a transparent green version of the patrol craft, indicating where to land. Anyone else on the police network would see the icon and know to stay clear.

"I thought she was the first Director?" Kirsten worked the control sticks with care, slowing to a midair stop before sinking straight down into her patrol craft's electronic ghost.

"She is. I was talking about pre-council days. Rumor has it we used to 'not exist' and take orders from The Old Man."

"The old man?" Kirsten grabbed her helmet and shot him a look.

"Head of Division 9." Dorian smiled. "People call him The Old Man because if you say his name, he'll find out about it and you'll disappear."

"Oh, stop." She got out and put her helmet on.

Faint hissing lingered for two seconds as it sealed to the neck ring on her armor. The visor filled with tactical displays, a small overhead view in the top left corner, and an ammo counter from a wireless link to the E-90. It converted the full E-mag's charge from a percentage to equivocate twenty-four shots remaining. Division 0 personnel appeared with blue glowing outlines in augmented reality, complete with their names and ranks floating over them as if she'd walked into a collision between Monwyn MMO and real life.

"Agent Wren, this is Lieutenant Commander Arroyo." A man's voice filled her helmet. "Come to the MCP."

Who is that? A part of her felt like a kid being ordered around by someone else's dad. Where was Captain Eze? Not that it mattered; Arroyo outranked him. She spotted the commander's name bar floating in space up ahead, and 'eye-clicked' on it. A small virtual panel opened with a handsome Hispanic man's portrait. LCMDR (O4) Arroyo, Miguel. Division Zero Tactical Operations. *Oh, no wonder I've never seen him... he's Tac.*

She jogged across the street-turned-parking lot, surrounded by staccato camera flashes of bright azure from all the patrol craft emergency lights. Lieutenant Commander Arroyo met her by the trailer of the mobile command post, near a ramp formed by a section of the sidewall that had lowered. She snapped to attention and saluted him. "Commander."

His return salute came crisp and abbreviated. "Agent Wren. I'm sure you are curious why I-Ops was called to a tactical event."

"The thought had crossed my mind, sir."

"Well. Most of your brethren are on crowd containment detail. Command has directed me to have you manage another problem."

"Sir?" She snuck a glance left at a cluster of tactical officers huddled behind two black A3Vs, one with Captain's insignia on his shoulders. The massive six-wheeled armored vehicles blocked them off from any possible attack originating from the building. "All due respect, but this seems like overkill for what's going on."

He set his hands on his hips. "I'm inclined to agree with you. How much do you know?"

"Only some of that jackass Harris's people have been taken hostage. Are we sure they're not staging this?"

"Let me verify." Dorian ran off.

"That is correct." Arroyo raised an eyebrow as Kirsten's head turned to follow her partner into the distance. "Is something... oh, wait. You're one of *those*. What did you see?"

"My partner is a ghost. He's going to scout the inside."

"Your partner?" He chuckled. "Please tell me that's not official..."

"No, sir. It is unusual. My particular skill set and assignments haven't been much for keeping a live partner willing to work with me. They'd have to be another astral sensitive and the only other one I know of who isn't prepubescent is assigned to East City. Been doing okay as is, so they haven't made a big deal out of it."

Lieutenant Commander Arroyo chuckled. "You're still a kid yourself." His casualness faded back to a military bearing. "Anyway. We have determined that between six and ten psionic suspects have abducted four or five individuals affiliated with the Reverend Harris's anti-psionic church. As you can imagine, the brass is highly concerned with the potential harm this could cause to public opinion. We can't afford to make martyrs of them. Your responsibilities here include damage control on the part of any NewsNet personnel who seem likely to spread false stories."

"Sir?"

"Agent Wren, you are hereby authorized on the order of the Command Council to utilize your suggestive abilities to prevent NewsNet employees from disseminating classified information to the public, especially if things go south. This includes, but is not limited to, ordering them to go home, turn over recording equipment, delete files, reveal anything they have learned, or forget what they have seen."

"I... they want me to make people forget?" She blinked. "Sir, that's not within my ability. I've only got a Grade 3 certification with Mind Blast... I can't erase memories... besides, isn't that... wrong?"

"At the moment, most people view Harris and his cult as crazy. You know how the NewsNet is. If they can splice together enough of a video feed to make it look like we went in there and killed them, they will. You are to prevent that. We're not asking you to make them lie."

"Yes, sir." A storm raged in her gut.

"This is probably a damn stunt to garner media attention. Past encounters lead us to believe they are fanatical enough to accept loss of their own lives to further their agenda. We've locked down all data feeds from the building, and so far, we haven't detected any attempts to breach the temporary firewall. If they were planning to broadcast a massacre, they haven't gotten started yet."

"Commander, Agent," said a woman with a deep, scratchy voice.

Kirsten stared like a deer facing a speeding car at a muscular woman only two inches taller than her in black psi-armor. Her hair, black on top, silvery-grey at the sides, had been cut short. She'd have thought it a pixie, but the woman looked too adult to be considered 'cute.' According to the augmented reality nameplate floating over her head, the approaching woman was Area Chief Helena Larson, equivalent to a brigadier general.

Both Kirsten and Arroyo rendered salutes, though the Commander's was almost casual by comparison, as was Larson's.

"What's this I hear about ghost recon?" Chief Larson's boots clanked on the ramp, falling silent once she reached the plastisteel ground.

Kirsten gave her a brief overview of Dorian and his plan to look around inside.

"I see." Chief Larson gestured at the cluster of tactical officers. "Our insertion teams have been evaluating an entry plan, and so far they're telling me they can't see a way in short of rushing the front door and kicking off the fireworks. It would be quite helpful if this ghost of yours happened to exist."

"I assure you, ma'am. He exists." She twisted left, watching the tactical squad argue with each other. One woman's voice rose above the din, pointing out an old access shaft from the building's boiler room down into the city plate. They crowded closer, poring over a large holographic screen. Dorian emerged from the front of the building and jogged toward her. "He's coming back now."

A shrill scream reminiscent of a classic horror movie bimbo rang out.

All eyes turned to an adjacent alley, where a man in a tattered coat sat up out of a pile of trash, one leg still inside a plastiboard box, his face a mask of sheer terror. He went cross-eyed as perhaps a hundred individuals scanned his surface thoughts—the telepathic chaos made Kirsten wince. The connection dropped as he fainted.

He's afraid of cops. She almost laughed, but felt guilty about it.

Dorian walked up next to her. "Well, it's not a setup. There are six people holding four hostages in a boiler room a level below the street. One of the hostage takers is operating a portable terminal tapped into the security system of the building. I eavesdropped for a bit. Sounds like their plan is to flee through the Beneath at the first sign of entry. The hostages are lined up against the left wall, secured to pipes with cheap physical handcuffs."—he mimicked someone forced to hug a column—"Probably ordered them on the spur of the moment from a sex shop."

Kirsten suppressed a shiver at the memory of Konstantin's 'dungeon,' and relayed Dorian's description to Larson and Arroyo.

"What sort of weapons do they have?" asked Larson.

"One of the suspects is a minor boy, who is not armed. The rest have an assortment of handguns, small automatic weapons, and one woman is carrying a katana. None of them noticed me, though they all reacted to my presence."

Kirsten repeated his assessment.

"Did your ghost hear any of their intentions?" asked Chief Larson.

Dorian nodded. "Yes. The boy appears to be a telepath who the others believe strong enough to erase the hostages' hatred of psionics." He shied away from Kirsten's glare. "He's about Evan's age."

"Something wrong, Agent?" asked Arroyo.

"Commander..." She took a breath to keep herself as calm as possible. "Dorian says the juvenile suspect is... only around nine or ten years old."

Both Larson and Arroyo mumbled curses under their breath.

"That's just fucking wonderful." Arroyo glared at the floor. "Wren, you're not to let word of this reach the NewsNet people."

"That's over her skill set, Miguel." Larson glanced at her armband computer. "Ashford is on the way, but we need to get everyone out of there first... preferably alive."

Arroyo's caramel-hued face paled several shades. "Understood, Ma'am."

"Any other kids?" asked Kirsten.

"One of the hostages looks young. Maybe twelve to fourteen." Dorian kicked the toe of his non-boot at the ground. "Of the four, she's the only one not spewing a steady stream of condemnation at them. She kept her head down."

"Probably terrified." Kirsten fumed to herself. "Her parents load her up with bullshit and then we have idiots proving them right."

"Hell with that," said a deep voice from the tactical team.

"It's the only way in." A female officer pointed at the schematic hovering in midair on a blue light panel. "Enter at this point, travel to this ladder, down to the surface, cross to this other ladder three hundred meters west, then back up here and here."

"For a bunch of bible beaters?" The big man shook his head. "Hell with that, Apps, I ain't risking my team down there."

The tactical group fell into a debate about the dangers of The Beneath, though it seemed only one of them—Tactical Officer II Appleton, E., according to Wren's display—was willing to consider the long way around. Comm chatter started up around Chief Larson looking for estimates on how long it would take a telepath of bare-minimum skill to reprogram the church members. Responses couldn't come to a consensus; everyone kept saying it would be impossible to tell without knowledge of the boy's ability... guesses ranged from forty minutes per person to five.

A clinical male voice with the tone of a university professor silenced the comm channel. "The crucial issue is how deep-seated the hatred lies. If an individual has a specific reason to dislike psionics, such as a prior personal trauma, it would take far longer to negate. Someone merely following the crowd could be made to forget in less than a minute. Of course, my mechanism is replacing memory with blank space... which is far more permanent than constructing fictional reality overlays transparent enough to avoid the slow erosion of dissonance from peeling them away."

Kirsten looked down as dozens of Division 0 personnel succumbed to fearful silence at the words of Lieutenant Commander Ashford.

"Ma'am." Kirsten looked over at Larson. It struck her odd not to have to peer upward at someone in a position of authority. Even kindly Director Carter, head of all of Division 0, made her feel tiny. "If the tactical team rushes the front door, the suspects will be gone before they make it to the basement. Even if we deprogram anything that boy does, it could give the impression of interference."

"You sound like Carter now." Dorian smirked.

"I'd like to try to get in from the Beneath." Kirsten glanced at the building. "I'm a suggestive, Ma'am. If I'm being ordered to skirt ethical boundaries already, I'd prefer to influence the HTs to stand down."

"You've no qualms about going under the plate?" Chief Larson blinked.

"No. The feelings of unease psionics get down there is due to a large amount of spirits. Most of the rumors of mutants and monsters, are fiction. It's not a problem for me... I've, umm, spent a lot of time down there before."

Arroyo waved at the air. "Appleton."

A woman in black psi armor jogged over. Like Kirsten, blonde, though her jaw and overall stature hinted at Nordic ancestry, leaving Kirsten eye-to-breast with her. She exchanged salutes with the three of them. "Sir?"

Kirsten's came slow. *Right. I'm technically a commissioned officer.*

"Still up for going underground?" asked Arroyo.

Appleton nodded without hesitation. "Yes, sir."

"This is Agent Wren, I-Ops."

"Agent." Appleton saluted her again. "It's a pleasure to meet you. I've been following your mission reports for some time."

"Looks like you have a fan club." Dorian winked.

"Uhh. Thanks. We're going through the Beneath. Ready?"

Tactical Officer II Appleton nodded. "Yes, ma'am."

"If anything looks like it's going out of control, we're kicking down the front door." Larson gave Kirsten a 'be careful' stare, then trotted back up into the mobile command trailer.

A nav dot opened in Kirsten's heads-up display as Appleton set up a waypoint to the hatch cover. The route required going all the way to the natural Earth below the city due to the presence of a 'hard wall,' a point where city plate construction had stalled for a decade or two when people believed the project to be finished, only to have construction pick up and keep going. The nearest passage in the barrier between plate interiors was over three miles away, a prohibitive trek on foot.

They hurried down the street, turned right two blocks later, and headed into an alley.

"What idiot designed this?" Kirsten grumbled. "No interior connections for miles?"

Appleton squatted over the access hatch leading down into the plate. "Probably the same geniuses who got the idea to build a city on fifty-meter stilts."

"Uniform flat surface." She rolled her eyes. "Something about maximizing efficiency to cram a giant nation's worth of people into two cities. I still think they brought so much asteroid-mined metal down here they threw off the orbit of the planet."

"So you're not afraid of the stories?" Appleton grabbed the rubberized handle, gave it a twist, and hauled the squarish hatch plate open. It rose on motorized struts with a soft hiss, emitting vaporous fog laced with a rotten-raspberry stink. "About what's down there?"

"Nope." Kirsten stared at the hole, out of nowhere feeling ten years old again. "First time I went down there, I didn't know any better, and I didn't have any weapons." She put a boot on the first rung of the ladder. *Or shoes...*

"Heh. What did they send you under the city for?" Appleton hopped on as soon as Kirsten had descended enough to make room. "Someone hiding out?"

"Yeah. Me. I was ten." Kirsten descended twenty-four meters of sticky metal rungs, caked with all manner of industrial chemicals.

"Aww. That's so sad. I kinda freaked out when Zero showed up at my door too, but I didn't run off."

"I wasn't hiding from them. I didn't even know they existed." Kirsten stepped away from the base of the ladder and checked her armguard. She turned to face the navigation trail, ignoring the ‹no signal› warning at the top of the holographic screen floating over her forearm. A few feeble LED bulbs in brick-sized cages dotted the dark maze of pipes and passageways. Her toes clutched the inside of her boots at the memory of how it had felt to walk on the metal grating barefoot.

Dorian settled at her left. "You okay?"

"Fine."

"What?" asked Appleton, jumping the last three rungs. The *clomp* of her boots echoed in the metal cavern.

"Talking to Dorian."

Appleton looked around. "That didn't go over comms."

"I know. He's right next to me."

"Oh!" Appleton laughed. "A ghost right? Hey, it's okay if you wanna hang back."

"I'm not afraid of anything in the Beneath. It's full of ghosts and I'm not worried about them." Kirsten stepped over pieces of a broken wire conduit and headed along the passage indicated by the computer.

"I meant once we get into the building." Appleton grumbled. "For what it's worth, I don't think it's right they send thirteen-year-olds into the field. Your parents must be worried to death."

Kirsten stopped.

"Oh, shit," said Dorian.

"I'm twenty-two." Kirsten glanced back at the taller woman. "I came down here to get away from my mother." She paused.

Appleton pursed her lips. "Well. Okay. I'm an idiot. I can't come up with anything to say back."

"The last thing you should think about right now is your mother." Dorian glided in front of her. Her shoulders chilled at his attempt to squeeze them. "Those hostages have simi—"

Kirsten stormed through him. "I know. I know."

He burst into a rolling cloud of silvery energy for an instant before he coalesced 'solid' again, facing her.

"What?" asked Appleton, jogging to catch up.

"Dorian is worried I'm going to do something stupid because these idiots are bible-beating shitheads like my mother. She almost killed me when I was little because she thought psionics were the Devil's work."

"Aww."

Kirsten whirled on her. "I don't need your pity. At least, not anymore... I'm over it."

Dorian shot her a disbelieving smirk.

"Sorry, ma'am." Appleton sighed.

"Okay, maybe I'm on edge. Sorry. I tend to get a little pissy around religious people."

Dorian made a pinching gesture in the air.

She couldn't quite laugh at the face he made, but it helped her mood. Kirsten resumed walking. Two minutes later, she paused at the top of the ladder leading from the bottom of the city plate to the natural ground about fifty meters farther down. "I was a pretty pathetic sight back then, but I'm not that terrified little kid anymore."

"Astrals are pretty rare. How old were you when you drew field?"

Kirsten lowered herself over the edge. "Sixteen. You?"

"Eighteen. Got discovered by accident at a varsity Gee-ball game."

"Gee-ball?" Kirsten stopped and looked up. "You played Gee-ball?" Before Appleton stepped on her helmet, she hurried downward again.

"High school, yeah. Everyone thought I was a phenom, until Coach Farkas from the *Star Smashers* watched the game video in slow mo."

"Star Smashers? The way you said that makes me think rival." Kirsten disabled the suit's active infrared night vision and concentrated on Darksight. In seconds, a narrow 'flashlight tunnel' of vision expanded to miles and miles of old, ruined civilization. Several high-rise buildings lay in ruins, no doubt victimized by century-past earthquakes that the floating city barely noticed. "Wow… This used to be a pretty big city here."

Appleton paused long enough to check her armband computer. "Uhh, Sacramento I think it was called, and yeah. Smashers were my school's primary rival going back like seventy years. Bastard shit all over my dreams and threatened to sue me and the school for cheating."

"Telekinetic?" Kirsten groaned at the expanse of ladder below, grateful that scaling the side of a fifty-meter tall support column as wide as a small house didn't trip a fear of heights. *Guess I left my fear of heights on an advert bot.*

"Nope. I've got a specialized form of precognition. It works subconsciously. Farkas saw me react to one of his players before the kid moved. He found like sixty video clips of me doing that and took it to Division 0 to complain I was cheating."

"Precognitive Imminence." Kirsten stepped off the base of the ladder onto rough macadam chunks, the carcass of a street that hadn't seen a functional car in centuries. She lost a few seconds staring upward at a dingy steel sky, fifty meters overhead, as far as she could see in every direction. At least thirty spirits popped up here and there, curious about the intrusion. A few recognized her and waved. "Ugh. Sorry."

Appleton slung a laser rifle off her back after letting go of the ladder. "Was a mess. Farkas wanted me charged with a crime, wanted the last thirteen games changed to forfeits, and tried to sue the school."

Dorian clucked his tongue. "Sore loser."

"That Farkas guy sounds like a real asshole." Kirsten frowned at the destroyed city. "Bet that ability comes in handy in a fight though."

"Yeah. Zero recruited me while I was still a junior. They let me finish school first. Turned out I'm a kinetic too."

"Predict often goes hand in hand with kinetics." Dorian exchanged stares with a few ghosts in gang regalia.

"Predict?" Kirsten took a long step over a puddle of black sludge. *Last time I trusted one of those to be only an inch deep, I went under.* She shuddered.

"You say 'precognitive imminence' ten times fast in a policy meeting." Dorian winked.

Appleton started to walk past her to take point, but stopped. "Your eyes are glowing white."

"Yep. I'm looking into the astral realm so I can see in the dark. Wider field than NV. Course, no color... but NV is all green so it's not much of a difference."

"You see anything?" Appleton swept her rifle around. "Supposed to be all sorts of crazy people down here."

"There are, but only spirits are near us now."

"I can feel them." Appleton shivered, but her expression gave off excitement. "That's pretty normal, isn't it? For psionics to 'sense' ghosts and stuff even if we can't see them."

"Yep."

"Why are you looking at me like that?"

Kirsten laughed. "I'm not used to people being so friendly. Somewhere between 'sees ghosts' and 'has a rating in Mind Blast,' people usually run like hell."

"Aww." Appleton gave her a sympathetic look. "Sorry. You're adorable. I feel lousy you get treated bad."

Kirsten clenched her jaw. *She means well.* "Thanks, but please stop treating me like a little girl."

"But you *are* adorable." Dorian grinned.

Appleton got up to a light run, following the old street. Few cars remained other than ones destroyed in the Corporate War. Anyone who'd had anything functional drove out as the city grew overhead a century and change ago. They passed old storefronts and office buildings on both sides, as well as a dentist's office and an ancient car dealership. Strange light shimmered around Dorian, wafting off his arms. The scent of wood-smoke and barbecue gave away a cook fire somewhere close, though Kirsten didn't want to know what kind of meat it was.

"What's that?" Appleton's voice quivered. "It just went from feeling a little creepy to feeling like a serial killer's sneaking up behind me."

"Dorian probably sensed someone coming, so he's throwing off fear."

"Six men, two blocks up on the right." Dorian pointed.

Kirsten patted Appleton on the arm and gestured at a group of men in shredded clothing made from old tarps and scrap cloth. They didn't look crazy-in-the-eye enough to be Discarded, probably only nomads. She made sure they saw her glowing eyes. "Up there. Bunch of locals. Shouldn't be a problem."

The men sank back into the darkness.

"What are they running from?"

Kirsten grinned. "The people who live down here have their own batch of stories and legends. Glowing eyes means I'm either a demon or an android that'll tear them apart. I even had someone call me an 'ancient goddess' once."

She glanced up as their progress dot on the nav map lined up with the 'hard wall' between city plates. From below, it looked like a trapezoid-shaped ridge running the length of the metal sky. Some committee of the past had expected the elevated city to stop here who knows how long ago... but the population kept on growing. *Why didn't they build on the ground? Guess it's easier to keep doing what you're familiar with even if it costs more.* She imagined the politicians spouting justifications—creating jobs, compatible with existing infrastructure, blah blah.

Appleton gestured to the right, raised her rifle, and soldier-walked into what had once been an alley between a café and an auto mechanic's garage. Kirsten left off a mental sigh at the coffee shop. Nicole had teased her with the suggestion of a strawberry latte that they never had the time to order.

The way up clung to the side of another of the massive support columns, which plunged down into the ceiling of a four-story retirement home. Appleton headed for the main entrance and kicked the door open on the first try, hard enough to cause it to fall off its hinges after slamming into the wall.

"Damn."

Appleton winked. "Kinetics. Playing sports in school, I never knew I had abilities... just always had this knack for anticipating what the other players were going to do. Training helped me tap other potentials. Good thing I didn't know how to use Kinetics in school or I'd have hurt people."

"So you're like a doll?" Kirsten stepped over the broken door.

"Hah. I wish. Not even close to that much power. I'm stronger than people expect me to be, but only in quick bursts. Probably could make myself stronger than a normal person could be... but I can't touch a doll for raw power. I use it more for speed anyway."

Two elderly women's spirits stood by the door to the stairwell, arguing over slippers. Each thought the other responsible for taking the other's footwear; both brandished colostomy bags as if about to use them as weapons of war.

Appleton tensed. "Feels creepier in here."

"Some ghosts arguing over shoes. One probably kicked them under the bed without noticing and assumed they were taken." Kirsten waved at them.

The ghosts exchanged a glance, ceased bickering, and hurried off down the hallway to a room.

"You are truly here to help everyone," said Dorian.

Appleton led the way to the third floor, where they found a twenty-five-foot wide city-support column in a long-abandoned cafeteria, spearing down into the basement. The floor near the hole looked iffy, but it tolerated their weight long enough for them to jump one after the other onto the ladder. Kirsten hurried to keep up with Appleton, who flew up the rungs at an almost superhuman pace. The woman relaxed a little once they'd reached the interior of the next plate.

"There's a lot of ghosts down there, huh?"

Kirsten offered a sad smile. "Yeah. Some of them were ghosts a long time before the war."

She checked the armband display. Sixty-three meters ahead, their target, an unoccupied residence tower, waited. Kirsten trotted along a corridor of blue-tinted plastisteel that flickered in the feeble glow from brick-sized LEDs every twenty feet near the ceiling. A bulkhead door at the end led to a crossing hall. She headed to the right, and ten meters later, ducked left past another door into another long straightaway. Storage cabinets on the left held jumpsuits, tools, and parts for city maintenance workers. Kirsten jogged to the end, where a metal door led to a chamber that connected to the underground portion of the building—well, underground in the sense of being below the surface of the city 'floor.'

The tall woman readied her rifle and slowed to a creep.

"What?" whispered Kirsten, hand on her E-90.

Appleton's reply came over near-channel comms, inaudible outside of her helmet. "Not sure what's waiting for us inside. If they're anticipating this as their exit route, they're going to have rigged it."

She glanced at Dorian and gestured at the door before a few eye-flicks at the HUD menu turned off her helmet's external speaker. "Dorian is checking."

"Can he spot cameras or electronics?" Appleton looked back.

"Yeah. He's a ghost. They can feel electricity, and he can kill any electronic gadgets he wants."

Appleton nodded and edged up to the door. Kirsten followed close. Distant shouting echoed from the other side, primarily a woman shrieking what sounded like biblical verse. The tone of it made Kirsten's blood hot within a microsecond.

Idiot. She's inches from being shot in the face and she's taunting them.

Dorian exuded out of the wall, stretching a little before he snapped free, looking blurry. It took him a second to shake it off and return to solidity. "Clean. They're not even watching the top of the stairs."

"Stairs?" Kirsten blinked. "Not a ladder?"

Appleton cringed at her speaking aloud. Over the comm, she whispered, "Quiet. They'll hear us coming."

"Looks like the property owner installed the water heaters, network room, and battery farm below street level." Dorian gestured at the door. "The physical plant is right through there."

Kirsten switched back to comms. "Clear inside. No electronics or people. Stairway at the far left. It's a basement."

"On three."

"Go." Kirsten pulled her sidearm and held it in two hands.

Three seconds later, Appleton flung the door open and speed-walked inside behind her rifle. Kirsten followed, aiming side-to-side at large boxy machines in two rows. Thick pipes came down from the ceiling to the ones on the left, a rat's nest of wires tangled around the smaller units on the right.

Dorian strolled by. "Give me a moment. I'm going to kill the batteries in their weapons."

Kirsten gave him a thumbs-up. "Apps?"

"Hmm?" The woman glanced back and chuckled. "Where'd you hear that?"

"The guy that didn't wanna go down here wasn't too quiet about it. Dorian's going up to suck the power out of their guns."

Appleton's eyes widened. "He can do that!? I'm stealing him."

Kirsten laughed.

A few minutes later, Dorian emerged from a plain metal door at the far end of the room, and nodded. He had a wild-eyed, overcaffeinated look about him. "I can't fully disarm the woman with the vibrosword. There's no juice left in the E-mag, so it's a normal blade now. About her height, thin, dark skinned."

Oh, he's going to do something bad with all that excess energy. Good thing he's not like Theo. "Clear. One woman with a sword."

"Vibro?" asked Appleton.

"Not anymore," said Kirsten and Dorian at the same time.

Kirsten eased the door open and peered up half of a switchback staircase. "Battery's gone. She could reload if she's got spares."

Dorian twitched. "They're dead too." He twitched again. "All five of them."

"Or not. Looks like he's got them under control."

A light banging came from above.

"Damn piece of shit," said a man with a trace of a Spanish accent.

"What's up?" asked a deeper voice.

"Damn terminal was freakin' out."

"I felt it too," said a quiet female. "Like we weren't alone in here. Felt that way ever since we went down the stairs."

"Will you cut that spooky shit out?" yelled a shaky voice that made her think teenaged boy. "It ain't funny at the dive, and it ain't funny here."

"It's not too late," wailed another woman who sounded older or at least huskier than the first. "The fires of Hell are lapping at your heels. You may be redeemed if you submit to Him."

"Stevie, get started on that hag first," said the deep voice.

"I don't wanna." A young boy sniffled. "She's crazy. There's a nightmare in her head. She wants me to die in a fire."

Kirsten crept up the stairs, anger pushing her ahead of Appleton. At the landing between the two sections of stairway, outside communications picked back up, and with it, Chief Larson asking for a status update.

"Chief," said Kirsten. "We're inside. You should have video now."

"Copy that, Wren. Proceed with caution."

"Understood, Chief." Kirsten tiptoed up the last ten steps, halting at a half-closed door.

The four-inch gap offered a view of a wall of old pipes in a room that housed the interface between the building and the city water/sewer systems. Two men in their thirties, one fair-skinned, one as dark as Captain Eze, stood with their hands cuffed around thick pipes. Both had the attire of office workers, light shirts with a strip of buttons leading from the left shoulder straight down to the beltline and plain blue pants. They glared at other people out of sight, muttering the occasional oath to God. To their left, closer to the door, a wild-eyed woman with semi-curly brown hair and a faux-denim jacket over a peach colored dress also had her hands cuffed around a pipe, but kept pointing while she shouted about how these people were sent by Satan and they had no power over her.

Nearest Kirsten, a young teenage girl with long, light-brown hair clung to another vertical pipe. She'd lost one flip-flop during the abduction, and her puffy green jacket and jean shorts bore numerous dark smudges the same shade of grey as a smear on her left cheek. The shortness of her arms and the size of the pipe kept the chain on her handcuffs taut and her hands red. She didn't seem able to move much at all, though she appeared the calmest of the prisoners. Eyes downcast, she almost gave off a feeling of boredom... or resignation that people she'd been brought up to think of as *creatures* would murder her for sure.

Electronics in Kirsten's helmet created amber ghosts where the system detected people inside the room. One man sat at a desk thirty feet away, two others paced about near the center of the room. A slender female shape with a katana handle sticking off her back lounged on a desk closer to the hostages, and a child-sized outline four feet away from the screaming woman fidgeted and bounced as if he really had to pee.

"You getting this, Apps?" asked Kirsten.

"Yep. You're sure your friend's trick works?"

Kirsten nodded. "Yep. There's at least six bullets I can think of that aren't in me because of him. The suspects are psionic though, so they're far from disarmed."

"Maybe they're all clairvoyants or telempaths?" asked Appleton.

"Hey, empaths are dangerous," said an unknown male voice on the comm channel.

"Yeah, Apps," replied the deep-voiced guy who refused to go into the Beneath. "Don't let Director Carter hear you say empaths are wimpy."

"No matter what you Hellspawn do, you will not be able to make me forget Him," shrieked the woman. She rattled her handcuffs, pointing. "Shame on you, taking the form of a child. I see through your lies. Begone, demon!"

Kirsten extended a fiberoptic from her left forearm and poked it around the edge of the door. The maybe-thirteen-year-old hostage looked up, made eye contact with Kirsten, but didn't react except to flash a faint smile.

Using the probe, Kirsten peeked at the room. A tall, blond man in his middle twenties and a Chinese man close in age loomed over a bookish looking child of about ten or eleven. He seemed a little older than Evan, and stood with his hands in his pants pockets, staring down. The woman on the desk had long, black hair and dark brown skin, delicate features hinted at Asian Indian mixed with African. The man at the desk had a deep tan and thick, black hair and such a look of focus at the screen in front of him she wondered if he'd even notice their entry. Near his workstation, a skinny man in his later teens paced back and forth, rubbing his face and emitting a repeating whine of "oh, man." All six had the grungy, shredded clothing of off-gridders.

"Apps... the girl with the sword's gotta be another kinetic. Only reason she'd be carrying a blade like that. Looks agile as hell."

"Don't astrals carry swords too?" asked another unknown voice on the comm.

"Dorian was walking all over the place and she didn't spot him. She's not an astral."

"Negative hits on any of them," said a female voice so young she sounded childlike. "They're not in the system."

"Put your mother on the line, sweetie," said a guy.

Lieutenant Commander Arroyo coughed. "Stop teasing the admin cadets, Sanchez, or I'll give you her dispatcher's terminal for a month."

"Sorry, sir."

"Shit," said Appleton. "No flashbangs."

"I got it." Dorian winked, a manic grin spreading over his face.

"On three," said Kirsten. "We don't need a flash. Distraction incoming."

Dorian sauntered over to the screaming woman, still rambling about hell and brimstone. He looked at Kirsten with an almost regretful stare, as though he wished he could've done something like this for her years before. After a three count, Dorian's body shimmered and became transparent—a sign he had manifested in the mortal world.

"Will you shut the hell up!" yelled Dorian.

Everyone froze, staring agape.

Kirsten burst in the door, E-90 raised. "Police! Division 0! Drop your weapons."

Appleton followed, covering the right side of the room. Her focus seemed to be the twitchy-looking kid about eighteen with a jacket on over no shirt, and ripped white pants. "Lasers are faster than psionics, people. Let's keep this from getting messy."

Dorian released the manifestation. To Kirsten, he seemed to stop glowing and went solid like a normal person. To everyone else, he must've popped out of existence. The room dimmed. The young hostage screamed and strained against the metal around her wrists. Both men gawked; the dark-skinned man looked about ready to tear the pipe down to get away. He shouted a continuous, repeating cadence of, "Oh, Lord Jesus Christ!" while hurling his weight against his restraint.

Urine spread out in a pool at the formerly ranting woman's feet; pale faced and slack-jawed, she continued to gape at the air where Dorian had appeared.

The boy held his hands up. "Please don't kill me!"

Appleton melted into a smear of color an instant before the sinewy woman blurred off the desk into a charge. The tall blonde darted in front of Kirsten in time to knock the katana aside with her rifle. Kirsten hurried to the right, swiveling to aim at the Chinese guy near the boy who stared at her with too much concentration. His surface thoughts gave away his intent to light her on fire with pyrokinesis.

She glared at him. *What are you doing? It would take you hours to generate enough heat to melt this armor.* Her eyes flared with psionic energy. "Surrender."

He raised his hands and got down on the floor.

The swordswoman recovered her balance. Appleton ducked a half second before the woman even moved; the katana swiped sideways over her helmet in a wicked slash, unbalancing her from so much force striking nothing but air.

Appleton lunged upward. She started a punch with her left arm, but grabbed her rifle in both hands and smashed it the other way forward into empty air; the sword-wielding woman jumped face first into the butt end in her effort to dodge the punch that didn't finish. The strike knocked the insubstantial woman off her feet, blood trailing from her nose, and sent the sword flying.

Kirsten floated off the ground. The skinny teen ran over, put his hands on her, and the air filled with the smell of ozone as little electric sparks danced about his fingers, but failed to have an effect thanks to the sealed psi armor. She pointed the E-90 at the blond man, who appeared to be the only one concentrating. When her surface thought skim confirmed him responsible for telekinesis, she shot him in the right thigh. The azure beam flickered for a quarter of a second, leaving a smoking hole on both sides of his pants and a glowing orange dot on the floor.

Her weight fell back on her feet as the man collapsed, clutching the wound and screaming. The skinny kid pulled a knife. Kirsten pivoted, letting his strike skim across the abdomen of her armored vest, and put the tip of her E-90 to his ear.

"Drop the goddamned knife."

Clank.

"Good boy. *Lie on your stomach.*"

Her suggestion overwhelmed his mind; protesting muscles shaking, he dropped to his knees like a malfunctioning robot before falling forward onto his chest.

A ripple of energy swam over Kirsten's brain. She latched on to it, trying to fight it off, but the incoming telepathy felt somewhat stronger than hers, slipping into her thoughts like a gradual loss at arm wrestling. Panic built up, but dissipated as the feeling stopped.

"She's not gonna hurt us!" yelled the boy. "Come on, guys. Stop."

"Bullshit," yelled the blond man. "She fucking shot me."

"In the leg," screamed the boy. "She could'a shot you in the heart."

Appleton pointed her rifle at the man by the terminal who'd gotten one hand on a submachine gun hanging over his shoulder. "Don't even."

"*No hablo Inglés,*" said the man in the chair.

She fired a green beam past his head into the wall. "Do you fuckin' *hablo* laser?"

Hands up, the small boy burst into tears. "Please stop!"

Kirsten glanced at the whimpering teen chained to the huge pipe. *Don't be afraid of what you saw. It's a ghost. He's a friend.*

The girl looked up, dark brown eyes set in skin the color of a porcelain doll brimmed with terror. She seemed to sense the concern in Kirsten and stopped trying to tear the handcuffs apart, though they kept her grip on the pipe so tight she couldn't slide down.

"*On the floor.*" Kirsten's eyes flickered as she fired a suggestion into the brain of the hacker.

He slithered out of the chair and got down.

Appleton cleared the distance to the howling blond man in three steps, kicked a gun away from him, and forced him over onto his chest before cuffing him and putting a psi inhibitor headband on him. He howled in pain the whole time. "Kirsten, you got any inhibitors?"

"One."

"Sword girl's probably the next biggest threat. She won't stay out forever."

Kirsten opened the belt compartment containing her inhibitor, a two-inch box. At the squeeze of a button, segments extended from both ends and formed a thin metal ring. With the blond man contained, the sword-toting woman unconscious, and the other three hugging floor under psionic compulsion, Kirsten lowered her guard for an instant to put the sword-bearer in binders and fix the psi inhibitor on her head.

"God sees through your lies." The frazzle-haired woman glared at Kirsten. "You try to deceive us. Both of you are just as demon-tainted as the beasts who have abducted us. We shall not fall for your treachery."

"*Shut up.*" Kirsten glared at her, barely containing her rage at encountering Mother all over again, only without the burning, beating, and locked closet doors. She narrowed her eyes.

A flurry of activity on the comm channel pierced the chaos of Kirsten's adrenaline-jacked thoughts. The tactical team was inbound, and would be on site in fifteen seconds. She kept a wary eye on the psionics, not willing to relax even though the situation seemed neutralized. At any second, one of the suggestees might shrug off her compulsion.

The boy walked over, keeping his hands up, and pointed at the blond man. "I didn't wanna do it. My brother Carl made me." Color faded from his cheeks. "Please don't put one of those things on my head. I swear I'll be good."

Dorian sighed. "The only way he'd be that scared of an inhibitor is if someone used one on him before… and left it there too long."

"Bullshit," muttered the black man tethered to a pipe.

Kirsten ignored the zealot. "I'm sorry, Stephen. Did someone hurt you with one of those before?"

"I saw into the head of a girl they put one on." He shivered. "I don't wanna go crazy. Please. I swear I won't do anything bad."

Feeling a bit like Nicole for her wanton disregard for personal ethics, Kirsten probed the boy's surface thoughts, and felt both a little surprised as well as relieved that he hadn't lied. She pointed at a desk. "Sit there and don't make eye contact with anyone."

"Yes, ma'am." He climbed up.

The interior double doors burst open, admitting over twenty Division 0 tactical officers in full armor with rifles. Since everything that had happened —except for Dorian—went over comms and video, Kirsten holstered her weapon, confident the troops knew what to expect.

"Ops, Wren. The male juvenile was coerced into using his telepathy. I confirmed intent with a shallow read. He's another victim here." She pulled her utility knife from her belt, a tiny Nano blade in a protective shroud, but couldn't pry the handcuff chain binding the girl away from the pipe far enough to get the end of the housing under it.

"Ow," whined the girl. "I can't feel my hands anymore."

"Dorian, is there anything in this pipe? Can I shoot it?"

Stephen looked over. "Roy's got the keys."

"Which one's Roy?" asked Kirsten.

The boy pointed at the Chinese man. Two officers struggled trying to secure him, but the scrawny man fought hard. After a few seconds, one of the officers tapped him on the head with a stunrod. Roy went limp, blue lightning flickering from his eyes. Kirsten trotted over and fished handcuff keys out of his pocket.

"That's much safer than doing it with an E-90." Dorian smiled.

She hurried back to the whimpering girl, who tried to keep both feet on top of her one flip-flop to avoid the spreading urine puddle. The woman beside her continued glaring at Kirsten, face contorted from her mental battle against the order to shut up.

"Wren, this is Chief Larson."

"Go ahead, Chief." Kirsten stuck the key in the cuff around the girl's right wrist.

"Keep the hostages secure for the time being. Ashford is on the way down."

"Chief?" Kirsten blinked. "The scene is secure."

"We appreciate your effort, Agent. Unfortunately, given the volatile nature of the individuals involved, we believe it best for them not to remember this incident."

Kirsten stared at the cuff for three seconds, and turned the key anyway. "Chief, all due respect, but this girl's hands are purple. She's going to have nerve damage if I leave her like this any longer."

As soon as the hasp opened, the teen fell to the side, and hopped a short distance to dry ground where she collapsed on her knees. Kirsten followed and unlocked the other cuff. She couldn't imagine such a young face hating her for being psionic, though the girl's expression held only gratitude.

"I understand, Agent. All I'm saying is make sure the members of that so-called church are still there when Ashford arrives."

The female hostage sneered. "You're going to burn. Demons, all of you."

The teen scowled at the woman, then whispered, "I don't hate you. I just act like it so they don't hit me. Please don't tell them. My grandfather will kill me."

Kirsten squeezed her shoulder before glaring at the shouting woman.

Cuffs rattled as the frantic, wild-eyed zealot pointed at her with both hands. "You're one of them. Oh, we are doomed. Satan's minions walk the face of the Earth. They have infiltrated the houses of power, and the masses are blinded by his charms and lies."

Kirsten glared.

"K... don't." Dorian glided over.

"Count down from one million." Kirsten scowled. *"In your head."*

The brown-haired hate-preacher took on a look of intense concentration.

Dorian chuckled. "That'll wear off long before she's anywhere near done, but nice."

A handful of tactical officers clapped.

Kirsten examined the teen's wrists and decided to give her a stimpak. A few seconds after tossing the empty autoinjector to the side, the nanobots did their magic, and bleeding lacerations faded to angry bruises.

Ashford swept in the door like Count Dracula himself come to take his blood tax. The pallid man couldn't have been forty yet, but he seemed older. Short, wavy black hair framed a face as pale as a dead man. Everyone in armor near the entrance shied away from him and found things to do in seconds. His too-serious expression softened a touch when he made eye contact with Kirsten.

"Who's that?" whispered the girl.

"He's our public relations man," said Dorian.

Kirsten smirked. "He's going to make sure that the people who kidnapped you haven't done anything to your heads. Implanted any long-lasting effects or anything illegal."

The girl shivered. "I'm scared. I'm only thirteen. Don't you have to get my parents okay first?"

Kirsten closed her eyes, feeling as much like a piece of shit as she ever had in her life. What they were about to do to these people, detestable as they were, bothered her enough. *Lying* to a child about it reached a new low.

Lieutenant Commander Ashford walked over and stood beside them. "Agent Wren, a pleasant surprise. May I ask why you look so grim?"

She didn't expect much from giving the doe-eyes to a man in his position. Not that he was cruel, but he had a reputation for obeying orders to the letter. A flicker of telepathy caressed her mind, so gentle she almost didn't notice. He looked at the girl, still sprawled at the floor, and smiled.

Don't feel guilty, Wren. This one's not a problem. He locked stares with the teen for a few seconds, and she nodded. *All set.*

Kirsten wanted to throw up. *What did you do?*

Ashford turned toward the other hostages, but paused in mid stride. *Merely asked her if she could keep what happened today a secret.*

Seriously? That's it? Kirsten blinked.

He smiled. *I trust her. She is good at keeping secrets.*

"Come on." Kirsten helped the girl up. "Let's get you out of here."

"Okay." The girl took off her remaining flip-flop and held it. She glanced at the others. "What's he going to do to them?"

"They won't remember being kidnapped. That's all. He's not going to change who they are."

The girl looked down.

"She almost seems disappointed." Dorian raised an eyebrow.

Kirsten looked around. "Where's the boy?"

"They took him out a few minutes ago." Dorian gestured at the door.

"I dunno," said the teen.

"Come on, kid."

"Ashley." She rubbed her wrists. "Thanks for, uhh, saving us."

"You don't believe the same as they do?"

"No. They're a bunch of assholes." Ashley kicked at empty plastic cartons in the hallway leading to the main entrance.

Kirsten glanced at Dorian. "Can we do anything?"

"Out of our purview unless the kid is psionic. She could file a complaint with Div 1."

"You wouldn't happen to be psionic?"

Ashley laughed. "Yeah right. My grandfather's in the Fundamentalist Church of the Redeemer. If I was psionic, I'd have been killed already."

"Are you being dramatic?" asked Kirsten.

Ashley padded along to the front door in silence, grimacing occasionally from stepping barefoot in something sticky. Once outside, surrounded by police, she stopped and looked up, shivering. "No. They wouldn't care about going to jail. If anyone in the church got found out as psionic, they'd be killed."

That kid is terrified. She's hiding... "If you're psionic, you can tell me. I can protect you."

"I... no." Tears ran down Ashley's face. She bolted to a run in the direction of a pair of medtechs walking over.

Kirsten fumed. "That kid is psionic... and scared shitless."

"Did you look?"

"No, but Ashford smiled. That's gotta mean something, right? The man never smiles."

"Wren," yelled Captain Eze. Fortunately, his tone sounded happy.

"We can't terminate custody because a dead man smiles." Dorian grinned. "Besides, she was just abducted by people she's grown up being told are evil incarnate. Of course she's terrified."

Kirsten folded her arms, watching Ashley escorted off by the man and woman in white medical jumpsuits. "This stinks." She trudged toward Eze's gleaming smile.

"Welcome back." Dorian winked. "I missed you."

4

ABERNATHY

Evan swung his feet back and forth at his desk, cheek mushed into his hand while using one finger to drag circles across a holographic screen that contained answers to questions on the left side about how plants converted sunlight into food. With every correct answer, the terminal played a one-to-two minute animation of the process. He knew if he got one wrong, he'd have to sit through a much longer rehash of the concept. If he got too many wrong, the teacher would pull him aside and ask a billion questions about how things were going at home. Tests and quizzes all had the same effect on him: sick to his stomach.

The teacher, Specialist Christopher Vasquez, paced back and forth in front of the desks, watching for suspicious gestures or fidgeting, which resulted in a surface thought skim to check for telepathic cheating.

Evan frowned while his screen displayed an animation of carbon dioxide molecules crashing into water molecules, bombarded by yellow arrows (sunlight). Evidently, the 'ethics' of warrantless brain diving didn't apply to school students suspected of cheating. He kept his head down, and guided chloroplasts into their place in the diagram while concentrating on bending reality to his will, attempting to stop Vasquez from looking at his head. No psionic could alter reality like that, but so much time in the Monwyn VR world gave him hope that some kind of magic might be real.

Every time he took a test, the same fear came back. Too many wrong answers equaled too many questions about home. Mom used to have nightmares and she was abused as a kid. If he failed a test, they'd assume something happened and no matter what he said, they'd take him away. He gulped down his fear. *Can't get any wrong. Why do they always think a failed test means problems at home?* A scowl formed on his face as he identified chlorophyll as what's necessary for the process to work.

Calm down, Evan. Specialist Vasquez's voice entered his mind. *No one is going to take you away from your mother for a bad test score.*

He looked up, meeting the man's grey eyes, wondering what he did to elicit a head poke.

The look on your face could've melted stone. Specialist Vasquez put on his most reassuring smile. *We can talk later if you like. It's far, far more complicated than one bad test. Please relax.*

Okay. Evan let the air out of his lungs and tried to stop worrying about being taken away. The judge lady had said Kirsten was legally his mother now. Maybe Vasquez had a point. Maybe he did worry too much. He pressed his left hand into his gut, trying to push down the unease, and took a few calming breaths. Minutes later, he'd finished three more questions, earning a perfect score, and pulled out his earbuds before curling over his desk with his head on his folded arms.

The classroom remained silent, save for the intermittent beeps of terminals registering other kids' touch commands. His class was relatively small, fourteen students total, and they'd likely be together as a group until they finished twelfth grade. Teachers would change, but the students wouldn't, barring new arrivals or 'bad stuff' happening.

At a strange feeling in the room, Evan sat up and looked around. A few seconds of concentration opened his eyes to the astral realm, and sure enough, the semitransparent figure of an older man entered wearing a black suit ripped up as if he'd been dragged over miles of thorn bushes.

The ghost looked older than Mom's father, about the same age as that creepy guy who had been trying to date her. Evan frowned at the memory of Konstantin as the apparition snuck up on the teacher. *I'm glad he went away.* Mom never said a word about what happened to him, but he stopped visiting and that suited him just fine.

The spirit pushed Vasquez's chair, making it spin a little and squeak.

Vasquez frowned at a dark-skinned boy in the front row. A second later, he looked confused. He gave a girl in the back row, another telekinetic, 'the eye,' but again seemed perplexed.

They're not TK-ing your chair.

The teacher raised an eyebrow at Evan's telepathic message.

Evan scooted down so he could hide his smile behind his arms. Abernathy the ghost pushed a plastic cup of e-pens off the edge of the desk. No one except Vasquez reacted, as they couldn't hear the clatter over the audio streaming into their ears.

Vasquez turned, grumbling, and paused when he faced Evan. The familiar tingle of surface thought skimming came on, but Evan didn't fight it. No doubt, the teacher had seen his eyes glowing white and by virtue of mind reading, knew what Abernathy looked like.

Rather than appearing scared, Vasquez sighed in exasperation. He left the pens where they landed, ignoring the event as though it hadn't occurred. The ghost stuck a hand into the teacher's terminal.

Oh great. He's messing with our homework again.

Vasquez picked up a small microphone, something that would relay his words into everyone's earbuds. "Five minutes."

Grumbling swept among the kids, with a few whines.

"Mr. Vasquez," yelled a girl in the middle. "Walter's trying to read my mind."

"Walter…" Vasquez frowned. "You've been warned once already to stop that. You know the tests are randomized. A class of four hundred could take this quiz six times and no two people will get the same questions. Not only does it betray a galling lack of ethics on your part, it's futile."

"Sorry, Mr. Vasquez." Walter looked down. "I didn't even get in. She's got a mind block on."

"Hailey's *always* got a mind block," said Shawn, a stocky kid with mocha skin and a body that belonged more in fifth grade than third. "She's so stupid she'd fail a pregnancy test."

Evan glanced at him sideways. *That's not fair. Girls have to take a test to get pregnant?*

The little black-haired girl whipped about in her seat and fixed Shawn with a glare that could've melted steel. Four seconds later, smoke began peeling from the boy's shirt, but stopped as soon as the teacher yelled.

"Hailey West!" yelled Vasquez. "No pyrokinesis in the classroom."

She burst into tears and faced forward. "But he called me stupid!"

Shawn swatted at his chest.

Vasquez pointed at her. "That is not how we deal with these situations. I'm slotting you in for a session with Dr. Yaz this afternoon."

Hailey pouted.

Shawn laughed.

"Mr. Fields." Vasquez's stare knocked the smile off the big kid's face. "You've earned yourself a debt of 50 citizenship points. Report to Sergeant Reed after class to clear some."

"Aww." Shawn grumbled.

"Well." Vasquez folded his arms. "Normally, this presentation is given a little later in the year, but I think it's probably close to time."

Abernathy wandered over to Evan and sat on the empty desk to his left. "Havin' fun, kid?"

"It's okay, I guess."

"Bah. You need to lighten up some or you'll grow up a serious old man like I was."

Vasquez went behind the teacher's workspace. As soon as he glanced at the terminal, his face turned bright red and he looked about ready to vomit or faint from embarrassment. He jammed his finger on a holographic button like a manic woodpecker until the glow of the one-way hologram panel on his face dimmed.

"What did you put on Vasquez's screen?" Evan wasn't sure what to make of a guy that looked like an old lawyer or banker, except for disheveled hair and sneakers that didn't belong with his expensive, though shredded, suit.

"Oh, just a few pictures with a farmer tending to his sheep and goats." Abernathy cackled. "Nothing interesting."

Evan squinted. "Why'd Vasquez wanna get them off his screen so fast if it was just goats?"

Abernathy whistled. "How should I know? Maybe the man doesn't like goats. Never trust a man who doesn't like goats, boy."

"Hey, look at Wren, talking to his ghosties again," said Shawn.

A few kids laughed, most remained disinterested. Hailey gave Evan an 'I hate that kid too' look.

"Stuff it, Fields," said Evan.

Vasquez cleared his throat. He hit a button on his terminal and a massive movie screen sized holo-panel unfurled in front of the class. Abernathy chuckled as soon as the title card 'Psionic Responsibilities' appeared.

"Oh, here comes the anti-bullying film." Abernathy overacted a yawn. "Seen it."

The mini movie opened to show a small Hispanic girl, black hair, light brown skin, perhaps six years old, trudging down the hallway of a school that looked much like their current surroundings. Words scrolled along the bottom: 'the following is a dramatization of actual events with actors.' According to the voice-over, Natalie Hernandez was placed in the dorms after being removed from a bad situation at home. Her parents were not prepared to deal with a psionic child.

Sullen, she kept her eyes aimed at the floor as she walked. Other kids teased her, pulled her hair, and seemed to want to give her a hard time.

"All of you possess special gifts. These gifts can be dangerous."

Natalie entered a classroom and took a seat in the front row. Small objects occasionally bounced off her head, thrown from behind. She never moved, flinched, or spoke. The camera panned in a slow circle around her.

"As you know," said the voice-over man, "our policy prohibits the public posting of information concerning a student's abilities, or past history." The camera panned around to reveal Natalie's face, her cheeks shimmering from tears.

Shawn sighed. "She's just sitting there and taking it. No wonder they pick on her. Crying never fixed anything."

About two-thirds of the class, and Evan, shot him dirty looks.

The image changed, flashing past different scenes of Natalie scurrying away from other kids, sitting alone, and hiding to avoid being teased.

"For most of the school year, Natalie hoped that ignoring the children tormenting her would make them stop. One boy in particular, William, sensed an easy target."

On screen, Natalie sat by herself at the corner of the outdoor play area while other students ran about in a light snowfall. William (or at least the actor playing him) stomped toward her with an enormous snowball. A few other boys got in his way, telling him to leave her alone.

"While some came to her defense, little Natalie remained shy and afraid to interact with others. William did eventually lose interest, and stopped bothering her for a few months."

The scene changed to the hallway again, where the girl kept her head down as she walked among other students. William lunged out of the crowd, grabbed the little girl by the arm, and threw her against a row of lockers. He pointed at her face.

"I almost got expelled because of you. You complained to the teacher," yelled William. "You know what I do to whiners?"

Natalie went wide eyed in fear and cringed. "I didn't—"

William drew his fist back, and the movie paused on his face, warped with anger and malice.

"Psionic abilities are often intensified by emotion. What William did not know was that innocent, tiny Natalie Hernandez had become an orphan by her own doing. In an instant of fear for her life, her telekinesis had surged, hurling her abusive father against a wall with enough force to kill him."

The class emitted a collective gasp.

When the film resumed, Natalie let off a terrified scream and William rocketed into the lockers on the other side of the hall, denting them. He peeled away from a divot and fell to the floor along with three mangled doors. The girl dropped to her knees and bawled, oblivious to her bloody nose.

"Walter survived, though he suffered numerous broken bones and spent ninety-seven hours in a medical tank. Natalie stopped attending class and received individual lessons for the remainder of her schooling."

The scene faded to reveal a dark-skinned man in Division 0 blacks, marked by a single silver bar for a rank insignia. "I'm Tech-Captain Moses Winter from the Admin Corps. You are all children with psionic talents, and it is vital for you to understand that the harmless easy victim next to you might just be able to kill if pushed too far. We live in a world that does not understand us, full of people who may fear or hate us for no reason other than what we are. If you learn anything from our schooling program, your classmates here are your only true allies. Any one of them might have a troubled past. Any one of them could do something terrible if pushed too far, so please... work *with* each other."

Captain Winter smiled, and the screen faded to black.

"Whoo. That man was angry," said Abernathy. "Glad he finally gave up and left."

Evan glanced at the ghost and whispered, "Who?"

"The father." Abernathy gestured at the holo-panel. "He came here looking for her. O'course, by the time he figured out how to leave the place he died, she was all grown up. Guess it took him awhile to get his butt out of that wall."

Vasquez touched his terminal, and the enormous holo-panel disappeared. "Would anyone like to offer up a thought on what that presentation means?"

"Don't make Hailey mad, she'll burn down the school... or at least my shirt." said Shawn, to a few hesitant chuckles.

"Well." Vasquez leaned against the front of his desk. "Despite your intention to make Hailey the object of ridicule, you come close to the point. There's something like ten or twenty thousand people to every psionic, and far too many of them are one bad experience with a psionic away from hating us. The point is, we shouldn't be hostile to each other."

"The point is," said Shawn, "if we're gonna pick on someone, make sure it's a kid like Wren who can't hurt anyone. What's he gonna do, see *more* ghosts if he gets mad?"

Evan glowered.

Abernathy stood. "I wonder what that boy's friends would think if they knew he couldn't fall asleep without clutching his teddy bear."

"Really?" muttered Evan, glancing at the ghost. He pictured everyone laughing at Shawn, but felt too guilty about announcing *that* fact out loud.

"No, Fields." Vasquez frowned. "There's no room for mistreating your fellow psionics in this school. The last thing we want is for anyone to get hurt, and you never know the full extent of what someone might be capable of."

"His mom's a mind-blaster," whispered Raven from the back row. She seemed afraid to even say the word.

"So?" Shawn laughed. "She's not his real mom."

Evan leapt out of his chair and got in Shawn's face. "She is!"

Shawn stood, towering over him.

Mr. Vasquez cleared his throat. "Boys..."

Evan narrowed his eyes up at the bigger kid. "What're you gonna do Shawn, hit me? Go ahead." Flashes of his stepfather's beatings replayed in his mind. This kid wouldn't even come close to that. "She is too my mom. Leave her alone and go hug your bear."

"Stop, Shawn," said Raven. "He's really not scared of you. Not even a little bit."

Shawn's bravado evaporated to a worried stare at Evan for a half-second before he laughed it off and pointed a thumb at the back row. "Oh, yeah... empaths. They're wimpy too, like astrals."

Raven raised an eyebrow; her fluffy hair wobbled as she cocked her head. "Wanna have everyone see you sucking your thumb and crying for your mommy?" She examined her purple-painted fingernails. "I could probably scare you enough to pee your pants."

"Uhh." Shawn looked between them.

"Fields... You're earning an appointment with Dr. Yaz as well."

A tingle of telepathy hit Evan's mind. He clamped down on it, resisting. Walter, Shawn's best friend, put a hand on the big kid's shoulder.

"Dude, let it go. Little guy's old man let him have it big time." Walter pulled Shawn back to his seat.

Evan backed up to his desk, unsure if he should feel angry or embarrassed, and clueless how to react to one of Shawn's buddies taking *his* side. No one knew about Mick but Kirsten and Doctor Loring. Now he had Walter to worry about telling everyone his crappy stepdad beat the hell out of him. He wanted to shrink into himself and hide, but never expected Walter to tell Shawn to back off. Maybe the other boy came from a similar situation. He looked to his left, but Abernathy had vanished.

"Mr. Vasquez," asked Mai, a girl on the far right of the room. "Is that movie real? I didn't think telekinesis was strong enough to kill someone."

The class fell quiet.

Vasquez smiled at her. "That's an excellent question, Mai. Jerome Harmon is the strongest telekinetic ever recorded, and was able to generate enough force to lift a small transport truck, or about twenty thousand pounds, at a slow crawl. He held it a few inches off the ground for nine seconds before the effort left him exhausted. It is true that Jerome could easily throw a person around with his ability, and he probably *could* inflict a fatal injury given enough room for the victim to accelerate. However, Jerome had been using his gift for forty or fifty years by then. What happened with the girl in the movie was the result of a spike of extreme emotional distress, built up over months and months."

"Is that why people are afraid of us?" asked Hailey. "Because they think we can hurt them?"

"That is a large part of it." Vasquez nodded. "Most people would be afraid of young children carrying firearms too. By law, a person has to be eighteen to carry a firearm... but they can't take away your abilities."

He zoned out as Vasquez droned on about how they should feel safe at the school, and learn how to control their talents. Evan spent the next ten or so minutes searching the school network for any mention of Abernathy, but nothing came up. Eventually, the period buzzer announced lunchtime, and the students queued up at the door and filed out.

On the way past the teacher's desk, Evan paused. "Mr. Vasquez?"

"Evan..." Vasquez looked up from his terminal, smiling. "What's on your mind? Is Fields giving you trouble?"

"Naw. I can handle him. Who's Abernathy?"

"Who?"

"The ghost." Evan crouched to pick up the spilled light pens. "You acted like you expected him to be messing with you."

"Oh, him." Vasquez chuckled with a slight shake of the head. "He's been around here forever. As far as I know, he's the first person to be killed by a mind blast."

Evan's eyes widened.

"He died over seventy years ago. I think they've got his brain in the archives."

"What, like in a bottle?" Evan squirmed.

"Something like that. They studied it for some years to try and understand how sensory overload burst telepathy-induced neuropathy worked."

"Huh?" Evan stared at him.

Vasquez grinned. "A hundred years ago, give or take a decade either way, that's what they called it. Well, scientists often use abbreviations in their notes. Someone had taken to calling it 'mind blast' for short, and it caught on. There's still some labcoats who hate the term 'mind blast,' thinking it sounds too much like something from a kid's cartoon... but no one wants to write out, or even say, its proper name."

Evan rolled his eyes with a nod. "Yeah. No kidding. Do you think Abernathy wants his brain in a jar?"

"It would probably bug me if I were him, but I'm not the astral sensitive... why not ask him?"

"Thanks Mr. Vasquez." Evan waved and scurried to the door, stomach growling. An idea came out of nowhere halfway to the cafeteria.

Mom helps ghosts all the time. I'm gonna surprise him! He got up to an eager run, following the smell of chicken parmesan.

5

HIGH PROFILE

Kirsten guided the patrol craft down out of the hover lane, heading for the street fifty stories below. The mechanical drone of the ground wheels unfolding ended with the reassuring *clunk* of them locking in place. She set the car half on the sidewalk to avoid sticking out into traffic. Passersby gave the car annoyed looks as the width of the vehicle crimped a six-foot wide stream of pedestrians to four feet.

Dorian leaned his head into his hand, one finger up to his temple while glancing at her from the passenger seat. "You know, you could've ordered."

"I could have." Kirsten opened the door, pushing it up on its hinge with a soft hiss, making swirls in the cryonic mist rolling out from under the patrol craft. "But this place doesn't deliver. Even if they did, it tastes better fresh."

"Like a two minute ride in a bot does that much damage." He chuckled. "Can you really tell?"

"Yeah. I can. Be right back."

Dorian waved her off. "Nothing for me, thanks."

Kirsten knew he teased, but couldn't help but feel a pang of guilt. The somber mood didn't last but a few seconds, gone by the time she walked into Cabrera's—the same place Nicole swore by for breakfast.

"*La habitual?*" asked a short apron-wearing man behind the counter. His thick black mustache parted with a warm smile.

"*Sí. Claro. Gracias José. Gran mocha así, por favor.*" Kirsten took her place at the end of a five-person line, behind three middle-management types and two university students. All gave her fearful looks, though their reaction struck her as simple trepidation of police. She put on her most unassuming smile. "Morning."

The other patrons seemed to relax, somewhat, but their body language continued to radiate nervousness. None acted so far from normal that she felt tempted to eavesdrop on their thoughts, and soon she walked out with a jalapeño omelet sandwich in a plastic clamshell carton and a large mocha coffee.

After looking both ways to make sure no idiot on Mishiro boosters would run her down, she navigated the river of pedestrians back to the patrol craft. She set the coffee in the cup holder, popped the case open, and raised the sandwich to her lips. The instant her teeth touched bread, the comm lit up with Captain Eze's six-inch holographic head. *Perfect timing.* Her eyes shifted to make contact, but she bit down anyway.

"Wren…" He smiled. "When you've finished your breakfast, I need you to investigate a possible paranormal event at the location I'm about to send you."

Kirsten mumbled into the second bite of her spicy eggs.

"No need to rush your food. There isn't an active manifestation, but be alert on site. You were requested by name."

She finished her current mouthful and furrowed her brows at him. "Are there any other astrals on the West Coast? Who else would they ask for?"

Captain Eze chuckled. "They don't know that." The Navcon beeped with an incoming waypoint. "Something happened at the home of Senator Preston Winchester."

Kirsten almost choked on egg crumbs. "Sector 19485? That's like in the woods… off the plate."

Dorian whistled. "Well, senators have to eat."

Yeah, and I guess they deserve multi-million credit houses, too. She closed her eyes and sighed out her contempt. *Calm down. Not every rich person is a piece of shit.* "Understood, sir. Any idea why he asked for me?"

"I wasn't privy to that information." Captain Eze grinned. "But you can ask him while you're there."

"What?" Kirsten's back muscles stiffened. "He's *here?* Aren't they supposed to be on the Moon?"

"Senate is apparently out of session at the moment. He's expecting you."

"Copy, sir." She flopped back in the seat as the holographic head dissipated into a spritz of dancing pixels. The NavMap shifted to display the incoming waypoint from dispatch, a bright red 'pushpin' stuck near the north end of West City. It took her a moment to summon up the urge to take another bite.

"You look like your cat died," said Dorian.

Kirsten chuckled. "I don't even have a cat."

"Anything you want to talk about?"

She nibbled. "Dealing with the wealthy is awkward enough. A senator is a whole other level of 'oh, shit.'"

"True. Though I somehow doubt you'll get on his bad side. You never cared about prestige. I'm sure you'll be fine. Just do what you always do, stick to your ethics, and stop worrying."

"Probably a Badlands ghost or something...." Kirsten took a huge bite, savoring it.

Dorian leaned toward the NavMap display. "There's nothing between that manor house and whatever might wander in except for a security team... and lots of snow."

"Great." She sipped coffee, forgetting her jalapeño-tenderized tongue. "Mmm!"

"I love the way you always do that." He winked.

She gave him a sidelong glare, then cracked up giggling. "Right... might as well finish my food before it gets cold."

About ten minutes later, she lifted off and climbed to join a northbound hover lane at the level of the fiftieth story. Since the call sounded more like a report of past events and not an active scene, she didn't bother with the lights or going faster than normal traffic. She engaged the auto-drive and leaned back, eyes closed, smiling while thinking of Evan cuddled up with her on the sofa last night doing his homework while she watched a vid. *I wonder what got into Evan yesterday at school. Usually, it's me who gets clingy.* He'd been extra affectionate, though she worried at what he didn't say. Not wanting to push, she'd waited for him to open up, but he hadn't said anything.

He would've said something if it had been serious. Maybe he just wanted to spend time with me.

Pinging from the console snapped her out of a nap. According to the clock, only a few minutes remained in the nearly hour-long ride. After a stretch, she resumed manual control and flew between shiny silver office towers. One bore the logo of NinTek Corporation, another had a green diamond on its corner marked with 'Orion Financial Services.'

She steered into a rightward banking turn, leaving the Northern Commercial District behind. Within minutes, the endless field of shining high-rise towers gave way to less-glimmery residence buildings, and eventually shorter structures: a mixture of stores, malls, low-income housing, and a few attempts at recreating pre-war suburban living. Soon, they shot over the northern wall extension by a checkpoint gate at the bottom of the half-mile long ramp to ground level. Traffic on the four-lane passage looked unusually heavy—three cars.

She gazed out on an endless field of snow-dusted pine trees. Here and there, one showed evidence of damage sustained during the corporate war. She spied a fragment of a wrecked warplane, covered in centuries of growth, and wondered if perhaps a dead soldier might be harassing the senator. While officially still within the legal boundaries of West City, those who dwelled here did so without the protection of the wall. Discarded emerging from under the city as well as any number of random atrocities might wander out of the Badlands at any time. It made for cheap, if not nerve-wracking, living. A manor house remained a manor house, but out here even they went for a fraction of the price.

The nav pin led her to a rectangular clearing in the pine forest, capped at one end by a four-story mansion. Two short extensions stuck out from the ends of an otherwise rectangular building, making it appear to hug the large courtyard in front of it. A military shuttle in green camouflage sat on an elevated landing pad about forty yards from the front door, likely the senator's quick ride back to Paramount City on the Moon.

"If I sit up here and think about it, I'm never going to wind up walking inside."

Dorian chuckled.

She landed next to a pair of silver hovercars, got out, and stared at eight intimidating white columns along a front porch almost as big as her old apartment. Trying not to think about who lived here proved futile. Being in the same room as Trade Commissioner Vernon got her shot over psionic paranoia… how much worse would an actual senator be? Then again, he did ask her to come here—unlike Vernon. Kirsten swallowed hard, climbed four steps, and crossed into shade on the way to push the buzzer.

The door opened two-ish minutes later to reveal a black-haired woman in her middle twenties. Between her delicate features and antiquated gown, she looked like a huge child's doll. Sure enough, Kirsten sensed no living mind within her, though the woman's mannerisms didn't come off as artificial.

"Hello. Can I help you?" asked the woman, peering down at her with a mildly condescending expression like she mistook Kirsten for a young teenager.

Kirsten already felt tiny in the shadow of the massive house, and being looked down at by a woman of 'average' height made her five-foot-nothing stature feel even smaller. She distracted herself by holding the senator in contempt for one man owning such a vast expanse of living space while so many others made do with cramped apartments little more than cells. "Agent Wren, Division 0. Senator Winchester reported an unexplained incident?"

"Oh, yes." The woman smiled and backed up. "Please come in. I'm Marguerite."

"It seems the good senator doesn't trust living help." Dorian clasped his hands at his back as he walked in, appraising the expansive foyer.

"Thank you, Marguerite." Kirsten stepped past the door, which the woman closed. Her first impression of the place conjured feelings of old land that had seen its fair share of spiritual events. Nothing paranormal stood out, and she attributed the weak sense of foreboding to the size and age of the building. "There's a report of something unexplained going on here... have you witnessed anything?"

Dorian scoffed.

"Well, as I'm sure you already know, I am not like you." Marguerite smiled, not a trace of shame in her expression. "I am in charge of the house and the staff. Though you think me young, I am almost sixty, and not as naïve as my appearance suggests."

Kirsten nodded. "I'm used to being on the receiving end of prejudice. Trust me. I have nothing against dolls. I'm not entirely sure how you would react to a paranormal entity."

"I'm synthetic, agent, not a doll. I do hear things sometimes." Marguerite tapped her ear. "Things *biologuiques* cannot detect without the aid of electronic devices. I have also experienced short periods of missing time, and once found myself on the floor." She glanced around at nothing in particular. "And the senator does trust me, though it is more due to my being here so long rather than I am not biological."

Dorian blinked.

Kirsten smiled. "Please forgive my partner. He's from a different generation. Hasn't gotten used to silicon-based life."

"Different generation?" Dorian frowned. "I'm not *that* old."

Marguerite giggled into her hand.

"Other than Dorian, what have you heard?" asked Kirsten.

The wisp of a woman gestured to the stairwell. "This way, Agent." She hiked up her long dress and led the way. "Various things, but most happened long enough in the past not to be the same as what I think the senator is concerned about. Two nights ago, I heard anguished cries, and a man's voice shouting impolite words."

Dorian looked about to say something, but hesitated. Kirsten winked at him.

Marguerite brought her to a study on the second floor, where she knocked in a series of rapid taps on a pair of wooden double doors, each decorated with eight pairs of bas-relief squares. She spoke in a demure, childlike voice. "*Monsieur Le sénateur? Votre invitée est arrivée.*"

Kirsten glanced at Dorian and mouthed 'what the hell?'

He shrugged, again biting back a comment.

"Please, come in," said a man's voice.

Marguerite opened the doors and stepped aside, smiling. "Please, go in."

A man with greying brown hair hopped to his feet from a chair behind a simple desk, which had the look of genuine wood. Shelves containing hundreds of paper books lined most of the walls, drawing an impressed whistle from Dorian. Quite against what she'd expected, the senator wore a sweatshirt and loose, nondescript blue pants. Perhaps in his middle forties, he hurried over to meet her halfway across the room by a pair of white wingback chairs facing a small, decorative table.

"Going to sniff around a bit." Dorian wandered off into the wall.

"Agent Wren? So good of you to come on such short notice." He gestured at one of the chairs and sat in the other. "Please."

The room reminded her too much of Konstantin, triggering an unsettling chill up her back. Nonetheless, she sat where he'd indicated. "Thanks."

"You seem… confused." He smiled. "Can I offer you coffee, tea? I'd mention wine, but you are on duty after all."

"I'm fine, thanks. I… was expecting someone older."

He laughed. "I had a highly-talented campaign staff. You're not the only one. A forty-year-old senator was a hard sell four years ago, but things worked out."

She hoped her smile didn't come off as too plastic.

"I'm sure you're wondering what all the fuss is about." He leaned back. "First, let me congratulate you for taking care of that awful business up in Paramount City a month or so back. I'm glad to see you're none the worse for wear."

Kirsten fidgeted. "Thank you."

"Something attacked me the other night. I thought I saw a figure in the corridor a little past one in the morning, but my physical security team failed to confirm an intruder."

"Attacked?" She opened a new inquest record via her armband computer and tapped in some notes. "Can you describe the event in detail, Senator?"

"Of course. It started as a sense of being watched… uhh, with malice. About an hour later, as I walked down the hall, I felt something grab my shoulder and pull hard enough to stop me. I didn't have any marks, and I can't say it even hurt… but the whole hallway didn't feel right, you know? Also, I noticed a cold spot."

She typed at the holo-panel floating over her forearm as fast as she could with one hand, while mumbling a summary of what he said.

"I hear cybernetic implants interfere with psionic talents. Is that true or a superstition? Or, do you find some manner of nostalgia in doing things the long way?"

Kirsten resumed eye contact. "With a few exceptions of individuals gifted with unusual aptitude toward technology, in most cases, significant quantities of cyberware reduce the effectiveness of psionic abilities and make it more tiring to use them... from what I hear. I'm not sure if it's true or the result of some purist movement, but I know I don't want anything put inside me. The very thought of it makes my skin crawl."

The senator covered his mouth with a finger to hide a sudden smile.

She blushed.

"I'm sure you didn't mean that as it sounded. Please don't be embarrassed. I've heard much worse on the Senate floor."

Unable to look at him, Kirsten stared at the burgundy carpet between her boots. "Have there been any other attacks?"

"Nothing that noticeable, though I have been feeling watched more often since. I can't tell if it's a spirit or if I am imagining it. And yes, before you ask, I do believe in ghosts."

She swallowed a bit of her embarrassment and looked up. "Well, that's refreshing. I'm used to working with people who think I'm crazy right up until they're covered with ice-cold slime. Mind if I walk around a bit and see if there's anything here?"

"In the middle of the day?" He raised an eyebrow.

"Spirits aren't weaker in the daylight. It's just easier for people to notice them when it's dark. If the spirit who touched you is weak or new, the energy it cost them to affect you physically might have sent them to their remains to recover, so they may not be around. If it's an older spirit playing games, they should still be here if they mean to continue haunting the place."

"All right." He stood. "I'll walk you."

Over the next forty minutes, Kirsten followed the senator room to room on the first and second floors, checking the kitchen, pantry, dining hall, ballroom, several sitting rooms, and a number of guest bedrooms. She stopped in a large library and watched an elderly man, glowing white and transparent, walk out of a bookshelf, cross the room, and drop to the floor clutching his chest.

"Sir?" asked Kirsten.

"Hmm?" Senator Winchester glanced at her.

"There's someone here." She eyed the empty floor.

The spirit appeared again a few minutes later, repeating the same walk and collapse. He ignored her attempts to get his attention.

"Oh. Never mind. It's a latent manifestation, not an intelligent spirit."

"I see." The senator shifted. "Any idea who?"

"Based on his clothes, he's been dead at least two centuries. Probably had a heart attack in this room. Only an imprint though, not a real spirit."

He cast a wary glance around the library. "Any chance it could've been that?"

"No, this is as harmless as watching a hologram. There's no intelligence here. It's basically 'ghost video.'"

Dorian swept in from the door and stopped beside her. "Place is clear. Curious a house this old doesn't have at least one lingering soul. I did pick up a strange feeling in a fourth-floor bedroom. Looks like a young woman in ill health. Severe enough for them to have an in-home medtech."

Kirsten nodded to Dorian before facing the senator. "There's a sick girl upstairs?"

Senator Winchester blinked, glanced at his left hand, then scowled. "Agent Wren, I was led to believe you were stringent in your application of ethics. I'm rather appalled that you've disregarded your principles."

"I didn't read your mind, senator. A spirit told me about her."

He froze for a second. Anger shifted to confusion and he tilted his head. "Did you not just tell me a minute ago that there's no spirits here?"

"None who are part of the house. My partner is a ghost. He went hunting for the spirit who attacked you while we were talking." She crossed her arms. "Do you want me investigating what happened to you or not? I need to check every possible angle. Angry spirits aren't the easiest things to track down."

He raised both hands in a placating gesture. "Very well. Please disregard my assumption of an ethical lapse. Let us continue."

The third floor contained nothing spiritual, and within ten minutes of wandering room to room on the fourth floor, he led her to a dark-stained wooden door and keyed a five-digit number into a pad on the wall. Once the door clicked open, he gestured for her to go in first.

Kirsten stepped past him into a massive bedroom with minimal furnishings other than a bed, two wardrobe cabinets, and a sofa by the far wall. Heavy, white floor-to-ceiling curtains blocked four windows, glowing from sunlight outside. Paranormal energy charged the air, subtle but noticeable.

A slim girl with snow-blonde hair lay unconscious on the bed, head turned toward Kirsten away from the windows. She appeared gaunt and sickly, and a faint phlegmatic wheeze accompanied each inhale. Kirsten guessed her between eighteen and twenty-two.

Electronic humming emanated from a columnar machine about the size of a mini-fridge by the couch. Holo-panels directed medical readouts to a thirtysomething woman with black hair and medium brown skin in a white medical jumpsuit bearing the logo of 'Expert-Kare' home medical services. Kirsten added it to the file notes, smirking at the purposeful mangling of the word care.

"She needs her rest, Senator," said the medtech.

"I won't be long." Kirsten opened her mind to the surrounding energy and walked in circles with her hand out.

"It's fine, Theresa." Senator Winchester addressed the medtech while staring somberly at the unconscious girl.

Kirsten walked past the bed, following her sense of a latent residue. She stopped nearer the medtech. "There is definite energy here. I'm pretty sure whoever grabbed you was in this room, long enough to leave a sense of their presence."

"Can you find it and deal with it?" asked the senator.

She observed the sleeping woman for a little while, glanced at the wall, and then at the waist-high medical device. "This is your daughter?"

"Uhh." The senator drew in a breath. He seemed ready to lash out for an instant, but wound up drilling a frustrated glare into the carpet. "I need you to understand the sensitive nature of my career. I trust, as a sworn officer, you will be able to exercise due discretion. Yes, Seraphina is my daughter, but I cannot publicly acknowledge that fact."

Kirsten glared. "She's psionic?"

He blinked, a surprised look on his face. "Oh... no." He bit his knuckle. "At least, not as far as I know. That's got nothing to do with it at all. Her mother." He shifted his jaw side to side. "She wasn't my wife."

Dorian smirked. "If having a kid from an affair is the worst thing this guy did, I'll be shocked."

"Hmm?" Kirsten glanced at Dorian.

He gestured at the man. "He's a senator. The only difference between them and organized crime is that they change the law to make what they do legal while the Syndicate pays people to ignore the law."

Senator Winchester stepped close and lowered his voice. "It's not that confusing, is it? Her mother was not my wife... she was someone else's at the time."

"Oh." Kirsten studied the girl's face. "The 'hmm' was for my partner. I... understand your situation."

"I hope you do. If certain people found out about her, it would give them fuel for pointless attacks. She's had a difficult enough time of it. I don't want her to have to suffer a media circus on top of it."

Dorian gestured at him. "Of course he couldn't be possibly worried about his own career." He paused with a pensive expression. "Though, I suppose no one would really care much about an affair."

"Senator," said Kirsten. "Did she have a friend or anyone close to her die recently?"

"Not that I'm aware of. Seraphina has never been much of a people person. She's spent more time in virtual worlds than the real one." He looked down.

"Is there something you're not telling me?"

The senator snapped his head around to glare at her.

She recoiled. "Umm. I mean... I'm only trying to find this ghost."

His sudden anger faded as fast as it manifested. He looked back at the girl on the bed and chewed at his lip. "I don't know the full details, but she spent a few months out on the street. She ran off while I was in session. Showed up about two weeks ago half dead."

"I'm sorry. Do you think she may have been involved with a gang?" Kirsten considered diving into the girl's mind while she slept, but decided against it as a deep read would be obvious, and the senator had already made his opinions of that sort of thing quite clear. Without an imminent threat of death or bodily harm, bending the rules with a senator involved would only bite her in the ass. "Is the mother still involved?"

"Unlikely. The woman was poor, and once she accepted I had no plans on abandoning my wife, she left Seraphina with me, expecting her life would be far better here."

Kirsten added to the notes. "I appreciate your help, senator. I will keep everything as quiet as I can."

"As you can?" He looked worried.

"I can't falsify a report. Command has the ability to see this."

"Oh." Senator Winchester relaxed. "Within Division 0... that's not a problem. What do you need in order to find and retire this spirit?"

She squinted at the walls. "I'm afraid nothing you can provide... At this point, there's no indication that the event you experienced relates to you in any specific way. It may have been a transient haunt, or perhaps a discharge of some old energy in the walls. I'm sensing something *was* here, but it's gone now. I'm sorry, senator, but I've got nothing to work with unless you can give me some clue as to who may have died within the past twenty years with a grudge against you. The best I can offer is to come racing back here if it happens again. Of course, the other possibility is that someone died a violent death on this property any number of years ago. *That*, I can research in the archives... but I don't think that's the case. Or they'd still be around right now."

He rubbed his chin. "There's nothing else?"

Kirsten looked up at him. "Do you have any reason to believe a ghost would want to harm you or Seraphina?"

"How am I supposed to know what motivates a spirit?" He fidgeted, tinted a bit red in the face, and jammed his hands in his pants pockets. "You're absolutely certain you have no way to find this thing?"

"Unless you can give me some idea of who is dead and might want to hurt you... I'll have to come back when the spirit is here. It may not even come back. The attack could've been random. Spirits do that sometimes. Many of them enjoy messing with the living for no reason other than to do it."

"I understand." He frowned. "I would like to hold you to that offer. If it does return, may I contact you directly?"

She nodded. *Yay. I'm on a senator's speed dial. This couldn't possibly go wrong.* "Okay. Umm. Do you mind if I ask what happened to her? If she is or was close to death, perhaps that attracted something curious."

"Seraphina is recovering from a serious injury and illness. She is not on death's door." Senator Winchester shot a look at the medtech.

"The young lady is delicate and requires medication to help with her recovery," said the woman on the couch while gesturing at the machine, aglow with eight or nine small holo-panel displays. "Her vitals are strong at the moment, but she is tired."

Kirsten bit her lip. *Ran off, probably got in with gangs, probably took a bullet or a blade. High chance of sexual assault.* The senator seemed agitated at the direction her questioning had gone, so she backed off. *Street crime wasn't the purview of Division 0 unless psionics had been involved. If he requested me here by name, he's probably got enough pull to send a Div 9 doll out there to kill everyone who even saw her.*

"Marguerite?" asked Winchester. "She will show you out, if there is nothing more you can do right now."

"That's fine, Senator." Kirsten headed for the bedroom door. "If you think the spirit has returned, I'll see what I can do."

The waifish housekeeper met her in the hall with a pleasant smile. Kirsten thanked her at the front door and made her way back to the patrol craft at a brisk jog against a chilly northern breeze. She hurried inside and stabbed a finger at the console to turn the heat up.

"So what do you think?" asked Dorian as he coalesced in the passenger seat.

"He's hiding something. I'm half tempted to think he caught her with some street tough she'd fallen for and had him killed… or maybe it's a political rival, and the girl's got nothing to do with this."

He rubbed his chin. "Might be the daughter got herself hurt doing something illegal and he doesn't want that blasted all over the Newsnet. I got the feeling he's genuine in his concern for her, but you're right—he is being evasive about something. Whoever this ghost is, I'm sure the senator knows them… That comment about 'retiring' tells me he's hoping you destroy someone specific."

She tapped her fingers on the control sticks. "I dunno. If it *was* that personal, why would the spirit have left? They'd still be in the house."

"Too new?"

"How long did it take for you to be able to touch a living person and have them notice?"

Dorian shrugged. "I can't say I tried much. Messing with people—Morelli notwithstanding—isn't my thing."

She powered up the patrol craft and pulled into the air. "I guess it's too much to ask that this was a one off."

"Yeah." Dorian settled in for the long ride. "I'd expect a call."

Kirsten plotted a course back to the PAC. With any luck, she could spend the rest of the workday relaxing at her desk.

6

SECRET MISSION

Evan carried his lunch tray away from the serving line and speed-walked into the seating area. Beige carpet, frosted seashell sconces around the walls, and beige curtains made it feel more like a hospital than a school, except for the one corner with cartoon figures on the wall and bright plastic chairs—where the preschool and kindergarten-aged kids went. Older children clustered in groups at circular tables that varied in size from seating four to twelve. He headed for one of the smaller tables by a window overlooking an enclosed yard that resembled a tiny version of Sanctuary Park.

Shani and another second-grade girl, Ruby Stanton, stopped chattering back and forth and looked at him as he took a seat. A scrap of pink peeked out from the top of her straight black hair. Shani's friend had the darkest skin he'd ever seen on a person; it made her seem to be a silhouette in the overly bright cafeteria.

Evan smiled at her. "Hey."

"Hey, Ev," said Shani.

"Hi." Ruby gave him a half-second look before staring at Shani. "If you don't do it. I'm gonna. I don't wanna get citizenship points for something I didn't do."

Shani huffed. "Even if you find who did it, you'll get in trouble for reading minds without permission."

Ruby grumbled. "It's not fair. She can't give us *all* points 'cause someone's stupid."

"Everyone thinks it's me anyway." Shani pouted.

"It isn't!" Ruby poked her.

"Uhh." Evan paused with a grilled chicken sandwich in front of his mouth. "Why doesn't your teacher just look at everyone's head? And what happened?"

Shani held both arms out to the sides in a grand gesture of exasperation. "She did! But she doesn't believe no one did it. She thinks someone's doing a trick to hide the memory."

"Only four kids have TK. It's not fair that *everyone's* gonna get points." Ruby grumbled.

Evan gave up waiting for an explanation and attacked his lunch. Four bites into it, the girls stopped quibbling about who deserved points and looked at him. He finished chewing the current mouthful and glanced between them. "What?"

"You're clairvoyant." Shani grinned. "You can touch the chair and figure out who did it, right? That's not invading someone's mind."

"Chair?" Evan took another bite.

"Someone pulled the chair out from under Mrs. Han when she tried to sit down."

Evan's sudden laugh sucked breadcrumbs into his throat, starting a fit of coughing. A red-haired teen in an Admin cadet uniform ran over to check on him. The boy patted him on the back until he resumed breathing normally.

"Crumbs." Evan hit himself in the chest. "I'm okay."

Cadet McPherson nodded. "Slow down a bit, and drink some water."

"'Kay."

The teen walked back to his post by the wall.

"It's not funny." Shani frowned. "Han's super mad."

"If you're sure none of the kids did it, I bet Abernathy did." Evan drained half his lemonade in one pass, then gasped for air.

"Who?" Ruby blinked. "That's a funny name."

"Ghost."

"Ooo." Ruby grabbed Shani in a hug, pretend hiding behind her. "Seriously? There's ghosts here?"

"Only one. He's a butthead. Plays tricks on people. He keeps changing my homework to like grade ten stuff." Evan took a bite of food before he remembered he had more to say. "Mmm!"

"Slow down," whispered Shani. "You'll choke again."

Evan rolled his eyes as he chewed, feeling as though the chicken took forever to reach a point he could swallow it. "I wanna help him. He's stuck here and I think I know how to set him free."

"This is too weird." Ruby held her hands up. "I don't wanna mess with a ghost."

"You're gonna get in trouble." Shani shook her head. "Like a million citizenship points. Let your mom fix it."

"I can't." He frowned at the 'healthy' substitute for French fries—baked zucchini sticks—but ate some anyway. "She's active duty. They won't let her do what we need to do to set him free. She'd get in trouble with Captain Ezzeh." He eyed a half-eaten bit of zucchini and dropped it back on the plate with a smirk. "She'd do it anyway, which is why I can't tell her about it."

"What is it?" asked Shani.

"He died like a really long time ago to Mind Blast. They put his brain in a jar so they could study it."

"Eww." Ruby dropped her fork in her salad. "*Really?* Tryin' to eat here."

"Yeah. I wanna get it and take it to Father Villera."

Shani bit her lip. "You're gonna get in so much trouble."

"I need your help." Evan flashed a huge, hopeful grin.

Ruby shook her head.

"Umm." Shani fidgeted. "I don't wanna get in trouble."

"We won't. They're not even looking at it anymore... they put it down in the archives and forgot him, that's why he's stuck here, 'cause they're treatin' him like a thing not a person. We gotta get in, find his brain, and save it."

Shani squirmed. "I dunno. Maybe if you tell Mrs. Han it wasn't someone wif TK and we don't get points."

"I can try."

He hurried to finish the last of his lunch, tossed the tray on the pile of dirty trays near a bank of trashcans, and followed the two seven-year-olds down the quiet, deserted hallway to their classroom. In stark contrast to the sterile white of the corridor, the room exploded with vibrant colors. Holographic cartoon characters paraded around the walls near the ceiling holding up the letters of the alphabet. Globes, rainbows, pictures of historic places, and hand-drawn student art covered every inch of the place.

Evan swelled with pride at being the 'big kid' coming to the younger kids' room. He headed to the teacher's chair and put his hand on it. Eyes closed, he opened himself to receiving any psychic imprints left in the fake wood. Miss Easley, a clairvoyant almost as old as Mom, had mentioned Epoxil was a poor conduit for emotional imprints, something about it being mostly plastic. He scrunched his eyebrows together, straining, and the soft whispering of the girls behind him blurred as though he'd gone underwater. Soon, a mood of annoyance came over him. He grunted, feeling trapped in the presence of people he couldn't stand to be around. The desire to go home hit him with such intensity he let go of the chair, fully intending to walk outside and get a PubTran car.

"Whoa." He blinked at his hand. "I didn't see who moved the chair, but I'm pretty sure your teacher hates kids. All she thinks about is going home all day."

"Is that so?" asked a woman.

Evan turned around, finding Ruby and Shani grimacing, and a half-Chinese woman in a uniform like Mom's (without the equipment belt, laser pistol, or forearm guard) standing there with her hands on her hips. The woman's nameplate read, 'Han, C.' She looked a lot older than Mom, but not quite enough to be a grandmother.

"Hello, Mrs. Han." Evan put a hand to his head and tried to clear the thoughts from his mind.

"Are you okay?" She eased back on the hostility a little.

"Yeah." He let his arm drop and gave her an innocent look. "Why do you teach if you can't stand being around kids?"

She frowned. "I'm fond enough of children when they can behave themselves. What are you doing in this room during lunch?"

Evan took a breath and sighed. "They said someone yanked your chair and wanted me to see if I can tell who did it with clairvoyance so you didn't give points to the whole class. I think it was Abernathy."

"There's no student in my class named that." She patted him on the shoulder, guiding him to the door. "Go on. Back to the lunchroom."

Shani and Ruby gawked in amazement.

Evan looked up at her for a second, glanced at the door, and back at her. "Mrs. Han?"

"What?"

"Does stuff happen in here a lot? Like things falling over or moving or 'lectronics not working?"

Mrs. Han let off an exasperated sigh. "I've got four or five telekinetics in here. Of course things happen."

"I think Abernathy knows you're not being nice to the kids, and he's giving you a hard time for it."

"Who exactly *is* this Abernathy?" Mrs. Han crossed her arms. "Some code word?"

"He's a ghost. Ask Mr. Vasquez about him. He knows."

"Oh, help me." Mrs. Han stared at the ceiling. "The last thing I need is nonsense about spirits. Do your parents know you believe in that stuff, or are you a ward?"

Evan clenched his jaw. "My mom knows that ghosts are real."

"Who is your mother? I think we need to have a talk." Mrs. Han fell into her chair and picked up a NetMini.

"*Agent* Kirsten Wren. I-Ops." Evan puffed out his chest. "She'd love to tell you all about ghosts, and Harbingers, and Abyssals."

The girls tried to stifle giggles at the face their teacher made.

Mrs. Han stared into space for over a minute before looking at him. "So you're trying to tell me that a ghost is haunting the classroom and doing things to annoy me?"

He shrugged. "I'd have to ask him."

"Is he here now?" Mrs. Han looked around again.

A few seconds of concentration opened Evan's senses to the astral realm. Mrs. Han gasped, staring at him. White light shining in his eyes glinted from a half-glass of water on the corner of the desk. Ruby drifted closer, mouth open, seeming fascinated. He turned in place, but the room held only the living.

"He's not here." Evan caught a glimpse of light behind Mrs. Han's shoulder. He crept over and leaned to peer at the chair behind her, at a glowing handprint. "Yeah. He did it."

Mrs. Han leapt from her seat. "How do you know?"

"Look at my thoughts." He kept his attention on the luminous residue. The tingle of incoming telepathy came and went. "He touched it here where it glows. Some of his energy stuck to the chair."

Another telepathic poke hit him, from Ruby. "Wow... that's *so* cool."

"Mrs. Han?" asked Shani. "Are we still gonna get points?"

Evan laughed and let his astral sight fade.

Mrs. Han shook her head, seeming too rattled to speak.

"Come on." Ruby grabbed Shani's hand. "We got like twenty minutes left on lunch."

The girls darted off. Evan walked to the door, glancing back over his shoulder at the teacher. Maybe telling her about ghosts hadn't been such a great idea.

"Mrs. Han? Next time I see him, I'll ask him to leave you alone, okay?"

She startled, as though she didn't realize he'd still been there. "Yes. Okay. Thank you."

Evan headed out the door, stuffed his hands in his pockets, and whistled. "Oops."

Two minutes later, he found Shani and Ruby playing holo-pong in the game room. He wandered over to stand beside the virtual table. The place had no 'cool' games, only variations of sports sims that kept the kids moving around.

"So you'll help?" asked Evan.

Shani didn't look up, too focused on the ball. "I guess."

Evan bounced on his toes. "Hey I got you out of cit points. And we're helping someone."

"Okay, fine... When?" Shani missed the incoming ball, which turned into a little dancing figure and held up a 'score' sign a few inches in front of her. "You're distracting me." She slapped the paddle over the animated ball, but it didn't react.

"It'll have to be after school... probably before we get a ride home. I wanna look up the archives to see how hard it'll be to get in first."

"Okay." Shani served the intangible ball. "If we get in trouble, I'm gonna be mad at you."

"We won't." He grinned.

Nine minutes later, the score had tied 11-11, and the class buzzer sounded. With a mission in mind, having to endure another two hours of school felt more like a burden than ever. A few seconds of grumbling gave way to resignation. Helping Abernathy would take planning. He didn't have to rush anything; the man had died years ago.

Not like he'd get any worse.

7

ALL FUN AND GAMES

Kirsten pounded away at a handful of old reports, wrapping up a few bits of bureaucracy from the incident with Konstantin she'd left hanging from a month ago. The mere thought of him made her want to shoot him all over again, but she had to admit, a demon devouring his soul topped anything she could do. *I don't think a person could get any more dead than that.* Thinking about his hand creeping up the inside of her leg almost sent her straight to an autoshower tube.

At 2:08 p.m., a text message popped up on her desk terminal:

[D0-Eze, J Captain-O3]: Ghosts are quiet today. You can go home if you want, but you're on call.

She bounced in her chair.

[D0-Wren, K Agent-W4]: Ok. Ty!

A tap on the holo-panel opened a new chat window.

[D0-Wren, K Agent-W4]: Nila, I got the all clear to bug. Want me to take Shani?

[D0-Assad, N Tactical Officer II-E4]: Ok w me. Up 2 her. Thx.

Kirsten waved at Captain Eze through his office blinds as she jogged out of the squad room, Dorian close behind. The opportunity to not make Evan wait around until her shift ended was a rare treat she couldn't refuse.

"What are you going to do with them when they call you in an hour?" asked Dorian.

Kirsten shot him a look. "Don't you dare jinx me."

"I'm serious, K. You can't leave a seven- and nine-year-old home alone.

You can't drag them to a scene with you, and there might not be enough time to drop them at the dorm."

She grumbled. "I'll ask Sam over."

"He doesn't get off shift until six."

Kirsten stopped in the middle of the hall. "In the six years I've been activated, I've only run into one entity that's been strong enough to be such a threat to the living that I wouldn't have time to drop them off here on the way, and if you've just jinxed another Wharf Stalker incident on me, I'm going to… I'm gonna…" She fumed. "Paint our pat-vee pink."

Dorian gasped. "You wouldn't dare. Besides, it's against policy to use a non-black vehicle in an official capacity." He grinned. "I think Charazu would've been strong enough to hurt someone."

"That thing didn't manifest until I pushed it. And what are the chances—" She pointed at him. "I'm not saying it."

She rode the elevator in silence, dreading the mere idea of another 'demon' showing up. When the doors finally opened, she walked to the front lobby of the education wing and used her NetMini to send Evan a message to meet her out front as soon as class let out rather than spend three hours in the rec room.

At 2:11 pm, Evan came sprinting down the main hallway and leapt into a hug, cheering.

Shani hurried along behind him, struggling with a bright pink backpack. "Hi, Miss Wren."

"Hi, Shani." She gave Evan a squeeze and set him down on his feet. "How'd it go today?"

Evan cringed. "Uhh, I think I broke one of the teachers."

Kirsten raised an eyebrow.

"She didn't believe in ghosts…" Evan explained what happened with Mrs. Han.

Shani smiled. "She's okay. She wasn't as mean as usual and kept looking around."

"Heh." Kirsten took them each by the hand and led them down the hall. "Abernathy was here when I lived in the dorms. He used to talk to me at night when I couldn't sleep."

"The man's crazy." Dorian tapped his head. "Acts like an overgrown child."

"He's harmless." Kirsten smiled.

"Can we go to a Funzone?" asked Evan.

"I'm technically still on duty, but I got the okay to take off. I might have to respond to a situation."

"Oh." He looked disappointed for a few seconds, but smiled anyway. "What do we do if you gotta go?"

"Well, if something happens before five, I'll drop you back off here. Otherwise, Nila's."

Evan looked out at nothing in particular. "Ghosts, please stay quiet tonight."

Kirsten laughed. *I wish it was that simple.* When they reached the garage, the kids ran ahead in a race to the patrol craft. She eyed the NetMini on her belt. *Whatever's haunting the senator... please take the night off.*

―――――――

NICOLE APPEARED AT KIRSTEN'S DESK AT 10:08 THE NEXT MORNING. A strawberry-mocha latte floated away from the box in her arms as she passed and glided to land in front of her. The redhead trudged, absent the usual spring in her step, and slumped in her chair at her desk against the left wall of the squad room.

Kirsten minimized the cheesy arcade spaceship game on her terminal and swiveled ninety degrees to face her friend's back. "What's wrong?"

"Nothing other than having been awake until almost six this morning." Nicole yawned. "Total Mongolian clusterfuck last night."

Dorian sputtered.

"Mongolian?" Kirsten lifted the seal off the lid of her coffee and took a long sip. "What's that mean?"

"It's a place in China," said Dorian.

Nicole stretched, yawned again, and opened a carton to reveal a breakfast burrito. "I dunno. It sounded more intense to add it. 'Mongolian clusterfuck' has a certain... *something* that a plain old run-of-the-mill clusterfuck doesn't. Heard one of the Div 5 guys say that." She lifted her egg-stuffed tortilla and let out an exhausted sigh. "It was a complete mess. Bunch of psionics decide to start a damned gang war in Sector 9924. Place turned out to be a ripper doc's lab. They found like four million credits in black market body parts. Div 1 went in, not realizing psionics were involved, and by the time we got there, at least four of them are shooting at anything that moves—even us."

Kirsten shivered. "W-what happened to them?"

Nicole flashed a weary smile. "I have three more images for the Wall of Derp. Just have'ta print 'em out."

"Hey, did you notice... when she's exhausted, she stays on topic for more than ten seconds?" asked Dorian.

"You disarmed them?" Kirsten let off a sigh of relief, glancing at all the photos Nicole had hung of the faces suspects made when she yanked their weapons away with telekinesis around her workstation.

Nicole spent a moment inhaling her burrito. Egg bits dribbled all over her desk. "Yeah. There was a pretty nasty pyro involved... chucking fireballs at us."

She winced. "Ouch. Was Nila there?"

"Yeah. She kept him busy. So we're like having this Mongolian standoff."

"Mexican," muttered Dorian.

"And like this massive dude comes running out, with two metal arms and huge blades sticking out of his fingers. He's screaming like a lovesick moose. Gets his hand under the front end of a damned Div 1 pat-vee, and flips it."

"Someone with that much aug had to be a pushover for a suggestive." Kirsten sniffed her coffee, unable to decide if she wanted to cradle the warmth or drink it.

"Yeah, if we had one that would'a been nice." Nicole grumbled. "So, Captain Torres is screaming over comms that we need Div 5 on site to deal with this insane borg, but the giant bastard takes off running. Benitez lifted a surface thought before the guy vanished, said it was all kinds of scrambled in there. The dude had the mental capacity of a 'smart gorilla.' Anyway, the guy was trying to protect some kid. He must've been on some wild chems; he thought the little girl's eyes were glowing blue."

Kirsten put a hand to her stomach to quell a churn. "Please don't tell me they found a kid in there."

"We did find bloody footprints going out the back door. Based on size, Div 2 estimated around ten years old."

Kirsten's heart sank. "Oh, no."

"Relax. Whoever it was got away. They only stepped in blood, didn't look like they were hurt. Jody tried to lift a psychometric reading from the procedure chair, but... ugh. I think she's *still* screaming. Lotta people died on that thing. So the borg runs off, no sign of any little kid—with or without glowing eyes." Nicole took two more bites, holding a finger up while she chewed. "Must've gotten away before we showed up. Wasn't much left of the ripper doc either. Total hamburger case. They think the psycho-borg pulped him."

"That sounds like a mess." Kirsten sucked on her latte like a baby with a bottle, feeling guilty at having a half-day yesterday while her best friend had to deal with that mess.

"Here's the best part." Nicole swiveled her chair around to face Kirsten, showing off dark rings under her eyes.

"It gets better?"

"Yeah." Nicole yawned again. "We fight our way inside, and pin the psionic suspects down behind this tangle of pipes and stuff. Div 1 is hanging back, watching the front door. Next thing we know, time jumps five minutes forward and all seven of the psionic suspects are gone."

Kirsten blinked. "Are you saying they like... teleported?"

"That's what it looked like, but they think something made us all black out at the same time. No one remembers anything but watching the suspects disappear. I can't even tell you what their faces looked like. Something even got into our armor cams and erased the recording. The cars outside are the only reason we know like five minutes passed."

"That's impossible." Kirsten blinked. "Telepaths can't make people forget things in an instant; it takes time and concentration... plus knocking a whole tactical squad senseless at the same time?"

Nicole's eyebrows formed a flat line across her head. "*That's* why we were stuck there 'til six in the morning. They kept trying to figure out what happened to us. We couldn't leave the scene."

"Had to be a chemical agent," said Dorian. "Maybe C-Branch got involved. They've got stuff no one knows about."

Kirsten turned her chair another ninety degrees to look at Dorian, seated at the desk behind hers. "Why would C-Branch care about an organ harvester?"

He shrugged. "Makes about as much sense as the idea of a telepath erasing the memories of multiple people in a few seconds."

"You should request the day," said Kirsten. "You're in no shape to go out there like that."

Nicole mumbled incoherently into her food while taking a bite.

"Wren," yelled Captain Eze.

"Someone should tell him they have these things called intercoms," said Dorian.

Kirsten laughed as she stood. "At least he sounds in a good mood."

She trotted to his office. "Sir?"

"We've received a report of unexplained phenomena. Sounds like an easy one." He touched one finger to his terminal and concentrated for two seconds. "There." Her NetMini pinged. "I've sent you the particulars."

"On my way." She started to leave, but whirled back. "Captain, Nicole's in bad shape. You should probably let her go home and sleep."

"Her and fifteen others." He shook his head. "Not practical; however, tell her to flop in the barracks. I'll leave her and Forrester alone if at all possible."

Kirsten saluted, smiling. "Yes, sir."

She stopped by Nicole's desk on the way to the door. "Eze said go to the barracks and warm a bed."

"Great." Nicole dragged herself upright.

When the elevator doors parted, Morelli stumbled into the hall looking dead on his feet.

"Tom?" Kirsten waved a hand in front of his face. "Eze's cleared you guys to crash in the barracks."

"That sounds like a good—" His eyes snapped open. "Kirsten."

"Boo." She frowned.

Morelli looked left and right.

She smiled. "Yes, he's right next to me."

He hurried out of the squad room. Kirsten headed down the hall to the elevator and hit the button for the garage level.

Dorian whistled to himself until the elevator stopped, then stepped out doing a full-circle spin around. "At least he's not afraid of *you*, per se. No demons following you today."

"Let's not bring that up. I'd like to go at least a year without running into another one of those things. On second thought, let's make that forever."

"Here's hoping," said Dorian.

She checked her gear on the way to the patrol craft. Satisfied, she climbed in and pulled the gull wing door down. With a *chirp*, the computer in her armband sent the information from Captain Eze to the car's terminal, and up on the screen.

The face of a middle-aged woman with coppery-brown skin and black hair appeared. To the right, text identified her as forty-nine-year-old Julia Dominguez. No criminal record, but three citations for operating a ground vehicle at 'speeds incompatible with public safety,' the most recent of which occurred over eleven years ago.

Kirsten poked the link to the recorded call, and listened to Julia explain that bizarre things have been happening around her home: her dog barking as if someone was inside, doors opening, lights going on and off, and the occasional feeling of someone watching her. She complained that the police didn't help, but they got sick of her calling so they gave her the link to contact Division 0.

"This one sounds pretty simple." Kirsten smiled. "Probably a previous tenant that doesn't like her in the place."

"She's lived there thirty years." Dorian pointed at another panel, with the woman's financial, employment, and tax records.

"Sometimes it takes a while for a spirit to learn how to do things." She shut down the file and drove out of the garage before hovering up to altitude.

Again, with no emergency code, she flew along with civilian traffic. While waiting at a red signal, she glanced up and left at a NewsNet bot. The thirty-yard wide holo-panel showed reporter Kimberly Brightman discussing a 'hostage situation' with Division 0 involvement.

"Our sources within the National Police Force have confirmed psionic individuals present, though we are unsure at this time if the psionics were the victims or the hostage takers. I am pleased to report that the situation was resolved without any loss of life."

Kirsten scowled as the screen cut to an advertisement for self-warming breakfast waffles.

"You do realize that three fourths of our job is PR, right?" Dorian held up a finger. "Amend that. Half. A quarter is filling out reports."

She couldn't quite bring herself to laugh. "Whatever happened to the truth?"

"Society doesn't want truth. They want safety. Command doesn't want truth either; they want people not starting a witch hunt on psionics."

Kirsten accelerated when the signal flashed green, fast enough to make the cars behind her appear stationary. "You don't think people would understand? Someone commits a crime with a gun, they don't blame guns. A psionic commits a crime, why do they blame all psionics?"

"Easy targets." He grumbled. "You missed a lot of school. Used to be they *did* blame all guns... or at least people who wanted to make things political did. Guy shoots someone and everyone went crazy about guns, ignoring a dozen other factors at play. Of course, no one really remembers that nowadays. A psionic commits a crime, so all psionics are ticking bombs. History is just repeating itself."

"So you think it's wonderful that everyone in the city is carrying weapons?" She slowed back to a reasonable speed, eyeing the navigation light-ribbon where it swerved to the right up ahead past a large office building shaped like three stacks of pancakes.

"If a guy really wants to kill someone, they'll find a way to do it, gun or not... but I suppose convenience plays a factor. The politicians don't care as much now. Civilian firearms can't penetrate police armor, and there's too many people in the city. I think the government's fine with everyone having guns because the people in charge *want* the poor killing each other. I suppose they look at it like a body ridding itself of disease."

"That's so wrong." She shuddered. "I hope you're just being cynical."

"Am I? Cramming three quarters of a billion people together on top of each other and giving everyone free access to weapons? Bullets are cheaper than social support services."

Kirsten glared at him. "I can't tell if you're serious or trying to torment me."

"Eh, maybe I am a little jaded. I've been working on my *dead*pan."

"Die." She scowled.

He winked. "Already did."

Eighteen minutes later, she landed on the roof of a residence tower in a middle-income area. A twenty-foot square enclosure allowed elevators up to the roof and offered the optional torture of a stairwell. Dorian, still smirking, followed her to the elevator and down to the 63rd floor. Kirsten kept her senses opened to her surroundings, but didn't get a read on anything by the time she arrived at apartment 63-33.

"Hmm." Dorian chuckled. "333. That's half the beast."

Kirsten rolled her eyes as she hit the doorbell. "Stop talking about demons."

A rainbow pixel glowed from a tiny camera on the face of the door about twenty seconds later.

"Oh, the police," said a woman's voice via a speaker. The door slid to the side with a pneumatic hiss, revealing the woman from the case documentation, only thinner and paler. Most of her shape vanished under a heavy blue sweater. "Come in. You are with the… special police?"

"Yes, Ma'am." Kirsten looked around at a living room done in shades of blue with white trim. A long, shallow cabinet of drawers on the right held something on the order of fifty tiny holo-bars displaying portraits of three boys and two girls all the way from infancy to early twenties. One lonely charcoal-grey disc bot made its way back and forth across the carpet, cleaning.

An oblong mass of black fur trotted out from behind a periwinkle blue sofa and yapped at Dorian. He waved at the miniature Schnauzer, but the dog only snarled louder.

"Oh, no! The spirit, it is back." Mrs. Dominguez clutched at her chest, eyes wide.

"Calm down, ma'am. I have a spirit with me. He's here to help."

The little dog continued barking, bouncing in place.

"Y-you bring a ghost *with* you? I ask you to get rid of one, not bring more." She fanned herself.

"He's Division 0 too, ma'am. Killed in the line of duty. You have nothing to fear from him."

"Well, all right, but… I don't know." Mrs. Dominguez snapped her fingers at the dog. "Bridget, quiet."

Kirsten put on her 'trust me' smile. "I understand you've been having things happen? Doors opening and closing, lights flickering… the dog barking?"

"Yes. All of that." She gathered her sweater closed. "Can you get it to leave me alone?"

Kirsten wandered deeper into the room, peering down a short hallway and into the kitchen alcove. "Is it okay if I look around?"

"Go ahead." Mrs. Dominguez picked the still-growling dog up and carried her to the sofa.

The animal squirmed to keep facing Dorian as he glided by, heading for the master bedroom. Kirsten explored a small dining area, the kitchen, a little bathroom and two sub-bedrooms (one peach and one blue) still decorated as if teens lived there. She stood in the hall, glancing back and forth between two sets of stacked beds necessary to allow five siblings to share two bedrooms. The excess of the senator's house annoyed her all over again.

"Anything?" asked Dorian. "Master bedroom's got a little feeling to it."

"Rest of the place is dead." Kirsten skirted around him and went in to the last room. Sure enough, the walls emanated a sense of latent paranormal presence. "This feels angry, but not too strong."

Dorian pinched the bridge of his nose. "I used to like dogs. Really. That one is driving me up the wall."

"Argh." She set her hands on her hips. "This is so frustrating."

"You think it's the same ghost from the senator's?" He looked around. "Maybe we have a serial prankster."

Kirsten honed in on the strongest source to a spot near the bed, by the nightstand. She held her hands out, palms oriented at the floor, fingers spread. "He—the energy feels male—was standing here for a little while."

"Think he was pulling a Theo on Mrs. Dominguez?"

She shook her head. "No, too angry. Also too weak for me to tell if it's the same entity."

"Husband?" asked Dorian.

Kirsten forced air past her lips as she shrugged. With nothing else to do, she returned to the living room. "Mrs. Dominguez?"

"Is the ghost gone?" The woman stood, holding the dog under her left arm like a purse. It snarled in Dorian's direction. "T-that's your friend, correct?"

"Yes. I was able to sense the presence of a spirit, but he's not here right now. I'm sorry if this is a painful question, but I assume you have or had a husband at some point?"

Mrs. Dominguez nodded. "Yes. Eric. We divorced four years ago."

"So he isn't dead?" asked Kirsten.

"Not as far as I know. I think they would have told me that." She appeared light-headed and lowered herself to sit, clutching the dog in her lap. "He didn't even visit when I was in the hospital."

Kirsten walked to the left so the woman didn't have to twist her neck to maintain eye contact. "Can you think of anyone who might've died within the past ten or twenty years who may hold a grudge against you or somehow blame you for their death?"

"No. I keep to myself. I work virtually, so I only rarely go outside."

"May I ask what you do?" Kirsten surveyed a holo-bar projector and coffee table full of small religious figurines. Much to her surprise, she didn't roll her eyes at them.

"I do logistics—clerical work for the military. Keeping track of uniforms, armor, drop buildings, vehicles, and such."

"Ask her if there's even a remote chance an error she made might've cost lives in the field." Dorian rubbed his chin.

Kirsten relayed the question.

"Oh, no." Mrs. Dominguez looked offended, but shot her disapproving scowl at the wall. "I suppose you must ask these things."

"I'm sure you're good at what you do, but I need to cover all possible angles." Kirsten bit her lip. "You mentioned you were in the hospital? Did you share a room with someone who passed away?"

"Yes, I was in the hospital, but no... no one around me died. Please, you must do something about this ghost. My new heart cannot take this much longer." She patted her chest.

"*New* heart?" Kirsten blinked.

"I was born with a congenital defect, but it was mild enough not to cause problems until last year." She coughed into a tissue. "My health plan covered regeneration, but my DNA would've come up with the same defect. The insurance people said that altering my DNA was too expensive unless I was about ready to drop dead. I got lucky. A donor organ became available. I'd been waiting almost eight months."

"Is that long?" Kirsten tilted her head.

"Well, not many people donate these days what with all that fancy regeneration. The donor organ wound up being much cheaper anyway. Something like three hundred thousand compared to two-point-two million for the DNA adjustment plus making my body re-grow a new heart." Mrs. Dominguez lost her grip on the dog, which ran circles around Dorian, barking. She waved at it. "Bridget, be quiet!"

The dog stopped only for three seconds.

Dorian gave the animal an 'I'm so tempted' look.

"Of course," said Mrs. Dominguez, "if I was going to die, they'd have had to cover it."

"Assuming they made the decision fast enough." Dorian grumbled.

Kirsten pursed her lips. "You think it might be the donor?"

"Organ donors are usually willing." Dorian chuckled. "If whoever the heart came from agreed to be a donor, I don't see why they'd be pissed off."

"They raided a ripper doc's place last night... What if it was an illegal donation?"

Mrs. Dominguez wheezed. "I went to the Empyrean Life Science Center. That is not a small hospital, officer."

Kirsten pulled it up on her armband display. The hospital campus took up almost a third of a sector, with three high-rises as well as a recovery park. "Well, so much for that."

"Zero for two. What about bringing in a clairvoyant? Evan?" Dorian raised an eyebrow.

"No. I'm not going to involve him in an official investigation." She ran a hand through her hair, scratching her scalp. "Maybe I'll get lucky and he won't wind up in I-Ops."

"And I might come back to life." Dorian put a cool hand on her shoulder. "They're going to lean on him. He's only the second Astral Sensate within 1300 miles. At least chasing spirits is less chances of him getting shot at."

"You *have* been with me the past couple of months, right? *This* is supposed to be safer?"

Dorian chuckled. "Point."

Mrs. Dominguez kept a polite silence, though her expression made it seem as though she regarded Kirsten as having a loose grip on sanity. "Can you remove the spirit? I am afraid for my life. Last night, I awoke unable to breathe. I felt like a weight sat on my chest." The woman blessed herself. "I think the new heart was ready to quit, but whatever was doing that stopped all of a sudden."

Kirsten paced. "I'm... There's no one who you think would be upset with you. The heart came from a respected medical facility. As far as I can tell, the entity has left. All I can do right now is give you a PID to call if it comes back and try to show up while it's still here."

"This sounds familiar." Dorian folded his arms, sighing.

Mrs. Dominguez looked down. "Will you be here fast enough to stop it from killing me?"

"I'm sorry." Kirsten cringed. "I wish I had more to go on. Can you think of *anything* else? Even if you had nothing to do with it, someone who might blame you for their death?"

Dorian feigned a lunge at the dog, which darted into the back room, crying.

"I..." The woman startled at the unexpected departure of Bridget. "Is it back?"

"I'm sorry. My friend was tired of hearing your dog bark at him."

Mrs. Dominguez frowned. "I don't know why it would want to hurt me."

Kirsten looked around. "I'll run the history on this apartment. Maybe it's a previous occupant. Sometimes it takes ghosts a long time to build up enough strength to affect the living. It could be as simple as a territorial spirit who views you as invading their home."

"Bridget has never acted out before. All the years I have lived here, there has never been anything strange."

Kirsten waved her NetMini at the one on the coffee table. Both devices chirped. "I sent you my contact tag. Vid me anytime it starts happening again, okay?"

"Thank you." Mrs. Dominguez stood. "Please tell me if you find anything in the records."

"I will." Kirsten followed the woman to the door. "Sorry I couldn't do more, but... ghosts aren't exactly routine. Every one of them is a different situation."

"I know you are trying your best." Mrs. Dominguez smiled. "I hope it's enough."

Kirsten sighed at the door as it closed.

"Feels like what happened at the senator's." Dorian started for the elevator, but stopped when Kirsten remained still. "Coming?"

"There's anger in that residue. I think the spirit wanted to hurt her. The heart's a weak point... vulnerable after an operation like that." She dragged herself away, shouldering a weight of guilt at not being able to do more. "If that woman dies, I'm going to feel like shit."

"Maybe Evan can learn something? I know you're trying to protect him, but it's not like this is a bad neighborhood."

"He's nine, Dorian. I told you: I'm not involving him in an official investigation. Who knows what sorts of visions he could get from spirit energy. What if it scares him senseless? I can't risk that. If I don't get anything from the records, I'll try to talk Easley into coming out here."

"Good luck. She's Admin for a reason. She'd probably pass out if you suggested going into the field. Evan's got more nerve than she does."

"I'd rather bring a twenty-five year old Senior Specialist scared shitless of her own shadow than a nine-year-old child who doesn't know enough to be careful." She punched the elevator call button. "This is pissing me off."

"What about beaconing for him?"

She stepped into the elevator, spun on her heel to face the door, and grumbled. "I need to have some sense of *who* first or I'll just get every curious spirit within a hundred miles showing up... and it would be my luck that one of them would like her apartment and stay there."

He pinched the bridge of his nose. "Endless barking..."

"Something like that."

"I hope you're right." Dorian clasped his hands behind him. "Perhaps this guy is weak and he's draining himself with these minor attacks. Could be why there's several days between reports."

"So you *do* think it's the same ghost as the one bothering Senator Winchester?"

"MO is similar. But bumps and bangs in the night aren't exactly unique. Even your friend Theodore did that when he was a new ghost."

She stormed across the roof to the car once the elevator opened. "Let's start with property records."

Dorian gestured at the patrol craft. "After you."

8

STRESS RELIEF

Kirsten darted along a darkened section of sidewalk in the shadow of a decaying warehouse, following the pale amber line of the waypoint provided by her helmet's HUD. Comm chatter offered sporadic updates regarding the movements of the Ridge Hill Crew. A force of at least forty armed gang members rushed a police line less than two blocks from her current position.

She leapt across a puddle to avoid making noise and ducked for cover in a spot where a recessed channel ran up the length of the building. The hollow disguised the gap between pre-fab sections of the high-rise as an architectural element, and she used it as a hiding spot to catch her breath and gain her bearings. Her helmet tracked her eye motions, dragging the minimap out and expanding it across the HUD. Blue triangles representing police moved in clusters of three to five, attempting to corral a disorganized swarm of red dots.

Why is he bothering with this elaborate scenario? This isn't tactical training.

After shrinking the map, she shoved off the wall and headed for the first possible right turn into an alley wide enough to be a four-lane road. Slick with rain, the plastisteel ground shone like a lake of blue light from the moon overhead, darkened in spots wherever grime or trash lay undisturbed. Despite knowing she essentially played a video game, the perceptible reality of her surroundings kept her on edge.

With a tremendous *crash* of metal-on-metal, a forklift crashed through the door of an abandoned warehouse up ahead, sending two dumpsters spinning and screeching, while a handful of smaller trash canisters went flying. Warped steel slats clattered to the ground, drowning out the murderous roar coming from a huge man hanging off the left side. Tires squealed as the somewhat smaller driver fought to get his ungainly vehicle to turn toward her.

On instinct, she drew her sidearm and fired five times into the front end of the lift before realizing the sim had given her a standard Class 4 ballistic weapon. The 10mm slugs bounced off the heavy loader with flashes of orange sparks. The driver raised the lift, using a shield plate to conceal himself as well as his hanger-on from further gunfire.

This isn't fair. My E-90 would've shredded that thing.

She dove into a sideways somersault as the forklift thundered by. The driver's attempt to stop became a flat spin. Rubber screeched over uncoated plastisteel as the forklift spun around and around while sliding until it smashed ass-end into the building across the street with an echoing *bang*. A stockpile of three-inch diameter pipes nearby collapsed onto it. The huge man flew into the wall, but bounced away and landed on his feet.

I guess I'm supposed to fight him.

"Why don't you be a good little girl?" asked the behemoth.

"Grr." Kirsten normally would've suggested him to get down, but the entire point of the sim was hand-to-hand training. She pictured Konstantin's face on him and charged, pulling a stunrod from her belt.

The driver scrambled to get out of the forklift, hampered by the avalanche of pipes. Hoping to avoid a two-on-one, Kirsten sprinted at the big man. He swung a wide haymaker for her head, but she dodged left and cracked him on the wrist with the stunrod. As he started to cradle his forearm, she threw herself into a jumping spin kick that drove her boot into the side of his jaw. He stumbled a step to his left, turning his back as his body followed where her foot sent his head. She recovered her balance and swung the stunrod up between his legs, holding it in contact while the blue tip glowed.

Growling, the giant whirled around in utter disregard of the stun electronics, using his thighs to torque the weapon out of her grip. He grabbed her throat with both hands. Kirsten put her forearms together and shoved upward, forcing his arms apart while thrusting her thumbs into his eyes. He flung her away and wiped at his face.

"Bitch."

She growled. Pipes rang in a cacophony of disharmonic bells as several dozen rolled off the forklift. Before she could look toward the sound, the big man tried to punch her again. This time, she spun under the attack while grabbing his bruised wrist and torqueing it with an aikido takedown that left him flat on his chest. She swung around, hooking his arm with her leg, and wrenched it backward at the elbow. The man roared and rolled onto his side, cradling his floppy limb.

Kirsten kicked a field goal into his nose, knocking him senseless not a second before the driver, the long-haired, perfect, beautiful man of a driver, ran at her with a crowbar. She leaned to the right to avoid an axe chop of a downswing. He followed through with a sideways slash, chasing her back from the abandoned stunrod. She ducked his next attack and grabbed his arm, trying for a shoulder toss, but he spun out of it and tried to bash her in the kidneys. Kirsten flung herself to the ground on her chest to avoid the crowbar, rolled, and swung her body around while kicking his legs out from under him, her hard armor sliding easily on wet plastisteel.

Gabriel's avatar landed flat, made an impressed face for a half second, and sprang upright. They circled, trading tentative attacks and grabs. Kirsten's heart pounded. All she could think about was Konstantin touching her, his coarse hand sliding up inside her leg, stopped by the symphonic blast of a ringing NetMini. That made her think of the ignored call from Evan. Somehow, whatever he'd done to that bracelet had made her regard the boy as unimportant. More than almost letting a seventy-year-old man have sex with her, more than getting locked up naked in a basement dungeon, more than anything physical he did to her… Taking her mind away, making her into someone she wasn't for weeks… Making her dismiss Evan…

Kirsten let off an enraged roar and lunged. Gabriel seemed unprepared for her aggression, and missed the block. Her armored fist crashed across his chin as an ill-aimed counterattack from the crowbar glanced over her left arm. As he reeled from the hit, she grabbed his right shoulder with both hands and drove her knee into his gut again and again while shouting, "Fucking… bastard…"

He let off a wheeze, abandoning any pretense of style to smash his crowbar down with a barbarian's wild swing into her left thigh. Again, the Division 1 armor bore the brunt of it, though the leg went numb and locked. Kirsten growled and shoved him forward while hooking his leg with her right heel. Gabriel slammed onto the ground, jacket flaring open to reveal a handgun in his belt. She favored her left leg for two steps and pounced on him, pinning his weapon arm to the plastisteel plate with her shin. She grabbed the pistol from the front of his belt and pounded him in the face with it over and over, bouncing his head off the metal ground. Not until the seventh hit did she realize she screamed, "son of a bitch," with every strike.

Winded, she froze, bloody handgun held high, the echo of her rapid breathing echoing inside her helmet. A droplet of sweat dangled at the tip of her nose for a second before falling, splattering against her visor and running down to the white strip of padding by her mouth.

Gabriel's mashed face liquefied into a blurry mass for a few seconds before returning to its former pristine state. "Ouch. Whatever they told you, I didn't do it."

She crawled off him and clamped both hands on her left thigh. Squeezing it didn't help much through armor. "Sorry."

Distant sounds of gang warfare stopped to silence. At the end of the alley, a few men stood with guns raised frozen in time, their faces in harsh shadow from azure muzzle flare. A passing pigeon hung motionless in midair between warehouses. Her police armor vanished, replaced by a white cheongsam and loose silk pants. Energy spread out from where she and Gabriel sprawled, overwriting the city. Plastisteel became the light-grain wood floor of a dojo surrounded by rice paper walls. The stink of trash and human waste gave way to the *much* more pleasant aroma of sandalwood. His grungy blue jacket and battered pants reconfigured into a black Chinese shirt with silver cuffs, a row of buttons down the center.

He sat up, elbows on his knees. "Are you up for more work on sword forms today or would that be taking my life in my hands?"

Kirsten rubbed her unarmored thigh until the memory of the crowbar strike faded. Staring at her bare feet reminded her of fighting her way out of Konstantin's mansion with only a thin black robe on. "Sorry. Just working out some leftover anger."

"Anything you want to talk about?"

She grumbled as she stood. "You wouldn't believe me."

A simple, straight jian appeared hovering in midair next to her, a matching one at his right. Both swords rotated on their long axis, narrow, mirror-polished dual-edged blades gleaming in sourceless light. Red and white paper lanterns swayed on a string by a door out to a snow-covered mountain. She lost a moment watching a gold tassel dangling from the handle sway.

"How can you know that? If it's too personal, I understand."

Kirsten grasped the weapon, which offered a little resistance as if she'd unseated it from foam. The blade felt heavier than she'd expected given its size. To her, it seemed about right, but in Gabriel's hand, it looked like a toy.

"Why do they always make these training sims so peaceful. It almost feels wrong to fight here."

"To clear the mind of all distractions." He walked closer, his stance casual enough not to get her guard up. "Stand like this." He adopted a posture with his arms wide, sword up, legs apart.

She mimicked him.

"The jian is an extension of you." He brought his weapon arm down in a slow, telegraphed gesture.

A few feet behind him, she recreated the maneuver.

"Do not think of it as a weapon in your hand, but your hand as a weapon." He completed the swing and moved through a graceful transition to another stroke. "As with Kung Fu, footwork is vital."

She followed his motions for a few minutes, feeling more like a dancer than a fighter. "If this wasn't meant to kill people, it would be pretty to watch."

He smiled. "Some masters do learn it for the sole sake of putting on displays."

"This man got into my head. Made me act like someone else... like a helpless little woman." She wobbled up on the balls of her feet, trying to keep balance, copy Gabriel's moves, and think at the same time. "Everyone kept saying he was wrong for me, but I couldn't see it... the... whatever it was— magic—wouldn't let me. I felt so defiled."

Gabriel paused, his face a mask of sympathy. "I'm sorry. That had to be—I can't even imagine."

Kirsten looked at her reflection in the flat of the blade. "It's worse than anything I can think of, to be someone's puppet like that."

"Mind control?" Gabriel reached a hand out to type on a little holo panel that appeared in response to his gesture. "You really look like you want to kill someone. I've started a melon chucker. If you let one in, you'll get a little zap."

"A melon chucker?" She glanced at him.

The answer to her question appeared in the form of a large cantaloupe with an angry cartoon face. Spaghetti-noodle arms dangling from its sides held small knives. It tilted forward in a mimicry of a human head, and came flying at her.

She sliced it in half with relative ease.

Another appeared, a second behind it. More melons phased in at a steady pace, varying in angle and elevation. By the fifth cut, she recognized the pattern of the form he had been demonstrating, and anticipated the seventh melon appearing at knee level. By continuing the motion, she cut the fake fruit as soon as it appeared.

After thirty, a gleeful chime filled the room and the melons stopped.

"Not exactly mind control. More subtle. Slight changes to my personality to suit him." She frowned at her seed-spattered cheongsam.

"Hope he got a long sentence." Gabriel adopted another stance, which she copied. He proceeded to show her a second form that included a few thrusting motions as well as a spin.

"Yeah. You can say that." She blocked out the image of Konstantin's body melting into the floor, and concentrated on how to move. "Karma's a bitch."

BLINDING WHITE LIGHT FADED TO THE CEILING OF THE TRAINING FACILITY AND A poorly positioned LED bulb cluster overhead. Kirsten moaned and scooted down on the padded, reclining chair to get her head out of a massive helmet more like a hole in the side of a computer cabinet than headgear. The pale blue material of her jumpsuit swooshed as she rolled around and sat on the side, sore and sweaty.

Gabriel sat up on a nearby bench and disconnected an M3 wire from behind his left ear. Kirsten glanced at the blinking lights and silver rods around the hollow where her skull had spent the last two hours. How it took something that big to replicate what a little wire could do…

"Ugh. I feel like I got hit by a PubTran." She looked down past her toes at her sneakers, the floor too far down to touch.

"Hey Gabe, you didn't tell me it was take your kid to work day." A muscular man in a dark blue Division 5 jumpsuit walked by with a swollen duffel large enough for Kirsten to sleep in over his shoulder.

Gabriel twisted to face him as he passed. "The short ones are usually the most dangerous." He glanced back at her and shook his head. "Idiots."

She sighed. "It's nothing I'm not used to dealing with whenever I'm around those meatheads. I think I'm gonna go back among my own kind where the knuckles don't quite drag on the ground so much."

"Really? Your Tac guys don't tease you at all for being so small?"

"I'm not *that* small. I'm five foot even." She jumped down to stand and put her sneakers on. "And no, they don't. When you've seen small children capable of throwing grown men around with Telekinesis, a person's size doesn't impress all that much."

"Five even huh? Are you sure you're not four-eleven?" He winked.

Her attempt to give him a playful shove ended with a submission grapple. She flung herself into him before he could complete the hold, tackling him over the padded chair with a forearm at his throat.

"You're getting better." He wheezed. "Use your opponent's strength and momentum against them."

She slid back to her feet, shaking her arm out. "Thanks. And… ow. How on Earth does virtual training make me sore?"

"The brain—"

"I know… I'm just complaining." She slouched. "Thanks. I gotta get back. Ugh. I know those melons weren't real, but I feel sticky."

Gabriel rendered a whimsical salute. "You are getting better, but remember… anger is a poor substitute for confidence."

Kirsten spun to face him, clasped her hands together, and bowed like a monk. "*Domo arigato, Silva-san.*"

He shook his head, chuckling. "You're working on *Chinese* sword forms, but points for trying."

"See you next week." She threw a small white towel at him and jogged out of the training room.

Preferring to avoid unwanted attention from some beat cop twice her size who thought her too small for service, Kirsten headed to the Division 0 wing to clean up. The barracks area for the active duty officers contained a military-style shower: zero privacy. Steamy air swirled around twelve autoshower tubes arranged in two rows of six against opposite walls with lockers and benches between them. Though not official, women tended to gravitate left while the guys went to the right. Two blurry figures occupied tubes on the left, while four men milled around by the other side.

Kirsten kept her gaze on the floor and headed straight for a locker, where she ditched her shoes before peeling off her sweat-soaked training suit and underwear, which she stuffed into a chamber in the center of the bank of lockers. Upon closing the hatch, the dirty clothes zipped off to a cleaning unit somewhere in the basement.

"Hey, Wren." A dark-haired woman with light brown skin stepped out of an autoshower behind her.

"Hey." Kirsten didn't look up. Shared showers were awkward enough *without* conversation, much less conversation with eye contact. When the woman sidled up to a locker four feet away, Kirsten couldn't help but take a quick glance left to see who it was. "Oh, Hey Kerrie." *Shit... is it Sanchez, Santana, Santiago?*

"Nice job with that hostage situation." Kerrie S-something opened another laundry chute and retrieved her underwear. "Real smooth."

"Thanks." Kirsten shut her locker and walked to the nearest open autoshower. *Wow. No 'oh crap, it's the mind blaster.'* She glanced over her shoulder at Kerrie, now half in uniform, felt grateful, and pulled the shower door closed.

Heeeeeeey!

Nicole's telepathic shout vibrated Kirsten's eyeballs. *Ouch.*

Water blasted her from all angles, a soothing, pulsating massage that made the imagined workout in a virtual reality scenario melt away. Nicole hopped in the adjacent tube.

The redhead blowfished the glass. *Hey, you okay?*

Kirsten grumbled, the sound lost under the whirr of spray jets. *Yeah fine.*

I mean about that jackass old man.

If I could kill him again I—

It's cool you and Sam are dating.

—would. Kirsten sighed as the soap phase started.

Evan is totally adorable! I'm so happy you found him.

Kirsten grinned. *I've been wondering if that really was chance or if there's—*

Oh, my God! You have to try this lime-avocado grilled chicken from this new place Morelli found.

—some kind of higher intelligence at—

I'm thinking of applying for a transfer to I-Ops. Nicole quieted for a few seconds while lathering her hair.

—*work.* Kirsten sighed. "Why do I bother?" She closed her eyes and basked in the feeling of the rinse cycle.

What do you think? Nicole wiped a patch of fog off the interior of her shower tube and peered at her.

Kirsten thought about sushi, the first thing her brain seized on in order to avoid killing the hope brimming in her friend's deep blue eyes. If she said great idea, and she failed the test, Nicole would think she could fix it with study. Heck, maybe she could. Maybe she wasn't *that* scatterbrained. *Uhh. Maybe. Are you sure you want to? I-Ops can be boring without the ghosts.*

You think? Nicole bit her lip. *That place has an awesome chipotle steak sandwich too.*

Sounds great. Maybe I'll—

So like what do they do if there's no ghosts?

Kirsten blinked. *Uhh, investigate crime committed by psionic indiv—*

Jaden wanted to take me to this expensive restaurant in a couple days. You wanna bring Sam and double-date it?

—*iduals. You know, police work? I'm in my own personal layer of Hell with the ghost stuff.* Kirsten shrugged. *I'll ask him, but if it's the Five Corners, no way.*

It's nice that they save all the ghost stuff for you. Nicole smiled. *You're like the best person to deal with it.*

Kirsten stared at her as the dry cycle whirred to life, surrounding her in a cyclone of hot air. *You're messing with me now.*

Nicole stuck out her tongue; a stream of water from the rinse in her tube ran from the tip. *Well you were worried about thinking I'm stupid. I'm not dumb. I have a short attention span.*

Kirsten looked downward. *Sorry.* The lock clicked on the tube door once the dryer fans shut off. She stepped out into the freezing air and trudged four steps to the lockers. She stood, staring at the hatch containing her cleaned-and-plastic-wrapped training suit and underwear, zoning in and out for several minutes.

"You okay?" Nicole put a hand on her shoulder. "I'd hug you, but it's against regs since we're both free-titting it right now."

Kirsten rubbed her face and slid her fingers up over her hair until she cradled the back of her head. "I went crazy on Gabriel. I thought about *him* and lost it."

"Understandable. If you wanna talk sometime... maybe get good and messed up." Nicole slipped around behind her and reached for a laundry hatch.

Kirsten glanced left, eye-level with Nicole's chin. "I'm trying not to drink now. My mother was always half in the bag. I... I'm afraid if I don't stop now,

I'll turn into her someday. Besides, the piece of shit that used to hit Evan drank all the time. He saw me reach for the SynVod once and gave me this heartbreaking stare..."

"Aww." Nicole snugged her underwear into place, flashed a mischievous smile, and pounce-hugged Kirsten, pinning her arms. "Oh, that's *so* sad! I'm really happy you found him. You sure you're okay after what that shithead did?"

"Uhh..." Kirsten went rigid as her friend squeezed. *Pretty sure physical contact with only one person being dressed isn't in the regs either.* "Thanks." As soon as Nicole let go, she swiped her fresh, still-warm underwear from the cleaning unit, leapt into them, and grabbed her uniform pants from the locker. "I'll deal with it. The worst part is I can't figure out why he went to all that trouble to get me to sleep with him."

Nicole's cherry-red hair burst out from the neck of her clingy black uniform shirt and settled around her shoulders. She tugged the garment down and worked her arms about to seat it. "He summoned the demon, right?"

"Yeah." Kirsten wriggled into her shirt.

"Is it true about the angel thing?"

Kirsten half-shrugged and grabbed her utility belt. "I think they'd consider 'angel' a simplification... or maybe an over-complication. They're not exactly the stuff the bible-thumpers think they are, but I guess they come close enough. And yeah. Something about them wanting me to stand between the realms or something."

Nicole held her hands out to the sides. "Well there ya go. I bet that jackass knew they chose you, so he wanted you disoriented so you wouldn't interfere with him. If he killed you, the uhh—Seraphim, was it? —would've chosen someone else."

Stunned, Kirsten gawked at her friend.

"See. I'm not an idiot." Nicole winked. "You wanna hit that place for lunch today?"

"Sure..." Kirsten stooped to click the fasteners on the outside of her boots closed. "Provided nothing goes bump in the afternoon."

"Huh?" asked Nicole.

Kirsten laughed so hard she cried.

"What?" Nicole folded her arms.

"Thanks... I really needed that." She wiped her eyes, giggling as soon as she looked at Nicole's clueless expression. "As long as I don't get sent on a call, sure."

"Great! You'll love the food there." Nicole looked around and lowered her voice as if passing along state secrets. "They say the guy who runs it grows his own veggies... like actual plants in the dirt."

Kirsten suppressed the urge to wince. "Sounds expensive."

"Nah, not really." Nicole winked and started for the exit. "I'll be back like ten after twelve. Gotta re-qual on the E-86."

"Okay." Kirsten left the shower room at a slow trudge, wondering why Captain Eze never made her requalify with the E-90. *I'm not tactical. I barely use it anyway...* She smirked and checked her armband terminal for any sign of incoming issues. No calls from the senator, nothing from Mrs. Dominguez either, and all quiet from the school. She pondered going anyway, frowning at herself for being unable to shoot down murderous orb bots. *Hmm. Why not. I could use some trigger time.*

Feeling more motivated than she'd expected, Kirsten strode off to the weapons range.

9

LATE

Pale, coral-hued walls glowed from LED bulbs set into a chrome-plastic track near the ceiling. Kirsten leaned on the bathroom counter, one hand on either side of the sink, staring at herself in the mirror. A baggy light-grey sweatshirt hung past her knees, the image of a 'cute' version of Monwyn the wizard on the chest. She straightened and slid a hand up under the fabric, tracing her fingers over her stomach. Worry flittered around her gut where the cramps weren't. As best she could remember, Konstantin hadn't done anything more than touch her with his fingers. She cringed and crossed her legs at feeling it again.

No. He couldn't have. She clenched her jaw. *After he drugged me?* She paced. That didn't make any sense either. He didn't want a child. Heck, the man probably didn't even really want to have sex with her… he wanted to keep her out of his way. If that meant playing the role of lover, so be it. Yet, anything could've happened to her while she was unconscious. Had Konstantin been the one to lock her in manacles, or did he have one of his thugs do it?

Feeling sick, she lurched over the sink but managed to keep in her dinner.

"Easy enough to find out."

Kirsten stormed out to her bedroom and grabbed her NetMini. She paced about while ordering a pregnancy test and marched up to the outer wall. Floor-to-ceiling window made up three quarters of the length of the exterior wall, an extended section like someone had stuck a glass box on the side of the building to form an enclosed patio. She gazed up past the curved glass roof at a hovercar lane nine stories overhead. Within three minutes, a little flying box glided to a stop outside. She opened the small section of window that could move, and the bot nosed in far enough to read her ID from the NetMini. It emitted a happy chirp and opened a hatch, from which she retrieved her order. After another pleasant sounding series of beeps, it rushed off to join the thousands of luminous dots swarming over the city in a band of dark beneath an indigo haze.

Silver residence towers glinted and flashed in an unending electric light show. She spent a moment mesmerized by it before trudging to the bathroom. "Window, dim full."

The amber-hued panes shaded to black, blotting out the city. She planted herself on the toilet and held up a white cylinder that resembled a stimpak autoinjector with an extra square bit about the size of an E-mag at the top. It projected a small holographic screen when she pushed the only button.

"Thank you for purchasing the RediMed home pregnancy test," said a female voice. "Step 1 – sync the test with your NetMini. This enables the nanobots to provide the most accurate results. Step 2 – after syncing, apply the autoinjector to any point on your abdomen or thighs you feel comfortable with." The three-inch square holo-panel played a demonstration animation. "Step 3 – Collect a urine sample with the lower end of the test device, on the provided pad. Step 4 – Approximately five minutes after injecting, the nanobots will transmit the results to the test unit, which you can access via your NetMini. Good luck!"

Kirsten held the white object up like a dagger about to be plunged into her heart, and stared a challenge at it. "Okay, listen up. You are going to make me a very happy girl right now... well in five minutes, right?"

It didn't react.

She exhaled, pulled the sweatshirt up to expose thigh, and hesitated. "Crap. Gotta sync it first."

Three seconds after holding the test unit up to her NetMini, both devices beeped. The NetMini opened a new app, which displayed a loading progress bar of a cartoon baby running on a treadmill. When it finished, the image changed to a status monitor showing a good signal strength next to a female outline with a yellow question mark in the womb.

Kirsten pulled up her sweatshirt again and held the device to her skin.

"Mom?" yelled Evan, probably from the door between her bedroom and hallway. "I made popcorn."

"Few minutes, hon." Kirsten pressed the autoinjector down. A brief flicker of pain preceded a cool numbness spreading under the skin. "Almost finished."

"'Kay."

She looked around to make sure Theodore wasn't peeking out from behind any walls, and tried to hit the little half-inch test square to collect a sample. Once finished, she leaned forward. Elbows on knees, she clutched the test unit with both hands, glaring at it. Her mind raced around what she'd do if it made her nightmare come true. She could have the developing embryo removed and grown in a medical tank, and adopt it away without ever laying eyes on the baby. Kirsten bit her lip. Despite the father being *him*, or even worse, one of his employees, some part of her couldn't readily accept giving the child up... half would still be her.

"Argh." She bowed her head, forehead to plastic. "Please tell me he didn't do that to me."

"You okay Mom? Sounds like you're goin' to war in there."

Kirsten's cheeks burned. "I-I'm almost done."

"You need me to get anything? Extra TP? A stimpak? Father Villera?"

She laughed. "Thanks... I'm okay."

His voice faded from shouting to an almost whisper at the bathroom door. "I don't think you need to be scared."

Does he know? Clairvoyant... She bit her lip, stood, flushed, and washed up. After sealing a sanitary cap over the bottom half of the test kit, she carried it with her NetMini and left the bathroom. Evan was nowhere in sight. She padded down the corridor, finding his room empty, but located the boy on the sofa. He grinned as she walked in. As soon as she sat next to him, he leaned into her, using her shoulder as a headrest. She left the NetMini and test on the cushion to her right, and put an arm over him.

"You've been acting weird for two days." He looked up at her. "You don't need to be afraid."

Kirsten kissed the top of his head and hugged him tight.

He raised a hand, pointing at the ceiling. "Play!"

Monwyn the Liberator, a new series, appeared on the 150-inch holo-panel. The show was set between the first and second movies, with a primary storyline revolving around the titular mage's initial meeting with Asara the Huntress. The story detailed how he'd become allies with her and assisted in the war that freed the Wild Elves from their servitude to the Shadow King. Kirsten had some doubts about how they could stretch something like that out to 138 episodes, but... Evan adored Monwyn, so she was going to find out.

The NetMini chimed. Kirsten glanced out of the corner of her eye at it and swiped a finger over the sensor. Its holo-panel scrolled into existence a few inches above the device, glowing violet. At seeing a negative result, her heart resumed beating. Not two seconds after she hit 'ok' to close the app, thirty-seven different mini-panels opened in a tremendous bloom of light. Most offered medical assistance with conceiving, some adoption services, and two showed ads for counseling—in case the negative result caused too much emotional stress.

She swiped her hand at the mess of floating micro-screens, scattering the intangible tiles apart. Images faded to blank amber squares, and they winked out of existence. Evan looked over with a sorrowful look that filled Kirsten with worry that the boy had become terrified she wanted to replace him.

"I'm... It's..."

He reached up and hugged her around the neck. "You only kissed Sam, and that doesn't make babies. I'm glad that demon guy didn't give you one."

Kirsten's composure faltered, and she found herself sniffling into his hair.

The NetMini emitted the modulating ring of an official call. She held on to him like a teddy bear, unwilling to let go long enough to answer. When it started ringing again, she'd gathered herself enough to pick up.

Captain Eze's hologram head faded in. "I hope this isn't a bad time. We've had an emergency call in."

She whined. "What happened?"

"We received a contact from the security team at the NewsNet office tower in Sector 1740. They are reporting unusual activity on the thermal scans, and one claim of an object moving."

"That doesn't sound like an emergency." Kirsten frowned.

"Does the name Robert Lamb sound familiar?" asked Captain Eze.

"Poor guy. Nope." She shook her head.

Captain Eze chuckled. "He's the assistant program director for Earth."

"Assistant?" She scrunched up her face.

"That means he does all the work and gets none of the credit." Captain Eze's hands entered the hologram as he held them up. "It's coming from higher up. Likely take you longer to get there than it will to resolve."

Kirsten grumbled.

"It's okay, Mom." He gestured at the screen. "It'll pause 'til you get back. Nothing bad happened for a couple weeks, sometimes you gotta work late."

"On my way, Captain."

Evan wiggled his toes. He looked disappointed, but smiled when she made eye contact. She felt horrible for leaving, despite not having a choice. Maybe she could go Admin and get normal hours... but they didn't have anyone else to deal with spirits. She called Nila on her way to the bedroom.

"Hey. How long?" asked Nila.

Kirsten laughed. "Am I that predictable?"

"*They* are." Nila's hologram-face smiled.

"I dunno, probably not long. This sounds like a case of a guy with an inflated sense of self-importance hearing a bump in the dark. Probably a half hour. Or so. Thanks."

"Anytime. He's too good to be true, ya know. Tell me he's got his bratty moments when no one's watching?"

Kirsten closed her bedroom door and tossed the NetMini to the

Comforgel pad so she could change into her uniform. "Not yet. Maybe I should be worried. Maybe it means he doesn't feel secure enough to let his guard down." She exhaled.

"Or maybe you got astoundingly lucky and he really is a perfect angel." Nila shrugged. "Stranger things have happened."

An ear-piercing shriek came over the vid call from the background.

"Dare I ask?"

"Shani's throwing a fit because some character in her game can't wear some dress." Nila cringed as another shrill wail shattered the silence behind her.

"Maybe Ev will distract her." Kirsten stepped into her boots. "I'll be right down."

"'Kay. See ya." Nila winked and hung up.

Evan met her in the hallway, still in his pajamas, but he'd put shoes on. "Do I need a sleepover bag?"

"Nah, this should be quick."

He tilted his head forward, staring past his eyebrows at her. "Never say that."

She held his hand on the walk from the 41st floor to the 39th, and Nila's apartment. After giving him a quick kiss on the cheek, Kirsten jogged back to the elevator and headed to the roof parking deck. By the time she reached the patrol craft, her mood had darkened almost as black as its armor plating.

"There'd better be something there for me to smack around."

She hopped in and brought the car online.

Dorian faded in as she lifted off, and yawned. "What's up?"

"Some asshat from the NewsNet got spooked enough to pull strings." She wrenched the sticks, launching them up and over the civilian hover lane at the fiftieth story. At about the eightieth, she opened up to 385 miles per hour, switched on the roof lights and activated the audible warning, a transmitter that forced any other car within about a quarter mile to simulate a siren with its sound system. Glowing traffic signals and advert holograms on the corners of high-rise towers formed a flashing zebra-stripe tunnel in bright bands, interspersed with the occasional smear of color from an advert bot.

Dorian stiffened, still seeming nervous with her driving at such speed. "Something bad's going to happen to the first person to say the wrong thing."

"I've been wound up the past couple days over Konstantin."

His look of apprehension relaxed to one of sympathy. "Anything you want to talk about?"

"Couldn't take it anymore. Bought a test today." She looked at him for a second before returning her attention to the front. "Negative."

"That's good." Dorian made a series of contemplative faces. "Nicole might've been right about that. It seems likely he was manipulating you by being exactly what you'd been dreaming about."

"He was *so* not my type." She slowed to a mere 290 to pull a left turn, rolling the patrol craft up on its side. For three seconds, she had a great view straight down out of the driver's side window. "The 'I'm so rich my money has money' thing was the exact wrong way to appeal to me."

"Well... he *did* have that much cash. I wonder how old he really was." Dorian tapped his chin.

Her eyebrows shot up. "You don't think?"

"All it takes is money, Kirsten. No magic needed. Genetic surgery. It's not cheap, but that wasn't a problem for Mr. Wrong."

"Ugh." Kirsten cringed. "Bad enough I think him seventy... if he's seven hundred?"

"Well... the oldest he could've possibly been is closer to two hundred. The technology didn't exist back then. Seven hundred years ago, they barely had flintlocks."

"You know what I meant." She craned her neck as the distant shimmering glow of the waypoint appeared from behind an approaching building. One good thing about having digital displays instead of transparent windows—getting lost was *quite* difficult.

The tall, rotating diamond came into view past the corner of the metallic green bulk of a ComTec International office tower. Every time she saw their goofy advert bot logo, she wanted to punch someone. More to the point, she wanted to find the guy who yelled at her for 'damaging' a bot after she jumped off a building to avoid getting blown up. The navigation crystal shrank from the apparent size of a fifteen-story building, resulting in a baseball-sized star shining at the dead center of the NewsNet complex.

Kirsten headed for the parking deck, the structure obvious from the air, and poked the windshield twice as if clicking the building on a touchscreen monitor. She shut off the bar lights and the audible warning system before landing in a parking spot close to the door.

The upper half of a late-twenties man with dark hair and light brown skin appeared in a panel at the center of the windscreen, wearing a light-grey NewsNet Security jumpsuit. "Evening, Officer. Is there a problem?"

"Oh shit," muttered Dorian, overacting a lean away from the imminent explosion.

The control sticks creaked under her grip. "Agent Wren, Division 0. We received a report about some unexplained events? Is there a guy named Lamb here?"

"Oh! Yes." The man's eyebrows shot up. "I'm *so* glad you're here. I'll meet you at the door."

"Now that is perhaps the happiest anyone's ever been to meet you." Dorian raised an eyebrow. "That makes me wonder what we're walking into."

"I told Evan it wouldn't take long." She hung her head. "Dammit."

With a grunt, she shoved the door up and open. A stiff, chilly breeze whipped her hair back, reminding her she'd forgotten her usual clip. Grumbling, she stormed across the roof. A faint pneumatic hiss from behind announced the patrol craft door sinking closed. Ignoring the out of control hair scattered around her shoulders, she headed for a bank of six elevators in a freestanding enclosure at the center of the roof. The second from the left opened, held by the same man from the call. A dark armored vest covered his jumpsuit over the torso. His belt supported a large ballistic handgun, several spare magazines, and a bevy of small compartments.

"Agent Wren." He offered a handshake. "I'm Curtis Parker, NewsNet security. Night shift supervisor."

She accepted his greeting and stepped into the elevator. "What can you tell me about the situation?"

The doors closed with a pneumatic squeak.

"Well… Lamb's been contacting us on and off for the past few hours. He thought someone was in the fish tank, and this late at night, everything's managed remote by work-at-homes."

Kirsten's eyebrows came together. "Fish tank?"

"Sorry." Curtis smiled. "There's a cluster of offices at the center of the 77th floor with frosted glass walls. Looks like a giant fish tank, so that's what people here call it. Anyway, with ops under the eye of the WAHs for the night, the area should've been empty."

Kirsten nodded.

Curtis glanced at the datapad he'd had tucked under his arm. "Mr. Lamb placed fourteen SRs between the… sorry, security requests, hours of 7 p.m. and 9:10. He insisted someone was walking around. At first, he thought Lewis or Martinez were trying to prank him, but his attempt to catch them failed. He was pretty sure no one could've possibly run from where he'd seen them to the elevators before he could spot them, but he still felt watched."

"Well, I suppose that could be caused by working ridiculous hours." Kirsten made a passing attempt to get her hair in order. *This guy isn't looking at me like I'm going to kill him.* She let some of her anger at being disturbed go. "Anything else? What made you call us?"

Ping. The elevator doors glided apart without a sound. Above the exit, a neon green hologram of the number 77 flickered. A dark room riddled with thousands of tiny light dots spread out before the elevator: a cube farm. Wires descended from the drop ceiling to desks here and there, glossy insulation glinting. At the center, an open space of about twenty yards surrounded a rectangular box of blue frosted glass that glowed from lights inside. Silver nameplates, too far away to read from the elevator, appeared as dark spots near doors.

She surveyed the area, sweeping her gaze from the desks at her left along the outer wall over the cubicles, to the right. The shadowed space at the outskirts of the room tugged at her consciousness with unease. A year ago, it might've unnerved her, but after getting up close with the energy around Charazu's ritual circle, it felt trivial.

Curtis held up the datapad and tapped it. "Well—"

Kirsten put a hand on his shoulder to stall him. "Wait. I feel something."

His expression lit up. "Really?"

Dorian walked off to the right, whistling. "Think you've got your first fan."

Focused on the far left corner, she disregarded his topic grenade. She advanced across a clearing in front of the elevator and followed a channel between the ring of cubicles to the clear area around the Fish Tank. The sense of a paranormal presence intensified as she entered the region where castoff light from the glass illuminated the grey-blue carpet. A trail led her to the second door on the left side, marked with the name Robert Lamb. She glanced at the dark corner near a red EXIT sign indicating a fire escape. Not until she looked back at the nameplate did a human-head shape in the shadow register in her mind.

Kirsten whipped around to stare at the spot where she'd thought she'd seen a man, and stared at a patch of pale wall, tinted pink in the castoff light from the exit sign.

"Is it still here?" Curtis walked around her, advancing closer to the corner.

I did see that... didn't I? She glared at the wall for a second more before facing Curtis. "If he is, he's not on this floor right now. What was it you were going to show me?"

"Clear," said Dorian, rounding the far corner of the Fish Tank.

Kirsten held a 'one moment' finger up to Curtis and looked at Dorian. "Can you check up and down a couple floors? I thought I saw something in the corner."

"Sure." Dorian sank into the carpet.

"Wow... that wasn't your comm was it?" Curtis's eyebrows ticked up a notch.

"No. So what did you have?"

Curtis worked his hand in a flurry over the datapad. "The last time Lamb sent in an SR, we pulled up the security vids. Check this out."

A holo panel appeared above the datapad, displaying a clone of the contents of the screen. Curtis opened an app, which split the secondary panel into six sub windows, views from security cameras. A pale blue vaporous mass glided across a black room. Lighter blue shapes hinted at cubicles, chairs, and pushcarts. The mass floated along, at times two whorl trails at the bottom swayed back and forth in a manner suggesting legs.

"That's a thermal anomaly, twenty-one degrees colder than the surrounding air."

Kirsten held back the urge to be sarcastic. "I'm familiar with the technology. I know something was here; I just can't tell who or why."

"Good grief," yelled a man on the other side of frosted glass. "I can't concentrate on anything with you out there talking. Either come in or go the hell away."

Kirsten gazed at the dark drop ceiling. "Lamb?"

Dorian poked his head up out of the floor. "No thanks, I'm watching my figure."

She exhaled out her nose. *He's not going to let that go.*

"Yep." Curtis nodded. "Oh, check this out." A few swipes of his finger changed to a thermal view of two bright orange bodies walking, with another pale blue anomaly to the right. On this screen, the cold spot had a far more humanlike shape.

"Damn, that's almost military grade… I didn't think civilians bothered with such high-res thermal units."

"You'd be surprised. Two or three times a year, we get people trying to sneak in and plant taps on our network. The ones who make it into the building invariably have some manner of thermal cloaking suit on. This can spot them."

"Wow. Who cares about news that much?" Kirsten pushed the door to Lamb's office open on her way in.

"Some want to inject their content onto our network to broadcast disinformation. Usually, it's people who make money on ads," said Curtis. "Other networks try to steal our feeds before we can broadcast so they get the ad revenue."

A thick-bodied man in a shiny silver dress shirt leaned over a desk formed of an inch-thick slab of the same cyan frosted glass as the outside of the Fish Tank. Dense, curled blond hair resembled a dead woodland creature draped over his head. His ruddy complexion strengthened her impression the hair didn't belong to the man. Trails of sweat glided down saturated cheeks. He leaned back in his chair, his face reddening even more as he stared at Kirsten. Eventually, the meaning of her uniform seemed to sink in and his demeanor went from irritated to tolerating. He grumbled before knocking back the last quarter-inch of brown liquid in a tumbler glass and setting it down, a pair of thermo-cubes rattling. Detecting no more liquid around them, they ceased glowing blue and went dark.

The other three walls had a grey tone not far removed from black, covered with motivational posters, bookshelves, and a few portraits of people that looked vaguely familiar. She might've seen one or two on the NewsNet as a child, and assumed them retired reporters.

"Mr. Lamb?" Kirsten walked up to the desk, taking note of a squarish bottle of JDH he leaned back in his chair Jack Daniel's Hydroponic, about ₡4,700 per bottle. "I'm Agent Wren from Division 0. We received a report of unknown activity here?"

"That's right." He wiped a hand down his cheek, pulling his jowls into a distorted caricature of a face. "I'm trying to finalize production schedules for the next broadcast period and I'm being constantly distracted. At first, I thought it was a couple of the day crew messing with me, but when I got up to look, I couldn't find anything. No way could anyone make it to the elevator that fast."

"Are you feeling all right, Mr. Lamb?" Kirsten tilted her head. "You look like you might be running a fever."

"Stress… and whatever atrocity those cafeteria people are passing off as food these days. Shit. I can't even tell what my lunch was supposed to be." The bottle of JDH wobbled in his hand as he poured himself another finger. "Been tryin' to cut back, but this is more than I can handle."

"I'd like to try something. It's going to look scary, but I want you to understand that it can in no way harm you." Kirsten concentrated on the Astral Lash, projecting a long tendril of blue-white energy from her right hand.

"Whoa," said Curtis. "That's the most amazing thing I've ever seen."

Lamb raised an eyebrow. "What is that?" Locking stares with a matching light emanating from her eyes, he froze.

"It's a psionic weapon that can only hurt ghosts. Please don't worry."

He rendered a mute nod.

She swept the lash at him, but it met no resistance. After a second swipe, she let it dissipate, darkening the room. "Whatever is making you feel sick is not a parasitic paranormal entity."

"That's good, I guess." Lamb picked up the glass, hesitated, and set it back down.

"Can you think of anyone who died within the past several years who might want to cause you harm?" Kirsten paced around the office, hand out like a paranormal antenna. Energy seemed at a constant elevated level. A glowing handprint appeared on a bookshelf, and a fist-shaped smear on the interior wall caught her eye. "Whoever this spirit is, he spent a lot of time in this room. And he was angry." She walked to the spot and traced her finger around it. "I'm thinking this is a relatively recent ghost who doesn't have enough power to affect you yet. He probably became frustrated and hit the wall."

"Uhh." Lamb scratched at the silvery frizz in front of his right ear. "I'm so damn busy with the day-to-days… I can't think of anyone. If an employee has been terminated from my group in the past three or four years, it would've been Sudha's call."

Kirsten added notes to the incident report. "Sudha?"

"Sudha Malhotra, Senior VP in charge of programming." Lamb waved his left arm at the wall. "Next office over."

Dorian glided in through the glass wall. "The one who gets credit for all the work the assistant VP does. Nothing around but a few former security officers hanging out in the café two floors down."

Kirsten glanced at him. "Former former? Or *former* former?"

"The latter. Couple years apart, but they were all killed by people trying to infiltrate the building." Dorian shook his head. "Sometimes, I think it's nicer on this side. No money to worry about. They didn't report noticing any other spirits, and they all confirmed each other's alibi at having been there the whole night so far."

She blew a sigh out the left side of her mouth. "Did you find out what's keeping them here?"

Curtis and Lamb exchanged a glance.

"One thinks 'haunting' is fun. Two are upset NewsNet cheaped out on their death benefits, and are waiting around until the lawsuits their families started are resolved. The other guy doesn't believe he's dead."

"There goes my 'be right back.'" Kirsten looked at Lamb. "Sorry. Looks like a couple of your security people are still haunting the cafeteria on the seventy-fifth floor. It wasn't any of them."

"Oh wow. I always did feel weird going in there." Curtis scratched his head.

"Well, Mr. Lamb." Kirsten closed the holo-panel floating over her arm. "I'm afraid there's not a whole lot I can do right now other than document my findings. While I am sure a paranormal entity has been here, and is likely the cause for your 'distractions,' I can't do much to track them down without some real-world information to go by. Unless you can think of anyone who might blame you for their death, even if it's untrue, I've got nowhere to start from."

Lamb grumbled and rubbed his chin. "Curtis, can you run by HR and see if there's any recent deaths of disgruntled employees?"

"Sure thing, sir. I just need you to reply to the trouble ticket with the authorization for that request." Curtis shifted his head toward Kirsten. "If you provide me the Inquest number, I'll attach it to the incident report so you'll get notifications whenever there's an update on our side."

"Can't you read some tea leaves or tarot cards or something?" asked Lamb, his deep voice making the glass wall vibrate. He heaved an exasperated sigh and rubbed his forehead.

She smirked. "I'm afraid I'm neither a witch nor a fortuneteller."

"Or a clairvoyant," whispered Dorian.

Kirsten narrowed her eyes at Dorian. "Mr. Lamb, has anything happened to make you feel in danger of harm?"

"Only from stress. I can barely concentrate on this crap. If I don't lose my job in the next two days, I'll be shocked."

Dorian smiled. "They won't fire the salaried idiot willing to work sixteen hour shifts."

Kirsten opened the Inquest via her armband display, poked her finger into the number: 24181108A1, and tapped a 'civilian agency filter' before flicking it in Curtis's direction. His datapad chirped. Pop up holo-panels appeared over both her arm and his device, and they synced the case record with the NewsNet security trouble ticket. Fifteen lines of text scrolled in on the incident report, detailing Lamb's numerous contacts with the security team. The thermal scan of the walking cold spot appeared last.

"Got it." She closed the screen and let her arm drop at her side. "Again, I'm sorry Mr. Lamb, but without *something* to go on… there's nothing I can do other than catching him here. Has this happened before?"

"Not that I noticed." Lamb shook his head. He rubbed his gut and stifled a belch. "Ugh. Excuse me. The worst part about not knowing what the hell I ate is I can't avoid it next time."

Dorian chuckled. "You'd think NewsNet could afford a decent cafeteria contractor."

"Everyone else orders delivery." Curtis shrugged. "Do you think they order because the café sucks, or does the café suck because no one uses it?"

Lamb almost smiled. "You might have a point about that… uhh…"

"Parker, sir. Curtis."

"Right, Parker." Lamb tucked up to his console and waved as if to dismiss him. "Thanks for the effort. I'll send another email if it comes back."

Kirsten bit her lip. As much as it vexed her to walk away empty handed, the desire to get home to Evan won out. "I'll do some research as well." *Tomorrow.*

Curtis spun on her with a broad smile. "I'll walk you out."

"You're not hitting on me, are you?" asked Kirsten as she left Lamb's office.

"No, officer. I've just got a lot of respect for you guys… and I'm fascinated by psionics."

"Translation: He wasn't accepted to the police academy, and he thinks you've got a perfect—"

"Dorian!" yelled Kirsten.

Curtis jumped.

Dorian held his hands up. "I was going to say job."

"Yeah, right." She narrowed her eyes, though smiled a little as she walked toward the elevator.

"So who's the ghost with you?" Curtis tucked his datapad under his arm again and hit the call button. "If you don't mind me asking?"

"My partner. He made the ultimate sacrifice in the line of duty a few years ago."

"That sounds much better than charged into a bad situation like an idiot." Dorian winked.

"Ahh." Curtis looked around as if trying to estimate where he'd be. "Sorry, officer. Hope they got the bastard."

"They did." Kirsten turned to face the closing elevator doors, trying to force the memory of Rene's head exploding out of her mind. "It was too quick."

Dorian blinked. "That doesn't sound like you."

She flashed a Cheshire cat smile. "I would've preferred he'd been arrested."

"Okay. *That* sounds like Kirsten." Dorian chuckled.

Once on the roof, Kirsten took out her NetMini to send Evan a message that she was on the way, but frowned at the time: 9:49 p.m. *He should be asleep now.* She glared at the building. It would've been one thing to lose the hour and change she could've spent with her son if something was happening… but a new spirit being an annoying shithead—no risk of harm—made her bristle at the total waste of time.

She shook hands with Curtis and returned to the patrol craft. Going Code 3 on the way home would probably get her 'talked to,' plus it wouldn't make any difference. She couldn't keep him awake past his bedtime. Feeling defeated, she brought the car into the air and slithered into a normal traffic lane. Dark buildings passed on both sides, covered in streaks of light from cars as well as an ant army of small advert bots ambushing drivers with targeted commercialism.

"You okay?" Dorian looked over.

"I'm worrying how long his ability to forgive me for disappearing on him will last. Is he ever going to resent me running off like this? I feel horrible even when he's okay with it… And this was a bullshit call. Some low-grade haunt waving his phantasmal dick in the face of some corporate manager." She fumed. "I already don't like him."

"The ghost?"

"No. Lamb." She squinted. "Pulled strings to get me here and it's nothing."

Dorian looked ahead at the steady stream of red taillights in front of them. "He couldn't have known that."

"Yeah, but the description of events would've been filtered out by Admin and not sent up to Eze as an urgent." She scowled. "Too late now. If I whine about it, I'll only look petty and emotional."

"Well, you *are* emotional." He winked. "But I wouldn't call it petty."

"What do you think is going on?"

He tapped his knee for a few minutes, tilting his head back and forth. "Could be one of the people who got killed trying to sneak in to steal data. Maybe it's someone generally going after anyone working for NewsNet? Messing with their production schedule would cost the company money."

"Hmm. Not a bad angle. I'll check that tomorrow. Right now, I have a pillow calling my name."

10

SCARY DREAMS

The grating buzz of the alarm clock dragged Kirsten's consciousness kicking and screaming out of the warm, dark place it had crawled into. Her eyelids peeled apart, revealing a mass of dense mouse-brown hair in front of her face. Sleep melted away from her brain, allowing reality to seep into her awareness. Evan had migrated into her bed at some point during the night, and pulled her arm over himself. He stirred, roused a moment later by the incessant noise.

"Morning, kiddo."

He shifted onto his back and turned his head, almost touching noses with her. The boy hadn't bothered opening his eyes yet. "Morning."

Kirsten pushed herself up to sit. After a yawn, she reached over him and waved at the alarm to silence it, then wiped her hands up and down over her face. "Bad dream?"

"Snooze, two minutes," said an electronic voice from the eight-inch silver bar on the nightstand.

"Not really." He went limp, as if about to pass out again. "You're not gonna sleep here tonight, so I wanted extra time with you."

"What?" She stared at him. A minute later when he didn't react, she traced a fingernail across a thin strip of exposed belly between his pajama top and pants.

He grinned. When she did it again, he laughed and opened his eyes.

"You dreamed it?"

Evan caught her finger in both hands when she tried to tickle him again. "Yeah... You're gonna call me to say you have'ta go somewhere."

Kirsten brushed his hair out of his face. "Are you sure? Did you see something you needed to warn me about?" *Precognitive episodes usually come on in the face of imminent danger. He's not strong enough to see meaningless things.* She closed her eyes long enough to hope he wasn't able to see the future. Or at least if he turned out to be a precog, that Director Carter would hide him from C-Branch.

He sat up, wrapping his arms around his legs and hugging them to his chest. The look on his face made her think he pondered lying, but resignation (and a touch of blush) replaced it. "I had a scary dream and I was afraid of you going." He picked at the sheet by his foot. "It's not bad... I'm just being a wimp."

She slid to the edge of the Comforgel pad and let her legs hang over the side. "Do you want to tell me about the dream?"

"I woke up back in that place you found me. I didn't know it was a dream right away... I thought I was still there an' you finding me was the dream." His lip quivered. "I..." He gave in to tears.

Kirsten pulled him into a hug and let him cry. When the loudest of it subsided, she rubbed his back. "Dreams can't harm you, Ev. The nannies at the dorms kept telling me that when I was younger."

He sniffled.

"Didn't help me much to hear it either." She leaned her cheek against the top of his head. "Those people can never hurt you again. How about I stay home today?"

Evan wiped at his tears. "I think someone's gonna get hurt if you don't go. I only had a bad dream." He took a deep breath. "I'm okay."

She held him to arms' length by the shoulders and looked him in the eye. "Are you sure? It's been quiet... mostly. I have so much vacation time saved up I could probably stay home for a whole year." *I may have to adjust my belief system.* She glanced at her NetMini on the nightstand. *Maybe there is a little old man in a white robe. The senator hasn't called me yet.*

"Yeah." He yawned and his mouth closed to a sour expression of protest at being awake. "I only dreamed about the call where you apologized for havin' to go, so it was just me bein' chicken."

"Ev. There is nothing wrong with admitting you're afraid. Trying to hide it or ignore it isn't going to help. It'll only make it worse... trust me." She grumbled. "Even when I was like eighteen or nineteen, I'd have nightmares about my mother and wake up acting like a little kid I was so scared."

He blinked, looking shocked and worried. "Am I still gonna be scared when I'm that old?"

"I don't think so. You're a tough kid." She ruffled his hair. "A lot tougher than me."

"Nuh-uh. No one's tougher than you." He hugged her, grinning.

The alarm buzzed again, and startled them both to screaming. Kirsten flailed at the nightstand until the noise stopped. They looked at each other; expressions of panic faded to laughter.

"Okay. If you're sure then... go get ready."

Evan ran off to the hallway bathroom while Kirsten used the autoshower in the one attached to her bedroom. Soon, they met in the kitchen. Grumbling, she had to climb up to kneel on the countertop to reach the overhead cabinets. Evan giggled from over by the 'sem where he dialed up coffee.

"Don't laugh. You need a chair to reach the 'sem."

He stuck out his tongue. "Yeah but I really am nine, you're only the size of a kid."

In a fit of spontaneous immaturity, she stuck her tongue out at him.

Laughing, she hopped down and took a gooey blob of Grandma Goodman's Easy Eggs from the refrigerator—essentially a protein-based water balloon filled with liquid raw egg. Kirsten dropped it in a pan, popped it with a fork, and whisked the slime into a scramble. Evan set a large coffee (smelling of pseudo-mocha) next to her, then leaned on the counter by the reassembler, swaying side to side. It took her a moment to wrestle open a silver foil pack with eight three-inch 'breakfast sausages.' They tasted far better than anything the reassembler could make from OmniSoy. However, exactly *what* they were, she had no idea.

"Mom, can I have coffee?"

"Decaf."

Evan folded his arms. "The coffee gods look down upon your transgressions."

"Make it a half-caf... and a small." She added another Omni-sausage and a little more eggs to his plate. *His metabolism is already nuts... I need to check with medical about giving him coffee at his age.*

The machine whirred and beeped. He took his cup and followed her to the table. A few minutes of quiet eating later, worry crept into her mind. *I've had him for months, and he hasn't had one nightmare until last night...*

"Ev?"

"Hmm?"

"Was last night the first time you've had a dream about before I found you?"

The way the happiness seemed to fade away from him punched her in the heart. He stared at his plate, no longer seeming interested in eating. "Yeah."

"Did something happen? Why would you have a dream like that all of a sudden?" She reached across the table to hold his hand. "For me, I'd see something little... the way one of the dorm attendants would stand over me would make me think of that bitch, or the way some other kid down the hall screamed in their sleep reminded me of a noise one of the ghosts made when I was too afraid to help them."

The sorrow in his eyes lessened. "Uhh, no. I don't think so. I, umm, did kinda feel watched before I fell asleep. Maybe some ghost was tryin' to scare me."

Kirsten clenched her jaw. The senator, Julia Dominguez, then Lamb… seemingly random attacks with nothing connecting them, and she had a strong feeling the same entity had been responsible for all of it. The idea that some asshat ghost targeted *her* instead of those people brought fury to her eyes. Did the spirit want to drive her nuts running all over the city? Regardless of its motives, they'd gone too far targeting Evan.

"Mom?" He leaned back. "You look like you're gonna tear someone's nuts off."

She let out a meditative sigh. "I've had a few cases of prankster spirits messing with people, but it's gone before I get there each time." *No connection between the victims. Maybe it's me.*

Weak white light glowed from Evan's eyes after a few seconds of him concentrating. "We're alone." He looked around in a full circle before tilting his head at her. "Mom? How long did it take for you to always see them? Having to turn it on is annoying."

She chuckled and stabbed her fork into a bit of sausage. "I'm not sure it's an advantage. There's some things out there you might not *want* to see… but, for me, it happened on its own after I kept using it so much. I never really thought about wanting it on all the time. I was maybe eleven or twelve… only a few months before the cops found me and dragged me back to civilization kicking and screaming."

"Dragged back?" He shoveled food in his mouth.

"I'd gone feral, living in the Beneath since I was ten. I was terrified of adults… unless they were ghosts. There's so many of them down there, having the sight on became routine. When the police found me rooting around a trash crusher for food, I thought they were going to take me back to that woman, so I panicked"

"Will I get in trouble for havin' it on alla time?"

Kirsten gazed down. *No sense bullshitting the kid.* "There are some people who won't react well to seeing your eyes glowing. When you're at school or here, it's not a problem. Out in public, it could cause unwanted attention."

He leaned back, his head a little to the side. "I'm not ashamed of being psionic."

Her heart melted. "Oh, Evan. I'm not saying you should be. But there are people out there who fear and hate us. I don't want anyone to hurt you."

"It's not my fault I have wimpy powers," he yelled. A second later, his eyes widened to a look of terror.

"Evan," said Kirsten in a tone that failed to hide anger. "I'm not upset with you for shouting. I'm angry with the people who treat us like that." She slipped out of her chair, taking a knee at his side and holding his hand in both of hers. "Please don't look at me like you think I'm going to hit you." Her rage collapsed into sorrow, and a tear ran down her cheek. "There's no way I—"

He looked at his lap. "Sorry. I didn't. It... I never yelled at you before an' whenever I used ta yell, I got hit."

She squeezed him again. "I'm not going to turn into my mother."

"*Pff*." Evan gave her an incredulous look. "She was crazy. *My* mother isn't crazy. She's awesome."

Kirsten dabbed at her eyes. "I love you too, Ev."

They embraced until a beep from her NetMini a few minutes later made her let go to look at a text message from Captain Eze.

‹Everything okay? You're usually on the way by now.›

He's watching my GPS? She blinked, and typed ‹Leaving soon. Kid issues. Nothing serious. Will explain once I'm in.›

Evan burst out laughing.

Kirsten raised an eyebrow.

"You 'member that vid with the ghost crawling out from under that girl's bed, and her mother kept looking her in the eyes and saying 'no scary dreams in there' when she wanted her to go to sleep?"

Kirsten racked her brain. The boy devoured movies at a frightening rate; they all ran together. "I think so."

"Well..." He leaned forward, eyes wide. "Psionic moms can really look."

She giggled. "Come on. Get your backpack. We're late."

SLEEPOVER

E van stopped at the double doors leading to the school wing of the Police Administrative Center. He hugged Kirsten, ignoring a few laughs from older kids making fun of him for having his mother walk him to school. It didn't matter what they thought. After she hurried off to the elevators, he swiveled around, faced the hallway, and concentrated on Astral Seeing. The grinning cluster of kids in the hallway traded in their huge grins for curious stares.

"Hey Wren," yelled a fifth or sixth grade boy. "You about to mind blast someone?"

"No." Evan kept walking. "I'm looking for ghosts. I don't have Mind Blast."

"Cool." A girl in a teal dress on his right kept pace with his stride. "I've never seen an astral before." She bit her lip. "Are there any here?"

"Not right now, but there *is* a ghost in the building." He thought of Dorian. "Uhh, wait. Two… but one doesn't come to the school."

"So what if he can see ghosts?" said Shawn Fields, forcing his way through the crowd. "No one's afraid of that."

"Why do you want people to be afraid of you? Half the world hates us already." Evan stopped and folded his arms, locking eyes with the much larger boy before continuing via telepathy. *Ghosts can tell me things… like about how you sleep with a teddy bear.*

Red flooded Shawn's cheeks in an instant. He grabbed Evan by the shirt with both fists and pulled him up on tiptoe. His brain seemed to still be grinding on what to say back to Evan's telepathic gauntlet; his lips twisted and parted, but he only made faces.

"Go ahead hit me, but you're wasting your time." Evan's eye-glow reflected back at him from Shawn's glare. *I wasn't gonna say anything out loud about the bear. That's like personal and stuff.*

"Yeah." Shawn let go.

Evan's weight settled back on his heels.

As the big kid stormed off, the girl—Michelle?—blinked at him. "You were really gonna let him hit you?"

Evan stuffed his hands in his pockets, trying to act nonchalant. Having the attention of a fifth-grade girl with long, black hair scared him, unlike Shawn. "Yeah." He choked back explaining about his birth mother's asshole boyfriend. That would sound like he tried to play the pity card.

Alas, he noticed the surface thought peeking too late.

"Aww." Michelle patted him on the shoulder. "It's okay. My stepdad tried to hit me with a sword."

Evan gawked up at her. "What?"

"Good thing I'm quick." She dashed in a blur from his right side to his left. "He was cheating on Mom. I ratted him out."

"You caught him or you peeked?" Evan resumed trudging toward class.

"Peeked." Michelle grinned. "It wasn't a psionic hate thing... he was mad at me for making her leave him."

"Sorry."

"Not your fault." She waved, and ran off ahead to her room.

Evan pivoted on his sneaker and loped down the hall to his classroom, then to his desk.

Mr. Vasquez raised an eyebrow at him. "Evan? Eyes?"

"Astral Seeing. I'm trying to practice so it works like my mom. Always on without glowing. She said I shouldn't do it out in public."

"Oh." He shrugged. "Don't let me catch you cheating on any tests with it."

"I won't."

Mr. Vasquez folded his arms, smiling. "You won't what? Let me catch you?"

"I won't cheat. Besides, Abernathy's so old computers stop working if he gets near them."

The class chuckled.

Kirsten passed fourteen people on her way to the squad room, two of whom returned her smile. The rest looked away or, in three cases, ran. By the time she reached the door to her unit's office, she resolved to scream at the next person to give her a fearful look.

Tom Morelli looked up from his desk as she entered, and paled.

"What?" she shouted. "Why does everyone look at me like that?"

Lieutenant Morelli fidgeted. "Demons."

"Well." She set her hands on her hips. "I suppose I should understand that more than mind blast paranoia. This isn't right." She paused to keep emotion from tinting her voice. "We're all on the same side here unless I missed a memo. And… and…"

"She's the sweetest, kindest, most innocent person in the entire building over the age of twelve." Nicole telekinetically levitated a cup of dark mocha coffee over. The café stuff made the sludge from her 'sem taste like ichor from a demon's nether regions by comparison.

"Tell that to them." Kirsten waved at the door she'd entered from. "Ever since word got out I have a rating in Mind Blast. Even if it is low."

"I heard Commander Ashford sneezed and knocked some guy back to mental infancy." Morelli shrugged. "Sounds like BS to me."

"That's because it is." Kirsten pointed at him. "And *no*, I don't know firsthand. I did a lot of research. Wiping a brain takes a *crapload* of concentration and time. It's not something you can do off a sneeze."

"Actually," said an icy voice from behind. "I did once make a man defecate by accident when I sneezed. Didn't even need to use my gift."

Morelli sat pin straight at attention. "Commander."

Kirsten turned slow, and managed a professional smile (and salute) at the pallid man in the doorway to Captain Eze's office. "Commander."

Nicole waved and emitted an *eep*; after two seconds of staring frozen, she saluted him. "Sorry, sir."

Commander Ashford glanced at Nicole with a hint of amusement dancing in his eyes. He waved Kirsten over. "A moment of your time?"

"Of course, sir." She walked past him into the office, brushing close in direct defiance of all the people who ran the other way when he showed up.

Captain Eze settled the handful of butterflies in her stomach with his calm smile. "This is merely a formality."

Ashford walked in behind her and took the second seat facing the desk. "The brass are curious about your dealings with Senator Winchester."

"There's not much to say. I put everything in the Inquest record. Some reports of paranormal activity, watched feelings, noises, whispery voices… I noted a latent energy trace in one of the rooms, but by the time I got there, the entity had already left." She picked at the coffee cup, desperate to drink some, but refrained. "I gave the senator my PID and asked him to call me if it came back… but so far, nothing."

Captain Eze nodded, smirked, and grumbled. "I respect you too much to beat around the bush, Kirsten."

"Sir?" She raised an eyebrow. "Is something wrong?"

"No." He raised a hand. "As you are well aware from your dealings with

Commissioner Vernon, there are certain people in high places who become nervous when psionic individuals, even sworn officers, get close to someone with a senator's position. However, it is on record that he requested your presence after specifically citing his opinion of your trustworthiness."

She nodded before taking a long swig of choco-coffee-awesome.

"What I am basically saying here is… Whatever the senator asks you to do, it would be best for us all if you did it… barring anything unethical of course."

Kirsten sighed. "Money gets special treatment again."

"More clout than money, but… kid gloves, Kirsten. Kid gloves."

"Tread carefully." Ashford's 'reassuring' look would've worked for a mortician sizing someone up for a box. "Chances are, he'll need a little special handling or TLC. Don't feel that you need to compromise your ethics, or those of the Division. We are behind you all the way if something goes south —but… make sure you can prove anything with enough evidence to survive a Senatorial Inquest."

"You expect something to go wrong?" She looked from Ashford to Eze and back again. "Is Winchester dirty?"

"If he is, he's a master at hiding it." Captain Eze chuckled. "Of course, only C-Branch would dare to even look… assuming he's not one of the Five."

Ashford chuckled. "Isn't that a rumor? Besides, even if true, Winchester's far too young. The old boys wouldn't let him anywhere near it."

Eze touched three fingers to his eyebrow before waving his hand. "Who knows?"

"The Five? What, that conspiracy stuff about senators so powerful they control C-Branch or something?" Kirsten took another sip.

"More or less. Unsubstantiated rumor." Captain Eze leaned back. "Please… just be careful."

"Okay." She glanced at her NetMini. "He might not even call. I have a new theory. So far, we've had three contacts with different victims with no apparent correlation. Last night, I think the same ghost gave Evan a nightmare. What if this thing is after *me*? Trying to play with my head by sending me off to chase shadows?"

"An interesting theory. Is he all right?" asked Captain Eze.

"Yes, sir. Whatever it did, it triggered a nightmare of his previous situation… in particular his birth mother's abusive boyfriend. Since I've had him, he's never had a dream about that, not even once. I'm sure there is an external influence involved. I was going to start running some pattern checks on all the vics to see if anything lines up."

"Nothing at all obvious?" Commander Ashford brushed a tiny speck of lint from his black trenchcoat.

"No, sir. Nothing I've seen. One woman in her early twenties. Another woman pushing fifty. A male in his later forties. Debutante, military logistics clerk, NewsNet upper manager, and possibly my son." Kirsten fidgeted. "Oh and I've received two inbound calls that terminated before I could answer. I had Sam check on them, and both came from virtual devices. He's still trying to track them down, but it's not easy."

Captain Eze nodded. "All right then. Anything else to add, Commander?"

Ashford shook his head and rendered a crisp wave of dismissal without lifting his arm from his lap.

Kirsten stood, saluted them both, and hurried to her desk.

An hour and ten minutes later, her terminal had exploded into an octopusine arrangement of holo-panels; eight satellite display screens hovered around the primary, each crawling with algorithms trying to pattern-match some commonality between the three people who had reported events. The software combed through everything from banking records to vid calling habits to work to GPS tracking of their ImDent chips or NetMinis to network activity... She'd even set up a sniffer to dredge the citycams system in the event they'd gone elusive and disabled their personal electronics to travel somewhere unnoticed. Senator Winchester didn't seem to spend much time at all in West City, much less on Earth. Kirsten watched screens churn, tapping her finger on her cheek. *Maybe it's not the senator.* Inspired, she opened yet another holo-panel and started searching for 'Seraphina,' filtering for women age 18-25. *Not much to go by, but there can't be that many people with that name.*

185,722 results.

"Crap."

Dorian sidled up alongside her. "Now you're grasping."

"Do you think I'm worried over nothing? This could just be a new spirit having fun." She crossed her arms. "No... it felt angry. It's gonna do something as soon as it's strong enough to."

"That could take decades." Dorian reached for her coffee.

She snatched the cup away before he could chill it. "That's cruel. And, not exactly. You're not that old and you're able to manifest and touch people sometimes."

He studied the floor, tapping his foot. When he lifted his head, his expression had become as serious as she'd ever seen him. "I was angry."

Kirsten concentrated for a second, infusing her body with psionic energy. Once solid to spirits, she rested her hand on top of his where he gripped the desk.

Dorian glanced away. "Feeling sorry for me isn't going to help any more than you already have." He sighed and summoned a weak smile. "I kept telling you to leave Rene alone, but you got him."

She squeezed his hand. "Technically, Div 9 got him, but... Yeah."

"Maybe you can do something." He shifted his jaw side to side. "Don't let

Nila throw her happiness away over me. I'd rather she find someone alive than wallow in what could have been."

Kirsten nodded.

"So." He slid off the desk and studied the screens. "Anything?"

"Just a big fat wad of nope." She melted back into her chair.

Captain Eze rushed out of his office, heading for her desk.

"Oh shit. That's not good," said Dorian.

Kirsten sat up straight, then stood when the captain made eye contact. "Sir?"

"We received a report of a 21-04 in progress."

"Are you sure?" Attempted murder by a spirit manifested visible to normal people was so rare she'd only seen it once before. "That's..." She checked her utility belt. "I'm on the way, sir. Send the nav to the pat-vee."

"Wait." Captain Eze put a hand on her shoulder. "You can't drive there."

She blinked at him.

"It's on the Moon." He looked as apologetic as he did worried. "Well, technically it's *near* the moon. An unexplained phenomena occurred on a lunar orbital platform operated by Gravion Interstellar."

Kirsten slid her NetMini off her belt. *He knew.* "Guess I'm spending the night. How dangerous is it? What's been reported?"

Captain Eze walked with her to the elevator. "As far as we know, there is one employee out on a berth who refuses to come inside and only screams over comm. I don't have time to give you a full briefing right now. They'll bring you up to speed on the DS2. This is as Code 3 as things get in space. I'll fill you in on the details over comms once you're airborne."

Kirsten flipped the NetMini over and over in her hand. "Is it even worth it? I mean, I hate to sound like that, but... It's going to take hours to get there."

His expression went grim. "We're not expecting the woman to survive. Primarily, you're going there to deal with the spirit so it doesn't kill anyone else. The DS2 is already on the roof waiting for you."

They stopped by a pair of armored gloss-white doors, which slid open with a faint hiss, revealing a large elevator. She entered, turned to face the doors, and dialed Nila Assad.

The woman's head appeared in hologram, black hair and olive skin stark compared to the bright area around her. "Hey, K."

Bands of light slid down the walls as the chamber flooded with the background thrum of machinery.

"Nils... I don't have a lot of time. Got a situation in Lunar orbit. I won't be back for at least a day. Can you *please* watch Evan? He's... expecting it, so he shouldn't be too upset."

"Oh, sure. He's no trouble at all." Nila stared up at her. "Don't do anything stupid out there."

"I'll try." *Now for the hard part.* She hung up and called Evan.

THE CLASSROOM MURMURED. ALMOST EVERYONE HAD TUNED OUT OF MR. Vasquez's boring lecture on the Battle of Laredo in the later stages of the Corporate War. Vast numbers of impoverished Mexican citizens as well as poverty-stricken Texans succumbed to promises of a better world run by privatization rather than a government concerned only with the enrichment of politicians and the elite. A conglomerate of multiple corporations—what would become the Allied Corporate Council—threw money at the people. The old United States government had appealed to patriotism, but cold, hard cash (and anti-government paranoia) proved the victor. For people who had been under the boot of 'the Man' for so long, the wages (tax free of course) promised by the corporations called a siren song.

"Of course," said Mr. Vasquez, "the ACC could not sustain that business model for long, but they knew they wouldn't have to. Most of the men and women involved in the Laredo battle wouldn't survive to be paid more than once or twice." The classroom's giant holographic screen displayed a map behind him, where a mass of maroon dots converged on a much smaller group of green ones over a basic geometric hint of a city's buildings. "Nine hundred and forty thousand or so people who had no training and no experience in combat hurled themselves at three professional military units, two US and one Canadian. About eleven thousand soldiers in total."

Evan winced, but not from Mr. Vasquez's story of how almost all of the million civilians-turned-corporates were slaughtered. He reached into his backpack and pulled out the NetMini. This felt like the dream. The classroom, the map, Mr. Vasquez's voice saying nine hundred thousand…

It vibrated, and the word 'Mom' appeared on the screen.

He poked the screen to answer. Kirsten's head appeared in front of a white wall where a thin strip of white glow passed from ceiling to floor in a rhythmic pulse.

"Ev…"

"I know, Mom. You gotta go, and won't be home tonight. Am I gonna go to Nila's?"

"Wren," said Mr. Vasquez. "Why are you on a vid call in the middle of class?"

"Yeah, she's going to pick you up." Kirsten's head swiveled to look at the teacher. "Specialist. Sorry for interrupting. I'll only be a moment."

"Agent." Mr. Vasquez saluted her.

"Be good to Nila and I'll see you as soon as I can get back. Probably tomorrow. There's a spirit trying to hurt people on a platform where they build starships."

"Okay, Mom. I love you."

"I love you too, Ev."

Despite expecting the call, heaviness settled in his gut as he put the NetMini away. Much to his surprise, no one in the class snickered or made fun of the mushy exchange. Four other kids whose parents were active duty Division 0 looked at him with that knowing, somber stare.

After a moment of silence, Mr. Vasquez resumed talking about how, despite their training and experience, the sheer numbers of citizens eventually overwhelmed the military detachment, forcing them to call in an airstrike.

"And that was the first use of tactical nuclear weapons in the corporate war. The old government woefully underestimated the threat, and by the time they understood, the situation had escalated beyond repair."

Evan huddled down in his seat, hoping his sense of trepidation at his mother's absence came from not wanting to be in his room alone instead of her being in danger. *Something* had been there last night. Something or someone that definitely did *not* like him. His mind filled with the image of Seneschal, the corporate guy in the long black coat staring at him in the parking lot in front of the 500th Street church.

Naw... Mom blew him up.

Mr. Vasquez's lecture swallowed time. The beeper made half the class jump when it announced lunch period. Evan shut down his desk terminal and slung his backpack over one shoulder as he stood. He caught sight of Abernathy at the far end of the hallway, standing near the wall with his hands clasped behind his back like a principal observing his students.

His worry vanished to a sense of mission and opportunity, and he ran to the cafeteria. It took almost ten minutes to get to the end of the lunch line, after four of the school staff stopped him to ask about his glowing eyes. Three believed him, but one needed a surface thought scan to make sure he wasn't 'up to no good.'

Evan bounced on his toes, impatient to get up to the serving station. As the line inched forward, child by child, he scanned the tables for Shani. He spotted her sitting with Ruby as she always did, at a little round table by one of the windows overlooking the garden. He frowned through the transparent barrier at the offerings up for lunch: a hamburger-like substance rendered in a frightening shade of bright green, cauliflower-crust pizza, and pink-grey fish pretending to be salmon. That looked the most natural in terms of color, so he pointed at it.

With tray in hand, he hurried over to the girls' table and sat next to Shani.

"Hey," said Ruby. "Whoa, your eyes are burning."

Shani nibbled on her greenburger. "He's looking at ghosts. Hey."

"Your mom's on a later shift, right?"

"Yeah." Shani lifted the top bun with her hand; salt and pepper shakers whirled about in a telekinetic dance for a second, dusting the patty before she set the bun down.

Evan scrunched up his face at it. "Does it taste as bad as it looks?"

"It doesn't taste like anything." Shani tried another bite. "She's off duty at seven."

"What is it?" asked Ruby with a suspicious stare.

Shani shrugged. "Veggie burger."

"I'm sleeping over tonight. Mom's going to the Moon."

The girls looked up.

Ruby whined. "Oh, that's *so* cool. I wanna go to the Moon."

"Are there ghosts on the Moon?" whispered Shani.

Evan shrugged. "Gotta be. Mom's going. I wanna help Abernathy tonight. We'll have time after school before your mom takes us home since she works later than my mom."

Shani shivered. "I dunno."

"You promised." Evan tried the fish. Much to his shock, it tasted okay. "I'll tell them we're hunting for ghosts. It's not a total lie. I'm looking for a part of a ghost."

"Mrs. Han quit," said Ruby. "We got this new teacher, Miss Heath, who's like *so* annoying."

Shani rolled her eyes. "Yeah, she's too happy. Keeps talking."

Ruby laughed. "Guess it's better than havin' a teacher who hates kids."

"Okay." Shani looked down. "I'll help."

"Uhh." Ruby's gaze shifted back and forth between them. "No way. I ain't gettin' in trouble like that. I won't tell on you, but I'm not gonna do it."

Evan nodded. "'Kay. It's just the archives anyway."

AFTER THE LAST CLASS PERIOD ENDED, EVAN WALKED DOWN THE MAIN SCHOOL corridor, head ducked, ignoring everyone racing over to waiting parents. Maybe one in fifteen kids only showed up for school and still lived at home with parents who had no problems with psionics. He shuffled along with the majority heading for the elevator down to the dormitory. Two older cadets from the high school accompanied the children on their walk. A few minutes later, Evan left his backpack on the couch in the dorm's rec area and ducked into the bathroom for some much needed relief.

Not two seconds after he sidled up to a wall urinal and let fly, the sound of breathing behind him made things slow down. He glanced over his shoulder, twisting to see behind him, and failed to stifle a yelp. Near the wall, a mangled mass of flesh in the approximate shape of a man paced back and forth. He looked way older than Mom, but not white-haired, and like he'd taken a dive off the top of a high-rise building. Bits of his insides hung out, dangling around his knees, and bright red bloodstains saturated his clothes.

Catching himself peeing on the floor, Evan reoriented himself at the urinal. After finishing up, he approached the spirit, not quite looking at him. A flat, silver disc-shaped bot zipped out of a slot in the wall, heading for the mess.

"Hi. I'm Evan. Are you trapped here?"

A gurgling noise emanated from the figure. He grumbled in Spanish and took a swing at him, but the fist had no substance. Evan shook off a mild case of brain freeze and stepped back. The ghost pointed at him and moaned. A series of unintelligible syllables followed before an icy whisper of "die" sent a chill down his spine.

"Uhh, no thanks. What's your problem?" The apparition tried to grab him by the throat. At the beginning of pressure closing off his windpipe, Evan jumped back and glared up at the spirit. "Why are you mad at me?"

The mangled visage pointed at his head. "Abomination."

Evan scowled. "You hate psionics."

A long moan accompanied a nod.

"Did a psionic kill you?"

The ghost nodded. Again, the whispery voice chilled the room. "Daughter."

"Oh no way..." Evan blinked. "Are you that guy from the video... Hernandez?"

He growl-gurgled.

I gotta tell Mom about this guy. Evan ran out of the bathroom, annoyed at himself for not having any way to threaten ghosts. Well, he could bind a knife or something, but he promised only to do that in emergencies. He raced down the long hospital-white corridor, sneakers squeaking as he slalomed around teachers on the way to the recreation room. Shani sat on the edge of the couch, more leaning on it, next to his backpack. He ran over to her.

"Are you sure we won't get in trouble?" Shani fidgeted with her beige dress, looking down.

"No. But if we do, I'll take all the punishment." He grabbed his NetMini from the backpack and sent a text to Mom: ‹*Bad spirit here. Wants 2 hurt kids. Weak. Bathroom B8.*›

"We've got like four hours. What do we do?" She exhaled past a hint of a frown.

Evan slung his backpack over his shoulder. "Let's go check out the door. I'm pretty sure it's gonna be locked, but I might be able to get a vision of the code."

"What if it's a swipe?" Shani fell in step at his left.

"Can you TK-borrow a NetMini from one of the history teachers?"

Shani glared at him. "I don' wanna."

"But, we're saving Abernathy from being stuck here forever. If that was your brain in there, wouldn't you want someone to help?"

Shani grabbed the sides of her head. "I don't want anyone takin' my brain out. My head doesn't open."

He sighed. "Okay, forget it. Hope it's a keypad."

Acting casual, he led the way to the school section and out the back end through the gymnasium to the Admin section. It would've been faster to take the hallway via the dorms to where they connected to the other end of the Admin section, but an hour of staring at maps told him the archives were on the west side, closer to the school. No one would bother kids walking around the school, but in the Admin section, they'd get caught.

"Oh, my!" said a woman's voice, high and chirpy.

"Uh, oh," mumbled Shani.

A spritely blonde woman in a standard uniform, sans utility belt, taller than Mom with longer hair and fuller cheeks, ran up to them. "You're so cute! Why are your eyes lit up?" The woman put her hand on Evan's shoulder. "Is it okay if I hug you?"

"Hi, Miss Heath," said Shani.

"Uhh, okay." Evan weathered an enthusiastic embrace, and explained about his astral seeing. "We're looking for ghosts."

"Be careful you two." Miss Heath patted him on the head, grinning. "Stay safe."

The over-energetic woman hurried off.

Beep. Evan fished out his NetMini.

‹Mom: Dorian isn't going to the moon. He'll check on it. Are you okay?›

He typed: ‹Yeah. Ghost is too weak to touch people, but he's super gross. Went splat. He tried to hit me, but it didn't hurt.›

Evan let the device slip out of his hand into the pack. "C'mon."

They hurried to the end of the school and snuck past the teacher's lounge area, from which the voices of several adults murmured. An open archway connected the school to the Admin section library, a too-quiet place full of brown carpet and shelves laden with holodisk cases. Twenty or thirty small tables and chairs littered the area around the shelves, each bedecked with terminals. High-school-aged cadets occupied some of the chairs, though none paid any attention to the intrusion by a nine- and seven-year-old.

Evan headed for an alcove past the seventh shelf on the left, where an old-style push bar door led to a stairway. Three floors down, they emerged in a dusty corridor painted pale hospital green. Aside from five disc bots zipping back and forth polishing the teal-and-white checkered floor tiles, it looked deserted.

"It's scary down here," whispered Shani.

"I don't see any spirits." Evan held her hand and walked in. "The archives are up ahead on the right side." He pointed at a slab of glass sticking out of the wall with arrows pointing different directions. One, labeled 'archive,' pointed right down an offshoot corridor. "See?"

"We shouldn't be here," whispered Shani.

"Correct," said another girl, behind them. "What are you doing down here?"

Evan froze. Shani clamped her hands over her mouth to mute a shriek.

He turned around. The girl behind him looked like a tiny version of an I-Ops detective: her close-fitting black Division 0 uniform would've been appropriate for field duty if not for her lack of weapons. Long, black hair hung in a single ponytail behind her; hands the color of caramel perched imperiously on her slender hips. He pegged her for a fifth or sixth grader. The girl's nametag read Peña.

"What are *you* doing down here?" asked Evan.

Shani made doe-eyes at the older girl.

"Following you two miscreants." Cadet Peña's head bobbed up with an air of superiority. "I saw you go into the stairway. I'm on watch, so I count as an officer right now. You two are kinda little to be up to no good. Are you lost?"

Evan shook his head. "No. I need to go to the archives to help a trapped spirit."

Cadet Peña looked at him like he'd spoken some ancient lost language. "Are you serious or are you pretending?"

"Yes. His name is Abernathy. He's the first person ever killed by a mind blast... and they're keeping his brain in a jar down here. He can't move on 'cause of it, so I wanna help him."

"If his brain is in the archives, it's the property of Division 0." Cadet Peña folded her arms. "You're planning to steal official property. I'm sorry, but I have to log this and report you."

"Are people property?" Evan stared at her. "They haven't even looked at the brain in like thirty years. It's been sitting in there forgotten. If you wanna 'rest me for stealing it, okay, but let me take it to Father Villera first. I'm just trying to help him."

Cadet Peña stared at him for a painfully long moment. "You're not lying to me..."

"She's a empath," said Shani.

"I dunno." A repetitive *thunk, thunk, thunk*, echoed down the hall from Cadet Peña's boots as she tapped one boot toe at the floor. "You should submit a request for funerary processing."

"What?" asked Evan.

"That means ask if they'll dispose of the brain properly." Cadet Peña shook her head. "You don't know what a funeral is?"

Evan gestured down the hall. "What if they say no? They don't think of him as a person, and they don't believe in spirits. They don't need his brain anymore. Come on, please? You can't let them treat a person like that. What's more important to you? Doing what's right or following the rules?"

Cadet Peña fidgeted. "The rules are usually the same as doing what's right."

Shani stared at her black ballet flats while swishing side to side, making her dress flare.

Evan felt worse about getting Shani in trouble than whatever punishment awaited him. "It's not her fault. I dragged her down here… can you say she wasn't here?"

"You got adopted by Agent Wren, right?" Cadet Peña seemed to sense the surge of warmth in his chest at the thought, and smiled. "Guess so. She's nice. Okay. Let's see this brain. If you can show me a ghost that wants peace, I'll stay quiet."

Shani looked up in shock.

"Yay!" Evan whirled back toward the archives. "It's over here, but I'm not sure how to get in. Can you open the door?"

He jogged to the four-way intersection and went right. About thirty yards down on the left side, an imposing set of double doors in plain brushed plastisteel bore the simple black word 'Archives.' The conspicuous absence of either a keypad or a reader panel twisted his stomach with the unease of his quest failing before it even started. A physical lock secured the doors, and the side without the keyhole had pins securing it to the floor and ceiling.

"Crap." Evan slouched. "No electronics."

Cadet Peña shook her head again, her long ponytail dancing. "Electronics are too easy for a psionic to get past… well, at least a technokinetic or an EK. I don't have the key."

Evan studied the doors for a few minutes and wound up staring at the locking bar between them. "Hey, Shan. Can you TK that open?"

"I wouldn't," said Cadet Peña. "If she's strong enough to break that door, all three of us are gonna be in deep poo."

"I can't break that whole door." Shani folded her arms.

Evan couldn't help but giggle. He backed up as Shani walked over. "She's strong, but she's got a sick amount of control. She can make her stuffed animals walk around like they're alive."

"Wow, really?" asked Cadet Peña. "I wanna see that."

Shani approached the archives and peered into the gap between the double doors. Seconds later, she let off a tiny grunt. A rattle of metal broke the silence, and the right side glided open. As soon as she stopped concentrating, the locking bar snapped out. "It had a strong spring."

Evan examined the stationary door for alarms, but only spotted levers to retract bolts into the floor and ceiling on the edge. Inside, an enormous two-story tall room yawned before them, lined with warehouse-style shelves.

"Wow." Shani walked in, gazing up and around as she spun with each step. "How are you gonna find it in here? There's *so* much stuff! We'll be grown up before you find it."

"Did you ask the ghost where it is?" asked Cadet Peña.

"Uhh, no... I didn't. I wanted to surprise him like for his birthday." Evan felt tiny in the face of such a huge room full of junk. "Maybe I can get a feeling for it... I'm clairvoyant."

"Samantha." The older girl smiled. "But only my mom calls me that when she's mad. Call me Sam. And I think you should ask him."

"Is that a sword?" Shani ran a few paces deeper among the shelves, pointing at a metal blade that looked older than the planet.

"Wow." He ran up behind her and somehow managed to resist the urge to pick it up. "We shouldn't touch anything except Abernathy's brain. We're gonna get in enough trouble already if we get caught."

Shani spun to face him. "We *got* caught." Her arm rose, pointing at Sam. "She's a cadet."

"I'm not 'catching' you yet... if this ghost is real, and he's trapped... I guess that kinda counts as kidnapping."

Evan smiled. He took a deep breath, closed his eyes, and tried to reach out with his mind to find what he needed. The soft scuff of Shani walking around distracted him far more than thin shoes should have. Or perhaps the worry she'd touch something bugged him; hearing her wander about only made that fear worse. Inexplicably, her being in this room worried him. He stared at the insides of his eyelids for a few minutes before an image came to mind of a folding table full of junk. His attention centered on a small statuette depicting a male figure with his arms folded over his chest, fingers splayed to grasp opposing shoulders.

"Hey, kid," rasped Sam. "Don't touch that."

"I'm not 'kid;' I'm Shani. And I'm not touching it."

Sam grumbled. "Telekinesis counts as touching... don't be literal."

"What's literal?" asked Shani.

Evan's eyes snapped open. His friend had drifted five shelves deeper into the room and stared up at a silly looking black helmet, which floated in midair above her. "Shan... please put that down."

The helmet glided to a position on a shelf taller than the ceiling of a normal room.

"Don't do that." Evan ran over to her. "If you knock something over that high up, it could hurt us."

She smirked. "Stop treating me like a little kid."

"You *are* a little kid."

"So are you," said Sam.

Evan glanced at Cadet Peña. "You're still a kid too."

"I'm almost twelve." She struck the imperious pose again. "And activated."

"Activated?" asked Shani.

"It means she's got some authority." Evan grumbled. "*Almost* twelve means you're eleven. You're only older'n me by two years. Did you see a table with junk on it? This little statue?" He sent the mental image on a telepathic burst into both girls' thoughts, one after the next. "The brain's gotta be somewhere near that table. I'll check the back, Sam the middle, and Shani near the door?"

"'Kay."

Sam smirked at him, probably for being bossy, but nodded. "Fine."

They split up. Evan lingered for a few seconds watching Shani, unable to get past that feeling bringing her here was a bad idea. When she disappeared around a shelf, he ran as far back as the central passage among the aisles allowed. The innermost wall also bore several shelves. He didn't bother digging among the relics, instead searching for the dead-end corridor from his vision. He checked three offshoots before Sam's yell broke the subdued squeaking of his sneakers.

"Got it."

He ran toward the voice, arriving a second before Shani, who looked annoyed.

"What's wrong?"

"You gave me boring hallways. It's full of dusty old gamepads." She leaned close and whispered, "They're heavy, and I couldn't turn them on."

He skimmed her surface thoughts, equally confused by stacks of rectangular objects that varied in thickness and size. Most had titles on one side and cover art that looked like video game boxes, but they turned out to be stacks of paper full of words glued together on one edge. "Weird."

"It's here," yelled Sam.

Evan darted down between the shelves toward her. She'd stopped by a folding table laden with statues, pyramids, clear orbs in wire stands, and a handful of decorative knives. At the dead end of the passage where the shelving wrapped around the wall, a few old-style composite alloy broadswords lay on a shelf. One lacked a sheath, and its shiny blade had been stained dark black by something that gave him a bad feeling.

Aside from the weapons, everything else here sat in boxes. He slouched. Even searching this immediate area would take hours, and he had no idea what a brain in a jar looked like.

"Well, it's around here somewhere, I think."

"You *think*?" Sam exhaled. "There's like hundreds of boxes here."

Evan shrugged. "Sorry. I saw this spot, not the exact box."

"Ask the ghost," said Shani. "I wanna go upstairs. I'm scared now. I don't like it in here."

"Yeah, I feel it too." Sam spun in place. "Something here is radiating like... anger and hate."

He gazed around at the shelves, boxes, and stuff on the table. No spirits showed themselves, but the little statue with folded arms gave off an energy as though it looked at him with sentience in its carved eyes. "Uhh, I think it's that statue. Don't touch it."

"What?" Sam walked over to it. Careful not to make contact, she leaned close to study it. "Wow. You're right. How can a lump of... whatever that is have emotions? It's radiating anger."

"Dunno." He looked at the shelf opposite the table. A dented metal box with a medical symbol on it caught his eye. He pointed. "That one. Shani, can you float it down?"

She looked up at it and concentrated. One by one, three other cartons on top of it lifted, moved to the side, and set down. Finally, the white box wobbled and rose into the air. Shani let off a grunt of exertion and seemed to hold her breath as she guided the container to the floor. As soon as it landed, she slumped to her knees out of breath. "That's heavy."

He walked around the waist-high box once before pushing on it to gauge is weight. Since he couldn't budge it at all, he gave up before the girls noticed him even trying. He peeled old tape from the lid flaps and pushed a button that caused them to open on motorized struts, revealing a canister of clear fluid with a metal cap on each side. A brain floated at the approximate center. He grimaced at the thought of what it might feel like to touch, and placed a tentative hand on the lid.

"Evan?" asked Abernathy. He faded in from the ceiling and glided to his feet among the kids. "What are you three doing down here? Get away from that!"

Samantha, staring up at the ghost, screamed and jumped back, bumping the table.

A few objects fell from the force of her hitting it, but Evan's gaze snapped to the statuette as it tumbled over the edge. He barely formed the thought to yell for Shani to 'catch' it before the figurine smashed to pieces on the floor. A wash of bright peach-hued light rolled away from the fragments and streaked off into the shelves.

"Uh, oh." Evan gulped. "We're in trouble."

CLOCKING OVERTIME

T he elevator doors parted, allowing a bastard of a breeze in, which
knocked Kirsten off balance. She grabbed for Dorian, but her fingers
couldn't get a grip on his intangible body and she fell against the
back wall.

Captain Eze reached down to help her up. "Bit of wind today."

"Thanks." She braced against the gale and stomped out onto the roof, hair
whipping at her ears.

At the far end of a metal grating walkway, a DS2 dropship perched on a
hexagonal landing pad. Drab green with a trefoil tail, it perched like a giant,
wingless dragonfly. The nose section resembled the cockpit of an attack
aircraft with the rear seat higher up than the one in front of it. However,
much like her patrol craft, armor plates covered it instead of clear panels. The
chamber in the main body held an armored personnel carrier, with only
enough room on either side to shuffle sideways to a ladder leading up into the
ship. Watching the ship sway on its landing struts made her feel less self-
conscious about being little enough to have the wind knock her over.

"Dorian," yelled Kirsten, over the sound of the idling ion thrusters. "I'm
glad you got over that 200 meter thing."

He cringed. "I'm not sure it's a great idea for me to attempt to leave Earth.
Last time, I was stuffed inside that damn gem, remember?"

"You're not coming?" She blinked.

He shook his head. "After what it took out of me to get back down here... I
would prefer not to."

"Oh... I..." She looked down. "Dunno what I'm going to do without you."

Captain Eze took a step back, seeming amused by watching her talk to empty space.

"I'm not sure I *can* leave Earth on my own power." He looked up. "Feels strange to think about. There's a force binding us here. As soon as that demon's influence faded, it felt like I'd been fired out of a cannon from the Moon to the Earth."

Kirsten tried to hold her hair down against the wind. "So you don't think this is the same entity?"

"Why do you assume I'm an authority on all things dead? Just because I happen to be a ghost doesn't mean I've studied up on them." He winked. "I suppose I could try and find out, but I'm a little hesitant. It's doubtful I have enough energy to go that far away from my attachment point. Most likely, whoever it is died up there. A starship production facility doesn't sound like the safest place to work. My guess is you've got a dead ex-employee looking for payback."

"Hmm. Are you sure? It's not like you'd be swimming. There's the ship."

"Maybe if I jumped inside a person for the ride." He shook his head. "Nah. This is pushing the two-hundred-meter thing a bit much, I think. The farther I get from the car... or my ashes, the more anxious I feel. If something took that spirit up there against its will... if his remains are on Earth, he might be completely psychotic with fear or rage."

"Great." Kirsten grumbled. "Can't be worse than getting slapped around by a thirteen foot tall demon with Konstantin's face."

"There, see? You've become an optimist." Dorian grinned. "I'll watch over Evan for you."

"Thanks." She patted his non-shoulder and jogged to the ship.

Captain Eze kept pace until the bottom of the ramp. "Vid me with an update as soon as you can. I don't care what time it is."

"Sir." She saluted him.

Fear gripped her as she looked into the dark APC bay. Going too far away from home was scary enough, but leaving the planet? Not like she hadn't been to the Moon once already... but still. After a breath of courage, she clenched her hands into fists and shimmied past the slab-shaped armored transport to the ladder.

A tall, skinny woman in an olive-drab flight jumpsuit and oversized helmet dangling with disconnected wires met her at the top of the ladder. Over her right breast pocket, a patch bore the word 'learner' in all caps.

"Please tell me that's your name and not your experience level," said Kirsten, saluting.

Lieutenant Learner laughed. "A sense of humor... that's gotta come in handy in your line of work. I need to ask you to unload your sidearm. E-90 might poke holes in my baby if it hits the right spot. That's not a great idea in space."

Kirsten drew her weapon and removed the E-mag, which she tucked into one of the little pods on her utility belt. "Not a problem. I'm kind of addicted to breathing."

"Yeah, same here. Pretty common addiction; someone should do something about it."

Kirsten chuckled.

Lieutenant Learner guided her down a cramped hallway to a little room with six fold-down canvas chairs on facing walls. Kirsten sat in one on the right side and the pilot helped her harness in before giving her a spare helmet from a cargo compartment. "Once we break atmo, you don't need to stay strapped. There's a head there if you need to piss or whatever."

Kirsten's cheeks lit on fire when the woman pointed at an exposed toilet opposite the passageway to the cockpit.

"Hah. I love that face." Learner patted her on the helmet and started for the cockpit. "You react like a civvie."

She grimaced. "Showers are bad enough... ugh. How long's this gonna take?"

Learner stopped and glanced back. "We'll be out of Earth grav in about sixteen minutes. Moon in about two hours."

"Great." Kirsten let her head fall back with a dull *clonk*.

A moment after Lieutenant Learner vanished down the cramped crawlway to the front, the thrum of ion engines built up and the entire DS2 shuddered. Kirsten's stomach lurched as gravity seemed to increase before pulling to the side. In time with a blast too close to sounding like an explosion for her comfort level, a violent acceleration hurled her left against the harness. Kirsten screamed, but someone in the chair next to her wouldn't have heard it over the roaring of thrusters.

Her weight shifted, dangling in the harness, suggesting the DS2 had pointed nose up. The shuddering airframe banged her helmet against the metal bulkhead in a rhythmic tapping. No matter how she tried to hold on, the forces on her body threw her about like a ragdoll.

She clenched herself as tight as possible, closed her eyes, and waited for it to stop.

Eventually, engine noise faded to a distant electronic hum, and all the turbulence stopped. It occurred to her that she more or less floated, held in the seat by the harness. Kirsten waited another twenty minutes before she felt confident the total stillness would remain. She unstrapped and removed the helmet before attempting to put it in the next 'chair.' It glided up and away. After a blink of surprise, she tethered it with the harness and tried to stand—and kept going. She flailed her arms at the air, floundering in zero-G.

Eventually, she glided close enough to the side to kick off the wall and launch toward the entrance of the crawlway leading forward. At the end of the passage, one olive-drab helmet peeked around the right corner. The cramped size made sense—the designers intended people to float horizontally rather than walk. She pulled herself along, gripping thin railings on both sides. In zero-g, the too-small passageway didn't feel so bad.

The tunnel ended at the top of a tiny staircase that descended between the left wall and a pair of pilot stations, the forward of the two seats much lower. From inside, most of the cockpit appeared to be window, filled with the star-dotted blackness of outer space. Sunlight glared and flashed from a handful of satellites and other space junk.

Learner had the nearer seat, and the voice muttering from up ahead sounded male.

The stars smeared into streaks of light, racing down and left. The Moon glided into view from the upper corner of the windscreen. As still as the craft felt on the turn, she could've been watching a video game on a holo-bar in her living room. Once the Moon centered on the windscreen, a faint sense of acceleration pushed her back. She grabbed the walls to hold still.

"Locked course," said the man up front.

"Copy." Lieutenant Learner glanced at her. "We're reading an ETA of one hour fifty five minutes."

"Okay. Wow that's fast. I thought shuttles took like eleven hours."

"*Civilian* ships do. You're getting the VIP treatment. You must be some kinda special shit for them to give us the detail of bussin' your ass out there."

Kirsten sat at the top of the little stairway and set her left arm across her lap to get to the computer. "I'm going to an orbital construction platform to investigate a report of a malignant paranormal entity attempting to kill the living."

"Man," said the guy up front. "I need to transfer over to the civvie police. I'm so sick of random drug tests."

Kirsten ran a hand over her head, smoothing her hair back. "Some days I wish it was only a hallucination, too."

She tapped her armguard to open a holo-panel. The case record Captain Eze assigned her hadn't made the transition from report to Inquest yet. Idle swipes of her finger leafed past a few pages and images, though none of the pictures contained unusual sights, mostly long silver hallways and people floating along in e-suits. An office with a view of the Moon in a window came next, followed by an exterior view of the station.

Gravion Interstellar's orbital platform resembled a bizarre comb made for a titan. The main body consisted of a loaf-shaped brick from which ten long tines extended. Four narrow spars made up each bay, a scaffold in which starships came to life. Five berths contained vessels in various stages of construction, attached to the spars by mooring lines. A large, rotating, ring-shaped section mounted on a spindle connected to the main body made the whole thing look like a windup toy.

According to the report, one of Gravion's employees had become stranded at the end of Bay Seven, refusing to come back inside and screaming nonsense like "he's out here" and "he's after me" as well as shrieking like a victim in a cheesy horror vid.

Kirsten brought up the personnel record. Lindsey Park, age 26, employed as a hull inspector/tester for the past seven years. The smile on the Korean girl staring back at her from the holo-panel made the flight feel intolerably long. She pressed a hand to her stomach, hoping Captain Eze's opinion erred on the alarmist side.

"Do you have comms with the installation?"

Lieutenant Learner glanced at her. "That's a civilian facility, but we can try to patch in. Best bet would be a relay to Earth to hop the laser... otherwise there's a bit of a delay." She pulled a small boom mic up to her mouth. "Control, this is 3-2-3 Delta, copy?" She waited a few seconds. "Requesting a patch to the..." She looked at Kirsten, who held up the armband display. "Uhh, Gravion Interstellar build platform in Lunar orbit. Right. Yeah, the Zero's asking. Okay." The pilot covered the mic. "They're trying."

Kirsten nodded. "I'm looking for a status update. Is the Park woman still out on the berth? Any other details?"

Learner fiddled with dials and buttons. "As soon as I hear anything I'll— Copy. Yeah, what's the sit-rep on station?" She "mm-hmm'ed" a few times. "Thanks, Control."

"Looks like your girl's still hiding out on the wire. They say she's panicking. One guy they sent out to pull her in got halfway down the spar before coming back in. All he'll say is 'nope.'"

"Ugh." Kirsten grabbed two handfuls of hair. "Not good. Two normals have seen it."

"That's bad?" asked Learner.

"Yeah. Usually takes a ghost ten years or more to feel their way around being a ghost enough to manifest to the living... unless they're really pissed. Thanks for that. I'm gonna go sit down."

The Lieutenant nodded.

Kirsten floated back down the narrow channel and struggled into the harness of the same seat she'd used for takeoff. With nothing else to do, and no way in hell able to sleep, she whipped out her NetMini and started up a Monwyn RPG.

THE DS2 SET DOWN ON A MILITARY PAD AT PLYMOUTH STATION. ALL SHUTTLES between the Earth and Moon landed here; the civilian starport sat a few hundred yards away at the end of a glimmering white segmented tube. This part of the station looked like an enormous hamster habitat.

Vibration in the hull startled her. Hours of utter stillness had become normal. She unbuckled and wobbled on shaky legs to the cockpit tunnel. Gravity had returned, though noticeably weaker than Earth's. Outside, the hexagonal landing pad revealed itself as an elevator, sinking into the Lunar surface. Soon, the ceiling closed overhead and a great hissing roar came from outside.

Lieutenant Learner flicked switches and buttons on her left and overhead. The pervasive thrum of electronics faded to deafening silence. "Shutdown complete, we're landed. Confirm all systems nominal." She hooked her thumb on a large plastic lever-switch. Hydraulic whine filled the air. "Opening ramp."

"Check," said the man up front. "We're green across the board."

"Out the way I came in?" asked Kirsten.

"Yep." Learner smiled at her. "You must have friends. Looks like we're going to be your ride home too... unless you'd rather fly civ. Food's better, but it's a long ass flight."

"I'd rather get home sooner." She patted Learner's shoulder. "Thanks for the ride."

Kirsten made her way back across the cabin, down the ladder, and past the APC. The landing bay air fogged in her breath and made her feel as though she'd walked into a subzero freezer. She swallowed the urge to 'eep' and ran to the only obvious door. The outer airlock closed on its own, and after a few seconds, the inner door opened to beautiful warmth.

A light-haired man of about thirty in a pale blue jumpsuit and ball cap met her inside. He smiled at her, his gaze went to her chest, and he shifted away with a bit of blush in his cheeks. "Hi. Welcome to Plymouth. I'm Rick with starport facilities. Sorry. I guess they forgot to warn you about how cold it gets in the airlock chambers. If you need a warm up, the coffee or tea at Luna's isn't too bad." He gestured at a distant café counter.

The thin uniform didn't do much to conceal her prominent nipples. She considered covering them, but decided against it thinking it would draw more attention. "How much time do I have before the shuttle leaves?"

"At least enough to grab a hot drink. They've been holding it for you." He walked off, heading for the café.

Beep.

Kirsten glanced down at her NetMini. Momentary terror tickled the underside of her heart at a message from Evan about a hostile spirit in the school who wanted to harm children. Naturally, her brain conjured up an image of a Konstantin-demon thing with claws stomping along the hallways.

She tapped the patrol craft in the contact list. After two rings, silence answered.

Not Vidmail? Oh, please be Dorian. "Dorian?"

An unintelligible whisper replied.

"Evan texted me… he said there's a spirit in the school who wants to harm the kids… can you please check on it?"

She listened for a few seconds before a hissing "Yeah, sure" came back, a trace of Dorian's voice recognizable in the sped up audio.

"Thanks." She waited a moment, but when no further reply came, she hung up. A flick of a finger switched back to the text interface and she sent Evan a message telling him Dorian would check on the school.

Rick kept quiet; his over-pleasant smile hinted he wanted as little to do with 'weird things' as he could get away with.

Worried to the point of her hands shaking, she shuffled over to the café counter. After grabbing a standard cappuccino, she followed him to a small security station in front of a waiting area where fourteen people—six women and eight men—sat scattered among four banks of attached seats. A nervous-looking man of Indian descent shot her an impatient look and muttered something. The man next to him, a hulk with a grey afro, seemed much happier to see her.

Kirsten ducked around the sensor, causing a woman with paper white skin and black hair to jump out of her seat at the console and get in front of her. Despite only being eye-level with the other woman's chin, the royal blue security guard uniform didn't intimidate her.

The guard shot a rather pointed look at Kirsten's E-90. "Sorry kid, but I can't let you skip the scanner."

"Thanks, but I'm not a kid." She held up her ID. "Agent Wren, Division 0."

"Uhh." The guard looked at Rick. "There's a zero? Is that a real uniform? This girl looks like she's thirteen."

"I don't think she's thirteen," said Rick. "And she came in on a military DS2."

"Argh!" An urge to go off on this woman welled up from deep within, but Kirsten fought it back down. She set her coffee on a baggage-inspection table. "Look" —she glanced at the woman's badge—"Landis, A, if I had ten credits for every time some idiot behind a security desk gave me shit about not being a 'real cop,' I could buy two of these starports. What do they pay you for if you can't recognize a commissioned officer of the National Police Force? If I wasn't in a damned hurry, I'd be half tempted to bury you in a mountain of bureaucratic horseshit it would take you three weeks to dig out from under."

"Ma'am. There's no need to become agitated." The guard went to grab her shoulder. "Perhaps we need to go to a quieter—"

Kirsten twisted the woman's arm up behind her back, slammed her chest-first over the security console, and held the tip of a stunrod within three inches of her right eye. "Does this look real?"

The pervasive din in the starport fell to dead quiet.

"Alia, she's genuine." Rick reached as if to pull Kirsten off her, but hesitated. "Psionic branch of the NPR. There aren't too many of them."

"Is there a problem?" asked a deep-voiced man in a similar security uniform, with more pins on his chest.

Kirsten shoved away from the woman. "You should stop recruiting from Mars and hire some people capable of telling the difference between a sworn officer and a kid in a costume. You're the supervisor?"

"That's right." He glanced at the female guard who scooted away while rubbing her arm. "I'm sorry for the disturbance, officer."

"Agent," snapped Kirsten. She closed her eyes and exhaled. *Evan's fine. He said the ghost was weak. Dorian's there. I'm on edge because I'm out of my comfort zone.* "Sorry. I'm not myself right now. I haven't gotten a lot of info about the situation I'm heading into."

"You didn't have to rip my arm out of socket." Alia grumbled. "What are you, augged?"

"Agent Wren is from Earth. Higher gravity equals higher muscle density." Rick offered Kirsten back her coffee.

She slid her stunrod back into its ring on her belt and took the cup. "Is she really that clueless or just messing with me?"

"You tell me," said Alia. "You're the psychic."

Kirsten stared at the coffee cup, daydreaming of an embarrassing psionic suggestion. *Not worth it.*

"That's enough, Landis," barked the supervisor. "Don't forget, despite that badge, you're still a civilian employed by a private security company."

"No problems." Kirsten forced a smile. "Neither being incompetent at one's job nor an asshole is illegal."

Alia wandered back to the security console, grumbling about how she thought she'd be 'safe' from psionics on the Moon since they'd 'taken over' Mars. Kirsten glowered at the windows overlooking a shuttle pad where an arrowhead-shaped vessel waited. Wisps of vapor lapped at ports around the landing gear, dissipating the instant they hit vacuum.

The nervous looking man who'd glared at her earlier approached Rick. "Excuse me. I couldn't help but overhear that you're letting a psionic on the shuttle? I demand an alternate flight."

A middle-aged woman still sitting a short distance away raised a hand. "I'm not comfortable being that close to one either."

Two more men nodded.

"She's probably reading our minds now," whined a slender pale man who scrunched up his face as if concentrating. "Think random thoughts so she can't get your bank information."

Kirsten pursed her lips. *Why do I try to protect these people? If they knew what—*

"All right, the lot of you need to secure that horseshit right now." The large dark-skinned man leapt to his feet. He pointed at the crowd, sweeping a forearm as big as Kirsten's thigh in a purposeful arc, a dark black UCF Assault Infantry tattoo clear as day below his sleeve. "You all's got some god-damned nerve. She took an oath to defend yer sorry asses. You think a normal cop is gonna be able to deal with some psionic dude who gone crazy?"

The people got quiet, all eyes on the huge retired soldier.

"You." The soldier pointed at one of the guys who nodded. "You carryin'?"

"Yeah," said the man.

"What about you?" he pointed at the nervous Indian. "Got a piece?"

"Yes."

"How many y'all got a gun on ya right now?" yelled the soldier.

All but two of the others in the waiting area raised hands, including two elderly women.

"Any you all killin' each other? You got guns; that must mean you just *itchin' ta* kill someone." He set his hands on his hips, glaring at the crowd. "You thinkin' 'cause she's psionic she's gonna use it just because?" He poked the whiny man in the chest with one finger hard enough to knock him back into his chair. "Havin' a tool and usin' that tool the wrong way ain't even the same thing. She's a damned commissioned officer. Might not be the same branch o' service, but she's my sister in spirit."

Kirsten smiled at him, though felt a little embarrassed at the overly loud display. Her chest warmed with a mixture of pride and gratitude.

"Now, you thinkin' it ain't the same 'cause anyone can buy a gun and they ain't got no store where ya can buy psionics. Even *more* reason ta want her around. If someone psionic lookin' ta use that shit for ill intentions comes by, y'ain't got a better thing than havin' her here ta stop 'em. That uniform means she's passed psych tests and has the trust of generals."

The Gravion terminal hung in awkward silence. People exchanged stares.

"Thanks." Kirsten sipped her coffee. "I'm sorry they made you wait. I don't expect you to be comfortable around me, but I'm not here to hurt anyone."

Rick walked to a small podium and hit a button, which opened the door to the boarding tube. "We regret the inconvenience of the delay. Please note that Agent Wren is responding to an emergency call on board the Gravion build station. Thank you for your understanding. Please board at your earliest convenience."

People formed up in a line. Kirsten hung back, sipping coffee. The soldier wandered over and offered a handshake, which she accepted.

"Thanks."

"Master Sergeant James E. Silver, United Coalition Front Marine Corps, retired. Shame watchin' stupidity like that in action."

"Yeah. Glad to see there's a few people out there who appreciate us."

"Damn straight." He ducked through the entry door. "What they sendin' you up here for? If you don't mind the askin'."

"Unexplained events with a high probability of being paranormal in nature have a woman stranded out on one of the construction bays. I'm trying to get up there fast enough to save her life... and deal with whatever it is."

"That like ghosts and shit?"

"Yep."

"Right on."

Whoa. He didn't even bat an eyelash. She sat across the aisle from him in the tiny twenty-passenger craft. The shuttle lifted off with a minute amount of sway. Aside from gravity increasing, the windows offering a view of the lunar surface falling away may as well have been monitors showing a flight simulator that remained on solid ground. The trip from the surface station out to the Gravion starship berth took sixteen minutes, which passed mostly listening to James talk about his years with a UCFMC expeditionary force hopping from one settled planet to another wherever a fire needed to be put out at a colony.

Kirsten shared a little of her story as well, which got him talking about an overly religious guy in his old unit, though his opinion seemed far more positive than her early views on the subject. Every time anyone mentioned 'the G word,' her mind filled with memories of Mother.

"Kinda hard not to hope for something when people lobbin' missiles at you." He grinned. "Figure it's like a teddy bear. Deep down, you know it can't do a damn thing for you, but holding it makes ya feel better anyway."

She smiled. "I guess some hope is better than nothing."

His lower lip stuck out with a frown as he shrugged. "Yeah, somethin' like that."

"Attention passengers," said a female voice. "We are on final approach to the Orbital Build Platform. Please secure seat belts at this time."

Most of the passengers had left them on, preferring not to float around the cabin. Kirsten tightened hers. *When they say to put it on, that usually means they're about to fly like idiots.*

The rush of maneuvering thrusters shook the shuttle. Stiff deceleration caused everyone to lurch forward. The whiny man who accused her of stealing bank information flew into the seat in front of him, flipped over it, and sailed ass-first into the wall separating the cockpit from the passenger cabin. Once the rumble of the maneuvering thrusters cut out, he groped his way into a seat in the front row, moaning. Seconds later, a *creak* groaned from the airframe as the shuttle's weight settled onto its landing struts.

Okay. Game time. She unbuckled and pulled herself upright as the glowing white interior of a docking bay engulfed the side windows. "I regret the inconvenience, but please remain seated for a moment."

"Is there really a ghost on the station?" asked the whiny man.

Kirsten clung to a handle by the exit door. "It's possible. All I know is there's a woman stranded almost five hundred meters out on a spar, and no one can explain why."

The passengers quieted. Kirsten stared at the clock on her forearm computer, which still showed West City Earth time at 4:56 p.m. Three minutes later, lights embedded in strips around the door glowed green, and it opened.

She jumped across a two-foot gap, not waiting for the boarding ramp to fully extend, and sprinted to a platform against a white wall decorated only with a Gravion Interstellar logo, a wedge-shaped spaceship pointing out of the top right of a round-cornered blue square. The shuttle bay came close to causing snow blindness, though the air wasn't near as cold as where the DS2 had landed.

The door at the end of the deck opened, admitting a woman her height with a round face, dark skin, and a sharp indigo suit. She extended a henna-covered hand. "Welcome, Agent. My name is Chandra Mitchell. I'm the public relations and legal liaison officer."

"Hello." Kirsten followed her to a warmer receiving area, which contained an information desk, food counter, and an automated kiosk with station maps and directions. "Is Miss Park still alive?"

"As far as I am aware, yes." Chandra took off at a brisk stride, possessing a masterful command of high heels that made Kirsten grumble. "I assume you don't wish to waste time and get right to it as they say?"

"I'm sure Miss Park would appreciate that, yes."

"You will need a suit to go EVO."

"Uhh. I've never done that before."

Chandra's wavy hair bounced over her shoulder as she snapped her head around to smile at Kirsten. "It's as easy as walking. I'll ask Benjamin to go out with you then. He's our lead instructor for new hires."

She wanted to protest, fearing what happened with the Division 1 officers at the church, but also terrified at the thought of screwing up and flinging herself out into space. *Please don't be a demon.* "Thanks…"

A pair of sliding glass doors parted at Chandra's approach. "Once we leave the ring, there won't be any gravity. I'm not dressed for that, so I'll be staying behind." She indicated her knee-length skirt. "Ben will meet you at the other side. Do you have any questions for me?"

"Can you give me any more details about what happened? Did anyone else see anything else? What's been going on?"

Chandra nodded. "Miss Park was conducting a routine inspection on IS4-1882, a recently completed colony transport vessel. When a ship is declared 'done' by the build crews, it undergoes several inspections. Lindsey is part of the team that does the exterior testing. It takes them a few weeks to go over every inch of the outer hull and scan for faults. They were about halfway through the procedure on yesterday's shift when her EVO-buddy screamed and lost consciousness. Lindsey began hyperventilating and complained of severe abdominal pain. Our medical team tells me that she showed an elevated heart rate, but the sensors picked up no other issues. She shouted about a man out there with them trying to kill her, and powered her way to the far end of the berth. The last we've seen of her, she's hidden in the mooring clamps and cables at the very tip of the spar. Her communications over the past twelve hours have been erratic and lapse in and out of coherence."

"She's been out there twelve hours? How long are those suits good for?"

"About twenty-four." Chandra stopped walking by an elevator and pressed the call button. "After we put in a request for your assistance, we sent Jonah out to try and talk her down. He made it about halfway before yelling something I cannot repeat and hurrying back inside. He proceeded to go directly to the cafeteria where he began to drink synthetic tequila. The only word he's said since has been 'nope.'"

"I'd like to talk to him after I'm done outside." *I have to know what he saw.*

"Very well. Aside from that, no one has reported anything unusual."

The door opened with a loud hiss. Kirsten entered the elevator and spun around to face out.

"Be prepared for a loss of gravity before it stops moving. You'll be traveling down one of the spokes of the wheel to the hub. Once you reach the middle, you'll be weightless."

"I understand." *I wanna go home.* "See you soon."

Kirsten glanced at the wall and hit the down arrow. The doors snapped closed, and the chamber whirred with motion. She tried not to think about being in an overgrown metal box floating out in the endless death of outer space, far from Earth, far from Evan.

Come on, K. Hold it together. You got this. That woman needs you.

13

ISOLATION

W ithin twenty seconds of hitting the button, Kirsten floated off the floor and hung in midair. She slid upward until she found herself flat against the ceiling. After a moment of stillness, she launched down and hit the ground flat on her chest, the wind knocked out of her.

The door opened with a hiss.

A tall man with a dense brown-blonde buzz cut and a moustache reached for her hand. Except for the helmet, he already wore a bulky EVO suit. Sections of glossy cyan metal protected the forearms, shins, and chest like armor, while bright white fabric covered everywhere else. The surprisingly thin glove had a coating of rubbery mesh. Still wheezing, she didn't try to move as he pulled her aloft like a human balloon.

"You okay?"

"Ouch." She coughed. "What..."

"The elevator stopped. You didn't. It was moving at about twenty feet per second."

She shivered.

"Not as bad as it sounds... that's about thirteen miles per hour." He looked her up and down. "You're on the little side. That uniform should be okay, but you'll need to lose the boots, belt, and that forearm guard. They won't fit in the Starstrider."

Kirsten let him rotate her into a standing position. "What the heck is a starstrider?"

"It's the armor." He tapped his chest. "As tough as anything the military uses, plus it's sealed and has a full RCS maneuvering system."

"Wow. It's only a little bulkier than our armor." Kirsten grabbed the ceiling to pull herself to a locker. She hurried out of her boots, curling into a ball while floating to undo the clips down the sides. "Guess you're Benjamin?"

"Yep." He smiled. "Please, call me Ben. Chandra tells me you've never done this before."

"Yeah." She winked and stuffed her boots/belt/forearm guard in the upper part of the locker above an empty Starstrider unit.

Ben pulled the stiff mannequin-like suit out of its bay, set it on its feet, and typed something on a forearm-mounted touchscreen. A four-inch disc at the center of the armored chestplate rotated a half turn before it opened like a mechanical claw, exposing the interior. "It's a single piece with attached boots and gloves. Only the helmet is separate."

Kirsten hurried into the suit, feeling a little small for it. "It's a bit big, but it works."

"The foot pads are magnetic. Sensors above your feet will react to you trying to walk and control the magnets. Don't try to pick up both legs at once or you'll go flying. It takes some getting used to."

She looked down at blocky cyan metal boots. "I feel like one of those guys in my kid's video game." Kirsten tried to lift her right foot, but it didn't move at all, as if bolted to the ground. A half-second later, the boot flew up with enough force to make her tilt over backward. "Gah!"

He pulled her upright again. "Take a few steps. Lindsey's doing fine... a few minutes more won't make a difference. No sense going out there unprepared. And whoa, you have a kid?"

"Yeah." Kirsten talked about Evan while she practiced walking for a few minutes, eventually going from 'drunk Frankenstein's monster' to 'tiptoeing giant.'

"Not bad."

"I need to test something. Don't freak out on me."

Ben folded his arms. "Try me."

She called the lash, which draped through the glove of her suit without an issue. She swung the luminous tendril of energy back and forth a few times before letting it recede. Her confidence swelled. "Okay. We're good."

"What uhh, what was that?" Ben handed her a helmet and grabbed one for himself.

"It's a projection of psionic energy, like a whip. It's how I fight paranormal entities. It can't hurt anyone who's alive. Wanted to make sure it would work with this heavy glove."

Ben lowered a helmet down over his head and gave it a slight twist to lock it in place. "Handy, that."

"What?"

"That it only hurts spirits. Guess that makes things easier in tight quarters."

"Yeah." She gathered her hair and fumbled with the helmet.

Ben helped seat it. Weak jets of cool air sprayed on her cheeks and the back of her neck, triggering a shiver. "Not bad for never doing this before. Gotta start it off two inches offset to the left."

"Oh." Soon after the neck ring clicked, her vision filled with a heads-up display, and her ears with a steady stream of whimpering and growling. "Lindsey?"

The growling stopped. Seconds later, a weary voice whined, "Go away."

A distorted rasp followed that made the hairs on the back of her neck stand up. While she couldn't make out speech, the tone came off angry. *That's a ghost... caught by the mic. Crap. Something's really here.*

"Okay, step two." Benjamin held his hands up. "Since you don't have an M3 plug to jack in with, the maneuvering jets respond to virtual joysticks. If you hold your hands like this" —he raised his arms and positioned his hands as if holding flight sticks—"the suit will react. The controls are pretty simple. Left stick moves you up and down, forward for up and back for down. Left and right cause rotation. If you squeeze a trigger and move the stick back and forth, instead of sliding up and down, you'll rotate longitudinally, head to toe."

Kirsten nodded.

Ben flexed the fingers of his right hand. "The other side is all lateral motion. Forward glides forward, back glides, back, left and right strafe to the side."

"Sounds easy enough."

Ben clipped a tether on her belt and attached the other end to his. "In case of emergencies."

"I'm not usually into that sort of thing, but I'll make an exception."

He laughed.

They tromped across the room to a six-wheeled cart with a flat surface and one little control unit mounted atop a strut at the front. After climbing on, Ben drove it down about a quarter mile of tunnel past a repeating series of receiving bays that appeared copy and pasted except for different arrangements of random boxes and carts. Each ended with a massive wall of triangular-paneled windows looking out into the vastness of space, and a few offered views of starship hulls in various stages of completion.

He eventually turned off the 'road' into one of the huge nine-story rooms full of heavy equipment, giant cargo boxes, and power-loaders. A huge black '7' decorated the center of the inner wall. Beyond the giant windows, an enormous starship sat in the berth, its eight massive engine cones frighteningly close. Something about staring into their gaping openings made Kirsten dread falling into them and not being able to escape. The craft had to be at least six stories tall and probably four or five hundred yards long. At the right and left corner of the recessed room, stairs led down to another chamber, from which the murmurs of several voices emanated.

Ben led her down into a room about half the size of the storage bay, where two huge airlocks took up most of the exterior wall, flanked by more windows. Kirsten approached, mesmerized at the sight of metal spars stretching off into space, so far they seemed to bend like noodles. Each one had to be ten meters thick, but their length made them look flimsy. She swallowed, second-guessing the idea of walking out on such a precarious place. *Uhh. I dunno about this.* She closed her eyes and wanted to wake up in her bed, at home, clutching Evan like a teddy bear. When she looked again, she still found herself a thousand miles above the Moon.

A small team huddled around a desk that seemed miniscule in comparison to the cavernous room. They had been staring since two Starstrider suits clanked down the plastisteel grating staircase. A man and a woman in business casual stood on either side of two Asian women in white coats.

Ben gestured at them. "They've been trying to talk Lindsey in for hours. Gene Michaels with our mental health team, as is Dr. Leslie Whitaker. Doctors Aya Shimura and Kimberly Nori are from health services. Everyone, this is Agent Wren from Division 0."

Kirsten tromped over and made a quick round of hand shaking. "Anything I should know?"

"Miss Park is showing signs of a psychotic break," said Dr. Whitaker, a confident-looking woman with auburn hair and steel-grey eyes. "I'm not wholly bought in to this whole spirit thing, but I suppose anything is worth trying as this point. None of the other crew will go out there."

"After Jonah came back in, no one wanted to go EVO." Ben fidgeted. "People who live and work on an orbital platform aren't too different from sailors. Superstitious as hell."

Kirsten looked at the medical doctors. "How's her health?"

Doctor Nori glanced at the terminal behind her for a second, then spoke in near-whispered Japanese before English emanated from a small silver device on her shoulder. "There have been several spikes of heart rate, and her blood sugar is getting worrisomely low. After her previous injury, this may create complications."

"Previous injury?" asked Kirsten.

"I'm sorry. I... shouldn't have said that much. I can't discuss a patient's file without an active investigation of Miss Park as a suspect, a binding order from a judge, or approval of next of kin." Dr. Nori let out a soft sigh. "It's not relevant to what's going on right now."

"Okay." Kirsten looked at Ben. "Any scanners pointed that way picking up cold spots?"

"In outer space?" He blinked.

She sighed. "Okay. Maybe blonde is more than hair color. Let's go."

Dr. Whitaker waved a datapad at Kirsten. "Miss Park has been one of the more stable personnel on board. The statistical probability of both her, Jonah, and Emmanuel having 'issues' at the same time are slim to none. That's why I asked them to contact you."

"Emmanuel?" asked Kirsten.

"Lindsey's teammate." Dr. Whitaker sighed. "He's still under sedation."

"Thank you, Doctor." Kirsten smiled at her; the woman had to be old enough to be her mom, but didn't really look it. *Who would I be if I didn't have a piece of shit for a mother?* She offered a pleasant smile, unable to wonder if the psychiatrist had picked up on the longing in her eyes, and headed toward her guide.

Ben waved to the support team and crossed to a fourteen-foot hexagonal airlock hatch in a single gliding leap. Two shiny white panels with yellow markings split apart down the middle and retracted into the walls, exposing a chamber ten yards deep to an exact copy of the inner door. Kirsten tromped over, gazing at the six-inch thick doors as she passed. Once inside the chamber, Ben approached a holo-panel near the exit and closed the inner doors.

"It takes about two minutes to reclaim the air."

She nodded. A readout at the upper left corner of the HUD flashed, warning the exterior atmosphere had become hazardous. About ninety seconds later, it showed 'vacuum.' Soon, the outer door opened, revealing a wider-than-expected path, a road paved out of plastisteel grating that ran the entire length of the spar. A huge dull-grey bot that resembled a legless titan with a tiny head sat parked near a wall that stopped a mere twenty yards from the exit. It didn't react to their presence, its single lens eye staring off into space. Dents and scratches on its chest plate suggested they used it to move around chunks of starship or large components too unwieldy for people.

For most of the walk to Lindsey, she'd have only the magnets in her boots to keep her from floating off.

"Ugh." Trying to concentrate on opening her mind to the presence of the paranormal proved somewhere between impossible and 'not happening' while her brain ground its gears on the terror of hurtling into nothingness.

"Agent Wren, we're reading an elevated heart rate. Are you feeling okay?" asked Dr. Shimura.

"Yeah. Other than scared shitless, I'm doing great." She lifted and placed her feet, falling into a meditative rhythm.

"I'm right behind you," said Ben. "It's going to take you an hour to get out there at that pace. We usually jet along, but it's okay if you're not comfortable with that."

"Lindsey, are you there? My name is Kirsten. I believe you. I'm with Division 0. They sent me up here to deal with the ghost who's trying to hurt you. I'm not going to let him touch you."

Snarling and whimpering came back over the comm.

"Oh, shit. Okay fine." Kirsten held her arms as though she had on a jetpack. "Don't let me kill myself."

Ben glided up at her left side. "I'm right here."

She unstuck her boots and pushed the right hand 'joystick' forward. A hit as though Gabriel had kicked her between the shoulder blades launched her forward. She screamed, watching the plastisteel spars fly past her. The illusion of a curve in the span stretching out in front of her made her feel like she'd gone from flying sideways to falling down a hole.

"Easy!" yelled Ben. "The sticks are super sensitive."

The tether went tight, snapping her to a halt and folding her in half. The cord sprang taut and recoiled, pulling Ben forward and her backward. They collided in a clumsy embrace. Kirsten screamed for a few seconds after, clinging to him for all she had. A torqueing motion came next, followed by a grunt from Ben.

"You're safe. Boots down."

She opened her eyes and blushed at her subconscious reaction to turn into a clinging koala bear. "Uhh. Sorry. Space is really not my thing."

"I'm sure Lindsey will appreciate your bravery." Ben held her out and spun her to face forward down the spar. "Okay. Give it a tiny little push."

Kirsten positioned her hands as if holding joysticks again. This time, she moved her glove about a millimeter. A faint hum sounded in the helmet, and she glided forward at a hair faster than walking. Another tap got her up to a running speed, a third, a little faster.

"That's good." Ben kept pace with her, one hand on her shoulder, the other at his side.

"You have a plug?"

"Yep. Doesn't everyone?"

"Oh, right. You said that already." She tweaked her course with micro-adjustments and tried to convince her mind that the sensation of going downhill came from a trick of the eye. Keeping the new starship in her peripheral vision helped focus on the truth of going in a straight line.

"Most psionics avoid cybernetics. Cutting into the brain messes with it. Plus I'm squeamish. Before today, my worst fear was having something sliced off by some crazy gang member and waking up with a metal hand or leg."

"I'm guessing your new biggest fear is drifting off into space and dying of starvation?"

She gulped. "If that was you trying to be funny, you failed."

The nose end of the ship passed, leaving her on the last two hundred or so yards of the berth strut. She peered over the side at the moon, wondering if its gravity would pull her in to a meteoric landing. This experience took the old pirate 'walking the plank' thing to a degree of ridiculousness she'd never imagined possible. Aside from a twenty-meter wide metal spar, only black void and stars surrounded her. The rasp of her gulping for air in the helmet plus a layer of fog forming in front of her face teased at panic. She held her breath for a few seconds in search for calm.

At the distant end, a boxy outcropping stood among spindles of metal cable and magnetized clamps, retracted since the ship parked here didn't reach all the way to the end. Capsule shaped tanks, arranged in a row on the right, framed some cabinets that held electronics. A rounded patch of glossy cyan stood out against the bland grey plastisteel.

"Visual contact," said Kirsten.

"You guys see anything on the way out there?" asked Gene.

"Nothing here, Gene," said Ben.

"I haven't seen anything either." Kirsten pulled back on the virtual stick to slow herself to a near stop, and tugged down on the left hand one to drop back on her magnetic boots.

"Nice landing." Ben clanked to a stop at her side.

"I need a minute." Kirsten focused on her breathing. She tried to put the idea of where she was out of her head. Having a solid grip on the ground with the energized boots helped. A faint glimmer of supernatural energy came and went, enough to sense as latent, but too weak to ascertain any sense of identity from it. *This is too damn familiar.* "Lindsey? We're here. It's going to be okay."

Kirsten tromped forward, grateful for a lack of gravity. If this metal noodle swayed, she'd lose it. Step by tentative step, she eased closer to where another Starstrider suit huddled behind a white cabinet with two doors.

"Hey, Park. It's Ben. You picked a shitty camping spot. Time to come inside."

"He's here," whispered a voice over comm. "He's watching me. He's out there."

Kirsten put her left hand on the electronics cabinet and pulled herself forward enough to grab Lindsey's arm. "Hey. We're here. You're fine."

Unable to see past the woman's gold bubble helmet, Kirsten didn't even try to dive into Lindsey's mind.

"W-where am I?" asked a weak voice.

"Lindsey?" Kirsten tugged. "My name is Kirsten. I'm here to help you."

"Who are you?" The other woman stood out from behind her hiding place. "Oh... I don't feel so good."

"Her vitals are all over the place," said Doctor Nori. "What's going on out there?"

Lindsey grabbed at her gut and screamed.

A glimmer of paranormal energy came out of nowhere. Kirsten stared at Lindsey for a half second before calling the lash and swiping it through her with a flick of the wrist. Her probing strike met a hint of solidity, a halfhearted slap to a weak entity. A smear of yellowish light melted out from the legs of the woman's suit and shot off to the left, heading for the blue orb of Earth. A flash near the edge of the floor took the shape of a hand in a desperate, but futile, attempt to hold on to something, but the entity rocketed off toward earth. Lindsey collapsed on all fours, moaning over the comm. Kirsten swiveled about and whipped the energy tendril at her a second time for good measure, but it found no solidity, so she ceased concentrating on the power.

She dropped to one knee and pulled the woman upright. "Lindsey, are you okay? What happened?"

"Felt like someone stabbed me in the lower back... Must be a cramp from squatting so long."

Kirsten grasped the other woman by the helmet, looking her in the eye as much as one could look someone in the eye past a visor of opaque gold. The reflection of her own faceless gold helmet stared back at her, creating an endless repeating tunnel of spherical headgear. "Do you remember seeing anything unusual? A spirit? They said you reported seeing a man out here without a suit."

"I..." Lindsey slouched. "Maybe. I'm not crazy. They're going to think I'm unfit and let me go."

"Well, they got my little trick on video too. Something *was* attacking you. I think it's a ghost but I didn't get much of a look at it." Kirsten glanced at the Earth in the distance. A momentary daydream of a ghost (or astral traveler) zooming down with such speed they exploded into a massive splatter of ectoplasm on impact made her smile. "You need to get inside right away."

"Yeah. My waste recycler is screaming at me." Lindsey lifted off her boots like a superhero, extended her arms out over her head, and flew off.

"Wow. She makes it look easy." Kirsten grumbled.

"It *is* easy when you've been doing it for seven years." Ben patted her on the shoulder. "For your first time out, you're doing pretty good... and I'm not just saying that to build confidence." He shook the tether between them. "I usually wind up flying rookie balloons on the first run."

"No offense, but the sooner I'm inside, the happier I'll be." Kirsten grabbed the 'sticks' again, and prodded herself up to a respectable speed with a few taps. Eagerness to reach safety got her going a little faster than she felt comfortable with, but Ben didn't say a word other than to suggest she start decelerating as the giant airlock door came up fast.

Whoever that was, they're not very strong. If I'd taken a real swing, that might've obliterated them. That doesn't make sense... if they're that weak, how could they affect the living, or manifest?

By the time Kirsten made it back, Lindsey had already gone inside. She waited with Ben for the airlock to cycle and rushed in as soon as the door parted. Filling the chamber with air took about a quarter the time of pumping it out. Only Doctor Whitaker remained from the support team when the inner airlock door opened, the rest evidently having gone with Lindsey.

"Agent Wren, are you feeling okay?"

Breathless, Kirsten nodded. "Yes, Doctor. Got a little scared for a moment there, but I'm okay now. I'd like to talk to Lindsey as soon as I can."

"Of course. She's been taken to the infirmary. That part is out of my hands, but I will let Kimberly know to contact you as soon as it's feasible to see her."

"Thank you." Kirsten twisted to face Ben. "Can I get out of this thing now?"

He extended his arm in an 'after you' gesture at the staircase. She trudged over to it and made the arduous climb up forty-five feet to the storage bay, and crossed it to the flat tram cart. Ben drove them down the enormous corridor, which she assumed ran the full width of the station, passing behind every ship berth. She removed her helmet on the ride, and soon after arriving back in the locker room, fiddled with the keypad on her left arm. The menu interface caught her off guard with its complexity. None of the options looked like anything related to opening it.

"How do I get out of this thing?"

"General > System Process > Suit > Disengage."

Geez, they really buried that. Guess it would be bad to open the thing by accident outside. She tapped through the sequence of menus, and then answered yes to two 'are you sure?' prompts. The disc at the center of her chest plate twisted and the metal claw around her torso popped open. She pulled her arms free and fell forward onto her hands before crawling the rest of the way out.

"Now that was one of the most graceful things I've ever seen." Ben chuckled.

Kirsten rolled over on her back and shook her head at him, smirking that he'd already finished changing into normal clothes. She got up before he could offer a hand for the third time and leapt into her boots, trying to avoid the freezing floor seeping into her socks. He took care of stowing the suit she'd used.

"Bet you can't wait to go out again." He winked.

"The next time I 'go out,' it's going to be in a much, much, much, bigger suit... like something the size of a shuttle."

KIRSTEN SAT AT A SMALL TABLE NEAR A WINDOW, WONDERING WHY PEOPLE bothered putting windows in space stations when the view only contained black and stars. Perhaps some found solace in staring at it... people had stargazed for as long as they existed. She sucked down the last tepid mouthful of plain, black coffee, cringing as it slid into her gut. The chicken/pasta thing she'd gotten from the company café tasted like warm raw OmniSoy with a dash of black pepper. Aside from having the consistency of pasta and noodles, she may as well have sucked it straight out of a packet.

Footsteps to her right broke the relative quiet. She glanced up at a wild-eyed man somewhere in his forties with disheveled greying hair and a few days' worth of beard. Silver stubble glinted on his cheek as his jaw shifted side to side. His demeanor made her tense; either he'd been electrocuted, or he meant to attack her.

"You that psionic girl?"

Kirsten gripped her stunrod and lifted his surface thoughts. Jonah, the man they'd sent to retrieve Lindsey. He wanted help. She relaxed. "Yeah. Have a seat."

The man went from menacing to frightened, and sank into the facing chair. "I can't stop seein' it."

"Seeing what?"

"Nope. Nope. Nope." He shook his head.

She peeked again into his head. In his memory, she looked out of his eyes at the spar gliding by as he flew out to where Lindsey hid. A man jumped out of nowhere in front of him, clad in ordinary street clothes instead of an e-suit. Blood welled out of his mouth and nose, oozing between teeth opened in a menacing roar below hollow, empty eye-sockets. Jonah fixated on the man's chest, a gaping cavity where the spine and surrounding tissue glistened in the sunlight behind a dangling clump of severed blood vessels. The figure grabbed at him, but Jonah felt nothing.

His memory at that point blurred into a mad dash to get back inside.

"I saw it in your thoughts, Jonah." Kirsten kept eye contact. "He's not out there anymore. I got a piece of him and he went flying back to Earth."

"Y-you're a psionic, right?" asked Jonah.

"Yes."

"Make me forget that." He leaned forward; the tequila on his breath scorched her nose. "I want it out of my head."

She looked down. "I'm sorry. I can't."

"I don't care if it's illegal. Please do it."

Kirsten took his hand. "It's not that. I don't have the ability to erase memories. Telepathy isn't my strength." *Technically, Mind Blast is what permanently erases memories... telepathy overlays can eventually fail. I don't trust myself to do that.* "Umm. I don't have any practice at deleting memories. I don't want to do more damage in there. Erasing memories requires a judicial warrant. Without that, it's considered highly unethical, but if the person is asking for it... I dunno how that works. How long are you up here?"

Jonah shivered. "We do a six-three rotation. Six months up here, three months off on Earth. I... uhh, got four left."

"When you get back down to Earth, you can contact Division 0 and ask about it if it's still a problem. I understand that guy looked horrible, but it's quite difficult for a spirit to hurt the living. Even on the off chance he comes back up here, the worst thing he could do is scare you into making a dangerous mistake."

Jonah wiped a finger back and forth under his nose, sniffling. His expression shifted past worry to disappointment to apprehension. "I dunno if I can go back out there. Keep seein' that thing when'er I close my eyes."

"You'd be a lot better off with Doctor Whitaker or her staff here than me trying to make you forget that. I've never done a memory deletion before and the... talent that does it can be dangerous. If I made an error, I couldn't fix it. I'm sorry."

"Mmm." He coughed and stood. "S'okay. 'Preciate you bein' honest. You sure that thing's gone?"

Kirsten stared at him and sent a telepathic glimpse of the spirit exuding from Lindsey's suit before zooming off toward Earth into his head. "I saw it go back to Earth. I have no idea how it got up here in the first place. Ghosts are usually tethered to the area of their death. Some can't even leave the room or spot where they died. I've never even heard of one going from planet to planet. The only thing I can think of is that it hooked a ride inside a living person who came up here."

"So it can't come back?" He perked up.

"If my theory is correct, he'd have to possess someone else who was coming up here. Seems like a freak chance that he picked a person headed for this base... unless he has a problem with Gravion."

Jonah shrugged. "Dey's not a bad place to work for. Aside from being stuck inside a giant lunch box for six months, they treat us pretty clear."

She smiled.

A Class 1 doll in a white shirt and matching short skirt entered at the door nearer the food counter. Lines around the mouth and exposed machinery at the joints announced its artificial nature in no uncertain terms. It hurried over to Kirsten.

"Agent Wren? The patient in bunk 23 is ready to talk with you."

"Thanks." She looked at Jonah. "Sorry."

He scratched at his beard stubble. "Oh... If you're sure that thing's gone, I'll try ta keep thinkin' on what you said 'bout it not bein' able ta hurt us. Maybe I'll get over it in a couple days. Do me a favor and tell the medics I really saw some shit and I'm not crazy? Maybe they'll give me a day or two to deal with it."

"Done." She smiled.

The doll led her out of the cafeteria to a corridor that bore a noticeable upward turn at the distant ends. At least in the spinning wheel, gravity felt Earth-normal. After a walk of about a quarter mile past offices, quarters, and systems' rooms, the doll ducked left into a tight hallway lined with doors on both sides. The air hung thick with the smells of sweating bodies, something minty, and floor cleaner. The fifth room on the right contained eight Comforgel slabs arranged in stacked pairs separated by curtains. Lindsey, in a clingy white and grey medical smock that covered from neck to mid-thigh, lay on the lower bunk in the second set. Three plastic tubes connected from a beeping panel on the wall to a patch stuck on her left arm.

Kirsten walked over. "How are you feeling?"

"Tired. Better after eating and showering." Lindsey rolled her head to the side to look at Kirsten. "You're younger than I thought."

"I'm older than I look."

"Sixteen?"

Kirsten laughed. "Twenty-two."

"Wow. Yes, I'm dodging the questions you wanna ask." Lindsey sighed. "Might as well go for it. I remember seeing a man out there with no suit on. Someone like hollowed out his whole body and he was coughing out blood. He had no eyes either... Whatever he was, he didn't say anything, but... I just *knew* he wanted to kill me." She curled up on her side, facing Kirsten. "I saw that light thing on your hand. Did you kill it?"

"What happened there? I didn't sense anything around us and you doubled over."

"Felt like I got stabbed." Lindsey grabbed her back an inch or so above her butt.

Kirsten frowned. If a paranormal entity had manifested scratches, the medical team would have removed them already. The vision of the spirit from Jonah's memory looked a lot like what black market organ harvesters leave behind... *The doc said she'd had some kind of procedure. I wonder.* "Is it okay if I touch you for a moment? I'm trying to get a read."

"Psionic stuff?"

"Yeah."

Lindsey nodded. "Okay."

Kirsten let her hand rest on the spot the woman indicated. She concentrated, feeling a trace amount of energy, about the same as she'd sensed on people after séances or visiting haunted places.

"What's wrong? You look pissed."

"There's a latent presence, but it's too weak for me to do anything with. I can't get a feel for who it is."

"What, like a dog tracking a scent or something?"

"Basically. Lindsey... the doctor mentioned you had some kind of injury before. Do you mind talking about it? They wouldn't give me any details."

"Uhh, sure." She rolled flat again. "A couple months ago, I was out doing an inspection. Some kind of electrical issue killed the mooring cables on the starboard side, and all the ones on port pulled the ship in that direction. I got pinned against the station. Crushed and broke both of my legs and my left hip."

Kirsten cringed. "Oh, gah... That had to be excruciating. I can't even imagine."

"I didn't feel shit." A somber smile played at her lips. "I passed straight out. Byron wasn't so lucky. He died right away when his helmet crushed. Before you ask, no, that guy I saw was not Byron. They told me later I was stuck there for a few hours before they got the ship off me."

"That sounds awful. I'm sorry."

Lindsey swished her feet back and forth. "They put me back together without cybernetics at least. Guess the damage wasn't *that* bad. Really, Gravion surprised me. You always hear about corporations screwing over their employees to save a credit or two, but they really pulled through for me. Ask most people up here, they'll say Grav is cheap. The TP is like sandpaper and the food's kinda shitty."

"Kinda?" Kirsten stuck her tongue out. "Bleh. How can you eat that?"

"Hell, they haven't even installed a relay for GlobeNet access up here. The food ain't that bad—when it's all there is." Lindsey sat up cross-legged. "I could kill for an Omni-burger right about now. The IV nutrients aren't doing it for me." She stared at the glowing blue Comforgel pad while combing her fingers down her long, black hair. "At first, I thought I saw Byron out there sometimes. You know, they say people who spend long hours EVO start to go nuts. Seeing things that aren't there, hearing voices and stuff. Even in two-person teams, the isolation sets in."

"I can see that. May I ask why you keep doing it if it bothers you?"

Lindsey sniffled. "I really saw that thing. I'm not crazy."

"You did. I saw it too."

"Good." She calmed. "I haven't had any luck finding a job on Earth, and I don't want to go to a colony. There's some stuff on the Moon but the pay is like half of this... and I get three months off, paid."

"Well... If it starts making you question your sanity."

Lindsey smiled. "They'll fire me before I go crazy. They have head doctors on staff here."

"Can you think of anyone who died within the past... twenty or so years who might blame you for it? Even if it makes no sense?"

"Uhh. Twenty years ago, I was six. I've had a boring life. Spent most of it online either in school or NOI."

"NOI?"

"Nothingness of Infinity. It's an MMO where the whole of North America is like West City—no Badlands. All cyberspace hacking and stuff. I've got a level 284 NetShade."

"So you log into cyberspace to play a game that's all about logging into cyberspace?"

Lindsey rolled her eyes. "Yeah, that's like the esoteric ironic part of it all."

Kirsten's gaze darted to a shadow passing by the door. "Some people can take those games too seriously. Did you have any experiences in the game that might have made someone angry enough to want to hurt you, possibly after killing themselves?"

Lindsey gawked at her. "Did you *see* that guy? How did he kill himself? By swallowing a gallon of acid?"

"Good point." Kirsten grumbled and tried to massage calm into the bridge of her nose with both hands. *Shit this is frustrating.* "It's gotta be the same guy."

"Hmm?"

"I've had a couple reports that are a lot like what happened to you, only yours is the worst so far. At least worst in terms of danger. In every case so far, I've come up empty handed. I can't connect any sort of motive and there's no common thread between the people being attacked."

"Sorry." Lindsey scrunched up her face, as if deep in thought. "I really can't think of anyone except for maybe this one girl. She was playing a boy character in NOI and we were like dating. I found out it was a girl for real and called it off. Not my thing."

"Did she take it hard?"

"Uhh, a little stalky type stuff, but she got over it." Lindsey looked over. "That was like ten years ago. I was sixteen."

"Do you remember the girl's name?"

"I never knew it... her character was Itsuko585."

"Well that's something." *That other woman could've been disturbed, killed herself, and now blames Lindsey.* Kirsten stood. "I'm going to be here until morning and the next shuttle leaves."

"I'd hang, but... I'm stuck on medical restriction. Not supposed to leave here 'til I'm cleared."

Kirsten sat on the next Comforgel pad. "Not like I've got plans. I can stay with you if you'd like someone to talk to."

"Sure if you want. At least until they kick you out at ten."

"So, what do you want to talk about?"

"Are you a cop now, or just some girl who flew four hundred thousand miles to drag my ass inside?"

Kirsten laughed.

"How 'bout a ghost story?" Lindsey rolled on her side and propped her head on one arm. "What's the funkiest thing you've ever seen?"

Demon-Konstantin... ugh, too soon. Pizza with eyes sliding down the monorail? Hmm. "Maybe the Wharf Stalker, but that's a—wait no. Getting covered by an army of Harbingers was probably the scariest moment."

"What's a Harbinger?"

Kirsten gazed into the distance. "Something you never, ever want to meet."

14

BROKEN FREE

E van looked back and forth from the smashed statue to Samantha Peña's face. She stared at the fragments, her expression cycling between panic, anger, and worry. Shani kept her head down and twisted the toe of her ballet flat into the floor. Samantha put a hand over her mouth and shot a glance in the general direction of Abernathy. Any trace of cadet authority faded, leaving her a terrified eleven-year-old.

"W-what was that?" Sam edged away from the broken artifact. "Did you see an old guy, all glowy and stuff?"

Evan gestured at Abernathy, several steps away from the spot at which Cadet Peña squinted. "That's Abernathy."

"Tell the kid it ain't her fault. I was a bit anxious when I felt someone fiddling around with my brain. I probably appeared."

"He says it's not your fault the thing broke. He didn't mean to scare you." Evan smiled at the ghost. "I wanted to surprise you by helping you."

"Help me?" Abernathy chuckled. "You can help me by putting that jar back where it belongs and leavin' it be."

Evan's mouth hung open. "Uhh, you don't wanna like... be free? I was gonna take it to Father Villera so he can give you a real burial."

"Pah." Abernathy waved. "I'm fine. I'm quite happy here. Maybe someday if they ever shut down the school and there's no life left in the building." A grandfatherly smile crinkled his eyes. "But for now, I'd much rather stay."

"Uhh. Wow. Okay." Evan fidgeted.

"What?" asked both girls at the same time.

"Abernathy doesn't wanna go away. He's happy."

Shani glared. "You butthead. We're gonna get in trouble an' he doesn't even want help."

"Sorry." Evan stared down. "I thought he was trapped."

Abernathy ran a tingly, cold hand over Evan's head. "It's all right, boy. I'm not trapped or anything. Matter of fact, I don't think any spirit is 'trapped' because a piece of their body is lying around in a jar or hasn't been 'buried right.' To me, that's my bed." He hesitated a few seconds, wagging his eyebrows. "Well, I suppose if the spirit believes it matters, it might. But I ain't seen nothin' on this side what leads me to believe I'm still here on account o' not followin' any mythological rituals over my remains."

Shani looked at Samantha. "We won't tell anyone."

"She didn't break it." Evan frowned at the pieces. "Abernathy scared her 'cause of my idea. I'll take the pieces to someone and say it was me."

Samantha bit her lip, a conflicted look on her face. "We should all go. Shani won't get in much trouble because she just followed us."

The seven-year-old fumed for two seconds before the tears started. "You said we wouldn't get in any trouble!"

Evan stooped, reaching for a fragment of the statue. Ice cold washed over his back. He cringed, head snapping up in Shani's direction. The world flashed to sepia tones, time frozen at the instant a broadsword fell on her from above, spearing into the top of her head and protruding from her belly. He screamed, and the horrible vision faded. The world once more returned to full color. Shani yelped in response to his scream, but at least she didn't have a three-foot long sword sticking out of her. Such fear for his friend's life gripped him, he almost threw up on her.

At the sound of metal rattling, Evan jumped at her. "Shani!"

He wrapped his arms around her, the weight of his body knocking her flat on her back. A loud *clang* preceded Samantha shrieking.

Shani coughed, shoved, and punched at him. "Get offa me!"

Evan twisted to look behind him. An ancient sword lay on the floor next to a large gouge where the point had dislodged a divot from the plasticrete floor. Shani went from pushing to clinging, and squealed in fright. Abernathy turned in place, eyes high.

"T-that thing just fell off the top shelf." Samantha pointed at it.

"Mommy!" yelled Shani.

Evan started to cry as well. Hearing the word made him want his mother here right now, but Shani whimpering gave him a little courage. He'd pretend to be brave to make her feel safer. "Abernathy, what happened?"

"Looks like a critter got loose." He walked sideways two steps, staring at something out of sight and high up. "Best guess, a poltergeist. Bet it was somehow trapped in that statue."

Cadet Peña stared at Evan. "Holy shit. You're a precog too! You like totally saw that com—" A box bounced off her head, knocking her to all fours, cradling her skull. "Ow." She rubbed the spot, mussing her hair. "Thanks for the warning."

He offered a helpless shrug. "I... it's not that strong. It only works when it's someone I like... uhh, care about a lot or something."

Shani looked at him and sniffled. "I still think you're a butthead."

Samantha crawled over to them and stood. "What's going on?"

"Poltergeist." Evan struggled to stand, but Shani wouldn't let go. "Ugh. Shan, get up."

She clung tighter. "I'm scared!"

"What's poltergeist mean?" Samantha pulled them both upright.

Evan put an arm around Shani. "A ghost. Like a little kid throwing a tantrum with TK, only you can't see them and they can fly."

"I gotta call this in." Samantha pulled a NetMini from her belt and held it up. Before she could do much more than glance at it, a phantasmal cloud of light raced by and yanked it out of her hands. The little slab of technology sailed off over the warehouse shelves. A few seconds later, a loud *click* echoed among the shelves. She jumped with a shriek.

"Run!" yelled Shani.

She started to sprint away, but Evan grabbed on and held the struggling girl back, not entirely sure why until a waterfall of boxes spilled from above. Cartons ranging in size from a few inches square to tall enough for him to stand inside of caved in, blocking them off in the dead end.

Shani recoiled from the towering pile, trembling. "T-that almost fell on us!"

"Oh, this one's angry." Abernathy jumped through the shelf. Bangs, clatters, and grunting came from the other side.

Evan caught a few glimpses of the old ghost jumping about as if in the midst of a brawl. His chest pounded with fear and dread; *Mom's gonna be angry.* He gulped. *If I'm alive to be punished.* "I don't wanna scare you, but I think this thing is trying to kill us."

Samantha eyed the sword. "Uhh, yeah I kinda figured that out. Why?"

"Prob'ly 'cause you broke his statue." Shani pointed at the statue bits with her foot.

A flash of pale amber/pink light raced out of the shelf, crossed the section of corridor, and vanished into the other side. For a fleeting second, Evan got a glimpse of a roughly humanoid shape: head, wispy claw-like hands, half a torso, all looking like a mass of tattered rags.

Abernathy stumbled into view a moment later, looking winded. "Blighter's fast. I can't catch the little fu—uhh, bastard."

Evan looked up at him. "It tried to kill Shani. I think the first word you wanted to say works better."

"What are we gonna do?" asked Samantha. "They won't give me a sidearm 'til I'm at least sixteen. Lasers hurt ghosts, right? That's what they said."

"Mom's got one." Evan shrugged. "I guess." He blinked. "I got an idea."

He scurried over to the broadsword and took a knee. A *creak* overhead made him look up at a huge plastisteel box tilting off the topmost shelf on the side above the table of junk. The apparition hovered behind it, pushing.

"Look out!" yelled Samantha.

Shani grunted and thrust her hands into the air.

The massive box fell, despite the girl's effort, but she shoved its path far enough to the left that it missed Evan by a good six feet. It burst open on impact, spilling holo-disks everywhere in a torrent of glimmering chromatic silver.

"What are you doing?" Samantha ran over to Evan. "You're gonna try to hit it with a sword bigger than you are?"

"No." Evan bit his lip. "Shani is."

"Maybe you can say sorry?" asked Samantha.

"Doubtful. Poltergeists aren't what you call full spirits. They're dumber than dogs." Abernathy tapped his head. "Raw energy without much of a brain to it. There's nothing to talk to, just a scrap of consciousness."

A flash of peach-pink light caught his eye. Evan cringed as the wailing apparition zoomed around a corner and came flying straight at him, skimming inches off the floor. He held his hands up and screamed. His desperate need to have the thing stop seemed to do something; a squishy sensation tugged at the back of his mind, and he *felt* the charging spirit's approach. Panic faded to determination and he shoved.

The poltergeist wailed again, slowing to a creep. It hissed, rolled over, and slipped sideways into a stack of tiny boxes, knocking several over. Evan gasped for breath. *Whoa. That was cool.*

"We can climb out." Samantha pulled herself up to the second tier of the shelf on the left.

"Don't do it." Evan reached for her. "It'll make you fall."

Cadet Peña's confidence melted out of her expression. After another glance at the dense arrangement of containers, books, scroll cases, and old junk, she hopped back to the ground.

Evan put his hand on the cold blade. Gritting his teeth, he slipped his thumb down the edge enough to cut it bleeding. Mick's beatings had hurt, but slicing open his finger was a new form of pain he hadn't become used to. An involuntary gasp escaped him, but he smeared his blood down the length of the blade while concentrating on binding it to the astral realm.

"Oh, hey now." Abernathy walked over. "That's an interesting trick. Where'd you get that from?"

"My mom showed me how to do it." Evan stuck his cut thumb in his mouth.

"Incoming!" yelled Samantha.

Shani grunted. Something else went flying and smashed in the distance.

"I got it," yelled Shani. "It's not that strong. It's pushing stuff over."

Bonk.

"Ow!" Shani burst into tears.

Evan looked up. The girl squatted with both hands on top of her head. An old-looking laser pistol that wasn't there before lay on the floor by her foot. The spot where an E-mag would go looked square instead of rectangular and about twice the size; whatever type of battery pack it took had to be obsolete, and probably impossible to find. He poured energy into the sword until he got the sense it couldn't soak in any more. With Astral Seeing turned on, the blade appeared to have a subtle glow around it that reminded him of dropped loot from the Monwyn MMO.

Abernathy leaned down and picked it up.

"Whoa…" Samantha backed away. "That sword is flying on its own."

"Abernathy's holding it." Evan rubbed the sore spot on his thumb. The cut had already reduced to a sealed cat-scratch; watching it disappear entirely over the next few seconds caused a twinge of hunger to murmur in his belly.

The old ghost swung the blade around in a cautious pattern, as if gauging its weight. "This thing's pretty damn heavy."

"You're too slow." Evan looked up at the old ghost. A shoebox-sized plastisteel carton rocketed from a shelf and slammed into his face, knocking him flat and seeing stars. "Ow."

An empty broadsword sheath flew out from the shelf and swatted Samantha across the rear end with a *pop* that sounded like a small gunshot. She went up on tiptoe, gasping. Shani yanked herself into the air with a burst of telekinesis to avoid a flock of knives scattering to the floor where she'd been standing.

"Ow," mewled Samantha. She took a step forward, holding her rear end in both hands while tears leaked down her face.

Evan rolled onto all fours, blood pouring from his nose. The scabbard that had whacked Samantha in the butt pivoted upright, the poltergeist holding it like a bat. It swung for her head, but Abernathy let off a war cry and thrust the bound broadsword in the way, blocking the strike. He lunged at the apparition, which abandoned the scabbard to glide backward in a blur. The blade *whooshed* through empty air. The keening wail of the poltergeist continued, trailing far away into the distance.

"Ev!" Shani ran to his side. "You're bleeding!"

Samantha, still cringing in pain, pulled him up to sit back on his heels. She pulled a tiny light from her utility belt and shined it in his eyes.

He raised an arm to block her. "Knock it off. I'm okay. Sam, are you hurt?"

She rubbed her backside. "That hurt so much I saw white, but I don't think it's serious."

Shani gasped and shoved her hands straight up. Another large box plummeted to a halt, hovering over the three of them. Sweat rolled down her face; her little legs wobbled.

"Sam, you're an empath right?" asked Evan.

"Yeah."

"Make her angry."

Samantha stared at Shani. Two seconds later, the seven-year-old growled and the giant box went flying back over the shelf it had fallen from. She slouched to her knees, panting.

"Nice!" said Evan.

Shani punched him in the eyebrow, yelling, "Butthead!"

"Ow." Evan grabbed his head. "Okay, that's too angry."

"Sorry," whispered Shani, both hands clutched to her chin.

"Not your fault." Evan blinked it off. Already, his nosebleed had stopped, though a dull ache settled in the middle of his skull from the box cracking him in the head. *Shan... use that sword. It can hurt the thing now.*

She looked at him as though he'd just suggested she give away all her dolls. "How? I can't see it. Butthead."

"Oh." He grumbled. "Wait." He jumped up. "Sam... when you see me start concentrating, gimme a boost. I don't think I'm strong enough to grab it on my own yet. Need uhh…"

"A high emotional state," said Abernathy.

"Yeah, that." Evan dragged the blade over to Shani and set it on the floor before locking stares with her. *I'm gonna try to hold it down by the statue bits. When it's there, make the sword slice back and forth as hard as you can.*

"Yeah, what?" asked Sam.

"I'm talking to the ghost." Evan pointed at Shani, the sword, and made a chopping gesture at Abernathy.

Shani nodded. *Why are you telepathing?*

In case it's smart enough to understand me. I don't want it knowin' what we're gonna do.

"Oh." Shani levitated the broadsword, held it a second, and set it down. "That's not so heavy."

Abernathy looked among the kids. "I'll go chase it out of hiding."

He ran off.

After telepathically explaining the plan to Samantha, Evan paced back and forth. His thumb looked unhurt, the dull ache in his nose had faded, only the dread of how much trouble they'd all get into remained. Of course, one had to stay alive to get in trouble. Given the option, he'd rather get punished.

"Incoming!" yelled Abernathy.

He spun to face the shout and sank into a stance like a Gee-ball goalie watching an offensive player charging the grid. As soon as the tattered phantasm streaked into view, he tried to seize it with his mind. Tingles and pulsating feelings spread over his brain. A sense as though his fingers sank into warm gelatin covered his hands. He grunted; the poltergeist clawed at the air, screeching and twisting like it mired in a bog.

"Now," grunted Evan.

Samantha put her hand on his shoulder.

An upwelling of courage and desperation exploded in his chest. His desire to protect his best friend grew strong to the point tears ran down his cheeks. Evan let off a war cry and wrenched all the energy he could summon with a twisting gesture that dragged the poltergeist closer before pushing it near the statuette fragments. It thrashed and clawed, knocking a few knives and an old utility belt off the bottom shelf where its hands could reach.

The broadsword left the ground with a metallic scrape. Evan twisted, fighting the poltergeist's sudden surge against his power. Inexplicable anger came out of nowhere, and he shoved the phantom back down. Samantha's fingers squeezed tighter into his shoulder.

Evan growled, forcing the spirit two feet closer to the statue fragments. Shani's levitating broadsword spiraled back and forth, swinging in ways no living swordsman could. After six agonizing seconds, a lucky random swipe sank most of the blade into the glowing mass. The poltergeist's 'body' split in half for an instant and drew whole again. After it reintegrated, it screeched a painful, glassy wail and slipped free of Evan's grasp. He tried to 'grab' it again, but it evaded his psionic hold and streaked out of sight into the floor.

"Ow." Evan swooned to his knees. All the raging emotions in his head levelled off to bland calm.

Samantha leaned forward, hands on her knees, and gasped for breath. "Wow. That was an awesome idea… how'd you come up with that?"

"Mom showed me how to bind a table knife."

"No, I mean the emotional surge."

Shani set the blade down and walked over. "Is it gone?"

Evan looked at Abernathy. "I dunno."

The old ghost winced. "That looked like it hurt. I don't think you destroyed it, but it'll be a while before it returns. Long enough for your mother to get back."

"Yeah. Umm." He looked at Samantha. "They made us watch a video about bullying. Some girl went psycho with TK when she was really mad."

"Oh, I saw that." Samantha biffed herself in the forehead. "I never even thought of doing it on purpose. You know she's still here? She's like almost thirty. She's part of the network ops team."

"That's kinda boring." Evan scratched his head. "Doesn't she use her powers?"

Samantha shrugged. "I guess she thinks about what she did whenever she does... probably doesn't like it."

"Oh." Evan looked down. "Yeah, that makes sense."

"You kids should get out of here now."

Evan looked up at the ghost. "Yeah."

"Maybe we won't get in trouble." Shani jumped up. One by one, boxes floated out of the collapse and glided back to shelves. She got about a third of the blockage back on shelves before swaying, dizzy. "I'm tired."

"It's okay." Evan took her by the hand. "We should go tell someone what happened."

Cadet Peña looked nervous, but nodded.

Shani cleared a few more containers out of the debris pile, enough to make a path. After taking a deep breath, Evan led the way out of the archives to the stairway. When he crossed the Admin section back to the school without approaching any adult in uniform, Samantha tugged on his arm.

"I thought you were gonna tell someone."

"I am." Evan pointed at an elevator.

Shani looked up at him with a doe-eyed pleading face. "Do we have to?"

"Who?" asked Sam.

Evan hit the call button and folded his arms. "Someone who will believe me about the poltergeist. Captain Ezzeh, and, yeah." He looked at Shani. "It'll be worse to lie on top of it."

Cadet Peña gasped. "But he's an officer... like a high-ranking one. You can't just walk up to a captain and talk to him like that."

"Why not? He's really nice and he likes me."

"But he's an O3!" Cadet Peña shivered.

"Right. He outranks a lot of people who'd be mad at us and not believe in poltergeists." Evan grinned. "C'mon."

"The last time I listened to you, we got in trouble." Shani pouted.

"I know. We're going to get in trouble, but it's an accident and we can't keep it secret. If that 'geist hurts someone, it's our fault."

She hung her head. "Okay."

Evan led them into the elevator and hit the button for the Operations level. "Don't be afraid of him. He's my mom's boss."

"Then why are you so scared?" asked Cadet Peña.

He stared at his sneakers. "If I get in too much trouble, I might get sent back to the dorms."

Cadet Peña frowned. "That sucks."

Shani squeezed his hand. "Nope. I shot her and she wasn't mad at me."

"What?!" Cadet Peña gawked.

The elevator door opened. Evan walked out, followed by Shani and Samantha at the end.

"A bad man made me do it." She sniffled. "I didn't wanna."

"Oh." Samantha scowled. "I hate suggestives."

Evan glared at her.

"You're a—"

"No. My mom is. And she uses it right."

"Sorry." Cadet Peña looked downcast.

Evan wandered into his mother's squad room and went over to Captain Eze's office. He knocked.

"Come in."

The deep voice made Samantha shiver.

He grabbed her hand and pulled them both inside. "Uhh, hi Captain Ezzeh. Can I talk to you?"

"Evan." Captain Eze smiled. "Of course. Your mother has gone to the Moon to help someone."

"I know. It's not about Mom." He took a deep breath and let it out his nose. "I did something bad."

"Oh?" He raised an eyebrow. His broad smile faded. "Is that blood on your cheek?"

"Yes, sir." Evan walked up to the desk. "It's my fault. I talked them into coming with me to help Abernathy."

"Slow down." Captain Eze got up and came around the desk. He guided the kids to the sofa at the back of his office and gestured at them to sit before pulling another chair over for himself.

"Sir, may I please stand?" asked Samantha.

Captain Eze gave her an odd look.

"Ghost hit her in the butt," said Shani.

Samantha blushed.

"All right." Captain Eze gave Evan a concerned look. ""Go ahead and tell me what happened. Start from the beginning."

"Yes, sir." Evan fidgeted. "There's this ghost in the school..."

15

GUILT

The DS2 hovered within a foot of the Police Administrative Center roof. Kirsten jumped down from the ramp, took a few steps, and turned to wave at the pilots. She pictured them returning the wave despite the opaque armor plated 'cockpit'. The ramp closed, and the aircraft rose into a banking turn. She watched it climb until the sun glaring down from the late morning sky became too painful.

Despite wanting to call Evan, she sent a text not to disturb him. At 10:26 a.m., he'd be in class. ‹Back safe. C U after school.›

A long minute later, ‹K› popped up on her screen.

He's probably afraid of getting in trouble. She sighed with a smile and went inside.

Dorian met her in the hallway of the Operations level. "Welcome back. How'd it go up there, and you were right. You're not going to like this, but I think you're going to have to destroy this one."

She cringed. "Same story." A rough explanation of what happened on the Gravion base kept Dorian's attention all the way to the squad room. "Destroy who?"

"The spirit Evan found in the boy's bathroom. Whoever he was, he's batshit insane now. I couldn't get a coherent word out of him other than enough to know he wants to kill psionic kids."

Kirsten glared.

"Well. Probably psionic adults too, but he's got a fixation." Dorian scratched at his hair. "I'm thinking a psionic child probably killed him during an outburst. From the looks of it, a telekinetic threw him off a building."

"Wren." Captain Eze emerged from his door. "How was the flight?"

"Okay, I guess."

"You don't sound too happy."

She pulled at a stray strand of hair over her right eye. "I could've gone to my grave happy if I never went into outer space in a suit. That, and more of the same. Whatever was up there slipped away."

He indicated his office with a sideways nod.

Kirsten followed him, sat facing his desk, and rambled about the entire experience. By the time she finished, her face felt as red as a fire suppression bot and she wanted to pull her hair out. "I'm so damn frustrated."

Captain Eze tapped his chin. "Might be a prankster, albeit a vicious one. There may be no connection at all."

"Oh, crap. Did my searches ever finish?" She looked out his office window at her desk. "I started a net crawl before I left."

"Kirsten... About Evan."

Her heart almost stopped. She looked at him as if expecting him to pull his sidearm and shoot her in the head. The din of activity outside faded, swallowed as if she'd slipped underwater. All the moisture in her throat vanished. "W... What?"

"Calm down, Kirsten. It's nothing too bad. He got into a little trouble."

She laughed. "He... got into trouble? It's not an adoption thing?"

"No." Captain Eze smiled. "He got it in his head that Abernathy needed 'saving,' and talked a couple of his friends into sneaking into the Archives in search of the brain. They made a heck of a mess down there, but it wasn't completely their fault.

"Thirty-two years ago, Division 0 conducted a raid on a mass-murder site where a number of doomsday cultists devoted themselves to an ancient demonic figure, Grachiel. The crime scene team recovered a small statuette that attracted the attention of a clairvoyant. He believed the statue had been infused with some kind of dark energy, and decided to store it away to keep it out of general circulation."

Kirsten shivered. "They found it and played with it, didn't they?"

"Not exactly. Evan said it was set out on a folding table. Perhaps a university-level student had been studying it and forgot to put it away. Abernathy manifested and startled a cadet, who bumped the table and knocked it over. A poltergeist seems to have been trapped inside... and it's loose."

"Oh." She exhaled. "That's all? Only a poltergeist. That's not so bad. Hard part is going to be finding it."

"You don't seem concerned."

"I was expecting you to tell me they let a demon loose." She exhaled into her hands. "Poltergeist is easy by comparison."

"Just be ready for that thing coming up at a bad time. The kids gave it a piece though. Something about a 'bound' blade?"

Kirsten squeezed her knees for a second before curling her fingers into fists. As much as it pained her to imagine him bleeding, he probably felt it the only option. "How much trouble is he in?"

"Well... He volunteered to help clean up the mess. A couple of items were destroyed beyond repair, but if you ask me, the stuff's been sitting down there so long no one will miss it. He wound up with 500 citizenship points."

Kirsten cringed. "That'll take him all year to work off."

Captain Eze smiled. "The penalty was 200, but he insisted on absorbing Shani's share of it, as well as the cadet's 100 points."

She failed at holding back a few tears.

"He's most afraid you'll be upset with him and send him back to the dorms."

Kirsten's heart sank. "He really thinks that?"

"I believe it's his worst fear, not what he actually expects you'll do."

The weight in her chest lessened a little. "I'm not sure how I'd handle it if he really thinks I could do that to him."

"How are the investigations coming?"

"I'm, uhh... Four attacks now without a pattern. I feel like I'm chasing my tail. I did get a glimpse of the spirit, but indirectly. A terrified witness's memory isn't the most reliable source when dealing with spirits. He might've exaggerated it."

"True. Well, you'll be happy to know the senator hasn't contacted us again."

She fidgeted. "He's probably waiting for a more annoying time. Oh, I need to deal with something at the school. Evan saw a spirit in the boys' bathroom that wanted to kill him, but it was too weak."

He blinked. "All right. I expect you'll be filing the usual reports."

"Yeah." Kirsten stood. "Reports."

"Dismissed." He smiled and saluted.

She returned the salute. "I'll let you know as soon as I have something."

"Great. Oh, Kirsten?"

"Hmm?" She paused at the door, glancing back.

"Whatever you're doing with that boy, keep on doing it. He's inheriting your integrity."

"Thank you, sir." She rubbed her naked right wrist, and wanted to kill Konstantin all over again.

KIRSTEN APPROACHED THE BATHROOM DESIGNATED B8, ALREADY ABLE TO SENSE a malign presence on the other side of the door. She glanced at Dorian then indicated the door with a nod. He walked in, re-emerging a moment later.

"Two standing one sitting." Dorian seemed torn between amused and angry. "The spirit is trying to choke the kid on the toilet, but the boy hasn't noticed."

She tapped her foot. Within a few minutes, a pair of boys a few years older than Evan emerged, looking pale. They startled at the sight of her so close to the door.

"Uhh, hi," said the shorter kid with dark hair.

"Hello." She smiled. "Did you feel anything strange in there?"

The taller one gestured at the door. "Yah. Been *extraño* in there for a while now. I, umm, hate going in there alone."

"Dude," said the other kid. "Girls go to the bathroom in packs, not us."

Another boy, younger and pudgier than the other two hurried out, coughing.

"I need you three to do me a favor. Stand here and don't let anyone come in," said Kirsten. "I'll be a few minutes."

"Why are you using the boys' room?" asked the heavy kid.

"I'm not using it… There's a malevolent spirit in there I need to deal with." She stepped closer to the youngest boy. "How's your neck?"

"Sore."

"May I?" Kirsten reached toward his shirt. When he nodded, she pulled back his collar, exposing three bruise-shaped fingerprints. "Oh, hell. I'm going to need to document that."

"Whoa," chimed the other two.

After taking a photo of the bruise, Kirsten slipped past them and went in. She hooked past an L-shaped alcove with wastebaskets and stood in the doorway to the bathroom proper with her arms folded. A row of urinals covered the wall on the right, stalls straight ahead, and sinks across the left side. The man wandering around in the middle looked as though he lost a bet with gravity. His shirt, pants, and sides had split open, oozing fluids as well as mushed up organs.

"So what's your story?" Kirsten glared at him as she advanced. "Got a problem with kids?"

He hissed at her, pointed, and moaned. At first, the tone came off questioning, then angry.

"Yes. I can see you. My son says you want to kill psionic children… is that right?"

The man gurgled and snarled. He rushed in, hands raised as if to strangle her.

She ducked to the side and called the lash as she whirled to face him. The ghost swung his arms together, grabbing nothing, and stopped a few steps past her. Stark shadows shimmered on the white walls, stretched forms of porcelain fixtures illuminated by the scintillating energy whip. Dorian pounced out of the wall and grabbed him in a compliance hold.

"Last chance. My partner thinks you're insane and can't be reasoned with. I am *not* going to let you hurt anyone. If you can be helped, I'll help you, but you have to tell me what's keeping you here."

He grumbled and growled, struggling against Dorian. The mangled ghost seemed stronger by a margin; the effort to hold him down showed on her partner's face. Kirsten thrust her left arm out, fingers splayed, and added her energy to the force holding the spirit still.

"Killed..." The ghost moaned unintelligible words. "Daughter... psionic."

"Okay. Your daughter killed you and she's psionic."

The spirit nodded.

"You're lingering because she got away with it?"

"Yrmmm."

"Who is your daughter, and why did she kill you?"

The mangled ghost slapped at the side of his head before twirling his finger around. The next gurgle he made sounded like "Natalie."

Kirsten blinked. "Hernandez?"

He nodded.

"You're the guy from that video they make us all watch. You tried to kill her. That was self-defense. There's no revenge for that."

He grumbled. "Kill her."

Kirsten closed her eyes, reaching out with the intent to beckon a Harbinger. *I'll know for sure if one of them is interested in him.* "Dorian, I think you were right. This guy's beyond help."

The spirit howled, twisted, and launched Dorian into the wall. Kirsten snapped her arm up, raking the last two feet of the astral lash across the ghost's chest the instant he charged at her. The hit resounded with a *crack* that knocked the mangled spirit over backward. Four of the LED light tubes overhead exploded.

All three boys she'd left guarding the door ran in, but stopped short gawking at the streamer of blue-white light coiling around her legs.

"Boys, get out. Something's coming you *don't* need to see."

The vengeful spirit collapsed into a head-sized orb of green light. All three boys stared at it, gasping. It darted into the middle boy, who took on a dazed look. Kirsten ran up on him, swiping the lash across all three as fast as she could. The shorter seventh-grader collapsed to his knees and vomited, spraying bile and ectoplasm from his mouth and nostrils.

Moaning, the crushed ghost rose from the puddle and dragged itself along the floor toward her. Chill settled in; the room dropped twenty degrees in a second. Lights flickered and dimmed, one emitted a twittering buzz. Black vapor welled up from the dark lines in the tiled floor, swirling about in a mass that coalesced in the distant corner by the sinks. Twelve drains gurgled with a hollow churning drone. The column of inky smoke clung to the wall, mounting higher and higher until it touched the drop ceiling. Two silvery sparkles appeared in an approximation of eyes as a Harbinger drifted forward out of the fog.

Dorian grabbed the spirit and struggled to haul him upright. It struggled at a stalemate, greater strength making up for a lack of combat training. Not wanting to risk hitting her partner with the lash, Kirsten circled. Dorian's hesitance at being near Harbingers resulted in him trying to throw the other ghost at the nine-foot tall cloud of blackness. The spirit darted left, but Kirsten caught it with the energy whip. The strike dispelled any vestige of humanity, reducing the apparition to a semi-formed puddle of slime.

The Harbinger bowed its head with a slight nod, and fell upon the writhing mass. Dark vapors billowed outward and engulfed the moaning spirit before seeping in a slow spiral down through the tiled floor.

Still coughing up vomit, the kneeling boy blinked at the room. "Thbt wmf coobl!"

Kirsten shot them a worried look. A quick surface thought peek made her feel better: none had seen the Harbinger, though they felt its presence as a dire chill that had paralyzed them with fear. She let the lash recede.

"You two can go back to class. I'll walk him to the medtech's station." Kirsten glanced at Dorian while helping the puking boy stand. "How long do you think that spirit was here?"

"No idea. Damn lucky thing Ev was messing around with seeing... Who'd have ever thought to look in here for a psychotic ghost?"

Kirsten laughed. "When I first arrived in the dorms, the girls had all sorts of stories about a haunted bathroom, but there wasn't anything in there."

"Did you break it to them gently?"

"No... I was too afraid to talk to anyone. Never said a word for almost a whole year." She rubbed her arms. "I was almost fourteen before I spoke to anyone who wasn't a teacher, doctor, or a counselor... Nicole. She wouldn't leave me alone. Kept trying to be my friend."

"Thanks." The kid went over to the sinks and spat a few times before grabbing a towel. "I'm okay. Can I go back to class?"

Kirsten let her building emotion out on a calming breath. "Are you sure? You just got possessed by a ghost and puked him out."

"Really?" He stared at her. "That's cool as shit. Yeah, I'm good."

"Okay then." She followed him out to the hallway. "I'm Agent Wren. If anything weird happens, please let me know. I deal with this sort of thing."

"Yes, Ma'am." He saluted and ran off.

Kirsten looked to her right at Dorian. "At least the reports will be simple. I think the daughter is still here. Should I tell her?"

Dorian shook his head. "Nah. Even if she does believe you, what's the point? Re-open an old wound. If your mother came back and someone destroyed the ghost, would you want to know?"

Kirsten raised both eyebrows. "Know? I'd want video so I could watch it over and over."

"You wouldn't try to 'save' her?"

"I..." She stared down, thinking back to the too-real nightmare and the way her eight-year-old self had looked. Phantom burning seared her hands; she crumpled them against her chest. "Some things... I don't think even I can forgive."

Kirsten walked into the school's rec room at 5:05 p.m. Evan ran around collecting unattended games and datapads, bringing them back to a table before sorting them onto a shelf and cubbies. She waited for about ten minutes until he noticed her. As soon as he did, he sprinted over and leapt into a hug.

"Mom!"

She hugged a wheeze out of him. "Hey kiddo. Are you ready to go home?"

"Yeah." His huge grin faded to a look of apprehension. He picked up his backpack.

"Sorry for going away."

"I understand. It's your job... helping people."

"Did you have fun at Nila's?"

Tales of video game conquests filled the walk from the school to the motor pool. Once in the patrol craft, his enthusiasm bottomed out and he stared at his lap. Kirsten offered a consoling smile. *I'll let him tell me on his own time. Unless he tries to go to sleep without saying a word.* A moment after they flew out of the garage and climbed into the hover lane, Evan looked up at her.

"What was the moon base like?"

"I don't think I've ever been more scared as an adult."

"*You* were scared?"

"Space is big. One little error and I was afraid I'd go flying off and never come back. All I could think of was not being able to come home to you."

Red appeared around his eyes.

Sixteen minutes later, she steered into the blinding orange glare of the setting sun, and climbed to the roof parking deck of their building. Dark cloud shapes blurred the horizon below thousands of moving spots—advert bots and hovercars. She headed for the closest open spot to the entrance, about halfway across the roof, lingered a few seconds at a hover, then set down.

Evan followed her to the door, head bowed, dragging his feet.

The elevator ride to the 41st floor passed in silence. Once home, Kirsten patted him on the head and went to her room to change. Minutes later, in panties and a knee-length white shirt, she walked to the kitchen and stared at the fridge. *Hmm. Do I dare practice necromancy today or should I just order something?*

"Mom?"

She turned to peer at the door. Evan looked so tiny and pathetic, she wanted to scoop him up and hold him forever. "What's wrong?"

He walked up to her, still looking down. "I got in trouble at school yesterday."

She took his hand, led him to the living room, and sat on the sofa so they were about eye-to-eye. "Evan. I want you to know that I will *never* get tired of you or get frustrated with you enough to send you back. You are not a holiday puppy." She grabbed him by the shoulders. "Do you understand that? There's nothing you can do that will make me give up on you."

Evan sniffled and wiped at his eyes.

"I've been wondering how long you'd stay perfect. I know you're a great kid... but you've been *so* perfect, you had me worrying you were afraid of being who you are. It's okay to be normal." She hugged him. "Not that I'm saying you should go off on a tear, but getting in trouble now and then is going to happen... you're a kid."

"You remember Abernathy?" He smiled, but tears kept falling.

"Yep."

Evan cuddled up at her side. "I wanted to help him move on. I thought if I got his brain and took it to Father Villera, he could be happy. We went into the archives but it made Abernathy mad when I touched the brain. He appeared and scared Sam so she bumped a table, and this statue broke, and a poltergeist got out. It was throwin' stuff at us. Almost hit Shani in the head with a sword. It was gonna kill her... I saw it." He shivered. "It trapped us behind all this stuff. We couldn't get out. I binded the sword." Evan explained how he held the thing down while Shani used telekinesis to swing blind until she hit it.

Kirsten clung to him for a few minutes before worry got out of the way of her voice. "That was brave of you, Ev..."

He sniffled. "You're not mad at me?"

"Well... Probably not as much as I should be, but... our life is far from normal. What you should have done is asked Abernathy first. Ghosts can be fickle and dangerous. The older they are, the more set in their ways they get, and they hate surprises."

"Guess they're kinda protective of their brains too." He grinned.

Kirsten brushed her hand over his head. "If that brain is his, umm, resting place, yeah. Ghosts are highly protective."

"Like the car and Dorian?"

"Right."

"So, I got like a million cit points."

"I heard. You took Shani's too. I'm proud of you."

He blinked. "You knew already?"

"Captain Eze told me. I didn't say anything because I knew I could trust you to be honest with me. I didn't want you to feel like I was coming after you."

His shock faded to a mix of guilt and relief. "It's still out there. Sam's afraid it'll come after her for breaking the statue."

"I think it's probably happy to be out of the statue. That could've been like a prison."

The doorbell chimed.

"Who's there?" asked Kirsten.

A holo-panel spread open a few feet to the left of the couch, showing a view of the hallway. Dorian's former partner, Nila Assad, hovered by her door, with Shani clinging to her. Both of them looked freaked.

"Open." Kirsten leapt over the sofa arm and ran to the door, which slid aside on its own.

"Kirsten!" Nila ran in.

Shani wailed. "I'm not doing it! I swear!"

"What's up?" She grasped Nila's shoulder in one hand and put the other on Shani's back.

"Stuff's flying all over the place. I almost took a damn steak knife to the face." Nila exhaled. "I thought it might be subconscious kinetic disassociation, but Shani's losing her mind screaming at me that it isn't her."

The girl stared at Evan. "It followed me!"

Kirsten and Evan made the same open-mouthed face of realization at the same time. They exchanged a glance.

"What?" Nila looked back and forth between them.

"The kids accidentally set a poltergeist loose at school the other day. Ev astrally bound a sword and Shani got a piece of the thing. It's probably coming after her."

Nila glared. "Why are you smiling about that?"

"Because if it *is* the 'geist, it saves me the trouble of chasing it all over the damn city." Kirsten ran to the master bedroom. "Lemme grab clothes."

She traded the oversized tee for a loose shirt, added baggy fatigue-style pants and hopped into her pink Nomz sneakers. Regulations demanded she bring the E-90, but she did *not* want to fire that thing in here... it could penetrate four or five apartments up or down, and the stunrod would only wind up turning against her.

Kirsten ran back to the living room where the kids were halfway done explaining the entire story again to Nila. "Okay. Is it still downstairs?"

"I think so." Nila eyed the door.

Evan's eyes lit up white. "Let's go."

"You three stay here."

"Mom." Evan marched up to her. "If it's after Shani, it's gonna go wherever she is."

She sighed. "Okay. Come on."

Kirsten followed Nila to the elevators at the center of the building, and down two floors to the 39th. Six apartments away from Nila's, the sound of stuff banging off walls and breaking became noticeable.

Evan looked up. "I think he's pissed."

"Sounds it," said Kirsten.

At Nila's approach, the door to her apartment opened. The living room looked like the morning after a frat party. In the center of the destruction, the upper half of a humanoid figure hovered. The body had only the vaguest hint of a person's features, consisting of pale white-yellow light in wispy tatters. Hands, a touch too large in proportion, ended with needle-like points of pure energy.

The instant Shani walked in, the apparition glared at her. It dove low to the left, grabbed a heavy transparent block (some service award Nila had won) and threw it at the child. Evan yelled a warning fast enough to allow Nila to turn and shield Shani. The block hit her in the back, knocking her a step into the hallway.

Kirsten charged, calling the lash at the same instant she swung her arm out. The energy tendril passed within inches of the poltergeist's head. It zipped low and darted between her legs. Kirsten whirled, drawing her arm back for another swing. The spirit dove under the couch, which flipped into the air, flying at her. She leapt to the ground, but the sofa landed on her—but didn't weigh much at all.

Shani let off a cute little growl, and the sofa stood up on end.

"K, does pyro work on ghosts?" Nila, wild-eyed, pushed her daughter behind her.

"A little, yeah… if you can see them." Kirsten sprang upright and ran after the glow in the kitchen.

The poltergeist hurled fistfuls of silverware at her. A puddle of apple juice complicated her attempt to duck, and sent her sliding ass-first into the cabinets. Dozens of OmniSoy packets fell off the counter on top of her.

"I really hate poltergeists."

She flipped over onto all fours, clambered up to her knees, and lurched forward with an overextended sideways swing of the lash. The poltergeist zoomed upward, evading her again, and tore one of the LED bulbs off the fixture before hurling it at her face. Plastic shards sprayed her cheek as she cringed away from where it hit the wall.

It pulled another bulb loose and threw it through a *passe-plat* between the kitchen and dining room, knocking over a tiny vase on the way. Shani let off a short, ear-splitting scream before something heavy thudded into the floor.

Kirsten slipped and wiped out again in a puddle of OmniSoy; her sneakers meowed with every strike against the floor or cabinets.

"Are you fighting an army of cats in there?" yelled Nila.

Evan ran in the archway right as she fell for the sixth time. He rushed over and grabbed her arm. Shani yelled again, followed by Nila letting off a stream of obscenities that made Evan blush.

"Come on, Mom. Before Nila burns the place down." He tried to pull her up, but his feet shot out from under him and he landed on his butt, drawing a pained hiss past clenched teeth.

Kirsten grumbled. "This crap is so fu—damn slippery."

Her Nomz finally found traction. She sprang upright, pulled Evan standing, and rushed into the living room where Shani levitated the coffee table as a shield against an endless pelting of random objects. The poltergeist raced around grabbing anything it could get its hands on, winging each item at deadly velocity.

Imma grab it. Evan's voice in her head sounded echoey, as if he stood inside a large, empty room.

She tried sneaking up on the poltergeist, but it whirled about, evidently sensing the energy of the lash. Kirsten slice at it, but the spirit streaked to the right, avoiding the whip by inches. A second later, it jerked to a halt and crept at a snail's pace. Evan let off a tangled snarl of exertion. Kirsten swiped the energy whip at the mired spirit. Unable to move out of the way, the phantom emitted a keening wail. The shimmering cord caught in its vaporous body like a knife snagging on flesh. A burst of focused energy brightened the lash as she poured on power, and the poltergeist drew inward to a light orb. Evan whined and gasped.

"It's... too strong, Mom."

She jerked the whip free, flipped her arm about, and caught the gliding orb with a sideward slash that detonated it into a spray of transparent goo. The sense of obliteration buffeted her with fatigue.

Kirsten let the lash recede and stared at the splatter. "Wow. Something's wrong."

"What?" Nila edged out from behind the levitating coffee table.

"Is it gone?" asked Shani.

"Yeah." Kirsten gestured at the goo on the carpet. "No one wound up covered in slime. That's never happened before."

"Check your pants," said Nila.

"That's OmniSoy, not ectoplasm." Kirsten shook her head at the mess.

Shani set the table down and plopped to a seat on top of it. "I'm tired."

Evan trudged over to Kirsten. He looked worn out as well, but happy.

Kirsten threw her arm around him. "Great job."

Nila groaned, hand on her forehead.

"Ev." Kirsten patted him on the shoulder. "You should've asked Abernathy if he *wanted* to be helped. As punishment, we're not going to watch Monwyn tonight. We're going to help Nila clean up."

He looked somewhat crestfallen, but nodded. "Okay. That's fair."

Going easy on him?

Kirsten glanced at Nila. *He didn't do it out of malice or even curiosity... he wanted to help a spirit in need. Did Shani tell you he took her cit points so she wouldn't get in any trouble?*

Nila smirked. *Yeah, but that isn't gonna save her from a little grounding here.*

She didn't really have much to do with it.

My kid opened the damn door. She broke into a secure room. Nila set her hands on her hips. *She's lucky all she's getting is a week without the Yume Koujou.*

She's seven. She doesn't understand the concept of secure rooms. Kirsten pointed Evan at a scattering of small items. *She thought someone needed help. You'd break into a place to save someone too.*

Nila held her hands up. *Okay, okay. I'll talk to her later.* "Thanks for helping. What a mess."

"Yeah." Kirsten chuckled. "For a poltergeist, this is mild."

AFTER HOURS

Kirsten lay flat on Nila's living room floor, gazing up at the ceiling. The faint clinks of glassware being rearranged came from the kitchen. Evan and Shani took up the sofa, both sleeping. Standing, walking upstairs, and going to bed seemed like far too much effort. Even sitting up to pull her sneakers off exceeded her threshold of tired.

"Incoming contact from Division 1," said her NetMini.

"Ugh, Suri… really?"

"Yes. The call is originating from Division 1."

Literal bitch. "One sec." She stuffed her hand in her pocket and pulled it out. A too-blonde twentysomething woman in a blue uniform shirt appeared in hologram. "Hello?"

"Am I speaking with Agent Kirsten Wren, Division 0?" asked the woman.

"Yeah." Kirsten yawned. "What time is it?"

"The current time is twenty four minutes past 10 p.m.," said Suri.

The woman in blue repeated the information. "Your presence is requested at the NewsNet office tower."

"What?" She woke up and sat up at the same instant. "Lamb?"

"Yes, agent. There are officers on scene. You were logged as having been there recently, so they wanted your input."

"That must mean they've got nothing." *I know how they feel.*

"I don't have that information, agent. Sergeant Patel is the senior on site."

Kirsten grumbled and stood. "All right. Tell them I'm on the way."

Nila breezed in with an armload of blankets. "Was that good or bad news?"

"Bad, but only in terms of sleep." She yawned. "I gotta go follow up on a case."

"They have the worst timing." Nila dropped the blankets on the kids and removed their shoes. "Hope it's quick."

"Yeah, me too." Kirsten leaned over and kissed Evan on the head.

His eyelids parted. "Mom."

"Official call. I'll be back soon."

He smiled and closed his eyes. "'Kay."

Well, he's not panicking... that's good. She smiled at Nila. "Thanks again."

Nila waved. "Anytime."

Kirsten ran upstairs, chased by the meows from her sneakers. She jumped into her uniform and hurried to the roof parking area. Dorian faded into visibility in the passenger seat as she pulled the car into the air.

"Sorry. Something happened to Lamb."

"Too much mint jelly?" asked Dorian.

"What?" She spared a two-second stare before looking forward again.

"Never mind. Think it's the ghost?"

"Div 1 called me in, so… probably."

He rubbed his forehead. "I'm going to run through the whole damn building this time. Maybe I can get those security guys back on duty."

"Here's hoping." She pulled up out of civilian traffic and hit the lights.

Thirteen minutes later, the patrol craft shot between a pair of century towers belonging to Sur-Stor Backup Solutions. Kirsten rolled her eyes at the crime against words. Ahead, the shimmer of emergency lights guided her to a sprawl of five Division 1 patrol craft, mostly identical to hers aside from being blue and white, not to mention the Starburst laser cannon mounted in a pod over the passenger seat.

She deployed the ground wheels early, and fought the drag on the control sticks down to a hasty landing. Two patrol officers walked up as she got out.

"Man, fuck this freako shit," muttered the one on the left. "This is all yours."

"Thanks." Kirsten jogged toward the door. "What's the situation?"

The men pivoted as she passed between them, then followed. Dorian flew off and vanished into the side of the building.

"Building security called us in about an hour ago on reports of gunfire. Turns out some manager had a meltdown and shot up his office. Far as we can tell, he tried to kill a hallucination."

"What happened to Lamb?" Kirsten waved her forearm guard at the door scanner, which beeped. The door opened. "He still alive?"

"Yeah. He's been transported to Ancora. He was still kickin' when they dragged him out of here."

A thin blond man in a black suit and purple ascot shot her a sour look as she strode to the elevator. "Figures. Always trouble around psionics."

Two women and another man standing in a cluster with him shifted, looking away from him and anywhere but at Kirsten.

She met his glare. "Trouble follows us like scandal follows the NewsNet, right?"

He whirled away with a petulant scoff.

Kirsten stomped to the elevator, fuming the whole way up to Lamb's office. Division 2 techs swarmed the area, boots crunching. Several of the Fish Tank's panels were missing, spread out over the floor in a glittering snowfall of bluish safety glass bits. The rug nearest the central enclosure resembled new fallen snow; tiny fragments sparkled in the glow from ion thrusters on a quartet of orb bots zipping around scanning for evidence. Energy charged the air, but again it felt like an aftereffect rather than a current presence.

An athletic man with coffee-toned skin and a prematurely silver buzz cut glanced at her as she strode up to the confusion. Silver sergeant stripes glinted on his shoulder. She drifted by the door to Lamb's office, but didn't bother trying to go in while six crime scene techs examined it. The energy, stronger in that room, had a hint of an identity to it. She grinned at getting enough of a feel for it that she could probably recognize the entity in the future.

"Sergeant Patel?" asked Kirsten. "Agent Wren, Division Zero."

He saluted; she returned it. "Sorry to knock you day job types out of bed in the middle of the night, but I'm getting some unbelievable reports."

She scowled.

"You are with I-Ops right?" He smiled. "Sorry. Bad detective joke… didn't mean anything about psionics there."

Kirsten exhaled. "Not your fault. Asshole downstairs. So, what happened?"

He brought up a holo-panel over his left forearm. "Security video caught something wonky."

She watched Lamb seated at his desk, still working on his terminal, and still spewing an endless stream of profanities. He repeatedly grabbed for a glass that wasn't there, and shot dire looks across the room at a cabinet.

"Was there any alcohol in his system?" asked Kirsten. "Looks like he's desperate for a drink but trying to quit."

"Not sure yet. He's not a stiff." Sergeant Patel tapped the bottom, by a progress bar. "Six minutes thirty three seconds is where you want to pay attention." He skipped ahead to six minutes flat. "First few minutes are just him getting more and more pissed off at some guy named Andrew."

At 6:33, a flickering speck of light glided across the office and disappeared into Lamb's side, an inch above his belt. By 6:35, his face had gone beet red. He grabbed his gut and let out a belabored bellow before collapsing over his desk and breathing hard. Sweat ran down his forehead in rivulets. Lamb wheezed and tried reaching for the Vidphone, but wound up falling out of his chair before he touched it.

By 6:39, his hand appeared at the edge of the desk and he pulled himself upright. After leaning against the desk for the span of a few breaths, he patted his belly and sat, seeming to brush off whatever happened to him as a non-issue.

"Dumb bastard doesn't call for a medic." The sergeant shook his head. "If he's a heavy drinker, his liver's probably on the way out."

Kirsten looked at him. *Oh, right... alcoholics have liver issues.*

"It doesn't get interesting again until twelve minutes. You ever see that little light thing before?"

"Orbs are pretty common manifestations on electronic recording devices. Even when spirits aren't visible to the eye, cameras sometimes pick them up as light spots. It's not conclusive evidence, but on top of the way it feels in here, I'm sure there's a ghost involved."

At twelve minutes, Lamb jumped. Hairline bands of static rolled down the image. He screamed and scrambled away from his desk to a cabinet at the back of the office, from which he produced a pistol. He aimed at nothing, screaming, "Go away," and "what are you?" A second later, he flinched back as though someone rushed at him, and fired. The handgun went off four times, creating a waterfall of sparkling glass bits out of the windows. Lamb spiraled to the floor and passed out. Another orb exited from the man's back and glided toward the door, but faded away several feet from it.

"What do you think?"

Kirsten set her hands on her hips, frowning at the screen. "I think I'm going to be up too late. Doubtful the techs are going to find anything. There's definitely a ghost out there who has a taste for Lamb."

Sergeant Patel moaned.

"Sorry. I've been hanging around Dorian too much." She grumbled, twisting to stare past the smashed-out window at the techs working over the office. *What on Earth could possibly connect Lindsey to Lamb? Other than Ls. Or either of them to the senator's daughter. Why would a senator want to keep his child a secret? Not like anyone gives a crap about affairs these days. Hell, he could probably have sex with his own daughter on a live NewsNet feed and it would only boost his approval rating.* She cocked her jaw to the side, exhaling.

"Something wrong?"

"I'm thinking. This is so random I'm having trouble putting the pieces together." The energy streaming out of Lindsey and racing back to Earth so fast made her think of astral projecting. She teased a finger at the spot between her eyebrows where the silver cord connected. Grabbing it triggered a near-instantaneous return to the body. *What if Seraphina is psionic and she's doing this? That memory Jonah had was like something out of a horror vid...*

something a teenager might have watched. Or... could this be connected to that organ harvester case Nicole responded to?

Kirsten pivoted on her boot heel and marched into the office. The techs gave her a cursory glance. One fortyish woman opened her mouth to say something but seemed to think better of it. It didn't much matter if they feared her rank or her being a Zero, as long as they stayed out of her way. She closed her eyes and opened her senses up to the room, detecting a residual presence stronger than the one by the doorway. She crept forward, honing in on the direction from which it seemed to grow the most potent.

I've felt this before... Seraphina's room. "Shit. No wonder I'm going in goddamned circles. I'm looking for a ghost when it's a person I should be after."

She checked the cabinet that Lamb kept glancing at. When she grasped the handle, a black square mounted to the center of the door projected a green-on-green keypad, looking for a six-digit code.

Dorian walked in. "Got some good news."

"Me too." She smiled. "Can you peek inside this cabinet and let me know what's in there?"

"Uhh, it's locked..." One of the techs sat back on his heels and looked up at her. "Is there an Inquest order?"

"I wasn't asking you guys."

"Two bottles of liquor and a tumbler glass." Dorian extracted his head from the small door and fixed his hair back into place. "Looks like he was serious about trying to give it up. That's not an easy albatross to get rid of. Something drastic had to have happened."

The tech muttered something suspiciously close to "bitch" under his breath.

Dorian went translucent. "Sorry, didn't catch that."

Kirsten had to look away to avoid laughing as the man screamed and fell over backward. By the time the others looked, Dorian had returned to looking normal (which meant he'd stopped appearing to the living). The other techs exchanged confused stares as she walked out.

"Idiot," muttered Dorian.

"What's an albatross?" asked Kirsten.

"Umm. An extinct bird, but it's a metaphor for a weight hanging around your neck."

She blinked at him.

"I'll explain later."

"So what's your good news?" She stopped halfway between Lamb's office and Sergeant Patel.

"One of the dead security guys spotted an errant spirit in the building about ten minutes before Lamb collapsed. Male, thirtyish, chest hollowed out and no eyes. Bloody damn mess."

"Same thing as that guy saw on the Gravion platform. Can astral projections change appearance?"

Dorian shrugged. "Don't look at me... Way out of my area of expertise. But... why? The only reason to do that would be to hide one's identity. There's probably a dozen people in the entire UCF who can see spirits."

"That we know of." She folded her arms and smirked. "I bet there's hundreds, but they all think they're insane and hiding it so no one puts them away. I need to go back to the senator's place. I think this might all be connected to that girl. She doesn't look scary at all. Maybe she's making herself look like that to scare people more. Perhaps she's doing an Evan thing and using projection to escape. Only in her case, she's escaping a body that can't wake up."

"Hmm. That might make sense. If she knows her father involved you in this, she might be trying to change her appearance to throw you off... but what's her motive?"

"She's a kid. Does she need one?"

"She's twenty." Dorian poked her in the side. "If she's a kid, so are you."

Sergeant Patel walked over. "Agent... Do you need to see the weapon? Touch it and get visions or whatever it is Zeroes do?"

"I'm not a clairvoyant. That wouldn't help me much, but... I'm sure Lamb was reacting to a ghost or... something else. Speaking of which, I need to talk to him too. Ancora Medical? Which facility?"

"Umm." Sergeant Patel checked his arm computer. "Sector 4491."

Kirsten shook his hand. "Thanks, sergeant. Nothing more for me here right now. I appreciate the heads up."

"Anytime." He waited long enough for her to take two steps toward the door. "Agent?"

"Hmm?" She glanced back at him.

"I, uhh, lost one of my guys last month. Real good man. His little sister called me the other day, said she thinks he's still there. Any chance I could ask you to swing by and check?"

"Sure. Send me the address and make sure it's okay with the family. I'd be happy to."

He nodded. "Thanks."

She walked out to the elevator door and hit the button.

Dorian smiled. "You're like a little kid, so eager to help people."

"It's more than that. For one thing, that guy might actually need help. Two... when people treat me like a person—that's rare enough—I automatically feel like I owe them something back."

"Sad." He shook his head. "Maybe someday people will get over hating psionics."

"Yeah right."

Ping. The elevator opened.

"A long time ago, they said that about skin color too." Dorian followed her in.

"Yeah well… under the skin, humans are the same regardless of what the environment did to their outer layer. Psionics actually *are* different." She tapped her foot, trying to move the elevator faster by sheer force of will.

"People have always feared what they don't understand."

"Doesn't make it any less degrading." She stormed out onto the roof and to the patrol craft. Once inside, she logged in to the D0-Net and started another comparison search looking for anything common between Senator Winchester and Lamb.

"The senator? Not looking for the girl?" asked Dorian.

She glanced at him. "She's a ghost in the other meaning, off the grid her whole life. I don't even know what last name she used in public."

"Great."

A couple of finger taps lit the dashboard and flooded the cabin with the subtle hum of electronics. The instant the status light went green, Kirsten pulled the car airborne. "Right now, I'm going the eff to sleep. Tomorrow, I'm dropping in on our little angel."

17

SERAPHINA

The next morning, Kirsten spent a few minutes holding Evan at the entrance to the school. He'd awoke on Nila's couch with an odd sense of fear about him, and didn't want to go back to his own room, even to get dressed. After leaving him to shower in a borrowed bathroom, she'd gone upstairs to check, but nothing at home seemed amiss.

"I'm worried."

Evan looked down. "Sorry. Just a bad dream."

"Don't apologize. It's okay." She hugged him. "I'm just not used to seeing you anything but fearless. Monwyn's not afraid of the shade goblins, right?"

He grinned. "Nope!"

"Okay, you're going to be late."

Evan gave her a peck on the cheek and ran off.

She headed up to the office to check on the data crawl. The only connection that popped up showed a pair of transactions occurring at a Morning Bean near the Allan Kantor Performing Arts Pavilion within two hours of each other. Kirsten smiled at the memory of meeting the man's ghost in the Beneath, and made a mental note to read up on him. A man famous enough to be dead for four centuries and still have buildings named for him had to be worth reading about.

"Crap." She typed a few notes in the case file about Lamb, and added a comment about heading to visit a possible suspect/witness. "Okay, Seraphina. What are you hiding?"

Dorian glided up alongside her. "I'm assuming you mean to find out."

"Yeah." She stood. "Coming?"

"You've got my car." He winked.

A HAIR OVER AN HOUR LATER, SHE APPROACHED SENATOR WINCHESTER'S MANOR house. Since no military security officer tried to comm her, she figured the senator himself wasn't here. The official transponder in the patrol craft would've been enough to get by the standing security detail. She spent a moment looking around at live trees, trying to contemplate having her boots on real earth rather than metal plates. A daydream came on of being ten years old, hiding in the Beneath with only a nightgown to her name. She remembered the feel of loose earth between her toes. It felt bizarre to have both genuine ground and open sky at the same time.

"What's on your mind?" asked Dorian.

"Nothing much… just enjoying a moment of nature." She walked toward the door. "Do you think it was right to build the plates? All the trees that destroyed?"

"Eco-alarmism." Dorian rolled his eyes. "Civilization abandoned the center of the continent. There's more than three times the amount of trees there than what died off after being covered by the cities."

"But they built the air processors."

He laughed. "You don't know how government construction works, do you? They build to budget. If they have money with nothing to use it on, they invent stuff to use it on. If they show a surplus, they receive less funding next year."

"You're making that up. That sounds so wasteful it can't be true."

"Poor, innocent girl." He patted her on the head.

She frowned.

The door opened, revealing Marguerite. Her dark blue eyes sparkled in the early sun. "Mademoiselle Wren, such a pleasure to see you again."

"Hello." Kirsten smiled. "I'd like to visit Seraphina. There was an attack last night and the energy I encountered at the scene felt like the same energy I found in her room."

"I'm… I…" Marguerite looked behind her for a second and bit her lip. "Senator Winchester is away and I'm not sure he'd approve."

"The only reason I'm here is because he asked for me to be involved in this case. The events so far aren't pronounced enough to warrant an investigation normally. It's a favor to the senator from Division 0 that we're looking in to this."

"Where did you learn to speak bullshit?" asked Dorian.

Marguerite glanced toward him for an instant before she raised her arms in a hint of a shrug. "Well, I suppose you do have a point."

Kirsten shivered. "It's a bit cold out here... if you'd like to vid him to make sure it's okay, would you mind if I waited inside?"

"Come in. My apologies." Marguerite stepped back, waited for her to pass, and closed the door behind her—through Dorian. She stared into space.

The idea of an implanted NetMini made Kirsten squirm, even if the woman in front of her was a synthetic, made entirely of plastic, metal, and silicon. She lost herself in wondering if bio-implants existed, would they bother her. Cyberware in a synth was like putting living organisms into a person.

"Mademoiselle?" asked Marguerite. "The senator is pleased you've come to call. This way."

"Thanks."

Kirsten followed her up a long, ornate staircase to the second floor, rounded a banister post, and up another set of stairs to the third. Marguerite stopped at a door and knocked twice with a light touch.

The medtech, Theresa, answered the door. "Yes?"

A weak female voice whimpered and grunted from behind her.

"I'd like to see Seraphina for a few minutes. I'm following up on some new evidence in the investigation."

"She is sleeping, officer." Theresa moved to push the door closed, but Kirsten blocked it.

"It doesn't matter if she's awake."

Theresa looked at Marguerite as if asking for support.

"Senator Winchester is aware. He would like the matter resolved as soon as possible."

The in-home medtech backed off, grumbling.

Kirsten watched her move back to the sofa near the bed, bracing for a sudden attack. The woman seemed to have something to hide, or at least an innate distrust of the police, or she feared psionics. Theresa sat, picked up a datapad, and resumed playing some game.

Seraphina remained in bed as she had been the last time, though she tossed her head from side to side, muttering.

"Has anything else unusual happened here?"

"No," said Theresa, not looking up.

"Hmm." Kirsten circled the bed, opening her thoughts to the ambient energy in the room. The latent presence felt stronger than the last time she'd been here, but not as powerful as what she'd found in Lamb's office. Her hand wound up on the waist-high obelisk containing all the medical scanning equipment hooked up to Seraphina. The charge of paranormal energy within it worried her. Not only did it feel strong, it had the same sense of identity.

She approached the bed and concentrated enough to establish a telepathic link to the woman. Seraphina dreamed of being adrift in churning water, slipping under in progressively longer periods of drowning. Stark moonlight made her arm and ancient-looking dress glow against an ink-black sky. The pale figure of Senator Winchester stood less than ten feet away, safe on shore. He stared down at his daughter with a mixture of guilt and hesitance. Seraphina's voice, screaming as if from a great distance overhead, pleaded with him to save her, but he paced as if afraid to get too close.

Ugh. Major daddy issues. Kirsten forced her way past the dream, sending her thoughts deep into the recesses of the girl's mind in a search for psionic ability. She shied away from peeking at full-formed memories, but caught glimpses of teenagers laughing in an alley, a child's vision bouncing down a dilapidated hallway strewn with toy dolls and trash, happily calling out for her mother, and an older teen voice sobbing on a VidPhone call, begging her father for help. The girl felt about as psionic as a packet of OmniSoy. When she let the mental connection fade, a cool minty flavor hit her in the mouth like a metal fist.

"Damn." Kirsten coughed and smacked her lips. "Not psionic at all."

"I could've told you that," muttered the medtech.

"Are you sure that nothing has happened here that you can't explain?"

"No." Theresa answered too fast.

Kirsten pondered for a second, and decided to peek. The medtech's thoughts betrayed three separate incidents where Seraphina had medical alarms, one where she nearly suffered a coronary, and one where Theresa spotted a shadowy figure in the room seconds before the health monitors went berserk.

She stomped over to the medic and swatted the datapad out of her hands, knocking it clattering to the floor. "Do I have your attention now?"

The medtech glared up at her.

"Three times, Theresa. You were supposed to notify us if anything strange happened. Like seeing a dark figure in the room? Or unexplained failures of medical equipment. Deliberately lying to an officer of the National Police Force is grounds for detention."

"Prove it." Theresa narrowed her eyes. "Isn't your mindreading voodoo illegal too?"

"Inadmissible, not illegal." *Okay, unethical, but not illegal.* Kirsten folded her arms. "All right. We can play that game too. Marguerite, please notify the senator that this medtech ignored his directions, possibly risked the life of his daughter. If I were him, I'd consider utilizing a different service entirely. It's well within his rights to pursue a civil lawsuit against her for negligence. I'm sure this equipment has logs that can be reviewed to prove Seraphina has had 'episodes' no one has been told about."

Theresa lunged to her feet, glaring.

"Oh, please take that swing." Kirsten loomed, as much as a short girl can loom. "You could've killed that woman."

"What happened?" asked Marguerite.

Kirsten kept staring at Theresa. "Her attitude bothered me, so I looked into her thoughts. There've been three attacks, one of which was definitely caused by the spirit the senator is concerned about, and she's kept it quiet. No wonder I haven't gotten a call yet."

"Please, don't." Theresa's bravado collapsed. She sank into her seat. "He will make such trouble for Expert-Kare, they will sue me for the contract, and I will not be able to pay. You must understand... I didn't believe it. I still don't believe it. If I speak of such things, they become real."

"I hate to break it to you, Theresa, but they *are* real." Kirsten let the venom out of her voice. "Seraphina's life is in danger. I need to know what happened."

Theresa kneaded her uniform in her lap. "She awoke screaming and gasping for breath. The machine goes crazy, but none of the alarms make sense. It say she has too much oxygen in her blood, but she cannot breathe so she should be hypoxic. Then it show her heart rate at nothing, but she is still moving."

"Could something attacking the machine have triggered her physical symptoms?"

"No." Theresa shook her head. "Is just a monitor. It can dispense pain medicine and antibiotics, but it cannot cause the heart attack or make her stop breathing. One time, I use the bathroom and come back here... there is a man standing by the window. I yell at him, and he rush at me." She raised her arms to shield her face. "I do like this, but he no hit me. When I look again, he is gone. Seraphina has recovering from a severe illness. The drugs to help her are giving her bad dreams. I think the attacks are normal for her condition, so I did not call you."

"What about the shadow man?"

"I no believe him." Theresa hid her face in her hands. "I no believe."

"You know what I 'no believe?'" Dorian glanced at Kirsten. "How she all of a sudden sounds like she's learned English a month ago. It's an act either for sympathy or to frustrate you out of talking to her."

Kirsten paced back and forth. "Well, so much for that theory. It's not her."

"I can take a look around the grounds again." He raised an eyebrow.

"Might as well." She glanced back to Theresa. "What was the nature of her 'severe illness?'"

Theresa looked down. "I'm sorry. I don't want to say. It is privileged information. I could be sued or dismissed for breaking confidentiality. The senator can tell you."

Kirsten gestured at the bed. "Medical confidentiality doesn't apply to law enforcement."

"I believe you, but please... ask Senator Winchester. I no want to be caught between this."

"What about Seraphina?" Kirsten wandered over to the bed again, watching the white-haired woman sleep. "Can't she tell me?"

"She is on medication to make her sleep until she is well enough to move around." Theresa made a few adjustments to the monitor device. "She is doing well, but must rest for another few days."

"Senator Winchester is in session." Marguerite shook her head. "I'm unable to reach him."

Kirsten glanced at Seraphina. *So tempting... I shouldn't. Damn, I hate politics.* "Can you leave him a message to contact me about it please? It may be vital to know for the investigation."

"I will." Marguerite smiled. "Do you need anything else?"

"Only for whoever's watching Seraphina to let me know if anything paranormal happens again."

Theresa raised her hands in surrender and nodded.

After a sweep of the manor house found no traces of malevolent spirits, Kirsten followed Marguerite down the hallway and two flights of stairs to the front door. The woman opened it for her, but stepped out onto the porch as well.

"Seraphina had been keeping bad company in the last few months prior to her becoming sick. Most of her 'friends' associate with wild gangs deep in the city. I think she may have been poisoned for stealing, perhaps even killing someone." Marguerite looked down. "I was nearby when Theresa saw what you called a shadow man. I heard a whispery voice say 'mine' or 'that's mine' before she screamed."

"Maybe her pimp got killed and he's coming for her?" asked Dorian.

"Thanks." Kirsten rubbed her hands up and down her arms; the supposed all-weather uniform didn't do too well in bitter cold. "Is there any chance you can tell me what happened to her, medically?"

"I've already said too much. The senator would not like it known that his daughter associated with street criminals. Bad enough he had her from an affair."

"The senator was married?" Kirsten blinked.

"*Is.*" Marguerite smiled with a touch of victory in her eyes. "Melody does not leave Paramount city on the Moon. I will ask him about the medical information. As soon as he gives me an answer, I will call you."

"Okay." Kirsten hurried to the patrol craft and cranked the heat. When Dorian coalesced in the passenger seat, she sighed at him. "I've got a bad feeling about this whole thing now."

"What are you thinking?"

She rubbed her hands up and down her thighs, savoring the little bit of warmth coming in from the vents. "Powerful guy has a daughter he doesn't acknowledge. That girl is desperate for his love or at least acceptance. Who knows what dirty shit he might've had her do or she decided to do in hopes of winning him over. Maybe she got messed up trying to infiltrate some place. Could be she's got some off-the-grid implants, murderware."

"Blood augs?" Dorian rubbed his chin. "She didn't look like the type. Too frail."

"Not all augs are juiced for combat. Maybe she's a spy. Her body's rejecting the implant so they're keeping her on meds." She drummed her fingers on the sticks. "I'm running in enough circles already. I'm curious how the senator reacts to me wanting to know what happened to her." She sat for a few minutes typing notes in to the case file. After updating everything she could think of, she plotted a course for Sector 4491. "Lamb?"

Dorian held up his hand. "No thanks. I'm considering going vegetarian."

She sighed.

18

OFF THE BOOKS

Strong sunlight at 11 a.m. made looking at the sprawling mass of polished plastisteel below painful, even via the digital windshield. Kirsten guided the patrol craft down an intermediary lane at 300 feet over the city surface. Civilian hovercar traffic rocketed by twenty stories overhead, individual cars melding to a stream of pulsating color and light. The occasional bright comet of an advert bot keeping pace with a car streaked along the edges of the blurry torrent.

Patches of green broke up the silver on the ground, park-like spots within the Ancora Medical facility up ahead, used for rehabilitation and relaxation. Her console lit up with a warning as a MedVan approached from behind. She slid sideways out of its path and hovered. Nine seconds later, a white brick-shaped vehicle festooned with flashing red lights on top and four cyan ion plumes beneath raced by.

Kirsten headed for the main roof and took one of the spots reserved for emergency vehicles. She fanned herself after getting out. Turning up the heat to compensate for the north had made the car too warm on the long flight from the senator's estate. She approached the roof access building, which resembled a Japanese pagoda done in white and brown with silver accents. Two security officers, a man and a woman in pure white jumpsuits, looked up from a desk inside a small receiving area.

She braced for the 'not a real cop' bullshit.

"Good morning, officer," said the man. "How can we help you?"

"Agent." She smiled. "I'm following up on an investigation. I need to speak to the attending physician for a Mr. Robert Lamb. Inquest 24181108A1."

"Hang on a tick." The woman's chirpy voice made her seem younger than she looked. "Right, there 'e is. Mr. Lamb is under the care of Doctor Grassley. Take the lift to the twenty-second, and hook right at the care station. You'll find him in section 22-0C. I'll let him know you'll be there in a jiff."

"Thanks." She hesitated a moment, waiting for the snide remark but all she got were smiles.

Kirsten headed for the elevator at the back of the room.

"You look shocked." Dorian grinned. "This is not a cheap hospital you know. Those two probably get paid as much as you do for warming a seat with their asses."

"Well at least they're polite."

The elevator dropped to the 22nd floor, paused, and slid sideways for a short distance before pivoting ninety degrees to the right and opening. Kirsten stumbled out into an immaculate hallway with soft blue-gel padded benches on both sides. *Okay. Was not expecting that.* She shook off the disorientation and walked about fifty yards to a nurse's station where six obvious dolls sat behind a curved desk in royal blue.

"Excuse me. I'm trying to find Doctor Grassley?"

"One moment." The nearest doll gave her a vacant stare while her violet glowing eyes flickered. The same voice echoed over the PA system. "Doctor Grassley, please come to the care station at 22-0C." She/it smiled. "He should be here soon."

Kirsten picked at her utility belt, glancing around. A heavyset older man with a few stalwart strands of grey still stuck to an otherwise bald head made eye contact from the bench about halfway up the next section of hallway. She offered a nod of acknowledgement, to which he leapt to his feet and ran over.

"You can see me?" He blinked.

"I can." She grasped for his hand, but her fingers passed through him. "Are you aware you've died?"

The man grumbled. "Yeah... Yeah. I know. I need you to help me."

She smiled. "If I can."

"Damn timing." He waved a trembling arm to the side. "I never got the apple pie they promised me. Kept saying they'd bring it Thursday. I waited all damn week for it."

"They never brought you pie?" Kirsten cringed.

"No. I kicked the bucket Wednesday. Can you believe that?"

Dorian covered his face with a hand.

"So... you want pie?"

"Yes, dammit! I waited for it."

Kirsten tilted her head, and tried to sound as pleasant as possible. "How do you plan to eat it?"

He blinked. "I… Uhh." The old man hung his head. "Dammit. Now I'm dead *and* stupid."

"Oh." Kirsten concentrated and made herself solid to the astral realm. She rubbed his shoulder. "It's not stupid. Odd things happen to people when they die. It was the last thing you were focused on with great meaning."

"Hmmf." He shook his head. "Thanks, but I still feel stupid." After a momentary pause, he squinted at her. "No way for me to have the pie, eh?"

"Well, I suppose you could wait fifty or sixty years until you figure out how to possess someone… then slip in when they're having apple pie."

"That there sounds like a damn lot of work for a slice of pie." He wiped at his face.

A silver shimmer stretched out of one of the patient rooms, near where he'd been sitting. The old man glanced at it. "Story of my life, young lady. Always seemed to wait for stuff and then bad shit happened."

Kirsten covered her mouth to stifle a giggle. What was so funny about old people cursing?

"Welp." He waddled off toward the light. "Thanks for slappin' me upside the head. Damn pie."

A few seconds after he disappeared past the doorway, the glimmering silver bands intensified and vanished.

Dorian grinned. "Well that was easy."

"Agent?" asked a male voice.

Kirsten whirled around, eye-to-chest with a tall man sporting perfect salt and pepper hair. She stared up at him, stunned by holovid-star good looks. *If he was twenty years younger…*

"Are you all right Agent?"

She wiped a tear from the corner of her eye. "Oh… I'm just happy for that old guy. I don't suppose you believe in ghosts?"

"Not really. I understand this is about an Inquest?"

"Yes, Doctor." Her brief fantasy of him dressed like a pirate disintegrated as her daydreamed virile sea bandit peeled off his face to reveal a withered old man. She coughed and put on 'cop voice.' "I'm investigating a paranormal event regarding a patient of yours. Robert Lamb. I need to know what happened to him last night."

"Why don't we adjourn to a conference room?" He gestured to the corridor opposite where the old spirit had been. "I've got rounds to attend, but I can spare you a few minutes."

"I'll try to be as quick as possible." She hurried after him, almost jogging to keep up with his lengthy stride.

He entered a room with peach-colored walls where four beige chairs surrounded a table. She gawked at the plush cushions, feeling like she didn't have enough money to touch one. After they sat, the doctor pulled up a holo-panel with some medical charts.

"Mr. Lamb suffered a severely bruised liver. To be honest with you, agent, I've never quite seen an injury like this. Tissue compression occurred with ridge patterns indicative of human fingers. Almost as though someone had reached inside him and squeezed the organ with their bare hands." He tapped the screen and a high-res scan appeared where the liver showed in color while the body and tissues around it rendered in grey tones.

"It looks like a hunk of raw meat someone tried to wring out like a dishtowel," said Dorian.

"Ouch." Kirsten braced a hand on where she assumed her liver was. "I'm guessing that would hurt. Enough to make someone pass out?"

Doctor Grassley flashed an appraising frown. "More than likely, with the possible exception of someone with an unusually high pain threshold."

"You have no explanation for how marks like that could've occurred?" She held her forearm guard up, taking an image capture of the screen to add to the Inquest.

"The most plausible theory I've been able to come up with involves a coordinated attack by nanomachines, but anyone capable of doing that could easily have killed him… and there's both no evidence of nanobots and no reason I could think of for the complexity of simulating finger marks. Oh, and there is something else."

Kirsten raised an eyebrow. "I hope it's good."

"Well." Doctor Grassley chuckled. "I doubt it will top inexplicable finger marks on an internal organ with no damage to the epidermis or surrounding tissues. Mr. Lamb's liver is a transplanted organ. I found evidence that the tissue was subjected to DNA manipulation to make it more compatible."

"That would explain why he seemed serious about not drinking." Kirsten closed her eyes and pictured the apparition from Jonah's memory. *If this ghost was killed for parts, he'd be pissed.* "I need to track down where that organ came from, Doctor."

Grassley's face tinted blue as he held up a datapad to read it. "Mr. Lamb's medical records do include several diagnostic procedures that indicate advanced liver disease as a result of alcoholism. Replacement or regeneration were advised, but there is no record of either procedure having been performed. The only possible conclusion I can reach is that he obtained an organ off the books. I ran the DNA profile in Ancora's system, but the anti-rejection treatments muddled the original genetics to the point where the liver is technically its own unique person."

Dorian read over the doctor's shoulder. "Finally something that makes sense."

Kirsten narrowed her eyes. "How long will it be before I can speak to Mr. Lamb?"

Doctor Grassley flipped three screens over on the datapad, his face tinted green, white, and blue again. "Likely not until morning. He's still undergoing surgery."

"Thank you, Doctor." She moved to leave.

"Agent?"

She glanced back over her shoulder. "Hmm?"

"Sometimes the realm of science doesn't have all the answers. I'm curious what your thoughts are on this most bizarre of injuries." Doctor Grassley's smile drew a little warmth to her cheeks.

"Well." She cleared her throat and resolved to stop staring at him. "I think you are right about his obtaining the liver from a street doc. I'm sure the former owner of that liver wasn't happy about 'donating' it, and my best guess is that those finger marks you saw are the results of a ghost attempting to tear it out of him."

"Interesting." The doctor seemed to think it over for a moment, and shrugged. "I suppose anything's possible. I hate to say it, but that sounds more plausible than vanishing nanobots."

Kirsten wasn't quite sure what to make of the doctor. No derision for being psionic, no ridicule for talking about ghosts... "There's so much more out there than most people believe."

"Well, I must return to my rounds. Is there anything else I can help you with?"

"Short of giving me a name on that liver, I think you've already done quite a lot to help." She smiled. "I'll be back tomorrow to have a chat with Mr. Lamb."

The doctor left after a handshake.

Kirsten exhaled and spun to put her back to the door, staring at Dorian. "That went well."

"He's old enough to be your father, and his good looks are probably a perk from knowing an aesthetic surgeon." Dorian winked. "Besides, aren't you seeing Sam?"

"Yeah. We dated twice. I'm only admiring the scenery." She rubbed her arms. "I like Sam, but I'm still a little freaked out by what happened with *him*, so we're going slow."

Dorian nodded. "Perhaps after Lamb, you should try some apple pie."

She laughed her way into a nervous stare at the floor. "Back to the office... I've got a few hours of data to sift through."

19

QUALITY TIME

The apartment trembled under the bass roar of six enormous starship engines. Some ridiculous massive spaceship version of an aircraft carrier lumbered across the holo-screen, surrounded by tiny fighters and streaks of blue and yellow lasers. Kirsten half slept on the couch next to Sam, smiling at Evan's frequent cheers. He'd started the movie off on her right side, leaning against her, but at the start of the battle scene, he'd leapt to his feet.

She couldn't even remember the name of the main character, but whenever the photogenic fighter ace got into a scrap, Evan twisted himself about as though he worked the controls himself, slapping imaginary buttons.

It occurred to her that she 'tolerated' Sam's arm behind her, and his hand on her shoulder. He'd been nothing but genuine with her, even when she'd shown no interest. Her hand migrated to her gut in an effort to massage away the twinge of nausea that came on. For days, she *had* been interested in the Division 2 tech who didn't run screaming from a psionic, who thought she was pretty, who helped her without expecting anything in return. She had been interested, but Konstantin's little pet bastard from hell hurt her whenever she felt attraction to anyone else. It had made her so painfully sick that even without the bracelet, her stomach braced for agony whenever she thought about him.

Kirsten glanced left and up at him. He smiled, though awkward disappointment showed on his face. She shifted her weight and leaned into him. *I'm sorry, Sam. I'm still trying to deal with what that demon did to me. I'm not trying to be distant on purpose.*

Sam opened his mouth, glanced at Evan, and nodded.

Kirsten stood and pulled Sam to his feet. "Be right back."

Evan shouted, "Pause!" The movie froze. He looked up at them.

"I'm going to get some real popcorn."

"'Kay." Evan smiled at Sam. "I gotta pee." He ran off.

Kirsten walked with Sam to the kitchen, tapping at her NetMini to order a bucket of hydroponic sourced popcorn. For butter flavoring, she chose some non-caloric 'healthy' option, since all the 'wellness' taxes made the closest thing available to genuine butter prohibitive. Fifty-two credits for a treat hurt enough already. Order complete, she let her arms flop down, still holding the 'mini in two hands.

"I understand." Sam smiled.

"No, you don't." She leaned her head on his shoulder. "You've got this look like you're expecting me to break up with you. I'm not. I'm... guilty as hell, but scared. You're a great guy, Sam Chang. I can't believe you're interested in me."

"Hey." He encircled her with his arms. "I can't even imagine what it was like not being in control of your thoughts. Yeah, I was wondering if you'd only gone out with me to be nice. Guys like me don't usually get a second glance from girls like you."

"Girls like me?" She gave him a coy smile.

"You're a beautiful person in every sense of the word. I knew from the first minute I saw you. Strength of heart, strength of mind, kindness, compassion, smart, and you're not bad on the eyes." He winked.

"Thanks, but I know I'm underweight, short, flat-chested, and have the face of a thirteen-year-old. I look like a refugee from an ACC prison colony."

He swayed side to side with her. "It's the big eyes."

"Big eyes?" She furrowed her brows.

"They make you look sincere and innocent. Stop being so mean to yourself. And you're not flat-chested. Nor do I think you look like you're thirteen. You are angelic."

She blushed and giggled. "Thanks, but I just pick up their odd jobs sometimes."

"Kirsten Wren, slayer of demons." He looked her in the eye. "I want to help you kill your own."

She leaned up and kissed him. He seemed surprised at first, fumbled around a second or two, and they both wound up laughing.

"I've never really done this before," she whispered. "Wow... it didn't hurt."

"This is your first kiss?" He smiled. "And, you expected it to hurt?"

"Uhh, remember when I got sick at your desk? That... thing was attacking me because I found you charming. I've been acting like this because I keep expecting it to tear me up inside again."

He put a hand on her stomach. "I didn't mean to—"

"You didn't hurt me." She leaned up and kissed him again. That time, they embraced for two solid minutes before the soft *pssht* of a pneumatic door came from the interior hall.

"Can I finish peeing yet?" yelled Evan.

Kirsten's eyes fluttered open. "*That* was my first real kiss. Please don't give up on me yet. I..." She looked down at his shoulder. "Might need a little more time to kill that demon, but I'm working on it... and I need all the help I can get."

His eyes lit up with love and hope; the way he looked at her made her shiver.

"Pee for another minute," yelled Kirsten.

Sam initiated the next kiss. Her eyes shot open and she moaned into his mouth when his fingers glided up her bare back under her oversized tee shirt. Her breathing quickened in time with her heartbeat. She slid her hands up his chest and held on to his shoulders while he pulled her close by the hips.

The doorbell rang.

Kirsten let her weight down off tiptoe. "Popcorn's here."

"We should probably get it before it's cold." He hugged her again, patted her on the back, and walked her to the living room holding hands. "'Mon Ev. You've been in there long enough."

Kirsten retrieved the delivery from a hovering bot at the front door. She'd expected the usual 'looks bigger on the screen' thing with the bucket, but she could barely get her arms around it. With her face in a mound of buttery goodness, she pushed the door button with her big toe and walked back to the sofa. "Well, we've got popcorn for two weeks."

Evan flopped on the couch again, clinging to her right side. Sam put an arm around her. Kirsten basked in the warmth of it. Evan seemed to like Sam. He'd never liked Konstantin. Maybe, in time, she could forget the withered demonologist altogether. *Bah. Go away.* She pulled Evan half into her lap and held onto him while leaning against Sam.

Two hours and eleven minutes later, the space epic ended. Kirsten walked Sam to the door, held hands and made goo eyes at him for a few minutes, and wound up kissing him again, not particularly caring if Evan saw.

"Hey Mom—eww." The soft thuds of him walking back to the living room faded to silence.

She chuckled.

Sam grinned. "I think we've got a good thing here. Don't feel like you need to rush anything. You're worth waiting for."

"I'm letting it get to me more than I should." She squeezed his hands. "This case is so frustrating it's hard to think of anything. Maybe after, I could see if Evan wants to spend the night at Nila's."

He wagged his eyebrows. "That will have to be a special night."

She nibbled on her lower lip. "I'm sure it will be."

They kissed again, more briefly than she'd liked, but part of her felt relieved he was leaving.

"Night, Sam. How much longer are you on that silly early shift?"

He shrugged. "No idea. Saunders makes it up based on a complex series of calculations and data analysis."

"So wherever the dart hits the wall."

"Basically." He caressed her cheek. "I love you, Kirsten."

Her heart did strange things that resulted in a pronounced moment of light-headedness. Her stomach muscles clenched in anticipation of a feeling like a knife slicing them up, but nothing happened. "Uhh, wow."

Sam tilted his head.

"Uhh, I mean... I..." She stared into his eyes. Her throat tightened. The butterflies in her stomach got into a dogfight using missiles. She grabbed her wrist—no bracelet, nothing on her to force these feelings from out of nowhere. No pain. "... think I love you too."

"After all you've been through, I'll take a 'think.'" He glanced at the floor, chuckled, and made eye contact again. "I can't wait to see you again. Why don't you bring Evan by sometime and we can check out the dragon."

"Dragon?" She fidgeted, still sure her face had gone bright red at chickening out and saying 'think.'

"Little China." He grinned. "Once a month, the dancers come out with this giant dragon costume. There's a street fair... food, fireworks, live performances."

"Sounds fun. I'll run it by little man."

"Night Kirsten." He kissed her again.

She bit her lip and waved. "Night."

Kirsten watched him walk until he went out of sight at the corner of the hall. She closed the door and armed the security system before dragging her feet back to the living room where Evan busied himself with the Yume Koujou. The 150-inch holo-panel showed a view remarkably close to how it felt to wear psi armor, though the HUD was different, and Kirsten had never even seen a rifle that large.

"Hey kiddo. You should've been asleep forty minutes ago."

He paused the game and stared down at the controller. "I know."

She sat on the sofa behind him. "What's wrong? Is it Sam?"

"No." He looked up, worried. "No... Sam's cool! He's not too good at *Colony Commando*; Shani's better. He needs practice."

Kirsten leaned forward and brushed his still too-dense hair away from his eyes. "You're white as a ghost. Ev, please... you're worrying me. You laughed Theodore off, what's got you frightened?"

He set the controller on the coffee table and crawled up on the couch next to her. "My room is scary."

"Do you want me to take down all the Monwyn stuff? The spiders and dragons?"

"No." He shook his head. "I love it. It's an awesome room. I don't wanna sleep."

She squeezed his shoulder and rubbed up and down his back. "You're still having bad dreams?"

"Yeah. I dream like I'm back at that other place and gettin' hit."

She cuddled with him, racking her brain for what she could possibly say. None of the platitudes or motivational crap the psychologists spewed at her ever helped get rid of the 'closet dream.' "For years, I had everyone telling me dreams can't hurt me. They were just images in my head, not real, my imagination."

He looked up at her.

The NetMini rang.

Kirsten growled, ignoring it. "They were wrong. Dreams can't injure you physically, but they *can* hurt. They kept me hiding… kept me terrified, not wanting to leave my room. I couldn't sleep, couldn't deal with the real world."

He squirmed into her, sliding one arm between her back and the cushions while clamping the other one around her stomach. "I don't like having bad dreams. I hate being scared."

Her NetMini went off again.

"It's okay if you gotta go." Evan sniffled.

Kirsten snagged the handheld device and glared at it for a half-second before answering.

A vaguely handsome twentysomething man in a grey dispatcher's uniform appeared in an eight-inch hologram. "Agent Wren, we've received a report of a suspected paranormal disturbance in Sector 9517."

Kirsten clutched the carpet with her toes. "Details? Is anyone hurt, being hurt, or about to be hurt?"

"The caller is identified as William Nuys." A smaller image of a late-thirties man with long brown hair in a ponytail and a goatee appeared to the left of the dispatcher. "He is reporting issues at a nightclub he owns, uhh… chairs stacking on tables, glasses falling on the floor, some canisters of synthetic liquor have been moved, and the audio system and lights are turning off and on at random."

"That's it?" She smirked.

"Mr. Nuys also stated that for the past month, whenever he's shown up to open the club, he's found tables upside down and liquor bottles scattered around."

"So basically, a ghost is being irritating?" She stroked Evan's hair.

"Dispatch, my son isn't feeling well. From what you're describing, this isn't an emergency call. Please tell Mr. Nuys I'll stop by tomorrow."

The tightening of Evan's hug killed any sense of worry about Captain Eze giving her grief over not going.

"It does seem like a low priority report, agent. I'll open a case file and send it to you. Shall I ask Mr. Nuys to provide an immediate update if he feels a life is in danger?"

"Of course. Thanks. I'll definitely check the place out tomorrow afternoon."

"Copy that, agent. Good night… and I hope your son feels better."

"Thanks."

The hologram went dark and she set the NetMini back on the table.

Evan looked up at her wide-eyed. "You stayed?"

"That isn't even close to an emergency. If I was still alone, I'd probably have gone out of boredom… but nothing is more important to me than you. I can't leave you right now."

"Sorry for actin' scared."

She ruffled his hair. "It's okay. You're nine. A couple of bad dreams are normal."

His eyes lit up white. "Do you think there's something in my closet?"

"Let's go look."

He gulped, but released the hug. "Okay."

She took his hand and slid off the couch. He showed little reaction to anything until she poked the silver square on the wall that opened his bedroom door with a muted *pssht*. His grip on her fingers tightened. The room looked dark, but empty.

Kirsten leaned in and brushed the switch on her left. Dragons winged above a nighttime meadow in his electronic window, and large fake spiders darted over the faux-castle-stone walls for cover when the room lights came on. Evan puffed his chest up and followed her to the closet. No spirits showed themselves, though the room *did* feel eerie. Something had been here.

Something malicious.

The closet opened without a sound, revealing toys, clothes, and coats.

"Do you feel it?" asked Evan.

She nodded. "Yeah. Did you mess with any others aside from Abernathy?"

"The guy in the bathroom who tried to hit me." Evan hurried over to his wardrobe and changed into pajamas.

"That ghost won't be attacking anyone again." Kirsten glared around at the room.

He walked up to her. "Can I sleep with you tonight?"

It's a bit early for me to crash… what the hell; I could use some extra sleep. "Okay." *Is it tied to this room, or will it try something if he's not alone?*

She backed out, killed the lights, and sent him to the bathroom to brush his teeth. Worry that the creepy abyssal he'd driven into a church on the hood of the patrol craft might have come back got her to bite her lip. *No... that bitch is beyond dead. Who would want to hurt him? This only started after we moved here... it's got to be a former resident going territorial.* She scowled. *That I can deal with.*

Evan raced out of the bathroom, shot past her, and dove onto the queen-sized Comforgel pad in her room. She smiled at him and headed for the attached bathroom. After brushing her teeth and emptying her bladder, she climbed in, unable to remember the last time she'd gone to bed at ten p.m.

20

SELF-INFLICTED

Despite going to sleep early, Kirsten struggled to wake up at the alarm. Evan jumped on top of her, straddling her stomach while shaking her by the shoulders. She groaned, grabbed him by the wrists, and pulled him down to the left while rolling onto her side. Nose to nose, they stared at each other for a few seconds before the laughing started.

"Get ready for school."

"You're gonna be late."

She yawned, rolled onto her back, and stretched. Evan darted off to his room. The effect of extra sleep kicked in, and she shrugged off the fog far faster than she usually did. A quick shower later, she got into her uniform and ran out the door with Evan in tow.

He looked up at her in the hallway. "We forgot breakfast."

"No time. I'm gonna order it on the way."

"Cool!"

"What do you want?"

"Where are you ordering from?" He raced her to the elevator.

"A place I used to get food from every day before I started burning my own. It's good."

"What'cha gettin'?"

"Omelet sandwich with jalapeños."

"Can I have that too?"

"It's hot. Spicy."

He shrugged. "I wanna try it."

"You can try a bit of mine first, and next time—"

"Aww. I can handle it."

She put in an order from the patrol craft, timing it so she parked in front of Cabrera's deli with about a minute to spare. Evan waited in the car while she ran in and picked up two white cartons, one large mocha coffee, and an orange juice.

After pulling airborne again, she set the patrol craft to auto drive and opened her food.

"You got him one of those abominations?" asked Dorian from the back seat.

"They're good!" Kirsten picked half her sandwich up. "Ugh, I hate it when they cut it in half. The owner leaves it whole."

"He's going to scream." Dorian smiled.

Evan opened the carton and took a hesitant sniff. "Wow. It's as big as my head." He got his fingers around a half, and took a bite. Within seconds, the look on his face sounded the alarm, but he soldiered on.

"It's okay if you don't like it." She took a huge bite of hers. "I can order you something else and give that one to Nicole."

He gasped for air. "It's okay. My mouth burns a little, but I'm not gonna scream."

Dorian laughed. "Takes a while to get used to spicy."

"I'm gonna eat it." Evan sucked in air and fanned his tongue.

By the time the Police Administrative Center came into view up ahead, Kirsten's sandwich was a distant, fond memory, and Evan had finished one half. His face remained pink, and he shifted an ice cube from his juice back and forth in his mouth. Kirsten reverted to manual flight control and brought the patrol craft down on the roof in the 'temporary' parking area.

"Going back out?" asked Dorian.

"Yep. Today I'm going to grill Lamb over liver."

Dorian winced. "You're having too much fun with that."

"*You're* gonna try to make lamb?" Evan's eyebrows went up.

"Oh hush." She poked him in the side.

Kirsten walked Evan to the school and returned to the car. Dorian had migrated to his usual spot in the passenger seat, and pored over three holo-panels scrolling with mugshots.

"What's that?" She pulled the door down and closed.

"I'm looking over Division 1 records of known black market organ dealers, as well as their associates—the ones who do the actual collecting. Trying to see if there are any electronic traces linking Lamb to the illicit trade of body parts." Dorian glanced at her. "And if you make another bad food joke, I'm going to cite you for assault on the English language."

"You started it." She laughed. "That poor guy. Must've been rough going through school with that name."

"No worse than being the one kid in Cairo who had a European father." Dorian chuckled. "Of course, I was like six when they moved here."

"Oh, Dorian... are you sure you don't want me to help you talk to your family?"

His expression darkened. "I'm not ready. I'm not sure I'll ever be."

"It might be easier on them if they know you're not 'gone.'"

"Trust me. You don't want my mother having your PID. You think the 'mini rings constantly now...'"

Kirsten laughed.

At 10:42 a.m., Kirsten landed at the Ancora Medical Pavilion. Six minutes later, she walked up to the same care station and smiled at the artificial nurse.

"Excuse me. I need to see a patient by the name of Robert Lamb."

The doll looked up at her, whirring audible from the neck joint. Emerald light surrounding the irises pulsated in an illusion of rotating motion. "Good morning, Agent. One moment." She/it remained eerily motionless for three seconds before the head tilted to the left. "I am sorry, Agent. Patient Lamb, Robert M., checked out at 9:23 a.m."

Kirsten's body shivered with the effort it took not to scream an impolite word. Aside from some color showing up in her cheeks, she concealed any outward reaction. "Thank you."

"Think he's running?" asked Dorian.

"For his sake, I hope not." She held her left forearm up. Sensing her hand approaching, it projected a holo-panel screen, rendered in lime green and black. She tapped the icon for 'police utilities.'

National Registry.

A text box popped open: *Notice: Use of police access to the National Registry is limited to official investigations and—*

Swipe.

NetMini registration database.

Swipe.

A virtual keyboard scrolled open left to right. She entered his name and age. After a brief search, she found the Robert Lamb she wanted and poked the entry showing his PID. Her touch initiated an outbound vid call at the same time running a location trace. A blue shield icon at the top right offered a shortcut to a pickup warrant that would send a notification to any Division 1 unit within ten miles of his NetMini signal.

"Hello?" The holographic face looked like death in a red bathrobe, a far cry from the neat and tidy manager.

"Mr. Lamb. This is Agent Wren from Division 0. I'm at the Ancora building looking for you."

"Oh. Sorry. Insurance guy said I was in good enough shape to go home.

Ancora's not cheap you know. If it was some other place, they probably would've let me spend a day or two. I can't swing it out of pocket."

"Ugh." She sighed, her anger fading as fast as it had appeared. "I need to talk to you."

"I have the day off at least. You're welcome to stop by." He rubbed his face. "If it takes me a bit to get to the door, I might be asleep. These pain meds are a bit more potent than I'm used to."

"All right. Thank you, Mr. Lamb. I'll be there soon." She hung up.

"Gotta love insurance." Dorian shook his head. "At least he's not running. Maybe he doesn't know you know about his discount body part?"

"Or doesn't care. It's not like they'd confiscate it. Considering his job, he might think of prison as a vacation. Also, I have no evidence proving a man was murdered to steal his liver... or that a man was murdered at all."

Dorian opened his mouth.

"*Proof.* I'm sure someone was killed. I can't prove it."

Dorian smiled. "Always in the details."

ROBERT LAMB RESIDED ON THE NINETY-FOURTH FLOOR OF A SILVER-AND-BLACK apartment tower in a glimmering, ritzy district full of micro parks and potted trees where the average resident occupied a niche between comfortable and wealthy. She didn't envy them, at least not if they all worked themselves to death like Lamb. A routine check of his finances, which seemed like a good idea while investigating potential illegal trade in organs, showed him claiming 2.1 million credits per year. Her salary, barely a quarter of that, made her feel a twinge of jealousy until she remembered the way he stared at the liquor, and how late he worked.

Yeah. I'd rather jump off buildings and have people shoot at me—as long as they miss most of the time.

Then again, starting Division 1 patrol officers only made about 200k a year. Much to her surprise, she did find a transaction that looked promising. He'd withdrawn C76,000 to a credstick nine weeks ago, the only time he'd transferred money to the less-traceable medium in the past eighteen years. It didn't prove anything, but it would back up firmer evidence if it came down to it.

She flew in a circle around the towers of Lamb's apartment complex, a pair of hundred-and-nine story obelisks flanking a cube-shaped central building less than half as tall. The middle building's roof consisted almost entirely of hovercar parking, except for a pyramid-shaped outbuilding of amber glass. Within seconds of her landing and exiting the car, a twelve-inch orb bot with the voice of a posh English butler zipped up into her face.

"Excuse me, Ma'am. Olympian Suites is valet parking only. I also do not detect a resident's transponder in your vehicle. I am going to have to ask you to move. As a courtesy, we will allot you fifteen seconds before assessing a convenience fee of two-thousand credits."

"Dorian, do stunrods work on bots, or should I just shoot this one?"

The hover-bot wobbled. "What? How dare you threat—" The orb fell straight down with a *clank*, dark and motionless. Tiny wisps of electricity crawled in a serpentine path across the roof to Dorian's shoes.

"Thanks." She sent off an email to Admin, requesting they 'fine the piss' out of the management company of this apartment for failing to install the proper equipment to detect and respond to official vehicles.

She stormed over to the pyramid at the center of the square roof. It contained a café as well as elevators. Each of the towers had separate entrances as well. Since Lamb's apartment was in the south tower, she headed for it.

Two men in navy-blue jumpsuits bearing the markings of 'Peerless Security Services' rushed out of the door and got in her way.

She glared at the one on the left for two seconds before aiming her contempt at the other. "Stand aside. I'm not in the mood right now, and I'd have no trouble arresting you both for impeding an investigation."

"I'm sorry, missy. We have to detain you for destroying property."

"Missy?" She gasped. "Who the hell do you think you are?"

The other man grinned. "She's in character. I love cop strip—"

"*Shut up.*" Kirsten's eyes flared with a momentary glow.

Dorian looked off in a random direction, muttering. "Oh, damn."

The security guard stared at her, his eyes as well as the tendons in the sides of his neck bulged.

She locked eyes with the other man. "Comm. Eze."

"Good morning, Kirsten," said Captain Eze in her earbud, three seconds later.

"Did you see the request I submitted regarding Olympian Suite's failure to maintain proper transponder recognition for official National Police Force vehicles? I just met a pair of genetic throwbacks who seem to think I'm a stripper. Obviously, adult entertainers in this part of the city routinely carry live laser weaponry. Can you send over a Div 2 team to deep dive the financial records of this place to make sure everything is in order? I'd also like your opinion on charging these two with impeding an investigation, plus anything Div 1 can rubber glove out of their records for the past, oh fifteen years?"

Dorian whistled, and grinned. "Division 0: the smiling face of psionics for the new century."

The guard not paralyzed by a suggestion glanced at his partner. "Sorry. Is that necessary? If we get arrested, we'll get fired. You, uhh, did blow up one of the orbs."

"Maybe you two can get work as strippers." She folded her arms. "Don't bother talking. Every time you open your mouth, you lose ten points of IQ. It's not destroyed; it's powered down."

Captain Eze's voice chuckled in her ear. "I hope you've scared them. The forensic accounting is an overreach. If you feel they've impeded your investigation, go ahead and call for Div 1 to pick them up."

"You're not that person, K." Dorian patted her on the shoulder. "You're the good cop remember? Let me be bad cop."

His body shimmered translucent. "Division 0. Stand clear."

The guards ran in opposite directions, one screaming, one attempting to scream with a clenched jaw.

Kirsten attempted a meditative breath. "I am *really* getting sick of people not recognizing the uniform."

"I'm sure they did. They were probably trying to be cute and make a pass."

"Do you think I should complain to their boss, or would that make me self-absorbed?"

Dorian shrugged. "Either that or kick their asses. But you're not that kind of cop."

She grumbled. "Lamb's waiting."

"Don't want it to get cold?"

"Go to hell." She sighed into a laugh.

ROBERT LAMB'S DOOR SLID OPEN FOUR MINUTES AFTER SHE'D HIT THE PAGE button for the fifth time. The towering figure leaning there looked somewhere between hung over and raised from the dead. Pale, unshaven, disheveled, in a too-tight white tee shirt that exposed his belly and oversized plaid boxers.

"Come in. Sorry if I'm not prettied up right now." He ambled inside, leaving Kirsten to close the door after entering.

Aside from the empty cartons of a recently-ordered breakfast abandoned on the kitchen counter, the expansive apartment looked immaculate. A square coffee table of smoky onyx glass capped at the corners by white plastisteel boxes hovered in the center of a C-shaped black sectional large enough for twelve people. She approached, wondering why anyone would want a table constantly emitting hover-bot thrum. The theme ran throughout the dining room and an interior hallway; anything not black or dark grey was metallic silver. He eased himself down on the sofa, letting off a heavy grunt as his weight settled into the cushions.

She sat at the tip of the C nearest the door. "How are you feeling?"

"I'd feel a lot better if Sudha would leave me the hell alone for more than twenty damn minutes." He cringed and pressed on his side. "Better than the other night, that's for damn sure."

Kirsten leaned forward, forearms across her knees, fingers laced. "I'm not big on going in circles, Mr. Lamb. I've got a pretty good idea of what's happened to you, and you're not going to like it. But, I need you to be honest with me if we're going to get anywhere."

He fidgeted at the bottom of his shirt, trying to cover his navel.

"I know you purchased a replacement liver from an illegal source. I'm convinced the person who was murdered to obtain that liver wants it back."

"Back?" asked Dorian.

"Back with his remains." Kirsten tapped at her armguard and projected an image of the squeezed liver. "Those are finger indentations, Mr. Lamb. A spirit stuck his hands inside you and tried to crush it."

Dorian slapped his leg. "That makes perfect sense. The ghost isn't that old, but because the liver is his, he can somehow interact with it more easily than other solid matter."

She glanced at Dorian.

"I-Is he here now?" Lamb broke out in a sweat.

"No, but there is a ghost in the room with us. He's with me. Can you explain to me why a man in your position has to resort to a street doc for spare parts? That's usually the domain of cybergang punks, corporate mercenaries, or Syndicate operating outside legal channels."

Lamb coughed into his hand. "Fucking insurance." He grumbled. "I've worked for NewsNet for twenty-one years, you'd think all that time paying into their system, they'd cover me for a regen. Oh, but that's how the whole insurance scam works." A grunt slipped out as he leaned forward to point at her. "All they really want is free money. The minute someone actually *needs* to use the goddamned insurance, they look for every damn excuse they can think of to deny you."

"Your employment record looked more or less spotless. What reason could they possibly have had to refuse?"

"Aside from the couple million credits regenerating an organ costs?" Dorian wandered off, looking around the apartment. "If they can get a lawyer to agree to it, they can make up any reason they want."

"They said it was a self-inflicted preventable injury." Lamb's fists shook; his face reddened for a second before he went paler than before. "I was, uhh, fond of the whiskey. Had maybe a bit too much. According to the Pantheon rep, they're not liable to pay out when a person injures themselves deliberately. They determined that my liver disease was 'self-inflicted injury' and refused to cover it."

"That's..." Kirsten blinked.

"Bullshit is what it is." Lamb grabbed his side again. "Shit... is that thing here again?"

"No."

"Bastard thing still hurts. You know that sanctimonious prick from Pantheon smiled at me when he hung up? Like we'd gotten into some kinda virtual Gee-ball game and he shut me out. I'll probably be chatting with your counterparts in blue if I ever meet that weasel in person."

Kirsten cringed. *Was that a serious death threat or was he venting?* "Mr. Lamb, you know I'm still an officer of the National Police Force, even if I am an investigator with Division 0... if you're seriously threatening someone's life in my presence, I have to—"

"Oh, for the love of... I'd only punch him."

"I see. Well, that won't be much of an issue if it's uncovered that you arranged for a man to be killed for parts."

Lamb somehow managed to grow paler. "N-no way. I'd have paid for the damn procedure myself before I killed someone. This guy I know in Investigative got a line on a person of interest. He's been doing a series of exposé pieces on so-called 'ripper docs,' and he knew I was having all sorts of problems with fucko at Pantheon. Turns out, he got in with this one 'doctor' who happened to have an extra liver sitting around with nothing to do. No way was I trusting my life to someone who works outta a black zone, so I checked around and found a place that'd do the procedure no questions asked, and they said the DNA didn't matter... they could 'make it work.'"

"So this guy grabbed a liver from a Nippy Nom and waltzed into a free clinic?" Dorian phased out of the wall on Lamb's right, and strode through the couch. "Not much here. I get the feeling he's not home too often."

"Where'd you get it?" asked Kirsten.

"I never knew the guy's name. Mole set me up with him."

"Mole?" Kirsten stared at her fingers, tinted green from the holo-panel over her left arm. "I hope that's a nickname."

Lamb flashed a grin tinted by wince. "Yeah. He's one of our better investigative reporters. Jim Burroughs. Everyone started calling him Mole after the 'Burroughs deep' jokes got thin. Anyway, Mole finds this thing... makes the deal. I show up in this broken down parking deck in a grey zone to do the swap. Wasn't even the doctor who showed up, some big guys with more hardware than most cops."

She typed as fast as she could with one hand.

"You don't have an implant? I don't think I've ever seen one of you guys use that arm thing before."

"I don't like cyberware. The mere thought of it makes my spine twitch." Kirsten shivered. "Can you tell me where you had the organ implanted?"

"Yeah." He picked at the fabric of his shorts. "Place called 1UP... with a number one in front of 'up' in caps. It's in Sector 5956, near the grey zone north of it. Doctor Simon something... tall woman with weird hair." He waved his hand around in thought. "Uhh... black and pink. Look, if the man was already dead, is buying that liver illegal?"

"Umm..." Kirsten entered notes about 1UP and a 'Doctor Simon?' to the file. "Technically it is, but assuming you had nothing to do with the procurement, it's somewhere between trading in stolen property and desecrating a corpse. Given the classification of the offense, it's unlikely command would pursue the investigation."

Robert Lamb exhaled with relief.

"Though, I don't think the former owner cares about legal technicalities." She shot a pointed stare at him. "He's only going to become stronger as time passes and he gets angrier. Considering the damage he did the other night, I think it's quite possible he could be able to kill you in six months or so."

"C-can you stop him?" Lamb shivered.

"That would require finding him. Are you sure you don't have any idea who 'donated' that liver?"

"I swear on my mother I don't. There's gotta be something you can do." He leaned forward; the look on his face said he'd have grabbed her like a begging child if she'd been within reach.

"Without being able to find this guy, the only thing I can suggest would be to get rid of the organ. He *might* not be angry with you anymore if the organ's not inside you."

"They still won't cover the procedure." Lamb deflated. "Two point nine mil to do a full regeneration, plus I'd be stuck in a tank for three days."

Kirsten stood and held her arms out to the side in a limp shrug. "Unless you can give me more information and I find this ghost, that's all I got."

"What if he comes after me again?"

"Put me on speed dial. He should be able to hear you. Try asking him to wait for me so we can talk."

Lamb struggled to his feet. "You think that'll work? Wait, am I seriously contemplating talking to ghosts?"

"You're offering that a lot," said Dorian. "Hope everyone doesn't all call you at once."

Kirsten folded her arms. "Do you have a better explanation for what happened?"

Lamb slouched.

She patted him on the arm. "Hey... You work for NewsNet. You could always threaten to do a week-long special on how the insurance industry rips people off."

A spark lit in Lamb's eye. "That might work."

"Or they'll have him killed." Dorian chuckled.

She glanced at him. "I'm going to see if I can track this guy down before he comes back. Call me if you have any more information."

"Thanks, agent." Lamb walked her out. He closed the door after she left, seeming energized while muttering about scheduling that special.

Kirsten looked at Dorian. "You're so cynical. Do you really think Pantheon would have him assassinated to stop a news report?"

"Would Intera send assassins after a cop to keep a secret?"

She shivered. "Thanks for reminding me of that mess."

"That's why I'm here." He smiled. "Though, I think you're more confident now... you'd probably handle that a lot better if it happened again."

"Don't jinx me." She hurried to the elevator and took it down to the 50th floor, where a connecting corridor led back to the roof of the cube-shaped central building.

A woman in a black business skirt-suit with a row of oval mirrored buttons on the front hovered by the patrol craft. She looked in her middle twenties, pale, blonde, and had the sort of severe look to her one might expect from an Eastern European spy—or dominatrix. As Kirsten approached, the woman offered an unexpected warm smile.

Kirsten stopped, gazing up at a woman who had to be more than a foot taller than her.

"Agent Wren?" Her voice had a chirpy, upbeat, almost teenage quality, at utter odds with her appearance. "I'm Katarina Burke, VP of operations for Hearthford Abbey Management Corporation."

Kirsten accepted a handshake, feeling wary. "Can I help you?"

"I'd like to extend the company's apologies for how some of our security associates treated you earlier." She removed a holodisk in a clear plastic case from the pocket of her blazer. "We found evidence that a former employee infiltrated the building's network and overrode the protocol responsible for detecting emergency service vehicles. It is our belief they were trying to initiate problems with law enforcement."

"Oh." Kirsten turned the square case over, letting the light gleam off it. "Thanks."

Katarina's pleasant demeanor hardened. "I reviewed security video of the... comment that was made to you. I also wanted you to know those two are no longer employed by us."

A twinge of guilt rose up inside her, but she decided to ignore it. "Thanks. Hopefully, they won't do that to anyone else."

"Please let me know if there's anything else we can do for you." Katarina offered a slight bow, and walked off toward the pyramid of amber glass in the center of the parking area.

Dorian walked around to his side of the patrol craft. "Now that was unexpected."

"I wonder what's on their network they don't want us to find." She got in.

"Hey." Dorian poked her in the arm. "I'm supposed to be the cynic."

She logged in from the car's console, and ran a search of a Jim Burroughs employed by NewsNet Corporation. Within three minutes, she had a fix on his NetMini location... a run-down sector somewhat close to a grey zone. According to the map, a Chinese restaurant known as the Fu-Sheng House. Kirsten studied the face on the monitor: later thirties, flat-topped afro, dark skin, and something about his face made him seem easy to trust.

"That place was awesome." Dorian sighed.

"Was?"

"Okay fine. *Is.* Was for me." He grumbled. "I'm surprised you haven't heard of it... then again, you're young and innocent. A lot of the local Div 1 guys go there three or four times a week for lunch."

"Thanks." Kirsten tapped at the control sticks, not quite sure she still deserved to be called '. She couldn't make up her mind at what point in her life 'innocent' no longer applied. Had Mother taken that from her, or did she give it away for food? Perhaps he meant her naïve tendency to search for the good in everyone. She let off a quiet sigh, and accelerated.

A MASSIVE HOLOGRAPHIC SIGN PAINTED HALF A BLOCK IN TWO DIRECTIONS FROM the Fu-Sheng House bright orange and red. Chinese characters taller than Evan blinked in and out in sequence along a board seven feet tall on the front corner of a building next to a tiny parking lot. Kirsten didn't even bother trying to squeeze the patrol craft in. Half again as wide and long as a civilian car, it wouldn't fit in the single available spot.

She landed on the roof of a building across the street, a five-story... something that looked abandoned. It might've been an office or an apartment, though the condition of the place left its former purpose a mystery. Kirsten jogged down a rickety fire escape ladder, basking in clouds of warm air tainted with the smell of urine. The flavor of rusting metal settled on her tongue with each breath.

The glare from the sign made her squint as she crossed the street, until she reached the shallow alcove sheltering the front door, covered in cracked, red paint. It opened with a jingle of physical bells, and she stepped inside. The powerful sign forced light through heavy curtains, tinting the entire room in shades of burgundy and orange. Metallic gold on the wallpaper shimmered wherever red felt didn't cover it, and a five-foot long carved-wooden dragon (also painted gold) gazed at her with a red lightbulb eye from where it hung at the back of the room.

A woman behind a tiny counter to the right smiled at her and asked something in Chinese.

Kirsten's NetMini translated, reciting, "Welcome to the Fu Sheng House, officer. Booth or table?"

She whispered, "I didn't come here to eat. I'm looking for someone… but it smells so good. Give me a moment?" into the device before a version of her voice, speaking Chinese, played out of its speaker.

The woman nodded. She said something else, which her NetMini echoed in English. "Okay. If you want to eat, you tell me."

Kirsten smiled at her and scanned the room. Jim Burroughs sat in a booth seat most of the way down the right-side wall, opposite a spritely ginger-haired girl with pale skin and freckles. Her short bob glinted with metal and flashing lights, some kind of headset with pods over each ear and moving antennas that made her seem to have metal rabbit ears. Jim had a napkin tucked into the neck of a beige turtleneck, with a few dribbles of dark red sauce on it.

She walked up to the end of the table, glancing back and forth between them.

Chopsticks in his right hand animated his conversation like a conductor's baton over a symphony, though he froze in place as soon as Kirsten arrived.

"Mr. Burroughs. I'm Agent Wren, Division 0 Police. I'd like a moment of your time."

The girl looked up at her with an eager expression. More tiny lights on her headgear came on. "That's the psionic cops, Mole. What's she want with you?"

"Great question." Jim wiped his hands and offered one. "Nice to meet you, agent."

She shook. "I need to ask you a few questions about your association with Robert Lamb. More specifically, how much you know about his recent health problems."

"He's at the upper end of middle management. I'm only a reporter. He and I don't really interact."

Grr. Kirsten squinted at him, unable to resist skimming his surface thoughts. He worried how much Lamb told her, and feared his cover being blown if he talked. The word 'Mardrake' drifted by, along with a scary-as-hell image of a cybered-up mammoth of a man who he'd apparently come to know as Nurse Bea.

"Mr. Lamb gave me a somewhat different version of events. He said you were doing an investigative piece on the recent surge in illegal organ sales. I got the impression you gave him some information."

"That's true about the story, and I'm still in the middle of it." His surface thoughts flashed a fast forwarded conversation with Lamb. Again, the name Mardrake came up, this time with the image of a man in a blood-spattered teal coat. The figure stood in harsh contrast at the edge of an operating room style lamp; half his face, pale as snow with a visible crow's foot entered the light, though much of him remained in shadow. Thick, black hair in a side part left him looking like a mad scientist from an old holovid.

"I see. I suppose Mr. Lamb may be trying to direct attention away from himself."

"How should I know what his game is?" Burroughs gave her a pointed look. *Come on... read my mind. You people do that all the time, right?*

Kirsten cringed inside, but responded telepathically. *Not all the time, but Lamb's life is in danger and I don't have time for bullshitting around. I appreciate your need to keep a distance. What do you know?* "Do you have any idea why Lamb would mention you?"

If you're listening to my thoughts now... Lamb was pretty messed up. His liver was gonna crap out and he couldn't afford to replace it. This guy Mardrake—I have no idea if that's his real name—did a job for someone else, and had a bunch of other shit lying around. They gutted some poor mofo but real. Took just about everything. You don't wanna go in there on your own, girl. He's got three hired bastards what do the 'unpleasant' parts. Spaz, Uri, and this cro-mag they call Nurse Bea. Burroughs shrugged. "Hell if I know. Like I said, I don't usually talk to the man. We're in different circles." He nabbed another piece of shrimp in dark orange sauce with his chopsticks and ate it.

"You're sure you're being honest with me? Lamb was pretty convinced you gave him some information." *Where can we find this guy? Do you have any idea who they killed or who uhh, 'commissioned' the harvesting?*

Burroughs shook his head. "No idea. On all counts." *Rumor says he's got his setup in Sector 6903, but I ain't know that for a fact.*

"All right." She sighed with a scowl. "Thanks for your time."

He took another piece of shrimp, and seemed to be fighting the urge to smile. "Sorry I couldn't be more help." *Damn. I wish all cops could do this. That's a damn sight easier.*

Kirsten tried to act frustrated. "I hope for your sake Lamb doesn't turn up any proof of your involvement." She glanced at the maybe-eighteen-year-old girl staring wide-eyed at her. "Since that would mean you've just been recorded lying to me." *Thanks.*

"Since when does Zero investigate ripper docs?" Burroughs waved shrimp and chopsticks about. "Not the usual sorta thing you guys get your hands dirty with."

"The former owner of Mr. Lamb's liver isn't too happy about it." Kirsten winked. "If you think of anything else, please contact us."

"Whoa," said the girl, her antenna-ears perking straight up. "Did you just imply that ghosts are real?"

"Yeah... sure will." Burroughs popped the shrimp in his mouth.

"They are." Kirsten smiled.

The girl leaned closer. "Can I interview you about that? A lot of my followers are into that stuff."

"I don't mind, but you'd have to go through the usual channels. I'm not really permitted to give interviews without the blessing of the higher ups."

"Right..." The girl sighed, antennas drooping. "Usual runaround. Is it okay if I tell them you're willing?"

"Sure. They like good PR." Kirsten headed for the exit, but paused at the front counter. "Can I get an order of shrimp lo mein to go?"

The Chinese woman nodded. Her voice repeated in English from the NetMini. "Sure. Thirty Eight please."

Dorian leaned up behind the redhead and whispered, "Ghosts are real, sweetie."

Her rabbit ears shot straight up.

Before she laughed, Kirsten turned her back on their table.

Six minutes after swiping her NetMini over the reader to pay, she hurried back to the patrol craft. Rather than try to fight her way up a fire escape, she summoned the car with her armband. It levitated, slid out over the street, and settled down at her side. She hopped in, lifted into the air, and hovered at the tenth story level. After engaging auto-hover, she opened her lunch.

"Now what?" asked Dorian.

"I got a name. Mardrake. He's a ripper doc." Kirsten stuffed her mouth with noodles. *Oh wow... this is amazing!*

A rattletrap of an e-bike whipped around the corner and skidded into the tiny parking lot of the Fu Sheng house. She smirked at the driver, a scrawny black-haired man, but didn't feel like 'slumming it' and giving him a citation for speeding or not wearing a helmet. She had bigger issues to deal with. As soon as he hopped off the bike, she recognized him—that guy from Division 9 net ops. Joey or something. He rushed inside as if he hadn't eaten in months.

Dorian shot her an astonished look. "After all the grief you give Nicole for that... I never imagined you of all people would play fast and loose with ethics."

She sighed out her nose while chewing, rushing to swallow. "I only surfaced him, and Lamb's gonna die if I don't do *something*. It didn't expose Burroughs to any trouble, legal or otherwise. I'm not going to rely on it directly for anything, and I have something to look into now. Besides, he asked me to do it."

Dorian remained quiet while she slurped up another chopstick load of noodles. "You're making justifications, but I suppose I can't disagree with your reasoning."

Kirsten grinned at him with a tangle of lo mein hanging from her teeth.

21

DEFECT

W ith the patrol craft on auto-drive, Kirsten attacked the terminal in the console and ran searches on the word 'Mardrake' as well as the 1UP clinic. The name search kept churning, but the clinic came back as a charity medical facility occupying a grey zone in Sector 6061. The system identified the chief doctor on site as one Petra Simonova, age twenty-six. Kirsten pulled up her records, finding images of a dangerously thin six- or seven-year-old girl with black hair from an immigration intake scan. She'd slipped into the UCF with her parents by way of Mars. Aside from a few pick-ups for illegal chems in her middle teens, her record was clean.

"They busted her for Sandman and Flowerbasket? Really?" Kirsten rolled her eyes. "Div 1 must've been bored."

"They usually only bother if someone's asking them to get involved. Probably her parents. Kid with a background like that, it's not surprising she had some wild years. Still, a medical doctor at twenty-six is pretty impressive."

"Yeah. Well, I'm not getting anything on Mardrake. Might as well go talk to our ACC émigré."

A flick of her finger tossed the record of the 1UP clinic from the terminal panel to the Navcon, and the map zoomed out to show the fastest route.

"She might know how to find Mar—"

Her NetMini rang.

"Oh shit. Maybe we're gonna get lucky." She leaned over in the seat to get the device off her belt. "Wren."

A frightened looking girl's face appeared in hologram, cloaked in shadow and a hooded sweatshirt. Muted color and lack of detail suggested she hid somewhere dark. Her voice came out as a whisper. "I'm sorry for hackin' your PID outta the system… I gotta talk to you. You're a psi-cop right?"

"Yes. Are you in trouble? How old are you? Where are you?"

The hood twisted to the left. "Uhh. Fourteen. I really need your help. Can you meet me here ASAP?" A glossy red pushpin hologram appeared, rotating next to the girl's head. "Please?" She pulled the hood back enough to expose a lock of light brown hair, pale cheek, and wide, terrified chocolate eyes, but a scarf covered the lower half of her face.

"Okay." Kirsten touched the floating pin, and it disappeared. The Navcon showed a second waypoint. "I'll be there in four minutes or so. Sector 9068? Pizza Heaven?"

"Yeah," whispered the girl. "I'm hiding in the bathroom." A trace of sniffles added to her voice. "Please… I escaped. If they find me, they're gonna kill me."

Kirsten flicked on the blue bar lights. "Two minutes."

The girl nodded and hung up.

"You gonna call it in?" asked Dorian.

"Shit." Kirsten grumbled. "I almost forgot. Ops, come back?"

"Copy that, agent." A blond male doll appeared in hologram over the console.

"A minor contacted my personal NetMini requesting help. She indicated her life is being threatened. Logging contact from the location of my current waypoint."

"Copy, agent. Noted. Do you need backup?"

Kirsten squeezed the sticks. "She looked skittish as hell. Might scare her off if we roll in there heavy. Can you have a tactical unit on standby, close?"

"You got it, agent. Be careful."

"Careful's her middle name." Dorian laughed.

Kirsten smirked.

Two minutes and nineteen seconds later, Kirsten dove out of the emergency hover lane at the eightieth story and flew almost straight down. Dorian closed his eyes, tensed, and muttered a series of Arabic words at the window to his right.

With the nose still pointed at the ground, she slowed to a near hover, levelled the car off, and set down in front of a restaurant built into the corner of an office building. Pizza Heaven took up about a quarter of the first floor of a hundred-story tower containing the offices of numerous different small companies.

She climbed out and jogged inside, finding about forty people (mostly business casual) arranged around red Formica benches and tables. A man with long, dark hair, a broad chest, and thick moustache waved in greeting from behind a counter full of glass-faced warming cabinets holding pizza slices, calzones, and plastic trays of French fries or onion rings. Despite having eaten not too long ago, the scent of tomato sauce and basil tempted her to get something to bring home for dinner later.

Kirsten headed for the back, but the bathroom door opened when she was halfway across the room. The girl from the vid call emerged, hands hidden in the sleeves of her too-large sweatshirt. Black tights concealed little about the shape of skinny legs, and bore smudges and a few rips indicative of having spent a brief time living on the street.

She forgot about food entirely and jogged up to the girl, who wound up being only an inch or so shorter than her. The kid pulled her scarf and hood down, allowing her long hair to fluff out over her shoulders. Red around her eyes hinted that she'd been crying. She grabbed Kirsten's hand, trembling.

"Where are the people who want to hurt you?"

The girl sniffled, eyeing the door. "They're not here. I ditched them. Can we talk?"

Kirsten followed her to an empty booth, and sat. "Are you hungry?"

"Not really… Thanks though." She wiped her face on her sleeve. "Can you guys help psionic kids whose parents would kill them if they found out? I don't mean like be pissed or disown me… literally drown me in the bathtub dead or tie me up and light me on fire."

Kirsten gasped, shock faded to anger. "If there's a determined threat like that, absolutely."

The kid relaxed—slightly. A nervous smile flickered across her lips.

Dorian frowned. "I'm inclined to believe her."

"Calm down. What's your name?"

The girl set her arms on the table, fingers half hidden in her sleeves, and picked at her nails while looking down. "Ashley."

Kirsten reached across the table to hold her hand. "Hi, Ashley. I'm Kirsten. Division 0 can protect you. I know what you're going through. My mother almost killed me for being psionic too."

"Really?" Ashley perked up.

"Yes. There's nothing wrong with you. It happens to… too damn many of us. Do you know what talents you've got?"

"Uhh. Sometimes when I touch things, I get visions of stuff. This guy that's always around, he left his gun on the counter once and I picked it up to check it out… I was like ten years old. As soon as I touched it, I like had a vision of him shooting a man in the head." Fresh tears ran down her face. "I never told anyone. The man was tied up on the ground, face down, and Terry shot him in the back of the head."

Kirsten gripped her hand a little tighter. "That had to be a hard secret to keep."

"Yeah." Ashley sniffled. "I think he knew I suspected something… I wasn't very good at acting casual around him. They kept asking me why I was all of a sudden scared of him. And, uhh, I read online that some psionics have like a weird thing with computers and machines and stuff? I'm good with computers but I never went to school for it... it's like I just know what to do."

"Could be technokinetic as well. Might as well give her the usual probe." Dorian glanced at the door. "She keeps looking at the windows... if she's clairvoyant, that could be an issue."

"Only about three percent of clairvoyants have precognitive ability."

"Huh?" Ashley looked at Kirsten for a second before following her gaze to about where Dorian stood. "Who are you talking to?"

"A ghost who helps me." Kirsten rubbed the girl's hand. The gesture brushed the girl's sleeve up a bit, exposing a red mark across a delicate wrist. "Ashley... Have you been abused?"

"Umm." The girl shivered. "Not like that, no. Just mental stuff. My grandfather didn't do *that*."

"Those are handcuff marks." Kirsten pushed both her sleeves up, finding a matching bruise on the other arm as well. "What happened to you?"

"You don't remember me?" Ashley fidgeted. "You came outta nowhere and saved us from that group of weirdos."

As soon as the girl said it, Kirsten felt like an idiot for not recognizing her right away. "Y-you're with that cult?"

"*Nooo*." Ashley whined. "I'm just related to them. I don't believe that bullshit! Uhh... I'm Ashley Harris."

Dorian cackled. Twice he tried to say something, but couldn't stop laughing enough to get words out.

Kirsten gawked. "You're that wacko's granddaughter?"

Ashley shrank in on herself. "Yeah. He doesn't know I'm psionic. *Now* do you believe me? He really would kill me if he found out."

"They didn't take you to a med center?" Kirsten brushed a finger over the red line.

"No. Karen thinks doctors are working for Satan too, but they don't hate them quite as much as psionics."

Kirsten glared. She took a stimpak from her belt case and offered it. "Here. That looks like it still hurts."

"You're awesome! Thanks!" Ashley fumbled with the safety cap and pushed the autoinjector into her forearm. "I think my wrist cracked. It's been hurting ever since. Those idiots left me hanging on that pipe for *so* long. We'd been there for like five hours before you snuck in. I was trying to run away, so I begged Grandpa to let me go shopping for some stuff for my birthday. I've only been fourteen for like a week. I acted like I was all into their religious bullshit for a couple months so they'd start to trust me, but Karen *insisted* on going with me, and Grandpa wound up sending Terry and Alex along to protect us. On the way into the mall, we saw that big blond guy doing tricks for tips—telekinesis or whatever—and Karen went off on him. Later, when we came out of the mall, they attacked us in the parking lot. I was waiting for them to make the others forget so I could tell them. I couldn't say I was psionic, too, in front of Karen and them. She'd have shot me herself."

"Ashley, would it be okay if I looked into your mind? To keep everything legal, I need to verify you're psionic, unless you have something visual you can do like Telekinesis."

The girl nodded, a flare of eagerness in her expression. "I can sometimes hear what people are thinking when I try real hard, but okay. You can do it."

Kirsten held eye contact with Ashley for a few seconds and pressed her thoughts deeper into the girl's psyche. Her surface thoughts swam with pure terror: that her grandfather would burn her alive. Probing with specific intent to detect psionic ability bypassed much of her cogent memories, though Kirsten did see enough to prove what the girl had been telling her. The Reverend Harris, fire-and-brimstone anti-psionic preacher, indeed had a clairvoyant, technokinetic, and possibly telepathic granddaughter.

When Kirsten dropped the mind link, Ashley's eyes fluttered and she swooned. "Wow that felt weird."

"Trouble incoming," said Dorian.

Kirsten sat up straight, tall enough to peer over Ashley's shoulder at three figures storming toward the front door. "Shit. Ops, this is Wren. That backup would be pretty handy right now."

"Copy, agent," said the doll.

A thin figure in a grey suit with a black shirt and priest's collar led the way, wispy white hair trailing off his head in the breeze. One of the two men behind him, the thick-chested guy with brown hair and an angry scowl, she recognized from the previous incident. The other man looked halfway between the type to go door-to-door with e-bibles and the sort of person one found selling firearms to street thugs. She spotted two handguns on his belt, and a suspicious bulge under his left arm.

Ashley whirled around in the seat when the door opened. She screamed and ducked under the table, shaking and sobbing.

Kirsten stood, one hand on her stunrod, as the men approached.

"Get away from my granddaughter, demon spawn." Reverend Harris's voice creaked through his teeth. The wrinkles around his mouth and eyes deepened. "Come now, Ashley Marie. You weren't given permission to go out today."

Kirsten edged closer to him, already seeing red. "I'm sorry, *Reverend*, but that's not happening. Ashley is now a ward of Division 0. I'm terminating your guardianship rights as of this moment."

"Out of my way, harlot!" His arms twitched.

Kirsten squeezed the stunrod handle tight enough to make the end glow, and subconsciously fell into a combat stance.

"You have no authority over the children of the Lord. Take your Devil-stained self out of my sight this instant!"

"You're wrong, old man. I do. Now, I'm giving you a direct command by the authority vested in me by the National Police Force. Turn around and remove yourself from my presence or I *will* detain you for interference of a sworn officer in the execution of their duties… and anything else I can find during the subsequent investigation."

"Liar!" roared the Reverend. He thrust his pointing finger at her face.

Kirsten parried his arm with the stunrod as though it were a sword coming for her head, knocking the old man to the side.

Reverend Harris spun into his two friends, cradling his arm and overacting pain. "Foul spawn of Hell. You and your kind recoil in fear at the True Path. You fear God and his children, and you seek to spread your lies and propaganda." He recovered his balance, wagging his finger at her from a safer distance. "No matter how hard you toil, your efforts are futile! *Futile!* Do you hear me, succubus? I shall not allow you to enslave humanity with your lies."

"Kirsten…" Dorian stared at her. "Hold it together. Backup is coming."

She tensed and relaxed her grip on the stunrod. "You're about as religious as that Stromboli over there. It's not about God at all for you is it, *Mister* Harris? Control is what you want. All it takes is a little ancient superstition to keep the idiots in line, right?"

Veins in his forehead bulged. "Destr—" He swallowed a growl.

Both muscular men behind him exchanged a glance. The one she'd seen cuffed around a pipe had the same wild-eyed glare as Harris, eager to lunge at her. His black-haired associate leaned away with evident trepidation in his eyes.

Harris started chanting Bible verses at her, ordering Satan back to Hell.

"*Stop!*" yelled Kirsten, a flare of white energy danced across her eyes.

Harris froze. Over the next ten seconds, the shaking tip of his finger trembled harder and harder. "Y-you j-just used your Devil power on me."

Rage swirled in Kirsten's soul. She found herself confronting Mother all over again, only in the guise of a man. She held her breath, searching for calm. Ashley crawled out from under the table and hid behind Kirsten.

"Wow. I've never seen him shut up before. That's awesome."

"Watch your tongue young lady." Harris glared at her. "What has this minion of Satan done to you?"

"Ashley has requested protection from Division 0. I have ample reason to suspect her life is in imminent danger in her present living conditions, and hereby terminate your legal guardianship. I will provide the official

Inquest number as soon as I trust taking my eyes off you long enough to do so."

"Go away," said Ashley. "You've never liked me. You treat me like a goddamn object and—"

"*Don't* take the name of thy Lord God in vain, missy!" screamed Harris.

"I'm not afraid of you anymore. I'm going with Agent Wren. I don't ever wanna see you again, you crazy old withered piece of shit." She squinted at him. "I'm psionic."

A second later, Harris recoiled as if burned. "H… her voice in my head. God!" Harris wailed and sank to his knees. He whispered, "My own granddaughter is one of *them*," before shouting, "Why have you abandoned me? Why do you mock me so?"

The same pathetic plea her mother used to bellow at the ceiling filled her with rage. Kirsten snarled and raised the stunrod. Dorian jumped into her with enough solidity to arrest her lunge and knock her back a step amid a freezing bath of air. She recovered her balance, angry tears streaming from the corners of her eyes. Ashley scurried backward three steps.

"Kirsten… don't. I know you think it'll make you feel better, but it won't." Dorian tried to grab her shoulders.

Reverend Harris pointed at Ashley. "You're flawed. Defective. Broken. Tainted. You always were a sinner, you little wretch. No wonder your mother killed herself. She knew you were unclean!"

Ashley glared back, her large eyes shaking in their sockets. "I bet you killed her! I'll prove it!"

Paper-thin lips peeled back with a grimace. Harris flared his eyes. "All of you should burn!" A hurled chocolate milkshake splattered over his back. "All of your kind should burn!"

"Shut the fuck up you crazy old bastard," yelled a man a few tables away.

The black-haired thug pulled a handgun out while the other one drew his jacket aside to reveal a submachinegun, which he gripped. Eleven patrons also produced weapons, including an ancient-looking man who appeared mostly blind.

The reverend's continuous calls for psionics to be purged mixed with prayers, blurring into a miasma of sound and fury in Kirsten's mind. She trembled from anger, trying to tune him out, trying to stop hearing the accusations in Mother's voice. Daydreams of bashing Harris's skull in with her stunrod advanced from idle whimsy to serious consideration.

She had to make the shrieking preacher stop.

22

THE ILLUSION OF CONTROL

Kirsten pondered trading the stunrod to her off hand and going for the E-90, but with so many people around, the laser was too dangerous. Reverend Harris swayed back and forth as if lost in some divine experience. Eyes closed, his invocations to God rose and fell from shouts to whispers.

"Purge them, my sons. Suffer not witches to live." His eyes snapped open, wild with mania. "That is no longer my granddaughter. She is not of my blood."

"Good!" yelled Ashley. "You're all crazy!"

Ka-chuck. "I got your back, officer."

Harris's thugs froze. They turned their heads at the same time, eyeing the pizza store clerk who had a massive shotgun leveled off at them.

"You've poisoned my own flesh." Harris pointed again at Kirsten. "You have poisoned her against God!"

Kirsten locked her eyes on his. "You're the biggest liar of all of them, Harris. The only thing you love is the spotlight. The only thing you believe in is controlling others. You use God as a weapon. You have no faith. What happened to you that you hate psionics so much?" The answer flashed in his surface thoughts, a too-fast-to-stop reaction to a question. As soon as she asked it, his brain considered it. His wife had read his mind and left him over what she'd seen. "What made her leave you, Harris? What did she find in your empty little head?"

A strangled gargling noise escaped his throat, too angry to form words, though his surface thoughts betrayed him again.

"Wow... your wife was psionic *and* religious. She really believed you followed 'the word.' Guess she couldn't take it when she found out the truth that you never believed. You knew a good con when you had one. Scream about God and people shower you with credits, adoration, and power."

"This creature is in my mind!" He twitched. "Kill her!"

Kirsten laughed. "You just admitted that I'm right, idiot."

"Don't!" yelled the pizza guy. "My finger moves a fuckin' millimeter and your brains are pudding on the wall. You boys ever see what a 42mm shotgun blast does to a head? These bad boys come with a free mop."

Both of Harris's thugs eyed the enormous rifle. People behind them cleared out of the line of fire.

Two Division 0 patrol craft came down hard outside; four bodies in psi armor charged out and ran for the front door.

"You..." rasped Harris. "You broke the law by doing what you did!"

Kirsten's gaze shifted back and forth between the thugs. *On the floor.*

The men, grunting and straining against the psionic compulsion, lowered themselves prone.

"And you, Harris. You disobeyed a lawful order to disperse, not to mention threatened the life of a member of the National Police Force in front of a room full of witnesses. That's a twenty year sentence, minimum."

"If you arrest him, it's going to be a media fiasco," said Dorian.

She sighed. "I know."

"Cast off the vile magic of Satan. Get up!" Harris waved both arms in an uplifting gesture at his cronies. "Take hold of my wayward granddaughter and let us leave this evil behind us. You shall be cleansed, my child."

"No!" Screamed Ashley. "You're gonna kill me just like you killed my mother!" She clutched her hands at her chest, shaking almost too hard to remain standing. "You're gonna tie me to a cross and light me on fire like you did to that guy a couple months ago."

"God! Why does she spew such vile lies and hatred! Why has my own flesh and blood embraced Satan?"

"He wants you to kill them," said Dorian.

Kirsten looked at the men on the floor. "This old con man wants you to attack me so he can turn you into martyrs. He doesn't care what happens to you."

"Police, Division 0!" shouted a man with a laser rifle. "Everyone, weapons down *now!*"

The other three officers made entry behind him, spreading out to either side and covering the room. Everyone who'd produced a weapon eased them down on tables, except for the old mostly-blind man who whirled to aim at the wall behind him. The gun jerked out of his hands, making him yelp, and floated over to the officer at the far left. The pizza man kept his shotgun trained on Harris and his friends.

"You too, Karl," said Nila. "Please."

Kirsten did a double take at the armored woman. *Nila! Holy shit; you showed up just in time. This guy...*

"God is watching, demon-spawn. He doesn't forget, and neither do I." Harris glared at her for a second before posing himself as if in prayer, but his hand went for the submachinegun abandoned by his bodyguard.

"*Drop it!*" yelled Kirsten.

The old man hunched forward, trembling with his effort to overpower the command.

Dorian swooped in front of Harris. A smoky aura of white energy billowed around him as he stepped across the veil, manifested. "Think carefully, Harris. The other side isn't what you're hoping for."

Reverend Harris fell backward, grasping his chest and wheezing. "She... she's forcing me to grab this weapon. The demons want an excuse to be rid of us." He struggled to look up at the patrons sitting at their tables. "Lies..."

Ashley let out a high-pitched shriek and pounced onto Kirsten with a hug from behind. Kirsten had her halfway into a ju-jitsu flip before she realized her 'attacker' was a teenager trying to cling for protection. She adjusted her grip from throw to hold, and carried the girl back around onto her feet.

"Sorry. Please don't come up behind me like that."

Dorian's energy aura faded with an audible *whuff.*

Ashley sniffled and nodded. "W-what was that?"

"Looked like a hip toss," said Dorian.

Kirsten shook her head at him. "A ghost. I'll explain later."

"Whoa," said Karl the pizza guy. "Was that a hologram?"

Reverend Harris lost consciousness with a gurgling rasp. One of the Tactical officers called for a MedVan while checking his vitals. Nila and the other woman rolled the thugs over and cuffed them before collecting their weapons. The Division 0 tactical team began the process of taking statements from the civilians in the room, though Nila walked over to Kirsten.

The old blind man grabbed at the air before patting around his table. "Ey, where'd my gun go?"

"Good to see you." Kirsten shuddered as her adrenaline rush subsided.

"Damn, girl... You keep walking straight into shit." Nila frowned at Harris. "Speaking of shit, where'd he come from."

Kirsten gave a quick explanation. Ashley offered "yeahs," nods, and whimpers throughout the story.

A trio of Division 1 cars swept in on clouds of cryo-fumes and settled down on their wheels out front. Five men and one woman in blue armor climbed out and filed in.

"You boys are late to the party," said Nila.

"These two are yours." Kirsten gestured at the thugs.

The Division 1 officers saluted her; about half of them muttered "agent" as a greeting.

Their sergeant, the woman, approached. "Agent. You okay? What happened?"

"I don't think I've ever been this angry before, but... I'm not hurt. This girl's psionic. She requested protection, fearing for her life."

"From these three?" Sergeant Ortiz indicated Harris with her thumb.

"Yeah. You recognize them?"

"Can't say I do."

Kirsten grinned. "That just made me feel a lot better." She indicated the room with a nod. "None of the civilians were involved. You can probably pin those two with a charge of brandishing a weapon in a public place. The old bastard tried to order them to kill me."

"Oof." Sergeant Ortiz shook her head. "Hope you got that recorded."

Kirsten tapped the name/rank/badge cluster above her left breast. "Yep. Probably on the building's security system too, plus witness accounts."

"They'll argue psionic compulsion even though its horseshit," said Dorian. "My bet is Command makes this go away quiet."

"All right. I'll send over our Inquest number when we wrap the scene." Sergeant Ortiz clapped her on the shoulder twice.

Kirsten bit back the urge to grunt under the woman's heavy-handed show of camaraderie. "Will do. I need to escort this girl back to the PAC."

"What's that?" asked Ashley.

"Police Administrative Center. It's where the dorms are. It sounds intimidating, but it's not bad. You'll be surrounded by other psionics. Kids, instructors, and mentors. No way in hell will any of those crazies be able to get to you." She froze. "Wait." Kirsten pointed at the thug who wasn't at the hostage situation. "That guy tried to give an explosive device to a six-year-old to blow up her psionic family."

Sergeant Ortiz nodded. "I'll add the appropriate charges. Any witnesses?"

"Yes, the girl. Ankita... Ravi. The poor kid's still terrified of being outside. I'll send you the file as soon as I can."

"Sounds good, agent." Sergeant Ortiz saluted, and backed off to oversee the rest of the Div 1 team.

"Hey..." Ashley raised her arms and let them drop at her sides. "If I don't get locked in my bedroom at night and have to live with the constant fear of being burned at the stake, it's an improvement."

Kirsten wanted to hug the air out of the girl. "Did they really?"

"Yeah. They always locked me in at night. My room even had bars over the windows... 'to keep the demons out.' If the building burned down, I'd have been dead." The teen's face paled. "I found burnt rope... touched it. Visions. Some guy on fire. I don't know who did it or who he was, but, uhh, yeah. Nightmares."

So much for the peaceful Reverend Harris and his 'faith' that prayer will get rid of us. She rubbed Ashley's shoulder. "My mother used to lock me in the closet when I was little."

"Really?" Ashley sniffled. "Why?"

"She was as crazy as your grandfather, thought psionics came from the Devil. One thing about ghosts, word spreads fast among them. It got out that I could see them, so they all started showing up to ask me for help. And Mother couldn't cope."

"Sorry." Ashley shivered. "Hey, if you guys want me to like testify or something about that burning, I will."

"We'll see. Clairvoyant visions aren't typically admissible in an Inquest proceeding. Come on. There's someone you need to meet." Kirsten took her by the hand and led her out to the patrol craft. "Doctor Loring's great."

She opened the door to let Ashley in the back seat, and glanced over at the hover-stretcher carrying Reverend Harris to the waiting MedVan. The old man shifted his head toward her, a hateful glare in his eyes even though he could barely breathe.

Kirsten contemplated sending an image of a Harbinger into his mind. She grumbled and dropped into the seat. Causing a fatal heart attack wouldn't be worth it. Not even for a miserable excuse of a person like Reverend Harris. His words, pure hatred masked in the guise of false religion, brought back memories of Mother. With the door closed, and the patrol craft between her and the world, she buried her hands in her face and wept.

Dorian rubbed her shoulder, a cool presence sliding back and forth. He didn't need to say anything.

Ashley poked her head between the seats. "You okay?"

"Not really..." Kirsten sniffled back tears, searching for composure. "Trying to get my mother out of my head."

"Sorry." Ashley held her hand. "Thanks for saving my ass... twice. Holy shit. I can't believe I'm finally out of that place."

Kirsten smiled.

Dorian glanced out at the sun gleaming off distant century towers. "I should probably zip over to the school and warn Evan to wear body armor tonight so you don't break his ribs from hugging him too hard."

She sighed. "What is wrong with this world?"

"I'll start that conversation once you're a ghost too. It'll take too long." He winked.

"Beats me," said Ashley. "Hey… can we get food on the way? I, uhh, haven't really eaten in two days."

"Yeah, sure. What do you want?" Kirsten grabbed the sticks and pulled the patrol craft skyward.

"Anything but oatmeal." Ashley shuddered.

23

INSERT COIN

After sitting with Ashley Harris during the forty some odd minutes it took to process her into the system, Kirsten traded hugs with the teen before trudging back to the operations area and her squad room. Lieutenant Commander Ashford looked up from the chair at the side of her desk where an interviewee would sit, and produced perhaps the warmest smile his corpselike countenance could muster.

She hurried over to her desk and saluted him as he stood. "Commander."

"At ease, agent."

"I assume you're here about the Reverend Harris incident?" She wasn't sure if she should remain stiff at attention or relax, and wound up somewhere between the two.

"Correct. It came down to a choice between taking a peek, or an exhaustive interview with a review board. I took the liberty of assuming you would prefer the expedience."

She relaxed. "Yes, sir. That's fine."

He gestured at her chair and sat in the side spot again.

She opened her mind, offering no resistance to his telepathic probe. Her brain seemed to writhe in her head as if massaged by a ghost's hands. Three minutes later, it stopped. When the room stopped blurring, Captain Eze came into focus at her side.

"Confirmation," said Lieutenant Commander Ashford with a nod at Eze.

"Of course." She smiled at Captain Eze, who repeated the mind read, though it took him seven minutes of a sensation closer to cool water pouring over her brain.

"I'm impressed," said Ashford once Eze broke contact. "Considering your history, you showed an almost unbelievable amount of restraint in that situation. I'm sure you were correct in your belief that Harris was attempting to provoke an incident, though I doubt the man wished to personally become the martyr. Command was concerned with possible ramifications of deliberate action against Harris and his followers, but you did about as well as could be expected."

"Thank you, sir. It wasn't easy to hear that same crap again. Based on what his granddaughter said, I have reason to believe he's committed or at least orchestrated two murders… but I have no proof. Also, I'd like to charge him with felony kidnapping and false imprisonment. They kept the girl confined to a small 'bedroom' with bars on the windows often twenty hours a day and slipped her oatmeal under the door. Harris might not be psychic, but he knew she wanted to run away."

Captain Eze nodded. "We are opening an investigation into those potential murders, though that case isn't going your way. Kurosawa drew that one."

"Oh, good. A clairvoyant is probably just the thing for that." Kirsten glanced at her terminal. "I've got some leads on the case I'm working. I think the victim of an organ harvester is trying to get his pieces back, or at least trying to take revenge on whoever got them."

"Ouch." Captain Eze cringed.

"Am I late?" asked a pleasant sounding somewhat familiar male voice.

Captain Eze grinned. Lieutenant Commander Ashford straightened his posture.

Kirsten glided around in her chair, stunned at the sight of Mikhail Kovalev, West City Regional Commander, strolling into *her* squad room. Despite his name and occasional (deliberate) Russian accent, the man looked Middle Eastern, and had the sort of disarming demeanor one might expect from a kindly neighbor rather than the man in charge of Division 0's activities in the entire city, his rank the military equivalent of a Major General.

"Sir." Kirsten jumped up and saluted.

Captain Eze and Lieutenant Commander Ashford saluted as well.

"At ease, all." Commander Kovalev smiled. "I'm not too late am I?"

"No, sir," said Captain Eze.

Kirsten glanced back and forth between the three men. "The girl called me, sir. I had no idea Harris was going to walk in there."

Commander Kovalev raised his hand in a calming gesture. "Oh, that's not why I'm here, agent." He nodded to Captain Eze.

The Captain produced a small, flat box with a black metal Division 0 logo in the center of the lid. "Kirsten, you've been active duty now for six years.

Your rank of agent was granted due to your unique skill set, and as you know, is only used for cadets who are activated out of necessity."

"Yes, sir." The Godzilla of butterflies rose up in her stomach and roared. She hoped no one heard the borborygmi.

"I know this is a bit late in coming, but I am pleased to be able to offer you a promotion to Second Lieutenant, effective immediately." Captain Eze lifted the lid of the box, exposing a full set of rank pins and insignia: a single black bar for her field gear and gold for her dress uniform.

Meep! Kirsten saluted him. "Thank you, sir. I hope I'm ready for it."

Commander Kovalev shook her hand, patting it as well. "Captain Eze certainly seems to think so. Congratulations, Lieutenant."

They exchanged salutes again.

"Now, if you'll excuse me... meetings abound." Commander Kovalev traded salutes with Eze and Ashford before walking out.

Kirsten stared at the box in her hands. *Guess I'm not a kid hanging out with the real cops anymore.*

"Congrats, Wren." Captain Eze patted her on the shoulder.

"Don't let it go to your head, butter-bar." Dorian winked as he gave her the traditional insult. "You're only a two-LT. You probably got more respect as an agent."

If not for Lieutenant Commander Ashford still being there, she'd have stuck her tongue out at Dorian. Captain Eze withdrew to his office with Ashford in tow. She sank into her chair, numb, and stared at the rank pins. Dorian took his seat at the desk behind hers and leaned back, fingers laced behind his head. She switched nametags with the one in the box and fiddled with it until it felt situated properly. The matte-black metal remained difficult to see against her sheer uniform top. The National Police Force had adopted military doctrine: field uniforms didn't conspicuously display rank to make it more difficult for hostile forces to target the command structure.

Kirsten tucked the box in her top left drawer. "Crap. I got sidetracked for so long with that idiot..." *Come on brain... stop spinning.* She pulled her NetMini off her belt and called Nicole.

The redhead's spritely grin appeared nine seconds later, rendered in six-inch hologram. "Hey, K. What's up?"

"Are you busy at—"

"Ooo. Your tag changed! Is that legit? You're a lieutenant!?"

"—the moment? Uhh, yeah I just—"

"Not really. Me and Forrester are on a patrol. Congrats!"

"—found out... You two mind meeting me some place for—"

"K, you have *got* to try the food at this place. I am *so* taking you out to dinner to celebrate!" The hologram Nicole leaned away, muttering low.

"What's the name of that place again? Oh. Right." She returned to the frame. "Sombrero's. It's south off the plates."

"—backup? My adrenaline's still spiky and I'd feel better with—"

"It looks like a tornado hit it, but the food is fawesome."

Kirsten sighed. "Some backup."

"Sure. Send us a pin, *Lieutenant.*" Nicole crossed her eyes and saluted.

Laughing, Kirsten returned the gesture. "Okay. See you there."

She unlocked her desk terminal long enough to log her intent to visit the 1UP clinic and send Nicole's patrol craft a nav pin. According to the map, their current location put them a third the distance to 1UP compared to Kirsten, so they would arrive first. Considering how Nicole drove, likely by a healthy margin.

"Coming?" asked Kirsten.

"Wouldn't miss it." Dorian dissipated into a cloud of fog and re-formed standing.

"Show off." She jogged to the elevator.

As expected, Nicole's patrol craft already waited in front of a cube-shaped four story building painted dark blue and covered with long strips of green, cyan, and purple neon mimicking the patterns of a printed circuit board. The logo 1UP flashed over the front door in a low-res pixelated manner, despite being a hologram.

"Guess they went cheap." Kirsten glanced up at it as she landed behind Nicole.

"I believe it's on purpose," said Dorian. "It's a reference to ancient video games. Fringers have an odd fascination with them. Probably because they don't require GlobeNet access, and you can fit several thousand different games on a device as small as your thumbnail."

Two figures wrapped in black psi armor emerged from the other car, one male and one Nicole. Squad Corporal Forrester approached and saluted her, while Nicole jogged up and gave her a quick hug.

"I know you two shared a bunk in the dorms, but you could get written up for insubordination," said Forrester.

"Zero's not that anal." Kirsten checked her E-90. After verifying a full charge, she re-holstered it. "Ready?"

"What are we doing?" asked Nicole.

"I need to talk to a doctor about a stolen organ. I have no idea how she'll react to questions, or what kind of augs she's got for protection."

They nodded.

Squad Corporal Forrester hurried to the trunk of their patrol craft and returned with a pair of laser carbines that looked as though someone stretched an E-90 to assault rifle size and painted it matte black. Small red lights swept forward from the area over the trigger guard to the tip of the barrel in a repetitious sweeping motion. He handed one to Nicole. "Damn, I hope we don't run into any augs."

"Yeah." Kirsten led the way to the front door. "Same here."

Bands of neon tinted the waiting room blue; drab green chairs stood against three walls. To her left, a brown-skinned man with waist-length hair sat behind a partition of bulletproof glass. Two terminals and stacks of holodisk cases occupied the desk in front of him. At the corner past the window, a door offered a way deeper inside. Her eyes watered at the mix of fart and sweat sock in the air. One of the chairs bore a suspicious stain. *Ugh. This stink would survive fire.*

Kirsten approached the window and held up her ID. "I'm looking for a Doctor Simonova."

"You got a 'pointment?" asked the man in a bored tone without taking his eyes off his terminals.

Before Kirsten could open her mouth, he flew up out of his chair and slapped into the window, face smushed against the glass, hands pressed on either side. Spit exploded from his lips in an artistic spray pattern.

"Look up, jackass. Police," said Nicole.

When she relaxed her telekinetic grip, the man bounced off the desk and fell back into his chair, wide eyed and staring.

"You are such a people person, Nikki," muttered Kirsten.

"Uhh, yeah... she's here." The man looked around with an expression as though he couldn't remember where he was. "What the fuck just happened?"

"Open it." Kirsten moved right, heading to the door. She pulled it aside when it beeped, and stepped through.

A short passage to the left led to the small office where the man continued to stare at Nicole and Forrester as they walked by. Ahead, a corridor led among six doors that had probably been white many years ago. Three gurneys, one blood-spattered, parked against sections of wall between them. To the right, another hall led to what appeared to be bathrooms and a third door labeled 'private.'

"Uhh, Doc? The cops are here. They wanna talk to you." Blue-green light from a terminal screen tinted the face of the man at the desk. He offered a weak smile and rubbed his cheek.

Nicole crowded Kirsten forward until she had line of sight on the man. "He's not gonna do anything."

Dorian came out of the wall at her side.

The third door on the right opened with a squeak. A woman with high cheekbones and long, straight hair, jet black with purple streaks, emerged.

Aside from the hair, her outfit looked reasonably professional. Black sweater and skirt, white doctor's coat, and black flats. Her face matched the file image of Doctor Petra Simonova, though the woman's height caught Kirsten off guard. Looking up at people made it harder to project authority.

"Doctor Simonova? I'm Age—Lieutenant Wren with Division 0."

Nicole giggled, but it only came over the comm channel, sealed from the outside world by her helmet. Warmth rode a wave of blush into Kirsten's cheeks.

"Lieutenant." The doctor offered a handshake. "This doesn't look like a clinical visit. What can I help you with?"

"I need to ask you some questions about a patient you recently helped. I have reason to believe the organ he brought in for implantation was stolen. I understand you were unaware of this fact, so at the moment, we are not looking at any investigation of 1UP directly, but your cooperation is requested."

"I see." Doctor Simonova turned on her heel. "Please, come in." She returned to the room she'd come out of and walked in without looking back.

Nicole and Forrester advanced as if expecting an attack, rifles up, stances tactical. They relaxed about three steps from the door, evidently monitoring the doctor via the amber 'ghost' projected onto their helmet displays.

Kirsten went past them and into a modest operating suite. Two medical tanks took up the far corners on either side of a gargantuan computer system connected to them by cables as thick as her wrist. A third line ran up along the wall and over the ceiling to an autosurgeon perched over a scary looking grey table with segmented black cushions and movable pads for arm support, upon which lay a bloody man in his early twenties, dark pants, shirtless, unconscious. His left arm from the elbow down consisted of gleaming plastisteel. Dark patches of metal on his head clustered at the temples, winking with tiny green and blue lights. His chest had been cut and peeled wide open, exposing his insides. One lung and his heart were missing—both of which floated in the tank on the right, and a tiny metal box sat on his spine with hair-thin wires running along the length of the vertebra out of sight beneath more tissue. A ghost of the same man paced back and forth by the head, muttering.

The doctor half leaned, half sat on a backless stool by a small workstation against the near wall, to the right of the door. She waved a hand at a holo-panel showing a little blonde girl in a white dress running barefoot across a sunny meadow, chasing yellow butterflies. The pastoral scene vanished, replaced by an array of small moving line graphs and one box of scrolling text. "What is the patient's name?"

"Finally," said Dorian. "Someone who doesn't bother with the whole privileged and confidential thing."

The other ghost regarded Dorian with a hostile glare. "Oh great. You fuckers get to give me shit on this side too?"

Dorian wandered over to him. "That depends. What'd you do?"

Forrester and Nicole tucked in behind Kirsten, holding their rifles sideways across the chest, pointed down. They glanced around the room, seeming comforted by the lack of anyone with cybernetic arms looking to tear people into smaller pieces. Nicole positioned herself to use Kirsten as a wall so as not to see the body on the table.

"Robert Lamb, though I'm not sure if he used his real name." Kirsten projected a holographic bust from her armband unit. "He had a liver implantation done here."

"Oh, that wasn't too long ago. I remember him." A black keyboard panel appeared under her hands, individual keys flashing bright cyan wherever her fingers touched. Seconds later, Lamb's face appeared on the terminal screen. "The liver was in an old container. From the condition of it, I figured it wasn't legally sourced."

"And you did the procedure anyway?" asked Kirsten.

"It sucks the guy died. I assumed the donor was unwilling, but he was already gone and I couldn't waste it and let Lamb drop dead on my floor. The man was in bad shape, Lieutenant Wren. I don't think he would've survived another month."

"Oh, a few more days on death's door and he'd have caved in and financed the regen." Dorian chuckled. "Lamb's not poor, he's just stingy."

The doctor waved her hand at the terminal, returning it to the animated display of the frolicking child. She crossed to the large computer between the tanks and tapped at a touchscreen. "Your heart is almost done, Zax." She smiled back at Kirsten. "Even though he's out cold, I like to talk to them."

Kirsten looked at the hovering spirit. "I'm sure he appreciates that."

"Come on, come on." The not-quite-dead man bounced on his toes. "The fuck you waiting for?"

"What happened to him?" asked Kirsten. "Does whatever you're doing usually take a while?"

"Our friend here decided to pick a fight with someone who had better speedware. According to his associates who dragged him in, he absorbed three bullets before he even got his weapon off his belt. He's fortunate to have a Phoenix blood pump, or he'd have been dead instantly."

"Right..." Kirsten scratched at her eyebrow.

Doctor Simonova smiled. "It's a mechanical blood pump that takes over if the heart is damaged. Lasts about six hours, assuming the nanobots it dispenses upon activation can close the damage to the heart to keep enough blood in the system."

"Man, that's *such* bullshit!" yelled Zax's ghost. "That dude was totally cheating."

"How is it cheating if the other man was faster than you?" asked Dorian.

Zax punched air. "Fuckin' lag man... I couldn't move."

"I'm sorry 'dude,' but I think you're confusing reality with a video game." Dorian shook his head.

"What can you tell me about the liver you put in for Mr. Lamb? I'm already aware it wasn't a good genetic match for him and had to go through some processing first."

"That's correct." Simonova hit a few buttons on the console in front of her. "The market for this sort of thing isn't what you'd expect. The NewsNet blows it way out of proportion. To hear them go on and on about it, a person's got a fifty-fifty chance of surviving the trip to work every day without having a harvester grab them. Most illegal organs are custom-procured by wealthy individuals whose proclivities present certain obstacles to health care of that nature. The vast majority of questionably-sourced organs are scraped up off the street after gang warfare."

"Rich people don't stay rich by spending big." Dorian shook his head. "Some of them probably get off on killing peasants to sustain themselves."

Kirsten glanced at him. "That's... a bit dark."

"It is, but it's true. My guess is that whoever Lamb purchased this liver from had recently accepted a job to source a specific body part for a specific client. The whole point of stealing organs is to save money, so it is in their best interest to find a genetic match for the desired organ to avoid the costly and not infallible need to run genetic conditioning on the tissue. Even with everything I did for that liver, there's a decent chance Lamb's body might reject it months or years down the road. Any tiny event might make his immune system wake up and realize there's foreign tissue. But to get back to the point, while your harvester was at it, they cleaned the victim out figuring they'd double or triple their money by sales of opportunity."

Doctor Simonova crossed to a small scrub station left of the door to wash her hands.

"Hey, why isn't he in the tank with the guts? I didn't think doctors still did work manually," said Nicole.

"His friends left him there and I'm not strong enough to manhandle him into the tank." Doctor Simonova held her arms into a dark purple energy field within a cube-shaped hollow to the right of the sink. "At this point, it's too dangerous to try and pick him up."

Nicole looked at the ceiling and sighed before approaching the table. "What about even pressure across his body?" *Ugh, this is so nasty.*

Kirsten looked away to avoid smiling in sight of Zax's spirit.

"If something like that were possible, it might work. However, any motion would need to be quite delicate."

Nicole handed her rifle to Forrester and held her hands out toward the body. "Open the other tank. I got him."

The doctor returned to the machine between the tanks. A few taps of her finger later, the left side tube drained to the halfway point and the cylinder wall sank into the floor, leaving about three inches of clearance above the top of the peach-colored gel.

Zax approached Nicole, leaning into her face. "What are you doin' to me, girl?"

"Back up." Dorian tugged him away from her by a firm grip on his arm. "She needs to concentrate. If you startle her, you could kill yourself."

"So you're saying that this guy had a buyer for some specific organ, and the killers took everything they could tear out of the victim because they'd already killed him." Kirsten hooked her thumbs on her belt and shifted her weight to her right leg. "So I need to figure out who initiated it."

Nicole made a soft grunt of exertion and Zax floated straight up off the table.

"Fuckin' what the fuck?" asked Zax's ghost.

"Truly a student of classic literature." Dorian golf-clapped.

"I would imagine so," said the Doctor.

Kirsten stifled a snicker at the doctor's response fitting Dorian's remark.

Zax's body glided at a creep to the other tank, reoriented vertical, and sank up to the waist in the goo. The doctor brushed her finger up in a sliding motion on one touchscreen control, which closed the cylinder wall. It sealed against a disc in the ceiling with a faint *squeak*. Another swipe triggered pumps. As soon as the gel filled past the body, Nicole sagged with relief. In seconds, the remainder of Zax's clothing disintegrated, destroyed by the nanobots in the fluid. Metal buttons and a buckle glided to the bottom of the tank.

"That was... impressive." Doctor Simonova smiled at Nicole. "Telekinesis?"

"Yeah." Nicole tried to catch her breath. "That guy's heavier than he looks."

"His major bones have been reinforced with indirium spars. These guys are all regulars... sometimes they're here three times a week."

"Idiots," said Dorian. "They live like they're in a game."

Forrester shook his head and handed Nicole back her rifle.

"Lamb couldn't have been the primary buyer or the liver would've been compatible with him." Doctor Simonova spoke without looking back. She tapped a command sequence that caused the floating heart and lung to rise to the top of the right side tank and disappear into a small opening. A short while later, they fell into the tank with Zax's body.

"Don't get too far away from your body, Zax. You might not be able to get back in." Kirsten winked.

The doctor glanced at her. "The way you said that..." She looked where Kirsten's eyes pointed. "It's like you're actually speaking to him."

"I am. He may or may not remember when he wakes up, but his spirit is outside his body right now watching. Not many people can handle that memory."

"Naw, I'm good." Zax grinned. "This is my fourteenth rez."

"Rez?" asked Kirsten. "What, like in the Monwyn MMO?"

"You're not being resurrected, Zax." Dorian rolled his eyes. "You're being prevented from dying in the first place."

"Whatever dude." Zax held his hands up. "Works the same for me."

"Thank you, Doctor." Kirsten shook hands. "I'll let you know if I need anything else."

Nicole shrugged. "Geez. That was kinda tame. You had me expecting mil-spec augs. You *never* ask for backup. Usually, Eze's gotta *make* you bring someone."

Kirsten walked out into the hallway. "Yeah... Figures the one time I bring backup, I don't need it."

"Better than the other way 'round." Dorian winked.

24

BLUE FLASH

The classroom blurred into a meaningless haze of colors and sound. Evan's head grew heavier against his palm until his elbow slipped across the desk, startling him awake. Moments later, consciousness faded as the process started over. Mr. Vasquez droned on and on about the Corporate War, tax evasion committed on a national corporate scale that blossomed into violence.

Evan's mind filled with the image of a blue van with guns firing out the open side door.

Hey! yelled Shawn's voice in his head. *Wren, wake up!*

Evan startled upright, blinking.

"... with their own armed and privatized security forces providing defense against civil unrest, the corporations felt they were in a better position to do what a so-called 'idle government' could not." Mr. Vasquez paced back and forth as he lectured.

Evan blinked and glanced to his right at the big kid three rows right and one desk forward. *Uhh, thanks.*

Shawn gave him a thumbs-up and shifted his attention back to the teacher.

It's boring, but don't let him catch you sleeping. A girl's voice drifted across his thoughts.

He looked to his immediate left at Annika, who resembled Shani to a degree, only with darker skin and thicker eyebrows. *Mom thinks I'm too skinny, but she'd freak if she ever saw Anni.* Her blue sweater had a pattern of white lines separated by flowers. For a second, the pattern morphed to resemble the front end of a van.

You okay? You're falling asleep with your eyes open.

Evan wiped his face. *I didn't sleep much.*

"... objected to paying taxes to a government they felt only wanted to sit back and collect money to be wasted. Major cellular providers were the first to declare themselves sovereign entities, not beholden to the government. Several major pharmaceutical companies followed soon after. Can anyone tell me what event occurred that the big three cited as a reason for their declaration?" Mr. Vasquez looked around.

A few hands went up; Evan's was not one of them. He shrank under Vasquez's probing stare, hoping the teacher would call on Mia in the front row who'd almost stood due to the enthusiasm with which she raised her hand.

"Mr. Wren?" asked Vasquez.

Crap. "Uhh. Blue van."

The class erupted with giggles and laughs.

"Try to stay awake please." Mr. Vasquez smiled at him before looking to his right. "Mia?"

"May 18th 2092, Corporations declare themselves independent from the government and refuse to pay taxes. July 4th 2092, since so many people were out of work 'cause they sent all the jobs overseas, armed citizens attacked the corporate headquarters of three major cell phone companies." Mia hesitated, tilting her head. "Mr. Vasquez? What's a cell phone?"

Evan forced his head to stay upright. The class's art projects shimmering over a shelf full of holo-bars all warped and shifted into blue cargo vans. He cradled his stomach in both hands to quell a sudden onrush of wanting to throw up, and stared down. Little blue vans peeked out from under backpacks and drove between the feet of the students around him. Innocuous in appearance, for some reason, they terrified him.

Evan let off an uneasy whine, attracting the attention of kids within two desks.

"Are you okay?" asked Annika.

"Blue van," said Brian.

"Blue van?" asked Mr. Vasquez.

Evan looked up; trickles of sweat ran down his face. The huge holo-panel behind the teacher emptied of its collage showing 300-year-old news coverage, and became a hulking cargo van with anthropomorphic features: windshield wiper eyebrows glared at him. Azure muzzle flare spat from the side windows like dragon's breath.

"Aah!" Evan trembled.

"Blue van!" yelled Annika, looking at Mr. Vasquez. "Blue van van van."

Evan stared at her, horrified. He needed Mom. Right now.

Mr. Vasquez waved to get his attention. "Blue van?"

Reality melted away in a swirl. The classroom gone, he floated as if astrally projecting in a scary-looking part of the city. All the buildings on one side looked shot up and abandoned, while the ones closer to him weren't so ruined. Mom, and two other cops in black armor, walked out of a doorway. Before he could yell to her, a spray of blood exploded from her head, chest, and left leg. Evan screamed as his mother died before her body could even hit the ground.

When the white flash faded, Evan found himself lying on the floor of the classroom, one leg up, sneaker snagged on the seat of his desk. Tears streamed down his face as his body shook from full-on sobs. Ignoring everyone around him saying 'blue van' over and over, he tore his backpack open to get to his NetMini.

Mr. Vasquez approached, a look of concern on his face. His shoes had become small blue vans.

Evan screamed and punched the icon to call Mom. When she answered two beeps later, the shock of seeing her alive lifted an unbearable weight from his heart and stole his ability to speak. He hugged the device and bawled.

"Ev? What's wrong?"

Trembling, he forced his hands away from his chest so he could see her holographic face. "M-Mom..." He sucked in a heavy, sniffling breath.

"Wren, please put that away..." Mr. Vasquez sighed. "You know you're not allowed to make calls in the middle of class."

"Mom. Look out for a blue van." He gave her an earnest stare, whining past a clenched jaw. "Stay away from it. I keep seeing it and it won't stop. Something *bad* is gonna happen." He shuddered and lapsed into crying.

"Oh..." Mr. Vasquez paused in mid-step. "You're clairvoyant. Agent?"

Kirsten's illusory head rotated to face the teacher. "Lieutenant, actually."

The class chanted "ooh, burn" at the same time.

"Mom. Please. The van is bad. It's gonna hurt you. I saw... I saw..." He choked up again.

She spun to look at him. "Hey, kiddo. It's okay. I'm all right. I'll watch for a blue van. I'll keep my eyes open, okay?"

He sniffled. "Okay. Please be careful."

Total silence settled over the classroom.

Evan ended the call and let the NetMini slide out of his hand into his backpack. Dread refused to release its icy claws from his heart. He wrapped his arms around his legs and hid his face against his knees, sniffling. He didn't care if they made fun of him for crying. The irresistible wave of fear permeated everything—worse than the way his room made him feel. Mom was in danger.

Annika knelt at his side and rubbed his back. The other students clustered around him. He looked up, surprised to find expressions of sympathy and curiosity. Even Shawn looked worried.

"He's really, really, scared," whispered a girl. "And sad."

Mr. Vasquez took a knee in front of him. "Ev, what's wrong, buddy? Do you want to go to the medical station or a quiet room?"

He pondered the quiet room... blankets and stuffed animals offered a place to hide, but the other kids around him had shocked him with their lack of mockery. He wiped tears from his cheeks.

"Is he a precog?" whispered Mia.

A hushed gasp passed among the students.

Evan stared at his sneakers. "Only for Mom... an' Shani. I guess me, too."

Class resumed on the floor, with everyone sitting in a circle around him.

Mr. Vasquez spoke in a soothing voice. "Some clairvoyants who develop strong emotional connections to other people have been known to have precognitive-like flashes of insight. The visions and feelings one can receive during these episodes are *too* real, as are the emotions associated with them."

He closed his eyes and tried to fight off the paralyzing fear that Mom would die. It didn't make any sense. The last time he'd felt this scared, the waking nightmare looked like a demon as big as a house. How could a boxy truck be so scary?

"Why is he still scared if he told his mom about it?" asked Shawn.

"A good question." Mr. Vasquez leaned down and right to make eye contact with Evan. "Still okay?"

"Yeah." Evan forced himself to look up. The urge to bawl like a four-year-old had passed, but he couldn't stop trembling.

"Assuming that we all just witnessed a precognitive event, there are different opinions on how it works," said Mr. Vasquez. "Some think we can alter the future if we become aware of it, while others think the vision leads to causing the very future we try to avoid. If the event were never to happen because we had forewarning, would the precog have had the vision of it in the first place?"

"Ow." Annika rubbed her temples. "My head hurts."

"His mom's out in the field now," said a dark-skinned kid named Byron. He scooted closer and put a hand on Evan's shoulder. "Couple of us got parents out there. My dad... We're with ya, man."

Evan managed a weak smile. *Come on, Mom.*

DEVIL IN THE DETAILS

Kirsten stood in the lobby of the 1UP clinic, three steps from the front door, tracing her thumb back and forth across the surface of her NetMini. Evan's worry about a blue van rattled around in her thoughts. Perhaps a traffic accident awaited her; a moment's hesitation might make the necessary difference. *He couldn't make himself say what he saw... did he watch me die?* Nicole's helmet turned enough to allow her to make eye contact. Squad Corporal Forrester edged past her and leaned out the front door.

"Well, I'll be damned," said Forrester. "There's a blue van parked two spaces behind your pat-vee. Uhh, reg is coming up to one Ron Santiago, forty-one."

The face of a brown-skinned man with short black hair and a 'hey, I just work here' expression appeared in hologram over her armband computer, receiving from Forrester's armor. A Division 1 cross-link in the database reported a handful of traffic citations and three pick-ups for assault. He'd served eighteen months for one, but got off on the next two.

"I'm gonna check it out." Kirsten stepped onto the street, hand on her E-90. "My kid's got good instincts so far."

"Didn't he say run *away* from it?" Nicole hustled up alongside her.

"He's also nine. He didn't say exactly what about the van was dangerous, but it's gotta be bad. He was terrified." Kirsten drew her weapon, keeping it aimed down and to her right in a two-handed grip as she approached.

Forrester advanced to within twenty paces of the back door. "I got three adults and one child about nine to eleven."

"I got 'em too." Nicole muttered something incomprehensible. "Can't get anything on metallurgical through the van... no idea if they have weapons."

"This don't make sense." Corporal Forrester shook his head. "Looks like a family out for a drive. Though, why they sittin' on yo' bumper, that's a damn bit of strange."

Kirsten reached for her comm. "Gonna check with Eze real quick. I wanna search it."

Nicole giggled at her. "Aww, that's cute, K. Police haven't needed permission to search for 200 years."

"Longer than that." Forrester raised his rifle, not quite aiming at the van. "Your call, Ell-Tee."

Crap. I know he didn't mean it that way, but that felt like a gauntlet being thrown. "It might be nice to live in that kind of world, but I guess it isn't the one we've got."

"Yeah, back then, everyone didn't carry guns either." Forrester chuckled.

Nicole overacted a gasp. "Your memory's better than I thought."

"Aww, go to hell, Logan. I ain't that old."

Kirsten walked up to the passenger door and locked eyes with a woman with light brown skin and long, straight black hair who appeared to be in her thirties. "Police, Division 0. Please step out of the vehicle, ma'am."

A pulse of fear flashed in the woman's eyes before she settled back to neutral.

"Wren," said Forrester. "Just got a hit back on Santiago's assault pops. All three were categorized as hate crimes. Every vic was psionic."

Kirsten tensed.

The woman opened the door.

"Slow," said Kirsten. "What are you doing parked behind our patrol craft, sitting here for so long?"

"We just pulled over to settle an argument." The woman slipped off the passenger seat and dropped a little more than a foot to land on her sneakers. "Place we wanted to eat ain't there no more, so we were tryin' to pick another one."

Ron Santiago eased out of the door, eyes locked on Kirsten. He startled and glanced to his left, no doubt at Forrester on the other side of the van. The woman's hands crept toward her belt, where a heavy green jacket possibly concealed a weapon.

"Don't," said Kirsten. "Turn around, hands against the vehicle."

"We haven't done anything." The woman got louder. "You're harassing us."

"Bullshit," said Nicole. "They were waiting to ambush you, K. She's freaked that you didn't just walk past them and she's got a Class 5 under her jacket. They're in Harris's cult."

"We are *not* a cult," screamed the woman. She grabbed for the gun on her hip.

Kirsten leapt at her, pulling the stunrod as she body-checked the taller woman against the van. The side door slid open, exposing a later-teenaged boy with a submachinegun. Three feet of azure muzzle flare erupted as he sprayed Nicole; a violet-blue energy field shimmered around her psi armor, sparking wherever projectiles hit the barrier.

"Shit!" yelled Dorian. He held his arms out and both guns lost power.

"Kid's in the way," yelled Forrester. "No shot."

Ron took advantage of Forrester's distraction and jumped into the van, climbing over the seats toward the sidewalk. Kirsten grabbed the woman's wrist in one hand, pinning her giant pistol to the fender. The woman spit in her face, but Kirsten twisted enough to get the stunrod up and touch it to the side of her attacker's head. Blue sparks danced around the woman's eyes and shot out of her nostrils. Kirsten held contact for perhaps a second longer than necessary. She used the woman's coat to wipe her cheek before letting go. The convulsing zealot collapsed to the ground.

Nicole let off an enraged roar. The submachinegun flew out of the teen's grip and smashed through the second story window of a building behind her. A second later, she snarled, and the boy's head jerked to the right, striking the side of the van door with enough force to cause an explosion of blood from his nose.

Kirsten kicked the woman's handgun away, knocking it skittering toward the front door of 1UP. Forrester ran around the tail end of the van, rifle pointed at the teen who staggered out onto the sidewalk as if drunk.

Nicole grabbed him and hurled him to the ground before locking his arms behind him in binders. "You better hope you're under eighteen."

Ron jumped out of the passenger door with a shotgun. Dorian's body erupted with blue-white energy and became transparent, numerous laser wounds in his torso and head visible. Ron managed a half second of scream before Kirsten jabbed him in the chest with the stunrod, causing him to lapse into a seizure on his feet. His eyes shifted to glare at her; foam seeped between his teeth with a clenched-jaw scream of rage.

Nicole yanked the shotgun away with a telekinetic pull, but took the liberty of cracking him across the skull with it. Kirsten caught his arm and flipped him over her hip into a chin-first landing on the metal sidewalk. She twisted his arm up in a chicken-wing, drilled a knee into his back, and reached for binders.

"K, these people tried to kill us. There's no point arresting them. Attempted murder on a cop is a death sentence." Nicole held her hand at the struggling teen, pinning him down with telekinetic force.

Kirsten locked the binder on the man's wrist and gathered his other arm.

"I... can't kill people like that, Nikki." She looked up at her friend. "One thing in the heat of the moment, kill or be killed... but execution? No. That's not who I am."

Boom.

Nicole flew back off her feet and skidded another ten yards into the side of 1UP, patches of blue-violet force field winking in and out beneath her.

Two small sneakers stuck up out of the gap between seats in the van.

Kirsten gawked. "Nikki!"

The redhead wheezed over the comm.

A boy, no older than ten, righted himself and pointed a hand cannon at Kirsten's head. Blood ran down from his nose, marred by a gun-shaped bruise. "Let my papa go. *¡Ahora!*" His angelic face twisted into a grimace of utter hatred.

"Kill the bitch, Julián," yelled Ron. "Do it!"

The little lights on the gun went dark. Dorian's spectral sigh came from somewhere behind her.

Kirsten stared into the child's eyes. *"Don't move."*

The boy froze.

She poked deeper into his thoughts; she was a creature, a demon, a *monster*... a psionic that deserved to burn alive. Seeing such animosity in the soul of a boy around Evan's age broke her heart. *"Drop the gun."*

His hand flicked open, the huge Class 6 pistol clattered to the street.

"Why do you hate us?" Kirsten's gaze lingered on him another second before she twisted to look at Nicole. "Nikki?"

"I'm hit. Fuck." A wet cough came over the comm. "That was a lung. Least we're already *at* a hospital."

"Calling this place a hospital is like calling CyberBurger a restaurant," muttered Dorian.

Forrester sprinted over, tackled the boy, and secured him hand and foot with plastic riot ties.

"You h-hellspawn... you used your demon m-magic on my s-son." The woman thrashed about in the aftershocks of a stunrod spasm, trying to pull herself onto her knees. "Julián! You can resist! Call on God to protect you!"

Nicole groaned and sat up. A silvery spot about an inch across unpeeled from her chestplate. Visual evidence that the bullet hadn't pierced allowed Kirsten to breathe again. Nicole wobbled upright, coughing up blood, and staggered over. Without a word, she punted the woman in the gut. "Ignorant bitch! You would rather she fucking *shot* him? Pull a gun on a regular cop, you get shot. You'd prefer that, wouldn't you? Sorry to fuckin' desecrate your kid with psionic power." She pointed her rifle at the restrained boy. "This little *angel* shot me and pointed a gun at another officer. You wanna see what usually happens when fucking morons—"

"Nikki, no!" Kirsten jumped into a tackle that knocked Nicole over into the open van door. Blood sprayed on the inside of her friend's visor, evidence of a punctured lung. She held her enraged friend down by the shoulders. "What's wrong with you?!"

In a second of eye contact, a telepathic link confirmed Nicole was only bluffing, planning to shoot the ground near the kid.

Ron bellowed and struggled to get up. Forrester ran over and pinned him.

Julián started screaming (mostly in Spanish) for God to help him before the demons peeled his skin off and ate him. His mother shook off the last lingering effects of the stunrod and pulled a knife from the back of her belt, out from under her jacket.

Kirsten pushed away from Nicole, who gave her a telekinetic boost back onto her feet. The supernatural speed of her motion caught the woman off guard, and allowed for an easy grab of the incoming knife-bearing hand. Kirsten wrenched the woman around and slammed her head against the side of the van. A little squeeze to the wrist caused enough pain to override her conviction. The zealot screamed and released the blade.

Seething, Kirsten pulled up on the woman's arm, making her howl in pain. "What you're doing to that boy is child abuse. Filling his head with such horseshit!" She rammed the woman's face into the van again by a fistful of hair. "You *do* realize you just tried to kill police officers, right? You *should* be dead right now. If I wasn't so goddamned *nice*"—she smashed the woman's face into the van a third time—"you'd all be dead!"

Dorian's icy hands tried to grab Kirsten by the shoulders. "Easy. You're about to break her arm."

"You got shit," said Ron Santiago. "You can't use your satanic mind reading in court. We were just sitting here minding our own business and you attacked us. Can't prove shit."

Kirsten hurled the woman to the ground and grabbed at where her binders weren't, already in use on Ron. *Dammit.* "Forrester." She held the woman down while the corporal ran over and applied cuffs.

Sirens approached in the distance.

"We don't have to." Kirsten smiled at Ron. "Everything you just said got recorded by at least three cameras—including your little boy shooting an officer in the chest."

Dorian wandered over to Ron.

"Dad! Mom!" screamed the hysterical Julián. "Don't let the demons eat me!" He bawled, struggling against the restraints.

Kirsten snarled. She pulled the woman up by her shoulders. "You think we're demons? You have no damn idea what a demon really is, do you?" An image of the huge onyx-skinned Hell-infused-Konstantin returned to the forefront of her memory, and she sent it into the woman's mind. *"That's* a fucking demon. Demons come from a place you can't even imagine."

Ron let off a tortured scream of terror. By the time Kirsten looked up, Dorian appeared normal again… and too innocent. Ron's courage looked as absent as the color in his face.

Four more Division 0 patrol craft raced in to land. Eight armored bodies swarmed the scene. One by one, they noticed Kirsten. Everyone seemed to be looking at her as if expecting orders. All Tactical officers, all enlisted.

Shit. Right. 'Lieutenant Wren' now.

"Someone call in a MedVan for Logan." She approached the panicking boy. "The three adults are charged with attempted murder on law enforcement personnel, but I don't want anyone going summary on me, understood? For one thing, I want information from them we haven't obtained yet. Second, this is complicated enough to warrant a full hearing. It galls me the most that these people were baiting us, willing to sacrifice their children to advance their hatred."

Nods came from all the armored figures.

She took a knee by the child as the Tactical officers dragged the murderous family toward waiting patrol craft.

"*Calm.*" Kirsten's eyes gleamed with psionic energy.

The boy went still, staring up at her, rapid breaths launching trails of spittle from his teeth.

"We are not demons. No one is going to hurt you. Please calm down and don't panic. I know you don't trust us, and this is hard for you to believe, but your parents lied to you." She pulled him around to sit rather than lie on his chest. "Your parents told you to shoot at one of us didn't they?"

Julián glared at her. His surface thoughts confirmed her fear.

"Do you know why they did?" She took a stimpak from her belt case.

"'Cause you belong back in Hell with the Devil." The boy squirmed, fighting his restraints, trying to get away from her.

"That gun you shot my friend with is as big as handguns get. Way too big for a little boy. You hurt yourself." Kirsten flicked the safety cap off the autoinjector. "Do you know what this is?"

He nodded, still glaring at her. Blood continued to trickle out from his nose.

Kirsten applied the stimpak to his shoulder. The device emitted a faint *hiss*, and within seconds, the bruises on his face faded. She held out her hand; her feeble telekinesis managed to pull the flattened slug that had fallen away from Nicole's armor into her grip. "See this? The gun your parents gave you isn't able to penetrate our armor. They *wanted* us to kill you."

He shivered. "No… you're lying!" The boy looked at his parents, who couldn't maintain eye contact with him. A glimmer of doubt spread over his mind, followed by nausea and fear.

Kirsten dropped the telepathic link as well as the projectile. "I'm sorry, Julián. My mother was nuts too." She leaned away as Tactical Officer Cortez came to collect the boy. With the scene under control, she joined Nicole sitting in the side door of the blue van, and held her friend's hand. "Sorry for jumping on you."

"It's okay." Nicole gurgled. "What's another inch of broken rib forced into a lung? I was too pissed off. Wasn't thinking. Forgot how you are with kids."

"They're Harris's people. I saw it in the bitch's thoughts. This is going to get worse." Kirsten leaned forward, head in her hands.

The rush of ion engines grew loud from above and left. Wind and bits of debris blew around both sides of the van, interlaced with small sparks and the taste of ozone.

"Lieutenant," said a female voice. "Medics are here."

Kirsten pulled Nicole's arm over her shoulders. "Come on, Nikki. Your ride's here."

Nicole closed her eyes and stifled a scream as Kirsten pulled her to her feet. She gasped with each step around the front of the van. Three Medtechs in white hurried toward them, pulling a hovering gurney along behind. A spot of pale cyan glow followed along the ground. Kirsten helped ease her onto it, and held her hand a moment longer.

"You get to go relax early. I'm stuck here for at least another two hours." Kirsten winked.

"Hey." Nicole coughed. "You better call Evan before he loses his mind."

Kirsten frowned over her shoulder at the van. "I'll be outside the tank before you're done cooking."

Nicole cringed. "Stop making me laugh. I'm good. Damn, I hate Class 6 weapons. Do what you gotta do… Lieutenant." She grinned.

Kirsten took a step back as the crew pushed her friend into the waiting MedVan, and muttered, "Okay, Harris. You want war?"

Dorian walked up on her right side. "Don't become what you've spent half your life hating."

"It doesn't make any sense." She tapped at her armband, calling in a crime scene team as well as some Division 1 units to cordon off the area.

"Hate never does." Dorian managed enough solidity to pat her shoulder with a clammy, sponge-like hand. "You've got a few minutes of quiet before the shitstorm swirls up again. She's right, you know. Go ahead and call your son now before it gets crazy."

She smiled and pulled out her NetMini.

PUBLIC RELATIONS

Kirsten sat on a bench in the hallway of the medical wing. The spot where Evan's face had been against her shoulder felt cold, dampened by his breath. He had limited time for his lunch break, and as much as she didn't want to be separated from him, part of her duties included seeing he got a good education.

She looked up when the door to the treatment room opened to reveal a gel-covered, naked Nicole. "What are you doing out there? Get in here."

Kirsten laughed. "I'm not hugging you until you're dry... and dressed."

Nicole showed off her chest, tracing a circle from collarbone, around one breast, down to almost her navel. "The bruise was *this* big."

She backed away from the door as Kirsten rushed in to push her friend out of sight from the hallway.

"I bet that little bastard had a busted nose." Nicole hopped in an autoshower tube. "Four ribs broken, one ripped my lung open."

Kirsten shivered.

"Yeah, no shit." Nicole stretched as the water hit her. "That thing hit hard enough to do that to me under rigid armor... don't wanna know what would've happened...." She stopped spinning about in the tube, looking at Kirsten. "I'm glad he picked me to shoot first."

"I should've sent Dorian into the damn van and had him kill weapons." Kirsten rubbed the bridge of her nose. "It's my fault."

Don't worry about it. Nicole switched to telepathy rather than shout over the dry cycle. *They'll think you're nuts if you start talking about ghosts. No other cop has that option, remember?*

Yeah, but I'm supposed to manage every resource at my disposal.

A towel jumped off a chair and draped over Kirsten's head.

She pulled it down.

Stop blaming yourself.

Nicole hopped out and looked around. "Where's my gear?"

The doctor shrugged. "Gone when I got here." He glanced at the medtech who looked fresh out of high school.

"Uhh." The woman bit her lip. "All she had was underwear, and we cut that off her."

"Dammit. Of course they wouldn't leave it sitting around. Psi armor's classified..." Nicole started for the door. "Fuck it."

"Nikki!" Kirsten grabbed her arm. "What are you doing?"

"Going back to the squad room." Nicole took a step for the door.

Kirsten gasped, blushing. "You can't streak the PAC."

"Why not?"

Kirsten pulled her back. "I'll run and grab you a new uniform... or use a towel."

"A towel would be more embarrassing than nothing believe it or not."

"I don't believe it." Kirsten folded her arms.

The medtech hurried for the door. "I'll get her a smock."

Nicole folded her arms and sighed. "Fine. Whoever stranded me here with nothing to wear needs to know it doesn't bother me at all so they don't do it again."

"Next thing I know you'll have cat ears and a tail installed." Kirsten rolled her eyes. "You can't run around the PAC naked!"

"I dunno." Nicole twisted around to look at her butt. "A tail might be cute."

Kirsten threw the towel at her.

"I wasn't gonna *run* around naked." Nicole laughed then put on a serious face. "Planned on walking."

A little while later, the woman returned with a patient's smock, a clingy white garment with super-short sleeves and legs. Nicole frowned at herself after putting it on. "This thing is so tight it's not much different than streaking. Whatever."

The redhead stormed down the hallways as confident as if she'd been covered in armor. Kirsten couldn't make eye contact with anyone. Eventually they got back to their squad room, and Nicole headed for the lockers to change. Kirsten went right to Eze's office, expecting he'd shout for her if she did anything else.

He looked up from his terminal as she walked in. "How's Logan?"

"Fine, sir. Back to her old self, though the painkillers haven't worn off yet. She's still communicating in full sentences before switching subjects."

Captain Eze laughed. "I read your report. The brass is concerned that acting against that little 'church' will trigger a backlash, and blow up in a big way. They do not want to give those imbeciles what they are hoping for. I need to commend you for again exercising great restraint. Most would've shot them as soon as they went for their weapons."

"Sir, are we just going to sit here and let them come after us? Attack random psionic civilians because of the ravings of a madman?" She paced in a three step back and forth. "I... We have to do *something*."

He raised a placating hand. "We are. I don't have the specifics of it yet, but rest assured this unprovoked attack will not go without consequence."

"Understood." She looked down.

Captain Eze gestured as if tossing something to her. No object flew, but her armband beeped. "I need you to check out this address. I know you're up to your eyeballs with the organ harvester case, but this just came in while you were waiting for Logan, and there's a child involved."

Kirsten's chest tightened. "How so?"

"We received contact from the parents of a five-year-old girl who's apparently seen a ghost. Sounds as though the child may require sedatives."

She exhaled. "I'm on it."

After trading salutes, she hurried out and ran to the elevator that would take her to the garage. Half of her hoped the kind of ghost that would terrorize a little child would do something to give her an excuse to smash it. It wouldn't be Reverend Harris's she'd be thrashing, but it would let off some steam. She tapped her foot and bounced as the blinding white capsule descended. When the doors opened, she sprinted to the car.

Dorian materialized in the passenger seat. "That was quick. New lead?"

"Different case." She shot out of the garage, keeping the car at an incline matching the exit ramp as she banked into the sky. "Some kind of haunt. It'll be nice to deal with a spirit on site for once rather than having to chase it all over the city. Scared the shit out of a little girl."

"Any idea why?"

"Not yet." She poked the Navcon. The pin Captain Eze sent indicated a residence tower 318 miles northeast of the PAC. "Ugh."

Kirsten turned on the bar lights and 'siren,' climbed to 1400 feet, and pushed the patrol craft up into the low 400 mph range. Forty-seven minutes later, she slowed and steered into a tightening spiral around the roof of the destination. So many residence towers clustered together here, flying above them made the ground look like an electron microscope view of carpet pile— if carpet pile were square.

She landed on the rooftop parking deck, half on the sidewalk by the door, and left the bar lights flashing. Three minutes of elevator brought her to the twenty-third floor, and apartment 23-09.

A haggard-looking man with a mocha complexion, goatee, and frazzled hair answered the door. "Hey, awright. You the psi cop?"

"That's correct. You are Mr. Short?"

"Da one and only." He smiled. "You know ghosts and shit, right?"

"Oh, I'm terribly sorry. She's never encountered one before," said Dorian.

She shot him a sidelong glare. "Yes, sir. Your daughter saw one?"

"Yah. Claire had a damn seizure in the bathtub."

Dorian blinked. "Wow… they have an actual bathtub?"

Ghost tries to drown the kid in the bathtub. Kirsten growled in her head. "Can I see her?"

"Sure. If you can get her outta the damn vent." The man backed up to let her in.

"She's in the vents?"

"Yah. Ran screamin' into the vents and hasn't come out since." Mr. Short walked with an arm-swinging, slow-ish gait that hinted he'd recently partaken of Flowerbasket or something similar. "My wife's tried everything from offerin' ta buy her crap ta threatenin' ta ground her 'til she's twenty. Girl still won't come out."

The deeper Kirsten walked into the relatively neat apartment, the louder the distant hushed mutterings of a woman's voice became. Halfway down a corridor leading from the living room to interior bedrooms, a woman who made Captain Eze look pale crouched down on all fours with her head stuck in a square vent along the floor.

"Ma'am?" asked Kirsten.

"Come on sweetie. Get on outta there."

"No!" wailed a tiny voice.

"Ma'am." Kirsten stepped closer.

The woman leaned out of the vent and sat back on her heels. Her red-tinted eyes had an exotic almond shape and inward tilt that recalled the desert-dwelling elves from the Monwyn world. She regarded Kirsten with fatigue and annoyance. "Who the hell are—oh, damn. Sorry. What took so long?"

"Apologies, ma'am. I'm the only astral in West City, and I'm stationed a bit of a ride away."

"Claire's been sitting in that vent for damn near an hour now. She crawled in there straight from the damn tub. She's gonna catch her death. Can you get rid of that damn thing so she'll come out?"

Kirsten looked around.

"I'll find the spirit. Get the girl." Dorian walked by, heading for the bathroom.

Kirsten knelt and stooped forward. About four feet in from the hall, two huge brown eyes peered out of a voluminous mass of hair. Grey dust covered a small shivering body.

"Hey sweetie." Kirsten smiled. "I'm here to make the bad ghost go away. I won't let them hurt you. Please come on out of there. Your parents are worried."

The child uncurled a little, but shook her head.

Kirsten peeked into the girl's thoughts. One second playing in the bathtub, the next, sharing it with a twenty-something woman with skin as white as a hospital wall and purple lips. The spirit bled from both wrists, smiled, and tried to hold the child's hand. It seemed like the spirit had attempted to say hello, but the little girl panicked.

"Well, that's not as bad as I thought."

"What do you mean?" asked the mother.

Kirsten looked up at her. "The ghost your daughter saw. I don't think the entity was trying to be harmful. The woman tried to say hello, but she looks pretty terrifying. I saw one like that when I was seven and I had a similar reaction."

"Are you saying my daughter is psionic?" The woman's eager look caught Kirsten off guard.

So far, every time she'd told someone their kid was psionic, it had become a 'get it out of my house' situation. Kirsten couldn't help herself and peeked at the mother's surface thoughts… This woman, and her husband, were into superheroes. To them, psionics were the same thing.

"I'm not sure. One second." Kirsten stuck her head back in the vent. "Claire, please come out. You need to get cleaned up and put some clothes on."

"No. I'm scared."

"I'm sorry Claire. If you don't come out, I have to get you out of there before you get hurt."

"I'm not hurt."

"*Come here.*" Kirsten's eyes glimmered.

Claire's stubborn scowl melted to a placid smile. After another second of staring into space, the child crawled forward to the opening. Kirsten leaned back and let the girl's mother collect her. The girl kept grinning. Kirsten stood and leaned close to her, eye to eye. A cursory mental sweep surprised her: the girl *was* psionic, but not an astral. From the way her brain felt, likely either electro or pyrokinetic, plus some telepathy she didn't know she had. Since Kirsten didn't have much in the way of the 'kinesis' spectrum, telling the difference was beyond her.

Kirsten patted the mother on the shoulder. *Ma'am. We'll need to talk once I address this ghost issue. Your daughter is psionic. I'm not enough of a telepath to tell exactly what, since her talents are still latent, but she's going to either be electrokinetic or pyrokinetic, maybe telekinetic. Telepathy is common as well.*

The woman's eyes swelled with excitement.

"Don't thank me yet." Kirsten patted her on the shoulder. "Children with kinesis abilities make for some *wild* tantrums. They're a handful. Tiny Pyrokinetics can even be dangerous."

Dorian walked out of the bathroom followed by a slender nude woman with grey skin, dripping wet, oozing blood from both wrists.

Claire fidgeted and whined, unsettled by the energy in the air, but didn't react as if she could see either ghost.

"Go on and take her to her room." Kirsten patted the mother. "I need a moment with your houseghost." She faced the suicide spirit. "Hi."

The suicide spirit ran over and hugged her... or tried. After a few seconds, Kirsten caved in and made herself solid to the astral realm. At the instant of physical contact, the ghost blew up in tears, sobbing and squeezing. Intense cold washed over Kirsten from the embrace, and it took a few minutes for the woman to gain control of herself.

"You can really see me..." Sniffle. "Please, help me."

"We really need to talk about a concept I like to call latent self-image." Kirsten clasped the woman's hand. "You're not required to keep the exact same appearance you had at the instant of death for eternity. If you concentrate, you can change how you look—like put on clothes."

"I didn't kill myself!" yelled the girl. "My name is Kylie Moore. I was twenty when I was killed fourteen years ago. I've been stuck in this apartment ever since. My girlfriend Gerri thought I was going to leave her for this boy from the Mars Academy of Tech, but we were just friends. That jealous bitch knocked me out with something and cut my wrists."

Kirsten cringed. "Is there any possible physical evidence you can lead me to? I'm sorry, but I can't do anything from a legal standpoint with ghost statements."

"Oh. No." Kylie sighed, casting a sad look at the ground. "Gerri killed herself already. Two years later... right here. Guilt got her. I forgave her, but she got pulled through this silvery thing."

"Why didn't you go with her?" asked Kirsten.

Dorian tapped his chin. "Parents. She doesn't want her parents thinking she killed herself."

"Wow. Yeah." Kylie beamed at him. "You're like smart or something. But please don't do it over the vid. Can they come here?"

Kirsten bit her lip. "That's not up to me. It's up to the Shorts, but I'm sure they'll be open to the idea if it lets you move on and stop haunting the apartment. Of course, I doubt your parents are going to accept me coming out of nowhere and telling them that their daughter was killed... you'll need to be part of the conversation and tell me things only you'd know until they stop thinking I'm trying to scam them."

"Yeah, I kinda figured." Kylie looked down. "I can appear in the bathroom… my energy is strongest there. I tried to say hello a couple years ago, but I think I killed someone."

"What?" Kirsten blinked.

"Old guy. I appeared in the mirror and he fell down. People in white came and took him out. I never saw him again."

Dorian cringed.

"Let me talk to them and see. Do you have your parents' PID by any chance?"

"No. I always used the contacts thingee. I don't remember it. Mom is Veronica and my Dad's name is Harvey."

"That shouldn't take too long to find. How many married couples with those names can there be?"

"Never ask that." Dorian winked.

AN HOUR LATER, KIRSTEN EMERGED FROM THE ELEVATOR. THE SHORTS HAD agreed to invite the Moores over next week, which of course meant Kirsten had to return to act as translator. Kylie promised not to scare the daughter again in the interim. Mrs. Short wanted Claire brought to the Division 0 facility as soon as possible for tests to determine what she could do, but both parents were so thrilled to have a psionic child that Kirsten felt sick to her stomach. Not that she begrudged the girl her family, but envy left a lingering heaviness in her gut.

The elevator doors closed with a hiss.

"What's wrong?" asked Dorian.

"Guilt and jealousy. Why'd I have to get such a shitty mother and that kid gets parents who adore having a psionic kid? And I feel horrible for feeling jealous."

She walked about thirteen paces toward the patrol craft before six orb bots flew out from behind parked cars. Her brain leapt back to a barefoot sprint across a grey zone while having orbs shooting at her, and she pulled her E-90. Before she could aim, a woman in a long red coat over an expensive looking suit ran out from hiding, followed by a pair of men. One had a backpack full of electronics, a huge beard, and appeared to have a knack for choosing cheap, ill-fitting clothes. An anticipatory air surrounded the other man, like a weasel looking for an opportunity to steal something.

Two of the orb bots sprouted microphones, the others glowed with spotlights.

Kirsten relaxed and let her E-90 slide back into the holster.

"Agent… Uhh, sorry, Lieutenant Wren," asked the woman. "I'm Andrea

Somers, NewsNet special reporter. Is Division 0 ready to destroy NewsNet property to keep their secrets?"

"The last time orb bots came at me, they had guns, not cameras. Maybe I should be asking you why you're sneaking around? Ambushing *any* officer of the National Police Force can be dangerous."

"Sorry." Andrea flashed a plastic smile. "What can you tell us about the recent declaration of war between Division 0 and the Reverend Harris's Church of the Redeemer?"

Kirsten sighed. "Well, if there's a war, it's a one-sided one. We are not at war with anyone. Those cultists are at war with reason and logic."

"What about the unprovoked attack on a small family only a few hours ago this morning?" asked Weasel.

"I'm sorry. I'm not able to comment on that at this time as it is still an ongoing investigation."

"Be strong, Kirsten." Dorian smiled. "I'm proud of you."

"We've learned that a family of four was taken into custody earlier today, with some violence. The Church of the Redeemer has released a statement claiming they were targeted for being faithful."

"Asking the same question in a different way isn't going to change the fact that I cannot discuss an ongoing case. You'll need to contact our media liaison, Captain Shanté Miller. Out of respect for the suspects as well as the officers involved, we are not speculating about anything at this time." Kirsten flashed an 'I wanna choke this bitch' smile.

Dorian clapped.

Weasel leaned in. Three of the camera orbs followed him. "What do you have to say in regards to reports that the Devil is involved?"

"Regardless of what exists on the other side, it's easy to get isolated, suggestible people who crave any sense of belonging to follow a cause when you scare them with words like 'devil,' and whip them into a frenzy of intolerance and hatred. I can assure you that even if such a thing as 'The Devil' exists, he, she, or it had nothing whatsoever to do with the creation of psionics."

Andrea glanced at a datapad for an instant before looking back up. "Isn't it true you have a significant bias against people of faith because your own mother didn't want you, claiming you were sent from the Devil?"

Kirsten shuddered with rage. The look on her face made the reporters lean away.

All six orbs fell to the parking deck with a resounding series of *clangs*. The lights on the backpack man's gear went out.

Dorian shimmered into transparency, his voice as icy as the energy wisping around him. "This interview is over. Go talk to the media officer if you want more. Now, get out of here."

Weasel screamed and ran. Andrea backed up for a few steps, wide-eyed, before she bolted without making a sound.

"Whoa. That's so damn cool." The equipment tech stared at Dorian. "Hey man… you fall in the line of duty?"

Dorian, trembling from exertion, managed a single nod before solidity crept back into his extremities. Once he ceased manifesting, he slouched, gasping as if out of breath.

"Sorry for us botherin' you. Thanks for your sacrifice." The NewsNet tech bowed his head, and walked over to the dead bots.

Kirsten stared down, caught between wanting to cry and wanting to scream and rant. She wound up staring without any visible emotion on her face. At a swath of cold across her back, she concentrated and infused her body with power, rendering herself solid to spirits.

Dorian put an arm around her. "Your mother is only going to haunt you as long as you let her."

She sighed. "Yeah, I know. I'm good. Thanks."

He held her for another two minutes. "Come on. It'll be almost three by the time we get back. After this morning, Evan needs you."

Kirsten closed her eyes and attempted to meditate away the last of her anger. "Yeah." Thinking of her son shattered any thought of religion, idiots, being shot at, or wanting to strangle stupid people out of her head.

The orb bots rebooted and zoomed off, careening around concrete pylons and parked cars.

Dorian shook his head. "Maybe I shouldn't have done that… who knows what they'll accuse you of now."

Kirsten slipped into the patrol craft. "You know? I'm not really that worried about it."

HEART ATTACK

I mages on the holo-panel moved about; voices murmured, but little reached Kirsten's consciousness. Some sitcom she'd never watched before continued as a background element to her reality while her brain chewed on too much information. She remembered starting to watch one of those viewer-submitted video shows where a crew of supposed comedians offered commentary on last week's best videos of people doing stupid things or making fools of themselves. At some point, the program changed to a sitcom about a human who'd married a synthetic woman.

Evan sat to her right on the couch, knees up so he could use his thighs as a desk for his datapad. He'd been busy with homework since they'd gotten back, except for the time they'd set aside for dinner. He caught her looking at him and smiled.

He's too pale... he looks worried and hiding it.

Her mind circled back to the ghost she'd been tracking. At Evan's unusual nightmare, she'd first thought the ghost had targeted her by going after random, unrelated people to drag her around the city and eventually drive her crazy trying to attribute a motive where there wasn't one. Now, at least, she had an idea of what went on. Someone had been killed for parts... but who? None of the net crawls, not even Sam's efforts had located anything usable yet. Between that, the Harris political shitstorm-in-a-box waiting to get out, and an upcoming meeting with two parents who'd spent the past fourteen years believing their daughter had killed herself, she wanted to go back on vacation. Well, technically not vacation. Eze had given her a month to 'recover' from Konstantin.

She wanted two more.

Of the victims so far, Lamb and Seraphina were the two most likely to have the resources to hire a ripper doc to source a matching organ. Lamb's new liver required tweaking, so it couldn't have been him, but maybe Julia could've done it. The Service Member's Medical Association had a reputation for being monolithic. The old joke went something like they save money by taking so long to approve treatment payouts, a third of veterans die before they had to spend credits on them.

Seraphina's been sick... live-in medtech. It fits, but I can't prove anything. I don't even know if she's had an organ replaced.

She slid a hand over the sofa cushion and onto Evan's ice-cold foot.

He laughed. "Your hand's warm."

"How's your homework going? You've been working on it for hours..." She tried to rub some heat into his leg. "You're freezing."

"I'm doin' extra work to burn off some cit points." He yawned, and his stomach growled.

Kirsten poked him in the tummy. "You're still hungry? We didn't eat that long ago."

"Nah." He shrugged, not making eye contact. "Guess I'm still digesting."

She encircled her grasp around his left ankle and pulled his leg straight, threatening his sole with a finger of her other hand. "Evan... please don't keep stuff from me."

He looked up; fear, shame, and worry in his expression drained her intention to tickle his foot.

She slid closer to him. "What is it?"

"My back hurts."

"Did you bend wrong or get hurt at school?"

He flopped the datapad up and down. "No, not that kinda hurt." With a defeated look, he sat up from leaning on the sofa arm and scooted to the edge of the cushion before pulling his pajama shirt up to expose his back, and a large yellow spot—a healing bruise.

"Evan!" Kirsten pushed his shirt up more. "Who did this to you?"

"A dream." He scissored his feet back and forth on the carpet. "No one hit me for real... I dreamed it."

Dreams don't leave bruises. "Did you fall out of bed?"

He shrugged. "I don't think so."

Kirsten pulled the shirt down before running to get a stimpak. She returned and sat next to him, debating if she should document the mark first. If something happened, not doing so might seem suspicious to the wrong people. "Let me get a good look at that, hon. I need to record it."

"Okay." He stood and peeled his shirt off. Another mark darkened his left shoulder, discernible fingerprints as though a large man had grabbed him about the neck from behind.

Directionless rage swirled in her. She pulled him into a hug and cried on his unbruised shoulder. "Ev... what's happened to you?"

"I don't know." He sniffled and started crying too. "Nightmares. I keep dreaming I'm locked in my old room and asshole comes after me."

She rocked him side to side for a few minutes before gaining the ability to let go long enough to retrieve her NetMini. After recording five images of the marks on him, she set the device on the cushion, and pulled him around to face her, hands cradling his cheeks. Kirsten held eye contact and peeked into his mind. Images of his former stepfather flashed by, a titanic figure looming in the glowing doorway of an otherwise dark room. Evan tried to run, but the man seized him in one hand and hurled him against the wall. The scene reminded her too much of Mother, only without all the religious shouting. The man simply loved to hurt this boy. As far as Evan knew, he woke up with bruises after going to sleep unharmed.

Kirsten stared into nowhere after dropping the link. He squirmed out of her grip on his face and grabbed her in a shivering hug. She held him, one hand sliding up and down his back. "It's okay, Ev. I'll figure out what's going on."

His hair tickled the side of her head as he nodded. "I know." When he leaned back to look at her, he wore a huge grin.

Kirsten pulled his shirt over his head. He hopped back up on the sofa next to her, wriggled into the garment, and resumed doing his homework. She bundled the images into a single file, and sent them to Captain Eze with a request for help, plus a description of what she'd lifted from his mind. As she typed out the message, she considered that a ghost might've attacked him in his sleep, but wondered why.

Never thought I'd do this. Eyes closed, she beaconed for Theodore. She smiled.

Theodore traipsed out from the back hallway about six minutes later, black semi-curly hair hanging wet down to his waist. His long, olive drab trenchcoat seemed drier than usual, and his baggy black shirt was thankfully free of bullet holes. Sneakers squished with each step across the room.

"Hi, Theo," said Evan without looking up.

"Hey, kiddo." Theodore smiled at him before winking at Kirsten. "And hey to you too, angel."

She rolled her eyes, and pondered taking the conversation out of earshot of Evan. *Oh, heck. It's his life too.* "Theo, do you know if spirits can inflict bruises on the living?"

He hooked his thumbs in the pockets of his dark fatigue pants, and rocked heel to toe. "Didn't that old doctor at that asylum come after you with a mace? Broke boards and shit, right?"

"That's different. That was probably an astrally bound weapon. I mean bare-handed."

Evan looked up. "I think somethin' hit me when I was sleeping."

Theodore's mirth faded to a grim scowl. "Now who would do a thing like that?"

"That's what I'm trying to figure out." Kirsten ruffled Evan's hair. "He wasn't awake for it."

"Any spectral traces on the spot?" Theodore raised both eyebrows.

Kirsten slid her hand up under Evan's shirt, making him squeal.

"Cold!" he yelled.

She concentrated, but didn't feel anything unusual. "No."

Her left breast exploded with pain. Kirsten clamped her hands over her nipple and yowled.

"Mom!" Evan jumped on her. "What happened?"

Theodore whistled innocently.

"Theo... You're a..."

"Pervert?" He grinned and bowed. "Why yes. Yes I am."

Evan concentrated until his eyes glowed, and glared at him. "You gave my mom a tittie twister?"

"Evan!" Kirsten tried to shout but wound up laughing. "Where did you hear that from?"

"Did it bruise?" asked Theodore.

Kirsten pulled the neck of her tee shirt away to look... sure enough. Purple. "Ow, dammit. What was that for?"

"You asked a question, and bein' the law-abidin', honest, upright, helpful soul I am, I had to provide you with the requested assistance." He smiled for a second before giving her a serious look. "Do you feel a trace on the spot?"

Kirsten held up a finger. "Wait. It's still throbbing. Ow." She grabbed her breast, cradling it until the pain subsided before concentrating. Indeed, a paranormal residue appeared in her senses, right where two fingers pinched. It even 'felt' like Theodore. "Yeah. Was that really necessary?"

"It was either that or slug you, and I ain't hittin' the kid." He raised his hands.

Evan shrugged. "It's okay. You could'a punched me to test. Mick hit me alla time, and I healed it."

"No way kid. Your mom would wrap that whip of hers around my throat."

Kirsten pointed at him, smiling. "You remember that." She blinked. *Healing.* "He's got healing abilities... Of course." Her throat tightened. *Probably the only reason he was still alive.* She grabbed him and squeezed, making him gurgle. When the overwhelming sorrow at what might've happened passed, she sniffled. "Can it go backward? Could he have caused the bruises himself, subconsciously?"

"How the fuck should I know?" Theodore shrugged. "When I died, psionics were only in movies. Ask me about ghost stuff, sure... mindwankery? I ain't got nothin'."

Evan's brows furrowed together. "Doesn't that mean you have something?"

"Smartass." Theodore swiped a hand across Evan's head, leaving a blot of clear slime.

"Aaah! That's cold!" Evan squealed.

Kirsten reopened the email she sent to Eze with the images, and added a question: "Captain, Evan's got a rating in accelerated healing... is it possible for it to work in reverse and cause an injury instead of repairing one? Perhaps driven by the subconscious in response to a nightmare of being beaten?"

She cradled her breast again. "Be right back."

"Anything else, girl?" Theodore tipped a nonexistent hat.

"Can a ghost induce nightmares?" She paused. "Specific nightmares?"

Theodore rubbed his chin. "Hmm. That's a good one. You know I've never rightly tried to do that before. Usually bein' 'round people is enough to give 'em the heebies. This kid's damn frustrating."

"You're not scary, Theo." Evan smirked.

"Let me do some, uhh, 'scientific experimentation.'" Theodore winked. "I'll get back to you."

Evan lowered the datapad against his knees. "Mom? You said with the psi 'hibitor, it made you hear what you're most 'fraid of, right? If a ghost caused a bad dream, maybe I just dreamed what scared me?"

"Hmm." Kirsten picked at the sofa cushion. "Theo, please don't do anything that'll generate a dispatch. I've got too much going on already." *Theodore's right... Evan's not afraid of ghosts. Damn. Another abyssal?*

Her NetMini rang. Expecting Captain Eze, she rushed over to answer. "Wren."

"Lieutenant," said a dispatch doll who looked eighteen, blonde and blue-eyed. The false girl projected as much professionalism as her cute face and oversized eyes could. "Your presence is requested at the General E. Evelyn Price Memorial Medical Center in Sector 9917."

Evan's smile evaporated. He went pale and stared at her.

She gripped his shoulder. "Is this an emergency? What happened?"

The artificial girl responded with a fervent nod and an expression like her parents had been shot; she had either a living brain or a fully sentient AI. "A woman connected to Inquest 24181108A1 has been admitted in critical condition. Before she lost consciousness, she kept repeating 'Wren... Division 0' over and over."

She looked at Evan, knowing she needed to go, but unable to bear the thought of leaving him right now. *Maybe I should stay... no, I can't. If that ghost is there, she's going to die.* "Okay. I'll get there as soon as I can." She hung up.

"Mom..." Evan's lip quivered. He reached up asking to be held. "Please don't leave me."

Kirsten took a knee and clasped his hand. "Someone's been hurt. You know I don't *want* to leave you." As much as it tore her heart into fine strips to see that face on him, that he finally expressed some level of resentment at her having to go away made her feel better. *He's coming out of his shell... he's not afraid I'll get rid of him.*

"I... Nila can't help." He swallowed hard and glanced in the direction of the hallway leading to the bedrooms. "I thought I heard Mick's voice."

That's what's scared him. Kirsten clenched her hands into fists. She'd seen horrors that would've probably left even Commander Ashford sucking his thumb, but if Mother ever came back, she might mentally turn into that terrified little girl again. *No.* Kirsten closed her eyes, remembering the not-quite-dream where she shattered the paddle with a lash. *I killed your hold on me, Mother.* She grabbed Evan by the shoulders and locked eyes. "Get dressed. You're coming with me."

Dread flashed to eagerness. He bolted for his room.

Kirsten looked at the ceiling after standing up. "It's only a hospital. Please be safe."

BUILDINGS RACED BY, SILVER AND GLASS LIT COBALT BLUE BY CAMERA-SNAP flashes from the bar lights on the patrol craft roof. Evan sat in the back, behind the passenger seat so he could see her. Once out of the apartment, he seemed to gain a measure of confidence as well as his usual color back. The change in him proved something had decided to invade their home. She glanced at the empty passenger seat. *Dorian must be worn out after those idiots. I wonder what he did to Ron. Bastard deserved it.*

Kirsten scowled at the lines on the heads-up display that traced a 'road' in the air toward the medical center. Shimmery highlights of bright lime green appeared on every century tower or advert bot that got close, helping her see in the dark.

"Wren?" Captain Eze's holographic head appeared in the center of the console. Rather than a uniform, he wore a dark blue top with a Chinese style collar. "I saw your message. How is he?"

"Fine now." She smiled back at Evan for a second. "I've ruled out direct paranormal contact, and if a physical person has done that to him, they're also telepath enough to remove it from his memory."

"I did some asking around concerning your theory of accelerated healing working backward." He pursed his lips as if whistling, but made no sound. "There's some hush-hush stuff circulating about an individual with a level of that ability never before seen. I am told this girl is supposedly able to affect other people with the talent… and has at least on one occasion admitted to using it offensively. Someone higher up the chain of command"—his hands drifted into the hologram and made air quotes— "did not tell me about it. It seems the girl managed to weaponize her healing ability during a moment of extreme emotional distress and the event is, according to that file I didn't see, not easily repeatable."

Kirsten's brain stalled at the mention of someone using accelerated healing on another person. "On other people? That's not supposed to be possible."

Captain Eze chuckled. "Neither are demons or ghosts. I think you might have a good theory there. Self-inflicted on a subconscious level. The good news is you're probably right. The bad news is, they want to take a closer look at him."

She cringed.

"It's okay, Mom. They're nice."

Kirsten exhaled. "Okay. I guess it's in his best interest to find out what happened. Sir, I'm about to land. Can I call you back in a little while?"

"Unless you've got something more urgent going on, we can talk in the morning. Have a good night, Lieutenant."

"Sir." She nodded. At least protocol didn't require salutes while driving hovercars.

The phantasmal roadway outlined by her HUD curved left and went down at an angle no wheeled car would've been able to stay on, plunging into a thick mass of green-tinged fog. She followed it to within a hundred yards of the parking deck attached to the medical center, put the patrol craft down in the emergency zone by the door, and left the bar-lights flashing when she got out. Evan darted after her before she could make up her mind if she wanted to tell him to wait in the car.

He pushed her and pointed at the door, which she took as an omen, whether or not it was merely the impatience of a boy. She zipped past the automatic doors, startling a group of standby medtechs waiting for arriving hover ambulances. Their odd looks faded as they processed her uniform, and settled back into their NetMinis and video games.

Kirsten ran the length of a white-floored corridor wide enough for ten people to stand abreast, and skidded to a halt at an information desk in coral orange-pink at the center of a large octagonal area loaded with bench seats, unused hover-chairs, and five carts full of dirty meal trays.

"Excuse me. Where is Julia Dominguez?" She held up her ID. "I received an emergency call?"

"Damn they start those Zeroes younger every day," said a bass voice somewhere behind her.

"One second, Lieutenant," said a living man, probably close to her age. Of the nine bodies staffing the desk, only he and a slender dark-skinned woman had surface thoughts. "Procedure room 33-E. I'm not sure you should go in there now, though. The system is showing an alarm state. Probably chaotic and best for her if you—"

"Best for her if I get there right away. Waypoint me, now."

The man gestured as if grabbing something from his holo-panel display and throwing it to her. Her forearm guard lit up with a minimap.

"Thanks."

She ran, following the holographic arrow over her extended arm. Evan sprinted behind her, clinging to his datapad. It led her to an elevator and showed a '33' for the floor. After riding down eight stories, the arrow brought her to another hallway, past a desk with three dolls—who all asked if they could help her at the same time. She ignored them and rushed up to a door much like the one she'd encountered when carrying young Brooke's spirit back to the medical tank in which her body floated.

A female security officer in a green military uniform with a black MP armband stood guard by the entry, hands clasped behind her back and a large sidearm at her hip. The nearly six-foot woman looked over and down at Kirsten as she ran up. "Evening, Lieutenant."

"Corporal." Kirsten leaned up to peer through a small window.

Julia Dominguez floated in a tank of peach-colored gel near the back of a modest-sized room. A man in a long brown coat stood with his back to Kirsten, arm thrust into the cylinder, forearm deep in Julia's chest. His short, black hair dripped blood, which disappeared a few seconds after the pats hit the immaculate white floor. A team of two women and three men in white coats scrambled at various terminals and consoles, shouting at each other, clearly at a loss to explain why Julia's heart continued failing.

"I need to get in there right now," yelled Kirsten.

The sentry swiped at the wall, opening the door. "Yes, Ma'am."

"Get away from her!" Kirsten shouted as she willed the astral lash into being. Ten feet of scintillating white-blue energy coiled out from her right hand.

Only one of the medical staff, a guy who looked like a teenager, noticed her, even with the shimmering energy tendril whirling around.

The ghost by the medical tank spun to face her. As she'd seen in Jonah's memory, the spirit had no eyes. Twin streaks of blood ran down his cheeks from the empty voids. His torso hung open and vacant, scooped clean of everything. Spine glistened under a layer of connective tissue, and the upper part of his pelvic cradle showed around a shallow puddle of gore.

As soon as he withdrew his hand, the alarms lessened.

"Stop," said Kirsten. "We need to talk."

"Whoa." Evan gulped. "Did he eat a bomb?"

The ghost roared, raising his hands as if trying to scare a little kid. Kirsten smirked. Evan folded his arms. After hesitating a second, the spirit sprinted left, disappearing into the largest computer core and causing a flurry of warnings to appear on every holo-panel in the room.

"I just lost nine process monitors!" yelled a woman. "All nanobots link-dead."

"Got it. Fail-safes are up." The youngest medtech forgot about staring at Kirsten and poked a few buttons. "Downtime nine hundredths of a second. Not seeing any appreciable damage."

Kirsten darted out and ran along the corridor, pausing by every room to peer in.

Somewhere behind her, the Military Police Corporal shouted, "Shit!"

Twenty seconds later, Kirsten skidded to a halt at a four-way intersection. A few old people in hover-chairs gave her suspicious looks. One toothless man grinned at her. An orderly got up from a chair along the hallway at her left and approached. Evan's glowing astral form emerged from the wall into the corridor at her right, as though he'd gone straight through all the rooms, following the spirit. He shot across the opening and went into the next wall.

Evan! Dammit! She looked around, feeling helpless. People with solid bodies had a distinct disadvantage chasing down a ghost.

"Can I help you, officer?" asked the orderly. "You look lost."

"No. I'm pursuing a suspect. Did you see a ghost go by?"

He stared at her.

Evan glided out of the facing wall and floated over to her. "He went outside and flew away. Want me to follow him?"

Kirsten forced her power throughout her body, rendering it solid to ghosts, and hugged his warm sponginess. "No... I have no idea what that man is capable of. Get back to your body."

"Okay." He grabbed the thin silver cord protruding from between his eyebrows and blurred into a streak of bright yellow light, vanishing back the way they'd come in an instant.

"Clearly, you got this." The orderly raised his hands. "I'm out."

Kirsten jogged to the room where Julia floated in the tank. The MP knelt, holding Evan across her lap. He wheezed and gave a thumbs-up.

"Please tell me this ain't your partner?" The woman shot Kirsten a horrified-and-somewhat-dirty look.

"No." Kirsten looked at her shirt. "Corporal Fuentes. He's my son, and he's fine. He was trying to help."

"By passing out?" The woman lifted him in her arms as she stood. Evan wriggled, trying to get down, but she held on. "I thought he fainted."

"I was in pursuit of a paranormal entity. My son is also an astral sensitive, and he thought it would help if he projected out of his body."

"Ghosts go through walls," said Evan.

"I'm going to have to insist a doctor check on him." Corporal Fuentes set Evan down on the bench seat outside the door to the procedure room.

Kirsten tensed. *They're not going to understand those bruises.*

Evan narrowed his eyes and made a face of extreme concentration. Right at the point Kirsten expected him to soil his pants, he stopped and smiled up at her. "It's okay, Mom." *I fixed it. I'm hungry now.*

"Fine. It's pointless, but fine. The body goes into a sleeplike state during projection." Kirsten pushed past the door into the room. "How's she doing?"

A woman her height with black hair and a nametag reading Dr. Amy Zhang looked up from a terminal. Bright amber light from the holo-panel saturated her white coat the same color. "Stable. It is peculiar that her symptoms disappeared when you walked in."

"Mrs. Dominguez was under attack by a ghost. I have reason to believe the man was murdered by an organ harvester, and logic leads me to believe his heart wound up in your patient."

Dr. Zhang frowned. "You just used logic and ghost in the same sentence. I—"

Kirsten projected a memory of what the ghost looked like into the doctor's mind. "I really don't care what you believe in or not. You saw her heart recover as soon as I showed up. Did it look like something was crushing it from the outside?"

"Umm." Dr. Zhang's eyes fluttered as she swooned into the desk. She paled. "W-what was that? Wait; don't answer that. Yes, the real time CT depicted what appeared to be a crushing pressure, though we were unable to figure out what caused the cardiac muscle to contract in that manner."

"I need to know where that heart came from." Kirsten folded her arms.

Dr. Zhang gestured at the wall. "Not here. We don't have the records. All I know is that her file shows the transplant surgery was performed at the Easley Military Medical Center, the VA's main facility near the starport. You'll have to go there for more information."

"Can you at least tell me what happened tonight?" Kirsten rubbed the bridge of her nose.

"Mrs. Dominguez was brought in partially responsive, suffering what appeared to be acute cardiac arrest. The paramedics attempted to defibrillate, but the unit died." Dr. Zhang shook her head. "Damn people can't be bothered to run the daily battery checks."

"Pretty sure it's not their fault. Ghosts tend to drain power." *Ugh. Whoever he is, he's getting close to killing her.* "Doctor, it's quite possible that this spirit is going to come back and try again. Can you keep her here under observation?"

"A couple days at most before the lawyers come into play. I can say there's a high chance of recurrence and we're keeping her close for treatment in the event of another attack."

"Then say it. It's true. She *is* at risk of another attack. Doesn't matter what's causing it." Kirsten thanked her and walked outside to collect Evan.

"There's a doctor waiting for him down the hall," said Corporal Fuentes.

"Come on, Mom. Don't argue. I'm okay. I wanna go home." He pulled her forward toward the exam room.

UNWILLING

Kirsten drifted in and out of consciousness, slumped over her desk. Staying awake while watching a terminal run a data-crawl would've been difficult after a full night's sleep and coffee. Doing it after four hours of sleep and no coffee had predictable results. Evan had been scheduled for a two-hour visit to the Division 0 medical facility for 'evaluation' of paranormal self-injury after school. It comforted her a bit thinking of Captain Eze's assurance they were only intent on finding out the mechanism of action of how his power inverted, and thankfully, no one had suspicion she had caused his injuries.

A uniform application of pressure about her skull lifted her head away from her crossed arms, seconds before a hot plastic dome lid pressed into her lips. The essence of strawberry-infused coffee wafted up her nose. Kirsten's eyes fluttered open and she grabbed the cup. The telekinetic grasp on her head dissipated.

Nicole walked by with a wave. "Two extra espresso shots in it."

Kirsten sipped, eyes closed again, savoring the warmth sliding down her throat. "Thanks. You're a life—"

"You get anywhere on that case yet?"

"—saver. Waiting for the—"

"Wanna go with me an' Jaden to a ZB show two weeks from now?"

Kirsten took her time with four consecutive slow sips. "—Scan to finish. I can't stand Zombie Ballerinas. Too damn creepy."

"Oh, it's just makeup." Nicole swiveled around in her chair. "How can costumes freak out the girl that fights demons?"

Kirsten leaned back in her chair, creaking the springs. "Well, for one thing, roaring with a microphone rammed down your throat isn't singing. Second, they look like undead children."

"Oh." Nicole cringed. "Yeah, they kinda do... if kids were five foot ten."

"Let me know if you ever go to an Antheus Rising show."

Nicole gawked. "You *do* have a thing for redheads."

Kirsten propped her head up on one arm, elbow on the desk. "I do not prefer women. She actually sings, and they're heavier than ZB."

Dorian glided in the door, which opened a few seconds after he passed. Morelli startled, staring at the empty hallway. He glanced at Kirsten, shivered, and buried his attention in his terminal. Dorian snickered and took his seat at the desk behind her.

"Good morning. You certainly slept in." Kirsten grumbled at the rapid flashing contents of three holo-panels over her desk. "You'd think they'd be able to make a computer search faster with all this tech."

Dorian grinned. "The faster computers get, the more data we force them to chew on. Hardware gains speed, software gains size and complexity. It's like running uphill in mud. As long as computers exist and as long as computers *will* exist, the people who use them will call them slow."

"I finally got a look at him last night."

"Oh?" Nicole perked up. "Who?"

Dorian grumbled. "Damn. Sorry I wasn't there. Burned a lot of energy with those idiots."

Kirsten inhaled her lungs full of coffee-scented air. "What *did* you do to that guy anyway?"

"Tried to scare him catatonic." I have no idea what he wound up seeing, but I tried to go over the top... skeleton, bloody wounds, and so on."

"The ghost wasn't interested in talking. I walked in on him trying to crush the heart of one of the vics. He ran like hell. I'm sure he's quite pissed off and taking it out on anyone who has his parts. I've gotta find that damn ripper doc."

"And do what?" asked Dorian. "You'll never be able to get official charges to stick based on a ghost's testimony."

She sighed, looking around at the walls for answers. "Maybe the ghost can lead us to physical evidence... *If* I can get him to talk. We have to try to do something. I'm so sick of waiting around for him to attack someone and hoping I can get there fast enough."

"Well you've got a number of people who've been attacked... they've all had organ replacements?"

"Two don't fit the pattern, but I'm not sure about Seraphina. The girl from the orbital construction platform *was* injured, but only had her legs broken.

That doesn't seem like it should require organ replacement. All the damage happened below the hips."

Nicole lost interest and opened a net crawler while munching on an egg sandwich.

"Maybe you can trace the heart from that Dominguez woman?" asked Dorian.

"That's what I'm trying to do." She scowled at the computer, and looked back at Dorian. *It stopped.* She whipped back around to face her terminal screens. "Hit!"

According to the records from the Easley Military Medical Center, one Dominguez, Julia R. was approved for a transplant heart received from a donor by the name of Darius Cook. Kirsten put a finger on that name and flung it at a holo-panel to the right of the one displaying the medical file. Within four seconds, a mugshot of a young black man appeared. Glowing blue NanoLED tattoos circled above both eyebrows and ran down the sides of his head in what appeared to be ancient runes.

"Pantheon," said Dorian.

"What?" Kirsten glanced back at him for a second.

"It's a street gang. Started on Mars, came down here about nine years ago give or take… or at least we noticed them nine years ago. They adopt a lot of affectations of very ancient pagan religions, but it's all for show and intimidation—no actual belief."

Kirsten swallowed. "I don't like this…"

"I'm ninety-nine percent sure this is not another Konstantin situation. There's no ancient mysticism going on here, just a lot of drugs and people who think that stuff is cool."

"Hmm." She swiped at the screen. "Darius… Age twenty-four. Died three months ago to 'gang violence.' No listed next of kin. Also no record of him being a donor. Looks like the hospital helped themselves to his parts. The spirit I saw didn't look anything like him." Kirsten narrowed her eyes at the picture of a dead man, tapping a finger to her lips. *Darius, you weren't trying to crush Julia's heart, so what happened to you? Did you even exist?* She turned to the left-most screen and the chat system, and poked Sam Chang's entry.

His face appeared in under a second, grinning. "Hey. Morning."

"Sam, can you—"

Nicole landed on her shoulder with one arm across her back, heads touching. "Oh, he is *so* in love with you."

Sam blushed.

Kirsten shoved her off, red-faced herself and giggling from nerves. "Nikki! Do you mind?"

"Nope. I don't mind." chirped Nicole. She took four steps backward and fell into her chair.

"Ugh. Sorry." Kirsten couldn't look at either of them.

"She's right." Sam cleared his throat. "What'cha need?"

Kirsten dragged Darius onto the chat window. "Can you tell me if this guy is real?"

"Oh, I thought you were going to ask me for something hard."

Nicole almost fell off her chair laughing.

Kirsten wanted to crawl under the desk.

Dorian coughed.

"Not you, too!" rasped Kirsten.

Her spectral partner raised his hands. "He said it."

"And you thought it!" She grumbled.

Sam looked down with the face of a scolded schoolboy. "I'm so sorry. I didn't mean it that way."

"It's not your fault my squad room is full of twelve-year-olds." Kirsten fumed from embarrassment.

"Got it." Sam glanced at something off to his right. "Darius Cook appears to be real, or at least was. Youngest son of Lawrence and Davina Cook. Guess he came along late. His next closest sibling is—oh, was, forty-three. Parents are listed deceased, natural causes. Oldest brother was killed in action on Mars, UCF Marines. Sister is apparently still alive. Her listing says she moved to a colony world, but doesn't specify which one. The middle brother died two years ago, also gang related."

Kirsten fidgeted. "Can you find any record of donating his organs? What facility processed his remains?"

"Easley got him... and no. No donor record."

She stood. "Can you go deep? I'm coming."

Nicole fell out of her chair, crimson-faced and gasping for air between laughs.

Kirsten glared at the ceiling. "I am on my way to where you are located."

Dorian battled a smile off his face, lost his composure, and snickered.

"You're both impossible." Kirsten stomped toward the door, shaking her head.

29

DATA MINING

Kirsten glared at the windscreen for the entire ten-minute ride to the Regional Tech Center. She landed the patrol craft and stormed across the roof to the entrance. As the doors slid open with a hiss, she pivoted toward Dorian.

"Thanks for not asking why I didn't just stay on the vid with him."

Dorian followed her in, smiling. "Well, I figured you were either putting some space between you and Nicole before you became seriously angry with her, or you wanted to see Sam. Shall I wait in the car?"

Kirsten smiled. "It's okay. Not like we're going to get cute in the middle of the network room. Besides, I think your friend Neal misses you. Sam said he's taken down all the ofuda and incense sticks."

Dorian snickered.

After a short walk to another elevator, and a longer corridor to a Division 2 network room, Kirsten resisted the urge to bounce down three steps into the sunken room. Fourteen workstations sat by spider-like arrangements of arms holding up holo-bars. Raised floor tiles clicked and shifted under her boots; gaps revealed a rat's nest of wires in the six-inch space between walking surface and actual floor. Five other men slumped over in their chairs, their consciousness lost via wires to the virtual world.

Sam grinned at her from his desk while the fuchsia-haired woman near the middle of the room shot radiated her usual territorial glare.

Kirsten glanced at her. *What's your problem? Not like you were interested in him.*

The woman jumped as if startled, and grabbed her neck. Once the initial shock wore off, she gave Kirsten a beckoning look and wandered down a narrow interior hall toward the ladies' room.

"One sec, Sam." Kirsten headed after her.

Dorian sauntered up behind the arrogant tech who'd assumed Kirsten clueless about computers. He cracked his knuckles, wiggled his fingers with anticipation, and stuck his hand into the terminal.

Kirsten entered the bathroom, treating it like an unsecured crime scene. Once she noted the pink-haired techie woman sat on a counter bearing a row of sinks a good fifteen feet from the door, (and didn't appear about to attack her) she relaxed.

"I don't trust blondes." The girl folded her arms. "Sam's a good friend, almost like my kid brother."

"I've barely seen you talk to him."

The girl sighed. "He's not great with soft skills. Some part of his brain was likely afraid he'd blow his chances with you if he acknowledged me in any way."

"Do you normally flash your tits in your brother's face?" Kirsten set her hands on her hips.

"Can we skip the catty shit please?" The tech let her arms drop. "I just don't want him to get hurt. You seemed so… out of it and snobby, like you were messing with him. You practically had this 'oh, gawd, the nerd is looking at me' thing going. They said you were an arm-hanger of this dude like richer than the whole UCF."

Kirsten slouched and walked over to lean her butt against the counter next to the girl. "That 'dude' is dead. I killed him, and the demon he turned into after he got back up." She traced a finger around her bare right wrist. "I wasn't myself. I don't know if you believe in supernatural things, but I had a demon *forcing* me to idolize that man. When I was near Sam, I got sick. The real part of me felt an attraction to him, but the thing in the bracelet hurt me."

"Is that why you threw up on his desk?" The girl covered her mouth to mute a gasp. "I thought you were like disgusted that a techie was into you."

"No." She smiled. "Sam's way more my speed than that old bastard."

"I'm Piper." She offered a hand. "Truce?"

Kirsten accepted. "Truce."

Piper pulled her closer, nose-to-nose, smiling. "Okay. But if you hurt him, I will motherfucking rule your life from the net. You won't be rid of me unless you're living in the Badlands, forty miles from anything plugged in. Got me?"

"I understand you, but you should know my partner's a ghost, and very protective. I imagine his response to that would be draining the power out of everything technological you tried to use, and leaving you stranded in a veritable Badlands of nonfunctioning hardware."

"Harsh." Piper shivered. "Look, just don't hurt him. He's brittle."

Kirsten shot a sad smile at the floor. "Maybe I'm taking things a bit too slow." *I should have that apple pie before it's too late.*

"Hey." Piper clapped a hand on her shoulder. "Sort your baggage, but be honest with him. 'Kay?"

"I will." Kirsten pushed off the sink. "Kinda in a hurry. Maybe we can talk more later? This case is kicking my ass."

"We'll see." Piper winked.

Kirsten left the bathroom and stopped dead in her tracks at the entrance to the tech room floor. Neal sat cross-legged on his office chair in the pose of a Buddhist monk with a large wireframe pyramid over his head and dozens of crystals arranged around his workstation, which displayed a series of crash dump screens.

Dorian had flopped in the chair next to Sam's desk, in tears from laughter.

Kirsten, shaking her head, hurried over. "Sam?"

He whirled about and looked up at her. "Hey. You two didn't kill each other."

"Nope." She leaned down and kissed him. When their lips pulled apart a minute later, she stared into his eyes. "I'm sorry I don't have more time."

"Yeah, it's cool. I found something." He gestured at the holo-panel. "Darius Cook was killed in a shootout with Diablos. I have the autopsy scans here." A fifteen-inch long holographic apparition of Darius's body floated over the desk, rotating to show wounds. "As you can see, he took three slugs center mass. Coroner's report listed them as 13mm hollow points. Class 5 pistol rounds. There wouldn't have been enough left of his heart to transplant into a mouse."

"They couldn't have repaired it?" asked Kirsten.

Sam shrugged. "I'm not a doctor, but look at it." A fist-sized mass of fleshy ribbons levitated away from the virtual Darius. "If they can remake *that* into a heart for transplant, it's probably as expensive as regenerating the patient's own tissue. There's no benefit."

"Looks like I'm going to Easley." Kirsten gave his hand a squeeze. "The first time I have a sane minute, I'd like you to come over."

Sam grinned. "I'd like that."

"Sane minute?" Dorian shook his head. "Poor boy's going to be waiting awhile."

Kirsten laughed.

"Uhh…" Sam looked terrified.

"Dorian said something funny. It's not you." She leaned down to kiss him. "You'll have to get used to me sometimes reacting to spirits."

Sam melted into his chair; the way his clothes flattened conjured the image of a deflated person. "Sorry. I understand. See you soon?"

"I hope so… Wish me luck." She walked backward two steps. *I'm as scared as you are about it, but I might be falling in love.*

His face reddened, though he grinned.

Dorian approached the meditating tech, holding his hand as if about to knock several crystals over.

"Stop," whispered Kirsten. "You're going to break him." She waved for him to follow. "We've gotta go."

He caught up to her by the door. "You know, Theodore might have something. There is a certain degree of amusement to be had in messing with idiots."

"That one's wound too tight." Kirsten jogged for the elevator. "If this turns out to be another dead end, I'm going to need Doctor Loring to talk me down from doing something stupid."

"I don't like the sound of that." Dorian slipped past the closing doors into the elevator.

Neither do I.

30

THE ART OF NEGOTIATION

Easley Military Medical Center sat within visual range of the Edmonson Memorial Starport. Bright lights from the ground cast three massive ships in a wash of harsh shadows, except for tiny dots of glowing windows. Kirsten shuddered at the memory of her last visit to the place, dealing with a man crushed under the landing gear of a Mars-Earth passenger shuttle. She looked away from the distant 'hole' in the city structure, where a safety-standoff prevented construction of anything too tall within a certain distance deemed necessary in case of an accident. It seemed ludicrous given the sizes of some of the vessels that landed there as well as the population density of the surroundings… plus the elevated city. If something went seriously wrong with a starship coming in to land, the death toll would be astronomical.

She set the patrol craft down in a spot labeled 'visitors' a decent walk from the main entrance, surrounded by warning signs indicating MedVan lanes were not to be blocked off. Within seconds of opening the door, the acrid burn of Cryomil fumes from the distant starport scorched the inside of her nostrils and throat. Kirsten coughed, sneezed, and spat twice on the textured plasticrete before getting out.

"Damn, it's stronger up here than it was on the tarmac." Dorian made a snorting noise. "Must be riding the wind up… I can taste it and I'm dead."

Her attempt to laugh caused her eyes to water. She jogged for the facility doors, eager to get out of the foul-smelling air.

A few two-foot wide orb bots, painted dark blue and white, glided around the parking area. Both had a single rotating yellow flasher on top of them, and the word 'Security' stenciled on their sides. Each carried a tiny version of a minigun canted upward at a safed angle on the front of the bottom half. The weapons appeared sized for pistol rounds, but the mere sight of it hurt.

Well, this is technically a military installation.

Unease gripped her. Thinking of soldiers reminded her of being shot three times. *I wonder how Commissioner Vernon is doing...*

A pair of doors opened at the western edge of the roof deck, allowing her entry to a corridor that descended at a gentle angle for at least fifty yards. The logo of the medical center—EMMC—interrupted a thick green stripe along both walls at about chest level.

Kirsten hurried past a few offices and another door marked security, jogging until the ground levelled out. Holograms floated near the ceiling, indicating 'emergency arrivals' were to go left, 'admitting' straight ahead, and 'gift shop,' 'cafeteria,' 'information,' 'physical therapy,' 'cybernetic services,' and 'other' all pointed right. She headed right, moving past a few skinny female dolls in white scrubs who stood motionless by hover-chairs, waiting to be needed. An antiseptic chemical fragrance finally displaced the memory of starship fuel from her nose.

"That is so damn creepy," said Dorian. "Why do they need to make machines look so much like people when they have them function like machines? Those 'women' standing around with vacant stares is just *wrong.*"

"I don't know." She diverted to an information desk staffed by two women and a man in camouflage uniforms. A petite woman with a cute face, dark skin, and cornrows sat closest, so she approached her. "Excuse me, sergeant."

The attendant looked up. Her expression betrayed momentary shock, presumably taking Kirsten for a young teenager before she spotted the badge. The instant realization set in, the woman stood and saluted. "Lieutenant. What can I do for you?"

"I need to see whoever is in charge of overseeing organ transplants. I'm here in an official capacity pursuant to an active Inquest."

"Umm... I've no idea who that could be." She sat behind her terminal. "Bear with me a moment."

Kirsten waited while the woman tapped away at her terminal for a few minutes.

"Okay, you'll want to talk with Doctor Drew Samuels. He's in the other tower, sixtieth floor at the offices. Looks like he's in now. Do you want me to let him know you're on the way up?"

"No rank?"

The young sergeant smiled. "Most of the medical staff is privatized. Some of the medtechs and a handful of doctors rotate in from active duty, but we need them out in the field where the civilian doctors don't want to be."

"Oh." Kirsten pointed to her right. "That way? Elevators?"

The sergeant leaned up over the counter and pointed, hooking her hand to the right. "Through the elevator lobby, 'round the corner, there's a bridge to the other building. Elevators on the other side."

"Thanks."

Kirsten jogged along, dodging two hover-chairs emerging from sliding doors. Beyond the glaring lights of the elevator lobby, a glass-walled tunnel spanned an eight-lane road to a century tower. Thousands of hovercars shot by, both above and below the tube. A similar blue stripe ran up the left side of the tower's face, with an EMMC that spanned four stories about halfway up.

She refused to look at the locust swarm of hovercars as she ran down the transparent tunnel, nor did she peer out the curved sides past the floor at distant ground traffic. She stopped running when she reached an elevator lobby inside the tower, and paused a few seconds to let her heart rate slow.

"I didn't know you were afraid of heights," said Dorian.

"I'm not." She hit the call button. "I'm afraid of being in a glass tube getting hit by a hovercar doing three hundred miles an hour."

Dorian chuckled. "I wonder what that phobia is called. Bet it's a really long word."

The elevator shot upward, reaching from the thirty-first to the sixtieth floor in the span of a breath and a half. She found the office of Doctor Samuels by following small green holographic signs jutting out from the walls near each door, and knocked.

"Come in, Lieutenant."

She entered a large, but modestly decorated, office. Shelves laden with holodisk cases, small statuettes, and plaques lined both sides. Digital windows covered the entire wall behind a stout brick-shaped desk of cherry red Epoxil, displaying a snowy forest. The man behind the desk stood to extend a hand in greeting. He seemed young for his position, perhaps mid-forties, and wore a silvery suit with a dark purple shirt, no tie. Traces of grey smeared across the sides of a short-trimmed afro, as though someone had highlighted him with an airbrush.

"Doctor Samuels." Kirsten shook hands. "I hope you can help me get to the bottom of something. Is it possible to compare organs used in transplants to find a common donor?"

"Depending on the amount of pre-implantation work done on the organ, it should be possible, though it can be data-laborious if there were significant compatibility modifications done."

He gestured at a wood-framed chair facing his desk with lavender cushions and back. "Please." Not waiting for her to sit, he settled into his seat and brought up a large fifty-inch holo-terminal.

"Thanks. I'm trying to track organs taken from a victim of a ripper doc. I believe a man was killed for a specific body part, but I'm not sure which one or how many of his organs have wound up in other people." She sat. "I know at least one of the organs, the heart, was involved in an implantation performed here in this facility. The patient's name is Julia Dominguez."

Doctor Samuels chuckled. "That narrows it down to a few thousand."

"Age forty-nine. Surgery was performed about four months ago in early July." Kirsten waved her hand over her armband and flung Julia's information at him.

"Illicit organ markets are dangerous business. People take too much risk. Never could understand how anyone could trust someone in an alley to do surgery, why they'd do that to themselves."

"Forty or fifty thousand credits compared to two million? Maybe if more than three percent of the population could afford it, they wouldn't have to." She tried to keep emotion out of her voice.

"People have insurance." Doctor Samuels's face took on a beige glow as the contents of his screen changed. "Here we are. Mrs. Dominguez received a transplanted heart from a DOA donor. Her insurance provider selected that option."

"Of course. Much cheaper for them, right?" Kirsten leaned forward. "Do you have any other organs listed as originating from one Darius Cook?"

"I'll check." He typed for a few seconds. "If you don't mind me asking, you seem a bit hostile to the insurance industry. This sort of investigation sounds like you're following up on a case they started."

Kirsten bit her lip with a little shake of the head. "I wish it was so ordinary. I don't have that kind of time. The ripper doc's victim is pissed off. I believe he is trying to kill everyone who received body parts taken from him."

Doctor Samuels froze. After a second, his eyes shifted to look at her. "Wouldn't that man be dead?"

"He is. I'm Division 0, Doctor Samuels. Specifically, an Astral Sensitive. I'm trying to stop a ghost from killing people."

His head swayed around as though his neck lost all strength. The most epic of eye-rolls came her way. "Ghosts?"

"Look, Doctor. I don't need you to believe me; I don't care if you do. Please, I need this information before someone gets hurt."

"I can possibly cross link that information, but there are matters of doctor-patient privilege to consider."

She sighed. *I was waiting for that.*

"His helpfulness seems to have given up the, uhh, ghost," said Dorian.

Her eyes fluttered half closed as she let out another sigh. "Doctor, the privilege rule does not apply to an official investigation. I'm operating under the authority of the National Police Force, Division 0."

"It applies to voodoo nonsense." Doctor Samuels waved his hand about as if casting spells.

"Want me to—"

Kirsten held Dorian off with a raised palm. "Perhaps you can explain to me instead why Darius Cook is listed as having suffered three high-caliber rounds to center mass which reduced his heart to a wad of bacon strips? And somehow, that lump of dog food wound up transplanted into Mrs. Dominguez and works just fine. Unless the insurance company decided to pay three million credits to regenerate the heart of a dead gangbanger so they could avoid spending two million credits to regenerate Mrs. Dominguez's own heart tissue, your records have been falsified. That gives me probable cause to have Division 2 come in here and tear the panties off every server cabinet in your basement and see what else is hiding in there."

Doctor Samuels's steely glare weakened after she refused to back down her challenging posture. "Ghosts... Wonderful. What's next? Will your office be doing a tax audit on Santa Claus? Very well." He poked a few buttons and the light tinting his face from the terminal shifted brighter. "It appears that the genetic profile of the heart also matches a pair of kidneys implanted around the same time."

"Who got the kidneys?"

He steepled his fingers. "I'm not comfortable releasing that information. I'm muddy on the whole police walking back and forth over privacy rights thing."

"If I was a nastier person, I could charge you with obstruction. I'm asking you as a human being. Someone's life is in danger."

"If you were a nasty person, you'd be slamming him against those fake windows." Dorian made a heave-ho gesture.

"I don't know if I can violate the patient's—"

Kirsten leapt to her feet. "Is the name on the kidneys as fake as Darius Cook belonging to that heart? If the DNA matches, and the names are different, that's only a little suspicious. I don't have time for games, Doctor Samuels. I'm not the armored-up sort of cop who'll mop the walls with your face to get what I want. I'm the sort of cop who's concerned about the bigger picture and who else is getting screwed. How much will Div 2 find when they're elbow deep in your network's rectum?"

Doctor Samuels shifted in his seat. "Please calm down, officer."

"Lieutenant," said Dorian, a trace of rasp in his voice hinted he projected it to the living.

The doctor twitched, staring at the approximate point where Dorian stood.

"Doctor?" asked Kirsten.

"Uhh..." He blinked. "I want to go on record as being opposed to this, but... another patient suffered renal failure as a result of acute blood toxicity, requiring a replacement of both kidneys. Apparently, they suffered a catastrophic crushing injury."

Kirsten blinked. *Lindsey?* "Where? Crushing injury?"

"The patient was compressed between two large solid masses, which broke both legs in multiple places, both feet, and caused significant damage to the pelvis. It seems the patient remained stuck for some time before they were able to be extricated. They developed 'crush syndrome' soon after."

"I'm... How does that work? Is the patient's name Lindsey Park?"

Doctor Samuels's expression gave away her guess as correct. "I can't confirm the name. When a limb is compressed with enough force to damage muscles, and the compression blocks blood flow through the tissues, releasing that pressure causes ischemia and frees toxins into the bloodstream. Myoglobin, potassium, phosphorous from rhabdomyolysis—the breakdown of skeletal muscle destroyed during the injury—gets into the system. The kidneys can't handle the rapid influx, may clog, and shut down. In this patient's case, the muscle damage and length of time trapped contributed to a massive influx of toxic breakdown products which destroyed her kidneys."

She typed as fast as she could with one hand, taking notes. "Was that the only other match?"

"Yes. Nothing else came up within an acceptable deviation from the genetic markers. The odds of there being another organ from the same donor in our system are about twenty-eight million to one."

"Shit. That means he *is* going to go back for Lindsey. I have to warn her. Crap! I might not be able to get to the Moon fast enough to matter."

"Is that all then?" asked Doctor Samuels.

She aborted her turn for the door. "How did the heart and kidney get into your system?"

"Both came in from one of our usual aggregator services, Life Vault Industries. They collect donor organs from various medical providers, sort them to a central storage facility, and send them out as necessary when matched to a recipient. It's likely a random chance that two of them came here. Then again, our hospital is among the top four in the UCF, so perhaps not so random."

"You may want to do some housecleaning before someone else comes looking." Kirsten grumbled, wishing she had more time (and the jurisdiction) to look into the records more. "Thanks for your help."

"Of course." He smiled. "I'll appreciate your discretion if either patient decides to take legal action against us for divulging their information. I am on record as objecting."

"Oh, if there's legal action, it won't be about divulging information." She rushed a handshake. "But that's not my case. I'm only trying to stop a ghost from killing people. They already cheated death once."

Doctor Samuels muttered, "Ghosts, hmph," and shook his head.

Kirsten leaned into her stride, walking a hair shy of a jog on her way back to the patrol craft. A few seconds after the door closed, Doctor Samuels shrieked.

She stopped, sighing. "Dorian!"

ON THE CHEAP

Cool air from the vents blasted Kirsten in the face as she cranked the patrol craft's fans to the highest setting. Even with military grade filters, it took about two minutes to remove any trace of Cryomil from the air. Either that, or the stink had been scorched into her mind. She coughed out the last of it and, still sitting on the parking deck of Easley Medical Center, swiped at the dashboard console while pulling up the Inquest file. After rearranging some frames around the holo-panel by fingertip, she grasped the one for Lindsey Park and pulled it to the forefront. Another tap initiated an outbound call to the Gravion orbital platform.

A pale blonde woman with bright blue eyes appeared a few seconds later. "Thank you for calling Gravion Corporation. How may I help you? Oh, Agent Wren. Hello."

Kirsten stalled, staring at the face. "Have we met?"

"Oh, only for a moment in the café when you were up here. You probably don't remember me... Mara Garcia?" She grinned. "I wanted to try blonde and blue. It's so rare, and you're so pretty."

Dorian leaned over. "Wasn't she a bit more tan?"

"Uhh, thanks." Kirsten smiled only as long as needed for politeness. "I'm sorry to rush, but I need to speak to Lindsey Park. She's probably in danger."

"Oh no..." The woman glanced to the left. Light flickered on her face from another terminal panel. "Uhh... looks like she rotated off two days ago on medical leave. She'd have to be back on Earth by now."

"I'll need her info."

"Of course." The newly minted blonde grinned. "Sending now."

A PID came up, associated to a physical address in Sector 4382 in East City.

"Thanks. I need to contact her right away."

Mara nodded. "I understand. Good luck and stay safe."

Dorian whistled. "Something's wrong. People are being nice and helpful to you."

She poked him, and tapped the PID to call Lindsey. It rang ten times and went to Vidmail.

"Lindsey, this is Lieutenant Wren, Division 0. We met on the Gravion platform. Please call me back immediately." Hang up. Retry. Vidmail again. She didn't bother leaving a second message. "Shit."

"Well, you can see the Statue of Liberty from 4382 if I remember right," said Dorian.

"The what?" She blinked. "Oh... wait, wasn't that destroyed?"

Dorian shook his head. "You should be in school, sitting at the desk next to Evan. Good grief, woman. And yes, it was. They tried to replace it, but a politician stole all the money allocated for the project by replacing the statue with a full-sized hologram instead of a physical object. Don't you remember the story about hackers making her do a strip tease a few years ago?"

"Uhh..." She rolled her eyes. "Don't people have better things to do with their time?"

"Apparently not." He grinned.

Kirsten powered up the patrol craft. It leapt off the roof of the Easley Medical Center and she headed right for the starport. "Outbound, Captain Eze."

The console made a *boop* noise. Three seconds later, his virtual bust appeared. "All well?"

"Sir, I need to go to East City. One of the victims isn't answering. The Park woman, from the Gravion station. I'm afraid I'm going to find another ghost."

"Understood. I'll have them either hold or expedite the next shuttle... unless you think it critical enough for a DS2."

Kirsten shook her head. "A military transport would take longer to set up. Even if it flies faster, I'd lose more time waiting for them to greenlight it."

"Funny how it takes three hours to fly over West City but like twenty minutes to go coast to coast." Dorian chuckled.

"Pat-vees don't do Mach 8." She glided in over a parking garage structure and landed in the emergency lane near the front of Edmonson Memorial Starport, programmed the auto-drive to move the car to the nearest open spot in the deck, and got out.

Two streams of civilians, one entering, one leaving, on a tall chrome-silver stairway slowed to watch her run up between them to the main entrance. Urgency coupled with getting pissed off at the expected static she'd get from a security person who didn't think she was a real cop hardened her expression and turned her jog to a stomp. By the time she reached the PubTran terminal, her demeanor had a chilling effect on people nearby, many of whom hurried out of her way.

Three security officers at the terminal saw her coming and stared in silence as she breezed around the sensor tunnel. One even saluted. She ducked down a corridor line with blue carpet specked with little black shuttle shapes, going downhill into a large waiting area, alive with the din of a few hundred people.

"Lieutenant Wren, please go to Intercoastal terminal 4B."

She looked at the ceiling as the voice came over the PA system. Twelve separate areas expanded from the walls, rounded sections where seats surrounded a boarding tunnel entry. She ran to the left, tracing signs until she spotted the one for 4B. No one but a PubTran employee in a blue skirt-suit and white folding hat remained. A good sign... people had already boarded. Kirsten, hand on her stunrod to keep it from banging into her thigh, sprinted past her with a wave and hurried along the tunnel connected to a shuttle.

Small windows offered a brief glimpse of a ship with a profile somewhere between bell and arrowhead, large enough to seat about two hundred. People inside grumbled and moaned about the delay, filling the air with an almost solid mass of sound. She greeted two crewmembers by the entry, shook hands with the woman, and followed her pointing finger to a seat within five steps of the door. Dorian took the spot at her left, closer to the aisle. Someone behind her started to bitch about the police doing whatever they wanted and damned everyone else's schedules, but a childish voice screamed at him.

"She's goin' ta help someone. If it was you, you wouldn't care who had to wait. Don't be a butthead."

Kirsten glanced over the seatback at a girl about six glaring at a fiftyish man in a dark suit. Her father, presumably the guy in the seat to the child's left, had the over-muscular build of a Gee-ball player. The other man whirled around, looking ready to scream, but at the sight of the enormous father, he backed down, grumbling to himself. The girl smiled at Kirsten and waved. She grinned back, and settled into her chair.

The shuttle lights flashed and dimmed.

"Hello everyone," said a female voice from speakers overhead. "We're sorry for the delay and will be taking off within thirty seconds. Please remain seated and fasten your belts. PubTran Corporation is not liable for any injuries sustained during flight due to not wearing your seatbelt. It should be safe to move around the cabin once we are at cruising altitude, but for your own safety, please remain seated during takeoff and landing."

Kirsten tried to vid Lindsey again, but the call went to her message inbox after eight rings.

The shuttle lifted off, going straight up while the world rotated past the windows. A heavy electronic *thrum* shook the cabin and her weight squished back into the cushions. The ground streaked away, soon replaced by bright blue, a flash of white clouds, and blue again.

For about nineteen minutes, Kirsten stared into the headrest in front of her. The same woman's voice announced they would begin descending in one minute, and again asked everyone to stay seated.

"Wren." Captain Eze's four-inch head appeared over her left arm. "Your ride is waiting by the main entrance. Tactical Officer Shah."

Crap. I totally forgot about what I'd do once we landed. "Thank you, sir."

"Since you didn't ask, I figured you were too wound up to think about the details." He chuckled. "Stay alert."

Kirsten smiled at him. "Will do, Captain."

The shuttle landed without incident three minutes later, and as soon as the docking collar clamped on over the door, she sprinted from her seat and rushed out into a terminal. An assault of food filled the air: hot pretzels, something sugary, frying chicken, and a good twenty yards of concourse filled with Indian and Middle Eastern cuisine. People milled around the shops making it seem more like a mall than a busy shuttle terminal. Despite her growling stomach, she didn't slow down until reaching the front entrance. A sudden change from appetizing to fetid air made the breath catch in her throat. This part of East City carried the stench of industrial waste mixed with the rotting diaper-pail aroma of low tide. Kirsten took small sips of air while she rode the moving stairs to the street level. A skinny armored figure with long black hair leaned against a conspicuous black patrol craft, with a helmet under her left arm.

The girl looked like she belonged in eighth grade.

"For the love of..." Dorian sighed. "That kid looks so fragile she probably needs that armor not to break bones riding in a hovercar."

For once, Kirsten felt large... it wasn't often she had a height advantage, even a half-inch.

"Lieutenant Wren." The small woman saluted. "Tactical Officer Riya Shah. I'm honored to accompany you. I read over some of your old Inquests. Amazing stuff."

Kirsten returned the salute. "Uhh, thanks."

Shah grinned. "I'm seventeen, and yes I'm still in Admin, but I'm training for a tactical squad."

Dorian shrugged. "Older than I thought. Still, she's young. Maybe you should drive?"

"Hi." Kirsten reluctantly took the passenger seat.

Riya yanked the door open with surprising ease and leapt in. "I've already got your case on the Nav."

Kirsten grabbed the 'oh shit' handle as the car shot straight up into a turn so hard they rolled beyond sideways for a few seconds. Fearless, Riya threaded the needle between a pair of billboard-sized advert bots and slalomed up and down while dodging a series of street-spanning walkways linking buildings.

Someone beeped; the horn lasted under a second. Riya flipped the bird over her shoulder, but didn't bother looking. "I swear… people can't drive here."

Kirsten glanced at Dorian. "Right…"

"Can I ask you something, Lieutenant?" Riya jammed the stick, causing the car to drop four stories in a split second to evade a crossing stream of traffic.

Kirsten's ass left the seat until gravity returned, then fell hard. "Ow. Shit. Uhh sure."

"Why's everyone freaked out about mind blasters?" The tiny woman looked at her for an instant. "I mean… we're on the same side right? I don't understand. When I asked 'what's the big deal?' I got the assignment to drive you around."

Kirsten frowned at the digital window. "Hypocrites. Every psionic hates that normal people fear us because of what we 'might' do, yet they simultaneously do the same thing to anyone with Mind Blast. Yeah, sure, advanced grades of 'Blast are horrifying to think about, and unless you happen to also have Mind Blast it's almost impossible to defend against." She made fists and tapped her knuckles together. "Fighting it with itself. It's so rare they think we're going to arbitrarily wipe their mind out if they piss us off."

"Oh. Yeah, you're right. That's hypocritical." She shook her head, making her thick hair fluff about. "They used to tease me for not being a 'real' psionic since I'm a bio-kinetic. I have a little telepathy, but I guess being able to bench 1760 pounds isn't all that impressive to them."

Dorian coughed.

"Damn." Kirsten laughed. "You're so small. I, uhh, really thought you were like twelve."

"You look like you're fourteen." Riya grinned and gave her a fist-bump. "Short girl power! Perps never expect us."

Cadet Shah steered into a torturous right turn that climbed forty stories in the span of about a second. The patrol craft cleared the edge of a roof parking deck with inches to spare, plummeted to within five feet of the ground, and skidded sideways down a lane between parked cars before slamming to a halt in midair and sinking onto its wheels as gentle as a landing feather.

"Was that necessary?" Kirsten couldn't quite will her fingers to release the handle above the door.

"What?"

"Coming in like you're putting a fighter craft on a carrier?"

Riya shrugged. "Guess people drive different on the West Coast. This is tame. I didn't want anyone stealing the spot before we landed."

"But this is a police car." Kirsten pushed the door open.

"Yeah, and?" Riya blinked. "They'll take the ticket. It's like paying to park. Plus they know if we're in a hurry, we probably don't have the time to cite them."

Dorian gestured at the elevator some fifty yards away. "Lindsey?"

Kirsten leapt out. "Shit. Come on."

She sprinted down the row of vehicles, entered a small glass-walled outbuilding on the roof, and raced to the nearest elevator. Two minutes nineteen seconds later, she pounded on the door to Lindsey Park's apartment.

A tiny light came on at about eye level (to a normal person) on the door. Kirsten looked up at it.

"Who is it?" asked Lindsey's voice from a tinny speaker.

Dorian walked through the wall. "She sounds exhausted."

"Lieutenant Wren. We met on the Gravion platform. I need to speak to you."

"Oh." The woman coughed. "Come in."

When the door opened via remote, Kirsten hurried in. Clothes scattered all over the living room floor and sofa made the place look like a teenager's bedroom had expanded to fill an entire residence. The air hung thick, overly warm and laced with the smell of cheap Ramen. Kirsten checked an empty kitchen and small laundry nook before heading to the right down a narrow hallway where a bathroom and bedroom door faced each other at the end.

Lindsey lay on the bed under a blanket, her shoulders and arms covered by white long-sleeved pajamas with a repeating pattern of grinning cartoon kittens. Half-closed eyes regarded Kirsten; she looked pale.

"What's wrong?" Kirsten rushed over, leaned one hand on the bed and put the other on the woman's forehead. "You're burning."

"Haven't been sleeping well. Lotta pain and I feel achy and shitty." Lindsey shrugged. "I'd say I had a flu, but my head's not stuffy at all."

Relief that the woman hadn't died lessened the tension gripping Kirsten's muscles. She sat on the edge of the Comforgel pad, but leapt up as though her butt settled on a hibachi grill. "Damn... you got that thing cranked."

"Hundred and two." Dorian pointed at the climate control panel.

"It's been so damn cold in here." She squirmed to sit up a little straighter. "Starting to get warm now. If you wanna turn it down, you can."

Dorian obliged by sticking his hand into the wall panel. Large green numbers shifted from 105 to 75.

"Whoa! How'd you do that?" asked Lindsey.

Kirsten took her hand. "Long story. Look... I need to tell you something that's going to be hard to hear."

Lindsey sniffled. "I got fired didn't I?"

"Oh, no... I, uhh, at least I don't think so. That's not why I'm here." Kirsten held eye contact. "Your kidneys were damaged as a result of your injury."

"Yeah. I know. They had to regenerate them. I was shocked. Gravion didn't even try to weasel out of covering it."

"Uhh. Lindsey, you didn't have a regeneration performed. You received transplant organs."

"What?" The little color remaining in her cheeks faded. "Transplants? Oh, no. Is that why I'm sick? Are they rejecting?" Tears ran down her cheeks. "Am I gonna die?"

"No. You're not going to die... at least not if I have anything to say about it. The kidneys you received were illegally obtained from a murder victim. Do you believe in ghosts?"

Lindsey shivered. "Uhh, before that thing happened on the platform, I would've laughed at you, but yeah. I think they're real now."

"That man you saw is the victim. He's angry that he was killed for parts, and he's trying to hurt you because you have his kidneys."

Lindsey convulsed, grabbing her face.

"Get a bucket," said Dorian.

Riya stood at Kirsten's side, fidgeting and looking awkward.

Kirsten put an arm around Lindsey and rubbed her back. "I'm trying to find the ghost. I won't let him hurt you."

"The pain's been... yeah. The kidneys. Those stingy sons of bitches." Crying shifted to snarling. "I thought they were being good to me, but they went cheap. They said they paid for regens." She dry heaved again. "I got a dead guy's kidneys in me?"

"A corporation took a shortcut? Gasp." Dorian shook his head.

Lindsey crawled to the edge of the bed and jumped down. Her pajama pants fell around her ankles as she landed, changing her attempt to run into a pratfall. Dorian looked away. Lindsey pulled them up, rolled onto her back, and tied the string at the waist before crawling to the desk. On her knees, she pounded a hand into the terminal until a login screen came up and she opened a Vidphone app.

Kirsten walked over and stood behind her.

Lindsey scratched the terminal like an angry housecat, tearing at an enormous contacts list until she hit the Gs. She punched her fist into the smiling round face of a heavyset looking woman with auburn hair.

Thirty-six seconds later, the same woman appeared in hologram. "Miss Park. Oh, my. Are you okay?"

"You lied to me." Lindsey started to cry, but wound up growling. She pulled herself up to her feet with both hands on the desk, grunting as though it took great effort to stand or hurt quite a bit. "You said Gravion would cover regeneration. I got fucking transplants! Not only transplants, illegal ones. I'm dying!"

The woman put a hand over her mouth and gasped. "Lindsey, are you sure? We... Hold on."

"Don't put me on hold!" screamed Lindsey.

"I'm not." The woman held her hand up in a placating gesture. "I'm checking records. Just give me a few seconds okay?"

Lindsey glared.

Green lit the woman's face from the side.

"Who's that?" whispered Kirsten.

Lindsey glanced back, whispering, "Trisha Breem. She's the HR benefits administrator. She's a VP, but she's got an open door policy and she's... well I thought she was nice."

"Lindsey," said Trisha. "Your record shows we paid out on a regeneration process. Two million four hundred thousand. I'm sending the file over to you now. Are you certain about this?"

"Miss Breem? I'm Lieutenant Wren with Division 0. I'm afraid it is true. Miss Park was given illegal organs."

"Someone at the hospital pocketed the difference I bet." Dorian paced. "That part of it isn't your problem, but you should flag the Div 2 corporate crimes task force in the Inquest when you file it."

Trisha's mouth hung open. "Oh, my God, Lindsey... I had no idea. I'm *so* sorry. Don't worry, hon. You get yourself to..." Patterns of light on her cheeks shifted; she glanced to the side as if reading something. "Go right to the nearest Amaranth Corporation facility. Give them my contact info. Umm, Lieutenant, would you be able to help her there? She looks too sick to even make it to a PubTran on her own."

Dorian stared, stunned.

Lindsey sniffled. "Really? You're serious? Amaranth?"

"Damn right I'm serious." Trisha scowled. "I'm going to send this down to legal as soon as we're off the phone. I hope you decide to stay with us here at Gravion, Lindsey, but after this lawsuit settles, you might not need to work."

"I like my job. It's fun." Lindsey slumped back to her knees, crying. "I don't wanna die. It hurts so much."

Trisha looked pained.

"I'll call in a MedVan." Riya tapped on a small holo-panel over her left forearm.

"K, look." Dorian squatted and pointed at a strip of bare skin between Lindsey's top and pants.

Kirsten took a knee and pulled the woman's shirt up. Two bruises on the small of her back approximated the shape of hands over the kidneys. "Shit. You could be bleeding internally." She pulled out two stimpaks and applied them one after the next, creating a small raised patch of skin where the nanobot-laced fluid collected.

Lindsey squealed. "That's cold!" Her body went limp; Kirsten caught her and eased her to the floor. "Oh... that's... nice." She passed out.

"I've never seen someone fall asleep after being shot full of synthetic adrenaline before." Dorian blinked. "She had to have been awake for days... pain preventing her from sleeping."

"Should we move her?" asked Kirsten.

Riya started for the door. "I dunno. Ask the medtechs when they get here. I'll go meet them outside and lead them down."

Kirsten rolled Lindsey onto her back. While waiting, she reached out with her mind. A supernatural trace lingered, strong enough to recognize as the same entity she'd seen with his hand in Julia's chest. She let her power ebb and opened her eyes. "Same guy."

"There's ethereal smears in the Comforgel. I think he was on top of her... no discrete 'prints,' the residual contact has diffused in the gel." Dorian looked around at the floor. "Doesn't feel like he's here anymore. This guy's new. It's taking a lot out of him to affect the living, even ones with his body parts."

Kirsten looked down at Lindsey's belly, rising and falling with her breathing. "Dorian... could he be 'sleeping' inside his old kidneys?"

"They might function like 'remains.' I've heard some spirits return to their bodies to recharge. Un-cremated remains are supposed to restore energy far better than ashes. Probably do in hours what it takes me days to do with the car."

"Why don't you go sleep in your urn?" Kirsten glanced over at him as he wandered into the bathroom.

"Too damn loud at that mausoleum. Imagine thousands of people living in apartments one cubic foot in size. Plus all the damn mourners."

There can't be that many spirits there... he's afraid of seeing his family. "Sounds annoying."

"You have *no* idea." He sighed.

Riya ran in a few minutes later, followed by two women and a man in white jumpsuits. The women guided a hover-stretcher between them; bright ion thrusters sent long shadows pivoting over the walls from the furniture as the techs ran over.

Kirsten gestured at the medics to wait. She pulled Lindsey's pajama jacket up to expose her stomach and rested a hand over where a kidney should be. A second's worth of concentration revealed a paranormal energy swirling around inside. She tried to force her will around it and draw it out. The spirit struggled, though its resistance felt weak—like she tried to pull a small child away from something they clung to. Annoyed, Kirsten concentrated, pouring more energy into her power. Lindsey's eyes shot open and she screamed in agony.

The spirit's 'grip' came loose, and Kirsten lurched away as though a tug-of-war rope had snapped. The same hollowed-out man rocketed up out of Lindsey and passed through Kirsten with the chill of a torrent of ice water, knocking her over backward. She shrieked from temperature shock and rolled onto her stomach, but the ghost raced into the wall before she could summon the presence of mind to oppose it.

Dorian sprinted off.

Two of the medtechs rushed to Lindsey while a dark-skinned woman with belt-length dreadlocks helped Kirsten sit up.

"You okay, officer?"

She forced the word "Lieutenant" out past chattering teeth. "I *hate* it when they do that."

Lindsey passed out again.

"Ruptured kidney," said the other woman. "We gotta move her now!"

"I'm good." Kirsten waved the medtech off. "She needs you more than I do. Damn ghosts."

The medtech nodded. "All right."

By the time they got Lindsey on the stretcher and out of the room, the paralytic chill had faded. Kirsten paced around, unsure if she should wait here in case Dorian caught the guy and dragged him back, or run around aimlessly searching for wherever a ghostly fistfight might be taking place.

"Are we going with them?" asked Riya.

Kirsten halted and looked at her. *If he gets away from Dorian, he's going to go after her again.* "Yeah. Good idea."

Six feet away from a medical tank, Kirsten fidgeted and tried not to watch the gory events occurring within. Amaranth Medical Corporation pumped pleasant music throughout the facility, and the procedure room even had a coffee machine. The staff hadn't protested her presence, though they did remain skeptical about spirits.

An hour and forty minutes after the tank flooded to the top, Lindsey Park's borrowed kidneys detached from all connections and floated free from her body. Nodules of developing tissue formed around the blood vessels in the region, lumps of grey-maroon proto-kidney that would—over the course of the next thirty to forty hours—grow into new organs made with her own DNA. For all intents and purposes, they would be her kidneys. She thought about using the removed organs as some kind of ritual object to force the spirit to show up, but the idea proved too grotesque to consider beyond a few seconds.

She forced herself to watch them swim to the top of the tank, propelled within the peach-colored gel by millions of microscopic robots. Minutes later, a medtech removed them from a hatch on the wall next to the tank, in a small canister of the same gel.

"What should we do with these, Lieutenant?" asked a young man with the name 'Hernandez' on his coat.

"My first instinct is to cremate them and add them to the rest of his remains, but I haven't found them yet. Give me a moment to finalize the paperwork. They'll need to remain as evidence during the investigation into the illegal procurement. I'm not taking chances. If you have a more discreet container, I'm going to maintain custody of them until I can turn them in back west."

"No problem, Lieutenant." Medtech Hernandez smiled. "I'll grab a tote. Coffee?"

"Sure. Mocha?"

He nodded.

Dorian poked his head out of the wall again. "No sign of him out here."

Five minutes or so later, Hernandez returned with a bioplastic cup in one hand and a white medical case in the other. "Coffee and kidneys to go."

"I'm hoping she's no longer at risk from spectral attack since the source of the spirit's anger isn't inside her. Maybe if I get lucky, he'll come after them right to me." She shied away from the tank and took a sip. *Not bad. Very not bad for a vending machine.* "I need to get back. There are others at risk. I'd love to stay to be with her when she's out of that tank, but... forty hours. The spirit might attack one of the other victims. Oh, please tell her if anything paranormal happens to say out loud that she didn't know the kidneys were stolen and they're no longer inside her."

"I'm sure she'll understand and will be quite grateful for your assistance, as strange as this whole thing sounds." Hernandez returned to a console and smiled at her. "I'll make sure she knows you were pulled away to assist someone else."

"I'll call her at least when she wakes up." Kirsten hurried out, eager to be away from the nauseating spectacle going on in the tank.

Riya looked up from the bench seat outside the room. "How'd it go?"

"She's having her kidneys re-grown. Going to be in there for almost two full days. The spirit's after these." She held up the cooler case. "I don't think she's in any danger now. If you don't mind, I could use a ride back to the starport."

"Yes, Ma'am." Riya leapt up and saluted her.

Riya drove somewhat more gently with a box of body parts in the car. For the duration of the ride from Lindsey's apartment to the starport, Kirsten kept her non-coffee-bearing hand on the case and tried to use the organs as a focus for a beacon, calling out to whatever spirit belonged to them.

Nothing showed up by the time they landed.

After yet another salute, Kirsten bade Cadet Shah farewell, and walked up the moving stairs into the starport. She dodged around a pair of young men trying to hand out plasfilm sheets bearing a religious message for some sect she'd never even heard of before, and hurried deep enough into the terminal for them not to bother following.

"You *must* be in a good mood." Dorian chuckled. "No sarcastic comments?"

"It's not my job to tell people what to believe. I just wish they'd stop trying to force it down my throat." She grumbled.

He squeezed chill into her left shoulder. "My little Kirsten has almost grown up. Lieutenant bars, now this."

She gave him a raspberry.

After booking the soonest shuttle flight to West City she could, she started walking to a CyberBurger halfway between the main atrium and the terminal area.

"You don't want to do that," said Dorian.

"What? That fast food is unhealthy thing is a myth someone resurrected from the pre-war days. It's all OmniSoy. No worse than anything else made from beige goo."

"Not that. You're in a starport. The prices are like triple what they should be, taking advantage of convenience and tourists."

Kirsten grumbled.

"Oh, come on. It's a twenty-minute flight. You can wait." He shrugged. "If you want to spend ninety credits for crap, go right ahead."

She walked into the place far enough to read the menu board. Sure enough, the prices looked more like a fancy hydroponic eatery that used chicken, beef, and pork grown in vats where specially trained caretakers read haikus over soothing music to the meat twenty-four hours a day. "Dammit."

"One of these days, you'll believe me."

Kirsten tromped to the terminal. She skipped the security scanner with a flash of her ID and took a seat in the waiting area. Having about a half hour to kill before the flight, she set the white case between her feet and got to work updating the report on the file via her armband.

Dorian's hand chilled her shoulder. "Heads up. About forty yards left by the advertisement for the blue dress. Stay calm."

Kirsten peeled her attention off the endless scroll of text and images. Even though the reports had to be done, watching the crowd appealed far more than the drudgery, especially on such a small screen and typing one handed. *Screw it. I'll finish this at the office. What the fuck?* She gawked.

The boy who'd shot Nicole, and his bitch of a mother, strolled across the starport as casually as could be. The child spotted her, pointed, and got an eager look in his eye. Before his mother could do anything about it, he darted away and came running at Kirsten.

She stood, barely suppressing a tremble of rage, her hand edging for her stunrod.

"Hi, officer," said the boy. "I wanna be a cop when I grow up."

Kirsten narrowed her eyes at him. "What are you doing here?"

His mother trotted over and grasped his shoulders. "I'm sorry. Cop this week, doctor last week…"

You spat in my face a few days ago and now you're smiling at me? Kirsten's knuckles creaked. *How the hell are they free?* "It's no bother…"

The woman pulled on him. "Come on, Julián. She's obviously busy."

"Are you mad?" asked Julián.

Kirsten, in an effort to not scream, broke her rule and plunged into his thoughts. He had no memory of her at all; aside from a little confusion as to why she glared at them, he thought cops were cool. She flicked her gaze to the woman. Again, no active recollection of who she was existed. The woman interpreted her scowl at being annoyed at the boy bothering her.

"Have we met?"

The woman shook her head. "I don't think so."

Kirsten swallowed a twinge of queasiness. "What's your opinion on people with psionic talents?"

Julián's eyes lit up. "They're awesome! Like superheroes from the vids. I wanna be one of those when I grow up too."

"No different than someone with another skin color," said the mother. "It's a shame people are so prejudiced against them."

"Wow," whispered Dorian. "I guess that's one way to deal with an issue."

"How's your husband doing, Vicki?"

The woman blinked. "How did you know my name?" She stared. "Are you psionic?"

"Yeah."

"Cool!" yelled Julián.

"Oh, nice to meet you." Vicki grinned. "I've never been married. Julián's father… I worked on Mars for a while as a waitress. He came in one night on leave; we had a fling. He was off planet before I knew Julián was on the way. I never could find him."

Kirsten put a hand on her stomach to hold back the sick. "Do you have any other children?"

"My brother Manuel is goin' to school on Mars." Julián beamed. "He's turning twenty in a couple of weeks. We're going up to visit him."

Vicki squeezed his shoulders. "He hasn't been on Mars since he was an embryo. I don't think he remembers it." She winked.

"Uhh. Sounds nice." Kirsten glanced to her left at Dorian who raised his hands in a 'not touching this' gesture. "I need to catch a shuttle. Nice meeting you."

"You too." Vicki started away, but paused as Julián snapped to attention and saluted Kirsten.

She returned it, awash in confusion, and stared at the two of them wandering off with the crowd toward the exit. "Dorian, what did I just witness?"

"That, my dear Kirsten, is why people run the other way when Lieutenant Commander Ashford walks by."

"That's… so *wrong*." She shivered.

"More wrong than executing her for attempted murder of an officer and orphaning that boy? More wrong than a ten-year-old hating psionics enough to want to kill them?"

"Do you think the older boy's really on Mars? Or did they sentence him and his dad to death?" She held her stomach, grateful Dorian had talked her out of eating.

"I'm guessing they sent him to Mars. Otherwise, they wouldn't remember him at all."

"Like the father…"

Dorian looked away. "Yeah. Like him. Of course, it doesn't necessarily prove they executed him. Maybe they split them up to prevent the memory overlay from peeling. I don't know."

"If Ashford did it, there's no overlay to peel. He erased." She bit her lip, refusing to allow herself to succumb to everyone else's fear for the man. A new personality did beat execution, at least from her perspective.

"Attention passengers," said a female voice over the PA. "PubTran shuttle to West City for 4:30 p.m. departure will be boarding in five minutes. Registered seat holders should proceed to Terminal 8A at this time."

Kirsten picked up the organ case and headed over to the terminal.

THE DEALER

Kirsten's eyes popped open. Her bedroom hung still and silent, save for the muted hum of the occasional hovercar out at—she rolled onto her side and stared at the holographic clock—4:05 in the morning. Worry tickled at her gut. She shook off the reins of sleep and slipped out of bed, tugging her nightshirt down around her thighs as she tiptoed out into the corridor. The huge windowed wall behind her let in enough ambient city light to illuminate the corridor to Evan's bedroom.

Soft whimpers and grunts came from within.

She pushed the door open, finding him curled up in the corner of the room in his boxers, cringing and shivering much the same way she'd found him in his birth mother's apartment. An angry bruise wrapped around the left side of his ribcage.

"Evan!" she ran over and fell on her knees next to him. "Ev!"

He startled awake, stared at her in stunned silence with the same expression he'd given her when she'd burst into his old room. It took him a second to finish waking out of his nightmare. He calmed, and cradled his side. "Ow. Ow. Shit."

Kirsten scooped him up. His hard little body tensed; muscles swelled out of his shoulders and neck. She whirled about to follow his line of sight. The closet looked empty.

"What?"

"Monster. I thought I saw a shadow."

She set him on the Comforgel pad.

"No." He clung.

"I'm going to look in the closet."

He seemed conflicted for a second, but kept clinging.

Kirsten picked him up again and crept up to the closet, opening the door with her left foot. Only coats, toys, and games. She let off a psionic pulse, but the feeble sense of energy in the area could've been nothing more than the aftereffect of a days-old blockade.

"If there was something here, it's extremely weak." She nuzzled the top of his head and kissed him.

He gritted his teeth. "Is that why it's giving me nightmares?" The bruise faded to a yellowish mark.

She bit her lip. If something external was responsible, that made her feel better and pissed off all at the same time. "Maybe. Do you think it's a ghost?"

He nodded.

"Have you seen it?" She carried him to the kitchen and shifted his weight to her left hip to free one arm. After dialing up a cheeseburger, she carried him and the food back to her bed. "Gotta pee. Be right back."

He devoured the late night snack before she returned, and cuddled up at her side when she climbed in. Kirsten wrapped her arms around him, glaring at the wall. *Come on, whatever you are. Try something when I'm here.*

AT 5:59 A.M., KIRSTEN REACHED OUT AND HOVERED A FINGER OVER THE ALARM. Having remained awake, she killed the blare one second after it started. Evan had a hand up to his face as though sucking his thumb, but fell short of putting the digit in his mouth. She let him sleep another two minutes, watching him breathe and worrying that he'd started to get too skinny again.

He's healing himself too much. Dammit.

Gentle tickling swipes of her fingernails over his bare belly roused him laughing. While he headed off to shower, she scoured his room for any traces of paranormal energy. Under his pillow, she found a sharp steak knife, with dried blood near the handle. It bore a weak imprint of energy, but no longer remained bound. She glared at it until the wave of anger gave way to worry. Against her better judgement, she put it on the little night table between a model castle and a dragon figurine. The idea of Evan cutting himself pained her, but not as much as him being helpless against a spectral force.

He walked in surrounded by the steamy smell of autoshower soap and wearing clean briefs. At the sight of the knife, he froze, looking frightened and guilty. Kirsten held her arm up, inviting him into a hug.

He ran over.

"Evan. I'm disappointed that you didn't tell me about it or ask."

"You would've said no."

"Maybe… but I need you to trust me."

He looked up, shocked. "I *do!*"

"I don't want you keeping a sharp knife under your pillow. You could hurt yourself in your sleep."

"Okay." He looked down.

"Until we figure out what's going on, I'm going to trust you to keep it here, but not under your damn pillow."

He blinked. "Really?"

She held him by the shoulders and nodded. "Yes. Really. But… I want you to come get me if something comes after you. Don't attack it if you can get out of the room, okay? That knife is only if you have no other choice."

Evan nodded. "'Kay."

"Get ready for school."

He ran to the wardrobe. She grumbled at the closet before getting up to go to grab a quick shower. Eleven minutes later and in uniform, she headed to the kitchen to make breakfast. Evan, dressed, sat at the table and checked his homework from the previous day. Over eggs and syn-bacon, he rambled about the testing. The Division 0 medical staff agreed with the theory that he'd caused the bruises himself, but as far as they could tell, he wasn't able to do it on purpose with his conscious mind.

"I think I was too scared. Whenever I thought about it, I was afraid of being hurt. In the dream, it's my sleepy brain doing it."

Kirsten wanted to devote every waking minute to figuring out what was going on, but the harvester ghost was getting stronger. She couldn't take days off now; if someone died, she'd never live down the guilt. "I'm going to ask Theodore to stay with you tonight, okay?"

"No way, Mom. I'll wake up with a wedgie so hard it'll be over my head."

She laughed, spraying eggs.

"Put an EM sensor in my closet."

"Those things are toys." She considered it for the span of a few breaths. "I'm not sure if they even work."

"Ask Dorian to test one." He leaned back in the chair, dangling an entire piece of bacon over his face with two fingers before dropping it into his mouth.

"Well, I suppose we could try. If it doesn't work, blockade your room."

"'Kay." He carried the empty plate to the dishwasher.

Kirsten tended to her dishes, then they made their way to the roof, and the patrol craft.

DORIAN LOOKED UP FROM HIS DESK WHEN KIRSTEN WALKED BACK INTO THE squad room. "What did you order?"

"Aside from coffee and lunch… a gadget." She handed sandwiches out to Nicole, Forrester, and Morelli before glancing at the six empty desks. "We're short staffed."

"Just waiting on a few more to ripen out of Admin." Dorian winked. "Unless you want to arm tweens."

"Tactical's overstuffed." Nicole mumbled past a mouthful of sausage-and-peppers sandwich. "That's why we're invading an I-Ops room."

Squad Corporal Forrester smiled, content not to talk over his turkey club.

"Ghost-tech EM pod." Dorian laughed. "Seriously?"

Kirsten unpacked a black box about the size of her fist with two collapsible antennas. "It's supposed to make noise and lights if a ghost comes within a few feet of it. Something's messing with Evan at night." She glared. "He suggested this as an alarm. Can you test it?"

She put it on her desk and turned it on.

"How does it work?" asked Dorian.

"Get close to it I guess." She shrugged.

Dorian, shaking his head, got up and approached it. Much to everyone's surprise, the device lit up and made a buzzing alarm noise when his hand came within a few inches of the antenna. "How 'bout that… it *does* work."

"Wow. I was not expecting that." Kirsten shut it off and sat down. She unboxed her cayenne pepper chicken sandwich and held it up to her mouth. At almost the exact second her first bite closed, her terminal and NetMini lit up. She mumbled, "Omf, fmmk ooo."

The image of a Division 1 patrol officer appeared over her desk. "Good morning, Lieutenant." The tag information on the right side of the comm window identified him as Senior Patrol Officer (E4) Warren Garber.

She waved the sandwich at him as a halfhearted salute. "Mmmng."

"It's not urgent, but… you're the woman who deals with the weird shit, right?" asked SPO Garber.

Kirsten nodded after taking another bite. Spice made her head sweat.

"I got a CI who says he's seeing all sorts of weird shit. Sounds like the kinda stuff from one of those ghost shows." SPO Garber waved his hand around in a circle. "You know… Banging in the dark, stuff moving around on its own. Scratches, unexplained pain."

She almost choked as she sucked in air. "Pain?" *Shit. Another organ case?* "Who's this CI?"

"It's confidential, so please don't put it in your records. The guy's name is Sanjay Rao, but he goes by Fizzle on the street. He's a chem dealer who's been feeding me info on some of the stuff we try to clamp a lid on: Nightcandy, Lace, Phindara, you know, the nasty shit. He keeps his own business strictly in the realm of tamer chems we couldn't care less about, but his info's good. He's helped us shut down two Lace labs already."

"Okay. Where can I find him?"

"He's squatting in an abandoned residence tower in Sector 6059. Grey zone near the 6060 black."

"That's ten miles from 1UP." Dorian waved at his desk terminal bar. A holo-pane scrolled open in midair already on a sector map. "6059, 6060, 6061 – where 1UP is."

Morelli jumped in his seat, staring at the 'empty' desk.

Kirsten eyed her remaining half of a sandwich. "Give me like ten minutes. Should I go in civvies not to rile up the locals?"

SPO Garber shook his head. "No offense, Lieutenant, but if those guys saw you in civvies you'd need an armed escort of assault infantry to keep the locals off you. You, uhh, look young. Better go in uniform. Those guys seem out of it, but they understand what the black means. They know you don't care about chems."

Yeah... even street thugs are terrified of psionics. "Nikki, Forrester, you guys free?" Kirsten glanced over. "I'd rather not have to kill anyone today."

"I don't wanna lose this CI, but we won't let anything go down. If you need backup, we'll be there." SPO Garber saluted.

"Appreciate it, Garber. You might've saved his life..." She swiped to end the call and inhaled the last few bites of her spicy chicken before heading to the locker room to grab psi armor.

Despite being bulky and annoying, she'd developed a fondness for the feeling of protection. It might not stop as much as the Division 1 armor could, but it also weighed about half. A little mental exertion activated the 'classified' stuff inside it, adding that field effect, so it wound up being more or less on par. Going into a post-haunting crime scene didn't bother her in the standard uniform, but for talking to a chem merchant in a dangerous area, she wanted something more between her and bullets than thin fabric.

THE CLOSER KIRSTEN FLEW TO THE NAV POINT, THE WORSE THE CONDITION OF the city around her became. At first, the decline manifested as fewer advert bots. Then, the thick garden of holographic signs mounted to walls thinned out. Twenty seconds more and some missing windows appeared sporadically on both sides. A block later, almost all of the windows were gone. Signs of life gave way to fluttering strands of plastic film trailing in the breeze from the locals' failed efforts to stop the wind from tearing through their squats.

Kirsten guided the patrol craft down to the level of the third story, skimming over a street jammed up with five-decade-old ground cars. An occasional spark crawled along the ruin below as the energized downdraft of ion engines blasted the ancient metal. Nicole followed at an uncharacteristic safe distance. As grey zones went, Sector 6059 tended toward dark, the kind of place Division 1 left alone unless they brought fifteen people and an armored vehicle.

"They're watching us," said Dorian. "I don't see anyone going for a weapon…"

She flicked her thumbnail at the crosshatch texture on the control stick.

Dorian kept his eye on the shadowed alleys. "They probably think we're chasing a psi criminal… Even fringers don't want to be cannon fodder for a rogue psionic."

"Heh. So they actually *are* afraid of something enough to tolerate police." Unable to decide if she felt insulted or comforted, she grumbled to herself until the digital windscreen showed a giant red thumbtack stuck in the roof of a building ahead on the left. "We're here."

"Copy that," said Nicole over comm.

The grime-darkened façade of a laundromat greeted her as she landed. Silver streaks in the muck coating the place showed where bullets had glanced away from the metal. Dim blue light glowed from within, glinting on jagged shards of grime-dusted glass embedded in the frame of a long-gone storefront window. Human shadows slipped away from nearby alleys, vanishing deeper into the urban deterioration. Kirsten stared into the building, her attention drawn to the small dark forms of rats crawling around the old washers and dryers.

Dorian blurred out of the passenger seat, coalescing a short distance away from her door outside. He walked through the knee-high front wall of the building.

Kirsten glanced down at the shiny black armor over her thighs. She teased a little psionic energy at it, causing the matte grey trim to glow violet for an instant. *Okay, it works. What am I so nervous about? It's really damn hard to kidnap a suggestive.* Dorian emerged from the building at the same time she put her helmet on.

"One guy inside. He's got three sentry guns. Small caliber, probably Class 1. More than likely intended for rats."

"Are they hacked?" She approached the door, with Nicole and Forrester two steps behind.

Dorian put on a used-hovercar salesman's smile. "They didn't fire at me."

She rolled her eyes. At the door, she paused to listen. A voice inside assured 'General Grok' that the fleet would fail if they dared to attack the Terran Alliance. *Holovid. Oh, that's Alien Armistice. Evan loves it.* The front door scraped plastic cartons and broken glass to the side in a clean arc over fading green tiles. She stepped into a wide room containing a counter with dry-cleaning racks behind it on the left by some benches for people to wait. On the right, the room stretched twice as deep, packed with old credstick-operated washers and dryers. A dense film of mold, dust, and chemicals coated the place, save for a discernible trail in the gunk that led around the end of the counter to the back room. Thick hanging ribbons of once-clear plastic obscured the room beyond, glowing in the flickering bluish light.

The ceiling shuddered under the roar of movie starship engines.

"Fizzle?" She drew the E-90, but held it down and to the side.

"Damn," said Forrester. "How can anyone live like this?"

"I wouldn't call this 'living.'" Nicole whistled, looking around. "I'd almost rather be in the Badlands."

"You'd look good on a leash." Forrester chuckled.

A plastic *crack* of armored fist on armored shoulder followed. "Go to Hell, Randy. It's not *all* like that out there. They have towns." Nicole grumbled.

"Yeah, but them towns get raided." Forrester shifted at sudden motion to the side. Whatever made the noise backed away from two laser rifles. "Man. This has got bad idea all over it."

"Fizzle," yelled Kirsten. She followed the path of clean floor to the end of the counter, freezing at the tiny sound of an electric motor whirring in three-second spurts. "Division 0."

The sound of a space dogfight cut out to silence. A second later, a nervous male voice called out, "Oh, that is being the awesome. Come in!"

"Turrets, Fizzle." Kirsten crept closer to the plastic curtain.

A metallic *creak* preceded the squeak of shoes and a few beeps. "Is safe."

Kirsten brushed the plastic strips out of her way with her left hand, and raised the E-90, following it into the doorway. The rails that once carried dry cleaned clothes passed overhead, uphill along a short corridor to her right, before hooking a sharp left at the end. Beyond the turn, another room waited, packed with tables covered in newish looking machines linked by hoses and tubes.

A skinny Indian man in a pink tee shirt and olive-drab fatigue pants waved at her from the top of the incline. The turret next to him came up to his knee, and looked more like a toy than a weapon; small as it was, the three-barrel rotary mechanism made it a threat. *6.5mm isn't too bad, but when there's eighty of them hitting you...*

The sentry gun had ceased sweeping side to side, so she relaxed—a little. "Fizzle?"

"Yep." He backed up, beckoning them with a wave. Her armor's HUD highlighted a handgun in the waistband of his pants behind his back, though his body language seemed nonthreatening.

He's happy to see us. Not a trap, said Nicole's voice in her head.

Kirsten bit back the urge to grumble at her for being free with surface thought skims. Perhaps the girl had a point. Being in *this* place tended to provide probable cause. She holstered her laser pistol and walked up to meet SPO Garber's confidential informant.

He offered a handshake. Only because of Nicole's assurance did she accept. When they clasped hands, she locked stares with bright blue eyes. For a second, the oddity of seeing an Indian man with blue eyes stunned her staring.

"Thanks for coming... I was afraid you guys might not wanna come out here."

Nicole scoffed. "You could've come to us. This place is a deathtrap."

"Yeah. Even without all these science projects." Forrester used his rifle to indicate at least thirteen boxy machines. Some sat quiet, others bore flickering LEDs, a few vibrated and thrummed. Twitching hoses carried neon-colored liquids between chambers. "First time I been in a drug lab."

Kirsten tensed. Of course... Garber had said chem merchant, but the true meaning hadn't hit her until Forrester's comment. This guy manufactured narcotics. Even if they were the sort of common cheapery that the police usually ignored, she didn't want to breathe anything in here.

"You guys are cool with it, right? I ain't brewin' nothin' serious." He smiled. "Little 'basket, some Smileys, Sandman... all low grade shit." Fizzle walked backward to a desk where a living-room-sized holo bar had been jury rigged as a monitor for a standard desk terminal unit. "I'm gonna take a gun outta my pants so I can sit down without hurting myself. Okay?"

Nicole and Forrester swiveled to almost aim at him.

"Easy and slow," said Kirsten.

Fizzle turned to show his back, removed the handgun with two fingers, and set it on the table before sitting down. "Damn thing ain't comfortable to sit on."

"So, our mutual friend said you've got some paranormal things going on here?" Kirsten approached him while looking up and around at the walls. Tattered plasfilm posters, mostly of sci-fi holovids and characters thereof, hid behind cobwebs so thick small children could probably climb them. "You really should dust once in a while."

Fizzle laughed. "You're funny for a cop. Yeah... I've been seeing some weird shit."

"Not to offend you or anything, but it's strange to see a person of your ethnic background with blue eyes." Kirsten took an image capture of his face via her helmet's electronics.

He grinned. "Not offended. 'Bout seven months ago, my previous lab blew up. Bunch of shitbags decided to muscle in on my operation and sent some bullets through the wall. Lucky spark set everything off. I caught a spray of glass in the face."

"Ow." Nicole sucked air between her teeth.

Forrester shook his head. "I thought you didn't make any of that nasty shit?"

"The phase one solution for Sandman is... vaporous. After it's been catalyzed, it's inert. They caught me at the perfect wrong time. Anyway, yeah, left me with a buncha glass where my eyes used to be. I had some cheap ass 'lectric ones for a while, but I hear from Deadcrow that some street doc had a set of eyes on the shelf he wanted rid of." Fizzle shook his head. "Now I kinda have a feeling why. Maybe I been samplin' too much of my own stuff, but I'm seein' shit."

Kirsten twisted to look at Nicole. *Watch this guy. I'm gonna close my eyes for a minute.* She opened herself to the surroundings, reaching out with a psionic feeler. Energy nearby had a surprising amount of strength. Perhaps the ghost had been about to attack him seconds before she walked in. She wandered a few steps forward, following an increase in charge, certain from the way it felt that the same entity had been here.

"You finding something?" asked Fizzle.

Kirsten opened her eyes and stared at a mattress so foul she didn't want to touch it even with armor on. Three transparent cartons on a plastisteel cargo box turned nightstand held something that may have once been pizza bites, but had separated into three layers of liquid, brown, clear, and yellow-orange. "Yeah. You're not imagining things. The man those eyes came from isn't happy about it."

"Shit." Fizzle folded his arms. "Shit twice."

Kirsten moved to his side and put a hand on his shoulder. "I need to know where you got them from."

"I met up with these bad dudes in 6851. We went into the black nearby, real skivey lookin' place. Like a basement outta some old mental hospital. Straight outta a slasher vid. Stank like old shoes. Ripper doc place... Mardrake I think."

"Dammit." Kirsten grumbled.

"What?" Nicole walked over. "What's a Mardrake?"

Kirsten ran a hand over her helmet and tapped armored fingers for a few seconds while thinking. "This guy gets killed by an organ harvester, his parts go all over the place, and the ghost is going from person to person trying to kill them or take his pieces back. It's the same spirit here."

"K..." Dorian waved from the far side of the nasty mattress. "Check this out."

He pointed at a silver holo-bar the size of a man's index finger, a standard picture display. When he poked it, a shimmery transparent image of Fizzle appeared, seated in the same chair. A naked Seraphina perched in his lap, teeth clenched around a chain attached to both of her nipples by clamps. She reached cuffed hands up behind her in an effort to 'hug' Fizzle's head. The young woman looked emaciated, pale, and snarled at the camera with an air of rebellious menace.

"Son of a bitch..." Kirsten stared at the picture a second longer before whirling on Fizzle. "How do you know her?"

He raised his hands. "She's freaky like that. Likes being tied up. Used to buy from me, but I haven't seen her in a while. Guess she finally got her wish." Fizzle looked downcast, and shook his head.

"Her wish?" Kirsten narrowed her eyes at him. "You're seeing that girl?"

"I..." He sighed. "I wanted to, but I guess she's not the type for a real relationship. I always thought she considered me nothing other than a casual fuck buddy. Didn't want more. She's all on the whisp so hard, like she's trying to fry her lungs and check the hell out." Fizzle pulled one leg up to hook the heel of his sneaker on the chair and rested his chin on his knee. "Sarah said she didn't 'want' to die, just didn't care if she did, but I knew what she meant. She wanted to, but was afraid to kill herself. Girl did so much whisp, she's gotta be gone by now. That shit'll chew up your lungs. I stopped making it 'cause of her."

Her thoughts were full of mint. Kirsten lowered her guard and put a comforting arm around him. "Hey. She's not dead."

Fizzle looked up, his eyes wet. "She's not? You know her?"

"Yeah. I've seen her." *Dammit! Son of a bitch!* Kirsten wanted to smash something, but kept an exterior of complete calm. "Now I know what her 'medical condition' was."

"New lungs," said Dorian.

She looked at him. "Yeah. And how much do you want to bet our ghost is genetically compatible with her."

"Motive, means, and resources." Dorian shook his head. "This is bad, K. It's going to get ugly if you butt heads with a senator."

She looked at him, mouth open, but couldn't think of anything to say before Fizzle grabbed her hand.

"Hey." He stared into her eyes. "If you see her, tell her I want there to be more for us. I'll leave all this shit behind if she'll stop hating herself."

"Aww." Nicole sniffled.

"Thank you, Fizzle. You were a big help. Bigger than you know. Now I have somewhere to go."

"Wait, what? You're leaving? What about the thing haunting me?" He stood.

"He's not here now. You might've just given me the means to find him. If anything happens again, let our mutual friend know, and he can contact me. Also, it might help if you said you had no idea the eyes were stolen."

"Doubtful," said Dorian. "I think this one's too angry to care."

"Yeah, maybe, but I can't sit here waiting." Kirsten started to leave, but paused by the little sentry gun. "Fizzle, if you're serious about Seraphina, you might want to consider getting out of here first. Show her you really mean it."

Kirsten stared at his sad smile for a few seconds, then hurried back to the patrol craft.

"Where to now?" Dorian's voice entered the car before he coalesced in the passenger seat.

Nicole and Forrester jogged to their vehicle. Muted *thumps* of closing doors came from behind.

"Morgue. I'm going to see how Oliver is doing."

PIECING TOGETHER

Kirsten banked the patrol craft to the left to dodge a green-camouflage DS2 lifting off from the roof of the Regional Tech Center. A light snow swirled about at altitude, though the ground below showed no accumulation. The DS2 flashed its lights twice, a gesture of greeting as it passed. She wobbled the car side to side in response, as it lacked running lights, and headed for the larger of three roof landing pads surrounding the dome-shaped main building of the RTC.

"I'm sure Seraphina has this guy's lungs. Attacks of being unable to breathe, the presence of the ghost in the room with her… Senator Winchester has the resources to set something like that up. What pisses me off is he could afford fixing her the right way."

"Good luck proving it." Dorian drummed his fingers on his knee. "And don't even think about compelling him to confess. One whiff of psionic manipulation of a senator gets out, and all of Division 0 is going to be in deep shit."

She glared at him. "You know me better than that. I intend to find proof. That's why we're here."

Kirsten landed in a spot reserved for police vehicles and sprinted through a light pattering of freezing rain to the entrance. Two white-walled corridors later, she rode an elevator down to the fourth basement level and emerged in air as frosty as the outside, only far less wet. Her boots squelched on the white linoleum as she passed dim freezer rooms, six per side. As it had the last time she'd been here, the place felt more like the set of a horror movie than an active medical facility.

The chill that spread down her back at the thought of Eli Hassan came from nerves alone. *He had to have been another shell.* She forced fear aside and hurried up to the large U-shaped desk in a room serving as a T intersection in the hallway. Oliver Murphy snoozed in his chair, headphones on, his puff of black, curly hair wild in all directions. Asleep, he looked even more like the pudgy frat boy everyone liked.

Kirsten tapped her hand on the counter three times fast. "Oliver."

He snapped upright. "Wabobo?"

"Wake up, Oliver." She tried to snap her fingers, but it didn't work well in the armored glove.

"Oh. Hey, Agent Wren." He smiled and rubbed sleep crumbs out of his eyes. "Crap. Sorry, Lieutenant. Congrats!"

"Thanks. Hey I need you to help me out with a case." She fished out her NetMini and opened the Inquest file. "Can you run a DNA comparison against a couple of stray organs? I'm hoping the body came here."

"Sure." He yawned, stretched, cracked his knuckles, and wiggled his fingers like a maestro about to play a piano concerto. "Give me a sec to get into the system." Four widescreen holo-panels shimmered into being around him, each a deep, royal blue. "Okay. Hit me."

Kirsten flicked data from her NetMini at his terminal including the DNA profile from the kidneys and heart she'd gotten from Easley, plus a file on Lamb's liver transplant Sam had 'stumbled across.'

Oliver poked, typed, and swiped, rearranging images onto the rightmost screen. "Well, it looks like all of these organs are from the same body."

"I knew that already." She smiled. "Is that body here? Can you give me a name?" *Come on. Please.* She looked up at the ceiling. *If you guys are listening, I could use a little nudge.*

"Might take a minute. You want some coffee?" Oliver stood.

She pulled herself up to sit on the counter. "Yeah, sure."

He hurried off to a vending machine between the bathrooms, down the same hall leading to the office where Hassan had shot himself in the head, or at least whatever that creature was who looked like a human named Eli Hassan. Kirsten swung her feet, idly thumping her boot heels into the Epoxil face of the desk. Distant whirring of the coffee machine foaming the brew broke the silence.

Oliver returned with two cups, sat, and slid one to her. He leaned back, taking a huge gulp from his cappuccino, seeming immune to its heat, and smiled a milk froth moustache up at her. "Looks like you've got the luck of angels. How long have you been on Earth?"

Dorian rolled his eyes. "At least he didn't ask if it hurt when you fell."

"Nice try. I only rent the wings." She sipped. For a 'sem in a morgue, it wasn't too bad. "Does that mean you got a name?"

"Yep. Looks like this guy came in about five weeks ago. Charles Prentice, age thirty-five." He swatted something from his screen at her, and a chirp sounded from her NetMini. "According to the file, they found him in a grey zone by chance while doing a burn and purge on a Lace lab."

"Still in a freezer?" She tapped the NetMini's screen, and a small panel appeared showing the face of a pallid man with short, black hair and green eyes. Despite his somewhat ghoulish coloration, he looked happy.

"Nope. He's got a sister. She claimed the ashes as soon as we finished the autopsy."

"Can't imagine that took long," said Dorian with a smirk. "Guy was as hollow as Nicole's head."

She swiped at Dorian with a playful slap. "Leave her alone. She's just got excess energy."

Oliver flicked his gaze up to her without moving anything but his eyeballs. "Ghost?"

"Yep. Thanks for the assist, Oliver." She slid off the counter and turned to face him. "Let me know if I can ever do anything for you, okay?"

"Dinner and a movie?" He smiled.

She cringed. "I'm not sure my boyfriend would go for that, but if you wanna hang out?"

"Story of my life." He leaned back in his chair, hands draped in his lap. "Take care of yourself, Lieutenant."

"You too." She felt bad for him, to the point her walk back to the elevator slowed. Once the doors closed, she glanced at Dorian. "Maybe I should try to set him up with Adrienne."

Dorian raised an eyebrow. "That's mean. What did Oliver do to you?"

"Will you stop?" She glared at him. "She's no different than if she'd been born a woman. Genetic surgery, remember. She can even have babies." Kirsten bit her lip with a mischievous grin and used her NetMini to set up a three-way chat, typing: "Hey Adrienne. This is Oliver."

"Don't you have enough to do?" He chuckled. "And why her?"

"They're both lonely and really sweet. Plus I don't know many other single women."

Dorian raised an eyebrow. "Didn't she have herself made sixteen again?"

Kirsten cringed. *Shit.* She cancelled the chat before sending the message. "Uhh… okay, good point. Way too creepy."

He nodded. "Just a little."

AFTER STOWING THE PSI ARMOR IN HER LOCKER, KIRSTEN SLIPPED INTO HER thin black uniform and sprinted to her desk. Three Cajun chicken salads (extra tomatoes in one) sat next to her terminal with a note from Nicole: 'you *have* to try this place and I know you love xtra tomz'. She unlocked her terminal and started a data crawl on Charles Prentice before sending Evan a text: ‹In the building. Want me to meet you at the school?›

‹5 mins of class left. Nah, we'll come up.›

She found it hard to resist the smell of the food, but managed to hold off while watching animated gears turn. Soon, Evan ran in dragging his backpack and flopped in the interviewee chair next to her desk. Shani followed at his heels, and telekinetically moved him over so they could both sit in the chair. They ate and chatted about the day at school while the search ran. Evidently, some big kid named Shawn who'd started off bullying him had decided to become friends. Evan wanted to know if he could come over some day to hang out. She didn't see any problem with that and gave him a nod, to which he grinned.

Information panels opened on the screen, containing every recorded bit of information the UCF had on Charles Prentice. For the four years prior to his death, he'd worked for a company named OnSite! – a subsidiary of ComTec International. Charles went to homes and businesses doing miscellaneous tech work on everything from NetMinis to terminals, to game systems, audio-video hardware, and high-end holographic alternate reality suites.

"Hang on, kiddo. Need to make a call."

Evan nodded, continuing to shovel chicken, croutons, and lettuce into his face. Shani amused herself by using telekinesis to levitate individual pieces of salad to her mouth one at a time.

Kirsten placed an outbound Vid to Prentice's former employer.

A company logo rendered in mirror silver appeared. "You have reached OnSite!, a subsidiary of ComTec International. How may we direct your call?"

"Human resources. This is an official contact from Division 0, National Police Force."

"One moment," said the artificial woman's voice.

The logo screen went black, and a coffee-toned face appeared above a cheap indigo suit. "Human resources, Bradley speaking. Thank you for calling OnSite!, a division of ComTec International."

"They've got to be required to say that." Dorian pulled at his hair.

"Hi Bradley. I'm Lieutenant Wren with Division 0. I have some questions about a former employee of yours. Charles Prentice?"

The man hummed to himself for a few seconds. "Lieutenant, there may be an issue here. We're currently engaged in legal action with his next of kin. It's a warrantless claim, but they are insinuating that OnSite!, a subsidiary of ComTec International, put him at undue risk by sending him on his last assignment."

"I'm trying to track down the people who killed him. There is reason to believe that Mr. Prentice was targeted specifically, and that reason is unrelated to OnSite."

"A subsidiary of ComTec International," said Dorian.

She shot him a glare.

Evan giggled.

"If I'm able to resolve this case, I'm sure it will prove that he would've been killed regardless of anything your company did."

"I can certainly help you with that Lieutenant." Bradley glanced at a screen to the left. He didn't move as if typing, which attracted Kirsten's notice to a thin silver wire draped down from behind his left ear. "Mr. Prentice was found dead some time ago. Sad. His employment record is exemplary except for one complaint, but we disregarded it."

"Oh?" She tilted her head.

"The last record in his file is a complaint from a customer saying that he never showed up or called. We believe the cause to be his untimely death, so we struck the complaint from his record."

"How nice of them." Dorian rolled his eyes.

"He was killed while on his way to an assignment? Where was the job?"

Bradley's glance shifted. "872 City Road 2444. Apartment 22-04. Sector 6796."

Kirsten brought up a sector map and grumbled. That address sat about ten miles southwest from the grey area spreading out from the black zone where Mardrake worked in Sector 6903. "Well, that's not particularly insightful, but it does back up my theory. Thank you, Bradley. Can you please send me that file?"

"I can certainly help you with that, Lieutenant." Bradley shifted his gaze to her. "Is there anything else I can help you with today?"

"Can you possibly display a unique personality?" asked Dorian.

Evan sprayed lettuce bits on a laugh before he could get a hand over his mouth. Kirsten ruffled his hair, adoring the way the psionic energy glimmered within his eyes. That she couldn't take him home right that second to enjoy a relaxing evening hurt. "No, that's it. Thank you."

Bradley blinked and gawked at her. "Uhh…"

Kirsten tilted her head at him for a second before she noticed four croutons orbiting her head like tiny moons.

"Thank you for calling OnSite!, a subsidiary of ComTec International." Bradley hung up.

Shani cracked up laughing; her concentration gone, the food fell to the floor.

"What now?" asked Dorian.

"I need to go talk to the sister…" She swiped a few data pages across her screen. "Laney. Hmm. Still Prentice. Guess she never married."

"You could set *her* up with Oliver." Dorian winked.

Kirsten rolled her eyes.

"Shani's gonna be stuck in the dorm tonight. Nila's on a stakeout." Evan swung his sneakers back and forth. "Guess you can't take me with you?"

"I don't know what could happen there, Ev. I'm sorry. I can't risk you getting hurt. You know I hate it when I have to work late."

The sadness in his expression retreated to a somber smile. "No, you don't. You hate leavin' me alone, but you love helping people."

She hugged him. "I'll pick you two up in a little bit, 'kay? Shani can sleep over."

"Really?" Shani blinked.

Kirsten patted her on the head. "Of course… as often as Nila lets Evan stay with you guys, it's not even a question."

"Okay." Evan hopped up and kissed her on the cheek before heading for the squad room door, pulling Shani by the hand. "Be safe."

"Hey, where are you going?" She cocked an eyebrow.

"Uhh, the dorms 'til you're back." He shrugged.

"Let me walk you down."

He grinned. "'Kay."

SCATTERED

Kirsten drove a little fast for not being Code 3, but Division 1 did it all the time… and faster, so she didn't let it bother her much. A few close calls with advert bots made her palms sweaty. Nothing existed but the twin yellow light trails on the windscreen display and moving objects she might bump into. She followed the navigation assist to the home of Laney Prentice.

Dorian kept quiet for the ride, protesting her speed with a hand over his eyes rather than words.

Worry about Evan stalked her. *What is in his room? Is this Konstantin seeping back into the world? Ev never liked him. Revenge? No. Giving kids nightmares could be an ordinary jackass move from some random new ghost.*

"Promise me you won't kill this woman?" Dorian lifted his fingers enough to look at her.

"I'm thinking about Evan. Keep going back to worst-case scenario. Konstantin trying to get revenge on him for snapping me out of his charm… or some abyssal…"

"If it was that, you'd have definitely felt something."

She exhaled. "Yeah. You're right."

A few minutes later, she guided the patrol craft through a wide portal in the side of the building at the fifty-fourth floor. This residence tower had a 'garden roof' covered in verdant greenery instead of a parking deck. Three stories at the midway point of the tower contained internal parking for hovercars. After finding a spot, she followed her armband computer's arrow to the elevator, and apartment 99-20.

The door squeaked to the side, revealing a wan woman pale enough to pass for a Marsborn, her skin pure white, devoid of even the slightest hint of color. Dark green eyes regarded Kirsten with a measure of resignation, as if she lacked the energy to protest whatever the police wanted to do to her. Ink-black hair framed a delicate face that reminded her a bit of Marguerite, though this woman looked less perfect, more like a real person than a sculpture of idealized beauty. An oversized beige angora sweater engulfed most of her body, two slim strands, black leggings, led down to bare feet.

"Can I help you?" Her voice had more depth than expected given her size, but also carried palpable sorrow.

"Miss Prentice?"

The woman nodded.

"I'm Lieutenant Wren, Division 0. I'm investigating the matter of your brother's death. Can we talk?"

"Wow. I thought they'd given up on Charlie. Come in." Laney walked away from the door, heading for the back of the apartment. "I suppose I should offer you coffee or tea or something?"

"That's not necessary." Kirsten entered, watching the door until it closed with a soft hiss. The smell of hours-old Earl Grey lingered in the air, dueling with something floral.

Laney aborted her fast walk to the kitchen and diverted to a dull blue sofa facing a holographic fireplace flanked by huge potted plants with leaves speckled two shades of green. Kirsten sat at the woman's left.

"The police have already said they have nothing to go on, and don't expect to ever find who killed Charlie."

"I'm sorry for your loss, Miss Prentice." Kirsten folded her hands in her lap. "I don't enjoy dredging up bad feelings or memories, but I want you to know I'm trying to help."

"You're one of those psionics, aren't you?" A hint of contempt underscored her voice, helped along by a 'get away from me' lean.

Kirsten's guilt at possibly causing emotional pain lessened. "Yes."

Laney seemed to let her brain take this in, chew on it, and blow fragments of thought out the other side of her head. "Well. I suppose since the normal police can't do anything, I'll take any help I can get. Do you really think you can find who did this?"

Dorian went for a walkabout.

"I don't want this to be any more unpleasant than it has to be given the subject matter. Might I ask why you dislike psionics?"

"I was abused by one when I was thirteen." Laney looked away. "I knew he was forcing me to do those things, but I couldn't stop. It went on for over a year before Charles finally came home early and caught the man in the act."

Kirsten's gut turned into a lead weight. "I'm so sorry."

Laney stared at the rug for a while. "He's dead now. Something happened to him in prison. I suppose I should be noble and not expect the worst of all of you. I... Charlie kept me going. I don't know what I'm going to do now that he's gone."

"Miss Prentice, nothing I can say will change what happened to you. I don't want to upset you, but Charles isn't quite gone."

"What?" Laney glared at her. "What are you talking about?"

Multiple cats in the distance shrieked, hissed, and yowled.

"Oh, babies!" Laney jumped up. "Excuse me."

Kirsten closed her eyes. "Your cats are okay. Trust me."

Laney looked between her and an interior archway for a few seconds before sitting again. "Are you sure?"

"Nothing here," said Dorian, emerging from the wall by the kitchen. "She's got the urn though, and she's storing enough chemicals to keep a forest preserve operational. Oh, and about thirteen cats. I'm guessing she doesn't go out much."

Kirsten cringed, and gave him a 'not now' glare. He raised his hands and backed off.

"What's going on?" Laney looked at the general area where Dorian stood. "What are you staring at?"

"Your brother was murdered, I suspect by a man who wanted to take organs for illegal sale."

Laney gasped; hand on her mouth, tears welled up.

"I'm an Astral Sensitive, Miss Prentice. I deal with paranormal events, ghosts primarily. I believe your brother is still here and he's attempting to harm other people who received his parts."

"I hope they die screaming." Laney scowled. "Bastards."

Kirsten bit her lip to stay calm. "Most of the people—possibly all of them —have no idea what happened. I only found Charles's name a few hours ago, and I've been hunting for this spirit for quite a while now."

"That stupid company he worked for sent him to a shitty area. They never should've let him go so close to all those bad people. If he had a real job, he'd still be alive." She crunched her hands together, making fists inside her sweater sleeves.

"I need to help him before he kills someone. There are things worse than death out there and I understand why he's angry. He deserves to be angry. I want to get the people who killed him and help him rest, but he won't talk to me. He keeps running away."

Laney frowned at her, red eyes glaring. "You're expecting me to believe this?"

"Allow me." Dorian approached and shimmered transparent.

"Eeee!" Laney leapt back against the sofa.

His body returned to its usual solid appearance. "Hmm. I was trying to project calmness."

"Laney, that's my partner, Dorian. He won't hurt you."

The woman shivered. "That wasn't a hologram, was it? I... *felt* him looking at me."

"No. Spirits exist, and right now, I need your help to find one in particular. You have Charles's remains?"

Laney sniffled and nodded.

"Would you mind if I held the urn for a little while? I'd like to use it to try and call him here."

The woman looked around at random objects for a few minutes, her expression shifted from frightened to sad to confused. Eventually, she got and padded off to the back. A chorus of baleful meows followed her deeper into the apartment.

"Can you ease back on the wiseass remarks for a bit please," whispered Kirsten. "She's been through enough."

"Okay... sorry." Dorian raised a hand in surrender.

Laney returned with a plain plastisteel urn, the size of a large synthbeer canister but rectangular, with an engraved portrait on one face above the name 'Charles Prentice.' Below, in block lettering, 'Beloved brother.'

She sat on the edge of the cushion, seeming not quite able to hand it over.

"It's okay. You can hold him. I only need to touch the urn." Kirsten set her hand on top of the rectangular vessel and closed her eyes.

Psionic energy swirled around in her head, concentrated on beaconing the spirit linked to the astral residue lurking in the ashes. Kirsten called out into the ether, radiating her desire for the ghost to seek her out. Another cat screamed, and something in the back of the apartment fell with a *thud* that jarred the floor.

At the sense of another person there, Kirsten opened her eyes.

The eyeless, hollow-chested apparition she'd seen before stood at the opening between dining room and hallway, under a white-painted arch. He 'looked' at Dorian, then Kirsten, with a grim expression of simmering anger.

"Charles." Kirsten stood, facing him. "Thank you for coming here. I want to help you."

"I don't trust you. That thing you did burned."

"Is he here?" asked Laney.

His rage faded, his expression became mournful as he glanced toward her.

"Yes he is. Charles, can you tell me who killed you?"

The spirit paced around, coming closer. "You're not going to trick me?"

"No. I'd like to ask you to stop hurting those people. They don't know where the organs came from. They have no idea you were killed."

He shuddered with anger. "The big bastard kept talking about 'be careful with the lungs.' He said that's the whole reason for grabbing me. Three of them. Big guy, bald, had silver eyes. The other guy was about his build"— Charles gestured at Dorian—"but his head was shaved. Same look too... Middle Eastern or whatever. The other guy was small, bright red hair, candy red. Purple eyes, and he kept twitching like he was on some bad shit."

Kirsten typed notes as fast as she could. "Did you overhear any names?"

"The big guy, they kept calling him Nurse B, or something. Little dude got called Spaz a few times, but I don't know if that was a name or just because he kept twitching."

"Okay." She added another two lines to the file. "I think I know where your lungs are."

"That rich girl. Senator's daughter. Seraphina or whatever. The one who tried to kill herself." Charles folded his arms. "I... Poor kid was so damn pathetic I couldn't do anything to her. She reminded me a bit of Laney."

Kirsten glanced at the woman who'd been staring open-mouthed into space.

"Careful, K. This guy's only been dead two months is it? He shouldn't be able to affect the living. Might be more than he appears. Remember Vikram?"

"He's technically affecting his own body." Kirsten looked from Laney to Charles. "It makes the most sense."

"Charles?" asked Laney. "Charlie? Where are you?"

"Here, Lane." He put a hand near her shoulder. "Tell her I saw Mom and Dad, and Goblin is with them."

Kirsten repeated it.

Laney sobbed.

"A dog we had as kids." Charles gazed down. "I can't let her see me like this."

"Spirits manifest most easily as they appear at the moment of death. It's perhaps the most powerful emotional imprint left on the psyche, being killed. It's not permanent. You can make yourself appear however you want, if you concentrate hard enough."

Dorian's attire changed to his dress uniform, and then to a tee shirt and shorts. After a smile, he let it go back to the standard Division 0 blacks. "Might take some practice, but you're years away from appearing to anyone but an astral sensitive, so you have time."

"I've got a lot of information to process now. Please give me the time to do this for you. I'll do everything I can to get the bastards who killed you, but I won't be able to if you kill one of those people."

Charles' presence darkened, becoming foreboding. Three cats shot out from under the sofa, blurry streaks of fur that disappeared down the hall. "You're threatening me now? Those people had no goddamned right to kill me for parts!"

Kirsten raised a hand. "I'm not talking about me, though I will try and stop you from harming the innocent. I'm talking about other things. Entities who come for dark souls."

"Innocent? They stole my life in little pieces!"

"Calm down and listen to me. Julia thought the heart came from someone who'd been killed in a gang war. Lindsey, the girl from the moon station, she believed new kidneys had been regenerated using her DNA."

"That NewsNet asshole knew." Charles glared at her. "And that chemist didn't seem to care much."

Kirsten cringed. "Okay. Fair point, but none of them were *responsible* for your death. Lamb's an asshole for not caring about it, but he didn't cause it. Did Seraphina know?"

Charles's anger faded. Again, he stared at his sobbing sister. "I don't think so. She saw me. She's close enough to death that she saw me. She told me to kill her. Welcomed it. Her father's the one who arranged for me to be killed. I'll leave those people alone, but you take him down. You also have to come help Laney if she wants to talk to me."

"Actually..." Dorian smiled. "You can do that with a NetMini on audio record mode. It's a bit slow to go back and forth with, but it's faster than waiting for us to get here."

"I can show you how to do that." Kirsten slipped her NetMini from her belt. "Laney, if you want to talk to Charles, you can use your 'mini. Go into Apps > sound recorder. In settings, turn up the microphone all the way." She demonstrated, pushing little sliders to the top of the touchscreen. "Charles can hear you speaking, but you can't hear him without something like this." She looked at the ghost. "Get close and speak into this."

Charles leaned his face to within inches of the device. "Hey, Laney-boo."

Kirsten paused the recording and wiped a tear from her eye. "Just, uhh... back it up and play."

After Kirsten's recorded instructions, a distorted whispery rasp repeated, "Hi, Laney-boo."

"What?" Laney jumped. "It's garbled."

"It takes a bit of getting used to... and Charles needs to concentrate on speaking slow. I understood it because I can hear him speaking like a normal person. He said 'Hi, Laney-boo.'"

The woman burst into tears. Kirsten looked away, choked up.

Laney sniffled. "Play it again, please?"

On the fifth replay, she looked at Kirsten with adoration. "He's really here..."

Kirsten stood and tucked her NetMini back on her belt. "I'm going to go start trying to track those men down. If you get angry or frustrated, please find me."

"How?" asked Charles.

"I'll stick around a bit and try and show him how to do some things," said Dorian. "On the condition you leave those people alone for the time being."

Charles scowled.

"Going after a senator for a contracted killing is going to be a delicate process. It may take me a while to gather enough evidence to nail him. If you want to go mess with him, feel free."

Laney ran off into the back.

He smirked. "Guess the law doesn't work for me anymore since I'm dead."

"That's my job, Charles. The law *does* help the dead, but it's an uphill march."

Dorian grumbled. "We're trying to turn the law back on one of the people responsible for making it. It's got to be done carefully, and will take time."

"It will be much smoother if I'm not racing around worrying about you killing someone." Kirsten summoned up her most reassuring smile. "Please?"

Laney jogged back into the living room, clutching a bright purple NetMini.

"Fine. I'll try waiting… but, if that girl dies, don't go pinning that shit on me."

Kirsten sighed. "So much for no longer having a timer running."

"I'll catch up." Dorian winked at her, and patted Charles on the arm. "First lesson, how to scare cats."

"Scare cats?" asked Charles, raising one eyebrow over a hollow eye socket.

Dorian walked over to him. "Oh sure. Every ghost works on that first. Ever see the little bastards lose their minds and zip around for no reason? Means there's a new ghost adjusting to life on this side. Extra points if you can get them to climb drapes."

"Be nice," muttered Kirsten as she headed for the door.

KIRSTEN FLOPPED IN HER SEAT IN THE SQUAD ROOM AND STARTED A DATA CRAWL with the descriptions of the suspects she'd gotten from the ghost of Charles Prentice, flagging Citycams within six sectors of the area rumored to be where Mardrake lived as well as any Division 1 contact with three men of similar descriptions.

She placed a vid call to Theresa. The live-in medtech answered in four rings.

"Hello, Officer Wren."

Sigh. Lieutenant. "How's Seraphina?"

"Sleeping."

Shock. "Please keep an eye on her. I think she may try to harm herself."

"Okay, I will." Theresa looked around for a second and leaned closer to her NetMini, making her holographic head enlarge. "She has already tried. I should not say this, but the senator, he should do right by her before it's too late."

"Yeah. I'm working on it." Kirsten offered a resigned smile. "Thanks."

"Good night, officer."

Kirsten left the data crawl going and locked her terminal. It wasn't *too* late yet, only seven. Hopefully, Evan would still want dinner. Grinning, she hurried off to the dorms, where she found Evan and Shani lost in a multiplayer *Colony Commando* game in the rec room. Both wore senshelmets, though the Yume Koujou device projected a holo-panel showing a rotating point of view that cycled among all 120 players. She sat cross-legged on the rug between them, and gave Evan a pat on the shoulder so he knew she was there.

"Ready to go home?"

"Match is over in like two minutes, okay?"

"Sure."

She grinned at the kids chattering back and forth like little soldiers. "Cover me," "going in," "flashbang left," and so on continued for about four minutes before the external screen showed a scoreboard split into two teams. Kirsten couldn't tell who was who, or where Evan's player name was, but based on the look on his face, his team had won.

Shani stood and stared down at her toes. "Night, Ev."

He furrowed his eyebrows at her. "Huh? You're coming over. Mom already said that."

Kirsten grasped Shani's bony little shoulder. "I am *not* angry at you. The man made you point a gun at me."

"Really?" Shani twisted side to side.

"Yes. Really." Kirsten patted her on the back. "Come on. Get your shoes on."

She grinned up at Kirsten and ran off down the hall. While waiting, Kirsten shot a text to Nila: ‹Bringing Shani home. Good luck on the stakeout.›

Nila's response appeared in six seconds. ‹Thanks! She hates the dorm so much. Hope bratling isn't a problem.›

‹Not at all.› Kirsten smiled as she typed.

Kitten mewls echoed from the corridor, emanating from the tiny pink Nomz on Shani's feet. She darted into the room, already wearing her jacket and backpack. Kirsten took the kids each by the hand and walked to the elevator.

HOME, AND OUT OF UNIFORM, KIRSTEN ORDERED DELIVERY CHINESE AND ATE with a child leaning against her on both sides while watching an animated movie about a planet ruled by giant robots. Once the movie ended, they played a holographic card game involving summoning creatures and managing land resources for a bit before the yawning started.

Kirsten ushered one child then the next through the cycle of changing and brushing teeth. Shani squealed in delight at Evan's Monwyn-themed bedroom. After an extended tour to check out all the stuff, the girl crouched to unroll her sleeping bag on the floor of Evan's bedroom. He sat up on the Comforgel pad and looked at Kirsten.

Think that box will work? I don't want the spirit to hurt Shani. His expression said he didn't want Shani to see him curled up in the corner, terrified.

Kirsten walked over and patted him on the head. *Dorian tested it. If something shows up in your closet, it'll make noise. Hey, why don't you blockade tonight? We can set the trap when Shani's at home and safe.*

He jumped up with an eager wide-eyed look. "Okay."

She backed out and let him hit the button to close the door. If a paranormal entity *was* harassing Evan, a blockade would let him sleep without fear, and from the grin on his face, he knew it too.

35

GHOST TRACE

A ringing NetMini woke Kirsten at 5:59 a.m. She rolled onto her side, moaned, and plugged her ears until it stopped. Before she could smile at the silence, her alarm went off. She sat up, rubbing her cheek.

"Son of a bitch." She grumbled, killed the alarm, and picked up the NetMini to see who called. She dialed Nila back.

"Sorry, did I wake you? I thought you got up at six?"

Kirsten feigned annoyance. "Twenty seconds to six is not six." Raspberry.

Nila laughed. "Your clock is slow. I'm on to you, trying to sneak in an extra half minute of sleep."

Children's giggles came from the hallway outside her room, making her smile.

"Still alive I see."

"Me or the kids?" Kirsten yawned. "How was the stakeout?"

"Both, and a waste of time. The guy never showed. I have better things to do than sit outside a residence tower waiting for a telekinetic pickpocket to go out on the stalk. Thanks for watching the bratling."

"Oh, she's adorable." Kirsten sighed, rubbing her foot through the sheet. "Still a little afraid of me I think, but I hope she'll grow out of it. Wanna pick her up before you leave or I can drop her at the school?"

"Would you mind? I'm off today. Least they can do for staying up all damn night. I haven't slept yet. I'll pick them up after school."

"Okay."

Managing two sub-ten-year-olds in the morning turned out to feel more than double as draining as one. Shani had *way* more energy than anyone had a right to possess that early in the morning and couldn't seem to sit still. Add Telekinesis to the mix, and Kirsten wanted to dive into a pillow by the time she reached the squad room.

"Did you sleep?" asked Morelli.

Kirsten froze. "Wow. Conversation. You feeling okay, Tom? And yeah, I did. Two kids this morning."

He looked like he wanted to say something sarcastic, but held it in. "You got another one?"

"No, just minding Nila's daughter. She had a stakeout last night."

"Isn't the kid seven? What's she doing on a stakeout."

Kirsten blinked at him. "I'm not awake enough to tell if you're making a bad joke."

He chuckled. "Yeah, I heard about that. They've been ignoring that guy for a while since he's hard to track down and isn't hurting anyone, but the NewsNet got him on camera so now it's like he's a serial killer."

"Oh, no!" Dorian faded in at his desk, overacting shock. "Someone caught a psionic crime on camera."

Kirsten grumbled over to her seat, and opened a panel to order coffee. Nicole's desk was empty, so she glanced at Morelli. "Want a latte or something?"

"Sure. Plain cappuccino with an extra shot."

Order sent, she pulled up the dreaded reports interface and got to work updating the official Inquest documentation with everything she'd learned. Much easier to do with two hands at a full computer as opposed to one finger picking at her forearm.

Her NetMini chimed, indicating a notice from a delivery bot hovering at the entrance to the parking area. Policy refused to allow them into the building under concern they could be used to bring dangerous substances or explosives inside. Kirsten hoofed it to the garage and back, carrying a tray with two cups. After giving Morelli his coffee, she cradled the double-extra-shot mocha latte in both hands and inhaled its aroma while staring at the data crawl she'd started last night.

The system continued to search for the three killers, though some information had popped up regarding Charles. She sipped as she read over it. The routine had discovered a hit on the name Charles Prentice from a network border router at a Morning Bean café near the same grey zone where he'd been killed. *I can't do much with that, but maybe someone at the store saw him.*

She got up and headed to the car, bringing the coffee. Dorian leaned against the fender waiting for her.

"Beat you."

"It's not an official race until I can go through floors too."

He laughed. "You can if you project."

"And then I can't drive, so there's no point." She hopped in. "How'd it go with Charles? I hope you didn't torture those poor cats."

"So-so. He's pretty weak, still. They got the hang of communicating with the 'mini, but I couldn't get him to manage noticeable physical contact. He can't tap his sister on the shoulder to get her attention, but we did get the lights to flutter." He smiled. "And the cats are fine."

"That's something. Do you think he's going to wait?" She pulled out of the garage and climbed to the hover lane, tapping the Navcon to set a waypoint to the coffee shop.

"He seems to want to, but you know how it goes with the 'purposeful rage' spirits. Eventually, the need for revenge is going to overwhelm reason. Of course, it could be years before his sense of who he was in life erodes that far."

"I hope this doesn't take years." She set the car on auto-drive and leaned back with her coffee, nursing it with small sips.

"Taking on a senator? You have better odds waiting for the clock to kill him."

She frowned. "He's a senator. He's not untouchable."

"You're Division 0. Strike one. Right there, everything we do is going to come under a microscope. Two, he's got power enough to cause trouble. One senator starts questioning the 'need' for an entire police division to be devoted to psionics and things might get shitty in a hurry."

"Carter wouldn't allow that." She twisted the cup around.

"Or Burckhardt... but what form would that take? They try to do something shady, it blows up in their faces, and then we're all getting hunted down."

"What's with the doomsday prophet stuff?" She glanced at him.

He shook his head. "I'm only being realistic. I've seen this happen before. If you make a run at the senator and miss, hell... if you gear up to make a run at the senator, expect to be told to walk away."

I can't see that happening. "You're being cynical again. Senator or not, he arranged for a murder."

"Of no one important." Dorian shook his head. "The machine isn't going to care."

"How can you say he's not important?" She blinked.

"I mean politically significant. Charles is a faceless citizen no one at the top would care to make a big stink over."

Her NetMini beeped. She spent the remaining eleven minutes of the ride reading a long email from Ashley Harris, thanking her over and over again for saving her from 'those psychos.' The girl explained she intended to join Division 0, but probably stay with Admin. She didn't want to be a 'cop,' but did want to help psionics who'd been abused—if she ever got out of therapy herself.

Kirsten held off on replying; the message she wanted to send would take too long and leave her too choked up to be done before going into a possible crime scene. A quarter mile from the Morning Bean coffee shop, she took manual control and brought the car in for a landing about half a block away and on the other side of the street—the only open spot.

Some people paused to watch her land and a few continued staring as if to see what happened. Most didn't pay any attention, lost to their NetMinis or own affairs. Six blocks separated the coffee place from the grey zone, enough for the general composition of pedestrians to be more or less civilized. A few who appeared to have gang affiliations paid the most attention to her, flagrant in their display of weapons. She walked past them, abiding a mutual sense of defiance.

Inside, the aromas of coffee, chocolate, maple, and cinnamon swirled, making the air outside bland and cold by comparison. She couldn't help herself and ordered a gingerbread latte. The kid behind the counter looked about seventeen or so, and bored.

"Kirsten." Dorian put a hand on her shoulder and looked her in the eyes with overacted concern. "I need to talk about your coffee problem. You're starting to go from one cup to the next without a break."

"Morning." She swiped her NetMini to pay and smiled at the clerk. "Got a minute?"

"Sure, need something else?" He smiled. "Running a ten percent discount on breakfast this week."

"I'm looking for information about some suspects involved in a recent crime. I have reason to believe they may have been in here within the past two months. Big bald guy, another with cherry red hair, and a third somewhere between the two with a deep tan."

The kid shrugged. "I don't really look at people. I barely remember who was in here an hour ago."

"Which one of those terminals is unit 001C?" She gestured at a small room of round tables, each with a holo-term.

"Do I look like I work in IT?" The kid glanced left as if hoping for someone else in line so he could stop paying attention to her.

"This guy looks like he can barely figure out how to get coffee in a cup." Dorian sighed.

"Never mind." Kirsten went to the nearest open table and waved at the gloss black plastic bar until a holo-panel scrolled open above it. She got into the system settings in a few key swipes and glanced at its local network identifier: 0018. *Shit. One-cee... that's twenty-six... no twenty eight. This one's eighteen. Crap, no that's hex... uhh, that's twenty-four.*

She backed out of the system window and moved one table over. That one showed 0017.

"Hey, you can't do that," said the kid from the counter. "How'd you get into that screen? Those things are supposed to be locked down."

Kirsten stood with a hand on her stunrod as he rounded the end and got in her face. "Police, kid. Get on back behind that counter."

"Nice try, sweetie. What are you fourteen? Where'd you get that *black* uniform anyway? Novelty store at 29P? I'm gonna have to ask you to leave."

When he reached for her, she torqued his arm around and flipped him onto his chest. The room fell quiet save for the sputtering hiss coming from one of the espresso generators.

"For your information, this uniform did not come from the Twenty-Nine Palms Mall. It came from the quartermaster of the National Police Force, Division 0. The same place that's about to issue you a nice orange suit. Since idiocy has yet to be written into law as a chargeable offense, I'm placing you under arrest for assaulting an officer as well as impeding an active investigation and possibly tampering with evidence depending on what I find in your system."

She wrestled him into binders.

The teen growled and squirmed. "What the hell is wrong with you?"

Dorian raised an eyebrow. "You usually let the little stuff slide. Getting tired of being called a kid?"

She grumbled.

"Is there a problem, officer?" asked a deeper voice. A man, fortyish, with traces of white in his black hair and four-day-old beard stubble hurried out of the back room behind the counter. "I'm Paul Collins. This is my place. Trevor, what did you do?"

"This kid's hacking into the terms, man. And she broke my fuckin' arm."

Kirsten leaned down. "If you're going to accuse me of breaking your arm, I should probably at least break it first."

Dorian looked shocked until she winked at him.

"Uhh, officer... is that really necessary? He's only fifteen."

"Good PR, K." Dorian smiled. "You can't arrest him for calling you a fake cop. That brings attention to Div 0. It'll bite you in the ass. Of course, you could make the assault stick. He did try to grab you."

Wow. Big for his age, unless that's bullshit. "I'll think it over. Someone used one of your terminals in the commission of a crime. You ever see three guys... big bald one, cherry red hair, third guy dark-ish skin with a shaved head?"

Gradually, the din of people working on terminals or chatting on vid calls picked up.

Paul offered a helpless shrug. "Can't really say. Couple of people—men and women—come in here with cherry red hair. Honestly the girl with the neon blue hair stands out most in my memory since she's always naked."

"Neko?"

He nodded. "Yep."

"Do you have security cams?"

He fidgeted.

"Look, I don't care if you're spanking it to a neko-cyber-junkie, I'm tracking down suspects."

"Whoa," said Trevor. "She *is* psychic."

Paul turned scarlet.

Kirsten sighed. "I'd appreciate it if you'd hand over a holo-disk with the past six months of operating hours." She removed the binders from Trevor and pulled him up. *Damn, this kid's taller than I am.* "Are you really fifteen?"

"Uhh, yeah."

His surface thoughts confirmed it.

"One, you never try to grab a cop. Two, black uniform is Division 0. I understand you're confused because there aren't all that many of us, but we're real." She pointed at the counter. "Please stay out of the way."

Trevor slinked back over to the coffee machines.

She looked at Paul. "Which one of these machines is 001C?"

He gestured at a table where a pair of tween girls sat. "That one. I'll go burn out a disk for you."

"Thanks." Again, she peeked at his thoughts, and relaxed a touch when telepathy proved his intentions were to do exactly that.

She walked over to the table. One girl continuously snapped her flip-flop against her heel while giving her the 'this table is taken' look. Fortunately, both had their NetMinis out and neither bothered with the table terminal. "Hi girls. I need this terminal for a little while."

"Go for it," said the thinner one. "We aren't using it."

The other girl's mood shifted at blinding speed. "Are you really a cop? Or are you doing that social engineering thing? You look adorbs. You're like twelve right?"

"She's too tall for twelve, plus boobs... hello?" The thin girl knocked on her friend's head. "Sorry, don't mind Andrea. She's obsessed with hackers."

The other girl scoffed. "And you're obsessed with boobs."

Andrea scoffed. "Oh please. I'm twelve and mine are bigger than hers."

"I'm a real cop, yes." Kirsten fought the urge to blush. She pulled over a chair from a nearby empty table and rotated the terminal to face her. "Don't mind me."

While the girls returned to a discussion about a school project they both dreaded having to finish, peppered with tangents about various holo-vids and bands, Kirsten dove into the terminal interface. One girl mentioned a boy she thought the other liked and the two got into a squealy debate about if 'Noah' really did like her. *Ugh. I am glad I won't have to deal with this when Evan's a teenager.* She checked the Inquest record via her armband and scrolled to the terminal activity log around the time someone entered 'Charles Prentice' on a search. The terminal showed an idle state for forty-five minutes prior, and an hour and ten minutes after. *Shit. Spoofed.*

She took her NetMini out and called Sam. He answered on the second ring. "Hey."

"Need your help here. Ran a crawl last night and I got a hit on this terminal, but I struck out with the log. Has to be remote, can you chase it down?"

"Oh he's cute," said the taller girl.

"Totally." Andrea leaned over to peer at Sam. "And he's like totally into you."

"He is!" the other girl cooed. "Look at the way he's staring at her."

Both girls made this 'aww' noise like they'd found kitten pictures online.

Sam turned crimson.

"Are you two dating?" asked the older girl.

"Blunt much?" Andrea leaned closer to Kirsten. "Don't mind Leslie. She's got this whole personal space issue."

Leslie rolled her eyes.

Kirsten's cheeks grew warm.

"They are!" Leslie squealed.

Again, they made the 'aww' noise. Fortunately, after that, they returned to their conversation about school.

Kirsten wanted to crawl under the table, but compensated by staring at the floor. Having Dorian's laugher in the background didn't help.

"I'll, uhh... start a ghost trace." Sam looked anywhere but at her.

Blink. *Huh?* "Wait, you can trace ghosts?"

Dorian's cackling reached the point where it sounded as though he couldn't breathe.

Sam's genuine laugh made her grin. "No. I wish. That would probably make your job a lot easier. We just call it a ghost trace. It's a cyberspace thing. Some interface decks are modified to mask the user's presence from the net, we call them ghosts. Not the paranormal kind. Ghosted connections route through dozens of network nodes, effectively concealing them. Sometimes the packet streams break up over several hundred connections making one user seem to be an army."

"Oh. Great." She sighed. "Proving myself a natural blonde."

The tweens made that 'aww' noise again. The smaller one whispered, "They're so adorable."

"You get like that around Bobby," said Leslie.

"I do not!" Andrea blushed.

Sam also looked like he wanted to find a quiet dark place. "I'm trying to reassemble traces of any connection from unpurged buffer logs over a few thousand separate routers, servers, and relays. Give me a few minutes."

"Minutes? Not hours? I had a data crawl running from last night and it's still going."

He smiled, forgetting his awkwardness. "You're probably running a search on user-entered parameters over a few dozen variables. I'm hunting down packets with a specific IPv12 in the header. Only need one thing…" A small sub panel opened, projected by her NetMini's holo-emitter, bearing the face of a rabid cartoon weasel. "Load that on the terminal and I'll get started."

"Right." She 'grabbed' the square pane and flung at the table. The same graphic appeared on the terminal's screen for a few seconds and faded away. "Done. What the heck was that?"

"I see it. Couple minutes now. And that's a Traceweasel soft."

A white hover-SUV landed double-parked out front and honked. A woman with brown-blonde hair and a leopard-print coat waved at the window. The girls jumped up, waved goodbye to Kirsten, and ran outside.

Dorian sat in one of the vacated seats. "At last, quiet."

She chatted with Sam about possibly doing something, though neither one of them had ever much considered anything even remotely social. Coming up with a plan to 'go out and have fun' turned into an awkward staring contest.

"Hey, Nicole once went on a Mars trip for a weekend." Kirsten bit her lip.

Sam's eyebrows went up. "Never been to Mars. Might be fun. Weekend trip? I thought it took days to get there?"

"Not if the shuttle jumps."

"That's not cheap," said Dorian. "Why not hit a museum or a restaurant or one of those blended reality VR games?"

"Maybe." Kirsten repeated the suggestions to Sam.

"Up to you." He smiled. "Oh, hey… shit." The color drained out of his face. "Why were you tracing this?"

"That ghost I've been after? The people who were searching for him used this terminal. Why?"

"I figured out where the source signal came from. Sector 213, an office building. Infinity Towers."

"Great." She smiled.

"Not great." Sam cringed. "That's a known Syndicate operation."

Kirsten glanced at Dorian who also looked as worried as Sam. "Shit."

"Yep." Dorian nodded. "This keeps getting better."

"If someone connected to the senator was arranging the attack on Prentice, they had to have gone through some high level channels."

"Indeed," said Sam. "This could just be a called-in favor or he hired a cyber-jockey to hit medical records and hunt for a compatible 'donor.' The Syndicate might not have much of a stake in this at all beyond getting paid or turning in a favor."

She stood. "Am I supposed to be comforted or frightened by that?"

Dorian flashed an appraising frown. "I'd say comforted."

A glance at her armband showed the data crawl still going. "Damn. I think it's time I had a serious talk with Senator Winchester."

36

BEHIND CLOSED DOORS

A feeling of ominous dread settled on Kirsten's shoulders as soon as she set the NavMap for Senator Winchester's manor in the north. She didn't expect much from walking into his office and threatening him. At best, she'd make a fool of herself. At worst, she winds up on the defensive facing a senatorial inquiry. Director Carter had her back when she confronted Commissioner Vernon, but that had been different. She hadn't been investigating Vernon. She'd been trying to protect her from an abyssal spirit.

This time, she had a mortal in her sights, and from what she kept on hearing, an untouchable one at that. There had to be something, some way. Maybe she'd prod him with a slight bend of the truth, say that it *appeared* someone was trying to set him up to look guilty and see where that rabbit hole led. His reaction might give her some clue where to take it. One thing did bother her though, a thought that wouldn't quite leave the tip of her brain.

He asked for me specifically. That might mean he fully expected the ghost. And he seemed pretty insistent that I destroy the ghost.

Her conundrum hadn't gone anywhere by the time she shot out from the area covered by the elevated city, and flew over natural ground. Snowy pine forest sprawled below, broken up here and there by silvery plastisteel and swaths of suburbia.

"It's beautiful up here, if not a little cold." Dorian took on a wistful expression. "I'd planned on living out this way after retiring."

She looked down at her lap. "Sorry."

"Oh, don't get all sad on my account. I'm still sort of 'here' to enjoy it.

Maybe I'll fall in among The Kind after you're a distant memory. Course, I'll probably stick around to keep Evan company."

"I'm twenty-two… couple months away from twenty-three. Are you going to torment yourself that long? You don't want to go be with your family? Whatever's on the other side?"

He glanced at her, his face a mixture of sad and serious.

"No, I'm not trying to tell you to go away. I want you to do whatever will make you the happiest."

"Right now, that's following you around and making sure you don't wreck my car." He wiped a finger across the dash, clucking his tongue at the dust smear. "And keeping you from joining me on this side."

She chuckled. "I don't know how I'd have gotten this far without you."

"Try not to say anything blonde in there." He winked.

"As if." She set down near the front door and groaned at the exterior temperature reading of forty degrees on the nose.

"The uniforms are actually fine in cold weather… if you're active. It's when you stand still in the wind they're frigid."

Kirsten hopped out and jogged to the front door. Marguerite answered the bell two minutes later.

"Agent Wren." The synthetic woman smiled. Her powder blue dress with white apron made her look even more like a huge child's toy doll.

Kirsten flashed a cheesy smile. "Lieutenant now actually. I need to have a word with the senator. It's about the case, and important."

"Oh, Senator Winchester is still in Paramount City. He spends most of his time up there."

"And here I thought he was a 'down-to-Earth' sort of guy." Dorian winked.

Kirsten gazed at the clouds. "Help me."

"I can send him a message if you like, Lieutenant." Marguerite half hid behind the door.

Dammit. Well, better than doing something stupid. She blinked. "I need to see Seraphina then."

"Now is not a good time. She's not feeling well."

"She's going to feel a whole lot worse soon when the ghost rips his lungs out of her."

Marguerite gasped, her accent grew thicker. "*Mon dieu!* You really do talk to the spirits." She backed up, opening the door. "*Entrez! Entrez!* It is freezing."

Not waiting to be led, Kirsten entered and raced up the stairs. Dorian rushed in before Marguerite could slam the door through him again. The synthetic muttered in French, hiked up her dress, and hurried after them. The sound of sobbing and shouted pleas of 'let me go' echoed down the third floor hallway.

Kirsten barged into Seraphina's room, halting in the doorway at the sight of the willowy snow-blonde girl struggling to escape padded wrist and ankle cuffs holding her to the bed like a patient in a mental facility.

Theresa retrieved a comforter from the floor and replaced it over the girl's lower body, though her continued thrashing promised to make it fall again soon.

"Seraphina," yelled Kirsten.

Theresa jumped and let off a half-second of scream.

"Great. Cops. Help! I'm being kidnapped!" Seraphina tried without success to sit up against a padded strap over her chest.

Kirsten, gawking at Theresa, ran to the bed. "What's going on?"

"Please, you must understand. The young lady attempted to kill herself. She was to jump from the roof."

"You're making that up!" yelled Seraphina. "They've kept me tied up for two days against my will."

Both women looked sincere. Kirsten skimmed Seraphina's surface thoughts. A large amount of terror at being restrained dueled with feelings of worthlessness. She did attempt to kill herself, though at that second, fear at being helpless dominated her thoughts, making it impossible for Kirsten to tell if she meant to try again. A flash or two of dark blue surroundings came and went, Fizzle's den. Walls swelled and sank back as if breathing, a cat-sized transparent purple phoenix circled near the ceiling, leaving a glowing trail in the air behind it. All around the room, warped versions of chairs and tables chatted to each other while sipping tea. The machines Sanjay used to make drugs grumbled and bickered like fantasy dwarves forced to toil in the deep mines. When the girl had been high on whatever chem made her see all that, she'd gotten a thrill from restraints—sober, being tied down scared her to death.

"If you're set loose, are you going to hurt yourself?" Kirsten kept listening to the girl's thoughts.

Seraphina stopped fighting and lay still, sweating and breathing hard. As the idea of being free danced in her head, the specter of wanting to die returned. "Of course not."

Kirsten looked down. "You can't lie to a telepath, Seraphina. I'm sorry. There's no legal right to suicide in the absence of a terminal diagnosis. If they have to restrain you to protect your life, they can."

"Please..." Seraphina cried. "Anyone could come in here and do whatever they wanted to me."

"I met the ghost of the man whose lungs you've got." Kirsten flicked a thumbnail at her utility belt. "He was killed to get them for you."

Seraphina looked away, a sour face aimed at the massive pea-green curtains to her right. "I didn't want to be saved, all right? You can tell him he can come get them back whenever he wants. Why do you think I did so much Icewhisper? I *wanted* to die."

"Why would you want to die? You're young, pretty, comfortable… you'll never have to work. *And* Fizzle is worried sick about you."

"Hah. Fizzle." She laughed. "My father would never let him within a hundred miles of me. He's a drug dealer just looking for a meal ticket."

"Are you sure?" Kirsten raised an eyebrow. "He seemed ready to go legit for you. Fizzle's already stopped making whisp because of you."

"You read his mind too?" snapped Seraphina. She twisted her arms, but the straps held her delicate wrists secure. "Please let me out. I hate this so much."

"Why do you want to die?" Kirsten sat on the edge of the bed and held the girl's hand.

Seraphina squirmed, but couldn't move enough to pull away. "Why the fuck do you think? You're the psionic."

"If I had to guess based on that dream you were having, I'd say you're most upset that your father won't acknowledge you. I know this sounds lame, but the only opinion that matters about you is yours."

"Ugh." Seraphina twisted her entire body, pulling at her arms and legs and trying to sit up. "You bitch." She scowled at Theresa. "Let me out right now. You work for me!"

Theresa folded her hands and looked down. "I cannot let you harm yourself."

"Grr." Snowy hair matted over Seraphina's face as she whipped her head to the left to glare up at Kirsten. "How would you feel if you spent half your life wondering who your father even was, then the rest being treated like half a person? He won't admit to being my father. Says it'd cause 'too many problems' for his political career."

"I think he's beyond that point now. When you ruined your lungs, he arranged for a man to be killed. He's gonna go down one way or the other."

Seraphina rolled her eyes. "See? He wouldn't even accept me to save my life. Has to keep everything hush hush. Probably won't put 'Winchester' on my tomb. Besides, he's a damn senator. You'll never touch him." She sagged limp, staring at the ceiling, her voice a weak whisper. "They own the world. You don't understand. The Senate, the ACC, they talk. They make deals no one knows about."

"That's called avoiding nuclear war and the extinction of humanity," said Dorian.

Kirsten squeezed the girl's hand. "Why not force him? Threaten to go public?"

Seraphina burst into tears, straining to get away from Kirsten. "No. I can't do that to him. He's an asshole, but he's still my father. I won't do anything to hurt him." She tugged at her arms to wipe her face, and cried harder when she couldn't.

Theresa leaned in and dabbed her tears with a white cloth.

"That man's public opinion of you doesn't matter. He obviously cares for you if he's gone to these lengths to protect you. What he says to the world means nothing."

Seraphina scowled through a tangle of hair. "How could you possibly know what it feels like? All I've ever wanted was for him to say he's my father. Fuck all this money."

Dorian sighed.

Kirsten kept quiet for a little while, still holding Seraphina's hand. "My mother hated me. No matter what I did, I could never be good enough. I made it to ten before she tried to kill me. I used to sit inside the closet she locked me in, listening to her scream and ask God why she was cursed with such a horrible beast for a child."

Seraphina seemed to melt into the pillow, jaw a little open, eyebrows furrowed. Theresa fussed at the young woman's hair to set it to some kind of order.

"My father... well, he did love me, but he was so afraid of the ghosts, he always went away on business trips. Every time his company needed someone to go somewhere, he'd volunteer. In three years, I think he might've spent a total of six weeks at home."

"I don't remember my mother. I was like three or four and she left me with one of her friends, who I wound up thinking of as Mom. I used to make dolls out of old autoinjectors while she got high and slept with whoever had credits to burn. I think I spent the entire fifth year of my life naked because we had no money, or that woman never bothered buying anything other than food and drugs. You wouldn't think it, but the johns were pretty cool to me." Seraphina took a wheezy breath and let it out. "One started buyin' me stuff. Clothes at first, then a toy or two... nothing too expensive because that woman would've sold it. Those guys took more care of me than 'Mom' did. I still don't know how she figured out Winchester was my dad... I was eight. She drags me here threatening to blast it all over the NewsNet."

Kirsten squeezed her hand. "I'm sorry."

"It wasn't all that bad. Could'a been way worse. None of the johns touched me. I didn't get shot whenever the idiots outside went after each other." She shrugged. "Course, Winchester assumed a paternity test would free him, but when it came back positive... That woman's probably dead. I never saw her again. Overnight I went from street trash to princess. All the time he said I had to promise never to tell anyone I was his real daughter. Anyone that found out about me got some bullshit story about me being a charity case and he didn't want publicity 'for my protection.'"

"I don't understand. Having a child from an affair is not a big deal to the political crowd. It happens all the time." Kirsten grumbled.

"I know!" Seraphina tried to sit up again, which triggered a fit of thrashing and growling. "That's why it's so much worse. It's like he's doing it just to be cruel!"

"It doesn't make any sense, which means it must be *who* her mother is." Dorian tapped a finger to his chin. "The only thing I can think of to scare him that much would be something that would jeopardize his position with the senate. I bet he had a tryst with a woman who held some kind of station in the ACC."

Marguerite twitched.

"Either an intelligence agent or one of their political elite. Either one would get C-Branch picking through everything the senator ever touched." Dorian glanced at Marguerite. "She knows a lot more than she's letting on, but it's not that he has a daughter. It's who he had her with."

"I think it's more complicated than you realize." Kirsten hesitated, trying to speak with care. "Did you consider the possibility your real mother's life might be threatened if you weren't a secret?"

Seraphina flashed a pained expression.

"I hope that's the crush of regret and stupidity," said Dorian. "She still suicidal?"

Kirsten patted her hand. "Seraphina? You've survived a hard start in life. I don't know how true Fizzle's feelings are, that's something you two will need to sort out. I can't say why your father did what he did, but it's not worth your life, especially if he's protecting your real mother. Can you tell me you won't hurt yourself and mean it?"

Seraphina stared at the tents her feet made in the comforter. "I don't know. Is that ghost going to tear my lungs out?"

"Technically, they're his," muttered Dorian.

Kirsten shook her head as she let off a weak chuckle. "He told me he came here intending on squeezing the air out of you while you slept, but he couldn't do it." An idea hit her. "He knows you tried to kill yourself. Considering he was killed specifically to keep you alive, he's going to be angry if you do it. Suicide ghosts tend to linger for decades, and he'd be hounding you the whole time. Do you really want to deal with that?"

"Really?" Seraphina looked up, horrified. "That's not true is it? You're just trying to scare me."

Dorian manifested amid a haze of whitish energy. "It's true. Suicides linger." He maintained visibility for a few more seconds before fading.

Theresa backed up. Marguerite twitched twice, blinking

Kirsten smiled at the trend in Seraphina's surface thoughts. "I think she's having second thoughts about rushing into the grave."

"Please let me out." Seraphina whined.

"Your father is sending a psychiatrist. Not until the doctor says it's okay." Theresa looked down.

Kirsten sighed. "I'm sorry. I can't do anything except send in yet another psych doctor. You're not a minor. You're not psionic. You *have* shown suicidal ideations, and your father is a senator." *Even if he is a murderer.* "Think about what I said. Killing yourself isn't an escape from depression. It just makes it last forever. It doesn't stop on the other side—and you get to have an angry ghost hounding you."

Seraphina squirmed more out of protest than any genuine attempt to escape.

Kirsten turned to leave.

"Hey," said Seraphina. Kirsten glanced back. "Tell that guy I'm sorry he died."

"I will." Kirsten bottled up rage and frustration, showing only a sad smile to the world. "I'm doing everything I can."

She plodded down the stairs and let herself out, finding it strange Marguerite didn't follow. "Great. The senator's probably watching a video of everything I said in there. He knows I'm on to him."

Dorian nodded. "Probably. Though I doubt he would do anything to you at this stage. He knows you've got no proof, but I'd expect some saber rattling."

AT ANY COST

Kirsten looked down at breasts smaller than she'd grown used to, almost nonexistent. The virtual elf body made her feel thirteen years old again. Her airy white crisscross top connected to a sigil-inlaid leather skirt she felt certain would show the world everything if she leaned even an inch forward or back. Laced leather boots came up to her knees, lined with fringe, and mystic sigils carved into the side of a wooden longbow in her hand glowed bright green.

"Are thee ready?" asked Evan.

She looked to her left at an indigo-robe wearing Monwyn. Longish black hair framed a chiseled face, surrounded by a thick black beard along the jawline. His intense blue eyes stirred a range of emotions from *wow he's gorgeous* to *danger: get away from him*. Hearing a nine-year-old boy's voice come out of the ruggedly handsome man in his thirties caused her brain to skip.

"Shani picked Asara the Huntress too. Most of the other girl characters are evil, 'cept for the elementalist and the healer."

"Like Xiana?" A twinge of headache spiked at the thought.

"Yeah. She's sorta both. She starts off as a bad guy, but winds up helping Monwyn by the third movie. You'd hate her armor; she's always in high heels."

Kirsten laughed. After a few steps to get used to 'bouncing' more than walking—the game translated elven speed and agility in disorienting ways—she rolled her head around, feeling almost drunk at the way the heavy Senshelmet pulled at her neck. "This helmet feels strange."

"You get used to it. Okay, Mom—uhh, I mean Asara! We've gotta go to the Cave of the Ancients and find the Ancestor Sword."

Is that the best storyline they can come up with? Go find a sword? Who leaves a priceless magic weapon just sitting around in a tomb? Why don't the monsters guarding it take the sword, sell it, and retire somewhere?

"Okay. How does this work?"

"We've only got a *Yume*, so we can't bypass the levels by knowing the words to the spells. You've got nature magic, but you're not high enough level to use it yet, so you gotta use the bow." Evan's attempt to flash a sheepish grin came out as Monwyn's 'let's go to the bedroom' smile. "I didn't mean the *Yume* you got us sucks. It's awesome! I mean this isn't like the Monwyn sim at the Funzone."

She raised her arm. "How am I supposed to hurt any of the creatures with a stick with a string on it? It's too light to hit anyone with."

Monwyn gawked at her, somehow inheriting Evan's expression. She laughed.

"Seriously, Mom? You don't know what a longbow is? We've watched like *all* the movies."

Kirsten studied the weapon. "It so big I thought it was a weak staff."

"You've got the level one weapon. Not Greenbriar. The real Asara's bow is smaller but super powerful."

She mimicked the gesture of drawing an arrow and one appeared. A few random shots at trees later, she more or less got the hang of aiming it. "Easy enough."

They trekked down the road, and soon found themselves attacked by hobgoblins—manlike creatures with green skin and intelligence about halfway between peasant and smart dog. She adjusted to the elf's technique of running and shooting, and it didn't take them long to fight their way past what felt like an endless amount of random creatures to a flat stone panel on the side of a moss-covered hill.

"Hmm. A rune of warding. It's a puzzle." Evan/Monwyn cracked his knuckles.

Kirsten stood behind him, though in the real world, he sat in front of her in their living room. She wrapped her arms around him and clung while he busied himself dragging glowing blue runes around a series of tiles. Frustration at a daydreamed Senator Winchester laughing at her, teasing her that he'd killed a man and she couldn't do anything about it got her growling. *Can I blame him? What would I do to protect Evan?* She debated if she could kill someone to protect him. *If they're threatening him, I wouldn't hesitate.* Could she do what the senator did and murder an innocent stranger to save her boy's life? She couldn't wrap her brain around the idea in theoretical terms. Murdering someone in cold blood went against everything she was. Thinking about it as an exercise sent her brain careening down a spiral of anguish. She imagined some corporation abducting Evan and forcing her to murder or they'd kill him, and kept trying to come up with ways to find a side door rather than dealing with the question.

Evan grunted. "Mom? What's wrong? You got squeezy again."

"Nothing's wrong." She cuddled him. "I'm thinking about how much I'd do to keep you safe."

He stopped moving. "Is something coming after me?"

"I don't know. I found the spirit I'd been chasing. No. He's not after you." She clung a little tighter. *Must be another spirit bothering him.* "Your blockade worked?"

"Yeah." He got back to moving runes around. "I didn't have a bad dream. Maybe it *is* a stupid ghost."

She held him in silence for a few minutes while he attacked the puzzle. He made up Monwyn-sounding curses along the lines of "by a shade-goblins balls" and "whoever designed this puzzle is dumber than an orc." Eventually, he figured it out and the individual blocks glided apart to reveal a passageway.

After an hour of slogging through a wearisome series of chambers packed with monsters that always somehow failed to hear the sounds of fireballs exploding and death screams past the flimsy wooden doors of the next room, they reached the end boss of the dungeon.

Clouds of sulfurous smoke rolled around the tail of a massive creature. Atop a thick, armor-plated serpent some twenty feet long, sat a humanoid upper body with four musclebound arms and the head of a bull. Torchlight flickered off the walls, glinting on irregular wet stones marked with violet moss. Kirsten grimaced at the slime everywhere and thanked the gods of video gaming that the Yume Koujou system didn't replicate smell.

"Okay. He can't see us 'til we walk into the room. You'll need to stay behind him because he's got a magic shield that blocks arrows. Asara's fast enough to run up his tail. Keep jumping over him. My elemental will hold aggro."

"Okay."

Monwyn the Magnificent chanted. Sparkles of amber light ran down his arms and cascaded to the ground, causing a ripple that spat out loose rocks. The stones levitated and stacked into a humanoid figure ten feet tall with glowing orange eyes.

The world froze. Yellow letters appeared reading, "Session timer 1:45:00."

"Bedtime, kiddo." Kirsten grabbed her helmet. "Save the game and we'll pick it up tomorrow."

"Aw, but he's the final boss of the map."

Kirsten tapped a finger on her Senshelmet. "How long does the fight take?"

He grumbled. "Awright. We can do it tomorrow. Boss fight's about a half hour if we know the strat, but you've never done it before so we'll probably wipe a couple times. You're learning fast, so maybe an hour and a half, and you're gonna say 'no too late.'"

Kirsten laughed and took her helmet off. "Well, since you've already decided to wait, I suppose we should."

Evan gawked at her. "You were gonna say yes?"

She kissed him on the forehead. "Not for an hour and change. It's already past ten."

"But it's Saturday."

"That's why you're up *this* late." She winked. "Go on, get ready for bed. I'm tired, too."

"Okay."

He ran to the hall, whipping his shirt off before he darted out of sight. Kirsten knelt on the rug, taking her time packing the Yume Koujou system into the cabinet by the living room holo bar. Every time she looked at the white boxy console, it made her remember the overwhelmed expression on Evan's face when she gave it to him. The whirr of the autoshower filled in the silence from the hallway. She savored this stolen moment of contentment, remaining motionless for a little while before closing the cabinet. When she stood, a familiar scent of spiced aftershave rolled past her. A scent she'd not encountered in too long.

Her eyes watered up. "Dad?"

"How're you doin', Hon?" Kirsten's father phased out of the wall. "Looks like you've settled in all right. That Sam fellow treating you okay?"

"He got stuck working this weekend, some kind of major server node upgrade." She pushed the cabinet door closed a little harder than necessary. "So far, so good. I think I like him. I tried to tell him I loved him once, but I couldn't say it without throwing a 'think' in there. Guess I'm afraid of commitment."

"Bah. You've known the boy a couple months. I have a good feeling about him, but don't rush yourself."

Kirsten concentrated, making herself solid to spirits, and buried her face in his soft flannel shirt. Her mind swirled with the last time she'd hugged him for real. She'd been ten, sitting in his lap after dinner, too full to move. Whenever he was home, Mother didn't starve her. Of course, he hadn't stayed long, leaving for a business trip right before she went to bed. That had been the night she had to run away from home. Ritchie had shown up and warned her that Mother would kill her.

Dad's familiar fragrance brought on a wave of anger and self-pity, blindsiding her with emotion. She sniffled into his shoulder, refusing to give in to tears while gagging on the memory of a turkey dinner, the last meal her mother ever made for her. She'd only eaten because Dad was home. Every time the fork went to ten-year-old Kirsten's mouth, Mother glared at her, thinking she didn't deserve that food because she had turned her back on Jesus.

"What are you doing to my Mom?" Evan, steam wafting from his hair, eyes glowing white, and a towel around his waist, stood in the gap between living room and hallway. "I heard her crying."

Kirsten sniffled and smiled. "Ev, go finish your shower. This is my father. It's okay. Bad memories."

Evan shot an accusing look at him. "The one who kept running away?"

Her dad cringed. "Yeah. I sure did, didn't I?"

"Sec, Dad," whispered Kirsten. She hurried over to Evan, put a hand on the back of his head, and guided him to the bathroom. "He's stuck coping with his choices. We've already made our peace."

He frowned. "'Kay."

"Hey." She poked him in the side until he smiled. "Thanks for sticking up for me."

Evan grinned dropped the towel, and jumped into the tube.

She trudged back to the living room, finding her father standing by the electronic window, watching hovercars.

"Dad?" She walked up alongside him. "Do you think it's right to kill someone to save your child's life?"

"A parent has an obligation to do whatever it takes to protect their child." His eyes bored guilt into the ground. "I don't expect you to ever forgive me."

"That's not why I'm asking." She wrapped her arms around him. "I do forgive you. In the ten years I've been with Division 0, I've met *one* person who handled ghosts like they were no big deal. It was too much for you. Primal fear, not thinking fear."

"She wasn't the mother you deserved. I should have done more to stop her."

"I'm alive. I forgive you, Dad." She exhaled, holding him for a little while in silence. "What about what Winchester did?"

"Who?" Her father looked up, chuckling. "Ghostliness doesn't come with omniscience. That Theodore friend of yours is always moving about, talking to other spirits. They all share information. I've, uhh, been keeping to myself."

"Sorry, Dad. You don't have to feel guilty anymore."

He let out a halfhearted chuckle. "Easier said... That's the curse of being human, isn't it? We see everything in perfect clarity only after it's too late." He sighed. "I could tell you were terrified of her, but I always rationalized it as the hauntings making me see things that weren't real. I can't stop seeing you as you were that night, the last time I held you. The night I chickened out for the last time."

Kirsten leaned against him. "It took me a long time to forgive you for leaving me there, but I understand. I think you were afraid of her too."

Her father chuckled. After a while of holding her in silence, he sniffed back tears and managed a smile. "So, who's this Winchester?"

She gave him a brief explanation.

"That man had the means to pursue other options. He didn't have to claim that woman as his daughter to get her proper treatment. Someone in his position… bribes, influence, lies… the man practically makes truth out of thin air. Sounds like he's either a stingy bastard, or maybe he feels entitled to harvest the peasants to prolong the life of the royalty."

"Now I think you're reaching a little." Kirsten tried to laugh but it carried little enthusiasm.

Evan's head and one foot poked around the corner of the hall. "I'm ready."

"Teeth?"

"Yep." He flashed an exaggerated smile.

"Okay. I'll be right there." She winked.

Evan scampered off to his room.

"What if someone takes your kid and threatens to kill them if you don't go murder some innocent other person?"

Her father took a deep breath, held it a second, and let it out slow. "I don't think it's possible to answer that question unless it's happening for real. That's the kind of choice a parent makes in the heat of the moment. Stop trying to drive yourself insane. I'm sure the boy knows you'd do everything you can to protect him."

"Thanks, Dad." She hugged him again. "Hey, would you mind hanging around tonight? Something's been bothering him. Something weak."

"Sure. I suppose that's the least I could do."

COMPLICATED

K irsten squeezed the control sticks while guiding her patrol craft down to the parking area reserved for official vehicles. The digital windscreen lit up red on the right side, warning her away from the exclusion zones around the Edmonson Memorial Starport. Despite its armored hull, most of the shuttles using those lanes would swat the hovercar aside like a flea if they collided.

For two days, she tried like hell not to think about Senator Winchester and focus on being Mom. By some miraculous stroke of luck, no ghosts decided to misbehave to the point Division 0 paged her over the weekend. Laney Prentice called once to ask for an update, apparently Charles wanted to know. For now, the woman had accepted the explanation that trying to line up a United Coalition Front senator under the crosshairs for a murder investigation was a sensitive project that would take time. With Lindsey Park no longer in possession of the offending kidneys, she assured the Prentices that the organs would be cremated and added to Charles's ashes once they were no longer needed as evidence in any cases or litigation.

She landed and walked on autopilot across the starport. This time, Command wasn't providing a DS2 for a personal flight. They had no idea she planned to confront the senator. She didn't even know what she'd say. *You're right Dad. Must be one of those situations you can't figure out until you're chest deep in it.*

The past forty-eight hours replayed in her head as she stood in the middle of the main concourse. Feeling wonderful for having time with Evan clashed with feeling guilty at making Charles wait... but in all honesty, he wasn't getting deader, as Dorian liked to say. The bigger source of guilt came from Seraphina. Not that her investigation appeared poised to offer any substantive change on her feelings for her father. No, perhaps the true drive pulling her to the moon came from that young woman—stopping another senseless death.

So far, hard evidence in this case left her looking at three unknown murder suspects working for a 'might or might not exist' ripper doc named Mardrake in a black zone that most cops didn't want to go near. The best thing she could do would be to kick the administration of Easley Military Medical Center square in the testicles for knowingly dealing with illegal organs.

What am I doing? Six hours flight time each way and he might not even see me.

Kirsten turned on her heel and ran back to the car. "I don't need to *go* to the damn Moon to talk to him. Might be better over a Vid anyway; he won't think I'm trying to use any abilities on him."

"I was waiting for you to realize that," said Dorian from nowhere. He faded into view a few seconds later.

Figuring out *how* to call the Senate Chambers in Paramount City on the Moon took the better part of twenty minutes. She finally got through to a public relations operator so unremarkable, brown-skinned, and happy, she looked like an avatar made from the average of the UCF's population demographics.

"Hello. I'm Mary. Which media outlet or entity do you represent?"

"This is Lieutenant Wren from Division 0. I need to speak to Senator Preston Winchester."

"I'm sorry, Lieutenant. Senators and their staff are unable to receive direct calls, with the exception of designated media liaisons."

"He's asked me to help him with a specific issue. I have information for him about his houseguest." Mary's right eye twitched. "Look, please tell him who I am and that I need to talk to him about the matter he's requested my assistance with. If he doesn't want to take my Vid, fine, I'll go away."

"Please hold for a moment."

The woman's holographic bust vanished, and a small 3D model rendering of the jade-green Senatorial Chambers appeared in her place.

Kirsten tapped her fingers and boots for three minutes. Dorian hummed some odd melody.

"What's that?"

"What?" He glanced over.

"That thing you're humming."

"Oh. It's from an old game holo-vid. They used to play that music while people filled out answers to questions. I think they wound up cancelling it about ten years ago. Guess most people weren't educated enough for it anymore... the show'd been around for centuries."

"Elitist much?" She chuckled.

"Truth is a harsh mistress." Dorian leaned back with a smug smile.

Senator Winchester appeared on the holo panel. The white hair over his ears seemed to have spread further up into the brown. "Good morning, Lieutenant now is it?" He smiled. "Nice bit of work the last time you visited Paramount City. Nasty little thing in the basement."

"Thank you, sir." A twinge of unease swam around in her gut. *Did he push my promotion through as a bribe?* She clutched her stomach with one hand.

"At least you're coming in over MilNet. Using Vid from your car, not too bad. Before we continue, I'll need to ask you to disable all recording and logging. Also, click this frame to start a secure channel."

A dark blue border appeared around the holo-panel, with a 'button' at the lower right full of hexadecimal numbers. Kirsten glanced at Dorian.

"He wants it off the record. I'm sure Marguerite has spoken with him already. Might as well, it's not like you're in any position to make a power play. Besides, it'll protect you from anything you might blurt if you get angry."

"All right. One sec." She keyed in an override code to shut down logging and recording. "You know by turning this off, I've just scheduled myself an intense meeting with my captain."

"I wouldn't worry about that." Senator Winchester smiled. "Please click the crypto link."

Kirsten hesitated for two seconds, but poked the blue button. The senator's image diffused into giant square pixels as big as her fingertip, shifted around, and resumed focus in eight seconds. His subsequent smile lasted three more.

"We now have privacy. There's a three to six second delay, so please allow a pause when you stop. What information have you found?"

She waited a bit to make sure he was done. "Senator... I'm not going to insult your intelligence by playing stupid. I know your daughter Iced her lungs to oblivion and you arranged for a donor to replace them."

"You're still dancing around it." Dorian winked. "You didn't say murder."

Kirsten kept her attention on the senator. "I tracked down the ghost... Other organs went to various individuals who have all experienced attacks. In short, the ghost is upset. He's been going after anyone involved, but as he's only weeks old, the only people he can affect are those who have his tissues inside them."

The senator nodded out of sequence twice. Four seconds after she stopped talking, he rubbed his chin. "Yes... I had a feeling. That's why I requested you. I did quite a bit of research on your career, Lieutenant. I chose you specifically to send this wayward spirit packing. Destroy it so everyone can get on with their lives. The man is dead. What goes on with the living is no longer of his concern."

She seethed, but kept her expression neutral. "Sir, I can't arbitrarily destroy a ghost on a whim because he's inconvenient. He hasn't done anything deserving of annihilation yet."

The placid face hovering at the middle of the console during three seconds of silence made her want to punch him dead in the nose.

"Well then you should destroy him before he does. If that ghost manages to kill anyone, you'll need to accept that you could have prevented it. It's on you. If the ghost harms Seraphina, there will be some other problems as well. Some rather serious ones."

She snarled under her breath. "Sir. You set all of this in motion. Why? You could have had her treated properly. You had no reason to do this. All of it circles back to you. She would never have inhaled that much whisp if you had simply acknowledged her."

His expression shifted from placidity to annoyance. "You must understand. Certain parties both politically hostile and legally dangerous... those who consider themselves above the law the Senate creates, monitor every single credit I spend. I could not run the risk of them going digging. I don't expect someone in your position to appreciate all the nuances of politics. Vid me again once our spectral problem has been dealt with. Kill it, pack it a bag and send it 'to the light,' whatever it is that you do with them. Make it gone."

"Even if I get rid of this ghost, she's going to keep trying to kill herself until you acknowledge her, you know. For some reason, she seems to love you a lot more than you deserve after leaving her in filth for the first eight years of her life."

Winchester's eyebrows rose. "Lieutenant Wren, at the time, I didn't even know she existed. The woman never bothered to mention her. When that leech of a prostitute decided to cash in, well... that's when I found out."

"Publicly acknowledge her as your daughter. You don't have to blast it over the NewsNet. Make up a mother. I get that you're protecting something sensitive here. You wouldn't go to these lengths to hide a simple affair. Senator, you've got connections. What about gene tweaking her to match your wife?"

"Seraphina is the most beautiful thing I have ever been responsible for creating. I couldn't bear to change anything about her."

"Ghosts aren't like the living. I have to help him break the fixation that's keeping him rooted here in our world. He needs his murder to be answered for."

"Lieutenant, I requested you specifically because I know what you're capable of. Deal with this ghost like you dealt with that mess in the decommissioned base. He's not a person. Ghosts have no right to existence under the law. You can't seriously tell me that you prioritize it over the living."

Kirsten shivered, anxiety made the car feel twenty degrees colder. "Sounds like you didn't read my file too well, senator. I can't just destroy a sentient spirit because his existence threatens to expose a murder. I have to see this investigation through to whatever result the evidence dictates. The relationship you have with your daughter, I can't begin to comprehend. You seem to love her a great deal, but I don't get why you felt the need to have a man killed."

Senator Winchester smiled, though his cheeks reddened. "We do what we must for our children. Isn't that right? Wonderful thing you did taking that boy in. It must be rough on him what with your schedule. One astral sensitive for the entire west coast? You're probably often working late, leaving him with friends or at the dorm. It would be quite a shame if some judge got it in their head he'd be better off in a more stable environment."

She glared at his widening grin, a dagger wrapped in silk. "If you go near him…"

"You'll what?" His bushy brown-grey eyebrows lifted. "Stop caring about laws? I see you finally understand. Now please, do what the taxpayers are paying you to do. Deal with that spirit before someone dies."

She dug her fingernails into the seat. "It wasn't necessary. You didn't have to have that man killed. You have the resources. Why didn't you have her lungs regrown?"

"It's complicated. An expense of that size would be noticed." Irritation bled from his smile. "You have a job to do, Lieutenant. Dismissed."

The call dropped.

Kirsten glared at the holo-emitter, trying to project anger into the fingertip-sized silver dome. "Tell me he can't do that."

Dorian studied his lap in silence.

She glanced over at him.

"I couldn't say that without lying to you. Do I think he *will* do it? Most likely not. Too much work, and he's confident you'll never prove he had anything to do with Prentice's murder."

She kept staring at him while powering up the patrol craft's drive system. "I'll prove it all right."

"If he thought you had any chance of being a threat, he wouldn't have remained so calm." Dorian looked at her. "And if he does think you're getting too close, I'm sure he'll do anything he can to survive."

She growled at the console and pulled the patrol craft into the air. "So you're saying I should let him get away with killing someone?"

"It's really not your case to worry about. Living man pays someone to kill living man, none of them psionic. You could file your report with Eze and let him make the call about escalating it. Stick to the paranormal."

"But…"

Dorian offered a wan smile. "Kirsten, you're far too honest to be in the NPF."

"Now you're making it sound like the whole thing is corrupt." She slammed the accelerator forward, mashing her body into the cushions.

"No, but 'normal' people bend before they break. Try to find a middle ground with Charles. Would you give Evan up to send Charles to the silver light? What if you make a run on Winchester and fail?"

"Oh, I *really* want to hop in the sim with Gabriel right now. I need to beat the shit out of someone and not feel bad about it later. Look, maybe I can get him. I won't make a damn move unless I know for sure it's flawless."

"There is one other thing you're forgetting." Dorian sucked at his teeth. "Men that high up on the losing end of a legal issue don't usually go to jail. They go to 'Miami.'"

Anger fell away to dread. "Division 9."

Dorian made a pistol gesture with his hand. "The appeals process is a lot more difficult."

Her stomach churned. Succeed in her investigation, a man dies. Dawdle, Seraphina maybe dies. Push and fail, she may lose Evan. Do nothing, any of the innocent people who received organs could die. To stop it, she'd either have to talk an unreasonable ghost into accepting an unreasonable compromise, or murder Charles Prentice for a second time.

Kirsten let her head thud back against the seat and stared at the black fabric overhead. *What am I supposed to do?*

39

GRASPING STRAWS

K irsten fumed to herself, the endless parade of what-ifs driving her near to madness. She faced a figurative circular firing squad where someone, or everyone, would die in even the best circumstance. She drove in literal circles for a while, trying to calm down, to find an out, a way to defuse the problem. Once she de-stressed enough to think, she picked a destination and headed for Laney Prentice's apartment. The temptation to squirm out from under the issue left a lead stone in her gut. *He got to me. That bastard's making me worry about Evan. Maybe Dorian's right. It isn't my job to take down a senator, but who would I be if I walked away?*

She swerved through the access door leading to the parking area at the middle of the residence tower fast enough that Dorian emitted odd noises. He half melted into the seat, bulging eyes glaring at her.

"Sorry." She set the patrol craft down hard in a cloud of cryonic mist and stormed to the elevator enclosure at the center of the floor.

Dorian followed in silence. Kirsten waited for him to walk in before hitting the spot on the holo-panel for the 99th floor. Neither spoke on the ride up. Grey carpeted hallways muted the thuds of her boots. Repeating patterns of black and red diamonds made her dizzy, so she stared at the bland white walls until reaching Laney's door.

The woman answered the buzzer looking as though she hadn't slept since the last time Kirsten visited. A huge teal-green smock, covered in hand-shaped smudges of potting soil, hung down to her knees. "Hi."

Charles ran into view, near the sofa in the living room. He had eyeballs and a non-cavernous torso, though his khaki pants remained blood-spattered. "Kirsten…"

"Come in." Laney offered an exhausted eyes-mostly-closed smile, and backed away.

Kirsten tried not to step on the woman's bare toes with her heavy boots and shifted sideways to scoot past her before approaching Charles. "I've run into a little problem."

"Problem?" Charles folded his arms. His eyes vanished and returned. "That's not what I need to hear."

"The man who ordered you dead is a UCF senator. In order for me to have any chance at making him answer for what he did to you, I'd need a mountain of non-paranormal evidence that no one could possibly question *any* aspect of."

"So you're saying this is going to take a long time." Charles let his arms drop and glided over to a bookshelf near the kitchen, where he stared at his urn. "How long?"

She exhaled. "I'm saying I might not be able to make enough of a case to convince the group who deals with crimes of that level to act. They don't do trials. If Division 9 becomes convinced that someone with too much power to convict at Inquest is compromised, corrupt, or guilty of crimes… they kill them."

"I'm cool with that. Dead is what he deserves." He leaned closer to the silver brick, as if trying to see a reflection in it.

Laney mumbled something, tripping over her feet on the way to the kitchen. She stubbed her toe on the doorjamb, but didn't react until four seconds later. "Shit. Ow. Uhh, you want coffee or something?"

Kirsten attempted a smile. "I'd feel guilty taking your coffee when bringing bad news, but sure." She walked closer to Charles. "He's threatened my son. I'm not saying I'm going to give up because of that, but I can't make a move until I've collected enough evidence to have a perfect case. I may not ever be able to do that."

"What am I supposed to do then? Follow this urge? Take back what's mine? There's a liver out there that belongs to me. Eyes… oh, and a heart too. Your partner was quite helpful teaching me how to do things. I should be able to rip it in half next time."

She leaned forward, eyebrows flat. "Charles, I want to help you, but if you kill someone, you're going to force me to do exactly what that pompous bastard wants."

"That'll make it easier on you." He glared at the wall.

"Until she has to explain it to Laney." Dorian approached him on the other side, a corralling position likely a result of training. "I hate to break it to you,

Chuck, but sometimes the big dogs shit on the little dogs, and the only thing the little dog can do is growl and shake it off."

Charles's horrific wounds reappeared; he held his fists up to his forehead, emitting noises as likely to precede sobbing as rage-filled screams.

Kirsten infused herself with energy, melding her astral and physical selves. She put a hand on his shoulder. "Calm down. I'm not giving up. I just need more proof that can stand up to a legal review."

He pounded a fist on the shelf, making one holodisk case fall over with a soft *plop*. Luminous off-white haze filled in the vacuous hole in his torso, and a hint of eyeballs reappeared. "What about the three miserable fucks that killed me? They're not senators."

"I haven't been able to find anything based on your description." Kirsten grumbled. "My terminal is *still* running a search."

Laney padded in, offering Kirsten a powder-blue cup. The coffee smelled like it came out of a reassembler, but she didn't flinch.

"Thanks."

"No problem. You're tryin' to help Charlie." Laney smiled, swayed to the side, and caught her balance.

"When was the last time you slept?"

"Uhh, two days ago." Laney made it to the couch before her legs quit. "Been trying to talk to Charlie at night."

"You may want to consider moving on for her sake." Dorian glanced at the delirious woman. "She's already becoming obsessive."

"Leave my sister out of this." Charles pointed at him. "We've always been close. Laney's not a social person. She can't deal with people. Likes plants and cats. Our parents ditched us, so it's only been me to take care of her, and I… can't handle not being able to."

"It's not impossible." Dorian smiled.

"Yeah." Kirsten smiled. "He's saved my ass a few times."

"Only because she gets reckless when she's emotional." Dorian winked.

She gazed at the ceiling. "If those men were ghosts, they'd be easier to find." Kirsten blinked as an idea hit her. "Charles, can you take me to the place where you were killed? I know it's painful, but I wouldn't ask if it wasn't necessary."

"Good idea." Dorian grasped his chin, staring into the distance. "Did they leave your body at the same place they attacked you?"

"Couple alleys over." Charles grumbled.

Kirsten sipped at her coffee. "I bet Div 2 missed the scene entirely."

"Of course. Body in a grey zone, they probably walked in a circle, took two image caps, and got the hell out of there." Dorian scratched the back of his head. "Can't say I blame them much."

"If you can take me to the exact spot you died, we might be able to get something concrete." Kirsten gulped down the remaining half mug."

Charles forced his appearance back to whole. "Fine. So how's it work?"

"It's quite complicated." Dorian grinned. "We ride in the car while she drives."

"Let's go then." Charles headed for the door.

"Hang on. I need to do something first." Kirsten set the mug on the table near the couch and leaned over the barely-awake woman.

"Mmm?" Laney's head lolled around. "What?"

Kirsten waited for her to open her eyes. "*Go to bed.* And when you get there, *sleep.*"

Laney slithered from the sofa cushions to the floor and crawled off down the hall.

"Okay. Now we can go." Kirsten shrugged an apology to Charles. "Try to make sure she takes care of herself."

"Yeah..." Charles stared guilt into the floor. "She's not listening, all wound up about talking to ghosts."

Dorian smiled. "She'll get used to it eventually."

Kirsten left the apartment, two ghosts following her to the elevator. She hit the button for the 52nd where she'd parked. Lights in the four corners pulsed from floor to ceiling, creating bands of illumination around the walls that kept pace with their descent.

"I'll show you something else once we're done at the spot," said Dorian. "Your ashes are your focus. That's the usual focus for a spirit, their remains. It's possible for us to move rapidly back to wherever they are."

Charles's voice took on an odd echo. "I figured that one out already. It's how I got to that woman near the Moon." He shivered. "I can pull myself to any of those people who have my pieces inside them, but that was a little scary."

Tell that to Jonah. "I was wondering how you got up there." Kirsten tapped her foot. The damn elevator seemed to get slower every time she rode it.

"There's some belief that spirits are also bound to the Earth." Dorian tilted his hand up in a half-hearted shrug. "Sucks to die on Mars if that's true."

"Maybe it's a planetary thing?" asked Kirsten.

"It felt like I was losing energy... being swallowed by nothing." Charles shot a guilty look at the floor. "That girl would've been safe up there. I don't think I would've bothered going back."

The doors opened.

"It's not her fault." Kirsten jogged to the patrol craft. "The only person who knew you died to obtain those organs didn't even get one."

"The senator." Charles scowled. "A guy you can't touch."

"Oh. I'm going to touch him." She yanked the door open and got in. "I just don't know how yet."

Dorian blurred to his spot beside her. "In all likelihood, it'll be Division 9 'touching' him with a small piece of high-velocity metal—assuming you can build a case strong enough to convince them."

She clenched the control sticks. "I should probably tell you that there's a chance taking the senator out isn't going to be possible. Can you settle for us nailing the men who carried out the actual killing?"

Charles let off a radiant burst of anger from the back seat, though with only two months' tenure as a spirit, it had little effect on Kirsten aside from announcing his mood. "Sounds like you're giving up already."

"She's beginning to understand things don't always work out clean between good and evil, if you believe in such concepts." Dorian gestured at the NavMap. "Sector 6796 is coming up."

"I'm saying I don't..." *want to lose my son.* She took a deep breath. "...know what's going to happen, and as you so keenly pointed out earlier, letting emotion take over isn't going to help." She looked at Charles. "I know you're angry. I would be too, but if I can't get him, please don't put me in a position to have to choose between you and someone who had nothing to do with this."

Charles's expression hardened.

Kirsten drove in low, twenty feet off the road. "Where?"

"That way." Charles pointed forward and left.

She extended the ground wheels, but kept flying at about thirty MPH. Charles gestured at a seedy-looking bar on the corner. A handful of young twentysomethings in mismatched clothing accented with strips of colored LED loitered out front, drinking and sucking on inhalant units. One guy with two dark metal legs whirled about in some manner of street dance that could've passed for an exotic martial art.

"Another block down, by that gun shop." Charles indicated a fortress-like building on the next corner with armored rolling doors over the windows. Bright neon green paint outlined an area on the sidewalk in diagonal stripes. Two metal spheres embedded in the wall on either side of the door flicked with tiny lights, gun turrets poised to fire on anything entering the boundary.

Kirsten gawked.

"If they're up to code, they won't fire on anyone unless the security system detects damage to the door or a network infiltration," said Dorian.

She landed at the mouth of an alley packed with giant plastiboard cartons that glowed in the glare of the patrol craft's headlights. Discarded cups and food boxes littered a narrow channel among them, leading deeper into the shadows. Every breath tasted like month-old hamburger and stale beer. Dirty plastisteel walls radiated an inexplicable sense of dread, as though she stood before the gates of the Abyss. Despite it being the middle of the day, the alley beyond the reach of the patrol craft's headlights remained dark. Her grip on the control sticks tightened, and she briefly debated changing her mind and going somewhere else. For once, Kirsten thought she'd found a place that would scare her at night.

"There's a bad energy here. I can feel it from inside the car." Against her instincts, she shut down the patrol craft and pushed the door up.

Charles headed for the alley. Kirsten followed, stepping with care among the various boxes, cartons, and wads of plastic wrap. Whispers teased at the back of her mind, chattering shades speaking too fast to decipher. Here and there, she caught a fleeting glimpse of a moving shadow, but nothing showed itself. She clenched and released her right hand, preparing herself to call the lash as a reaction to something bursting out from the walls.

Evidence related to Charles's murder, traps left over from gang warfare, or a sleeping vagrant might lurk under anything. The stink grew worse with each step deeper into the alley, the air thickening with the essence of human waste. A warm, musty breeze rustled the trash, tossing her hair about and making her cover her mouth to keep from tasting whatever funk had collected on the ground. Charles rushed on ahead and stopped near a small, square yard in the hollow of a low-income housing tower. Solid plastisteel walls surrounded it on three sides and a chain-link fence on the last. The heavy presence of dark energy worsened, though she couldn't tell if a mere Harbinger lurked in the area, or something darker.

Dorian fidgeted. "One of *them* has been here recently."

"Let's hope." Kirsten edged up to the gate in the fence. "I wonder how many people died here?"

"Hey." Dorian pointed up and left. "Citycam." He spun in place. "Another one there."

"What are the odds they work?" Kirsten held up her left arm. "Ops. I need a crime scene unit to my current location."

The face of a Hispanic boy, maybe fifteen and in a Division 0 cadet's uniform, appeared. "Copy, Lieutenant."

A quieter voice murmured, its owner not rendered by the hologram. "Panel 2, hit the locator there and drag it to the dispatch request board."

She'd have smiled if not for being on edge from the pervasive doom in the air. "I really don't like it here."

"Yeah." Dorian hooked his thumbs on his utility belt. "This is the kind of place that puts clairvoyants in mental care. A lot of agony in these walls."

She shivered as she moved about in a slow turn, gazing up at a point about thirty stories overhead where an unnaturally stark border between dark and light ran the length of four city blocks. Even the Sun didn't seem to want to filter down to this particular corner of Hell. To her astral sight, the darkened walls shifted with trails of ebon vapor, gathering thickest around broken windows that appeared as portals to infinite blackness howling with a driving wind. "The veil is thin here. It's like the astral realm is touching reality."

"The astral realm *is* reality." Dorian wagged a finger at her, mocking a teacher. "It's not imaginary."

"You know what I mean." Unease left her breathing shallow. Harbingers probably traversed this 'hole' on a regular basis.

"On the way, Lieutenant," said the cadet. "They're insisting on a Div 6 escort. Looks like you went to the nice part of town."

"Thanks." As soon as the cadet disappeared, she called Sam.

"What's up?" He grinned.

Kirsten took a breath and put on cop face. Now was not the time to worry about Evan, Sam, her feelings for Sam, or any trepidation at what might wander between worlds at any moment. "Can you hit a couple of Citycams near me? I don't know if they're even working, but they might've recorded a murder."

"They're on. I can feel the electricity inside them," said Dorian. "They stand out like torches."

"Checking." Sam's holographic head shrank as he leaned away and typed on another panel. "I'm connecting to the three nearest units to your position... got it. What time frame am I looking for?"

"August 26, 2418. About 4:20 p.m." Charles looked down. His figure lost solidity here and there; small patches of him dissipated into ethereal wisps and re-formed.

"You should do that thing now." Dorian made a 'get outta here' gesture with his thumb. "You've not been around so long as a ghost. The scene of your death might wind up becoming a trap." He pursed his lips. "Ask me how I know... later."

Charles nodded. Concentration showed in his face for a second or two before he exploded into a silvery-yellow cloud, which dissipated onto the street.

Kirsten kept her mind away from the mood in the air by talking about random nonsense with Sam. Monwyn, possible restaurants to go to at some point, other things to do, what kind of music he liked... Nine minutes after she'd called it in, the ground rumbled with the arrival of a huge A3V. The dark blue six-wheeled Advanced Armored Assault Vehicle pulled to a stop next to her patrol craft with a dull squeak of brake pads. Five men and two women in blue armor exited a side door, past tires taller than their helmets, and jogged over as a rear ramp wound down with a hydraulic whine.

The crime scene team, three women and an older-looking man with a pale grey afro, unloaded gear from the back end.

"Lieutenant." A six-foot-four man with a silver visor for a face snapped off a crisp salute. "Sergeant Vanris, Division 6. What's the situation?"

"Hopefully just babysitting Div 2. They got nervous based on where we are. Possible gang hostility, but I haven't seen anything. I think the energy in this place is chasing them away. If any of you experience unexplained feelings of dread, vertigo, or sadness, please tell me."

"Those three things do not exist in the Marine Corps, Lieutenant, except for what we leave in our wake." Sergeant Vanris spun with a quick heel turn and barked orders and tactical map coordinates to the rest of the team, who hustled off to establish a perimeter. He took up a position fifteen yards away, closest to the alley mouth—the first target for any incoming problem.

"K, I think I'm going to make you very happy." Sam's holographic head grinned.

"Can you talk about the case, not later tonight?" asked Dorian.

Kirsten's face burned with blush. "What'cha got?"

"Three men dragging an unconscious figure into that little yard behind you and... oh my." Sam blanched and covered his mouth. He averted his gaze and flailed at the holo panel to transfer the file, trying not to look at it.

She brushed his holo-bust to the side to make room for the video feed. In green monochrome, the Citycam night vision revealed a huge man, an average man, and a little man dragging an unconscious Charles through the gate into the yard. They cleared a spot and flung him down. The massive bald man performed the 'surgery,' while the little guy ran back and forth with gel-filled organ transport boxes, holding them open to receive each piece.

"How can you watch that?" Sam gurgled.

"Being able to watch it with a straight face doesn't mean I enjoy it. I've seen ghosts in far worse shape." Kirsten swallowed a little bile and waved the Div 2 lead over.

The older crime scene tech finished pulling on a set of blue gloves before he approached. "This is going to take a while, you realize."

"Tech..."

"Tech four. Bill Finch." He saluted.

Dorian snickered.

Kirsten gave him the side-eye while returning the tech's salute. "Hopefully, this will make things easier on you." She held her arm out and replayed the video of the murder.

"Wren... Finch..." Dorian snickered again. "Birds of a feather."

She rolled her eyes. "You need to get out more."

"Sorry?" asked Tech Finch.

"Not you." Kirsten smirked at Dorian. "A very bored ghost."

"K." Sam waved to get her attention. "I missed your birthday last year, so I got you something."

She shook her head, almost able to smile. "I didn't even know you then."

"The feed from cam 0AC1:44F0 was good and clear. I have hits on all three suspects. Hank Bren, aka 'Nurse B,' Uri Sarkov, and apparently the other guy's legal name *is* Spaz. If you give me about a half hour, I can probably tell you where they are, provided they're not in a black zone or the Beneath and out of the range of cams."

"Finally, some damn good news." She smiled. "I could kiss you."

"Later." Dorian winked. "Little advice? Those lugs aren't psionic. Kick it over to Div 1. Let them deal with the pickup. About time you started acting like a detective and stopped getting shot at."

She closed her eyes and thought of Evan. "None of them are psionic. Okay. I'll send it to Eze to make the request." After creating a sub-Inquest, she bundled the video from the cams and a placeholder for the eventual crime scene information together and shot it off to Eze with a request to have Division 1 round up the suspects. "Sent."

Dorian smiled. "Now we wait… and hope one of them talks to save their own ass."

"Think they will?" She snuck a quick kiss on Sam's hologram before she hung up.

"My money's on the little guy." Dorian backed away as a Div 2 woman approached with a trio of fist-sized orb bots in tow, scanning the ground. "Of course, you can always cheat to see what they're most afraid of. Surface thoughts rarely lie."

"That's not ethical." She scowled at him.

"Oh, and slicing Charlie up for spare parts stands on moral high ground?" Dorian raised an eyebrow. "A little skimming during an interrogation isn't even close to compelling some punk to confess to molesting his friend's sister, even if it happened to be true. The girl's still alive. Charles…"

"Okay, okay. Point taken."

She shifted her weight from one leg to the other, 'supervising' the crime scene people; small hovering bots glided over road-hugging mist, projecting lasers here and there while the technicians crept about with glowing visors. Everyone scoured the area to find useful evidence in all the trash and muck.

Please work faster. She eyed one of the black-and-white patches. *I want to get out of here before something notices me.*

40

DELICATE ENGAGEMENT

O atmeal swished back and forth in Kirsten's square bowl, perfect cubes of 'peach' sinking and surfacing in an endless cycle. The tapping of her spoon against the sides clicked as rhythmic as a clock. Sleep had been elusive due to nerves about something stalking Evan as well as the imminent raid Division 6 would conduct based on her warrant. Listed addresses for Mardrake's thugs sat close enough to an unpleasant grey zone that Division 1 kicked it down the hall.

Except for the crew that had played bodyguard when Intera Corporation had sent assassins after her, she worried whenever Division 6 became involved. Blue instead of green armor seemed the only difference between them and front-line assault troops. Dorian had once commented that calling them in on a civilian area should be a last resort, tantamount to attempting brain surgery with a battleax.

She'd showered as soon as she got home and spent almost two hours with Evan de-stressing in the Monwyn game before attempting sleep. At 3 a.m., she almost talked herself into trying Theodore's suggested cure-all for not being able to pass out, but couldn't quite summon the courage or desire to pleasure herself. The last thing she'd need would be for Theo (or some other ghost) or worse yet—Evan—to walk in on her in the middle of that.

Twenty minutes on the treadmill didn't do much but make her want to shower again. Attempting to stare at herself in the bathroom mirror and use psionic suggestion with the one-word command 'sleep' skipped the clock to 5:42 a.m. and gave her a bloody nose. After cleaning up the sink where her face met it on the way to the floor, and forcing a stimpak into her cheek, she showered again, dressed, and prepared the oatmeal she had yet to eat, the same oatmeal gathering against her spoon in a back-and-forth tidal wave across her bowl. She imagined tiny sailing ships on the churning sea of beige nothingness, microscopic sailors screaming for their lives as each 'peach-galleon' went under.

No call yet. I hope that's good news. She lifted a spoonful of the tepid mush to her mouth. A piece of pseudo-fruit between her teeth started out with consistency, but devolved to something akin to the sensation of biting raw egg yolk as soon as she closed her jaw. *Ugh.* She forced the mouthful down and let go of the spoon. Reassembled oatmeal was bad enough when eaten right away. Twenty minutes later, raw OmniSoy seemed tasty by comparison.

Motion at the door made her look up.

Evan, eyes closed, stumbled into the kitchen in his floppy Monwyn pajama pants and no shirt. He stopped about halfway to the table, swayed on his feet for a few seconds, and shucked his pants to the floor. One arm out, he zombie-walked forward, grabbed the knob of a tall closet to the left of the refrigerator, and climbed inside before pulling the door closed behind him.

Kirsten covered her mouth to stop from giggling.

Tapping evolved to thumping. Two minutes after he shut the closet, Evan yelled from inside, "Mom! The autoshower's broke. It won't start."

Laughing, she got up and walked over. "What's on the screen?"

"It's dark."

She pulled the door open. "Ev?"

He twisted around to squint up at her, shrinking from the kitchen light like a vampire staring at the sun, only with less hissing and smoke. "Mom?"

"You're too young to be nonfunctional before coffee."

Evan looked around, let his head sag, and rubbed his eyes. "Ugh." Still kneading crumbles away from his face, he stepped down out of the closet and yawned.

The lack of bruising anywhere on his body reassured and worried her. "Did you stay awake all night to avoid a bad dream?"

"No." His arms dangled limp; his left eye seemed stuck closed. "Was up late talkin' to this lady who died 'neath our building."

Kirsten took his hand. "Come on. The bathroom's this way."

"Like way 'neath. Under the city 'neath."

She stooped to grab his pajamas from the floor on the way to the corridor. "Does she need help?"

Evan shrugged. "She wanted someone to talk to. Her family's all gone 'cause she died a long time ago. 'Fore they made the city. I asked how she died, and she said she couldn't tell me on 'count'a me not bein' old enough." He stopped at the bathroom door and looked up at her. "I think she died without pants on. Why'd the killer steal her pants?"

"Uhh." Kirsten couldn't look him in the eye. "Uhh... The man that killed her was *very* bad."

He scrunched up his face. "Stealin' pants isn't that bad. Not as bad as killing someone."

"I... Umm..." *Can't tell a nine year old about rape.* The idea she'd been only three years older than him when she'd let a man use her filled her head with a brief waking nightmare of Evan's life had she not found him. She took a knee, holding his hand in both of hers. "Evan, the man who killed her did something very evil to her. He probably killed her so she wouldn't tell the police what he'd done. When a woman loves a man, sometimes they show their love in a physical way."

"Like kissing?" He yawned.

She smiled. "Yeah. Like kissing. When someone makes a person who doesn't love them do that, it's one of the most evil things imaginable."

His lips twisted into a frown of contemplation. "Not more evil than what your mother did to you. I think that's the worst. Moms are s'posed to protect their kids."

She wrapped her arms around him and squeezed, too choked up to speak.

"Ghosts wanted to talk to you when you were little too, right?"

"Yeah." She swallowed the lump in her throat. "They did. Most of the time they wanted me to pass messages or warnings to their families. Sometimes, they thought I could give the police enough information to solve their murders. I never really managed to help any of them when I was small. Mother saw to that."

Evan smiled. "It's okay if I talk to them, right?"

She put his pajama pants on him like a hat, and grinned. "Yep. But tell me if anything sounds dangerous or wrong."

He pulled them off his head, laughing. "Okay."

Kirsten shooed him into the shower tube and returned to the kitchen. After ditching the gelatinous mass of not-oatmeal, she whipped up a quick breakfast, blending liquid OmPlus with synbacon bits to make a pair of omelets. Evan, dressed for school, darted in seconds before she transferred the food from pan to plate. He sat at the table before shrugging out of his grey-and-red jacket, which he draped back over his chair.

A conversation about strategy for the giant boss they'd gotten stuck on last night slipped in between mouthfuls. Before long, Kirsten collected the plates to the dishwasher while Evan got his coat back on and retrieved his backpack.

"Hey, Mom. Maybe you could ask Sam to come over. That fight would be a lot easier with three people, and he's really good with Halek."

Kirsten grinned to herself. "Well, having a knight to hide behind would make that ogre-king a lot less scary."

Evan led the way to the door. "Yeah. Unless you get three lucky crits in a row again. I didn't know Asara's got such a big multiplier." He cracked up laughing. "The mino-naga wanted you *bad*. Chased you around in circles no matter what I hit him with."

Kirsten hit the elevator button for the roof. "Ugh, yeah. I ran so much in VR I got tired for real."

"Oops!" He looked up at her, color draining from his face.

"What?" She grabbed his shoulder.

"I uhh…" He fidgeted. "Forgot to do one of my assignments. But it's short. It's just some questions I gotta look up the answers for. I can do it on the ride."

"Okay." She ruffled his hair. "Don't get so upset over one assignment. If I got in serious trouble every time one of my reports was late…" She shivered. "As long as they get done."

He grinned and rummaged a datapad out of his backpack.

Kirsten kept a hand on his shoulder as they strolled across the roof to the patrol craft. Once inside, he got to work amid a trio of small holo-panels. Violet, green, and blue light saturated the interior and made his hair glow. She suppressed the urge to laugh at his expression; he looked like a little mad scientist about to take over the world.

Four minutes into their flight, Captain Eze's virtual head appeared over the console. "Glad to see you up and about a little early today, Wren. I've got some good news for you. Div 6 managed to keep two of your three suspects alive, not for lack of trying."

"Let me guess, the big guy's gone?"

"Nope. That's what I meant for lack of trying. They put enough rounds in him to kill half the ACC on Mars, but he's still alive. The little man with the red hair didn't make it. Whatever stim he took traded all his common sense for misplaced confidence. He came out shooting."

"Idiot." Kirsten grumbled. *That guy didn't look like he knew much anyway.* "Okay. Where are they holding them? Can you set up an interrogation session?"

Captain Eze smiled. "Don't have to. The Prentice murder is technically not in our scope. Detectives from Div 2 got them to talk. Mr. Sarkov gave up Mardrake's location, and a couple of network addresses. Div 5 is going in."

"Five?" Kirsten blinked. "Six didn't blow enough up so you're sending in the cyborg interdiction team? What happened?"

"The thugs mentioned Mardrake has at least one full-conversion bodyguard, and a handful of augs working for him as protection in exchange for free maintenance and installs whenever they get new hardware."

"Dammit, sir. If Div 5 goes in there, they won't leave a piece big enough to interrogate."

Captain Eze raised an eyebrow. "Not expecting their ghosts to remain?"

"I need living testimony to go after Winchester. A spirit won't help me. I've gotta get there before Five flattens the place."

"The tone of the interviews leads me to believe that Mardrake isn't going to surrender." Captain Eze's hand entered the hologram, rubbing his chin. "This engagement is going to need care."

I'm sure Winchester's gotten wind of this. He'd much rather have Mardrake turned into a smoking crater than arrested. No wonder it got pushed to Div 5. "I understand."

"You're not to go in there alone, Wren."

"I wouldn't try, not with that kind of hardware. Suggestion only goes so far." She looked at Evan. "Hey kiddo. Feel anything bad?"

He looked at her, tilted his head, and returned to his assignment. "Nope."

"I'm two minutes out, Captain."

"All right. I'll have an A3HV waiting for you in the garage by the time you drop little man at school."

Evan saluted him without looking up from his work.

"Yes, sir." Kirsten stared past her HUD, the numbers, lines, and icons, a meaningless blur. Her sudden dose of luck in the arrest and interrogation of the men who killed Charles Prentice all but guaranteed an immediate portion of bad. She glanced at Evan. *I hope you're right, kiddo.*

41

DON'T FEAR THE RIPPER

E xpecting a long day, Kirsten decided to trust the advice Nicole gave her a few weeks ago. In the locker room, she stripped down to her underwear before donning a mesh stim suit and psi armor. It felt odd putting on the armor with so little cloth between it and her skin, but her friend did have a point. The material connecting the protective plates was essentially the same stuff (plus cushioning) as the Division 0 blacks, only less flexible. Putting the armor on over the uniform did amount to doubling up. Spending more than an hour or two in the armor plus the uniform would be dreadful.

With the equivalent of five stimpaks strapped to her body, she enjoyed a degree of confidence; the system would trigger them even if she lost consciousness. She re-checked her arm guards, gloves, and leg plates. Satisfied, and feeling invulnerable, she hurried down to the garage where Nicole, Morelli, Nila, Cortez, and Forrester waited by an enormous, gloss-black hover van with sinister lime green searchlights.

The A3HV resembled a MedVan, only larger, black, and armored. Wheels, tiny by comparison to the vehicle, remained fixed behind thick shrouds while in flight, unlike the retracting ground tires of patrol craft. It looked imposing, but it traded protection for mobility and speed. An A3V couldn't fly, but it could drive through buildings.

Captain Eze emerged from the A3HV's side door and climbed a ladder to the ground level. "Good morning everyone. Has anyone not read the briefing?"

Kirsten looked among her friends, and Morelli. None of them reacted. Dorian appeared next to her patrol craft, walked over, and stood at her side.

"Good," said Eze. "Division 5 is already en route to the location, but they're on the ground. You will fly into a disavowed sector, proceed straight to the designated waypoint, and attempt to detain the primary suspect with minimal loss of life. It's important to bring him in alive. Lieutenant, you are cleared to use Suggestion to encourage compliance with lawful detention. The only reason I'm going along with this is you have advantages Division 5 does not. Suspects with major cybernetic enhancements lose their natural defenses against psionic abilities."

Kirsten nodded. "Understood, sir."

"How much time do we have?" asked Cortez.

Captain Eze raised his datapad. "Five will be on site in approximately sixty-one minutes. Factoring in your flight duration, you'll have about a half hour of quiet time with Mardrake."

A bust appeared in hologram over Eze's datapad of a pale-faced man with wrinkles on both cheeks, one purple cybernetic eye and one blue living one. Thin black hair hung to his shoulders, split by a central part. His face had an overall squarish shape, and the teeth-baring grimace of a smile on his face hinted at a man who enjoyed inflicting pain.

"This is the primary suspect. Ian Mardrake, presumed age fifty-nine. We have no record of his arrival in the UCF, though we were able to get some information via Division 9's connections with the United Kingdom. He fell off their radar four years ago, at which point the assumption is he set up operations here."

"All due respect, Captain," said Nila. "This suspect's dossier had no mention whatsoever of psionics. Why are we involved?"

"That," said Captain Eze, "is a question for the Lieutenant. We have minimal intelligence on his facility or what defenses you may encounter. Indications are that he has at least four augmented individuals providing security, none of whom are of the type inclined to respect law enforcement. Time's running short, people."

Kirsten jogged to the rear ramp door of the A3HV. The interior seemed too cramped for the massive size of the vehicle, though armor, electronics, and ion engines made for thick walls. A giant of a man in a green tank top and blue-camo pants leaned into the narrow doorway leading from the back to the driver's compartment. A large Division 6 tattoo covered both shoulders.

"Morning, Lieutenant." His salute could've been mistaken for shooing a gnat from his eyebrow. "Guess none of your Tac boys have the balls to fly into the black. You psi-ops people ready for the ride of your life?"

"You're about eleven years late, son." Forrester chuckled as he flopped on one of the benches running along the inside walls. "This lunchbox ain't got nothin' on a DS2 goin' down Lucifer's throat."

The driver blinked. "You slalomed Io?"

"Ganymede too. That bastard made Io feel like a nice Sunday drive. Whoever got the bright idea to put the damn base in the middle of that canyon oughta be shot." Forrester shook his head. "Goddamn fourteen years in before they realized I had 'the touch.'"

"Touch?" The Division 6 sergeant hit a switch to raise the ramp once Morelli took a seat.

"Technokinesis." Forrester wiggled his fingers. "Probably the only reason my ass managed to pull off forty seven landings on Gany without clipping a wing. Got sent over here when they figured out I 'had the psionic.'"

"Heh. All right then, maybe you're not all cube dwellers."

The big man focused his attention forward. The A3HV rose off the ground slow enough not to feel much inertia. Kirsten held her helmet in her lap and leaned her head against the cushion behind her.

"Okay, spill it, K. Why are we going after a ripper doc?" asked Nila.

"I was wonderin' that too." Cortez smiled.

"Because I need a living suspect to turn witness against the man who ordered a murder. He's pretty high up the food chain. If Div 5 gets there first, the biggest piece of Mardrake left is going to resemble a potato."

"When was the last time you saw a potato?" asked Dorian. "The synthesized growth ones are bigger than Evan before they're cut up."

"Something doesn't feel right. I'm not sure this hop is a good idea." Morelli fidgeted.

Kirsten smiled at him. "That's just because Dorian's making faces at you."

"I am not." Dorian feigned offense.

Morelli broke out in a sweat.

"Tom. Hold it together please. I know you two didn't see eye to eye when he was alive, but try not to let your superstition get the better of you."

He gazed up at the dim blue-grey LED bars recessed behind an armored mesh overhead.

Nila kept tapping her fingers. Nicole wore a face like a six-year-old about to be grounded. Forrester slumped a little to the left, seeming about ready to fall asleep.

"Okay guys, I know you're all… well mostly all nervous," said Kirsten.

Forrester smiled but left his eyes closed.

"We're expecting augs and at least one full-conversion cyborg."

Nila shivered.

"Oh, crap." Nicole stared at her.

"Shit." Morelli checked his laser rifle. "We're going to need something bigger than these E641s."

"Not true, Tom." Dorian clucked his tongue. "That thing'll go right through a Class 4 cyborg chassis, and I highly doubt Mardrake has those kind of parts. Granted, little holes, so you'll actually have to hit the right spot. I know you've never been big on marksmanship."

Forrester laughed, and Morelli scowled before going pale.

Kirsten gawked at Dorian.

"Every helmet has speakers." He winked.

Kirsten checked the charge indicator on her borrowed E641. She'd only used one twice, both times at the training course. While it was one step up from her E-90 pistol, most of its energy went to greater range, some three thousand meters (with appropriate optics to see a target) as opposed to the two hundred or so for the pistol. That, of course, and the rifle was capable of rapid fire. Twenty pulses per second. "Don't worry about the cyborg. If it's got a living brain, I'll mind blast it. If it's an AI, Dorian will turn it off. I'm less worried about cyborgs than normal people."

"Heh. Don't say that too loud or we'll wind up doin' Five's job," muttered Cortez.

Being reminded he shared a small chamber with a mind-blast-rated psionic seemed to make Morelli even more nervous. Rumor had it a cyborg reduced to a 'brain in a jar' had almost no ability to resist it, as the body's natural protective auras and psychic energy fields were absent.

The A3HV wobbled, jostling them.

"Two minutes. We're about to cross into the black zone. Gonna come in high, skimming rooftops. Orient on target, and do a hundred ten story drop. You may experience a slight period of weightlessness." The big guy up front held out a thumbs up in the doorway.

"Slight period of weightlessness." Forrester buckled his harness. "That means you'll be French-kissing the roof."

Everyone strapped in and put their helmets on. Amber HUD elements flickered to life before Kirsten's eyes, and the sound of her breathing grew loud in the enclosed space around her head. The faces of Nila, Forrester, and Nicole glowed yellow out of their visors, behind a thin layer of fog. Nicole still looked terrified.

"Killjoy," said the driver. He laughed.

Forrester smiled.

"Wren," said Eze over comm. "Division 5 is reporting twenty-eight minutes out. Looks like traffic was light. If you encounter more resistance than expected, wait for them. I recognize what you're trying to do, but this case is not worth your lives."

Kirsten closed her eyes. *Evan didn't seem scared. I'll make the right call.* "Understood, sir."

"One minute," said the driver.

Are you sure this is a good idea? Nicole's voice entered her head.

Kirsten looked at her friend. *What's wrong, Nikki? I've never seen you afraid of anything before.*

You know how some people are like phobic of psionics? I'm the same way with cyborgs. Saw this stupid vid when I was like eight. I shouldn't have watched it. It was for adults, but this cyborg killer... Nicole shivered. *I still have nightmares sometimes about that. Metal skeleton tore a woman's spine out.*

Kirsten cringed, but grinned. *Bet that girl wasn't a badass telekinetic with an attitude.*

"Nope." Nicole laughed.

The driver flashed another thumbs up. "Ten seconds." The interior lights went out, and came back on red.

Forrester looked up at the roof. "Damn, what is this, a spec ops drop?"

Gravity inverted, slamming Kirsten upward into her harness. The rifle almost flew out of her grip, but she clamped it to her chest. Morelli and Nila screamed. Nicole's scream changed to cheering after a second. Forrester looked bored. Kirsten grunted, clenching her jaw. After about four seconds (though it felt like twenty), her ass hit the bench. The sudden switch in gravity twice in rapid succession made her regret eating breakfast. She tried to resist the urge to vomit by fearing what throwing up inside an enclosed helmet would be like, though that pushed her closer to erupting.

The ramp door deployed so fast she thought it had blown off. Forrester jumped up first and jogged down, yelling "Go, go, go" over the comm.

Kirsten shook off a mild sense of panic and hurried out into a scene that could've been a set from a post-nuclear war disaster vid. The street they'd landed on occupied a canyon of smashed buildings, most of which had no walls on the sides facing the road. Bare floors dangled in chunks from rebar; wires, pipes, and snapped cables swayed like whiskers.

Standard procedure put the nose of the A3HV toward the target, so as not to create a situation where the crew wound up as fish in a barrel to incoming fire. Four panels on the van's exterior opened outward and angled to touch the road, providing cover barricades. Kirsten rushed around the left side and took a position behind the rear flange, which came up to her chest, and aimed her rifle over it. Nila ran past Kirsten and tucked in behind the forward one. She also sighted her rifle over the two-inch thick armor slab.

Mismatched hunks of plastisteel plates covered the windows of a long-ago abandoned commercial property in front of them. From the general design of the ground floor, it looked much like a Nippy Nom convenience store. The improvised protection bore as much graffiti as it did dents from bullets. Two large gouges surrounded by scorch marks suggested someone in the area had shoulder-launched missiles. Vacant windows covered the bulk of the remaining sixty some odd stories, some with tattered curtains billowing outward.

Three men in long coats, one with two metal arms, popped up inside, concealed up to the waist by the reinforced windowsill. One pointed at the van and shouted as the man next to him sprinted deeper into the building.

"Attention," said the driver over a loudspeaker. "This is the National Police Force. Place your weapons on the ground and walk outside in a single-file line, hands in the air."

The thug with metal arms raised a rifle.

Nicole grunted, and the weapon lurched, but didn't break out of his grip. Her attempt to telekinetically disarm redirected his shot into the ground.

Morelli, Nila, and Forrester opened fire with rapid pulses. Blue-violet laser streaks left finger-width holes ringed by glowing orange in the metal plates grafted to the building. The man fell, landing out of sight behind the plastisteel wall, screaming in agony.

Kirsten aimed at the remaining man, a clear picture of his chest appeared in zoom courtesy of her HUD, a floating-point aim dot glowing red at its center. *Don't do it. Don't.*

When he raised a ballistic rifle, she triggered twice, putting two laser streaks center mass. The dead body fell out of his ghost, who remained standing there attempting to fire a nonexistent rifle at her.

"Incoming," yelled Forrester. "Two tank bots and a class 3 'borg with a god damned Nano sword."

Kirsten shifted her aim a few degrees to the right. A six-foot tall humanoid shape made entirely of dull unpainted plastisteel stomped down the main central aisle of the old store. Like something out of the Monwyn fantasy, he carried a giant clear-bladed greatsword. The sight of it froze the blood in her veins. A Nano knife in her tiny arm cut a one-inch thick steel pipe like hard ice cream. A sword that size in the hands of a cyborg could take big pieces out of the A3HV, and shred psi armor without even slowing down. He could probably cut all four of them in half in one swing if they stood close enough.

On either side of the cyborg, a pair of tracked bots, each about the size of footlockers, rolled forward. Both had miniguns mounted on struts, flanked by a pair of two-pack missile launchers loaded with 60mm 'soda can' rockets.

"Now it's a party," yelled the Division 6 driver. He stormed out of the back of the A3HV carrying an enormous machinegun with a backpack for an ammo supply. He didn't bother putting it on, dropping the pack on the ramp before grabbing the squad-support weapon in two hands.

Kirsten reached out with telepathy, confirming the metal figure had a living brain. "The 'borg is alive. I got him. Dorian, zap the bots before they fire those missiles."

"On it." Dorian blurred forward.

Drop the sword and stand down. I don't want to kill you, but I will melt your brain if I have to.

The telepathic message made the cyborg stop. He tilted his head at Kirsten. Yellow-glowing cybernetic eyes whirred wider. All four of the bots' missile launch pods angled toward her.

Kirsten snarled. Her friends were in danger because she *had* to go after the senator. Her eyes flared with white light as a barrage of rapid, random sensory input erupted from her brain at the speed of thought. She focused on the presence of a sentient mind within the metal skull, and tapped her resolve to protect her squad. Mental energy streamed forth, with a sensation like warm snot flowing around her eyeballs, peeling away from the inside of her skull.

"Ngggh!" roared the cyborg. The enormous sword fell from his grasp. His body twitched and convulsed in a rapid jittery rotation to the left. Metal hands slapped and pawed at his face for three seconds before he collapsed over backward, lost in an endless repetition of shouting a word like "nyarp" interspersed with groans and high-pitched trilling noises. A panel on his thigh opened, spitting out a giant pistol, which flew to the ground a short distance away. Claws sprouted and retracted from his forearms over and over, and his right leg locked immobile at the knee.

Hair-thin threads of blue lightning snapped from both tracked bots, lapping at Dorian's outstretched arms.

One missile fired from the bot on the far right, though it veered almost straight up the second it cleared the windows, leaving a trail of white smoke fifteen stories up to an orange fireball. The *boom* of its detonation reached ground level seconds after the flash.

"Fuck." Nicole gasped. "That was a missile."

"Nice catch," said Forrester.

"Hey, that was me." Cortez grumbled.

"That was both of us," said Nicole.

Kirsten pressed the heel of her armored glove into her helmet, failing to soothe a sudden, intense headache as though a metal spike had pierced her brain. *Ngh. Mind blast...*

Four more men came from a back hallway, armed with rifles and copious amounts of cyberware. The Division 6 driver unloaded with his machinegun, peppering the interior of the store with 8mm rounds. Fist-sized holes appeared in the metal walls, the high-velocity projectiles shredding steel, pulverizing concrete, and causing machinery inside to explode in showers of sparks. Three feet of dark azure muzzle flare erupted from the front end of the weapon, glimmering off nearby metal. Despite her helmet, the gunfire punished Kirsten's eardrums and pounded on the air in her lungs. With any luck, the local wildlife would be more afraid of a weapon that loud than interested in stealing it.

Mardrake's thugs dove for cover amid a rainfall of shredded steel, as the machinegun chewed apart shelving and interior walls. Despite the driver's immense size, firing a continuous burst forced him to inch backward.

"Covering fire," yelled the driver. "Go!"

Forrester jumped out from behind the retractable flange, sprinted to the front of the building, and aimed in the broken window. He pivoted and fired a short laser pulse at a downward angle.

Kirsten ran up to the other side of the door, followed a second later by Nila. They both aimed at the cyborg, who'd ceased screaming and had fallen into a tic-like twitching fit accompanied by *nguh* sounds every few seconds.

"I don't think he's going to be getting back up," said Dorian. "You turned his brain into OmniSoy."

Kirsten frowned. His surface-thought reaction to her warning was a panicky 'shit, psionic, kill it' desire of wanting all four missiles to fire at her. She wouldn't let herself feel guilty about it. A *ping* overhead made her duck as a bullet ricocheted out into the city. Nila put a laser pulse into a metal shoulder, but the aug ducked before she could take a fatal follow-up shot.

"Dammit." Nila growled and stared.

Four seconds later, the mountain of trash by where the augs hid burst into a burning conflagration. When two of the men jumped up to flee, Nila and Forrester mowed them down in a barrage of bright violet laser streaks. Kirsten aimed, but decided not to fire as their ghosts already seeped away from their remains.

Kirsten jumped in the window, letting some psionic energy leak into the armor. Matte grey trim glowed purple as the armor's bizarre electronics converted mental energy into a force field. No one ever talked about how that worked or where they got the technology from. Rumors abounded, most of which pointed at devices discovered on Mars. Fewer people believed in aliens than ghosts. *Demons are real... why not aliens?* She took an abbreviated breath of air reeking of carrion and chemicals.

Kirsten aimed at a moving shadow. "Drop it!"

A stocky man with medium brown skin and long, shaggy hair stood with his hands raised, assault rifle dangling on a strap from his left elbow. His surface thoughts contained an image of Kirsten's helmet superimposed over a targeting crosshair, and the inclination to fire the laser weapon installed in his cybernetic right eye.

"*Stop.*" Kirsten's suggestion hit him hard enough to make him drool. "*Come outside. Surrender.*"

The man shuffled like a zombie toward the front door.

She pulled the rifle away from his arm as he went past her, and tossed it to the side. "One exiting, compelled. Watch him; he's got a laser embedded in his eye."

Cortez tackled the guy as soon as he left the building, putting him in binders and plugging a Medusa into his M3 port before the compulsion wore off. "Secure." He dragged the suspect out of sight behind the A3HV.

Nicole and Morelli rushed in, taking up cover behind a shelf on the right. Trash shifted, and a man with four arms, two made of flesh and an extra pair of metal limbs sprouting from his shoulder blades, popped up holding four submachine guns. A hail of bullets peppered Kirsten, Morelli, and Nicole. Kirsten screamed, but more from fear. With the psi armor charged, the attack hit her with a force like a disorienting barrage of fists from an ancient warrior monk.

Nicole and Morelli shouted and hit the ground. Uncharged psi armor had weak spots, and from the sound of the screams, bullets had found them.

Kirsten slumped back into the shelves, gasping for air. Dorian ran at the four-armed gunman, drawing the power from his weapons' firing circuits as well as the mechanical limbs.

"Son of a bitch!" screamed Nicole. She picked herself up a second before the Nano greatsword levitated. The six-foot weapon whirled like a thrown dagger across the room. It seemed to pass the man without effect; a second later, blood exploded in a sheet out of a hair-thin line that ran from the top of his head down through his left eye to his groin. Two pieces of body with glass-smooth edges slid apart and fell.

"Nikki!" yelled Kirsten. She ran across the aisle, taking two rounds in the left side when she broke cover. Based on the tremendous *boom* of the shot, plus finding herself lying on the ground, she guessed Class 6 pistol and at least a cracked rib. Her voice went from scream to croaky rasp. "You okay?"

"Two hits. Stimsuit's got it." Nicole growled while pivoting to fire at the man who'd shot Kirsten.

More laser streaks, as well as a stream of orange tracer bullets passed over her.

The driver reached the front door and looked at the cyborg. After two seconds of watching the man-machine twitch and emit *nrk* sounds, he fired a long burst into the metal skull, denting it and sending a scattering of tiny parts dancing across the floor. The borg kept twitching and making sub-vocal noises. "Damn. That ain't right."

Metallic clunking came from the rear hallway, filling her mind with visions of another huge cyborg. Kirsten crawled back to her knees before standing, and pointed her rifle down a dingy corridor lined with thick, ribbed hoses and electrical cables. Morelli and Nila hit the shelf on either side of her, also aiming toward the approaching monster.

Nicole busied herself cursing and further mauling the four-armed man's corpse with the floating Nano sword.

A pair of robotic walkers, spindly and covered with exposed actuators and wires, emerged from the darkness, each holding a large assault rifle. The tactical computer in her armor provided helpful HUD tags, indicating Class 6 assault rifles chambered in 15mm, a weapon capable of punching holes in psi armor with ease if she didn't charge the field.

Doctor Mardrake walked behind them, wearing a surprisingly clean powder-blue jumpsuit and white lab coat. A surgical mask hung loose below his chin, exposing an irritated sneer. He brandished a two-pack over-the-shoulder missile launcher. "I'm not unreasonable." Seven fourteen-inch diameter orb bots dropped into view out front. Iris doors on their front faces opened, revealing solid glass transparent barrels—laser weapons. "I understand you are police and suffer from a unique brand of idiocy borne of a perceived sense of power you do not possess here. For this, I shall forgive you the deaths of these fools, and not demand one of your number as spare parts."

"He's worried," said Dorian. "Bluffing."

"Mardrake," yelled Kirsten. "I'm willing to offer you a deal in exchange for testimony against Winchester?"

"Who?" asked Mardrake.

Forrester crawled over to one of the inert tracked bots and put his hand on it while using its mass as cover.

Shit, those cyborgs don't have thoughts. She whispered, "Dorian... those 'borgs don't have brains. All yours."

He nodded. "Technically, they're 'bots, not 'borgs. No biological tissue."

She scowled and shouted, "The person who hired you to kill Charles Prentice?"

Mardrake's expression looked pained. "Who? Why would I remember the name of a meat sack?"

Kirsten grumbled. "The lungs that Senator Preston Winchester hired you to find?"

"Oh, dear girl..." Mardrake laughed.

"He's thinking proxies," said Nicole. "He never knew a senator was involved. Holy shit, a senator's involved?"

Mardrake's eyebrows shot up.

"Now he's thinking, 'oh shit, psionics'." Nicole giggled for an instant before she looked worried. "And now 'eek, psionics, die!' He's triggering the orbs!"

Nila dropped in place, spinning to put her back to the shelf and aim at the floating spheres. Morelli did likewise. Dorian seemed torn between the orbs and the two androids.

Mardrake raised the missile tube at Kirsten.

Nicole let off a war cry.

Simultaneously: Mardrake's weapon reoriented downward, releasing a missile at the ground between his shoes; Nila and Morelli opened fire on the orbs; the orbs shot back; both androids took aim; and the minigun on the tracked bot Forrester touched sprang to life, spewing bullets at the orbs.

An explosion flooded the interior hallway with smoke, metal fragments, and gore. Two mangled androids lurched forward, falling as their massive assault rifles chugged at a laborious rate of fire into the floor and walls.

Kirsten whirled around, ducking behind a shelf away from the onrush of exploding debris while firing her laser rifle at the orbs. Sparks sprayed from one then the next as the minigun Forrester overrode tracked and spat bursts with the accuracy of a computer. Three spears of burning agony ripped into her, one in the left bicep, one an inch below her left breast, and one about a hand's width above her left knee. She staggered to the right, her left arm more of a brace to lean the rifle against than a useful limb, and kept firing at orbs until she fell on her side. Though she fed mental energy to her armor, the lasers from the orbs didn't seem to care.

Heavy thuds outside signaled the driver opening up again with the huge machinegun. One orb bot after the next burst into clouds of metal shrapnel and the flashes of dying ion thrusters.

The stimsuit went off, pumping her bloodstream full of synthetic adrenaline and nanobots. Within a second, she felt wired and pain free. The chemicals made time seem to slow around her, and all sound hit her ears as though she'd slipped underwater. Individual bullets streamed from the minigun like a solid rope of lead cutting apart one orb after the next. When it ran dry, Forrester leapt and crawled to the other tracked bot.

Fragments of Doctor Mardrake littered the floor, the most recognizable piece a hand on the pistol grip formerly attached to a missile launcher. Heavy cannon fire continued outside, and the last two orbs disintegrated like clay pigeons. More shots came from deeper within the building, followed seconds later by a billowy cloud of dust.

Silence.

Kirsten took three breaths before she dragged herself out of the open aisle running along the center of the old Nippy Nom and leaned against the twisted ruin of a display shelf. Men laughed outside amid the clap of a handshake. Figures in bright blue Division 5 armor approached the front of the store, most carrying ABR20 rifles, weapons that resembled antiquated pump-action shotguns, but far larger.

A man with silver sergeant's stripes on his shoulders walked in, glanced around at everyone, and headed over to Kirsten.

"Lieutenant." He eyed the man cut in six pieces by a giant sword, the twitching, babbling cyborg, and finally at the corridor painted with Mardrake. He whistled. "I thought you raced us here to be subtle."

Kirsten stared past the fog on her visor, not quite sure why she no longer had red hot needles piercing her body. It didn't seem likely the stimsuit shots could completely fix three laser hits, but she didn't feel a damn thing. Nicole kept muttering curses, a sure sign she'd been shot again. Morelli huffed and whined, cradling his right arm. Nila lay motionless, her chestplate slick with blood. "Nila! Nila!" She struggled to get up, but neither her left arm nor leg obeyed.

She'd made Shani an orphan.

Kirsten slumped forward, sobbing in silence.

"Aw, shit." Nicole grunted in pain and dragged herself over to Nila.

Morelli stared at the floor.

The idea of having to look Shani in the eye and tell her that her mother died for nothing drained any willpower to move. "I'm sorry, Nila. This is—"

"I'm good," rasped Nila over the comm. "At least I will be after a dip in the tank. *Shit* this hurts."

"You looked dead!" Kirsten leaned forward as she screamed, more anger than she intended in her voice. The breath she sucked in afterward chattered, her tears not quite done.

Nila groaned. "Don't kill me, but I was praying. I know you hate that."

Morelli limped over and offered Kirsten a hand up. A scrap of light brown matter clung to the left pectoral region of his armor.

"Something on your chest." Kirsten let off a fluttering whimper when she tried to put weight on her left leg, and almost blacked out from a sudden, blinding pain.

"I believe that's a piece of Mardrake," said Dorian.

Kirsten gagged. Morelli flicked the scrap of skin away.

Mardrake's hollow voice emanated from the left, asking no one in particular what had happened. Dorian pounced on the ghost of the former ripper doc, and dragged him over to Kirsten.

"Any more questions for the suspect?" Dorian cocked an eyebrow.

She grumbled. "Ops, need a MedVan."

Dorian blinked. "I think he's a bit beyond that."

She frowned at him.

The operations dispatcher replied with a long "ummmm."

"They're not coming here," said the driver. "Black zone remember? Can you walk, Officer Assad?"

"Fuck no." Nila groaned. "Feels like my hip's in three pieces and my right lung's half full of blood."

"I got her." Nicole wobbled upright and levitated Nila, keeping her as flat as possible.

Darkness settled over the area. Kirsten sensed it first; about four seconds later, Dorian glanced at the north wall.

Nicole looked around, pausing in her effort to carry Nila out. "Uhh, anyone else feel that?"

"Yeah." Morelli looked at Kirsten as though she were about to sacrifice them all to the Devil. "What are you doing?"

Billowy black vapor melted out of the plain wall, accompanied by thin trails of ichor running to the floor. The eight-foot tall apparition of a Harbinger exuded forth, head tilted back and arms wide. Its body tapered to a wispy point at the bottom rather than legs, and glinting onyx talons glinted from its outstretched hands. Sparkling silver flecks of eyes amid the impenetrable void approximating its head regarded Mardrake with cool detachment.

"Ooh," muttered Nicole. "I think one of her shadow fluffies is here."

Dorian raised an eyebrow. "Shadow fluffies?"

"Me? What am I doing?" asked Kirsten. "Nothing except feeling like shit for getting everyone hurt. We're not the worst thing to happen to Mardrake today. Oh, Doctor, your ride's here." *Wow, he must be dark... I didn't even beckon them.*

Dorian faced the approaching Harbinger, standing his ground with a resolute expression while containing the flailing Mardrake in a headlock. When the Harbinger stopped at arm's distance away, he flung the ghostly ripper doc into its waiting embrace.

"What's going on? Psionic freaks! What are you doing to my mind?" Mardrake's ghost wailed, frothing at the mouth as a shadowy hand covered his face.

The vaporous specter engulfed the screaming Mardrake, and sank into the floor. Astral screams faded to silence a few seconds later.

Boom.

One of the Division 5 men stood over the cyborg out front, white smoke peeling from the barrel of his gargantuan rifle. Nothing remained of the borg's head but a sparking stump of neck and a burning hole in the ground. "Sorry, that *nygh, nygh, nygh* shit was getting annoying."

A ghostly brain zipped around in a panic before racing out through the back wall, trailed by about two feet of spinal nerve.

Kirsten closed her eyes. "Ugh. Now *that* is going to haunt my dreams for a while."

Nila gasped over the comm. "Thanks, Nikki."

"Got her loaded," said Nicole. "Can we get out of here now?"

"Yeah." Kirsten flailed at the air and clung to a shelf to keep from falling over when she tried to walk. She winced as a searing rod of agony flared in the laser wound, all her weight on her fingertips. "Damn. My leg's all torn up. I... don't think I can walk."

A Division 5 man hurried over and picked her up like a child. "Gotcha, Ell-

Tee." He carried her outside and up the ramp of the A3HV. Once inside, he eased her onto the bench seat before securing her harness and planting her laser rifle next to her. Kirsten clamped her mouth shut, crying from the pain, but refusing to scream.

"Not calling in a crime scene team?" Dorian phased out of the wall at her right.

"Don't rub it in," she muttered, off comms. "Okay, everyone. Let's go home. Five, would you guys mind grabbing that Nano sword before some crazy fringer finds it? If there's a terminal back there somewhere, bring that too please?"

"Got it," said a female voice. "Holy shit... someone really objected to this man's existence. Looks like someone ran him through a food processor."

"He *shot* me," said Nicole, in the tone of an annoyed child.

The ramp whirred closed. Kirsten couldn't reach Nila to hold her hand and lacked the energy or the willpower to undo her harness.

Sorry, Nila. I'm so, so sorry.

Nila held a thumbs-up, and let her arm drop limp.

Kirsten closed her eyes. "Ops, this is Lieutenant Wren. We're coming back with multiple wounded. Please have medical standing by."

"Copy Lieutenant," said a male voice.

"The only difference 'tween us and the military is the color of the uniform," muttered Forrester. "Bus load of wounded mother—umm, wounded people. Feels like old times."

Her head rolled back against the armor plating, leaving her staring at the digital windows on the far wall above where Nila lay. Passing buildings blurred as the A3HV picked up speed and altitude; muzzle flare flickered in the darkened spaces within crumbling buildings. One or two *clanks* sounded on the hull. Soon, the condition of buildings improved and the natives stopped firing at them. The adrenaline from the stim shot wore off, leaving her short of breath and acutely aware of the laser that hit her under the left breast. Ragged breaths took on a metallic flavor.

I fucked up. The continuous grunts and groans of her wounded friends made her cry. *That was too close. That wasn't Division 0's job. That was stupid.*

Nicole gave her shoulder a telekinetic squeeze. *Hey. You didn't know he had a missile.*

She jostled in the harness as the A3HV climbed higher. Pain and exhaustion left her trembling. *Yeah, I guess, but I should've known better than to think Winchester dealt with him directly. I'm such an idiot.*

Nicole lifted her faceplate and stuck her tongue out. *Maybe, but you're a righteous idiot.*

'Righteous' can be taken two ways there. Kirsten furrowed her eyebrows for a second before smiling; she would've laughed if not for tasting her own blood.

THE MACHINE

K irsten sat on the edge of the Comforgel pad in the treatment room, not having bothered to dress or even wipe the powdery white residue of dried gel off. Elbows on her knees, she cradled her head in her hands and stared at the floor. Her mind swam with frozen instants of a decaying Nippy Nom lit in reds, greens, and blue-violet smears of laser. She'd been hit five times, but hadn't noticed the grazing burn on her hip or the hole two millimeters under her left collarbone.

Adrenaline's a bitch.

Nila had taken seven, Morelli three, but all in his right arm. Forrester managed to evade the laser fire from the bots, walking away with only a couple of bruises from the four-armed machine gunner; the small caliber rounds hadn't penetrated his armor. Any of a hundred tiny things happening differently could've killed them. Of course the senator would've had proxies do his dirty work for him. Men like that don't leave trails. Stupid people don't make it to the senate in the first place.

No, stupid was reserved for idealists.

She frowned at the boots and fresh uniform waiting on the end of the bed, next to her armband computer, wondering if she deserved to touch them.

The door opened with a soft pneumatic hiss. A dark-skinned medtech with hot pink hair approached, bearing a cup of honey-lemon tea. "Is something wrong, Lieutenant? You've been sitting there for an hour."

Kirsten sat up straight and accepted the tea. "I almost got people killed and the whole thing was a waste of time." She stared for a few seconds at bands of glare from overhead lights undulating across the dark brown surface. "I guess Division 5's protocol of walking in shooting really is better sometimes."

"There's a Captain Eze looking for you. I bought you a couple minutes saying you're going through some last tests to make sure you suffered no complications re-inflating your lung."

"Thanks." She sipped the tea; lemon-honey-warm slid down her throat. *People mess up. Deal with it. They sent me out there at sixteen. I'm surprised it took me this long to pull off a major error.* "Suppose I should clean up then."

"Do you need any assistance?"

Kirsten stretched her legs, admiring a tiny pink spot where the laser hit her. Dried breathable gel had formed a second-skin layer that wrinkled and peeled away as she moved. "Pain's stopped, but I still feel like an idiot. Suppose I shouldn't make him wait."

The medtech nodded. "If you do require assistance, just tap the call button."

"'Kay. Thanks for the tea." Kirsten set the mug on the table near the bed and crossed the room to the autoshower.

"You're welcome. I know you like it." The medtech let herself out.

Kirsten walked straight to Captain Eze's office upon returning to the squad room. Dorian materialized in his usual seat and jumped up to follow her in. She knocked at the doorjamb. Captain Eze looked up with a neutral expression and waved her in before going back to whatever he'd been reading on his terminal screen.

She entered with her head bowed and hands clasped in front of her. *Lieutenant* Wren should've known better. *Agent* Wren wasn't really an officer… *Agent* Wren was a child given a pay grade; no one expected much from the teenagers assigned to Investigative Operations based on rare abilities or unusual power. As a lieutenant, she was supposed to be trusted and she'd blown it the first time out.

Captain Eze looked up a little over a minute later after tapping the terminal in such a way as to make her think he'd fired off an annoyed email. "You're still standing and you look like you're expecting a beheading."

"I'm sorry, sir. I should've known Senator Winchester wouldn't have dealt directly with Mardrake. It was dumb, and I rushed in there before thinking."

He pondered, fingers steepled in front of his face. "Well, I suppose I should shoulder some portion of that, since I mentioned Division 5 was on the way. Going after a sitting senator is a project unto itself, something best left to Division 9. It takes them months, years sometimes, to gather enough information to act."

"Have they investigated senators before?" Kirsten lowered herself into one of the chairs facing his desk. Still unable to look him in the eye, she stared at the collection of four-inch African tribal masks along the edge.

"A few times, but they've only acted once."

Dorian made a quiet gunshot noise.

He leaned back, hands on the desk, and exhaled. "There's an audit coming down the pipe. Procedures, personnel, policies. I'm sure it's Winchester sending us a warning."

She picked at her nails. "He arranged for Charles to die so they could steal his lungs. Seraphina Winchester tried to commit suicide with heavy Icewhisper abuse. The senator can afford the best care. He could've taken her to Amaranth Medical, Ancora if he wanted to spend a little less. There was no need to have the man killed. I'm not sure how Charles will react if I tell him Winchester's out of reach. He hasn't done anything worthy of obliterating him. I don't want him to kill people who received his organs."

"If a person threatens the life of another, and you believe they are about to do so, you are perfectly justified in using whatever force necessary to safeguard life." Captain Eze looked around. "Is Dorian here? I'm sure he'll say the same."

"He's right, K. If you think Prentice represents an imminent threat to an innocent life, you're obligated to stop him."

A wave of resolve lifted her spirits, and her chin. She looked Eze in the eye. "What if he's only venting off steam in a rage? I'd have to be there at the moment he's trying to harm someone. I can't stay with them constantly, wondering if he'll show up to kill someone."

"It seems likely the two men Division 1 has in custody will face charges in connection with his murder. Senator Winchester is, as you put it, out of reach for now. You don't even have enough evidence to justify looking for more evidence." Captain Eze laced his fingers together, hands against his gut. "At least, nothing anyone outside of Division 0 would be open to hearing."

Dorian shook his head. "He's initiated an audit as a warning. The Captain's right, K. I think you're better off letting this one go. Pick your battles and all that. Forget the senator and focus on convincing Prentice you got the men who killed him. Maybe he'll see reason."

"But..." She leaned up in her seat, wide-eyed at Dorian. "Walk away? I can't—"

"Kirsten..." Eze's tone sounded less like Captain and more like big brother. "You're treading into thick mud. The kind of thick mud you don't have the temperament to get involved with. Crossing horns with people at that level requires lowering yourself into a pit of corruption."

"Not every senator's corrupt." She looked back and forth between Dorian and Captain Eze. "They can't be."

"The honest ones never make it past being district governors." Dorian chuckled. "They might be honest when they get to the Moon, but ideals never last long once they settle in. It's like dropping an ice cube in boiling soup and expecting it to stay frozen."

"But..." She clenched her hands into fists.

"Wren, your raid on Mardrake was hasty, but all things considered, probably went about as well as could be expected. I'm not advising any disciplinary action. The whole team, even Morelli, said you handled yourself like an officer out there."

She bowed her head. "Thank you, sir. I won't rush in like that again."

"Sometimes rushing in is the only way to get something done. Hell, that's practically the Division 5 motto." Captain Eze's smile stood out stark white against the deep brown of his face. "You'll have to trust yourself."

Kirsten exhaled out her nose.

"Now, in regards to this audit... You've got about eighteen Inquest reports that need some cleaning up. Perhaps you should reconsider your habit of working on them at two in the morning."

"I'll hop on that right away." Again, she found herself staring downcast. Despite his words, the meeting had the mood of a scolding. Perhaps the others' praise had kept it to an off-the-record warning, or maybe Eze felt he should've told her to stand down before they went in.

"That look in your eye." Dorian tilted his head closer to her face. "I see it. You're not planning to give up. If you push, the fallout is going to land on more than just you. He'll come down on all of Division 0. He'll make life as miserable as possible for as many of us as possible until you back off."

"That's such bullshit!" Kirsten whirled to face Dorian. "So a senator can do whatever the heck he wants and get away with it? What's to stop him from killing random people next? Or... or..."

"Turning the tide of public opinion against psionics," said Dorian. "You've read how it is in the United Kingdom. Mandatory government registration and implanted cerebral detonators."

"... what about Division 9?" She looked around as if some answer might be sitting on one of the shelves. "And that detonator thing stopped like a few years ago."

"Detonator thing?" asked Captain Eze.

Kirsten rubbed her brow. "Dorian mentioned the UK."

"Oh. Yes. That policy was suspended. Something about an attempt on the life of one of their Parliament people five years ago."

"I don't know. Can't Division 9 take this over then? Are *they* afraid of the senator too?"

Captain Eze's eyebrows drooped. "They'll need more evidence than you have to open an investigation on a senator. I know it's infuriating, and I'm frustrated right there with you, but... how many people are you willing to hurt to make a point."

She cringed.

Captain Eze held up a hand. "I wasn't referring to the raid. There are a shade under four thousand people affiliated in one capacity or another with Division 0, and every one of them could potentially suffer the consequences of an angry senator."

Kirsten fumed. "That's so... *wrong.*"

"That's politics." Dorian grumbled. "Those who write the rules, by definition, can't cheat."

"It's not 'making a point.' He *killed* a man." Kirsten glared at him for an instant before directing her fury at the wall. "Uhh, sir."

"Kirsten, they want me to order you to back off on the senator."

She deflated.

"I won't... yet." Captain Eze held up one finger. "But... I'm asking you not to cause trouble until and unless you find enough tangible, non-paranormal evidence to survive an Inquest at the highest levels. Officially, Senator Preston Winchester is no longer considered to have any involvement with the murder of Mr. Prentice. As far as Command is concerned, you are not investigating him."

She stared at her boots. "Yes, sir."

"Please, Kirsten." Dorian put a hand on her shoulder. "One ghost isn't worth losing Evan. It isn't worth who knows how much damage he'll do to us all."

Bastard. Her hands shook from anger, her stomach churned. *He can't win... that's just not right.*

"I won't tell you not to collect evidence in secret, but if the senator complains, they will ask why you disobeyed a direct order... that I haven't given yet. If you're sloppy, you'll take us both down."

"I understand, sir." She lifted her head and made eye contact. Guilt worked better than any order could have. "It's disheartening to hear Command takes his word over ours, but I won't do anything to get you in trouble. You've always been there for me."

"Oh, I'm sure Command believes you. But when you're armed with a table knife and the other guy's holding an E-90, the man with the E-90's right."

Kirsten nodded.

"Well, if you've got nothing else..."

"No, sir."

Captain Eze gave her an apologetic look. "Dismissed."

"Sir." She saluted him and walked out.

Once out of eyesight of the captain, her walk became a trudge until she fell into the chair at her desk. Her simultaneous desire to kick something, burst into tears, scream her throat hoarse, and kill someone crashed together and left her staring mute into space with a non-expression.

Nicole swiveled around in her chair to Kirsten's left. "That went well."

Kirsten stared at her hands, limp in her lap. "Yeah. Got slapped on the knuckles."

"That wasn't your fault. I thought you did great out there."

"Not about the raid. I'm not allowed to go after the senator." Kirsten glanced at her. "Not unless I—"

"Wanna come over tonight and marathon *Galaxy Chronicles*?"

"—have enough evidence to—"

"We haven't stayed up all night watching that since we were fifteen." Nicole beamed.

"—convince all the brass he's guilty. I've got a—"

"Better idea. Weekend!" Nicole giggled. "We can sit around all day in our underwear and drink."

"—son to look after. *Galaxy Chronicles* will bore him to death." Kirsten sighed.

"But it's got spaceships and aliens!" Nicole flailed.

Kirsten laughed. "It's about romance triangles and who's scheming against who in the Terran Council. In two hundred and fourteen episodes—"

"I need coffee. Mocha or strawberry? Wanna Jalapeño Omwich?"

"—they get into *two* space battles. And we are not lazing around in our undies with Evan in the apartment." Kirsten massaged the bridge of her nose. "Sure. Mocha."

Nicole whirled to face her desk and grabbed her NetMini.

The rest of the day promised only the 'tantalizing exhilaration' of editing old reports. Busy work. Kirsten leaned back in her chair and covered her face. Had that been Eze's call or was this a 'sit down and behave yourself' from higher up? Charles Prentice would probably wait a little longer before getting restless. Waiting would give the Division 1 case time to percolate against the two remaining men who did the actual killing. *I hope it's enough.* "It's gonna have to be."

"Hmm?" asked Nicole.

"Nothing, just whining to myself." Kirsten swatted at her terminal to open the Inquest database. Eighteen of her old case records had amber gems glowing from the left side of the dim green row, flagged by Captain Eze for additional attention. "Ugh. I hate reports."

43

BEYOND DEAD

K irsten leaned against the doorjamb of Evan's bedroom, arms folded, watching him sleep. After hours of tedium spent reading and filling in small details of old reports, the Monwyn game had proved to be wonderful stress relief. They'd finally taken down the ogre boss, and she'd come out ten thousand and change damage points ahead of Evan on the end-of-battle report. She'd braced for him to freak, but wasn't prepared for the awestruck look he'd given her.

"My mom's a Monwyn badass" would echo in her brain for years, and bring a smile every time.

Grinning, she crept in to kiss him on the forehead. He looked angelic, and she couldn't help but hover for another few minutes. *Back off the senator or he'll get taken away.* She closed her eyes and let off a silent sigh before walking out. *I can play along, Captain. Winchester won't see it coming until I can nail him to the wall.* She walked to her bedroom and glanced at the nightstand. Though it had no bottle of SynVod in it, the day she'd had made her want some in a bad way. She gnawed on her finger while pacing. *Am I an alcoholic already?* The first two years on the job had been rough. Some of those spirits were not meant for the eyes of a sixteen-year-old. Somehow, she'd wound up reaching for a bottle... the same way Mother had when she couldn't cope with her Devil-sent daughter.

Kirsten pondered ordering a small one, not enough to get drunk but enough to maybe find sleep without staring at the ceiling for hours. *Evan...* The look he'd given her when he saw the bottle... She flopped on the Comforgel pad, back against the wall, NetMini in hand. For some time, she stared at the blank, black screen and the weak reflection it cast of her face. She smoothed her oversized pink nightshirt over her thighs, frowning at her lack of hips. The designers had created the Monwyn character Princess Asara as an exaggerated depiction of a super-thin female, a high-elf... but aside from Kirsten actually *having* breasts, their shapes weren't too different.

The warmth of blush in her cheeks, she swiped down her contacts list and called Sam.

His holographic bust appeared a few rings later, in a blue tee shirt with dual white stripes along the arms. A Division 2 tech logo adorned the area where breast pocket would've been. "Hey."

"Hey yourself." She bit her lip.

"It's nice to see you." He smiled. "You look beautiful, if not a little sad."

"Rough case. I wanted something too much and rushed in. We got shot up pretty good, but no one died." She rubbed her neck to massage a lump out of her throat. "I thought Nila got killed, but..."

"Sorry." His gaze flicked from eye contact to his lap and back. "Want me to come over?"

She looked down. *I dunno. Evan's here; we both have to be in early.* "If you had like a two percent chance of finding concrete evidence of something, but attempting to get it and failing would cause a lot of people to get hurt, including people you care about, would it be wrong to let a murderer get away with it?"

Sam's eyebrows crawled together. "Well, that whole 'needs of the many' thing. How many people died? How many could be hurt? If the murderer gets away with it, will he kill again?"

Guilt refused to go away. "One dead. I don't think they'd kill again since it wasn't a random act, but we swore to uphold the law. Besides, it's *wrong*. If we give in to powerful people only because they're powerful, they win."

Sam clasped his hands together in the posture of a Shaolin monk. "A wise warrior strikes at the moment of greatest success." He dropped his arms out of frame. "I'd say never stop looking, but don't do anything stupid. Everyone's bound to mess up sooner or later, no matter who they are. When they do, you'll be there."

Kirsten traced a finger back and forth over the empty queen-sized Comforgel pad at her side. Whenever she looked at Sam, the urge to hold him reared its head. Also, revulsion at the memory of what Konstantin did to her. Maybe she didn't need SynVod to cope with her day after all. "So what does Samuel Chang do when he's not at the RTC?"

He grinned. "Well, I've got a couple of large model starships. The CSS Saratoga's about six feet long. It's meditative to work with such delicate pieces. Sometimes I fiddle around with a little hydroponic garden. It's not much, but I've managed not to kill any plants yet."

She laughed. "I've been playing *Forests of Wrath* with Evan lately. I think I'm getting the hang of Asara. He's been suggesting you join us."

Sam nodded, smiling. "That would be great."

Kirsten flexed and relaxed her toes a few times. "Sam?"

"Hmm?" He tilted his head.

"If I, uhh…" She twirled a strand of hair around her finger. "Theoretically speaking, if I said maybe I didn't really want to be alone right now, would you umm, maybe wanna stop by for a little while? I mean, I know we've both gotta get up at six."

"It's only quarter to nine." He leaned closer to the holo-cam, making his head enlarge. "I don't mind. Even for an hour or two. I'd love to be able to spend time with you."

She crossed her feet, toes curled. "Uhh. Okay." *Geez, what am I thirteen?*

"See you soon." He winked and hung up.

Kirsten let go of the NetMini, which slid over her hip into the gap between her thighs. *I am not inviting him over for sex.* She closed her eyes. *I need not to feel alone.* She leaned her head back, picturing Evan. He was way too young to burden with her insecurities. As much as he tried to offer her comfort, hugging him always felt like the protection went from mother to child. When he towered over her in about six or seven years… maybe not.

"Mommy!" screamed Evan. "Mom!"

Raw terror in his voice launched her upright. She leapt off the bed, the NetMini bouncing off the top of her right foot on its way to the rug, and sprinted down the hall to his bedroom door, arriving as he wailed "Mommy" again, distorted by crying. The boy cowered in the corner of the room, shaking and bawling. Tears glimmered from the glow of astral seeing in his eyes.

A tall man with a shaved head and an orange hospital tunic loomed over the foot of the bed. Paranormal energy radiated from him, flooding the area with a sense of anger and malice. The clingy smock bore the word 'corrections' along the back with an inmate number, P044CD83, below it in block letters.

"You worthless little shit." The man growled.

Wailing, Evan raised his arms to guard his face. Snot bubbled out of his nose.

Kirsten called the lash; the blinding-bright tendril unfurled and coiled around her feet. "Get away from my son."

The man came about in a slow turn and glared at her. Dark brown stubble covered his scalp as well as his cheeks, where a glittering snot train ran from nostril to chin. It took a second for her to recognize him without a disaster of a moustache and beard, but the way he glared at her brought the memory back.

Mick.

"Bitch. You're the one who fucking killed me." He took a step toward her, pointing. "Left me in that goddamn bed, unable to fuckin' move or think straight. You got any idea what a septic infection feels like? I'm gonna love sharing it with you for the next, oh, sixty years."

Kirsten glared at him. "Don't even go there. You tried to kill me. You've got four seconds to cross over, or I'm going to kill you again." Her hands shook with rage. *The bruises... he's been beating Evan in his dreams.* "I will not allow you to hurt him again."

Mick laughed. "I'm already dead, you blonde whore. I ain't goin nowhere 'til I drive the both of you fuckin' batshit nuts. I'm gonna watch them lock you up in a nice little padded—"

She let off an incoherent scream of rage and lunged forward, bringing the Astral Lash around in a wide overhead swing. Never had Kirsten felt such anger before; the look Evan gave her before he showed his bruises, the fear she'd felt at possibly being blamed for them and losing him, the steady whimpering from the corner right at that moment... all of it set loose a surge of emotion that flared the energy stream more white than blue.

Mick crossed his arms defensively and tried to jump backward, but her downstroke ripped him in half from shoulder to groin. A sense of striking a weak gelatinous mass stalled her hand for an instant before she growled and yanked the whip out of the spirit.

The ghost flickered between solid and transparent, crying out with a keening, inhuman wail that lasted all of a second before his form dissipated with a muted *whump*. A cloud of luminous fog hung in midair for a few seconds before blasting outward with a ripple of paranormal energy, leaving behind a lingering odor of beer and belch. Lights in the hall outside flickered, as did the digital window showing a fantasy landscape.

Evan screamed.

Despite feeling the obliteration of a soul, Kirsten slashed three more times at the fading cloud before trusting that she'd destroyed him. The energy tendril coiled low to the floor around her feet, lofting distorted shadows of furniture on the walls. She glared at the spot of carpet where the apparition had been, arms shaking, breathing hard, her entire body trembling from rage. A few minutes later, her anger faded, and she relaxed her power.

The room darkened with the absence of the whip.

Evan bolted from the corner and plowed into her, not quite standing, sobbing against her stomach. She wrapped her arms around him, letting him cry. *I barely felt him... He couldn't have been dead long.* Kirsten pulled Evan to the bed and up into her lap.

"I'm sorry," whispered Evan between snivels.

"There's nothing at all for you to be sorry about, Ev." She squeezed him. "Nothing."

He sniffled. "For acting like a baby."

She palmed his head and pulled him against her shoulder, rocking him. "If my mother's ghost came here right now, I'd probably wet my pants."

"Nuh-uh." He looked up at her. "You're not scared of ghosts."

"It's not the ghost I'd be afraid of. Seeing her again would bring back all the memories. It would make me feel like a little, powerless child all over again."

Evan wiped at his face and leaned against her. "You're just sayin' that to make me feel better. If your bad mom walked in here you'd be like"—he snapped his arm as if using a whip while making a *whoo-pssh* sound effect —"Back, foul minion!"

Kirsten grinned. "Okay, maybe I would get angry instead of scared… but I'm grown up now. You're nine."

"It felt funny when you hit him. What was that?" He tucked his knees up to his chin and put his feet on her leg.

"I call it obliteration. The longer a ghost is around as a ghost, the tougher they become. When I hit them with the lash, it hurts them like… I guess like lasers hurt people. If I hit them too much, it destroys the ghost."

"Like abyss? He's dead again?"

"No… Ev. He's way beyond that. There's nothing at all left of him." She exhaled, guilt settling on her shoulders. Who was she to make that judgement call? Final obliteration for a soul… had that left a stain on hers?

"He oblirated instantly. You only hit him once." Evan sniffed and wiped his nose.

Kirsten stroked his hair. "He threatened my son. I was angry. I guess you could say I cast Meteor Rain at a giant rat."

Evan hugged her tight. "They showed us this vid… 'motion makes psi stuff work better. When Cadet Peña used empathy on me, it made me stronger. You didn't need a empath."

"Nope." She grinned.

His lip quivered; tears gathered in the corner of his eyes. "That means you really love me."

"Yes."

"You're not gonna make me go away if I do somethin' bad on accident?"

She choked up, shaking her head. "No. Never."

He smiled. "You pasted Mick in one hit."

The doorbell rang.

Oh, Sam…

Evan gave her a quizzical look.

"I asked Sam to come over."

He ground his left hand into his cheek, wiping at his eyes. "'Kay."

She picked him up and carried him to the door. Sam's huge smile dimmed to a concerned look at the sight of them.

"Is he okay?" He fidgeted. "What happened?"

He might be too embarrassed to let you see him like this. Kirsten cringed. "It's a long story."

"Hi, Sam." Evan still hadn't stopped trembling, but he waved.

"It's all right." He glanced down at an overnight bag. "Another time then."

Kirsten stared at her feet.

Evan looked up at Kirsten. "Can I sleep with you guys tonight?"

She gripped the rug with her toes, staring at Sam. *He's... wow; he must trust you.* "Don't go... Please, come in."

Elation spread over Sam's face. He dropped his bag inside the door and walked up to them. Kirsten shied away from eye contact and looked at his chest. When she leaned into him, he embraced her. Evan reached out and got his arm around Sam's neck. Kirsten closed her eyes; Evan's breath at her neck and Sam's heartbeat in her ear.

You can kiss him if you want. Evan's voice drifted into her mind.

She laughed and looked up at Sam.

After a lingering stare, their lips met. Her pulse quickened. With Sam, she didn't at all feel like the helpless girl running to the powerful man for protection. His presence reassured without diminishing, an equal at her side to face the world.

When Evan squirmed, she pulled back and smiled up at Sam. He followed her to the living room couch and sat at her left with an arm across her shoulders. Evan curled up on the other side, using her lap for a pillow. It seemed he'd taken it to heart that the source of his nightmares had been destroyed in every sense of the concept, and fell asleep within seconds of them settling in.

Kirsten tugged a blanket off the armrest and draped it over him, before resting her head against Sam's chest. "I have no idea how to do this."

"How to do what?" Sam's fingers squeezed her right shoulder.

"Be with a boyfriend, do the whole relationship thing." She chuckled. "I spent so long trying to find a man who wouldn't run away screaming when he found out I was psionic... I never actually made it past the first date before. Now that you're here, I don't know what to do. I haven't had much experience."

Sam grinned. "You may find this difficult to believe, but I haven't either."

"Naw..." She poked him in the side.

"Alas." He feigned a sigh. "You're the first woman I've ever felt at ease around enough to talk to. I thought it was my luck that you were involved already."

She scowled at the ceiling. "I don't remember most of it anymore. I know he took me to these places. One embarrassed the hell out of me, but I can't recall why. All the dinners and functions, everything's just become this nauseating blur and mostly faded away. It must've been the influence. The one piece I *do* remember I wish I could forget." She shuddered. "That and his old-ass face smiling at me before he knocked me out."

Sam winced. "I'd give anything to take that all back like it didn't happen."

Evan's mouth popped open in his sleep.

She grinned at him before looking up at Sam's face. "Oh, there's other things in my past I'd rather you use that wish on. But, there's no point in lingering. I'm glad I met you, Samuel Chang."

He brushed his hand over her hair. "I am the luckiest man in the world."

"Let's see if you still feel that way after a few months of weird things happening." She tapped him on the nose.

"Oh, I think I can handle it. Your pal Theodore's been by a few times. He seemed rather keen on warning me not to hurt you."

Kirsten gasped. "You saw him?"

"Yeah. He hung out the other night for almost an hour. I got the feeling he liked me at least."

Wow. An hour of manifesting? How old is Theo? Could he really be 400-plus like he claims? "He's a… strange guy."

Sam kept teasing his fingers at her hair. "How'd you run into him?"

She blushed. "He stuck his head up through the toilet when I was on it and yelled hello. He amuses himself by doing embarrassing things to women, and making men shit their pants."

"He likes scarin' kids too," muttered Evan, sounding half-awake. "Makes him mad 'cause I'm not scared of him. I know he's only playing, an' won't hurt me."

Kirsten giggled. "Do you remember about four years ago when the City Arts and Recreation Commissioner was giving that speech in Sanctuary Park, and her pants flew off and got 'carried away on an unusually strong breeze?'"

Sam laughed. "Yeah… The NewsNet played that over and over for months. That video's cropped up in ads for belts too."

"Well, Theodore objected to her plans to relocate the park to make room for more commercial space in that district." Kirsten glanced down at Evan. "I've never said this to a man before, but do you wanna go to bed?"

"Sure."

She smirked at him. *I want to share the bed with you. Forget that sleeping bag. Is it okay if we just be together tonight? Ev is freaked out.*

Sam kissed her again. "That sounds great."

44

WALK AWAY

For once, Kirsten wasn't upset at Nicole's habit of casual surface thought reading. It prevented a prolonged argument about her sharing a bed with Sam and nothing happening but cuddling. Nicole didn't believe her at first, even when she mentioned Evan had a bad fright and wanted to sleep in the same bed. Though Nicole did spot the six minutes of heavy kissing and roaming hands the next morning when Evan had hopped in the shower.

Kirsten leaned on her desk, flicking a finger at the empty coffee cup next to her. Her brain shifted gears between wondering if she should cave in and take her feelings for Sam in a more physical direction, dreading finishing updating the reports, and worrying about the situation with Charles Prentice and the whole Winchester mess. She batted around the thought of asking Nila to watch Evan someday soon so she could see what happened with Sam, or if that would lessen what they felt for each other.

I'm not a princess waiting for the knight. Dammit, I've wanted someone in my life so long, I am not gonna screw this up. She smiled, decision made. Dread came next. *Ugh. I should really tell him about what I did when I was twelve.* She bit her lip, considering Father Villera's words. *No. What that man did.* A scowl formed on her face. *Sam deserves to know, but I don't want him thinking I'm looking for sympathy. I need to tell him, but not yet...*

Grumbling, she unlocked her terminal and got to adding more details wherever Captain Eze had put little stars in the report on the poltergeist at the Green residence. *Ugh. That guy was such an asshole.* The look on his daughter Alexis's face when he thought the girl was psionic and didn't want her made her fume.

Morelli had pulled a case tracking down a telepathic thief who had enough talent to erase himself from the memory of those he victimized. Nicole ran off only three minutes after breakfast arrived, a tactical mobilization in response to some gang warfare involving psionic fringers.

Kirsten sat alone in the squad room for over an hour, pecking away at old reports until angst about Senator Winchester got the better of her. She decided to see Director Carter. The woman might've been the head of all Division 0, but she supposedly had an open door policy, not to mention being one of the stronger telempaths on record.

She locked her terminal and got up. Fourteen minutes of corridors and elevators later, Kirsten approached a security checkpoint on the fifth floor. What the Police Administrative Center lacked in height, it made up for in width. A man and a woman in psi armor flanked a set of double doors leading to the Command offices.

"Good afternoon, Lieutenant," said the man.

"Morning, Sergeant. I'd like to see Director Carter. Is she available?"

"One moment." A short conversation with someone on the other end of a comm didn't leave his helmet. Once his lips ceased moving, he nodded to her and swiped his forearm unit past a sensor to open the door.

"Thanks." She smiled at him and the woman on the other side of the door before going in.

Director Carter's office sat at the end of a long hallway that curved to the right, close to another set of double doors at the end, which led to an auditorium. She announced herself with two soft knocks.

"Come in, Lieutenant," said a confident sounding voice, tinged with a hint of grandmother.

Kirsten entered when the door opened with a soft *squeak*. A pair of four-foot tall spiral silver 'leaf' sculptures flanked a wide floor-to-ceiling window looking out over a small octagon-shaped park in the central hollow of the PAC building. At the center of the room close to the window, the director occupied a huge desk of glossy onyx.

She quick-walked up to the desk, and saluted. "Ma'am."

Director Carter had her pewter hair up in a bun, and aside from her rank pins and lack of utility belt, wore the same uniform as Kirsten. Clingy black fabric with a high neck covered everything but her face and hands. It did have the added embellishment of two gold stripes on the outside of each sleeve, a 'dress' uniform not meant for field duty that identified her as part of the command staff.

"At ease, Lieutenant." Carter returned her salute and gestured at one of three chairs facing her desk. "You're quite troubled. How can I help?"

Kirsten blushed at Carter's subtle reaction to her sudden upwelling of gratitude and loyalty. Having the top commander of Division 0 pick up the emotional sense of regarding her as the mother/grandmother she'd always wanted was only slightly less mortifying than Nicole's suggestion of walking from the medical wing to the squad room stark naked to convince pranksters to leave her alone.

Carter cleared her throat, failing to suppress a smile.

"Ma'am. I wanted to talk to you about a case I'm working on. I've been ordered to stand down on one aspect of the investigation, but it amounts to letting a murderer get away with it."

"This is about Senator Winchester, isn't it?" Carter's eyes narrowed, though the focus of her ire didn't seem to be Kirsten.

"Yes, Ma'am. He… via proxy hired a ripper doc to procure replacement lungs for his twenty-year-old daughter, whom he refuses to publicly acknowledge as his. I have no idea why he won't. Because of that, she tried to kill herself with Icewhisper. The ghost of the man who the harvester's thugs killed had been attacking anyone who'd received organs taken from him. That spirit came close to killing two of them: Robert Lamb and Julia Dominguez. I finally tracked him down, and his attachment to this world is wanting his murderers prosecuted."

"So this spirit cannot rest until Winchester faces some form of justice for precipitating his death." Director Carter's jaw crept forward in thought. "That's a delicate process. I'm sure you're aware he's already tabled an audit of our policies and procedures."

"Yes, Ma'am. All I have right now is a ghost telling me he did it, a girl with replaced lungs who will probably come up as a compatible match for transplant with the murder victim who lives in his manor house and is supposedly his illegitimate daughter. She won't cooperate with an investigation against her father. The ripper doc, Mardrake, didn't even know the job came from the senator. Everything happened via proxies. I can't prove it. And, I've been ordered not to even try to go after him. Is it wrong to let him go? The senator has all but told me he requested my attention to destroy that ghost, like I'm some hired assassin cleaning up a loose end. I don't feel right doing that… unless the spirit becomes a danger to the living."

Director Carter leaned back, finger curled around her chin. "I agree that, given the limited tangible evidence you've discovered, any legal action against the senator will blow up in our collective faces. We have a fair amount of influence over things, including the military, but interfering with senators gets everyone's panties in a knot."

Kirsten would've laughed if not for the dead-serious look in the Director's eye. "Yes, Ma'am."

"It's the sort of thing everyone's so afraid of. Psionics manipulating government. In matters of psionic individuals, I have authority. I could tell even C-Branch to go diddle themselves if they wanted to 'recruit' one of ours. There isn't much I can do to stop a vengeful senator from conducting a witch hunt." Director Carter sighed. "While regrettable, one man's death doesn't outweigh the good Division 0 does for the population at large."

"We can't get Division 9 involved, can we?"

"I'm afraid not. We'd need irrefutable evidence before we could hand it off to them."

Kirsten stared at her lap. "Ma'am… what should I do? Every choice feels wrong. Can we really just let him kill a man like that?"

"You feel genuine guilt about destroying that ghost." Small wrinkles formed at the corner of Carter's eyes as she smiled.

"I do. I know it sounds lame, but I've seen some spirits go to silver doors while the Harbingers drag others away screaming. I've also seen… other beings. Destroying that spirit is wrong. His anger is justified, and as long as he stops harming the innocent who had no idea they received stolen body parts, I have no moral grounds to destroy him. I have to do something for this spirit, but I'm afraid of what the senator might do if I don't give him what he wants. He threatened my son, Ma'am."

"What?" Carter raised an eyebrow. "Did you get that on record?"

She sighed. "No. He demanded I shut everything off. He didn't threaten to harm him physically; he inferred my duties obligate me away from being able to properly care for a boy, and he said it would be a shame if someone decided he should be put in a better home."

Carter offered a sympathetic look at the maelstrom of anguish, guilt, and sorrow churning in Kirsten at the thought of losing him. "Well, he certainly knows the best way to hurt you. Wren, you've got three choices. Which can you live with the most? You can destroy the ghost so he cannot harm any of those people. You could spend the next few years searching for evidence and hoping no one catches you doing it; maybe the person who proxied the deal between the doctor and the senator could be persuaded to testify. Or, you could accept this is beyond your grasp and wait for the universe to sort things out. Assuming your Harbingers are out there, it sounds like they would have a keen interest in the senator. Aren't they supposed to be the judges of souls?"

"Yeah." Her heart sank. "He's a murderer, Ma'am."

"He's also a senator with strong connections. I doubt he will act on his threat toward Evan if you keep your distance. I can feel your concern for everyone here as well, Lieutenant." Carter offered a reassuring smile. "It pains you greatly that this man could retaliate against Division 0 for us trying to uphold the law. I think you should trust the universe to work things out. We engage in many battles throughout our lives. Some are difficult, some easy, and some situations present no way to win no matter what we do. Sometimes, the only reasonable option we have is to walk away."

Kirsten sat straight, trying to ignore guilt, fear, and worry. "Thank you, Ma'am."

"If it helps your conscience, you are responsible for dealing with crimes and events of a psionic and paranormal nature. While you have had contact with a spirit resulting from a crime, the function of said crime did not involve psionics. Unless your spirit harms the living, your responsibility here is done. What does or does not happen with the senator is on the shoulders of the brass outside of Division 0. This isn't even your battle, Kirsten."

"I understand, Ma'am, but I still feel…"

"Disillusioned." Carter leaned forward, arms folded on her desk. "Our government isn't perfect. Far from it. As long as there is government and people in power, there will be those who abuse that power. It's happened since the days of organized politics, crowns and swords and it will continue to happen until the fundamental psyche of humanity changes. Our system has its flaws, but there's no denying we've got it better than those poor bastards in the ACC."

"Dorian called me a dreaming idealist."

Carter chuckled. "They thought that of me too when I was your age. Don't give up on that outlook, Kirsten. But you'll need to accept that few people share it, and often us idealists are the ones who wind up disappointed. You probably had it in your head that this whole machine of the National Police Force was some kind of white knight championing the cause of the little guy. Most of us are just trying to do what we can to make things a little better for as many people as we can. You'll drive yourself into the ground trying to do everything for everyone all the time. Focus on that little boy of yours." Her eyes sparkled as she smiled. "To him, you're the world."

Kirsten took a deep breath and smiled. "Thank you, Ma'am."

"You're quite welcome, Lieutenant."

She stood, traded salutes with Carter, and walked back across the halls of the Police Administrative Center in no great hurry.

How am I going to face Laney with this?

45

CAN'T LET GO

Her mood alternated between numb and like a kid who'd been beaten at a video game she loved for months by someone who'd never played it before. Kirsten trudged down an immaculate corridor of blinding white. By the time she reached the elevator, she'd swayed most of the way to being angry.

Sometimes, the only reasonable option we have is to walk away.

Carter's words repeated on a loop in her memory. Kirsten scowled at the elevator doors as they closed. *Okay, Senator. You win at your game. Let's see how well you play mine.* She stormed out on the ground floor, heading for the garage. A boy and a girl of about eleven in Admin cadet uniforms pushed a hovering cart with two cube-shaped network storage drives, three holo-terminal bars, and a box of datapads. Both kids halted their discussion of nested neural-memory arrays and saluted as she passed.

Kirsten smiled while returning it, went grim-faced to salute a pair of Lieutenant Commanders from Tactical, and exchanged neutral greetings with six other enlisted adults before she made it to the garage entry.

Dorian appeared within seconds of her closing the patrol craft door. "Hope you've got a good reason for waking me up."

"Hah." She powered the car on. "Sam gave me an idea."

She powered up the car and drove to the exit gate.

"Well, he seems like a smart guy." He looked around. "Where are you planning to get shot at today?"

Kirsten waved at Samir in the booth by the ramp, and switched to hover mode as soon as the fourteen-year-old cadet opened the gate. "Random acts of street punks aside, this should be quiet."

"I'll believe that when it happens." He winked.

She reached forward and tapped a nav pin in for Sanctuary Park. "I need to have my idealism stepped on a little more before I believe I can't do the right thing here."

The patrol craft climbed up to the level of the fiftieth story and levelled off.

He laughed. When the fit of mirth subsided, his expression became serious. "Be careful."

"Yeah." She stared ahead at a canyon of silver, black, and blue-tinted plastisteel buildings agleam in the late afternoon sun. An advert bot came up alongside, bearing holo-panels advertising high-end coffee, so-so sushi, and Monwyn products. "Damn. They're getting better at this."

Dorian glanced out his window, curling two fingers over his cheek. "I won't think less of you if you order coffee. That rune-rabbit plush though…"

"What? It's cute." She grumbled.

"Mm hmm. The thing's the size of a small car. I can just picture you hugging it. You'd look *adorable*. Heh. You'd probably sleep wrapped around it."

She scowled at him, but wound up laughing. "Yeah… I guess I would look like a big kid."

Dorian opened his mouth, but closed it on a smile without words.

Kirsten eyed the delivery bot, already tasting coffee.

CUPS AND SCRAPS OF PLASFILM POSTERS DANCED OUT FROM UNDER THE PATROL craft as she landed at the edge of Sanctuary Park, five square miles, one whole sector, covered in humanity's best approximation of nature. Trees, grass, hiking paths, some 'rocks' to climb, and two lakes. She pushed the gull wing door open and got out, earning some worried looks from a pack of teens in garish clothing, some see-through, some blinding neon. They started stuffing things in pockets and preparing to run, but the worry in their eyes became confusion when she walked past them into the park.

She followed a trail deeper into the woodlands, past a rounded clearing with a statue of Loretta B. Deacon, the senator who'd established the park seventy-some-odd years ago. Evidence of last night's frivolities—empty synthbeer cans, a few sets of underwear, and crumpled up snack chip bags— littered the area. Kirsten wandered out of the circle, heading northeast.

"This place is almost peaceful during the day," said Dorian. "I hear there's a couple of Yoga classes and one guy teaching meditation as well."

"I dunno. I think I get enough exercise right now." She smiled at the bench she usually parked on with Nila while watching Shani make Evan fly around. "This is a good spot."

Dorian raised an eyebrow. "For what? Planning to fling off your uniform and go catgirl?"

Kirsten laughed. "Uhh, no."

She sat on the bench, closed her eyes, and concentrated on an astral beacon, calling Theodore. Within a few minutes, coolness spread around her body, centered on her breasts. She looked down at Theodore's arms encircling her from behind. He squeezed each breast twice quick, as if testing oranges.

"Nice and firm. Bit small for my liking, but perfectly shaped."

"Hi, Theodore," said Kirsten, deadpan.

He walked around the bench with an exaggerated frown on his white-painted face. Black star pattern makeup over his eyes smeared his cheeks; wherever he'd been when he died, it had been raining hard. Despite hanging in loose curly strands, his long mop of hair ignored the breeze. Puddles gathered at his boots, and without the appearance of blood, his baggy pants turned dark blue-green.

"You've been around a long time, right?"

Theodore winked. "You can say that." He sat next to her, left arm draped along the backrest. "What's goin' on?"

Kirsten took a deep breath. "I'm stuck, Theo. Not sure what to do."

"She's recently discovered the government isn't all unicorns and rainbows." Dorian scratched at his eyebrow and squinted at an odd yelp in the distance.

"Guy with a dog," said Theodore. "Almost stepped in it. Ahh, yeah. Government. It was a right mess when I was sucking on air too. It is what it is, yanno? You're a cog in their machine. 'Course, you're far enough deep in your little niche dealin' with the likes of us not to see it."

"It feels futile. How can I trust in anything when the supposed law won't stand up to someone in power?" Kirsten recounted the story of a man killed for parts, a spirit seeking justice, and innocent victims caught between it all. "My entire command structure is afraid of him. He's responsible for a murder and they don't even care. It's too hard to prove anything, so they don't even want to try." She fumed, glaring out over the grassy field at a lone tree, and an older man walking a giant chocolate-brown mastiff.

"Division 0 is as much a public relations engine as a law enforcement organization, K." Dorian let off an exasperated sigh. "Psionics are something like eight to ten percent of the population. We're still at the point where a bad shift in fear and paranoia could hurt a lot of innocent people."

Theodore's wheezy chuckle sent a chill down her spine. His hair danced with a resigned shake of the head. "You're a rare breed, Kirsten. Sometimes, the people with all the money and the power win. Your friend Ritchie... the cop what offed him never faced charges. That fucker killed another ten or so people before he retired. Mostly the Seattle drug crowd, but he opted for the cheap divorce twice, too."

She scowled.

"Don't get too mad. Your little black puffballs got him." Theodore winked.

Kirsten cocked an eyebrow at him. "Did you just refer to Harbingers as 'puffballs?'"

"Yeah. Cuddly li'l things, ain't they?" He grinned. "Or do you prefer 'shadow fluffies?'"

She almost smiled. "So you think I should let it go?"

"That's what you came here for right?" asked Dorian. "To get told the same thing a third time by someone else. I don't understand women."

"It's not being a woman." She glared at him. "It's seeing something *wrong* and not being able to do a fucking thing about it. I..." Kirsten deflated with a sigh, leaning on her knees.

"Hey." Theodore patted her on the back twice before squeezing her ass. "You're too cute for language like that."

"Die."

"Too late, honey." Theodore pulled his shiny black trenchcoat off his chest and let it fall back in place. "Already did. A long ass time ago."

Absurdity of what she said made her chuckle despite wanting to choke Senator Winchester with her bare hands. "You think you'll ever get tired of it? Want to go on?"

Theodore sat up straight and made whistling, smoochy noises at the mastiff, over a hundred yards away. As soon as it looked at him, his head went transparent and glowy, and he yelled "Boo."

Howling, the animal bolted off into the trees, dragging the old man by the leash like a ground-skimming kite.

Theodore laughed himself to tears. "Nah. This never gets boring."

"Theo! You could've killed him." She tensed to stand and go after him, but relaxed when the old man walked back out of the woods, dusting his muddy pant legs off and cursing his idiot of a dog. "That's not funny; that was mean."

"You are adorable." Theodore patted her on the head.

She settled into the bench, grumbling. "I guess I came looking, hoping you or The Kind could maybe sniff out enough evidence for me to give to Eze."

Theodore shrugged. "I suppose I could try, but people don't do a lot of talkin' to me these days. More like runnin', screamin', and loadin' up their pants." He grinned.

She chuckled. "Haven't seen you in a while."

He winked. "Bah. That's 'cause you don't flip out anymore. When'd you start liking having an audience in the shower?"

Her back muscles tensed. "Liking an audience and becoming desensitized aren't the same thing." She grumbled. "Damn."

"Best thing you can do, kid." Theodore reached for her left breast, but changed his mind when she made no move to avoid his hand. "Let the puffballs deal with him. You want some help talkin' to yer errant ghost, gimme a shout."

"Harbingers." She smirked. "Sometimes I wish they'd take an interest in the living."

"Hah." Theodore grinned.

Kirsten sat up and blinked. "I just got an idea." She channeled a minute amount of power and grabbed Theodore's hand. "Will you help?"

"If yer takin' this where I think yer takin' this..." Vodka fumes leaked between his teeth as his lips curled into a dark grin. "I'm in."

―――――

KIRSTEN TAPPED THE SILVER PANEL TO THE RIGHT OF LANEY PRENTICE'S DOOR. Dorian paced behind her, muttering. A few seconds later, the nondescript grey slab slid to the side, revealing the slim figure of Charles's sister in a clingy emerald green shirt and loose, black shorts. Seven of her toenails were pink, three green, and a Nanochroma wand dangled from her fingers. Kirsten's gaze went to a pair of black cat ears on a headband, with dim cobalt blue light emanating from within.

"Uhh, those are cute."

Laney grinned and bounced in place. "I know! I can hear Charlie with them. I'm thinking about getting cybernetic ones put in. Not sure if I'd go for cat ears or just normal augmented hearing, which doesn't look different on the outside."

"How long is she expecting Chuckie to stay around?" asked Dorian.

"His name is not 'Chuckie.'" Laney smirked. "Where else would he go?"

Dorian winced. "Heh. Guess her electronics work."

"Can I come in?" Kirsten offered a placating smile. "Is Charles here?"

"Yeah." Laney backed up, let her pass, and shut the door. "He's getting a little impatient. I'm glad you stopped by."

"Wren..." Charles phased out of the living room wall near the holo-bar, which displayed a pause-frame image of a middle-aged man in a greenhouse. He'd managed to rearrange his appearance to something close to how he'd been in life. "I was starting to wonder if you were going to come back."

Kirsten met him by the coffee table. "Sorry. This case is *so* frustrating. I have some good news and some not so good."

Charles folded his arms. Laney sat on the edge of the sofa, leaning forward, gaze off in a random direction as though she focused every ounce of her attention on hearing. She tapped the Nanochroma to one of her pink toenails, turning it green.

"We got the three men who killed you as well as the ripper doc who processed your organs and ran the harvesting operation. The little guy with red hair didn't survive his arrest. Citycams caught the entire thing. We've got video of your murder. It's all but guaranteed those two will be convicted." Kirsten studied the tips of her boots. "The senator… I can't touch him. It's like having a gun to my head. Command won't support an investigation because he's got enough influence to possibly disband Division 0. He's already threatened to have my son taken away from me if he thinks I'm even trying to go after him."

Charles glared. "You can't let him kill me and laugh it off."

Laney looked worried and a touch angry as well. "Charlie, maybe it's not so bad? She got the men who actually killed you. You're still here for me. What if she's telling the truth? The man's a senator. What's one cop gonna do?"

"Especially without any real evidence," said Dorian. "The kind of foundation you need to take on someone that high up can't be built on the backs of ghosts. The legal system won't admit psionic evidence, and ghosts, they'd laugh straight out of a courtroom."

"So you're saying your kid's more important than making him pay for a murder?" Charles leaned toward her. "You said taken away, not hurt."

Kirsten hardened her glare. "I'm sorry, Charles, but yes. My son *is* the most important thing in my life. If I thought I had a reasonable chance of nailing that bastard, I would, but all I'm going to do by going after him is cause a lot of people to drown in a river of shit." She stormed two steps to the left, growling. "I don't like it either. Is there any way you can find peace with two of your actual killers facing charges, plus one dead as well as the organ-harvesting doctor? Will that let you move on?"

"No," whined Laney. "I don't want to be alone."

Charles sighed. "She's been like a different person with me here all the time. Even spoke to the woman in the adjacent apartment yesterday. I can't be happy with you walking away, Wren. That girl, Seraphina, is tilting suicidal again. I don't want you to give up. If she kills herself, my ass died for absolutely no reason whatsoever. You think I'm angry now, watch me if she dies."

Kirsten put her hands on her hips and shifted to face him. "I know… I know… I can't kill the senator."

"I'm stuck here until he answers for what he did." Charles scowled.

"He eventually will answer for it when the Harbingers come for him."

Dorian glanced at Kirsten. "That's assuming he's got their attention. No offense, Charles, but one murder in this city might not stand out."

"He's a damn senator," spat Charles. "They should already be after him."

Dorian stifled a laugh. "I like this guy."

"You want me to wait around until he dies and hope they get him? I don't know if I can contain myself that long. This… anger is pulling me to take what's mine back from those who stole it. I don't know if I can wait."

"That's your anger or attachment, Charles." Kirsten concentrated for a second to align her body with the astral world, and put her hand on his shoulder. "If you can focus on letting go of it, you could transcend."

"No," whispered Laney. "Please don't leave me alone."

"I can't." Charles stomped over to the window and grumbled. "I know it's not their fault, but I am *not* a box of spare parts for some senator to help himself to." He whirled around, pointing at her. "I'll try. *Maybe* I can get over the want to pop Winchester's head like a zit, but you can't let me die for nothing. Do something about that girl and I'll see how I feel."

Kirsten gazed at the ceiling and took a few meditative breaths. She tucked her trembling hands under her armpits to warm numb fingers and hugged herself. "I've got a backup plan. I was hoping I could find some compromise with what I've been able to do so far, so you could be at peace. It's a giant risk, Charles."

"What are you going to do?" He drifted back toward her.

Dorian shook his head. "I don't see this working. He's not the kind of man to be reasonable."

"Oh, this isn't reasonable." Kirsten narrowed her eyes. "The problem is that as a Division 0 I-Ops officer, I'm stuck operating within a set of rules that the senator, and people like him, make. I'm going to switch things up and play a different game, one Winchester doesn't have the instruction manual for." She looked at Charles. "If I do this, you might wind up owing a favor to some… people."

"People?" asked Charles.

"Ghosts." Kirsten fidgeted. "Old ones."

Dorian smiled. "Maybe you'll get lucky and Winchester will drop dead of a heart attack."

"Oh, hell." Kirsten shivered. "No. That wouldn't be lucky. That would come back to bite me square on the ass."

"Will it make him go away?" asked Laney.

"No, but it might involve some occasional extra house guests." Kirsten chuckled. *Okay, Winchester. No recording when you threatened Evan. No way to record my response either. Ghosts don't exist at Inquests, asshole.* "I'm not going in there expecting the senator to roll over and confess to murder, but I'm not going to let him have a total win."

Charles moved to stand near Laney. "Do what you have to."

"Okay, perhaps you aren't as idealistic as I thought." Dorian winked.

Kirsten marched out into the hall. "It's not the senator I'm worrying about. It's his daughter."

Dorian leaned his head next to hers when she stopped to wait for the elevator. "There you are." He smiled. "Promise me you won't change."

46

BREAKING POINT

Sick with anxiety, Kirsten clenched the control sticks as the patrol craft breached a pocket of turbulence. Flying at 1490 feet afforded the opportunity to avoid both advert bots as well as buildings. Except for a twenty-mile swath around the starport where she had to stay under a thousand, she cruised high and straight at 510 MPH to Senator Winchester's manor house.

Speed wasn't so much an urgency as getting there faster would reduce the chances of her chickening out and changing her mind. She didn't know what she'd do if the situation deteriorated and the threat of losing Evan became more than theoretical. *He's going to want to meet off the record. Can I get away with Suggestion?* Her stomach protested with a loud warble. *Captain Eze would be horrified. Suggestion will wear off in minutes and he'll know I did it. Division 9 might see me as a threat. I'd never know it was coming.* She sighed. *No, I can't go that far... I'm not that person. I'm... going to do whatever I have to do to protect my son.*

"I'm not sure I want to know what's rattling around in your head to result in a face like that."

She glanced at Dorian. "I don't understand how some people can play chess and see the whole game unfold in their head after like four moves. I'm trying to think of an endgame and I can't pick which pawn to move yet."

"That was more a 'can I get away with killing him if he goes after Evan' face."

Kirsten nudged the patrol craft into a descent and slowed. Snow-scattered forest filled the windscreen as the car tilted forward. Whirring came from numerous airbrakes flaring out to slow the vehicle. Thin corkscrew contrails spiraled off the corners of two large flaps on the hood. "Sometimes I don't like how well you can read me."

"Well, Since he is aware that you know about his involvement, he is going to want to keep your meeting secret. If he threatens Evan, you could mind blast him into a guava and make up any story you wanted. Say he threatened to dismantle Division 0 because you won't destroy Charles." Dorian shot her a grim stare. "Burckhardt would back you."

"I hope you're not seriously suggesting that." She levelled off and sank the last hundred or so feet straight down to land.

"Why do you think everyone's so afraid of us?"

She gawked. "It happened already?"

"Not that anyone's proved. It *could* happen. Some people think it has. Burkhardt's cut from the same cloth. He'd do whatever it took to keep Division 0 intact. She looks like your kindly grandmother, but even Director Carter is a 'needs of the many' pragmatist."

Kirsten's lips thinned with anger. "I guess I'll have to make sure he doesn't think that threatening Evan or Division 0 can help him."

Dorian grinned.

She climbed out of the patrol craft and approached the door. Marguerite opened it the instant boot touched porch.

"*Bon après-midi, lieutenant.*" Marguerite offered a slight bow. "Senator Winchester has asked for a few minutes before he can meet with you. He is wrapping up a policy meeting."

Her cheeks grew cold; she all but felt the blood drain from her face.

"Do not fret, *mademoiselle*." Marguerite smiled. "They talk of taxes on Earth-Mars shipping."

"I'd like to see Seraphina." Kirsten walked in.

"She is not well." Marguerite shut the door and clasped her hands in front of her. "But, she has asked for you... so."

Kirsten followed the synthetic woman upstairs to the third floor, and the quiet bedroom where the willowy figure of Seraphina Winchester squirmed and wriggled against the same soft restraints she'd been strapped down in last time. "Theresa? Has she been tied down for days?"

"Agent Wren!" Seraphina sobbed. "Please help me! I wanna file kidnapping charges against this awful woman."

Theresa, eyes downcast, muttered something.

"Following orders my ass." Seraphina stopped crying long enough to scowl at her live-in medtech. "Would you do it if he told you to rape me?"

"No, Miss." Theresa flinched.

Kirsten ran over and took Seraphina's hand. "Are you still going to hurt yourself?"

"No." Seraphina looked away.

The young woman's surface thoughts debated trying to get Kirsten's E-90 and offing herself with it as soon as her hand was free.

Kirsten shook her head. "Stop trying to lie to a telepath. I'm not going to let you kill yourself over what that man thinks of you."

Seraphina thrashed. "I can't take this anymore. I've been tied down a week! He doesn't even treat me like a *person* anymore. I'm a possession."

"As soon as you decide not to harm yourself, I will insist they release you." Kirsten sat on the edge of the Comforgel pad. "The ghost of the man whose lungs you have said he's worried about you. If you die, he was murdered for nothing."

Seraphina scowled at the wall. "I didn't ask to be saved. I don't want his lungs. He can come back and take them." She looked around before attempting to thrust her chest upward in defiance of the padded strap around her armpits. "You hear me? Come take them back. Rip them right out if you can." Grunts and squeaks came out of her as she pulled at her legs and twisted. "Argh! Kill me already!"

"Seraphina, please calm down." Kirsten squeezed her hand. "You don't need his approval to have value. My mother wanted to kill me and my father didn't have the balls to stop her. He kept running away. I took things into my own hands when I was ten. I missed my dad, but I didn't need him to survive."

"If you don't care, why do you look ready to cry?" Seraphina stopped struggling and stared at her.

"He ran from ghosts, not me. They were as normal to me as living people are to you, and I couldn't understand how they scared him for a long time. I was fifteen or so when he died, and I'd never seen him again since the night I ran away from home. Your father isn't afraid of ghosts. I don't know what his excuse is."

"Why does he hate me?" Seraphina convulsed with wracking sobs. The straps holding her by the wrists went tight as she tried to bury her face in her hands. Sorrowful bawling morphed into enraged shrieking, and she flung all of her slight weight back and forth in protest of being tied down.

"What's going on here?" bellowed the senator from the door. A band of metallic sheen ran down his black suit as he leaned in. "Seraphina! Calm yourself."

Kirsten glimpsed into the woman's thoughts; blind panic at being immobilized had overcome all reason. She put a hand her cheek, pulling the girl's head to make eye contact. "*Calm.*"

Theresa gasped at the flicker of light in Kirsten's eyes.

Seraphina went still.

Kirsten pointed at Theresa. "Undo the straps. Now. They're making it worse."

Seraphina sniveled as the medtech unlocked her right wrist. "Daddy…"

Kirsten held her by the cheeks. "I want you to give me a half hour. Can you do that? I'm trusting you not to hurt yourself for at least that long. You'll be free in a minute. Okay?"

"Okay." Seraphina wiped at her face and nose as though she'd been itching for hours.

A surface thought skim let Kirsten breathe. For a little while at least, elation at being set loose made the girl happy enough to forget wanting to die. Winchester stomped over. "Lieutenant? I trust you have some good news for me?"

"Senator…we need to talk." Kirsten slid off the bed and faced him, doing a masterful job of hiding her fear. Staring a challenge at a senator would've been difficult at eye level, much less his being a full head taller.

He gave her a look as though preparing for an argument with a tween daughter. "Very well. Downstairs. My study."

Theresa opened the padded cuffs around Seraphina's ankles and came around the bed to her left arm.

Kirsten moved out of the way. "Please make sure she stays in this room." She put a hand on the medtech's shoulder to get her attention. *Neither one of you is going to want to be downstairs.*

Theresa's cheeks faded a few shades at the telepathic voice in her brain. "I understand."

Facing off against demons had been frightening, but at least in that battle she had the safety blanket of believing Division 0 had her back. Here in Senator Winchester's manor, she dangled out on a thread, far past any legal authority or backup. What she planned on doing didn't even exist in any policy documentation. She had no doubt Division 0 brass would let her hang herself rather than see the entire organization go down. *This is the right thing to do.* Hands clenched into fists, Kirsten composed herself with military bearing, and followed Marguerite down the stairs.

KIND WORDS

Marguerite glided along without a sound. Kirsten stared at the paper-white skin between the woman's shoulder blades, half an inch above the lacy frill where her dress clung at the armpits. To distract herself from worry, she tried to deduce if the synthetic chose to dress in such fancy things or Winchester demanded it. Perhaps the man had a thing for delicate women who looked like someone lifted them out of a thousand years ago. For that matter, would the senator's wife (who never set foot on Earth) consider it cheating if anything happened between them?

By law it would be adultery. Sentient AIs were granted the same rights and privileges as the living.

She glanced at Dorian, knowing what he'd say. He found dolls creepy as hell, inhuman, and if he dreamed, he probably had nightmares about them. Synthetics fell into the same group, perhaps even worse since no one could tell them apart from humans without telepathy, or a portable medical scanner.

"This way, *Mademoiselle*." Marguerite flashed a genuine smile with a trace of a giggle, as though she led a childhood friend into a place they'd been told not to go.

Kirsten kept her hand close to the E-90 as Marguerite stopped by a bookshelf where one section had opened like a door. Raven hair framed an innocent face that could've been carved from snow; her dark blue eyes sparkled with mischief, but she had no surface thoughts to see. Innocent in appearance, but Kirsten couldn't know for sure.

The synthetic woman stood to the side, hands clasped at her waist, seeming to have no intention to enter the room beyond. "Can I bring you anything, Lieutenant?"

"Thank you, Marguerite, but I don't think I'll be here long enough to impose. Hopefully, Senator Winchester will find my information agreeable."

"Very well." The woman curtsied.

Kirsten stepped into the narrow end of a rectangular room with blue carpet. Dark wood wainscoting covered half the walls, the rest a bright Washington blue. The senator stood behind a brick-shaped onyx desk, austere in comparison to the surroundings. Books, busts of former senators in white on Roman columns, and animated electronic paintings decorated the perimeter.

"Come in, Lieutenant." Senator Winchester gestured at a pair of dark grey wingback chairs facing his desk.

"Your housekeeper had the strangest smile. I'm not walking into an ambush, am I?"

His surface thoughts found it amusing, but alleviated her fears. The senator's attention leapt to a prickle of pain spreading over his hand, and he gave her an intense stare. "Lieutenant, please explain what you just did."

Kirsten walked up to stand between the chairs, her knee almost touching a tiny wooden table bearing tea service. "Forgive me, Senator. I was just prodding you with a quick question to make sure I wasn't walking into a dangerous situation. Would you like an explanation of surface thought skimming? No, I do not plan to continue... extenuating circumstances, concern for my life."

He held a deep breath for a second before releasing it. "I've got an implant capable of alerting me to psionics affecting my mind. Since you didn't experience any pain, I'll assume you are being truthful in that your 'peek' was limited to shallow foremind thoughts. Need I advise you that the use of invasive telepathy or suggestion on a sitting member—"

"No, sir." She smiled. "I'm well aware that touching your brain is a criminal offense, but then again, so is contract murder. I have no plans of that nature. I merely wanted to make sure you didn't have a pair of large men with big guns waiting behind that bookshelf."

A saccharin smile spread across Winchester's face.

She gave Dorian the side-eye.

"Off?"

Kirsten smiled at her ghostly partner.

"Well, what is it you have to tell me then?" Senator Winchester sat and leaned back in creaking leather.

Dorian walked through the desk and put his hand into the senator's ear.

Winchester's left eye twitched, and he rubbed the eyebrow.

"Are you all right, Senator?"

"Mild headache. You've been causing a little stress lately, as well as my daughter."

Kirsten nodded. "I understand. I'd like to make a deal with you."

"What manner of deal?" He raised an eyebrow. "I wasn't aware you had anything to negotiate with. Here I thought you were coming to apologize and humbly ask me to call off the audit. We do have to make sure our taxpayers' credits are being used properly."

Dorian made faces as if reaching around inside the man's head looking for something. He winked and smiled once his hand stopped moving. "Found it. Internal power cell has a lot of juice. I can't kill it, but I can turn it off as long as I'm touching it."

"Of course, Senator. We appreciate your concern that our books are in order. It is true that my attempt to investigate the murder of Charles Prentice has encountered some difficulty in establishing a concrete link back to you. However, I did have a little help from one of your colleagues in the Senate. Alas, I'm not at liberty to say who." The name 'Susan Forsyth' leapt to the tip of his brain, followed by a fleeting daydream of his unfulfilled desire to punch a fiftyish woman with thick brown hair after she threatened to expose a shady connection between him and Intera Corporation. "Sh—the person seemed rather interested in learning about this little situation."

Senator Winchester glared; redness spread across his face. "You think I don't know you've made contact with Forsyth?"

Dorian chuckled.

Kirsten thought about her mother whipping open the closet door to help her appear genuinely frightened. "Uhh. How could you possibly know that?"

A trace of victory glimmered in his eyes. "You don't get to where I am without being able to find things out." He pounded his fist on his desk and pointed at her. "Whatever you think you're going to accomplish working with her, think again. Forsyth is only looking to use you. As soon as you give her what she wants, she's not going to help you survive the fallout."

"Nice, umm, 'accidental' slip there." Dorian winked.

"You don't give her enough credit," said Kirsten. "She's pointed us at a few individuals who might've been your proxy dealing with Mardrake. Division 9's got their ears perked."

The senator's lips peeled into a rictus grin. *That bitch doesn't know Flynn. She probably thinks I used Ludwig or Bale.* "You don't think I'm concerned about Division 9 do you? Is that supposed to unsettle me? What's your endgame, Lieutenant? I understand you're blonde, but you don't actually expect me to publically admit to having anything whatsoever to do with some dead home electronics technician, do you?"

"Well, I suppose since you're so well connected, you'll find out anyway. Carter's got some friends in C-Branch, and they sent me a nice little dossier on a couple of people who've done some work for you. Ever hear of a guy named Ludwig? What about Bale?" She held her arm up and opened a holo-panel. While she read over her notes concerning Lamb's liver diagnosis, she tapped the intangible screen (and tried to ignore Dorian's laughter). "C-Branch poked Ludwig with a sharp stick and he mentioned another name we haven't quite been able to put a face to yet. They're after someone named 'Flynn' now. If he talks to Div 9, game over."

Senator Winchester's eyes seemed about to explode out of his head. He pointed at her again; his surface thoughts leapt between the start of tirades threatening to do everything from get her thrown out of Division 0 to charged with treason and executed, but he felt certain Niall Flynn would never admit to anything. The man was a consummate professional.

Kirsten frowned at her holo-panel, and turned it off. "There can't be too many guys named Niall in the UCF. I will give you credit, Senator. I never saw the reason you went to such obtuse lengths to hide that Seraphina is your daughter coming."

The face of a woman formed in his mind, early forties, light brown hair, delicate... she could've been Marguerite's mother. His dread fear of an affair with a sitting CEO—Jeanette Favreaux—one third of the power in ACC-controlled France going public plunged his brain into chaos and pulled all the color from his cheeks.

"I warned you..."

"Yes. Yes you did." Kirsten nodded. "You threatened my son. I've been going over and over what you said about understanding your reasons for doing what you did, about how laws don't mean anything when you're protecting your child."

He glared, still-pointing finger shaking.

"Are you trying to give him a stroke, Kirsten?" Dorian indicated a thick vein pulsing in the man's forehead with the hand not embedded in the man's skull.

"I've decided to bend the rules a little bit today, Senator, because I'm protecting my child. You, on the other hand... there's a problem. You're not protecting your child. You're protecting your own ass. She looks a lot like Marguerite. Favreaux?"

Dorian cringed. "Ooh. Direct hit. His brain just got warmer."

Senator Winchester rubbed his forehead, grimacing as if from a pounding migraine. "You really think you'll be able to do anything with that information before it's too late? I tried to be pleasant with you, Lieutenant... but you kept pushing. Six months from now, I guarantee you all psionics will be off world or hiding in the Beneath. Division 0 will be a memory. And that boy of yours—"

"About that..." Kirsten glared. "I realized something else, Senator."

Winchester folded his arms. "Oh, what's that?"

"I've been trying to play your game." She raised her hands as if in surrender. "You win. I don't have enough evidence to survive an Inquest. Even with the new information I've discovered, I don't think Division 9 is going to be confident enough to act over, as you said, one lowly home-electronics tech." Kirsten tapped her finger on her chin. "Though, that mess with Intera might get their attention but that's way out of my scope. I want you to know that my mistake was playing your game. You make all the rules in that game. Laws. Judges. Police. Society. All of it is under your thumb. I can't beat you, and I don't intend to try."

His right eye twitched as a grin bared his teeth. "So, you just came here to get my blood pressure up? I said that blonde thing as a jab, but I never expected you to prove it correct."

Kirsten held her arms to the sides. "I'm not playing your game anymore, Senator. There's something you need to know."

Theodore walked in through the wall. He looked normal to her, except for an aura of wispy energy around him.

"What the—?" Senator Winchester blinked. "Who the fuck is that?"

"Senator," said Theodore, offering a hand. "Name's Theodore. I hear you're quite the asshole. Nice ta meet'cha."

Winchester didn't reach up, staring with an open mouth.

An old man with silver hair and a bodybuilder's physique hidden under an expensive ancient suit walked in and stood on Kirsten's right.

"This man used to be Governor of California." Kirsten smiled at the older man. "A long time ago. Centuries in fact."

A dark-skinned woman in military fatigues arrived next, also surrounded by the strange energy. The assault rifle in her hands predated caseless ammunition.

"Private First Class Anita Shaw. Killed in action on May 19th, 2017, Iraq."

"Am I late?" asked a thin, balding man in a turtleneck. He cocked an eyebrow at Winchester and glanced at Kirsten. "Is this the fucking dickless asshole threatening your kid?"

"Meet Steve," said Kirsten. "He's been a ghost since 2011."

"Ghosts..." Winchester's eyes snapped left and right as four more of The Kind faded near the outer wall.

A cloud of strange herbal fragrance surrounded a long-bearded man in jeans and a cowboy hat who looked every bit as ancient as he probably was. "Politicians never change." He took a long pull on a hand-rolled cigarette.

"What is that?" asked Winchester.

"Marijuana, jackass. Figures you bastards don't legalize it until after I kick off."

"Hi, Willie," said Kirsten.

Senator Winchester broke out in a cold sweat, eyes bulging. "Ghosts? What's the meaning of this?"

"You need some new lines," said the Governor. "Even mine were better than that."

"Senator." Kirsten walked around the desk and loomed at him as much as a short girl can loom. "I'm not playing your game anymore. If you do *anything* to hurt my son, no lawyer, no judge, no soldier, no politician is going to be able to protect you."

Theodore seized the Senator by his lapels and lifted him out of his chair on tiptoe. "This yer first time seein' a ghost?"

Winchester punched and flailed; his hands disrupted Theodore's body to vapor for an instant wherever they passed.

"I'm only solid when I want ta be. An' if that's breakin' yer skull open"— Theodore leaned nose to nose, and snarled—"So be it." He flung the senator against the shelf behind the desk, knocking several small statuettes and plaques over. "Fuck wit that boy, you're gonna answer to The Kind."

"I'm the only astral sensitive within two thousand miles," said Kirsten. "And the only one on record capable of harming a ghost… but you know that already, don't you, Senator. Tell me what you think the odds are that I'll get here in time to stop them, and you know traffic can be such a pain in the ass sometimes."

Winchester fixed his shirt and adjusted his suit jacket smooth with a sharp tug. "You're daring to threaten me? A sitting senator?"

Kirsten smiled. "I didn't threaten you. A four-century-old ghost did. Make that a couple dozen ancient ghosts. I suppose you could pen some legislation to declare ghosts dangerous and illegal."

Willie and the old veteran laughed.

"This is what's happened to politics?" asked the Governor. He waved dismissively at Winchester and scowled. "Bah. It's a good thing I'm already dead."

"You broke the law to save a daughter you supposedly care about, but you won't even admit to having." Kirsten rounded the desk and poked him in the chest with her finger. "She's going to kill herself because she thinks you don't want her. You say you love her, but you don't. You give her cheap organs and you're going to sit here and watch her take her own life because you love your political career more than your child." Kirsten looked away and down. "I don't have enough to send a damn thing to Division 9. The evidence I *do* have would raise some eyebrows, but that's about it. You're right. I can't make legal trouble for you, but there's worse waiting for you on the other side."

She locked eyes with him. Her mind filled with the memory of a swarm of Harbingers engulfing the soul collector ghost from the Saguaro Asylum. The man in the tattered doctor's coat screamed and reached out from the roiling mass of vaporous black bodies, a tornado of infinite darkness that dragged him down through the old, dusty floorboards.

Telepathy shared the images.

Winchester wheezed, clutching his hand with the psi warning device as he slid down the shelf to sit on the floor. "W-what did you do to me. You… did something, I know it."

"I let you see one of my memories. I don't know how much you believe about what happens after death, but those entities are Harbingers. They gather the souls of men like you, Senator. I don't want to know what happens after that." Kirsten looked down. "I can't make legal trouble for you. Honestly, I can't do anything at all to you. But it's not me you should be worrying about."

"What do you want?" He shivered.

"That it for this then?" Steve checked his watch. "I've got a thing."

Kirsten smiled at The Kind. "Thank you all so much. I'll always be there if you need me."

One by one, the ancient spirits waved, and walked off into the walls.

Dorian attempted to grab the Senator's arm. He glared with severe focus, clamped his hand shut, and succeeded only in making the man shiver again.

"I want your daughter not to kill herself. If she does, Charles is going to come after you. It might take him ten years to build up the strength to do anything, and again, you'd have to hope I got there in time." Kirsten offered him a hand. "Accept her publicly. She won't care if you keep the identity of her mother a secret."

"Better to set up a fake," said Dorian. "Less temptation to find the mystery woman and discover the truth."

"Good point."

"What?" asked Winchester. "I didn't say anything."

"I was talking to a ghost. You're worried they'll find Favreaux. Hire someone to be the mother. Hell, have your wife claim her. You've obviously got a thing for waifish French women… maybe your wife would enjoy a trip to Reinventions to make her look a little more like Seraphina."

Dorian laughed.

Winchester let her help him up. "That's it? All this was to get me to claim Seraphina?"

"Well, yes. That and leave my son alone… and back off on Division 0. Also, you'll have her own tissue regenerated like you should've done in the first place. Once Charles's lungs are out, they'll be cremated and returned to his ashes. You'll contact Robert Lamb and arrange for his liver regeneration as well, the same with Julia Dominguez and her heart, and a man named Sanjay your daughter knows. In return, I forget everything I never found about your involvement and we can both keep smiling for the cameras."

Winchester flopped in his chair, hand over his mouth in thought.

"He's either going to accept, or pull a gun out of that drawer and shoot you before taking his own life," said Dorian.

She tensed her legs, ready to pounce.

"And those..." He waved his hand around at the empty room. "Things won't bother me? You'll stop them?"

"They came here to protect Evan. All it takes for you never to see them again is not to fuck with my child." She narrowed her eyes. "Understand?"

"What about that... Harbinger nonsense."

Kirsten raised her hands and shook her head. "Way above my pay grade. I have no idea how dark your soul is or how bad they want it. That's all on you. How interested they are in someone depends on that person and that person only. I can ask them to come and look, but I can't make them pounce on anyone who doesn't deserve it."

Winchester looked up at her. The silver creeping over the hair by his ears seemed to have spread farther up. "Any more demands? Nothing for you?" He cocked an eyebrow with a sarcastic sneer.

"No thanks, Senator. I'm good. Take care of your daughter."

He grumbled and let his hand fall away from his chin to his desk. "Fine. Give Marguerite the information to contact those people."

"Sir?" Marguerite leaned in.

"Please tell Seraphina to clean up and make herself presentable for travel. I will be taking her to Amaranth Medical. Also, schedule an appointment for my wife at Reinventions of Paramount City."

"Shouldn't you ask her first?" Kirsten blinked.

Winchester chuckled. "She's been trying to talk me into it for months already. She wants to be thirty again... might as well."

Dorian grumbled.

"Also, prepare a press release. Come up with something about my daughter having spent her childhood in protective seclusion to keep her away from the news hounds."

Kirsten fought the urge to grin, allowing herself a contented smile. "Thank you, Senator. I think you should go tell Seraphina yourself. On a deep, internal level, not seeing you charged for Charles's murder bothers me, but I know there's nothing I can do about it. If you take care of what I've asked as you say you will, I'll keep everything quiet."

"I should hope so." Winchester smirked. "This entire meeting wouldn't look good for you if it got out either."

Kirsten smiled. "Probably not, but who'd believe there's so many ghosts in West City? Judges and Inquests are funny like that. Say the word 'ghost' once, and everyone starts looking at you like you're insane. Oh, you also might want to avoid mentioning Harbingers on the NewsNet. Somehow, I doubt that will go over well."

He gave her a flat look.

"Good afternoon, Senator. Thanks for making the time to meet with me." She saluted him, and exited without waiting for any reaction.

MEMORIAM

Kirsten walked at Laney Prentice's side, passing a long, curved wall of burgundy marble squares. Each twelve-inch tile bore a grave number and name as well as birth and death dates. Many had holographic candles flickering in front of them. Gloss black floor came alive with shimmering blobs of light reflected from the LEDs in the ceiling; to the right, a grid of window squares formed the outer wall of the ring-shaped mausoleum complex. The vaulted atrium carried the hushed voices of mourners visiting loved ones.

Laney carried the rectangular urn, to which they'd added the ashes from Charles's lungs, heart, liver, kidneys, and eyeballs.

Charles's spirit followed at a distance, looking around at random whispers, reacting to the voices needling at Kirsten's eardrums. Perhaps a third of the cubbies held spirits annoyed at the constant visitation of other people. Kirsten caught herself smiling at Dorian's remark that it reminded him of a nursing facility for the elderly—some spirits complaining that no one visits them, but everyone else has family coming all the time.

"I can't believe he paid for everything... how did you do that?" Laney looked at the ash container. "Are you sure it's better to put his ashes here? I'd rather keep him home."

"She's going to mistake me for fertilizer," muttered Charles.

The electric cat ears on Laney's headband swiveled to face rear. "I heard that."

Kirsten smiled at the floor. "That's up to you."

Approaching sharp *clicks* triggered Kirsten's ingrained hatred of high heels. She glanced back at the sound. Seven other mourners in the section all watched an athletic woman with a black bob in a formal black gown that sparkled silver when the light hit it; the effect reminded her of Harbinger's eyes. The approaching woman seemed at once dainty and powerful, and her violet lipstick and downcast eyes conveyed her mood.

Kirsten blinked when recognition finally hit her. She patted Laney on the shoulder. "Excuse me a moment." She took three steps toward the windowed wall, waving as the woman got closer. "Nina?"

Nina stopped. "Oh. Agent Wren. Hello. Sorry… Lieutenant."

Kirsten saluted her. "Lieutenant. I'm sorry about Vincent."

"Thank you." Nina nodded. "I know he's gone on, but I still come here at least once a month."

"I'm sure he knows." She clasped her hands and looked out the window. "Sorry for interrupting."

"What brings you here? I hope you didn't lose anyone."

"No. Part of a case. Helping a spirit say their final farewell before they transcend." Kirsten bit her lip thinking of the woman's doll body. "If, uhh, anything strange happens to you, it's the crossover."

Nina's smile seemed more sad than anything. "Noted. Take care of yourself, Lieutenant."

"You too, Lieutenant." Kirsten returned to Laney's side.

She fidgeted with the urn. "Who's *that?*"

"Another cop. Different department, but we've worked together once."

Laney clutched the urn to her chest, and cried. "I-is he gonna go away now?"

Charles put an arm around both women's shoulders. "I'm not sure. You know, I think maybe I'm going to hang around for a while."

"Really?" Laney's eyes widened. "Can I take you home? I swear I won't put you in a flowerpot."

He offered a resigned shrug. "If it makes you feel better. Meh. Might let me sleep easier. So much chatter here."

"So I hear." Kirsten glanced at the grave cubbies. "Guess I'll drive you home then."

"Thank you." Charles offered a hand. "Not a perfect result, but… I guess I'll take it. Having all of me in one place did weaken that overwhelming pull of anger. Hey, one question."

"Hmm?" She stopped walking and looked up at him.

"That 'transcending' thing. If I hang around to keep an eye on Laney, am I going to be stuck here when her time comes?"

Kirsten raised her arms and let them flap at her sides. "It's different for every spirit. Some think they've got only one chance to enter that door, and they're stuck here forever if they miss it. Some say they can go whenever they feel like it; they only need to want to. If you *do* stay though... that whole Harbinger issue remains. You might be clean enough to transcend now, but if you do soul-staining things even as a ghost, that doorway might not open again when you want it to." An idea raised her eyebrow. "Maybe you're still here now because you want to protect her."

"I get it." He smiled.

"Thank you!" Laney leapt into a brisk hug, jabbing the corner of the rectangular urn into her breast.

"Ngh." Kirsten pushed her out to arm's length, moved the urn aside, and pulled her close again. "Better. And, you're welcome."

On the walk around the mausoleum ring back to the parking area, Kirsten gazed up through the windows where the outer wall curved inward, forming a portion of the ceiling. Billowy clouds glided across the blue.

What am I going to put in the report for this one?

THE HUNTRESS AND THE KNIGHT

K irsten balanced on tiptoe atop a stone pillar only six inches in diameter. While standing on one foot, she loosed arrow after arrow at a monster resembling a four-clawed crab the size of a small building. After seven shots, her pedestal cracked for no apparent reason. She leapt to the next one, emitting a high-pitched elven war cry at the height of her rolling jump. One foot landed with perfect precision on the next sturdy pedestal, and she kept firing, aiming for one of eight stalks tipped with black eyeballs as big as human heads. Below her, a rippling pool of bright green acid waited. She couldn't shoot from solid ground on the left half of the room; if the crab saw the arrows coming, it would invariably 'close' the eye, causing the shot to bounce away from hardened carapace.

Sir Halek, aka Sam, in glowing fiery armor, stood at the edge of where catacomb floor met the acid pool. He absorbed the brunt of the massive creature's claws with a round shield studded with saw teeth. Each time the beast hit him, he slid away twenty or thirty yards, but blurred back into place between the creature and Monwyn (Evan) before the next claw could smash the wizard.

Evan shouted the words of spells from the more elaborate sim at the Funzone, despite speaking them having no effect on the home system. Hearing the voice of a nine-year-old come out of the adult-looking mage left her grinning.

Monwyn raised his hands and threw a retina-searing lightning bolt into the crab's roaring mouth. The *crack-a-boom* of the magic slammed into Kirsten's eardrums, hurting in reality as well as the game.

The monstrous crustacean leaned back, raising its claws. Gaps in its underbelly shell stretched open a few inches as it began to channel a regeneration effect.

"Mom!—uhh Asara!" Monwyn hurried another spell and made a grabbing gesture at her.

An invisible 'hand' closed around her, making her feel like a tiny child's toy. Force flung her off the pedestal in a clean trajectory for the stone floor behind Halek. Kirsten rolled over, flying sideways while aiming. She touched the rune on her bow for 'speed shot,' and her arms blurred. In the three seconds it took for her to fly from the pedestal to the safety of solid cavern floor, thirty-seven arrows flew.

Only two missed the narrow gap in the shell plate.

The progress bar floating over the crab for its self-heal stuttered back every time she inflicted damage. A constant stream of '1357' scrolled over its head. Sir Halek leapt into the air, a ghostly image of him separating from the more solid metal-armored knight to ram a broadsword to the hilt in its shell.

Evan conjured up a rolling sphere of flames, and hurled it into the crab's face as the two copies of Sir Halek coalesced once more into a single entity. The fireball hit the crab in the mouth, sending a crisscross of burning lava lines across the carapace. It roared, waving its claws, and proceeded to do a belabored, two-minute long death animation as it gradually sank into the bubbling green liquid. The entire cavern shook, knocking huge rocks from the ceiling that thudded to the beach and splashed in the lake.

Scrolls appeared floating in front of them, offering a choice of loot rewards. Evan made faces at his as though he'd gotten stumped at his homework. Sam jumped up and down cheering. It took him less than a second to reach into the scroll and grab a new sword, made of a solid chunk of blue gemstone infused with lightning.

Kirsten looked back and forth between gauntlets with a small agility boost, a bow about the same as what she had now (slower rate of fire, but more damage per hit), and a necklace that almost doubled her mana reserve. "Hey, Ev? What do you think? Huntsmaster's bow or the Charm of La'astra?"

He held up a hand. The animation included Monwyn raising the 'do not disturb a wizard in the midst of critical decisions' eyebrow. After some minutes, he grabbed a ring from his scroll and put it on. "Sorry, Mom. What?"

She repeated her question.

"Uhh. The bow. Asara's best special shot is slow, and it scales with the weapon's top damage. The Huntsmaster does an extra sixty-six damage per arrow. With the multiplier on 'Slay,' it winds up being a lot more."

"What about the charm? It almost doubles my mana. I could use the middle-range specials more often."

"We can run this boss again and farm the necklace. That bow's got a lame drop rate... like one in two thousand."

"Sounds like the Sapphire Hand." Sam raised his blade with an adoring stare. "Been after this guy for nine months."

"Okay. Bow it is." Kirsten grasped the weapon, which became a solid object in her hand while the scroll faded away. She thought about 'inventory,' and her old bow disappeared in a cloud of pixels."

The sound of the real world doorbell made all three of them jump.

"Save, Logout," said Evan.

Monwyn vanished.

Sir Halek walked over to Asara the Huntress. "My princess, thine bow has surely turned the tide in service of the kingdom. It was an honor to fight at your side."

Kirsten couldn't speak without giggling, so she merely extended her hand to be kissed.

Sam obliged.

"Mom!" yelled Evan from reality. "Nila's here."

Kirsten winked at Sam. "Save, logout."

The lava cave faded to darkness infused with the soft 'lobby music' of the game. Kirsten took the Senshelmet off and blinked a few times to adjust to seeing the real world again. Sights and motion blurred for a few seconds while her brain acclimated to getting its input from biological sources instead of the helmet beaming electrical signals straight into her skull.

Nila, in all her relaxed sweat pants glory, padded barefoot into the living room with Shani in tow.

"Hey." Kirsten detangled her crossed legs from her over-long tee shirt, stood, and ran over to hug her and Shani in turn.

Sam pulled his helmet off and packed the game console away in the cabinet.

"All set?" asked Nila, winking at Evan.

Ugh. I'm so nervous. Kirsten put a hand on Evan's shoulder. "Are you sure this is okay?"

Evan rolled his eyes. "Yeah, Mom. I like hanging out with Shani." *And you and Sam wanna get all mushy and eww.*

Kirsten laughed. Sam walked up behind her, and she smiled over her shoulder at him.

"Relax." Nila bit her finger and made sultry eyes at Sam. "Who'd have thought one of the D2 network wonks was so cute."

Sam's eyes bugged. His mouth opened, but no words came.

"It's like right out of one of those stories. As soon as I saw him the first time, he broke through that thing controlling me."

"Eww," said Evan. He grabbed a small bag and marched toward the door. "I'll be downstairs."

"That's why it hurt so much." Kirsten put a hand on her stomach. "What, no hug?"

Evan dropped the bag and ran over to jump into an embrace.

She closed her eyes, squeezing him while swaying side to side. "I love you so much, kiddo. Have fun tonight."

"I will." Evan leaned up to whisper, "I love you too, Mom" before running out.

Kirsten waved at Nila and Shani. When the door closed with a squeak, she turned around and put her arms around Sam. "I meant that. You really did break through. 'Course, at the time, I didn't know which way was up."

"Well, I *am* a knight." He smiled.

She stood on tiptoe, kissing him for a while. She let her weight back down on her heels and stared up into his eyes. "Feels like we're getting away with something."

"Kind of." He smiled, and started another kiss.

Minutes passed as they kissed and held each other. She walked backward, tugging him by the hand toward the bedroom. Once he realized where she was going, his eyebrows climbed. The excitement and worry on his face made her giddy.

She backed into her bedroom, let go of his hands, and held her arms to the sides.

"Umm..." Sam glanced past her. "What's that?"

Kirsten twisted to the right. An enormous plush rabbit took up half the bed, an inch or two over four feet tall. Bright azure runes decorated its snow-white fur. "Uhh, it's a rune rabbit."

"I know *that*." Sam chuckled. "Why do you have a life-sized rune rabbit on your bed?"

She pouted. "It's *so* cute!"

"Yeah, that seventy-second level creature is real cute when it one-shots you."

Kirsten smoothed her hands down the front of her long tee shirt and walked up to him. "I'm not really thinking about the Monwyn game now." She nibbled on her lower lip and gave him a coy smile.

"Ever hear that thing about how it's impossible to get romantic when there's a dog watching? That rabbit takes it to the next level."

"Oh, fine." She rolled her eyes. "Come on Binky." Kirsten carried the giant plushie to the corner, putting it down facing the wall. "Is that okay?"

He looked down. "Sorry."

Kirsten giggled and sashayed back over. "You're right. It is too cute."

Sam grasped her hips and pulled her against him. "Are you sure about this?

You look nervous. I don't want you to feel pressured. I want to be with you no matter how long it takes you to be ready."

She kissed him long and gentle, pulling away with her mouth half open a minute or so later. "Yeah... I want this." Kirsten stared into his dark brown eyes; time slowed to a standstill. Her breath resonated in her ears over the *thump* of her heart. She drew her arms into her tee shirt and pulled it off over her head, standing before him in only panties. Her brain leapt back to the moment she'd removed the ratty scrap of canvas serving as a garment for the man who wanted sex in exchange for feeding her.

Long-past shame came over her. Without being charmed, the last time she'd disrobed in front of a man while alone with him, she'd been twelve and starving, willing to do anything for something to eat that had never been trash. The beginnings of tears welled at the corners of her eyes as a surge of love gathered in her core. She stared at him; an overwhelming sense of trust dispelled her shame, and she stopped trembling.

He looked worried. "What's—?"

"Bad memories." She pushed the taste of military ration stew out of her memory and smiled.

Sam removed his shirt and stepped closer. Kirsten clung to his warmth, threading her arms around his chest to savor his presence. He caressed the back of her head and let his hand glide down her back.

"Sam?"

"Hmm?"

"I love you, and yes. I want to do this." Kirsten guided him to the bed. "I need you to do something for me."

He kissed her neck, sending a shudder down her back. "Anything."

Kirsten held him in silence for the span of a few breaths. "I want you to give me some *good* memories."

---

fin

ACKNOWLEDGMENTS

I'd like to thank everyone who'd read the Division Zero series up to book 3 and kept asking me what happens next. Initially, I had planned on letting the series rest after Thrall since it seemed to be a nice place to leave Kirsten... but so many people mentioned it, I set to thinking about a story until this book came about. So, to everyone who asked for it – thank you!

Additional thanks to Alexandria Thompson for the cover art!

ABOUT THE AUTHOR

Originally from South Amboy NJ, Matthew has been creating science fiction and fantasy worlds for most of his reasoning life. Since 1996, he has developed the "Divergent Fates" world, in which *Division Zero, Virtual Immortality, The Awakened Series, The Harmony Paradox, and the Daughter of Mars series* take place. Along with being an editor at Curiosity Quills press, he has worked in IT and technical support.

Matthew is an avid gamer, a recovered WoW addict, Gamemaster for two custom RPG systems, and a fan of anime, British humour, and intellectual science fiction that questions the nature of reality, life, and what happens after it.

He is also fond of cats.

Visit me online at:
  Facebook: https://www.facebook.com/MatthewSCoxAuthor
  Amazon: https://www.amazon.com/author/mscox
  Pinterest: https://www.pinterest.com/matthewcox10420/
  Goodreads: https://www.goodreads.com/author/show/7712730.Matthew_S_Cox
  Email: mcox2112@gmail.com

OTHER BOOKS BY MATTHEW S. COX

Divergent Fates Universe Novels
Division Zero series
Division Zero
Lex De Mortuis
Thrall
Guardian

The Awakened series
Prophet of the Badlands
Archon's Queen
Grey Ronin
Daughter of Ash
Zero Rogue
Angel Descended

Daughter of Mars series
The Hand of Raziel
Araphel
Ghost Black

Virtual Immortality series
Virtual Immortality
The Harmony Paradox

Divergent Fates Anthology

(Non-Divergent Fates novels)
The Roadhouse Chronicles Series
One More Run
The Redeemed
Dead Man's Number

Faded Skies series
Heir Ascendant
Ascendant Unrest
Ascendant Revolution

Chiaroscuro: The Mouse and the Candle

Temporal Armistice Series
Nascent Shadow
The Shadow Collector

Wayfarer: AV494

Axillon99

Vampire Innocent series
A Nighttime of Forever
A Beginner's Guide to Fangs
The Artist of Ruin

Operation: Chimera (with Tony Healey)

The Dysfunctional Conspiracy

Winter Solstice series (with J.R. Rain)
Convergence
Containment

Alexis Silver series (with J.R. Rain)
Silver Light
Deep Silver

Samantha Moon Origins series (with J.R. Rain)
New Moon Rising
Moon Mourning

Maddy Wimsey series (with J.R. Rain)
The Devil's Eye
The Drifting Gloom

Samantha Moon Case Files series (with J.R. Rain)
Blood Moon
Dead Moon

The Far Side of Promise anthology

Young Adult
Caller 107
The Summer the World Ended
Nine Candles of Deepest Black
The Eldritch Heart
The Forest Beyond the Earth
Out of Sight

Middle Grade
Tales of Widowswood series
Emma and the Banderwigh
Emma and the Silk Thieves
Emma and the Silverbell Faeries
Emma and the Elixir of Madness
Emma and the Weeping Spirit

Citadel: The Concordant Sequence
The Cursed Codex
The Menagerie of Jenkins Bailey
Sophie's Light

www.ingramcontent.com/pod-product-compliance
Lightning Source LLC
Chambersburg PA
CBHW060216030726
47499CB00004B/1067